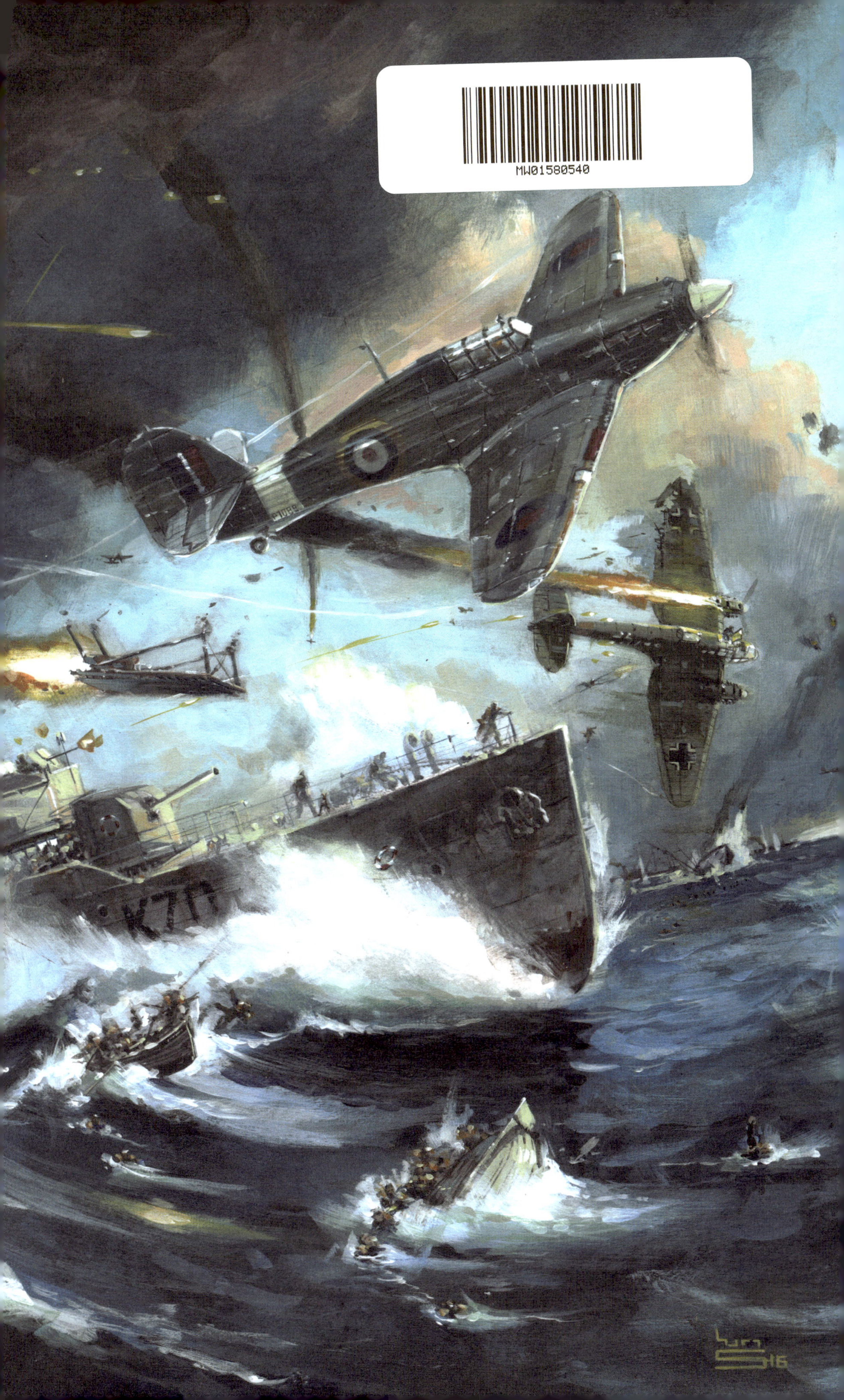
K70

Writer Garth Ennis **Artist** Keith Burns **Colours:** Jason Wordie **Letters:** Rob Steen

Originally published as **Johnny Red: The Hurricane** issue 1-8
Copyright © 2023 & 2024 Rebellion Publishing IP Ltd.
All Rights Reserved.

Creative Director and CEO:
Jason Kingsley

Chief Technical Officer:
Chris Kingsley

Head of Publishing:
Ben Smith

Publishing Director:
Beth Lewis

2000 AD Editor in Chief:
Matt Smith

2000 AD Brand Manager:
Michael Molcher

2000 AD and Graphic Novel
Marketing Manager:
Steve Morris

Production Manager:
Dagna Dłubak

Rights Manager:
Sam Birkett

Trade and Special Sales Manager:
Owen Johnson

Archivists:
Charlene Taylor & Tom Duckham

Senior Graphic Novels Editors:
Keith Richardson & Oliver Pickles

Graphic Novels Editor:
Jonathan Stevenson

Junior Graphic Novels editor:
Chiara Mestieri

Graphic Design:
**Oz Osborne, Sam Gretton
& Gemma Sheldrake**

Reprographics:
**Joseph Morgan, Richard Tustian
& Scarlett Willow**

ISBN: 978-1-837864-20-1
Published by Rebellion, Riverside House,
Osney Mead, Oxford, UK. OX2 0ES
www.rebellion.co.uk

Printed in Malta by Gutenberg Press
Printed on FSC Accredited Paper.

First printing: January 2025
10 9 8 7 6 5 4 3 2 1
A CIP catalogue record for this book is
available from the British Library.

Johnny Red and all related characters, their distinctive
likenesses and related elements featured in this publication
are trademarks of Rebellion Publishing Ltd. The stories,
characters and incidents featured in this publication are
entirely fictional. No portion of this book may be reproduced
without the express permission of the publisher.

For information on other Rebellion graphic novels
visit **treasuryofbritishcomics.com**, or if you
have any comments on this book, please email
books@2000ADonline.com

MIX
Supporting
responsible forestry
FSC® C022612

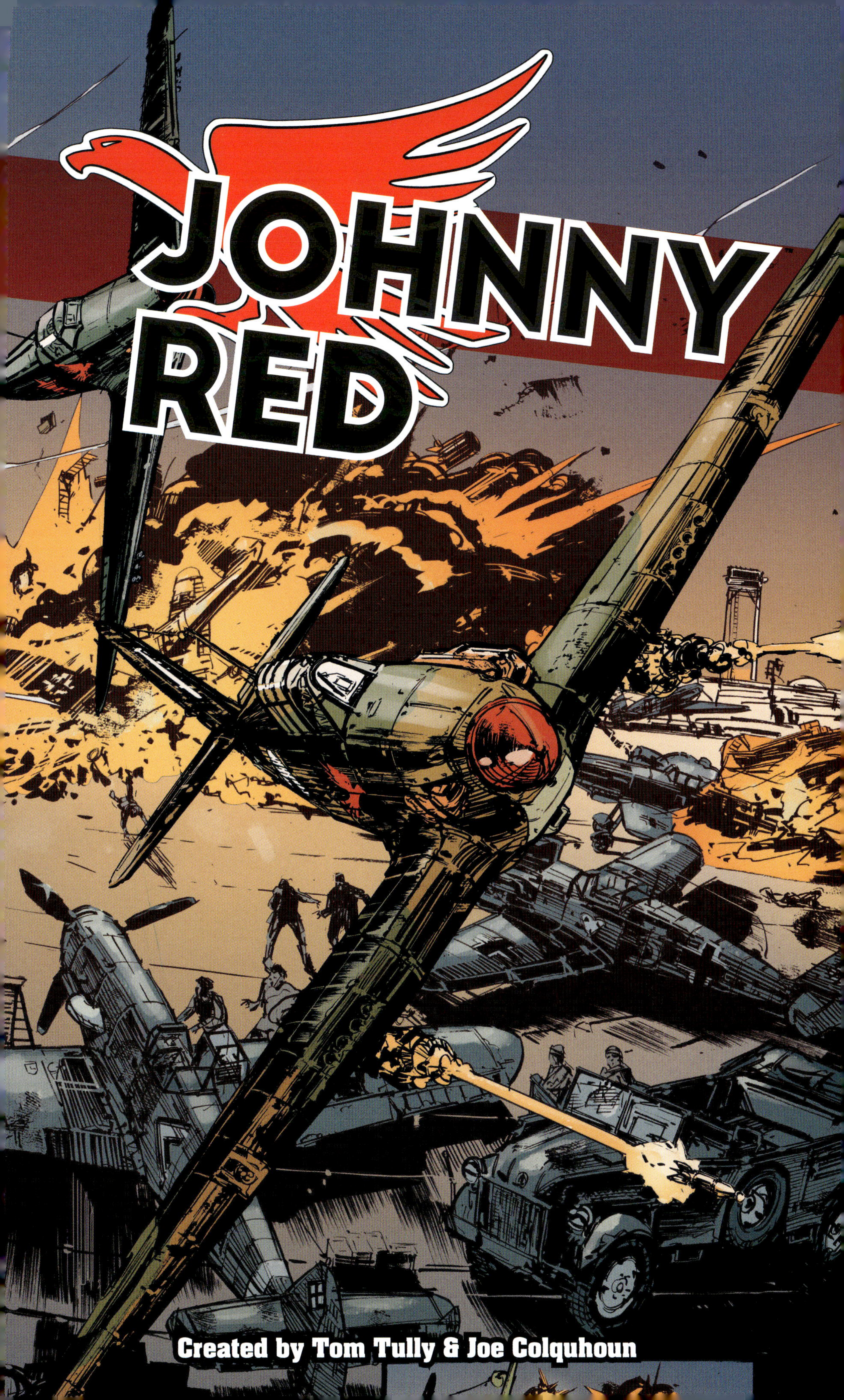
JOHNNY
RED
Created by Tom Tully & Joe Colquhoun

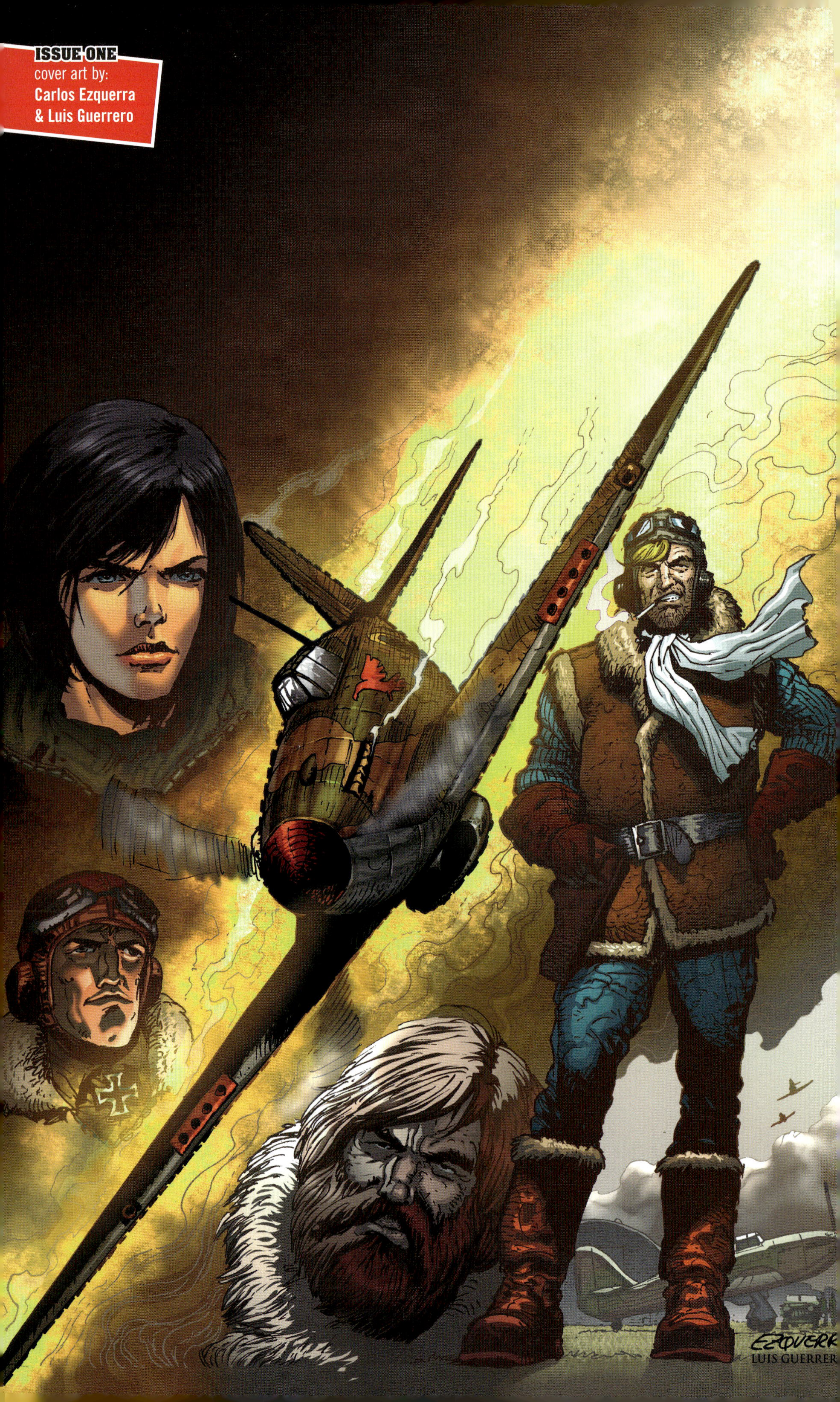

ISSUE ONE
cover art by:
Carlos Ezquerra
& Luis Guerrero

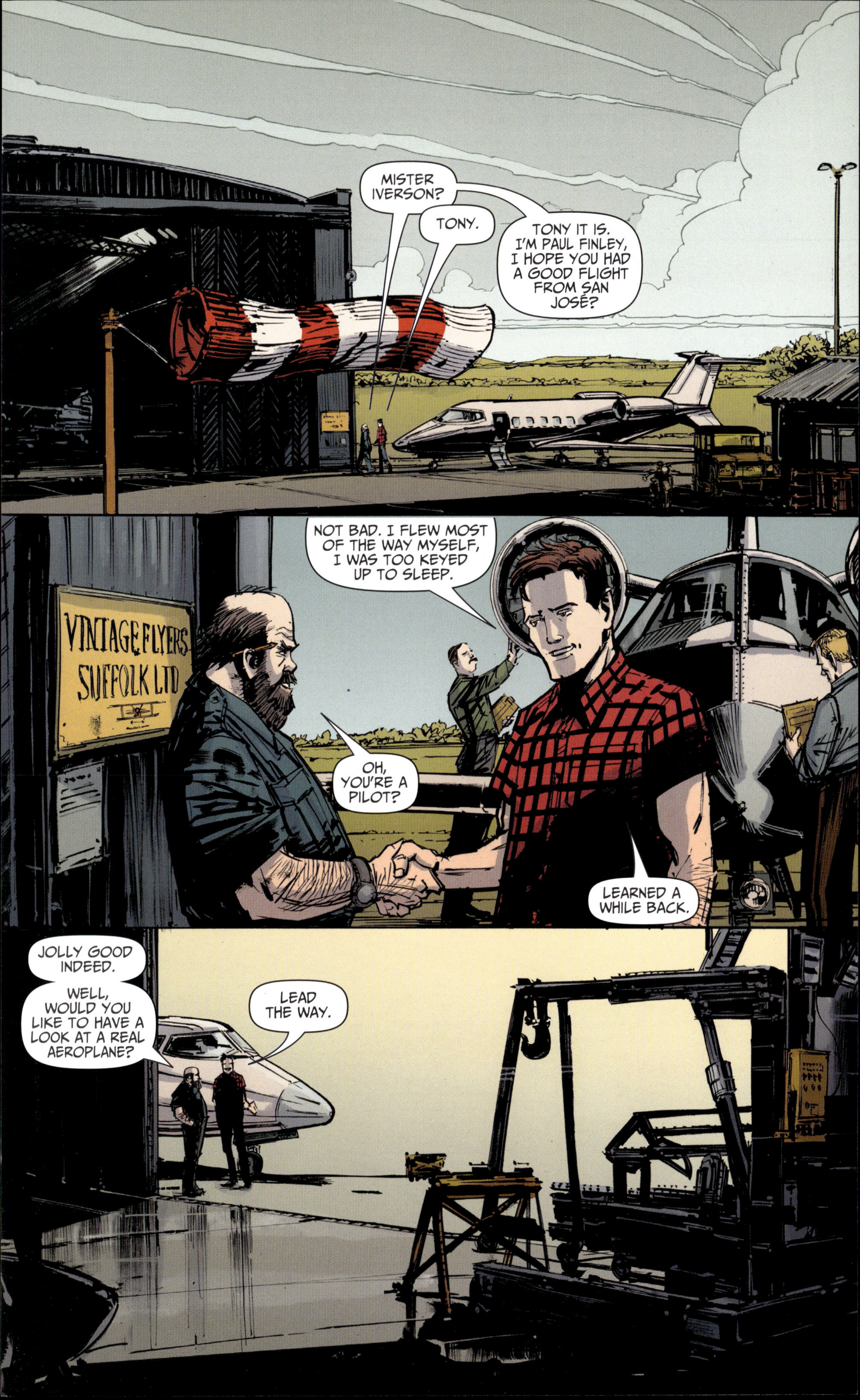
MISTER IVERSON?
TONY.
TONY IT IS. I'M PAUL FINLEY, I HOPE YOU HAD A GOOD FLIGHT FROM SAN JOSÉ?
NOT BAD. I FLEW MOST OF THE WAY MYSELF, I WAS TOO KEYED UP TO SLEEP.
VINTAGE FLYERS SUFFOLK LTD
OH, YOU'RE A PILOT?
LEARNED A WHILE BACK.
JOLLY GOOD INDEED.
WELL, WOULD YOU LIKE TO HAVE A LOOK AT A REAL AEROPLANE?
LEAD THE WAY.

ONE: P7089

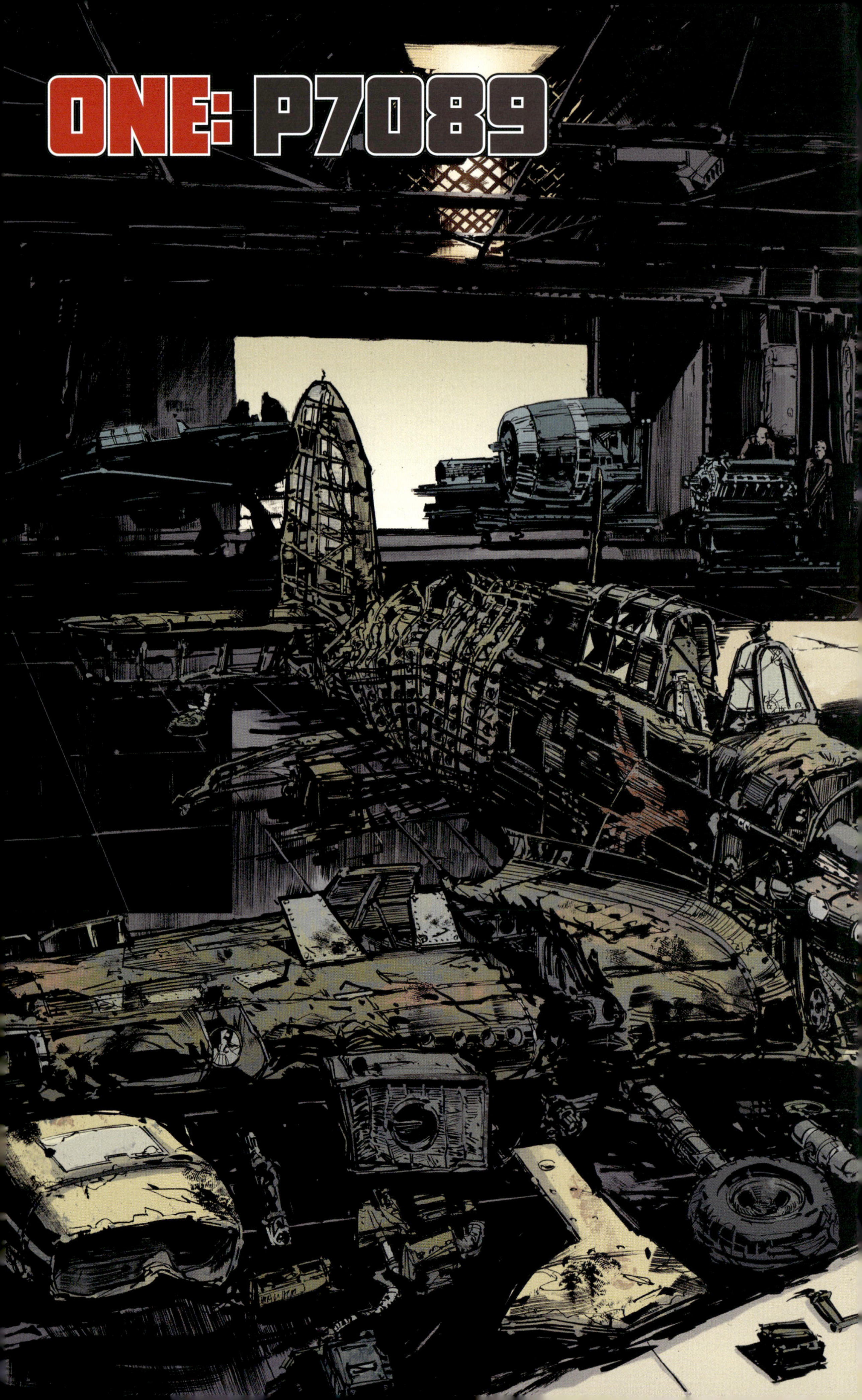

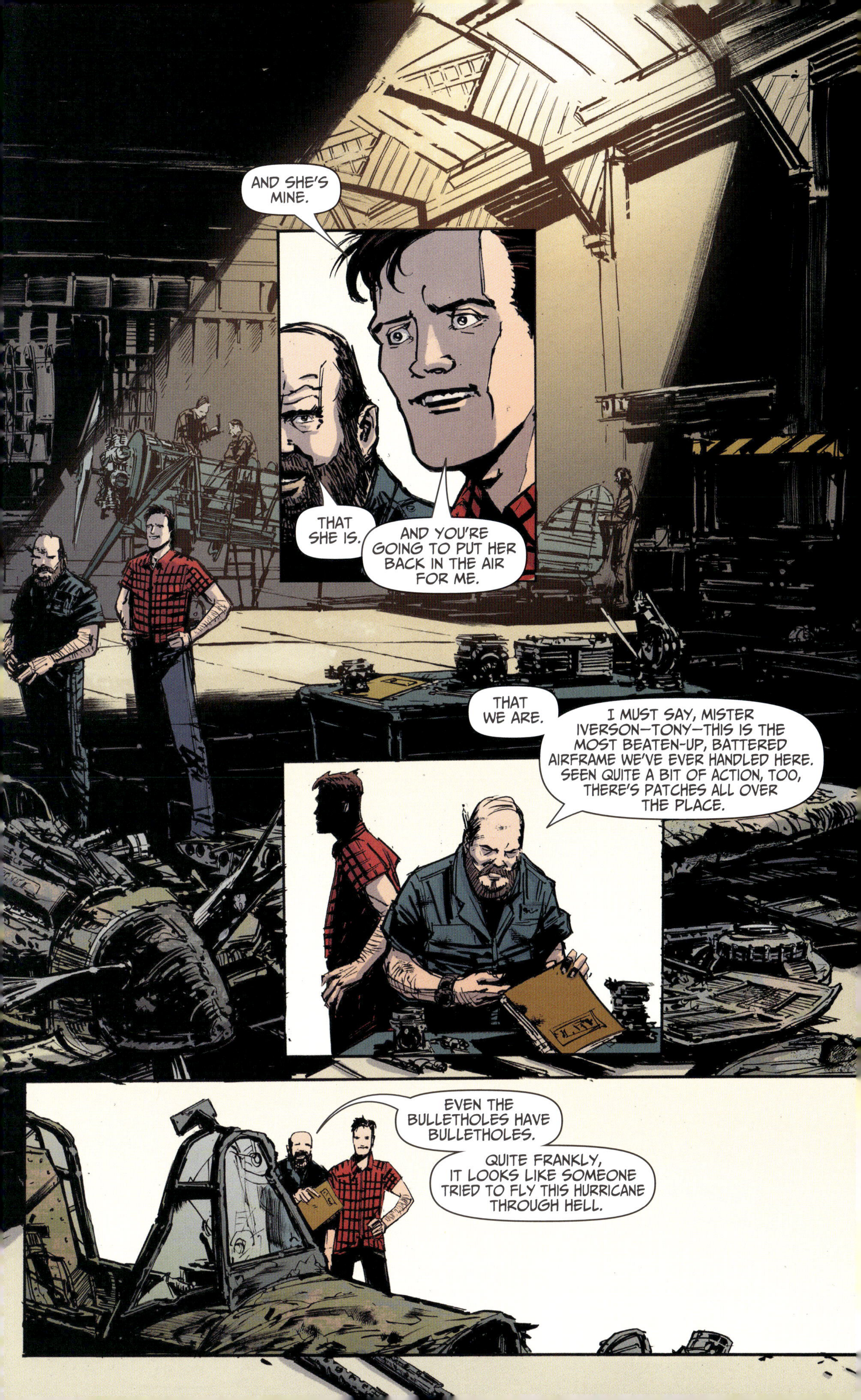
AND SHE'S MINE.
THAT SHE IS.
AND YOU'RE GOING TO PUT HER BACK IN THE AIR FOR ME.
THAT WE ARE.
I MUST SAY, MISTER IVERSON—TONY—THIS IS THE MOST BEATEN-UP, BATTERED AIRFRAME WE'VE EVER HANDLED HERE. SEEN QUITE A BIT OF ACTION, TOO, THERE'S PATCHES ALL OVER THE PLACE.
EVEN THE BULLETHOLES HAVE BULLETHOLES.
QUITE FRANKLY, IT LOOKS LIKE SOMEONE TRIED TO FLY THIS HURRICANE THROUGH HELL.

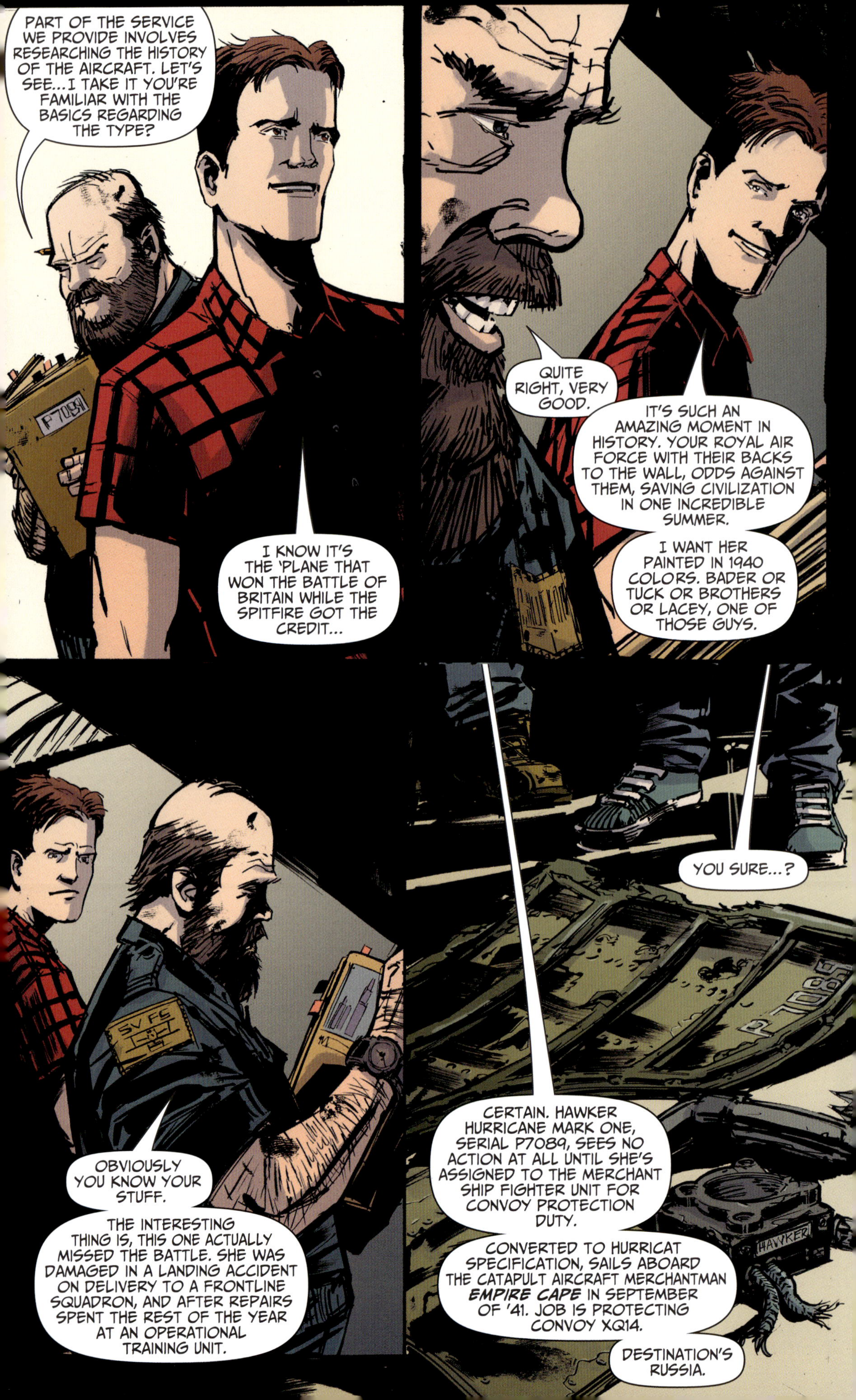
PART OF THE SERVICE WE PROVIDE INVOLVES RESEARCHING THE HISTORY OF THE AIRCRAFT. LET'S SEE...I TAKE IT YOU'RE FAMILIAR WITH THE BASICS REGARDING THE TYPE?
P7089
I KNOW IT'S THE 'PLANE THAT WON THE BATTLE OF BRITAIN WHILE THE SPITFIRE GOT THE CREDIT...
QUITE RIGHT, VERY GOOD.
IT'S SUCH AN AMAZING MOMENT IN HISTORY. YOUR ROYAL AIR FORCE WITH THEIR BACKS TO THE WALL, ODDS AGAINST THEM, SAVING CIVILIZATION IN ONE INCREDIBLE SUMMER.
I WANT HER PAINTED IN 1940 COLORS. BADER OR TUCK OR BROTHERS OR LACEY, ONE OF THOSE GUYS.
SVFS
OBVIOUSLY YOU KNOW YOUR STUFF.
THE INTERESTING THING IS, THIS ONE ACTUALLY MISSED THE BATTLE. SHE WAS DAMAGED IN A LANDING ACCIDENT ON DELIVERY TO A FRONTLINE SQUADRON, AND AFTER REPAIRS SPENT THE REST OF THE YEAR AT AN OPERATIONAL TRAINING UNIT.
YOU SURE...?
P7089
CERTAIN. HAWKER HURRICANE MARK ONE, SERIAL P7089, SEES NO ACTION AT ALL UNTIL SHE'S ASSIGNED TO THE MERCHANT SHIP FIGHTER UNIT FOR CONVOY PROTECTION DUTY.
CONVERTED TO HURRICAT SPECIFICATION, SAILS ABOARD THE CATAPULT AIRCRAFT MERCHANTMAN *EMPIRE CAPE* IN SEPTEMBER OF '41. JOB IS PROTECTING CONVOY XQ14.
HAWKER
DESTINATION'S RUSSIA.

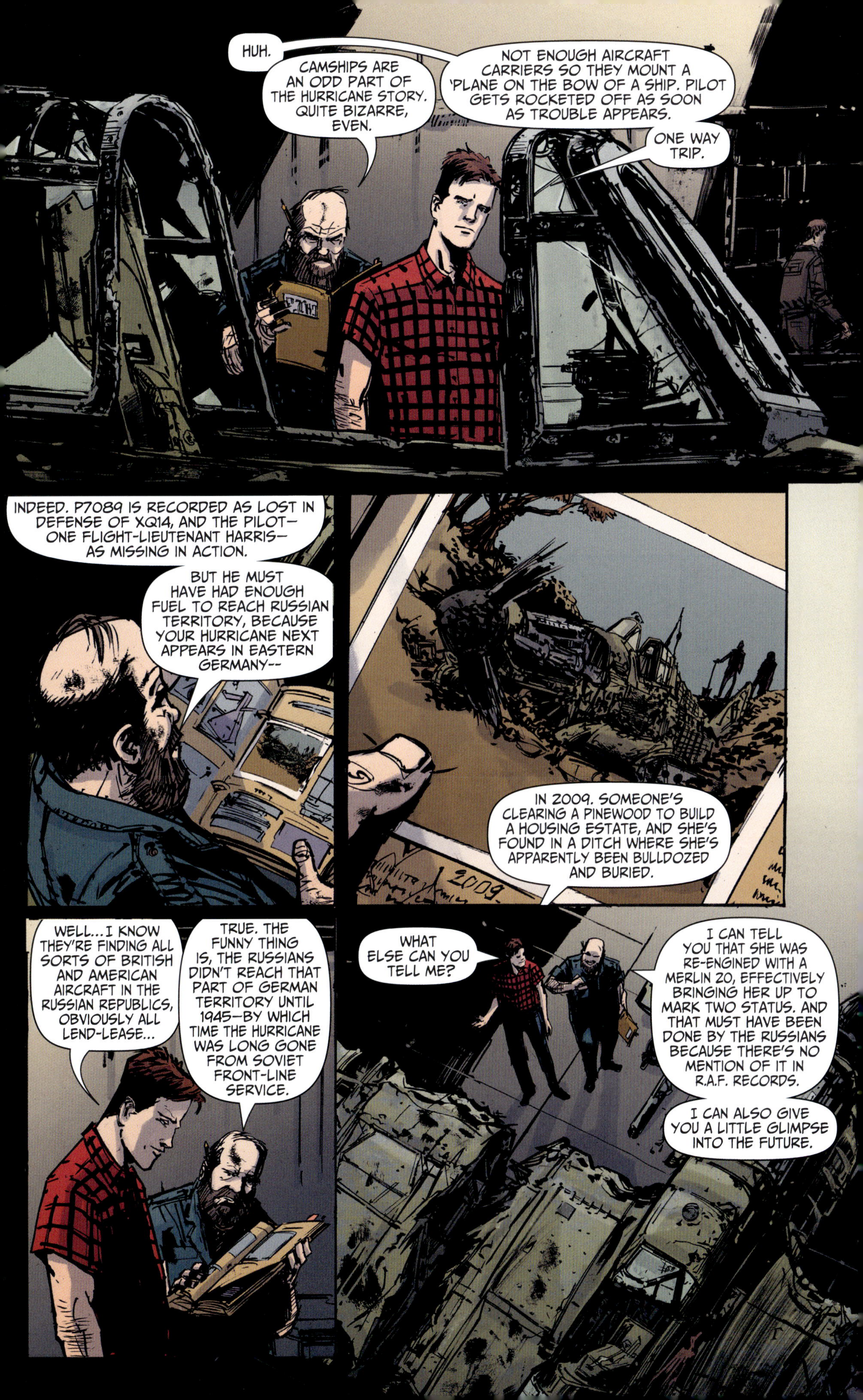

HUH.
CAMSHIPS ARE AN ODD PART OF THE HURRICANE STORY. QUITE BIZARRE, EVEN.
NOT ENOUGH AIRCRAFT CARRIERS SO THEY MOUNT A 'PLANE ON THE BOW OF A SHIP. PILOT GETS ROCKETED OFF AS SOON AS TROUBLE APPEARS.
ONE WAY TRIP.
INDEED. P7089 IS RECORDED AS LOST IN DEFENSE OF XQ14, AND THE PILOT—ONE FLIGHT-LIEUTENANT HARRIS—AS MISSING IN ACTION.
BUT HE MUST HAVE HAD ENOUGH FUEL TO REACH RUSSIAN TERRITORY, BECAUSE YOUR HURRICANE NEXT APPEARS IN EASTERN GERMANY--
IN 2009. SOMEONE'S CLEARING A PINEWOOD TO BUILD A HOUSING ESTATE, AND SHE'S FOUND IN A DITCH WHERE SHE'S APPARENTLY BEEN BULLDOZED AND BURIED.
WELL...I KNOW THEY'RE FINDING ALL SORTS OF BRITISH AND AMERICAN AIRCRAFT IN THE RUSSIAN REPUBLICS, OBVIOUSLY ALL LEND-LEASE...
TRUE. THE FUNNY THING IS, THE RUSSIANS DIDN'T REACH THAT PART OF GERMAN TERRITORY UNTIL 1945—BY WHICH TIME THE HURRICANE WAS LONG GONE FROM SOVIET FRONT-LINE SERVICE.
WHAT ELSE CAN YOU TELL ME?
I CAN TELL YOU THAT SHE WAS RE-ENGINED WITH A MERLIN 20, EFFECTIVELY BRINGING HER UP TO MARK TWO STATUS. AND THAT MUST HAVE BEEN DONE BY THE RUSSIANS BECAUSE THERE'S NO MENTION OF IT IN R.A.F. RECORDS.
I CAN ALSO GIVE YOU A LITTLE GLIMPSE INTO THE FUTURE.

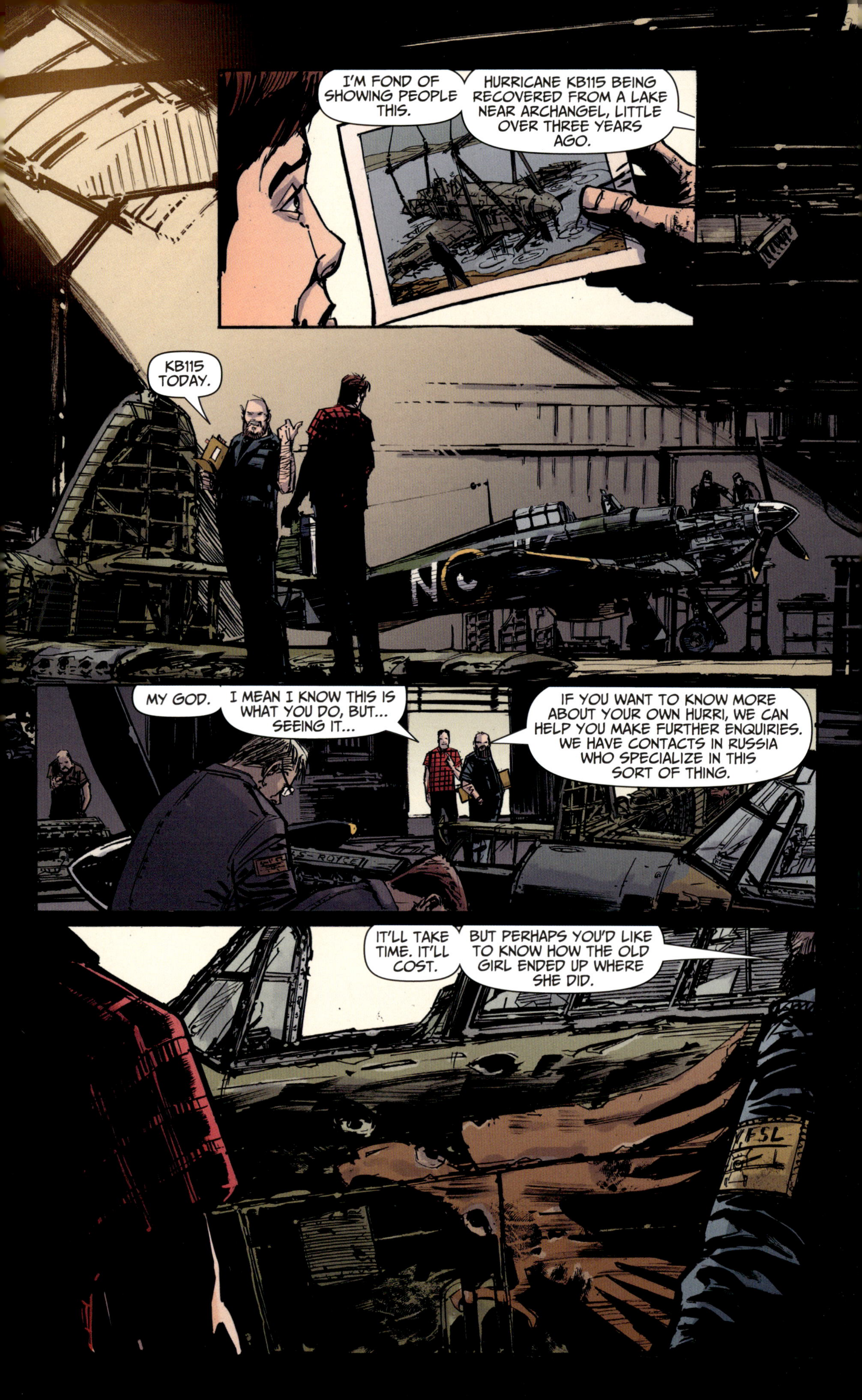
I'M FOND OF SHOWING PEOPLE THIS.
HURRICANE KB115 BEING RECOVERED FROM A LAKE NEAR ARCHANGEL, LITTLE OVER THREE YEARS AGO.
KB115 TODAY.
MY GOD.
I MEAN I KNOW THIS IS WHAT YOU DO, BUT... SEEING IT...
IF YOU WANT TO KNOW MORE ABOUT YOUR OWN HURRI, WE CAN HELP YOU MAKE FURTHER ENQUIRIES. WE HAVE CONTACTS IN RUSSIA WHO SPECIALIZE IN THIS SORT OF THING.
IT'LL TAKE TIME. IT'LL COST.
BUT PERHAPS YOU'D LIKE TO KNOW HOW THE OLD GIRL ENDED UP WHERE SHE DID.

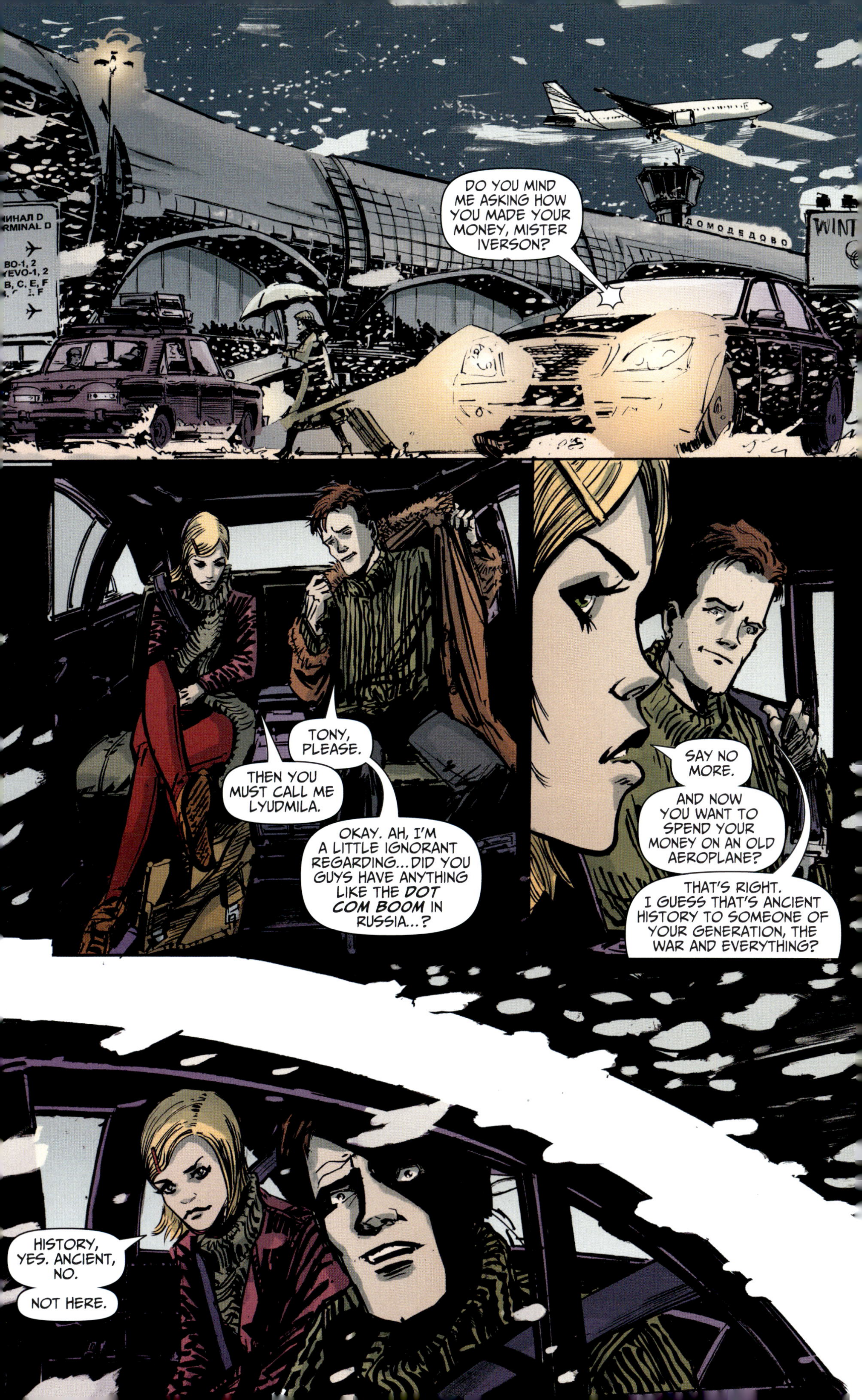
ДОМОДЕДОВО
DO YOU MIND ME ASKING HOW YOU MADE YOUR MONEY, MISTER IVERSON?
TONY, PLEASE.
THEN YOU MUST CALL ME LYUDMILA.
OKAY. AH, I'M A LITTLE IGNORANT REGARDING...DID YOU GUYS HAVE ANYTHING LIKE THE *DOT COM BOOM* IN RUSSIA...?
SAY NO MORE.
AND NOW YOU WANT TO SPEND YOUR MONEY ON AN OLD AEROPLANE?
THAT'S RIGHT. I GUESS THAT'S ANCIENT HISTORY TO SOMEONE OF YOUR GENERATION, THE WAR AND EVERYTHING?
HISTORY, YES. ANCIENT, NO.
NOT HERE.

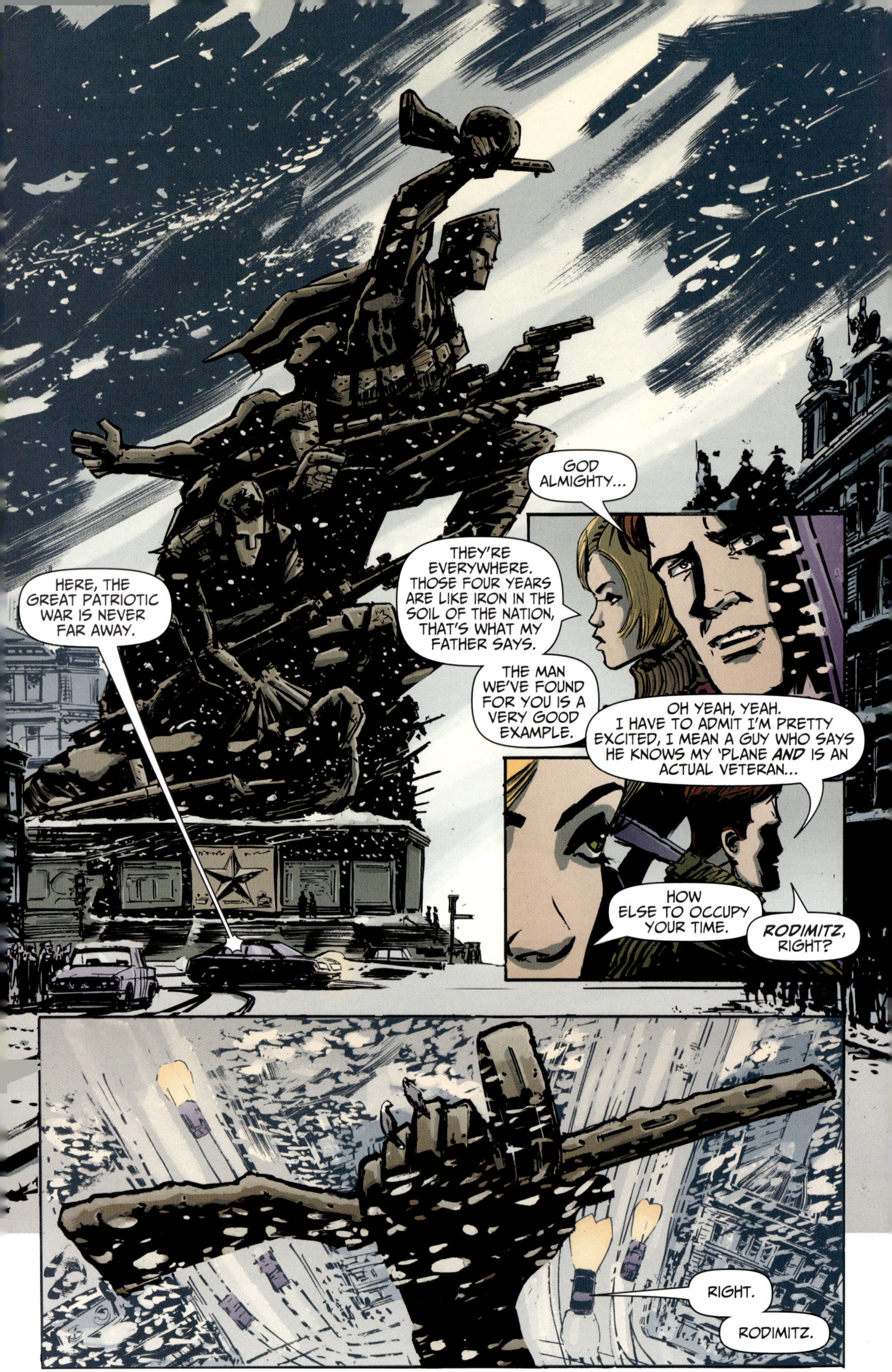

HERE, THE GREAT PATRIOTIC WAR IS NEVER FAR AWAY.
THEY'RE EVERYWHERE. THOSE FOUR YEARS ARE LIKE IRON IN THE SOIL OF THE NATION, THAT'S WHAT MY FATHER SAYS.
THE MAN WE'VE FOUND FOR YOU IS A VERY GOOD EXAMPLE.
GOD ALMIGHTY...
OH YEAH, YEAH. I HAVE TO ADMIT I'M PRETTY EXCITED, I MEAN A GUY WHO SAYS HE KNOWS MY 'PLANE AND IS AN ACTUAL VETERAN...
HOW ELSE TO OCCUPY YOUR TIME.
RODIMITZ, RIGHT?
RIGHT.
RODIMITZ.

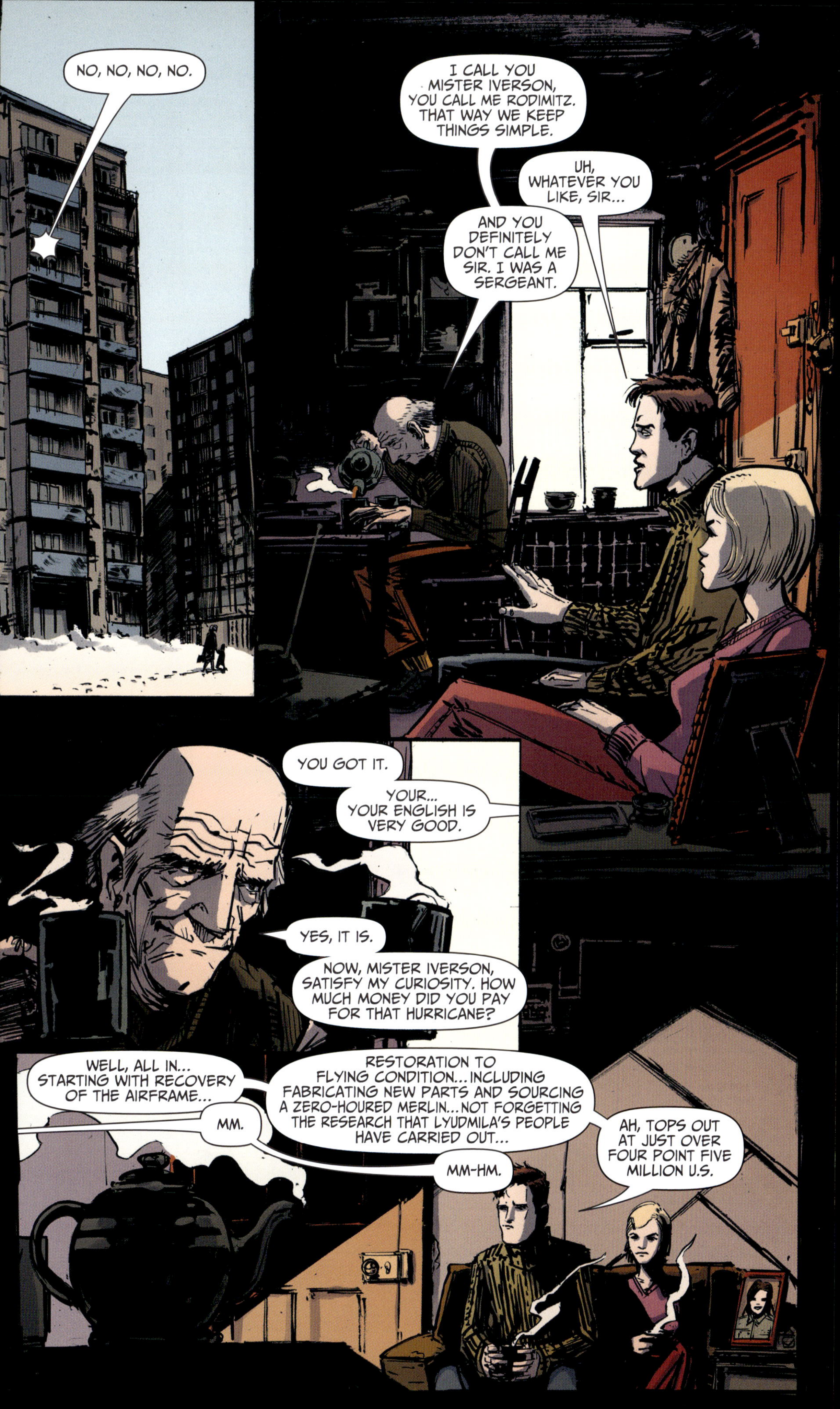
NO, NO, NO, NO.
I CALL YOU MISTER IVERSON, YOU CALL ME RODIMITZ. THAT WAY WE KEEP THINGS SIMPLE.
UH, WHATEVER YOU LIKE, SIR...
AND YOU DEFINITELY DON'T CALL ME SIR. I WAS A SERGEANT.
YOU GOT IT.
YOUR... YOUR ENGLISH IS VERY GOOD.
YES, IT IS.
NOW, MISTER IVERSON, SATISFY MY CURIOSITY. HOW MUCH MONEY DID YOU PAY FOR THAT HURRICANE?
WELL, ALL IN... STARTING WITH RECOVERY OF THE AIRFRAME...
MM.
RESTORATION TO FLYING CONDITION... INCLUDING FABRICATING NEW PARTS AND SOURCING A ZERO-HOURED MERLIN... NOT FORGETTING THE RESEARCH THAT LYUDMILA'S PEOPLE HAVE CARRIED OUT...
MM-HM.
AH, TOPS OUT AT JUST OVER FOUR POINT FIVE MILLION U.S.

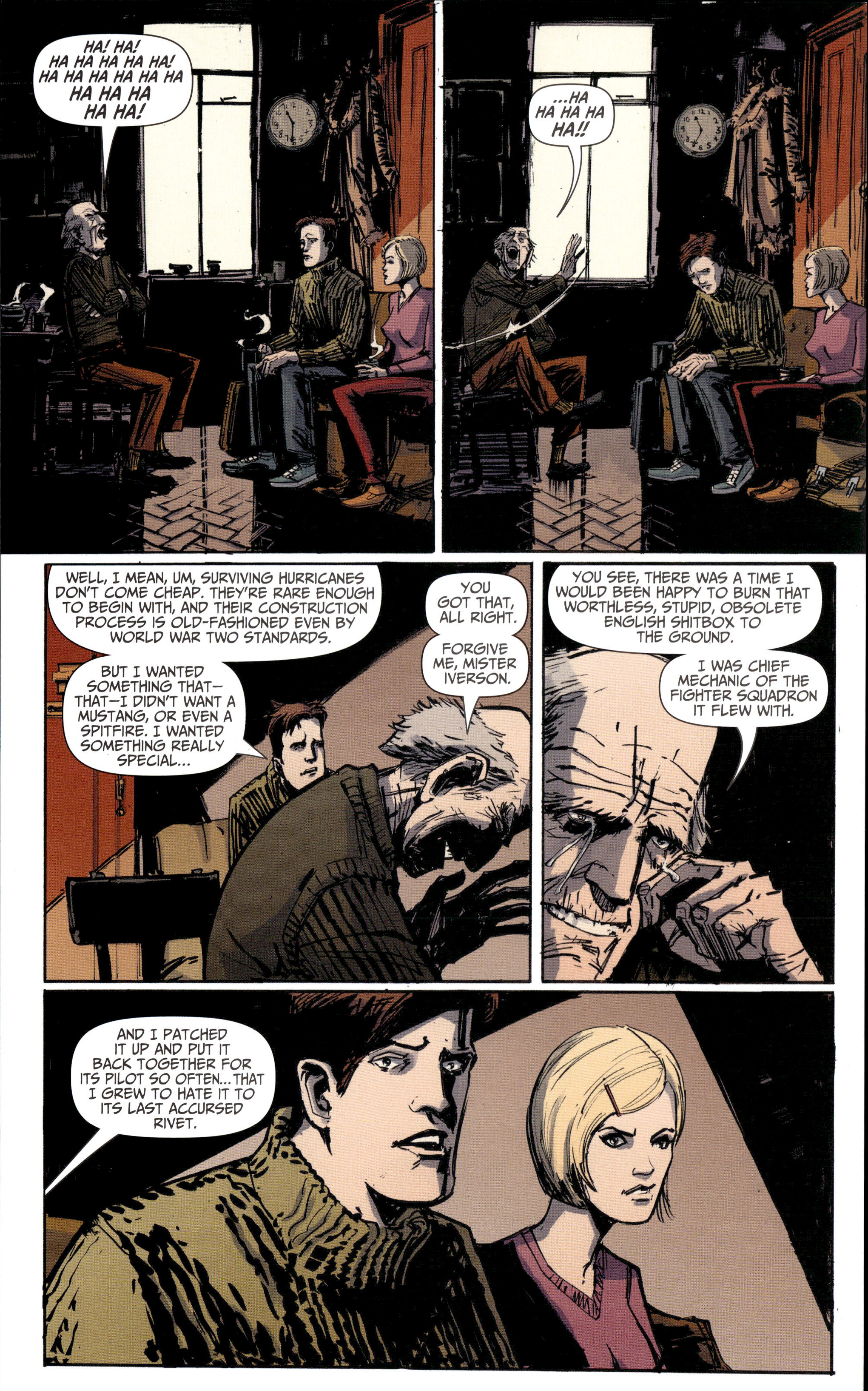
HA! HA!
HA HA HA HA HA!
HA HA HA HA HA HA
HA HA HA
HA HA!
...HA
HA HA HA
HA!!
WELL, I MEAN, UM, SURVIVING HURRICANES DON'T COME CHEAP. THEY'RE RARE ENOUGH TO BEGIN WITH, AND THEIR CONSTRUCTION PROCESS IS OLD-FASHIONED EVEN BY WORLD WAR TWO STANDARDS.
BUT I WANTED SOMETHING THAT—THAT—I DIDN'T WANT A MUSTANG, OR EVEN A SPITFIRE. I WANTED SOMETHING REALLY SPECIAL...
YOU GOT THAT, ALL RIGHT.
FORGIVE ME, MISTER IVERSON.
YOU SEE, THERE WAS A TIME I WOULD BEEN HAPPY TO BURN THAT WORTHLESS, STUPID, OBSOLETE ENGLISH SHITBOX TO THE GROUND.
I WAS CHIEF MECHANIC OF THE FIGHTER SQUADRON IT FLEW WITH.
AND I PATCHED IT UP AND PUT IT BACK TOGETHER FOR ITS PILOT SO OFTEN... THAT I GREW TO HATE IT TO ITS LAST ACCURSED RIVET.

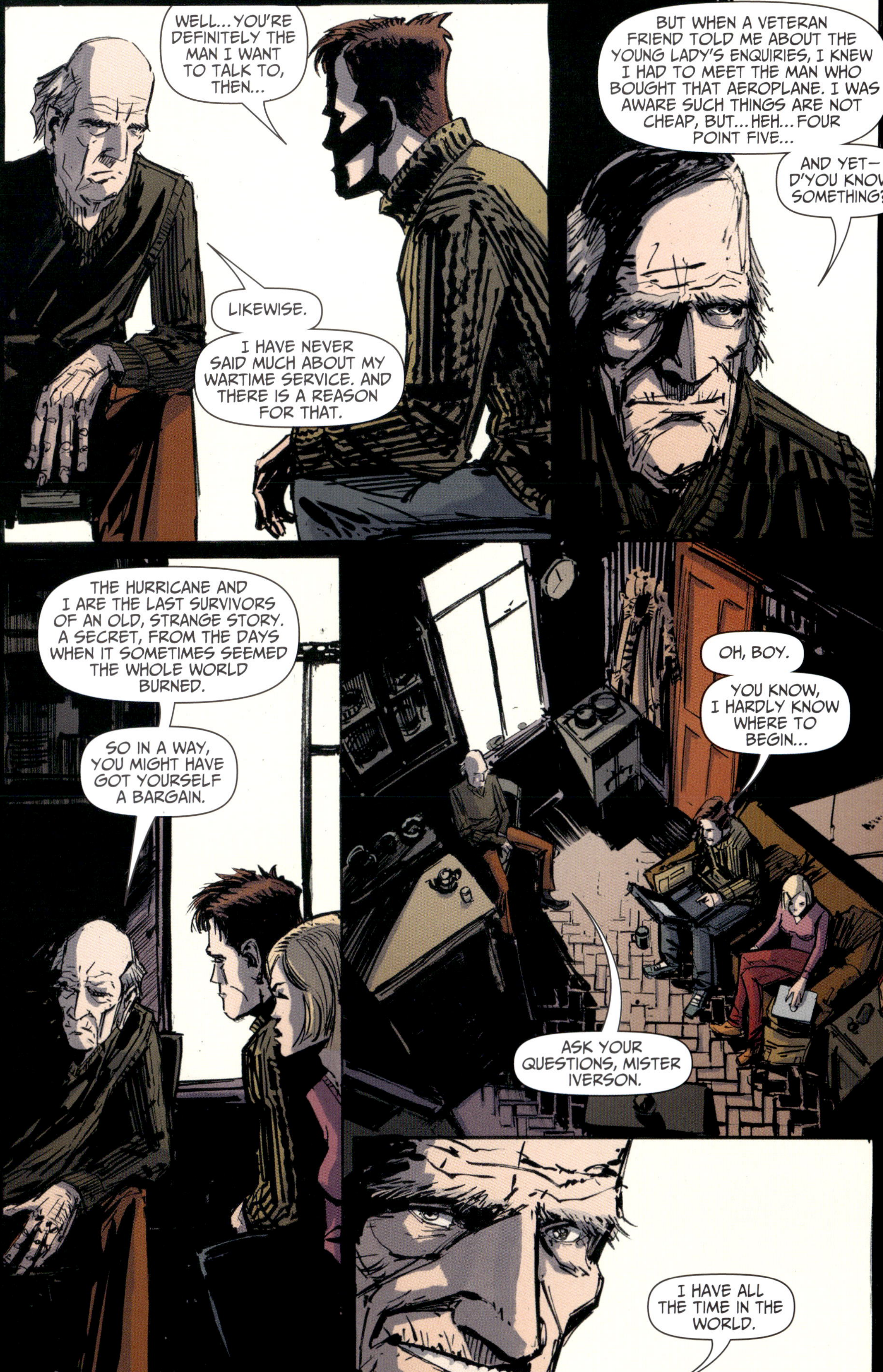
WELL... YOU'RE DEFINITELY THE MAN I WANT TO TALK TO, THEN...
LIKEWISE.
I HAVE NEVER SAID MUCH ABOUT MY WARTIME SERVICE. AND THERE IS A REASON FOR THAT.
BUT WHEN A VETERAN FRIEND TOLD ME ABOUT THE YOUNG LADY'S ENQUIRIES, I KNEW I HAD TO MEET THE MAN WHO BOUGHT THAT AEROPLANE. I WAS AWARE SUCH THINGS ARE NOT CHEAP, BUT... HEH... FOUR POINT FIVE...
AND YET— D'YOU KNOW SOMETHING?
THE HURRICANE AND I ARE THE LAST SURVIVORS OF AN OLD, STRANGE STORY. A SECRET, FROM THE DAYS WHEN IT SOMETIMES SEEMED THE WHOLE WORLD BURNED.
SO IN A WAY, YOU MIGHT HAVE GOT YOURSELF A BARGAIN.
OH, BOY.
YOU KNOW, I HARDLY KNOW WHERE TO BEGIN...
ASK YOUR QUESTIONS, MISTER IVERSON.
I HAVE ALL THE TIME IN THE WORLD.

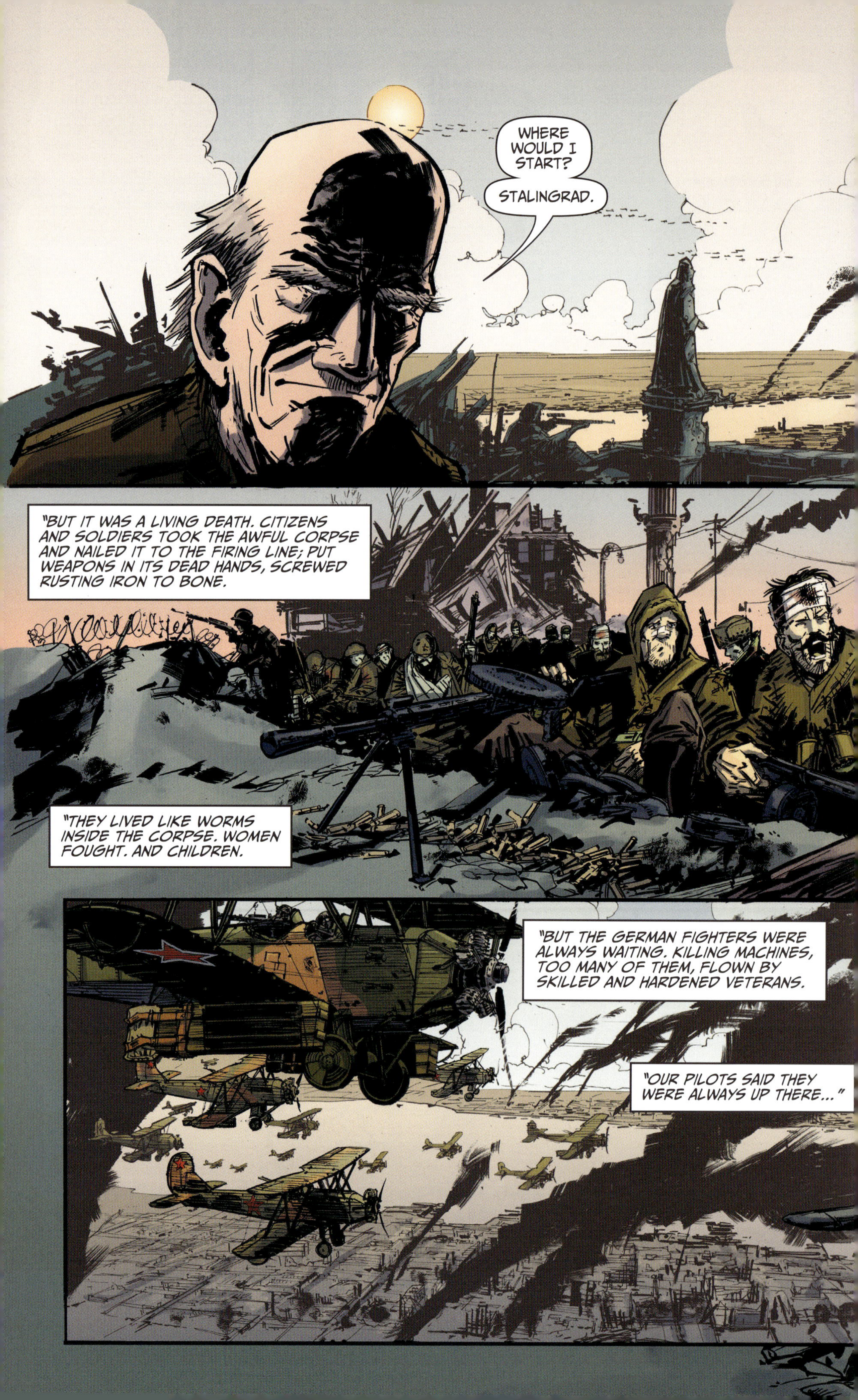
WHERE WOULD I START?
STALINGRAD.
"BUT IT WAS A LIVING DEATH. CITIZENS AND SOLDIERS TOOK THE AWFUL CORPSE AND NAILED IT TO THE FIRING LINE; PUT WEAPONS IN ITS DEAD HANDS, SCREWED RUSTING IRON TO BONE.
"THEY LIVED LIKE WORMS INSIDE THE CORPSE. WOMEN FOUGHT. AND CHILDREN.
"BUT THE GERMAN FIGHTERS WERE ALWAYS WAITING. KILLING MACHINES, TOO MANY OF THEM, FLOWN BY SKILLED AND HARDENED VETERANS.
"OUR PILOTS SAID THEY WERE ALWAYS UP THERE..."

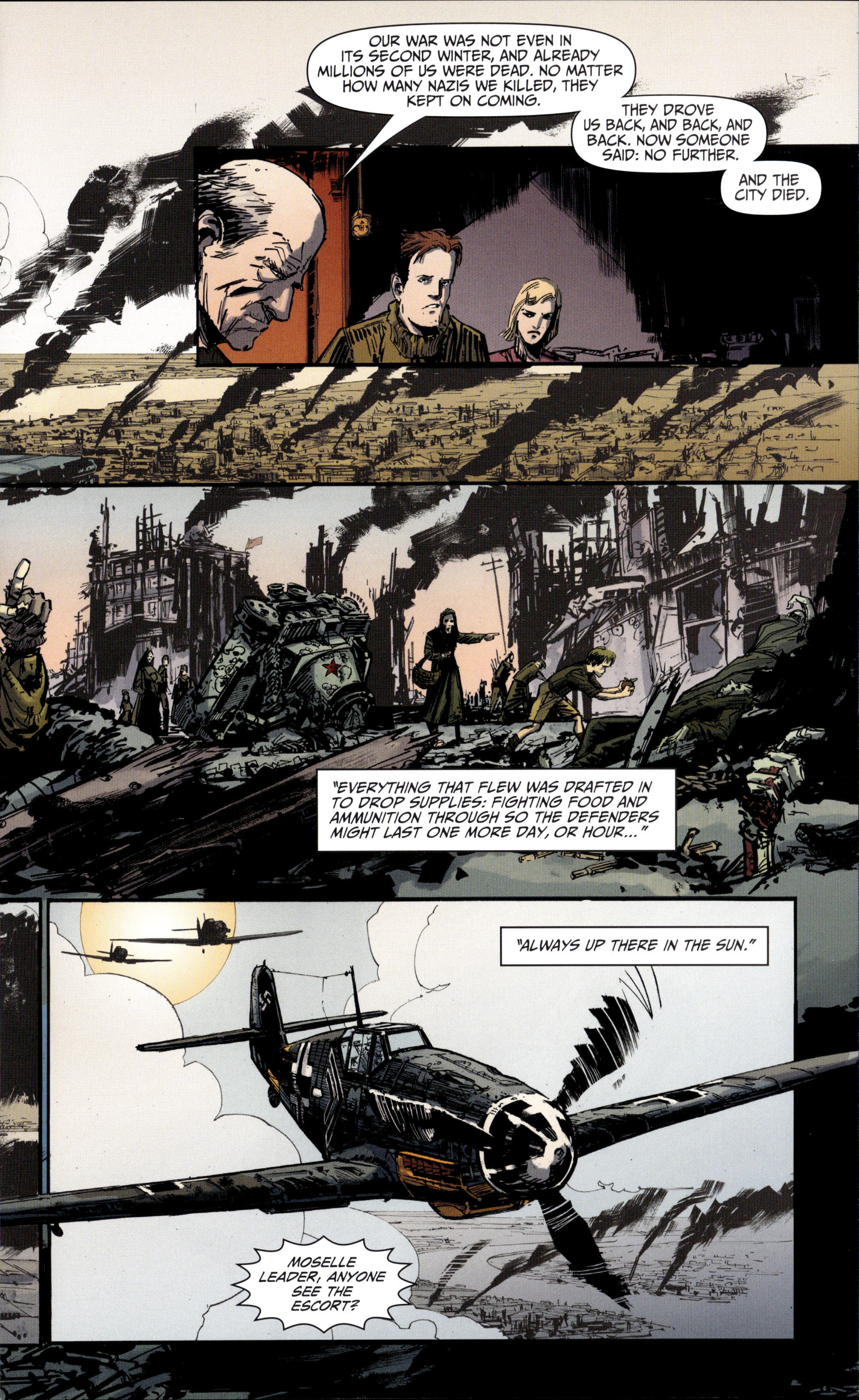
OUR WAR WAS NOT EVEN IN ITS SECOND WINTER, AND ALREADY MILLIONS OF US WERE DEAD. NO MATTER HOW MANY NAZIS WE KILLED, THEY KEPT ON COMING.
THEY DROVE US BACK, AND BACK, AND BACK. NOW SOMEONE SAID: NO FURTHER.
AND THE CITY DIED.
"EVERYTHING THAT FLEW WAS DRAFTED IN TO DROP SUPPLIES: FIGHTING FOOD AND AMMUNITION THROUGH SO THE DEFENDERS MIGHT LAST ONE MORE DAY, OR HOUR..."
"ALWAYS UP THERE IN THE SUN."
MOSELLE LEADER, ANYONE SEE THE ESCORT?

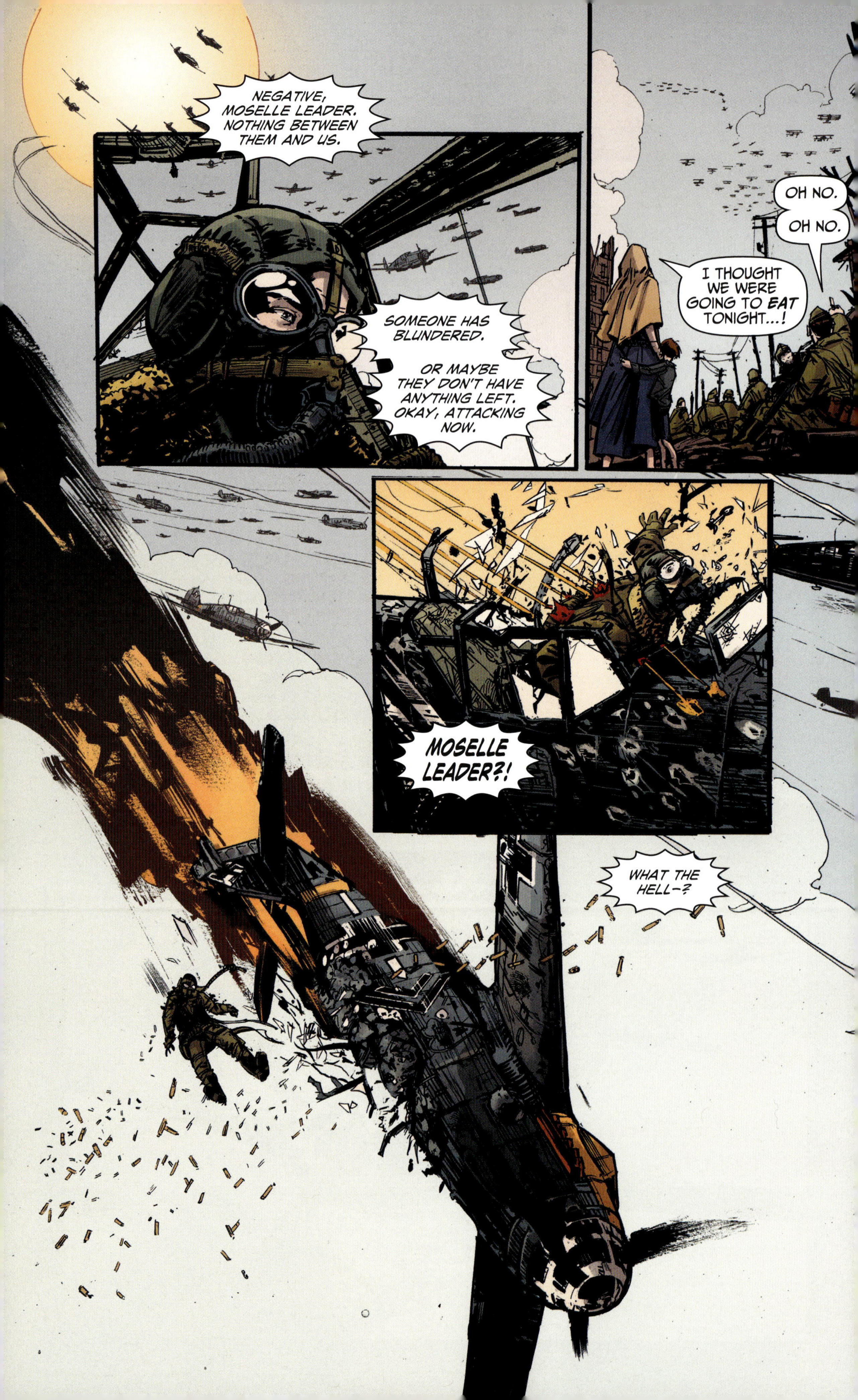
NEGATIVE, MOSELLE LEADER. NOTHING BETWEEN THEM AND US.
SOMEONE HAS BLUNDERED.
OR MAYBE THEY DON'T HAVE ANYTHING LEFT. OKAY, ATTACKING NOW.
OH NO.
OH NO.
I THOUGHT WE WERE GOING TO EAT TONIGHT...!
MOSELLE LEADER?!
WHAT THE HELL-?

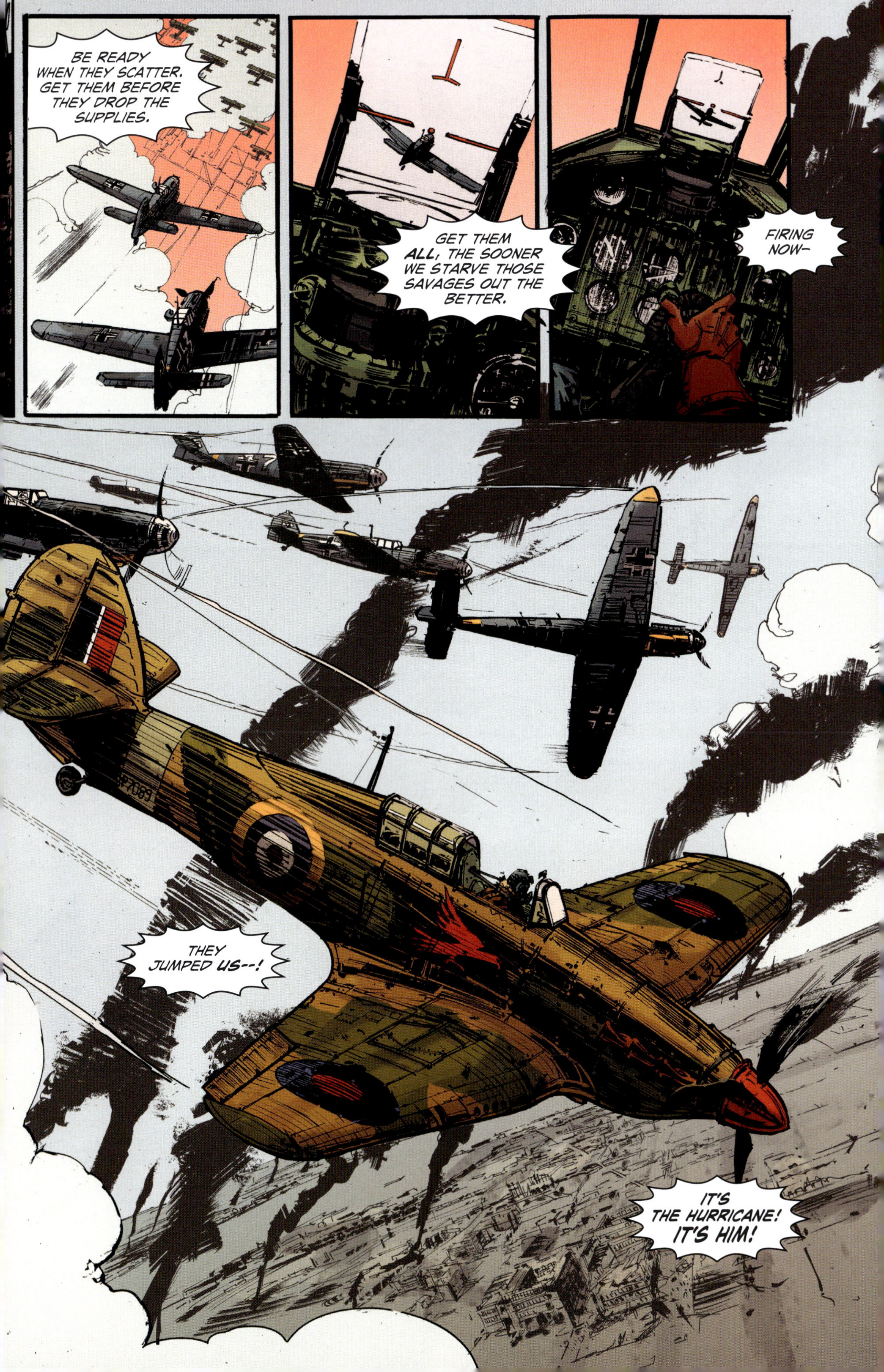
BE READY WHEN THEY SCATTER. GET THEM BEFORE THEY DROP THE SUPPLIES.
GET THEM ALL, THE SOONER WE STARVE THOSE SAVAGES OUT THE BETTER.
FIRING NOW—
THEY JUMPED US--!
IT'S THE HURRICANE! IT'S HIM!

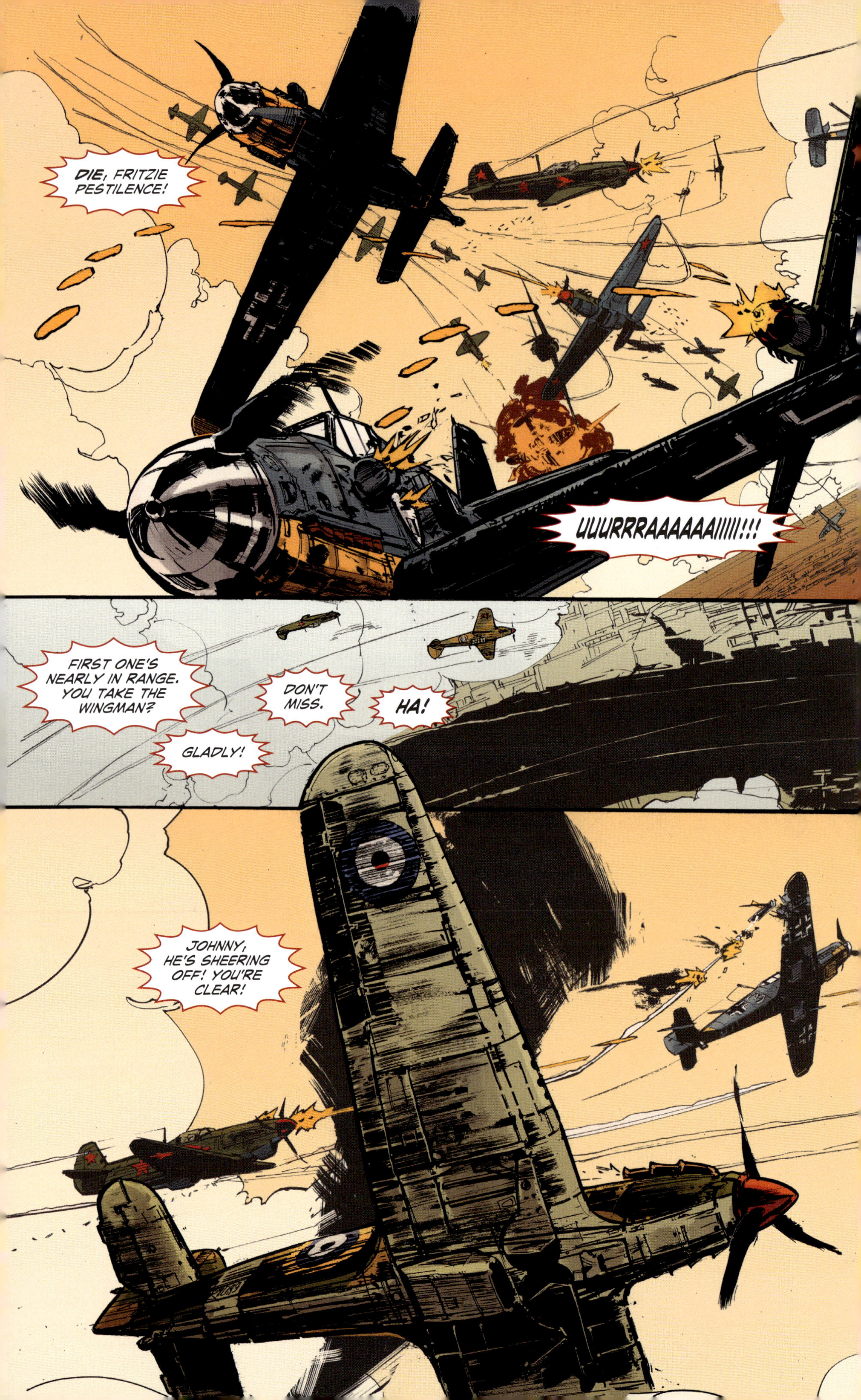
DIE, FRITZIE PESTILENCE!
UUURRRAAAAAAIIIII!!!
FIRST ONE'S NEARLY IN RANGE. YOU TAKE THE WINGMAN?
GLADLY!
DON'T MISS.
HA!
JOHNNY, HE'S SHEERING OFF! YOU'RE CLEAR!

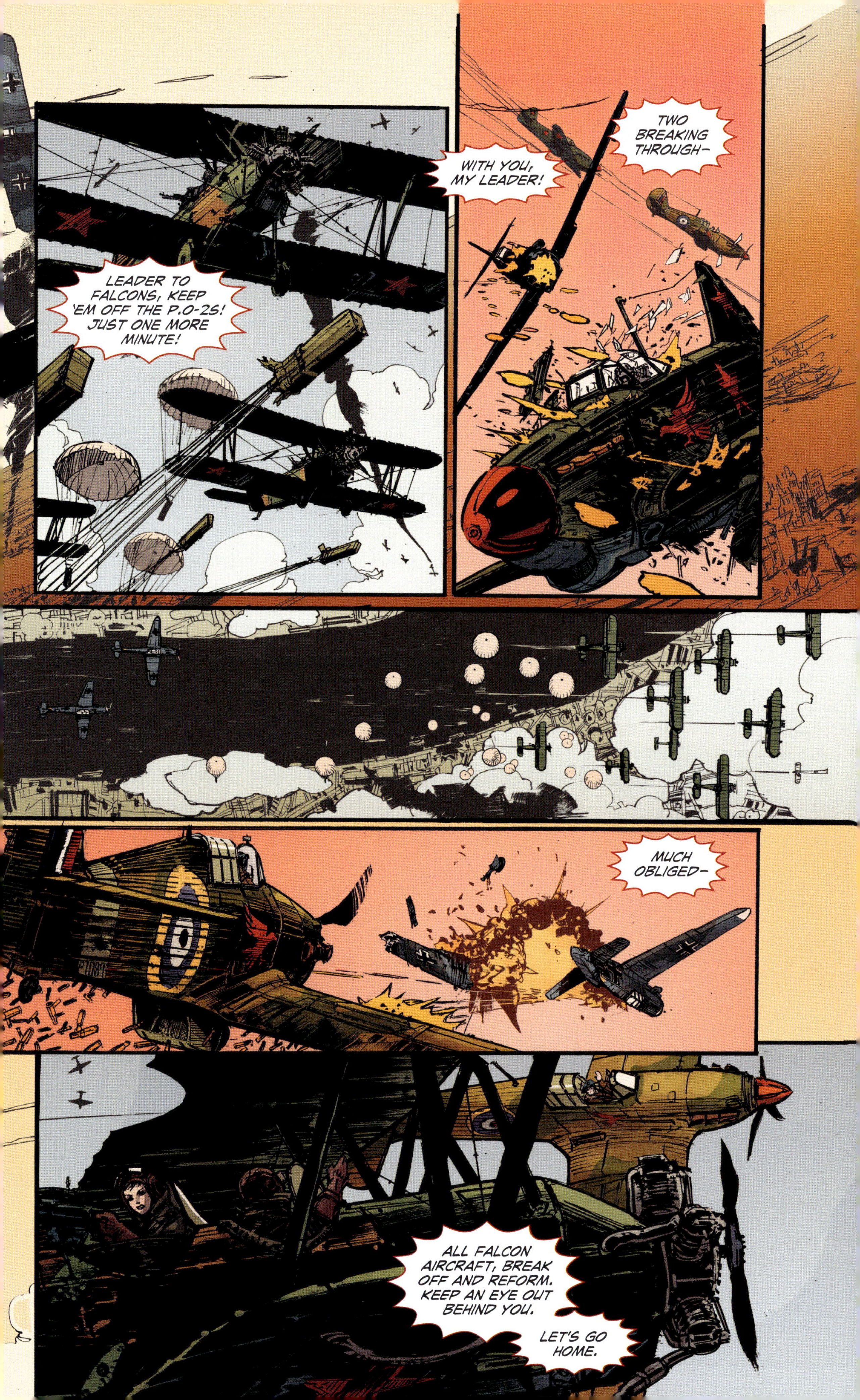
LEADER TO FALCONS, KEEP 'EM OFF THE P.O-2S! JUST ONE MORE MINUTE!
WITH YOU, MY LEADER!
TWO BREAKING THROUGH–
MUCH OBLIGED–
ALL FALCON AIRCRAFT, BREAK OFF AND REFORM. KEEP AN EYE OUT BEHIND YOU.
LET'S GO HOME.

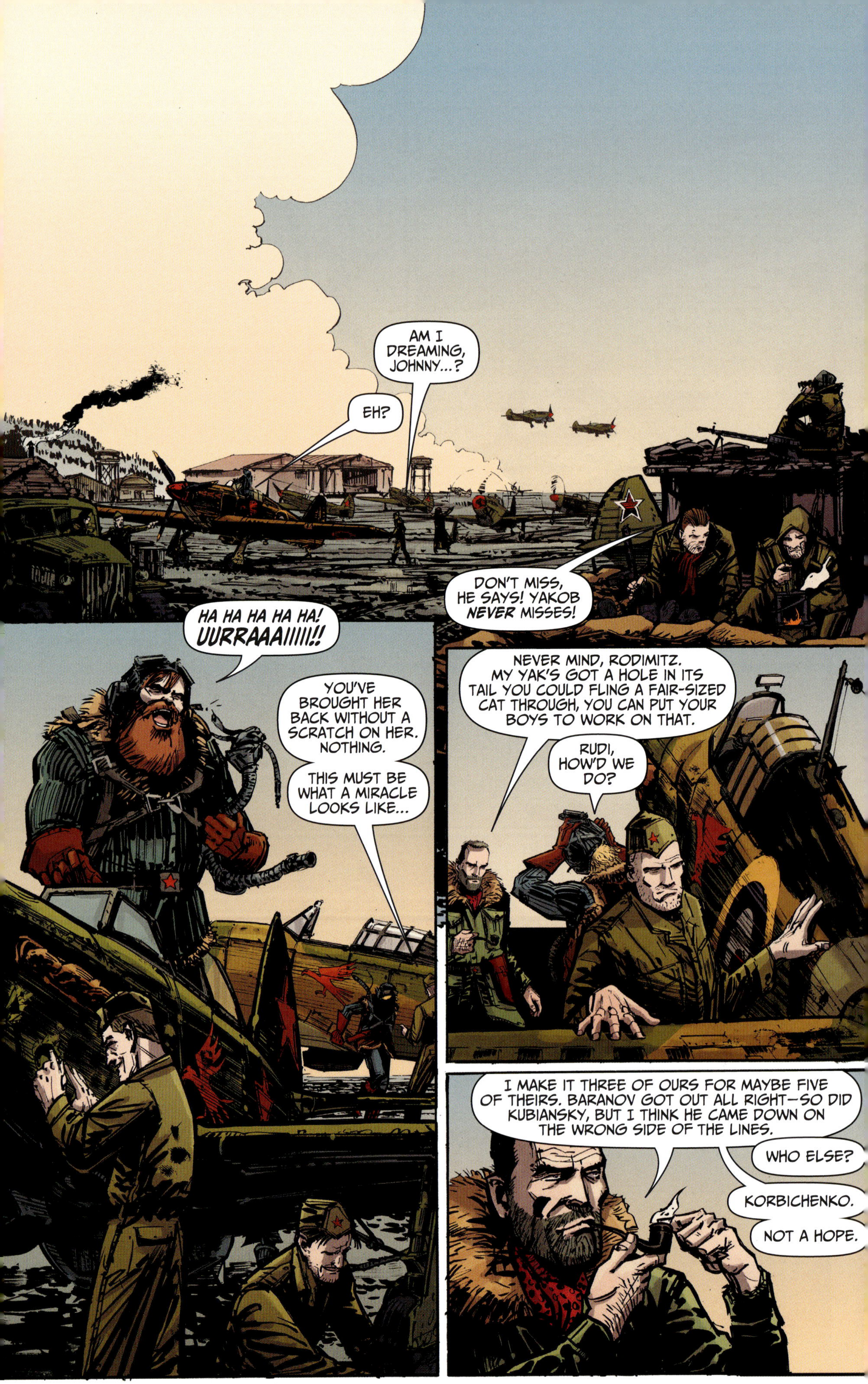
AM I DREAMING, JOHNNY...?
EH?
DON'T MISS, HE SAYS! YAKOB *NEVER* MISSES!
HA HA HA HA HA! UURRAAAIIIII!!
YOU'VE BROUGHT HER BACK WITHOUT A SCRATCH ON HER. NOTHING.
THIS MUST BE WHAT A MIRACLE LOOKS LIKE...
NEVER MIND, RODIMITZ. MY YAK'S GOT A HOLE IN ITS TAIL YOU COULD FLING A FAIR-SIZED CAT THROUGH, YOU CAN PUT YOUR BOYS TO WORK ON THAT.
RUDI, HOW'D WE DO?
I MAKE IT THREE OF OURS FOR MAYBE FIVE OF THEIRS. BARANOV GOT OUT ALL RIGHT—SO DID KUBIANSKY, BUT I THINK HE CAME DOWN ON THE WRONG SIDE OF THE LINES.
WHO ELSE?
KORBICHENKO.
NOT A HOPE.

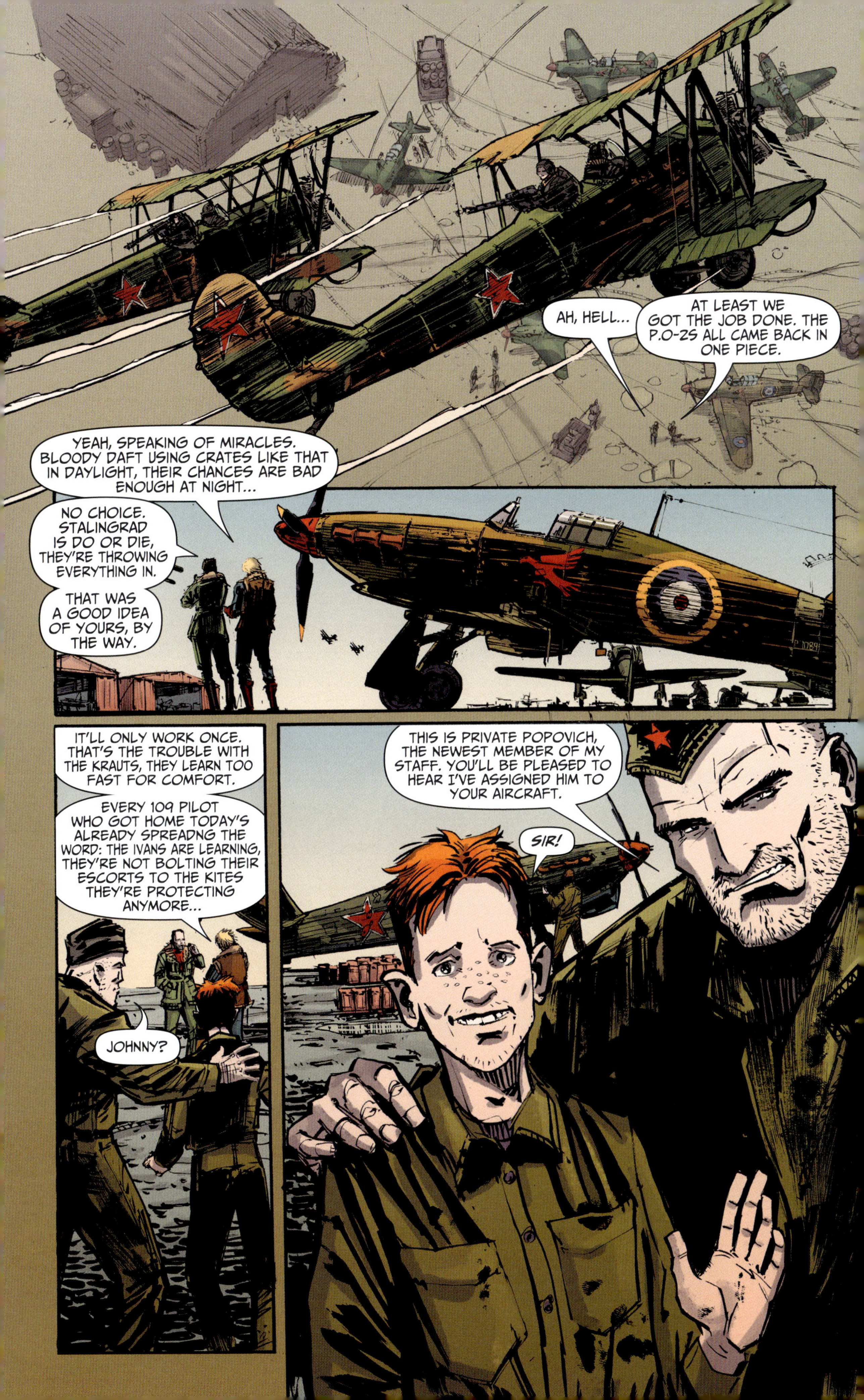
AH, HELL...
AT LEAST WE GOT THE JOB DONE. THE P.O-2S ALL CAME BACK IN ONE PIECE.
YEAH, SPEAKING OF MIRACLES. BLOODY DAFT USING CRATES LIKE THAT IN DAYLIGHT, THEIR CHANCES ARE BAD ENOUGH AT NIGHT...
NO CHOICE. STALINGRAD IS DO OR DIE, THEY'RE THROWING EVERYTHING IN.
THAT WAS A GOOD IDEA OF YOURS, BY THE WAY.
IT'LL ONLY WORK ONCE. THAT'S THE TROUBLE WITH THE KRAUTS, THEY LEARN TOO FAST FOR COMFORT.
EVERY 109 PILOT WHO GOT HOME TODAY'S ALREADY SPREADNG THE WORD: THE IVANS ARE LEARNING, THEY'RE NOT BOLTING THEIR ESCORTS TO THE KITES THEY'RE PROTECTING ANYMORE...
JOHNNY?
THIS IS PRIVATE POPOVICH, THE NEWEST MEMBER OF MY STAFF. YOU'LL BE PLEASED TO HEAR I'VE ASSIGNED HIM TO YOUR AIRCRAFT.
SIR!

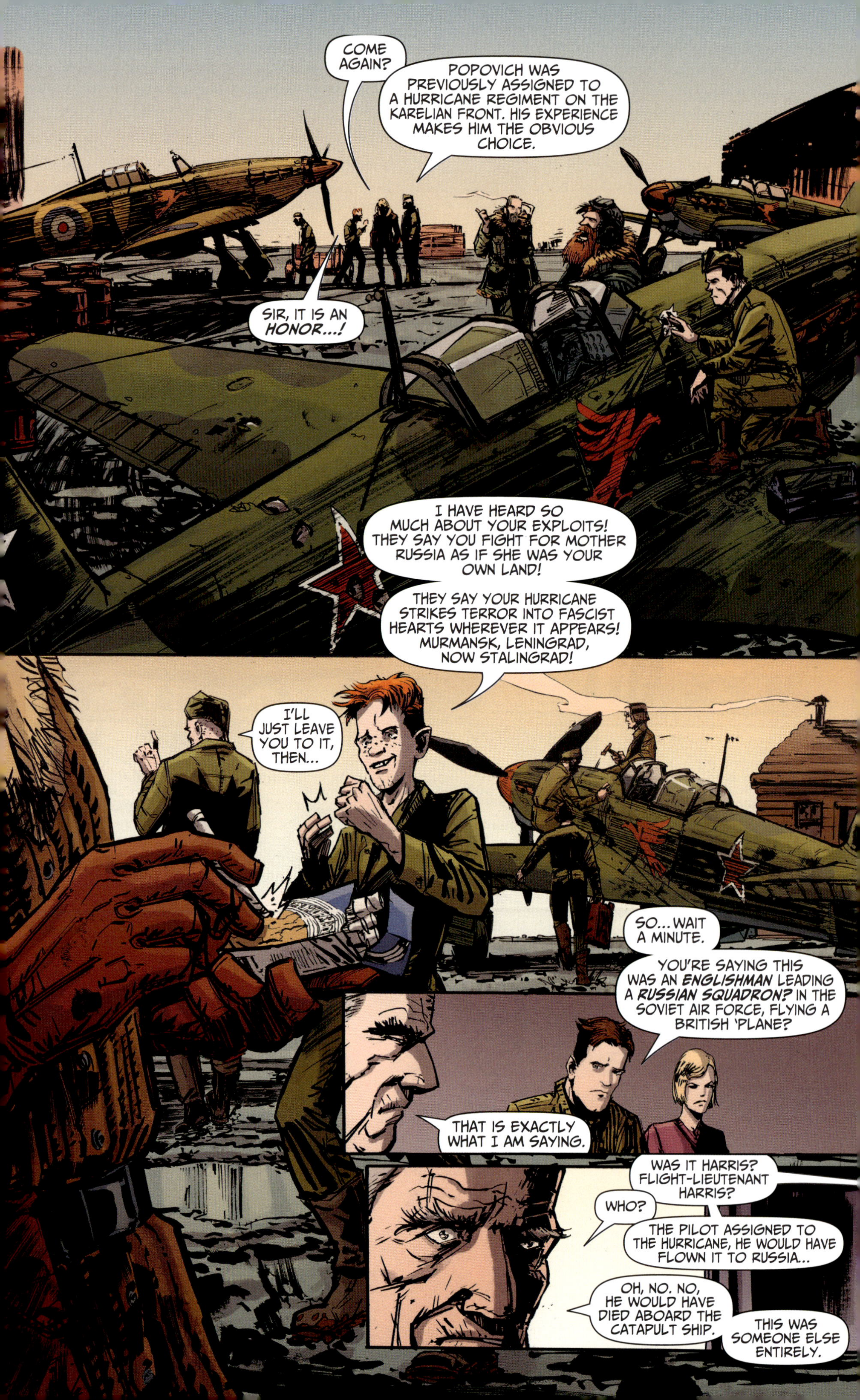
COME AGAIN?
POPOVICH WAS PREVIOUSLY ASSIGNED TO A HURRICANE REGIMENT ON THE KARELIAN FRONT. HIS EXPERIENCE MAKES HIM THE OBVIOUS CHOICE.
SIR, IT IS AN *HONOR...!*
I HAVE HEARD SO MUCH ABOUT YOUR EXPLOITS! THEY SAY YOU FIGHT FOR MOTHER RUSSIA AS IF SHE WAS YOUR OWN LAND!
THEY SAY YOUR HURRICANE STRIKES TERROR INTO FASCIST HEARTS WHEREVER IT APPEARS! MURMANSK, LENINGRAD, NOW STALINGRAD!
I'LL JUST LEAVE YOU TO IT, THEN...
SO... WAIT A MINUTE.
YOU'RE SAYING THIS WAS AN *ENGLISHMAN* LEADING A *RUSSIAN SQUADRON?* IN THE SOVIET AIR FORCE, FLYING A BRITISH 'PLANE?
THAT IS EXACTLY WHAT I AM SAYING.
WAS IT HARRIS? FLIGHT-LIEUTENANT HARRIS?
WHO?
THE PILOT ASSIGNED TO THE HURRICANE, HE WOULD HAVE FLOWN IT TO RUSSIA...
OH, NO. NO, HE WOULD HAVE DIED ABOARD THE CATAPULT SHIP.
THIS WAS SOMEONE ELSE ENTIRELY.

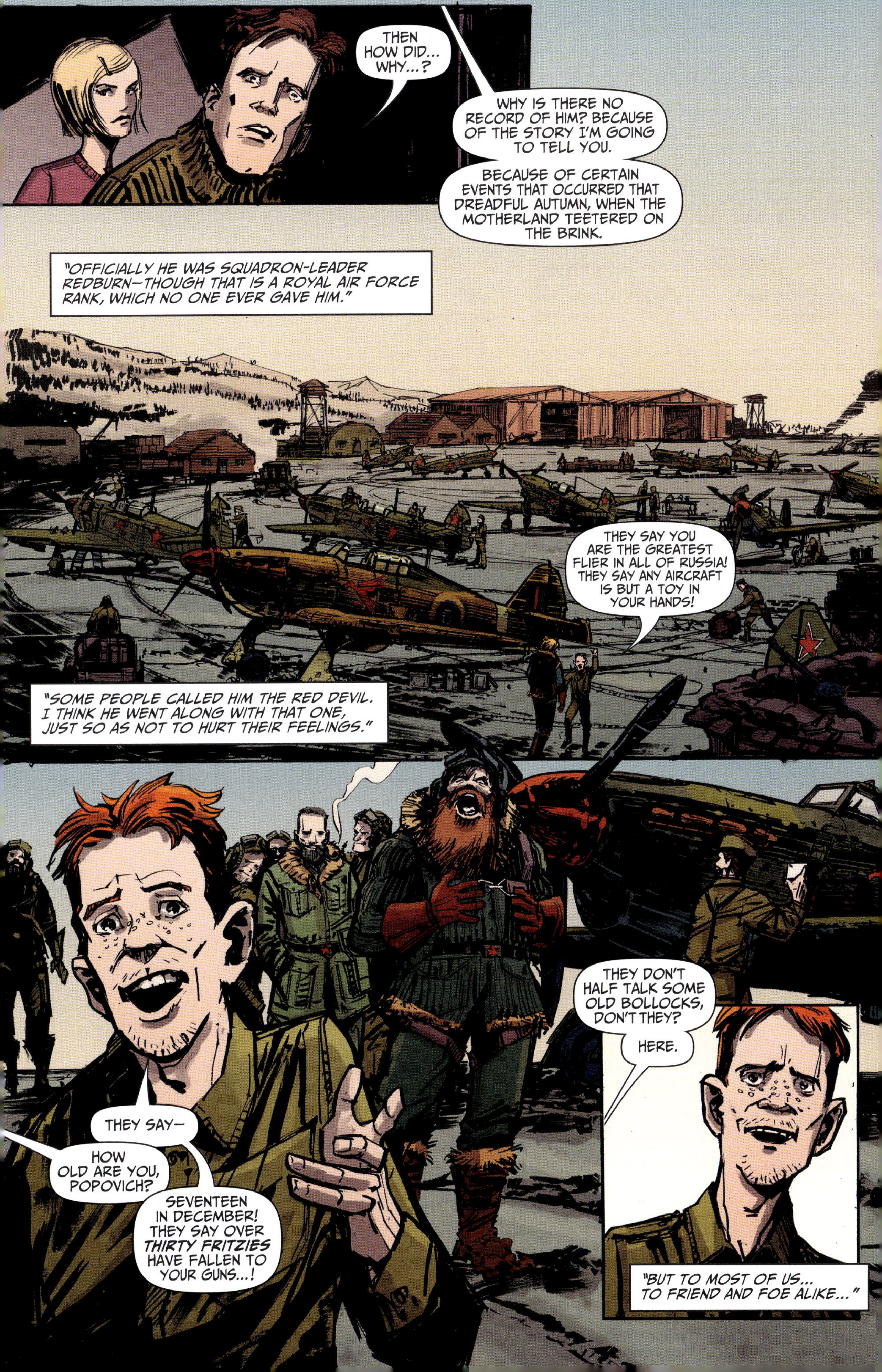
THEN HOW DID... WHY...?
WHY IS THERE NO RECORD OF HIM? BECAUSE OF THE STORY I'M GOING TO TELL YOU.
BECAUSE OF CERTAIN EVENTS THAT OCCURRED THAT DREADFUL AUTUMN, WHEN THE MOTHERLAND TEETERED ON THE BRINK.
"OFFICIALLY HE WAS SQUADRON-LEADER REDBURN—THOUGH THAT IS A ROYAL AIR FORCE RANK, WHICH NO ONE EVER GAVE HIM."
THEY SAY YOU ARE THE GREATEST FLIER IN ALL OF RUSSIA! THEY SAY ANY AIRCRAFT IS BUT A TOY IN YOUR HANDS!
"SOME PEOPLE CALLED HIM THE RED DEVIL. I THINK HE WENT ALONG WITH THAT ONE, JUST SO AS NOT TO HURT THEIR FEELINGS."
THEY SAY—
HOW OLD ARE YOU, POPOVICH?
SEVENTEEN IN DECEMBER! THEY SAY OVER *THIRTY FRITZIES* HAVE FALLEN TO YOUR GUNS...!
THEY DON'T HALF TALK SOME OLD BOLLOCKS, DON'T THEY?
HERE.
"BUT TO MOST OF US... TO FRIEND AND FOE ALIKE..."

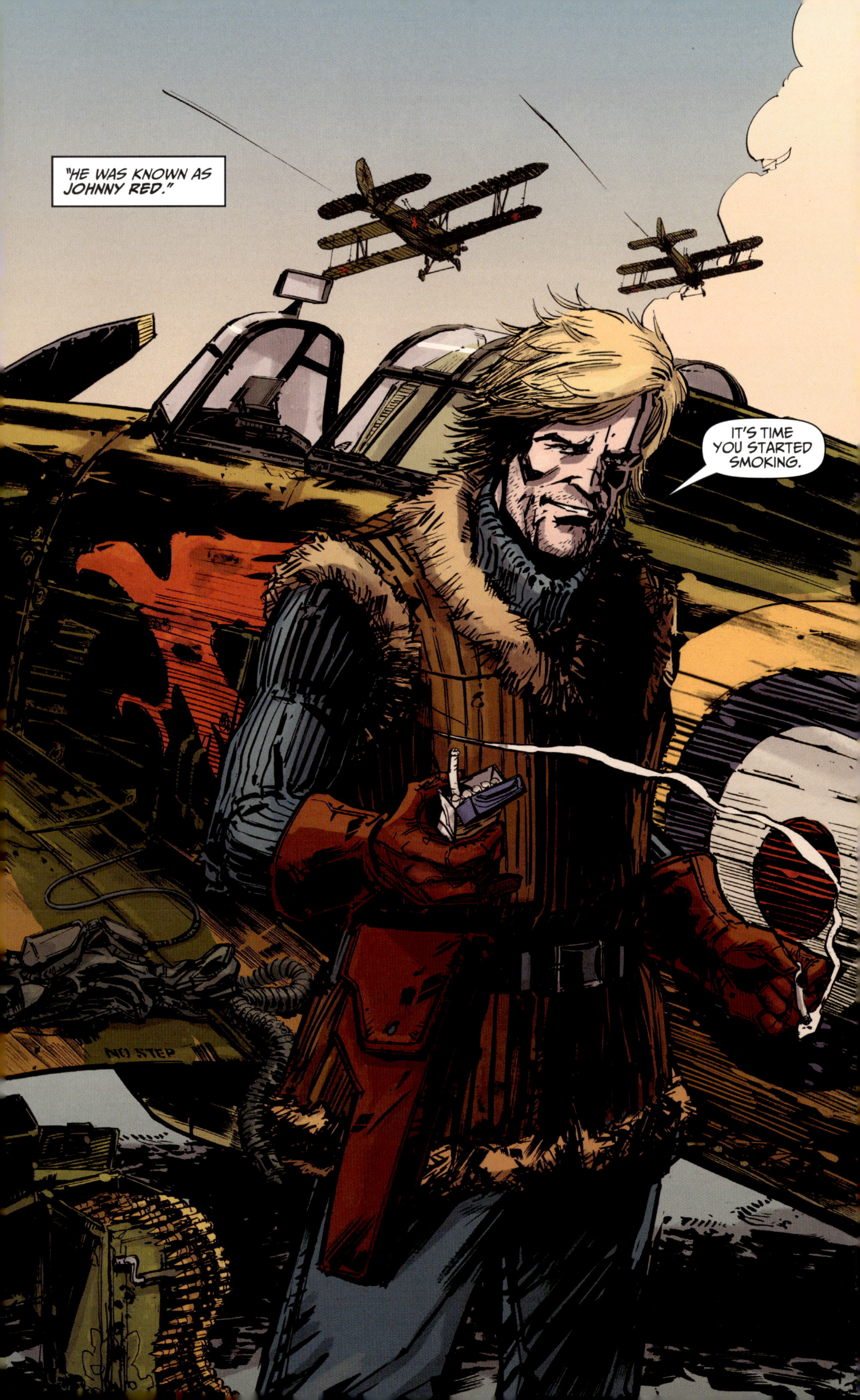
"HE WAS KNOWN AS JOHNNY RED."
IT'S TIME YOU STARTED SMOKING.
NO STEP

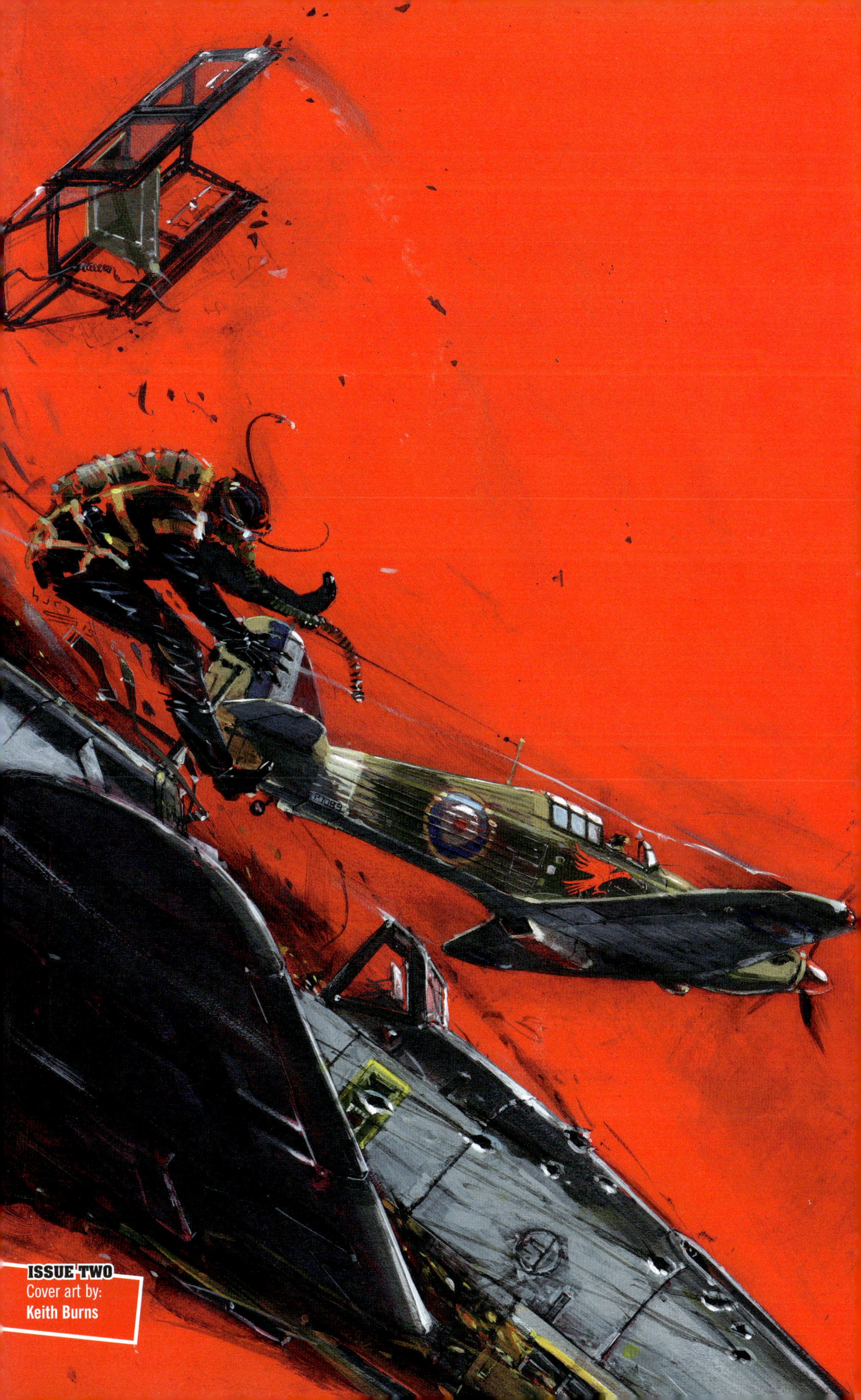

ISSUE TWO
Cover art by:
Keith Burns

VARIANT
Cover art by:
Ian Kennedy

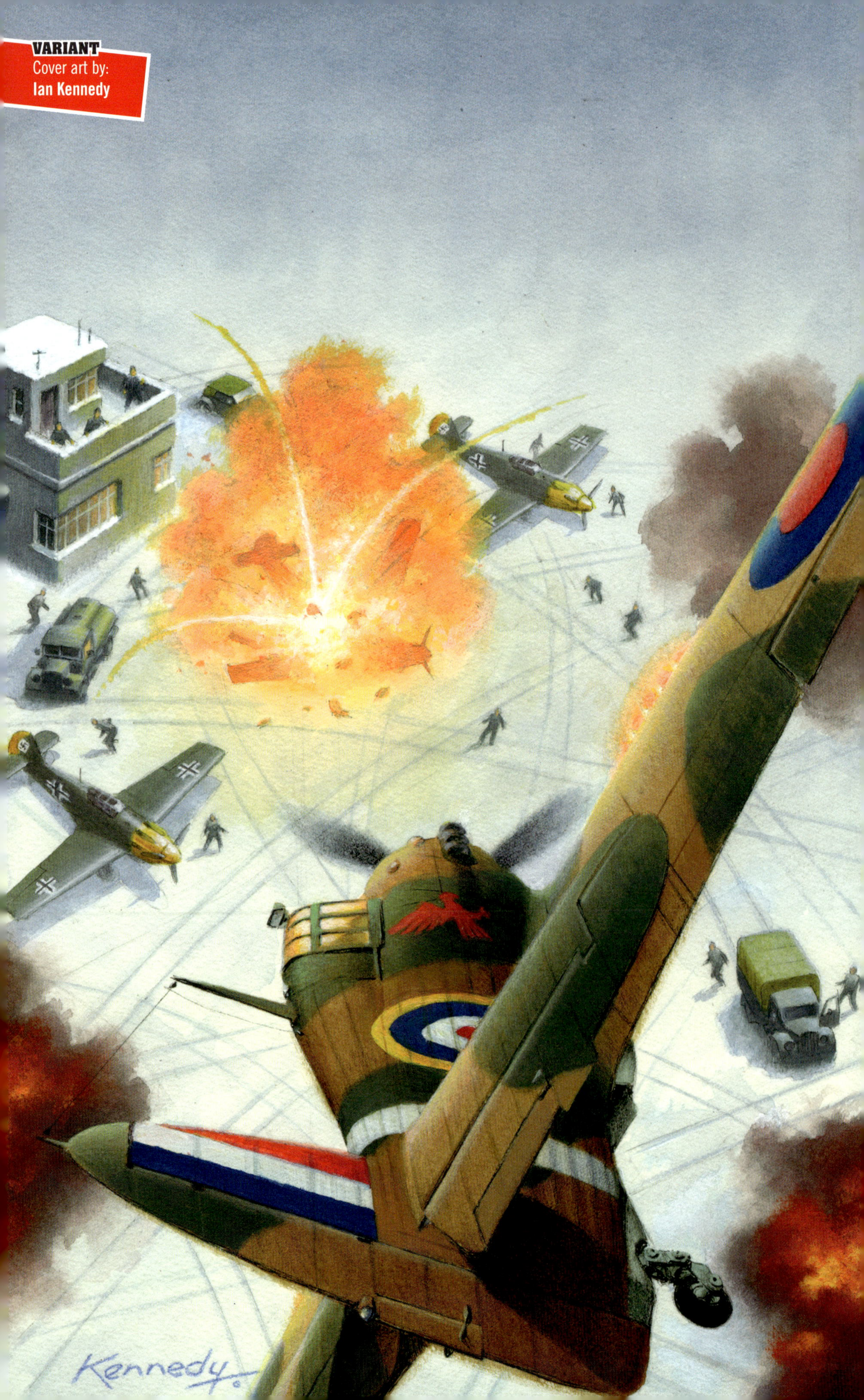
Kennedy

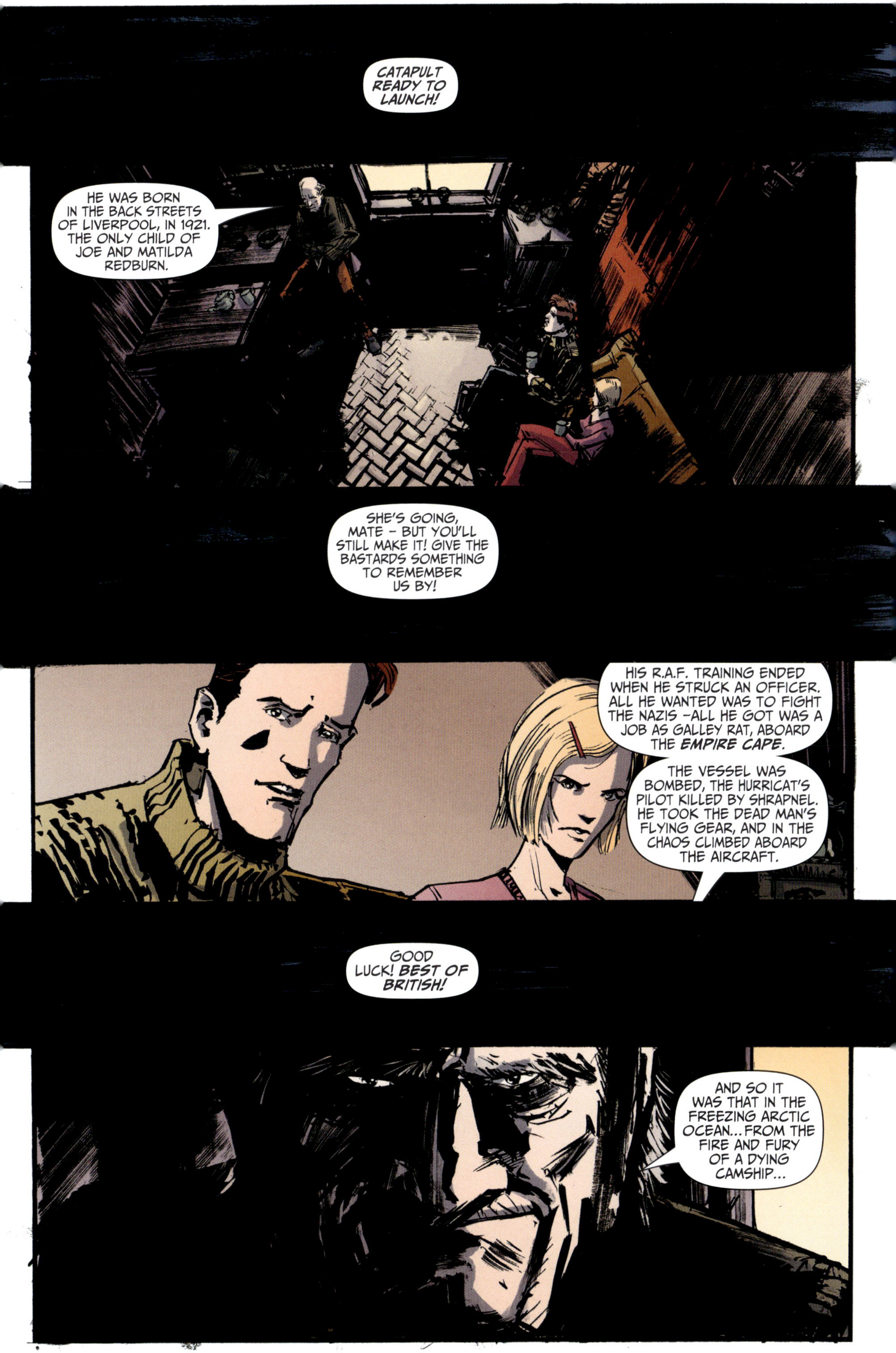
CATAPULT READY TO LAUNCH!
HE WAS BORN IN THE BACK STREETS OF LIVERPOOL, IN 1921. THE ONLY CHILD OF JOE AND MATILDA REDBURN.
SHE'S GOING, MATE – BUT YOU'LL STILL MAKE IT! GIVE THE BASTARDS SOMETHING TO REMEMBER US BY!
HIS R.A.F. TRAINING ENDED WHEN HE STRUCK AN OFFICER. ALL HE WANTED WAS TO FIGHT THE NAZIS –ALL HE GOT WAS A JOB AS GALLEY RAT, ABOARD THE EMPIRE CAPE.
THE VESSEL WAS BOMBED, THE HURRICAT'S PILOT KILLED BY SHRAPNEL. HE TOOK THE DEAD MAN'S FLYING GEAR, AND IN THE CHAOS CLIMBED ABOARD THE AIRCRAFT.
GOOD LUCK! BEST OF BRITISH!
AND SO IT WAS THAT IN THE FREEZING ARCTIC OCEAN...FROM THE FIRE AND FURY OF A DYING CAMSHIP...

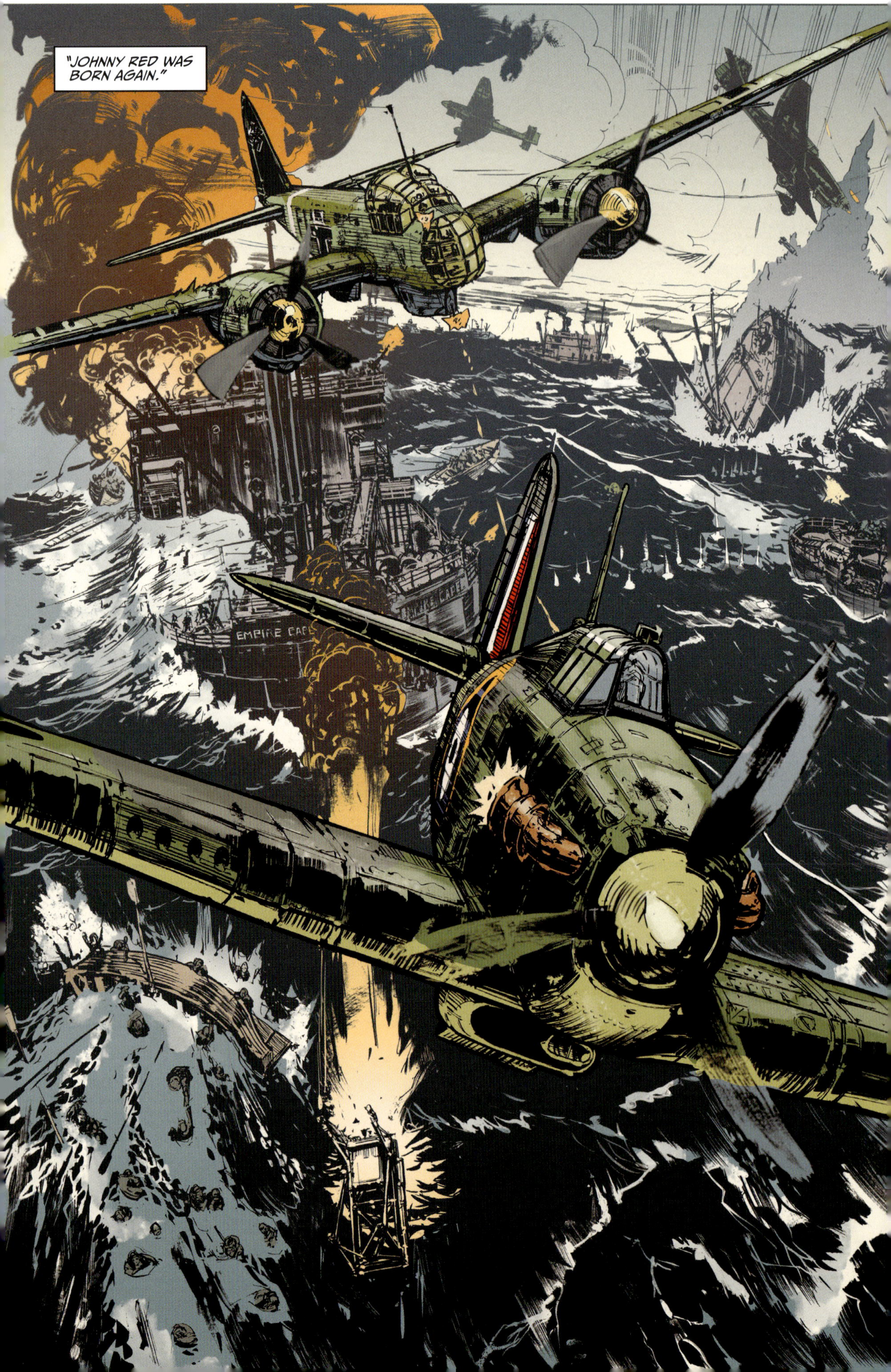
"JOHNNY RED WAS BORN AGAIN."
EMPIRE CAP

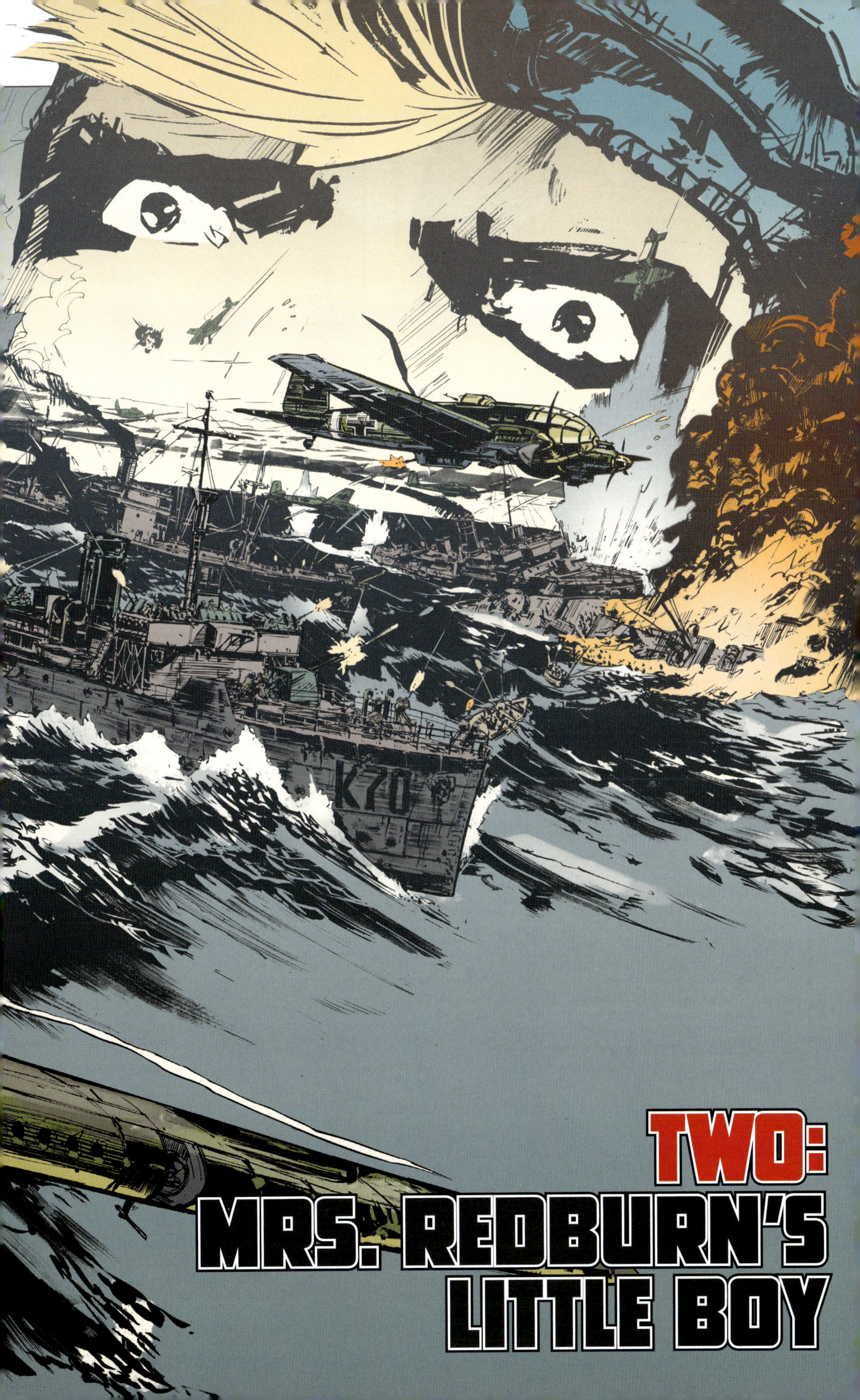

K70
TWO:
MRS. REDBURN'S
LITTLE BOY

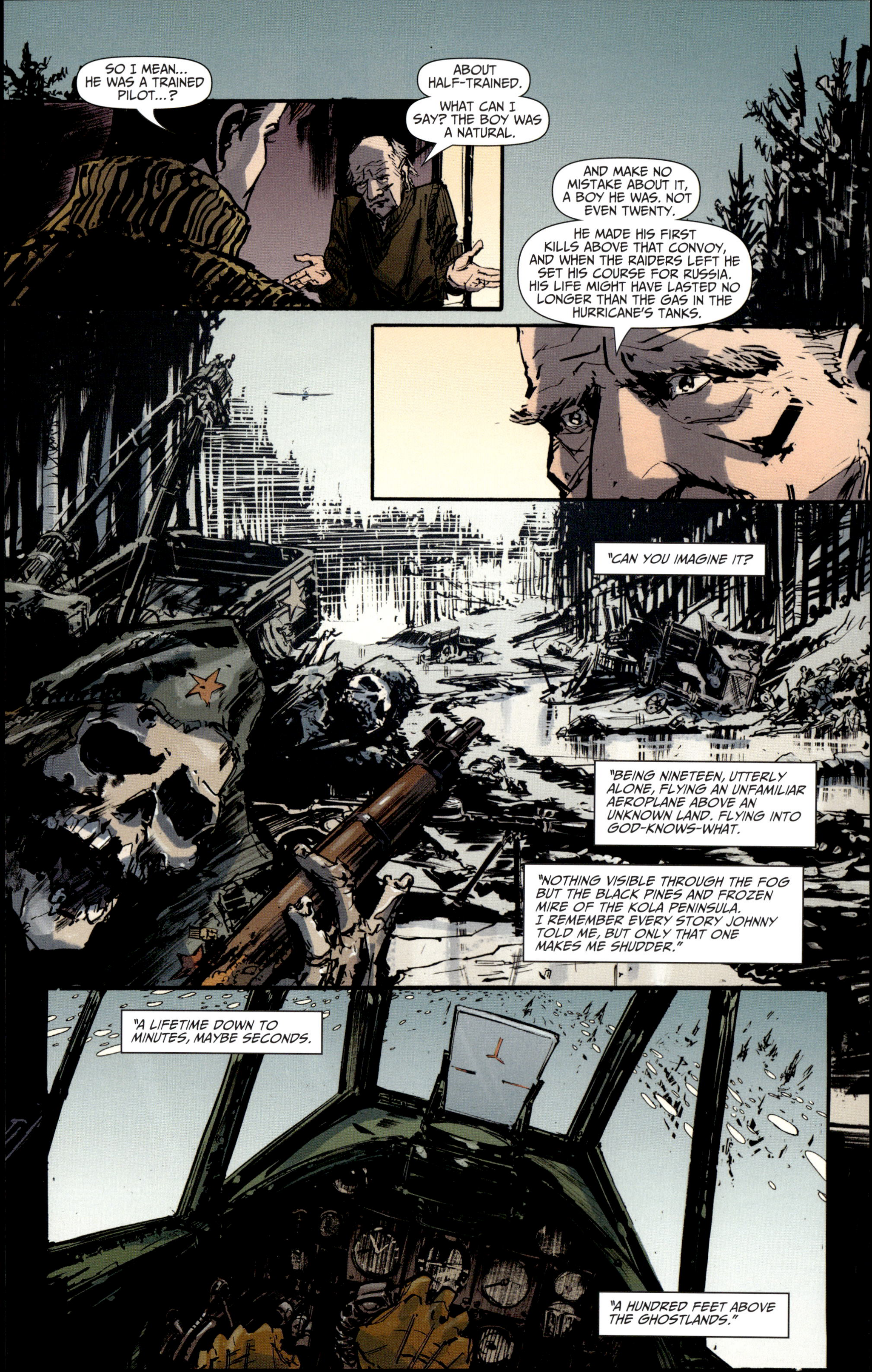
SO I MEAN... HE WAS A TRAINED PILOT...?
ABOUT HALF-TRAINED.
WHAT CAN I SAY? THE BOY WAS A NATURAL.
AND MAKE NO MISTAKE ABOUT IT, A BOY HE WAS. NOT EVEN TWENTY.
HE MADE HIS FIRST KILLS ABOVE THAT CONVOY, AND WHEN THE RAIDERS LEFT HE SET HIS COURSE FOR RUSSIA. HIS LIFE MIGHT HAVE LASTED NO LONGER THAN THE GAS IN THE HURRICANE'S TANKS.
"CAN YOU IMAGINE IT?
"BEING NINETEEN, UTTERLY ALONE, FLYING AN UNFAMILIAR AEROPLANE ABOVE AN UNKNOWN LAND. FLYING INTO GOD-KNOWS-WHAT.
"NOTHING VISIBLE THROUGH THE FOG BUT THE BLACK PINES AND FROZEN MIRE OF THE KOLA PENINSULA. I REMEMBER EVERY STORY JOHNNY TOLD ME, BUT ONLY THAT ONE MAKES ME SHUDDER."
"A LIFETIME DOWN TO MINUTES, MAYBE SECONDS.
"A HUNDRED FEET ABOVE THE GHOSTLANDS."

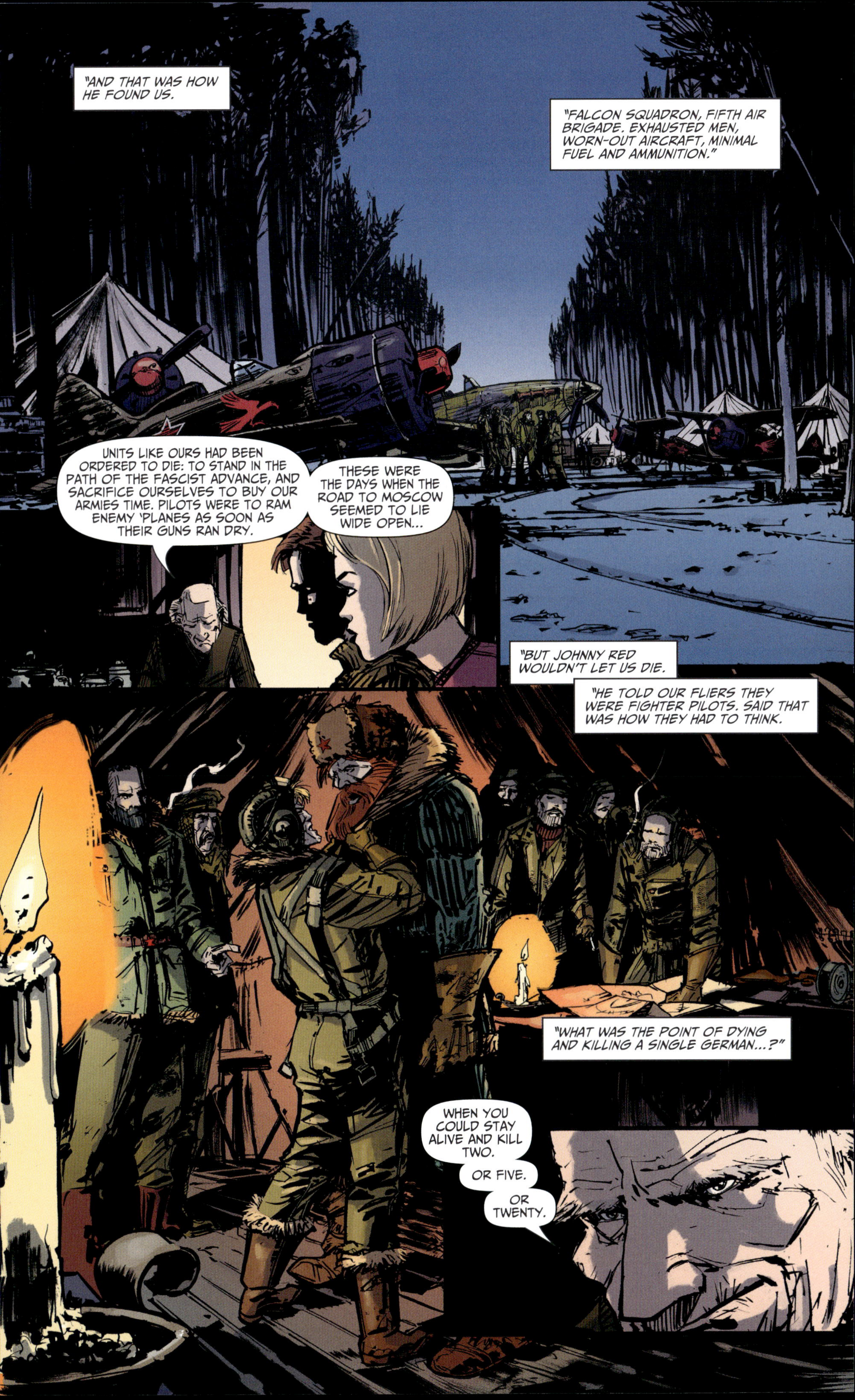

"AND THAT WAS HOW HE FOUND US.
"FALCON SQUADRON, FIFTH AIR BRIGADE. EXHAUSTED MEN, WORN-OUT AIRCRAFT, MINIMAL FUEL AND AMMUNITION."
UNITS LIKE OURS HAD BEEN ORDERED TO DIE: TO STAND IN THE PATH OF THE FASCIST ADVANCE, AND SACRIFICE OURSELVES TO BUY OUR ARMIES TIME. PILOTS WERE TO RAM ENEMY 'PLANES AS SOON AS THEIR GUNS RAN DRY.
THESE WERE THE DAYS WHEN THE ROAD TO MOSCOW SEEMED TO LIE WIDE OPEN...
"BUT JOHNNY RED WOULDN'T LET US DIE.
"HE TOLD OUR FLIERS THEY WERE FIGHTER PILOTS. SAID THAT WAS HOW THEY HAD TO THINK.
"WHAT WAS THE POINT OF DYING AND KILLING A SINGLE GERMAN...?"
WHEN YOU COULD STAY ALIVE AND KILL TWO.
OR FIVE.
OR TWENTY.

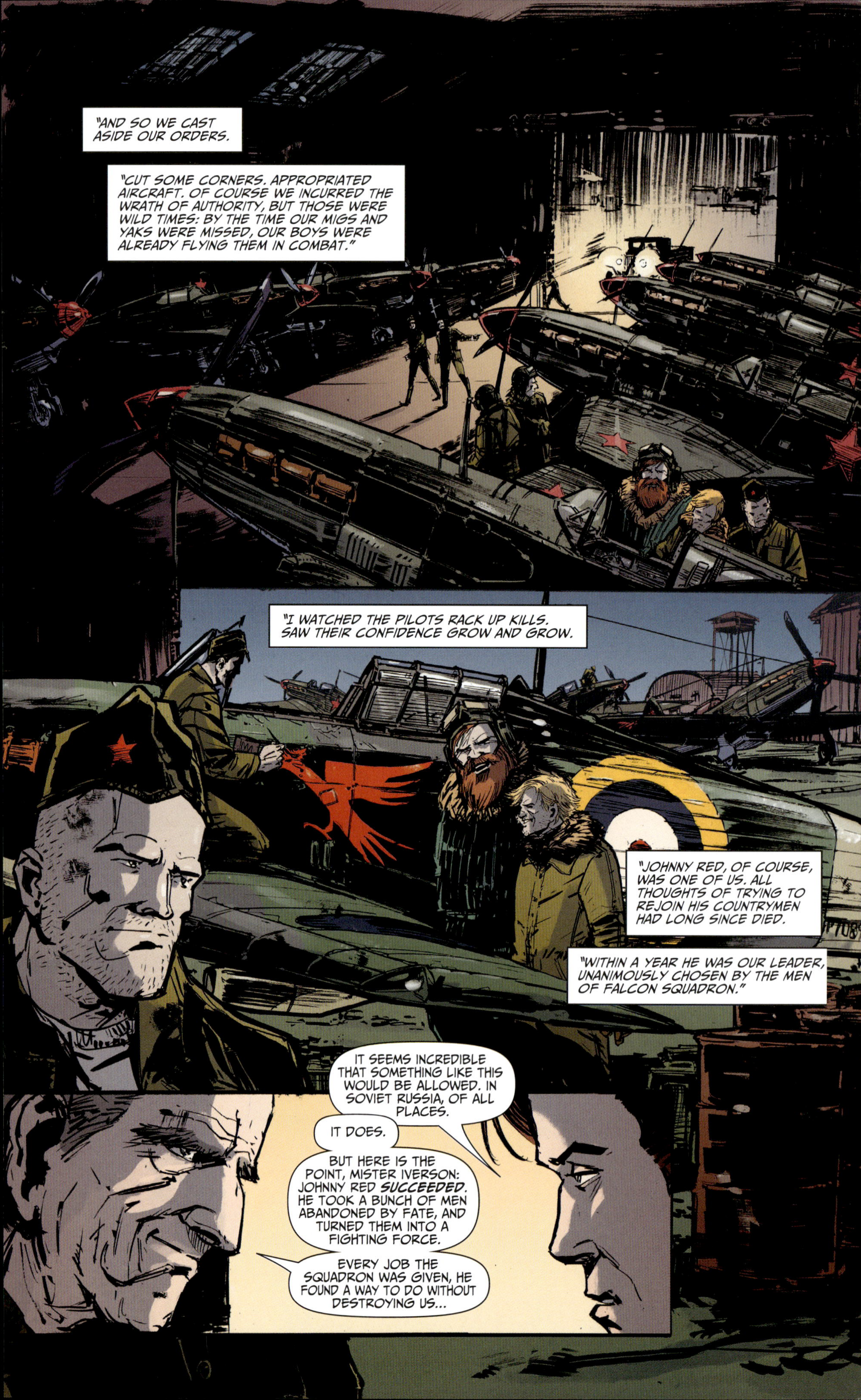
"AND SO WE CAST ASIDE OUR ORDERS.
"CUT SOME CORNERS. APPROPRIATED AIRCRAFT. OF COURSE WE INCURRED THE WRATH OF AUTHORITY, BUT THOSE WERE WILD TIMES: BY THE TIME OUR MIGS AND YAKS WERE MISSED, OUR BOYS WERE ALREADY FLYING THEM IN COMBAT."
"I WATCHED THE PILOTS RACK UP KILLS. SAW THEIR CONFIDENCE GROW AND GROW.
"JOHNNY RED, OF COURSE, WAS ONE OF US. ALL THOUGHTS OF TRYING TO REJOIN HIS COUNTRYMEN HAD LONG SINCE DIED.
"WITHIN A YEAR HE WAS OUR LEADER, UNANIMOUSLY CHOSEN BY THE MEN OF FALCON SQUADRON."
IT SEEMS INCREDIBLE THAT SOMETHING LIKE THIS WOULD BE ALLOWED. IN SOVIET RUSSIA, OF ALL PLACES.
IT DOES.
BUT HERE IS THE POINT, MISTER IVERSON: JOHNNY RED *SUCCEEDED*. HE TOOK A BUNCH OF MEN ABANDONED BY FATE, AND TURNED THEM INTO A FIGHTING FORCE.
EVERY JOB THE SQUADRON WAS GIVEN, HE FOUND A WAY TO DO WITHOUT DESTROYING US...

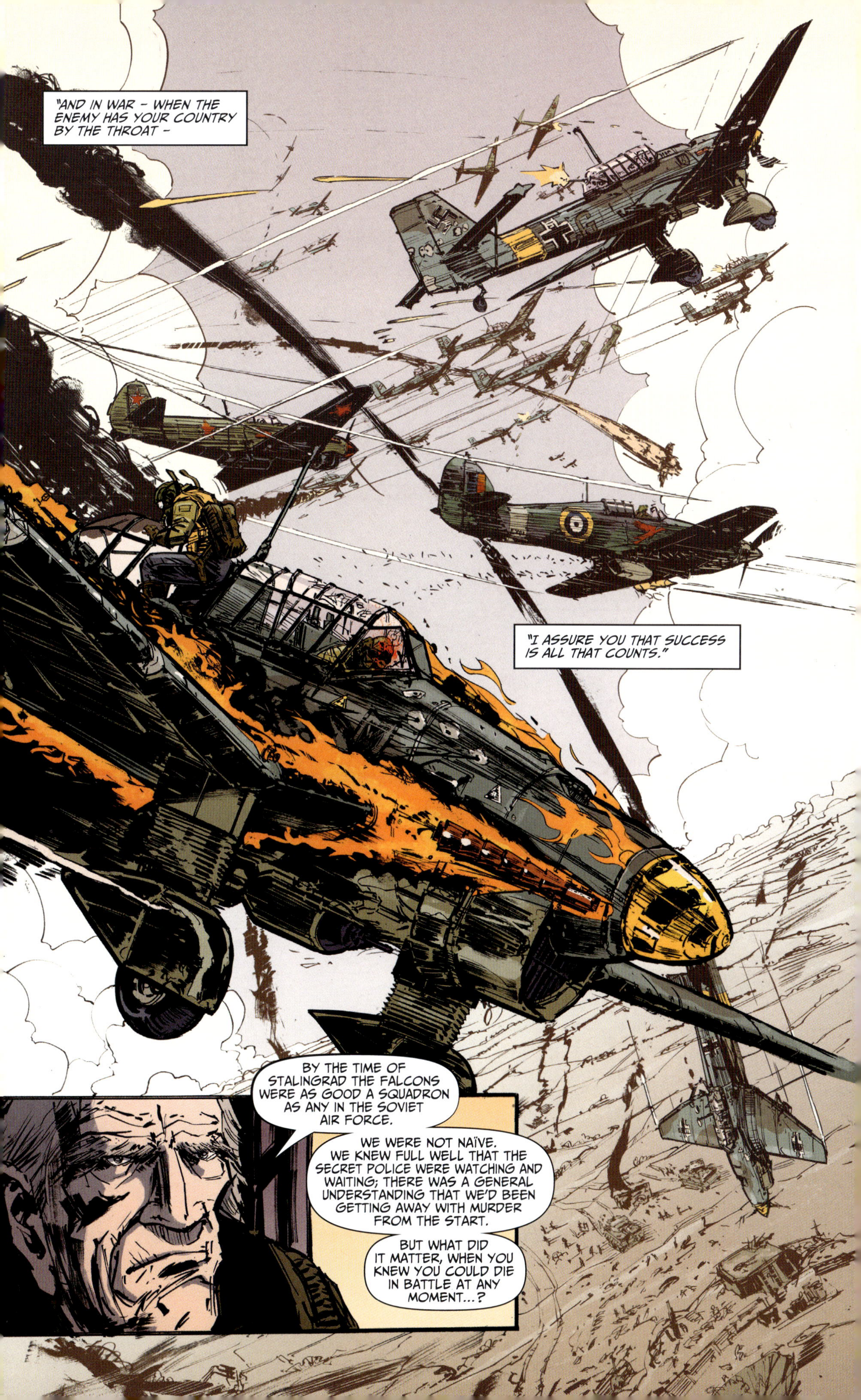
"AND IN WAR – WHEN THE ENEMY HAS YOUR COUNTRY BY THE THROAT –
"I ASSURE YOU THAT SUCCESS IS ALL THAT COUNTS."
BY THE TIME OF STALINGRAD THE FALCONS WERE AS GOOD A SQUADRON AS ANY IN THE SOVIET AIR FORCE.
WE WERE NOT NAÏVE. WE KNEW FULL WELL THAT THE SECRET POLICE WERE WATCHING AND WAITING; THERE WAS A GENERAL UNDERSTANDING THAT WE'D BEEN GETTING AWAY WITH MURDER FROM THE START.
BUT WHAT DID IT MATTER, WHEN YOU KNEW YOU COULD DIE IN BATTLE AT ANY MOMENT...?

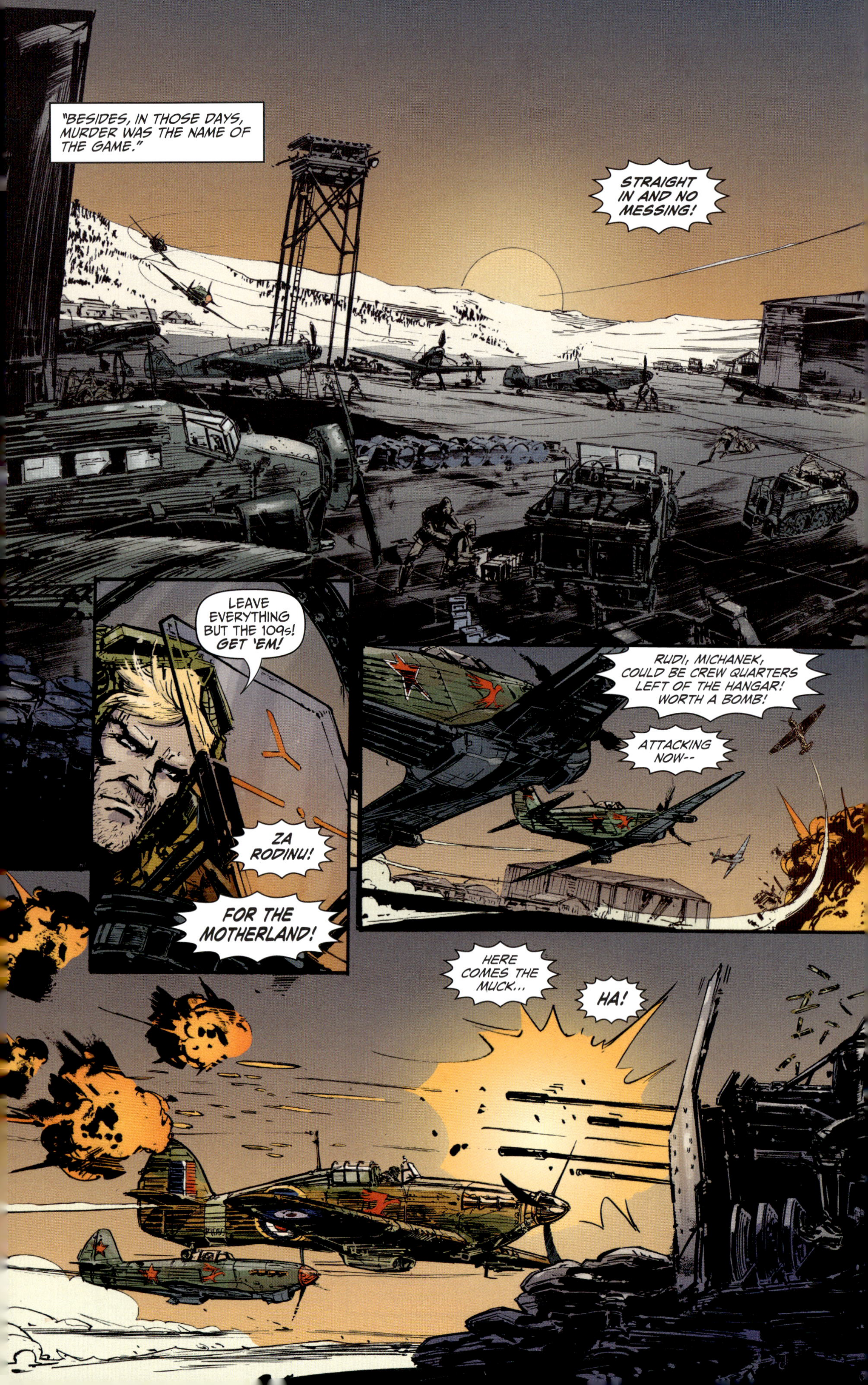
"BESIDES, IN THOSE DAYS, MURDER WAS THE NAME OF THE GAME."
STRAIGHT IN AND NO MESSING!
LEAVE EVERYTHING BUT THE 109s! GET 'EM!
ZA RODINU!
FOR THE MOTHERLAND!
RUDI, MICHANEK, COULD BE CREW QUARTERS LEFT OF THE HANGAR! WORTH A BOMB!
ATTACKING NOW--
HERE COMES THE MUCK...
HA!

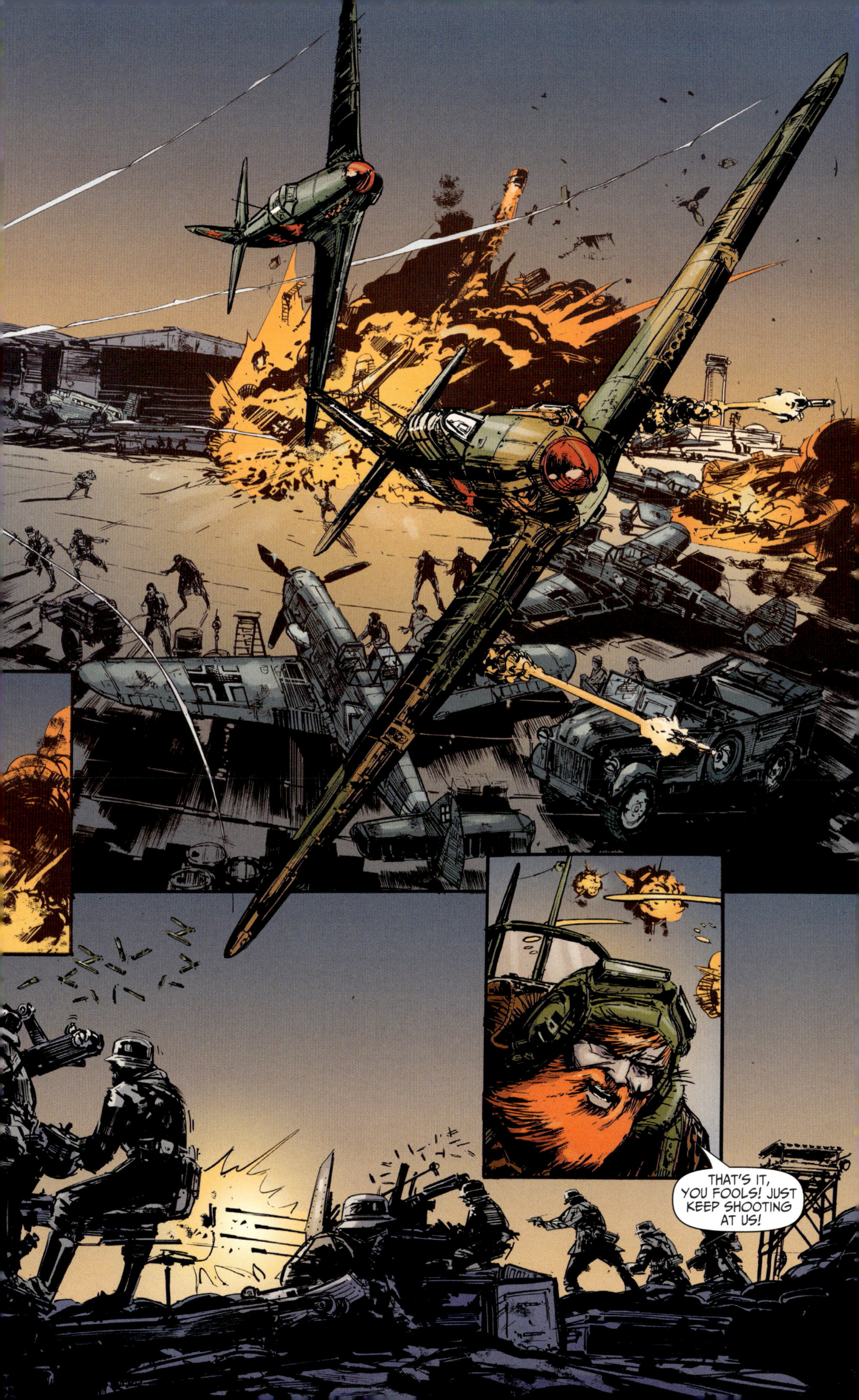
THAT'S IT, YOU FOOLS! JUST KEEP SHOOTING AT US!

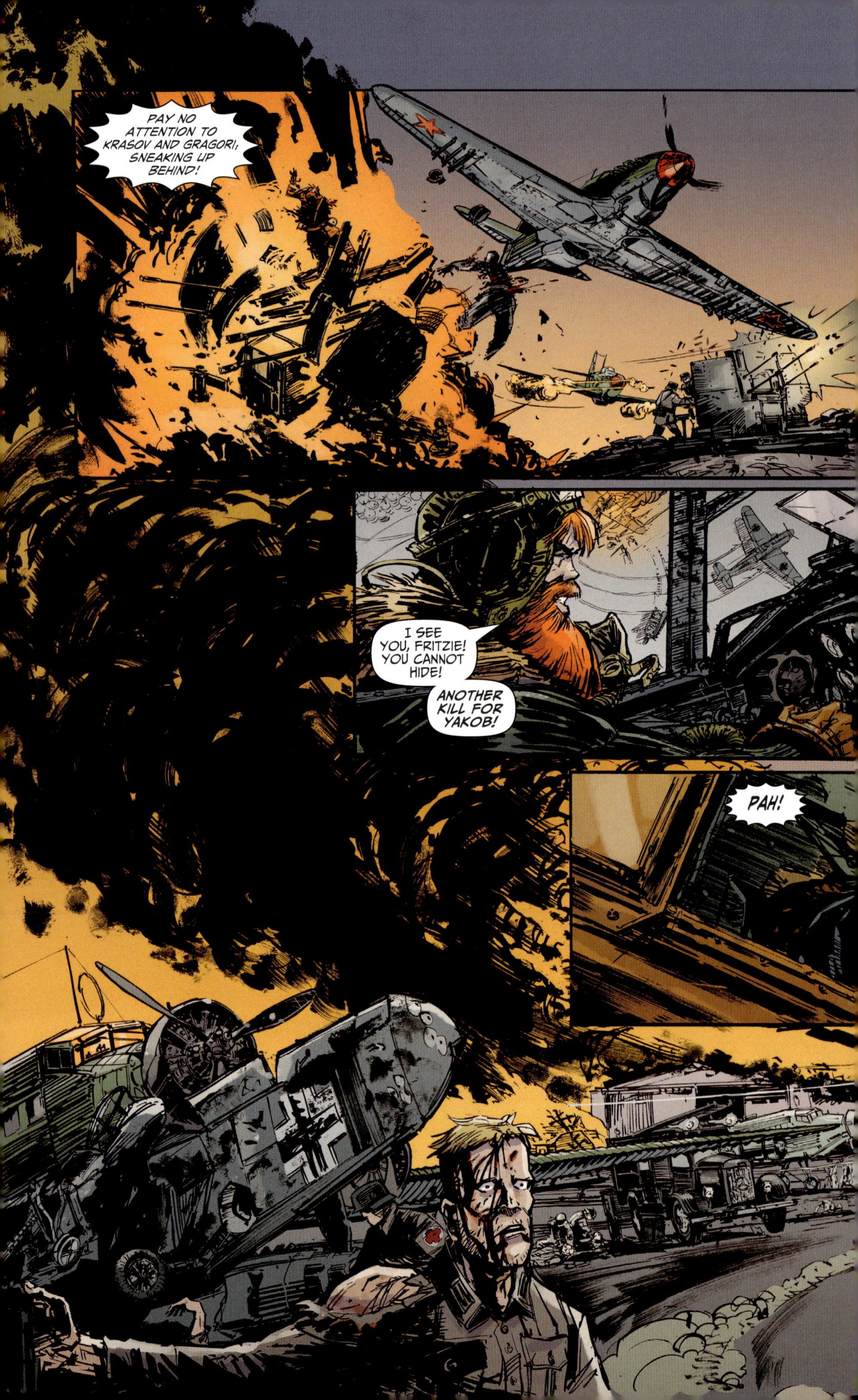
PAY NO ATTENTION TO KRASOV AND GRAGORI, SNEAKING UP BEHIND!
I SEE YOU, FRITZIE! YOU CANNOT HIDE!
ANOTHER KILL FOR YAKOB!
PAH!

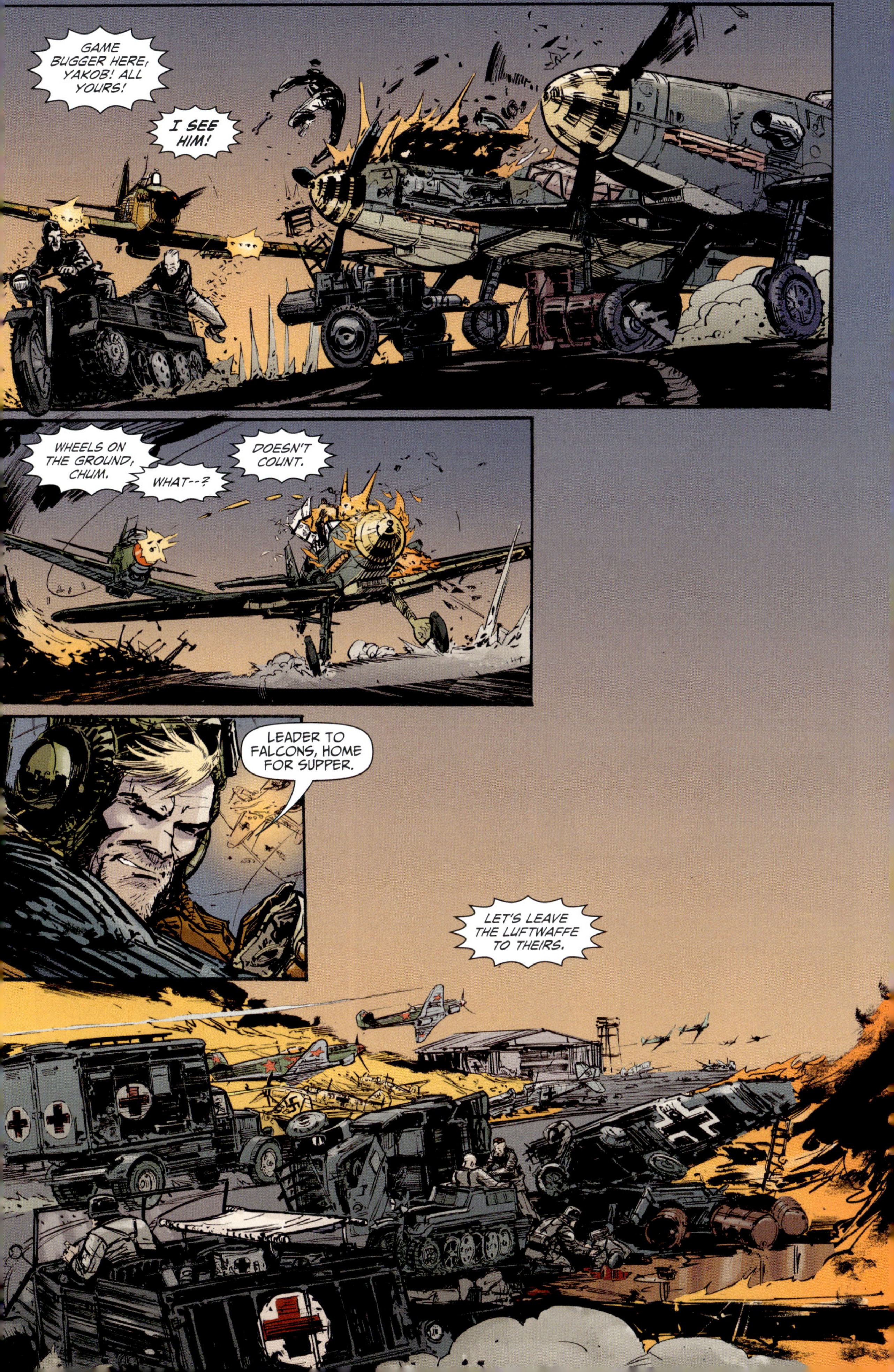
GAME BUGGER HERE, YAKOB! ALL YOURS!
I SEE HIM!
WHEELS ON THE GROUND, CHUM.
WHAT--?
DOESN'T COUNT.
LEADER TO FALCONS, HOME FOR SUPPER.
LET'S LEAVE THE LUFTWAFFE TO THEIRS.

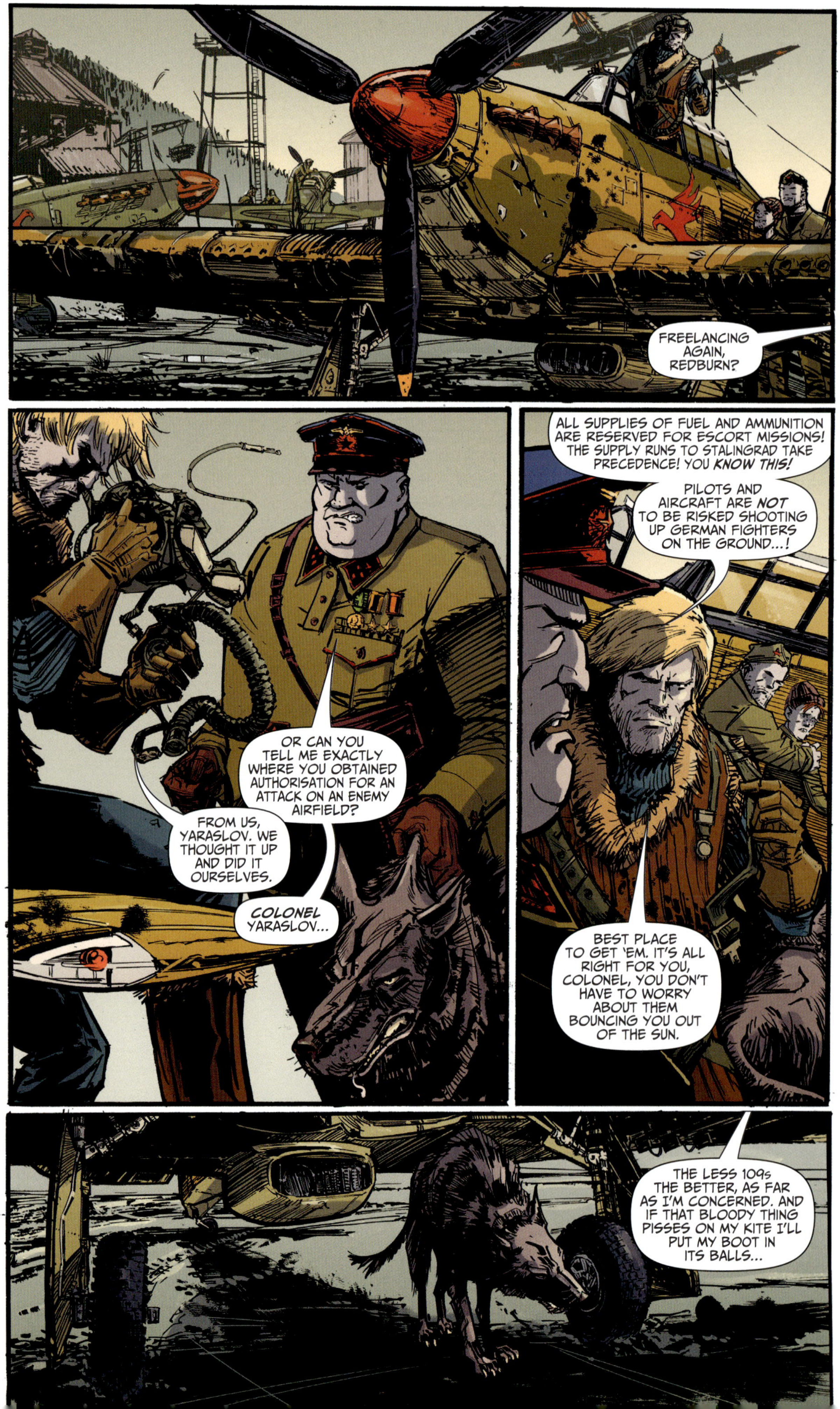
FREELANCING AGAIN, REDBURN?
OR CAN YOU TELL ME EXACTLY WHERE YOU OBTAINED AUTHORISATION FOR AN ATTACK ON AN ENEMY AIRFIELD?
FROM US, YARASLOV. WE THOUGHT IT UP AND DID IT OURSELVES.
COLONEL YARASLOV...
ALL SUPPLIES OF FUEL AND AMMUNITION ARE RESERVED FOR ESCORT MISSIONS! THE SUPPLY RUNS TO STALINGRAD TAKE PRECEDENCE! YOU KNOW THIS!
PILOTS AND AIRCRAFT ARE NOT TO BE RISKED SHOOTING UP GERMAN FIGHTERS ON THE GROUND...!
BEST PLACE TO GET 'EM. IT'S ALL RIGHT FOR YOU, COLONEL, YOU DON'T HAVE TO WORRY ABOUT THEM BOUNCING YOU OUT OF THE SUN.
THE LESS 109s THE BETTER, AS FAR AS I'M CONCERNED. AND IF THAT BLOODY THING PISSES ON MY KITE I'LL PUT MY BOOT IN ITS BALLS...

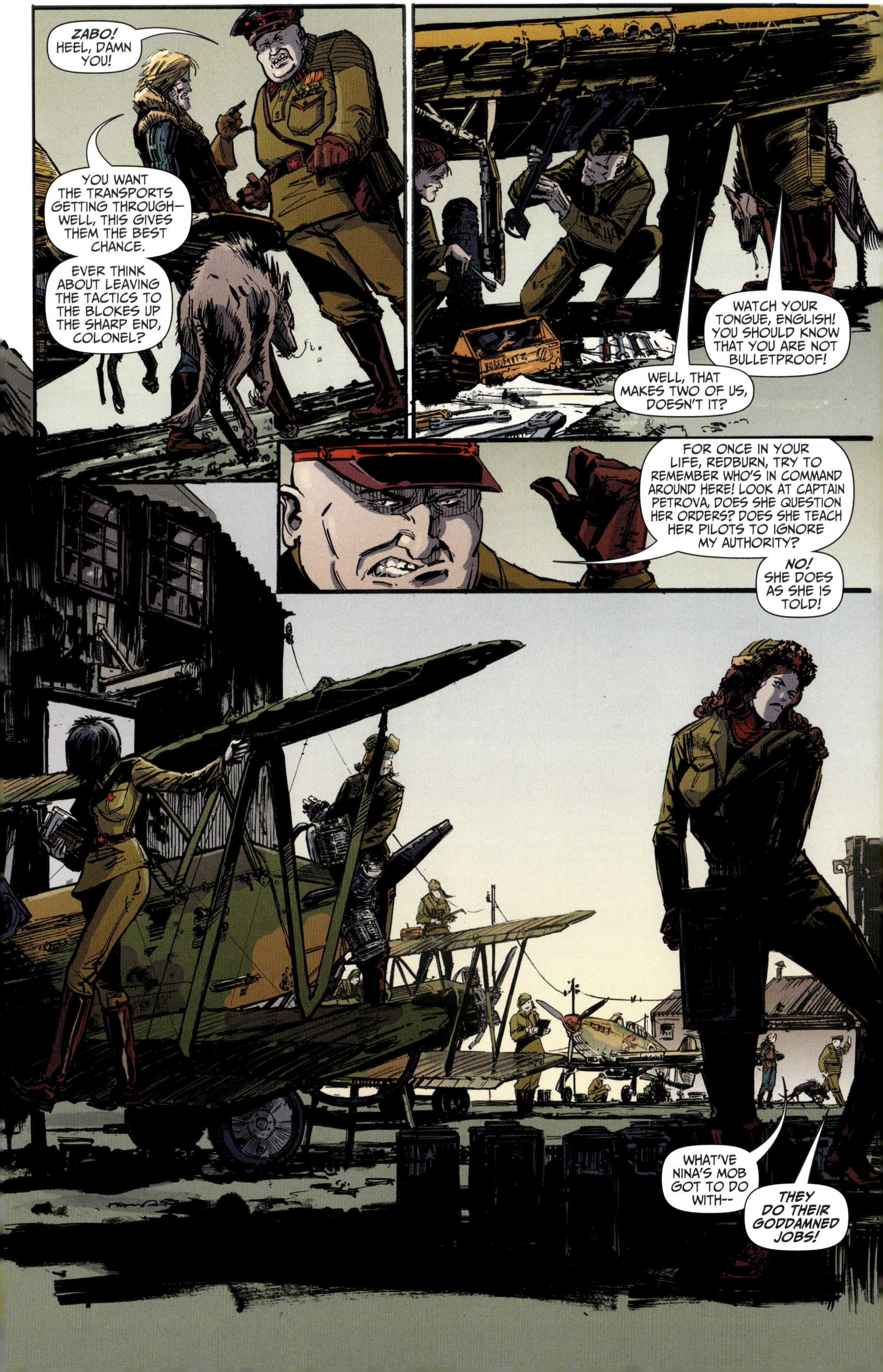
ZABO! HEEL, DAMN YOU!
YOU WANT THE TRANSPORTS GETTING THROUGH— WELL, THIS GIVES THEM THE BEST CHANCE.
EVER THINK ABOUT LEAVING THE TACTICS TO THE BLOKES UP THE SHARP END, COLONEL?
WATCH YOUR TONGUE, ENGLISH! YOU SHOULD KNOW THAT YOU ARE NOT BULLETPROOF!
WELL, THAT MAKES TWO OF US, DOESN'T IT?
FOR ONCE IN YOUR LIFE, REDBURN, TRY TO REMEMBER WHO'S IN COMMAND AROUND HERE! LOOK AT CAPTAIN PETROVA, DOES SHE QUESTION HER ORDERS? DOES SHE TEACH HER PILOTS TO IGNORE MY AUTHORITY?
NO! SHE DOES AS SHE IS TOLD!
WHAT'VE NINA'S MOB GOT TO DO WITH--
THEY DO THEIR GODDAMNED JOBS!

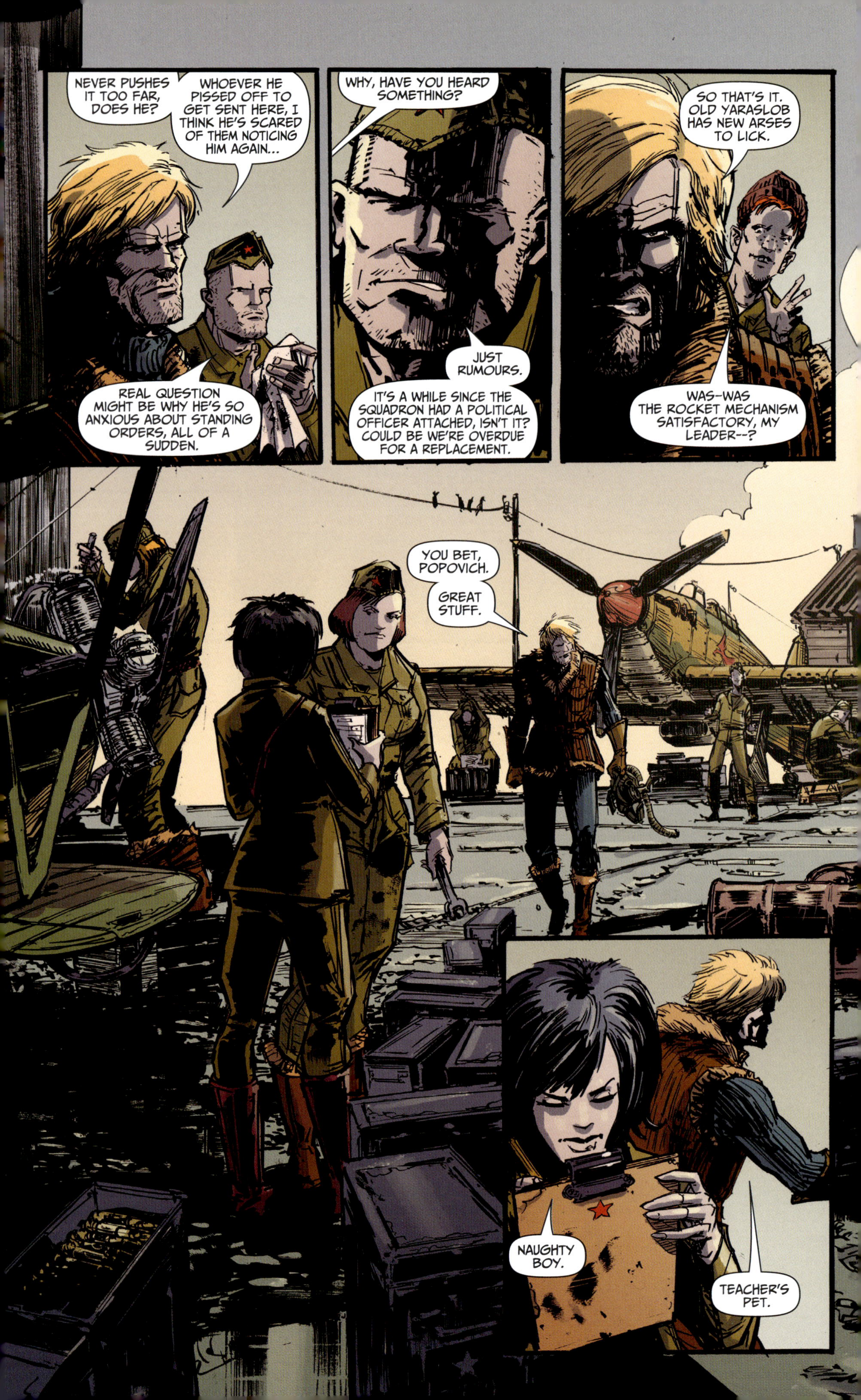
NEVER PUSHES IT TOO FAR, DOES HE?
WHOEVER HE PISSED OFF TO GET SENT HERE, I THINK HE'S SCARED OF THEM NOTICING HIM AGAIN...
REAL QUESTION MIGHT BE WHY HE'S SO ANXIOUS ABOUT STANDING ORDERS, ALL OF A SUDDEN.
WHY, HAVE YOU HEARD SOMETHING?
JUST RUMOURS.
IT'S A WHILE SINCE THE SQUADRON HAD A POLITICAL OFFICER ATTACHED, ISN'T IT? COULD BE WE'RE OVERDUE FOR A REPLACEMENT.
SO THAT'S IT. OLD YARASLOB HAS NEW ARSES TO LICK.
WAS-WAS THE ROCKET MECHANISM SATISFACTORY, MY LEADER--?
YOU BET, POPOVICH.
GREAT STUFF.
NAUGHTY BOY.
TEACHER'S PET.

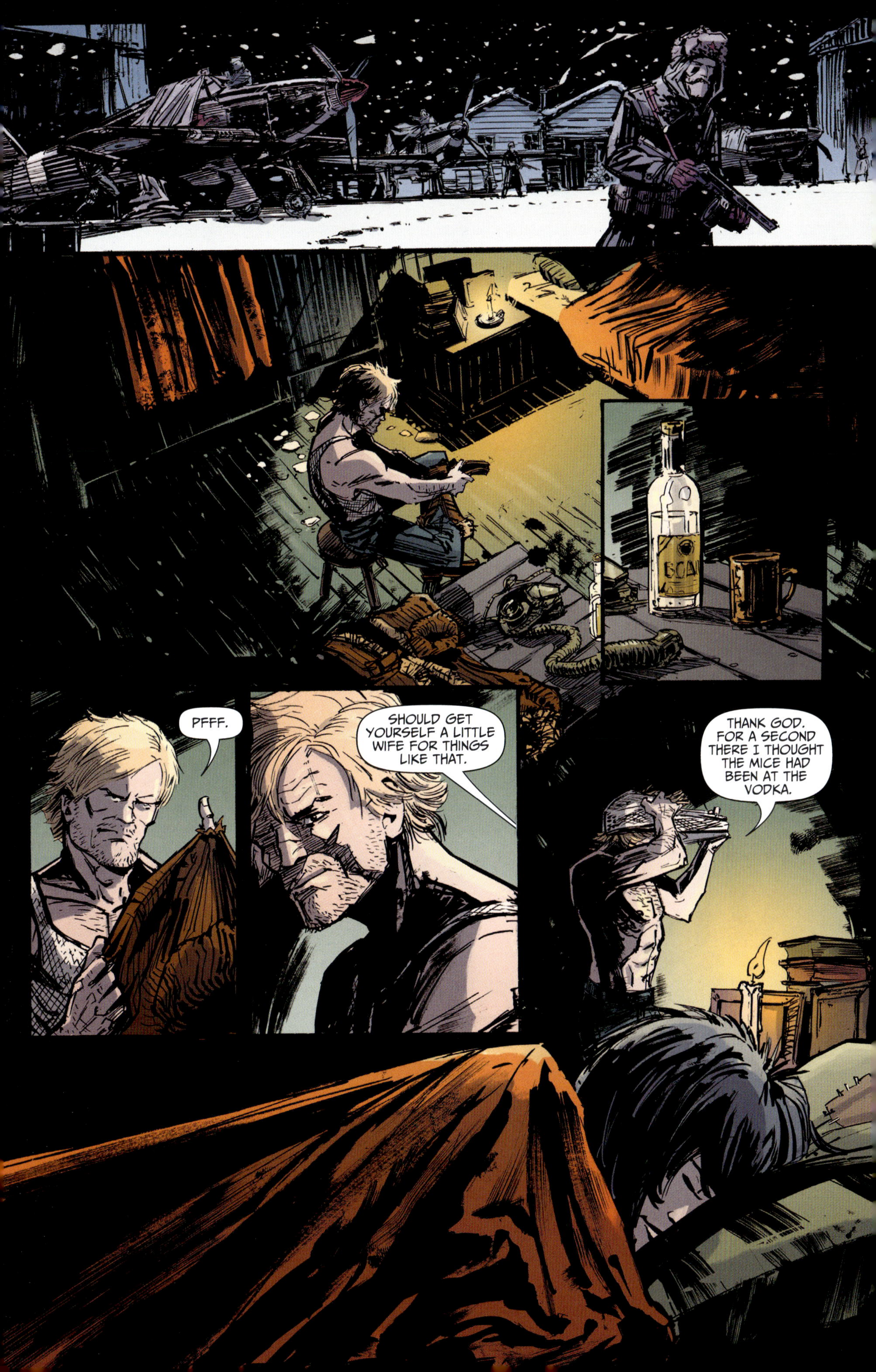
PFFF.
SHOULD GET YOURSELF A LITTLE WIFE FOR THINGS LIKE THAT.
THANK GOD. FOR A SECOND THERE I THOUGHT THE MICE HAD BEEN AT THE VODKA.

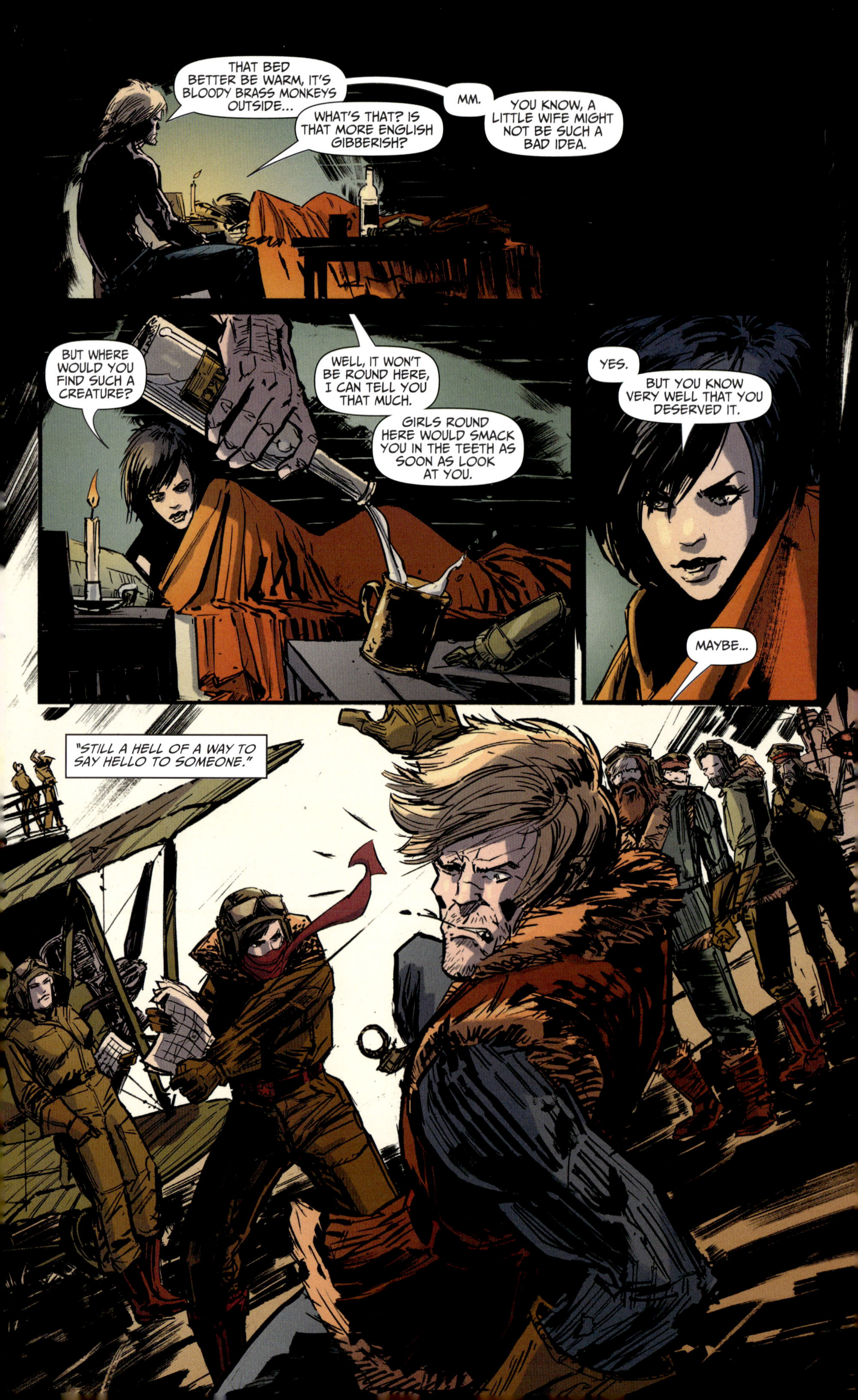

THAT BED BETTER BE WARM, IT'S BLOODY BRASS MONKEYS OUTSIDE...
WHAT'S THAT? IS THAT MORE ENGLISH GIBBERISH?
MM.
YOU KNOW, A LITTLE WIFE MIGHT NOT BE SUCH A BAD IDEA.
BUT WHERE WOULD YOU FIND SUCH A CREATURE?
WELL, IT WON'T BE ROUND HERE, I CAN TELL YOU THAT MUCH.
GIRLS ROUND HERE WOULD SMACK YOU IN THE TEETH AS SOON AS LOOK AT YOU.
YES.
BUT YOU KNOW VERY WELL THAT YOU DESERVED IT.
MAYBE...
"STILL A HELL OF A WAY TO SAY HELLO TO SOMEONE."

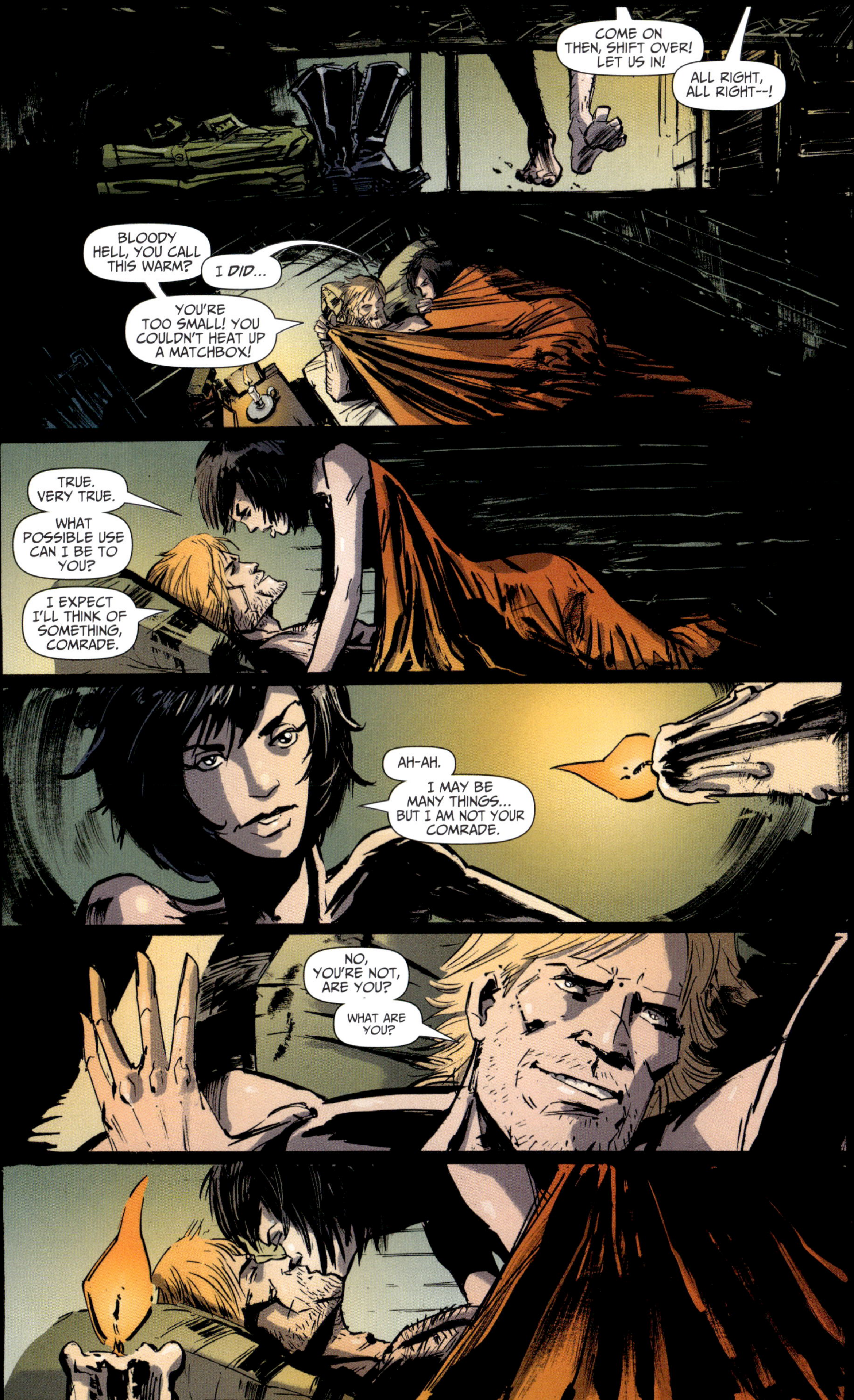
COME ON THEN, SHIFT OVER! LET US IN!
ALL RIGHT, ALL RIGHT--!
BLOODY HELL, YOU CALL THIS WARM?
I DID...
YOU'RE TOO SMALL! YOU COULDN'T HEAT UP A MATCHBOX!
TRUE. VERY TRUE.
WHAT POSSIBLE USE CAN I BE TO YOU?
I EXPECT I'LL THINK OF SOMETHING, COMRADE.
AH-AH.
I MAY BE MANY THINGS... BUT I AM NOT YOUR COMRADE.
NO, YOU'RE NOT, ARE YOU?
WHAT ARE YOU?

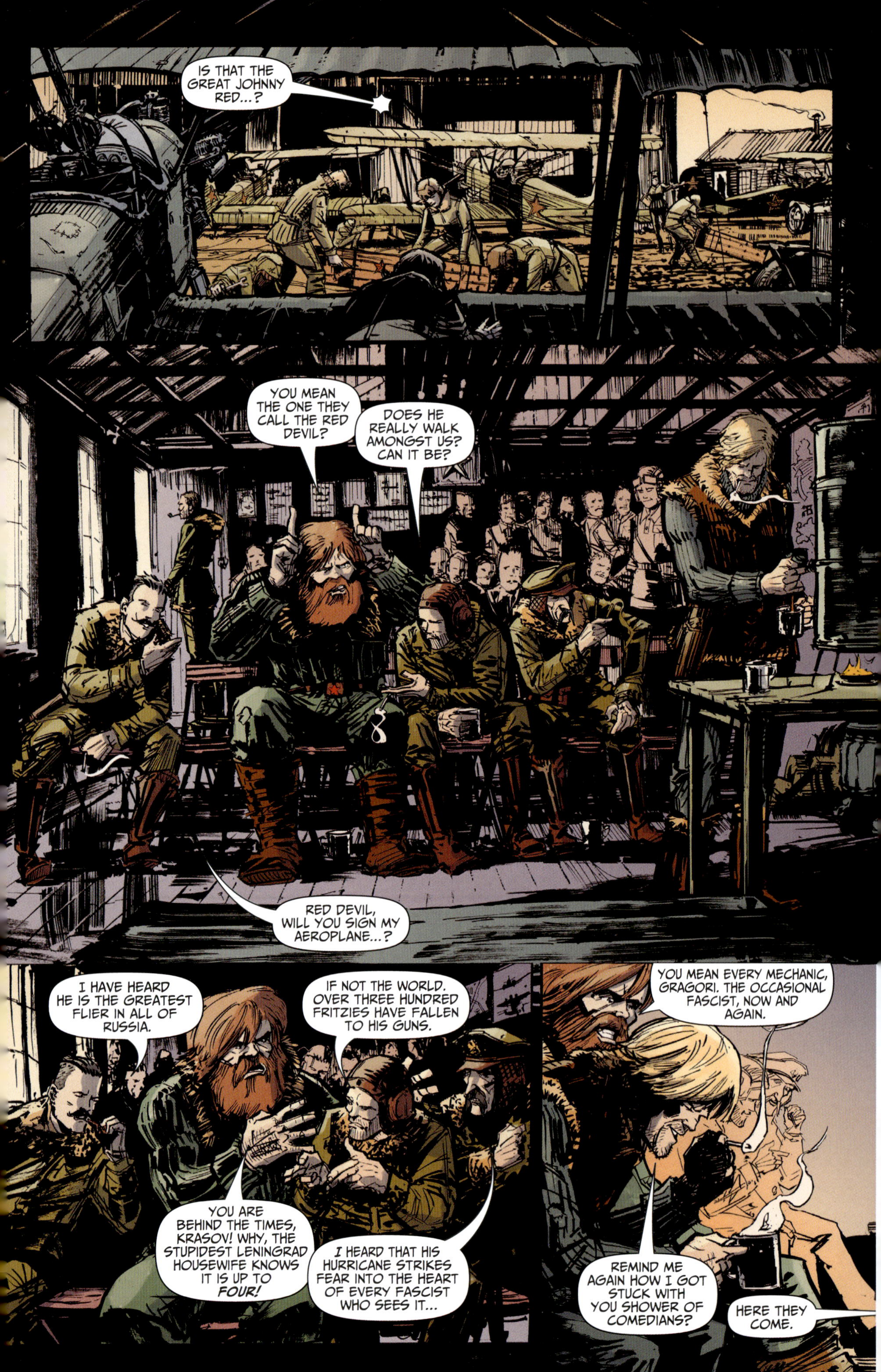
IS THAT THE GREAT JOHNNY RED...?
YOU MEAN THE ONE THEY CALL THE RED DEVIL?
DOES HE REALLY WALK AMONGST US? CAN IT BE?
RED DEVIL, WILL YOU SIGN MY AEROPLANE...?
I HAVE HEARD HE IS THE GREATEST FLIER IN ALL OF RUSSIA.
IF NOT THE WORLD. OVER THREE HUNDRED FRITZIES HAVE FALLEN TO HIS GUNS.
YOU ARE BEHIND THE TIMES, KRASOV! WHY, THE STUPIDEST LENINGRAD HOUSEWIFE KNOWS IT IS UP TO *FOUR!*
I HEARD THAT HIS HURRICANE STRIKES FEAR INTO THE HEART OF EVERY FASCIST WHO SEES IT...
YOU MEAN EVERY MECHANIC, GRAGORI. THE OCCASIONAL FASCIST, NOW AND AGAIN.
REMIND ME AGAIN HOW I GOT STUCK WITH YOU SHOWER OF COMEDIANS?
HERE THEY COME.

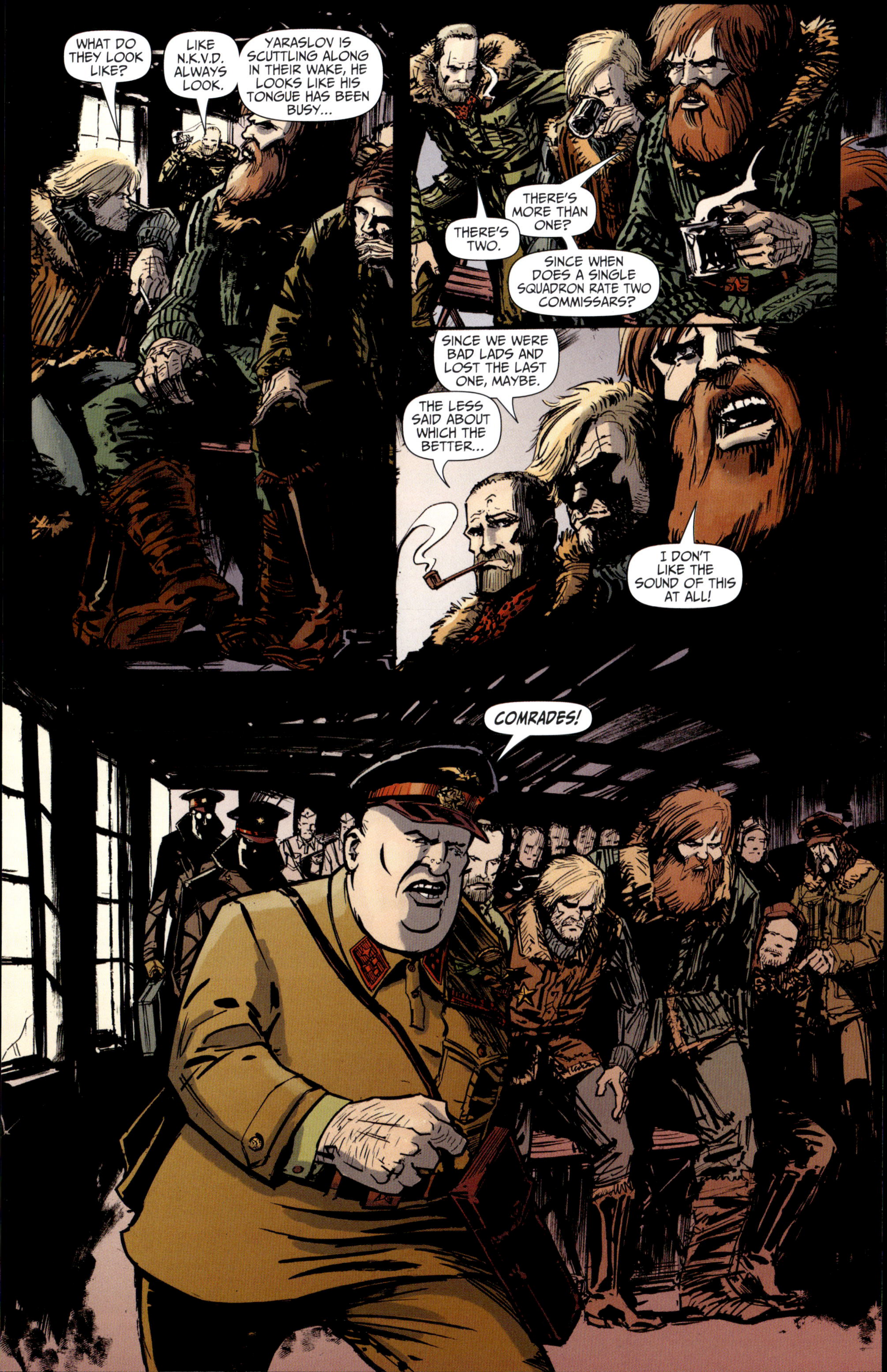
WHAT DO THEY LOOK LIKE?
LIKE N.K.V.D. ALWAYS LOOK.
YARASLOV IS SCUTTLING ALONG IN THEIR WAKE, HE LOOKS LIKE HIS TONGUE HAS BEEN BUSY...
THERE'S TWO.
THERE'S MORE THAN ONE?
SINCE WHEN DOES A SINGLE SQUADRON RATE TWO COMMISSARS?
SINCE WE WERE BAD LADS AND LOST THE LAST ONE, MAYBE.
THE LESS SAID ABOUT WHICH THE BETTER...
I DON'T LIKE THE SOUND OF THIS AT ALL!
COMRADES!

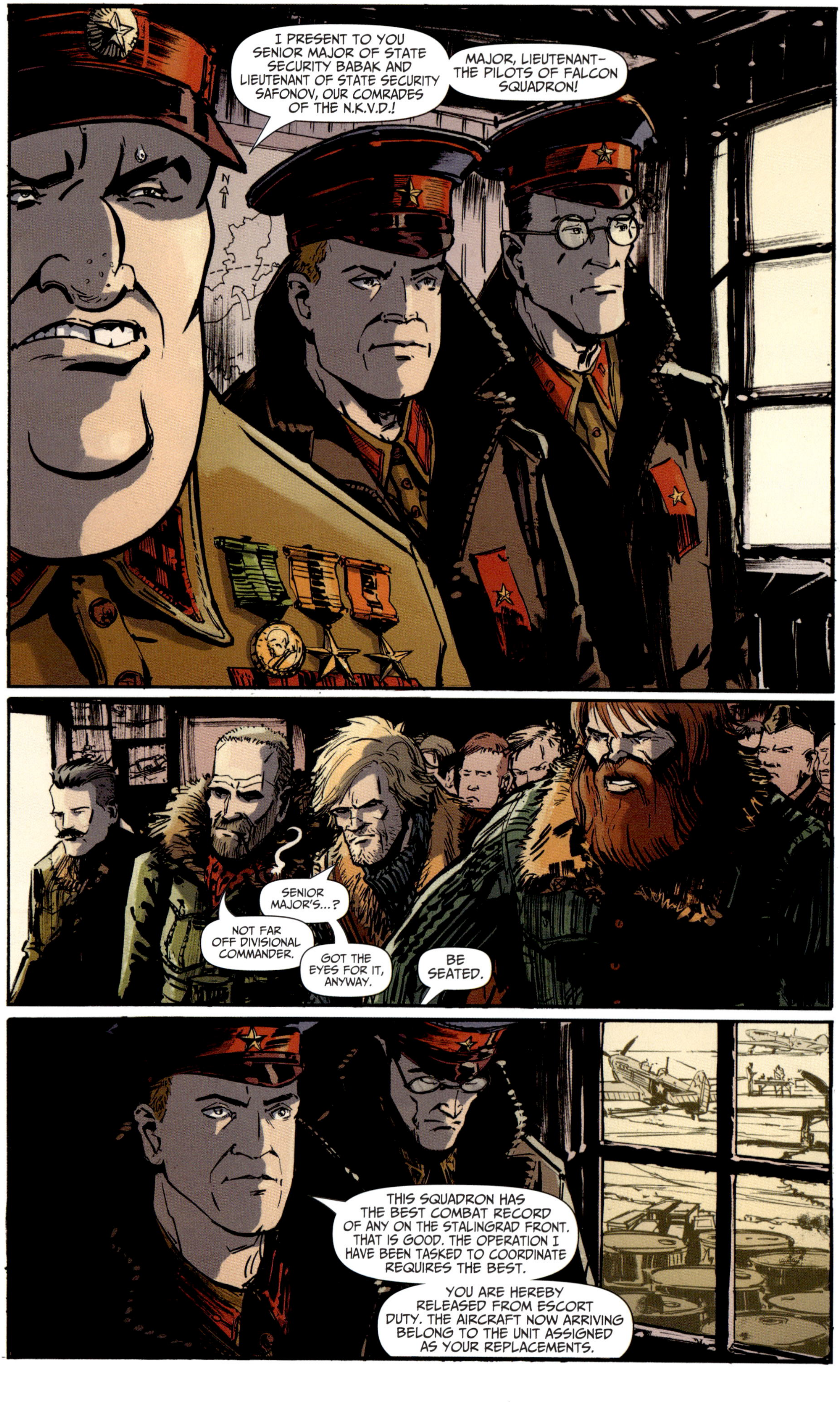
I PRESENT TO YOU SENIOR MAJOR OF STATE SECURITY BABAK AND LIEUTENANT OF STATE SECURITY SAFONOV, OUR COMRADES OF THE N.K.V.D.!
MAJOR, LIEUTENANT-THE PILOTS OF FALCON SQUADRON!
SENIOR MAJOR'S...?
NOT FAR OFF DIVISIONAL COMMANDER.
GOT THE EYES FOR IT, ANYWAY.
BE SEATED.
THIS SQUADRON HAS THE BEST COMBAT RECORD OF ANY ON THE STALINGRAD FRONT. THAT IS GOOD. THE OPERATION I HAVE BEEN TASKED TO COORDINATE REQUIRES THE BEST.
YOU ARE HEREBY RELEASED FROM ESCORT DUTY. THE AIRCRAFT NOW ARRIVING BELONG TO THE UNIT ASSIGNED AS YOUR REPLACEMENTS.

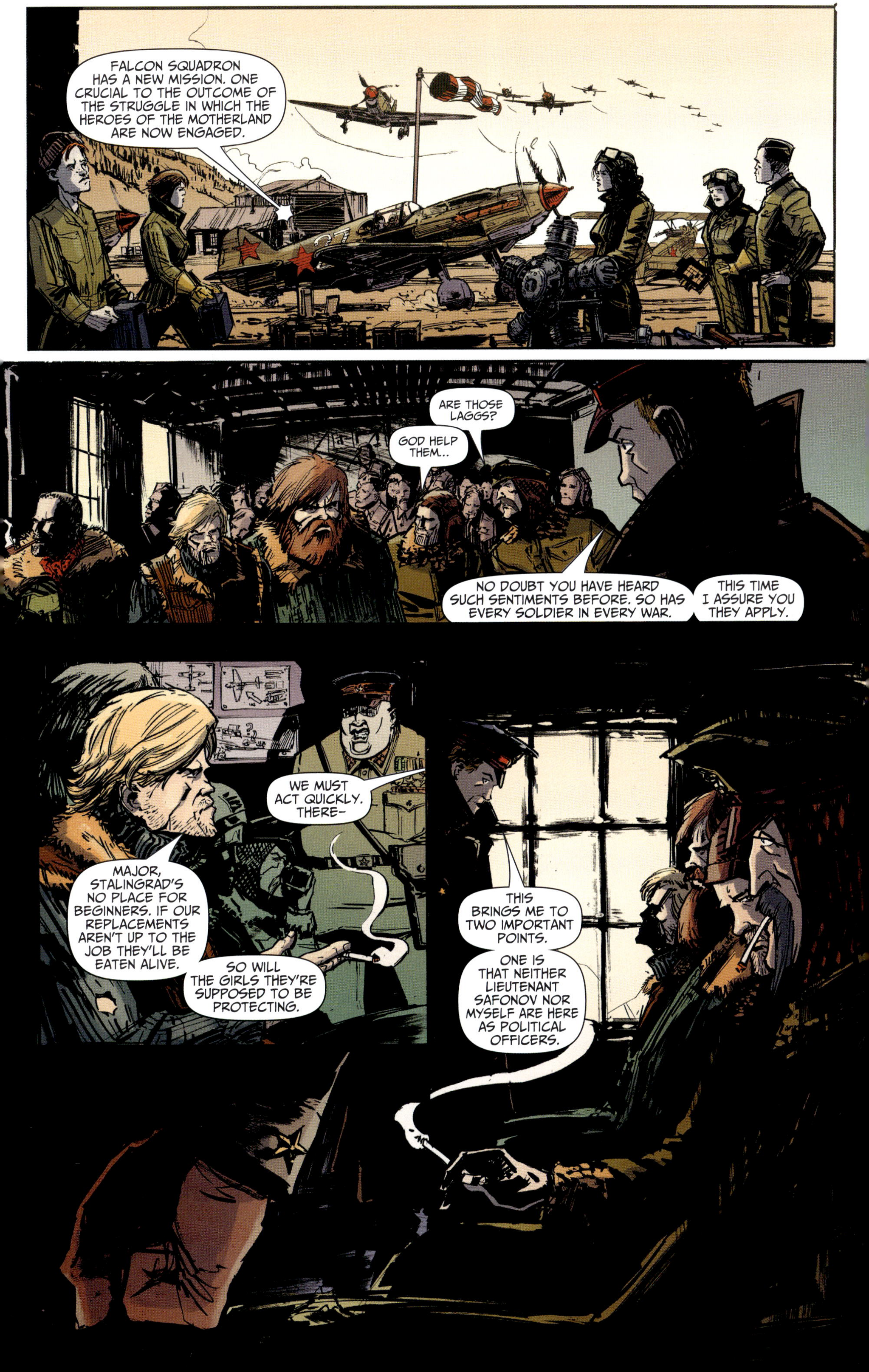
FALCON SQUADRON HAS A NEW MISSION. ONE CRUCIAL TO THE OUTCOME OF THE STRUGGLE IN WHICH THE HEROES OF THE MOTHERLAND ARE NOW ENGAGED.
ARE THOSE LAGGS?
GOD HELP THEM...
NO DOUBT YOU HAVE HEARD SUCH SENTIMENTS BEFORE. SO HAS EVERY SOLDIER IN EVERY WAR.
THIS TIME I ASSURE YOU THEY APPLY.
WE MUST ACT QUICKLY. THERE-
MAJOR, STALINGRAD'S NO PLACE FOR BEGINNERS. IF OUR REPLACEMENTS AREN'T UP TO THE JOB THEY'LL BE EATEN ALIVE.
SO WILL THE GIRLS THEY'RE SUPPOSED TO BE PROTECTING.
THIS BRINGS ME TO TWO IMPORTANT POINTS.
ONE IS THAT NEITHER LIEUTENANT SAFONOV NOR MYSELF ARE HERE AS POLITICAL OFFICERS.

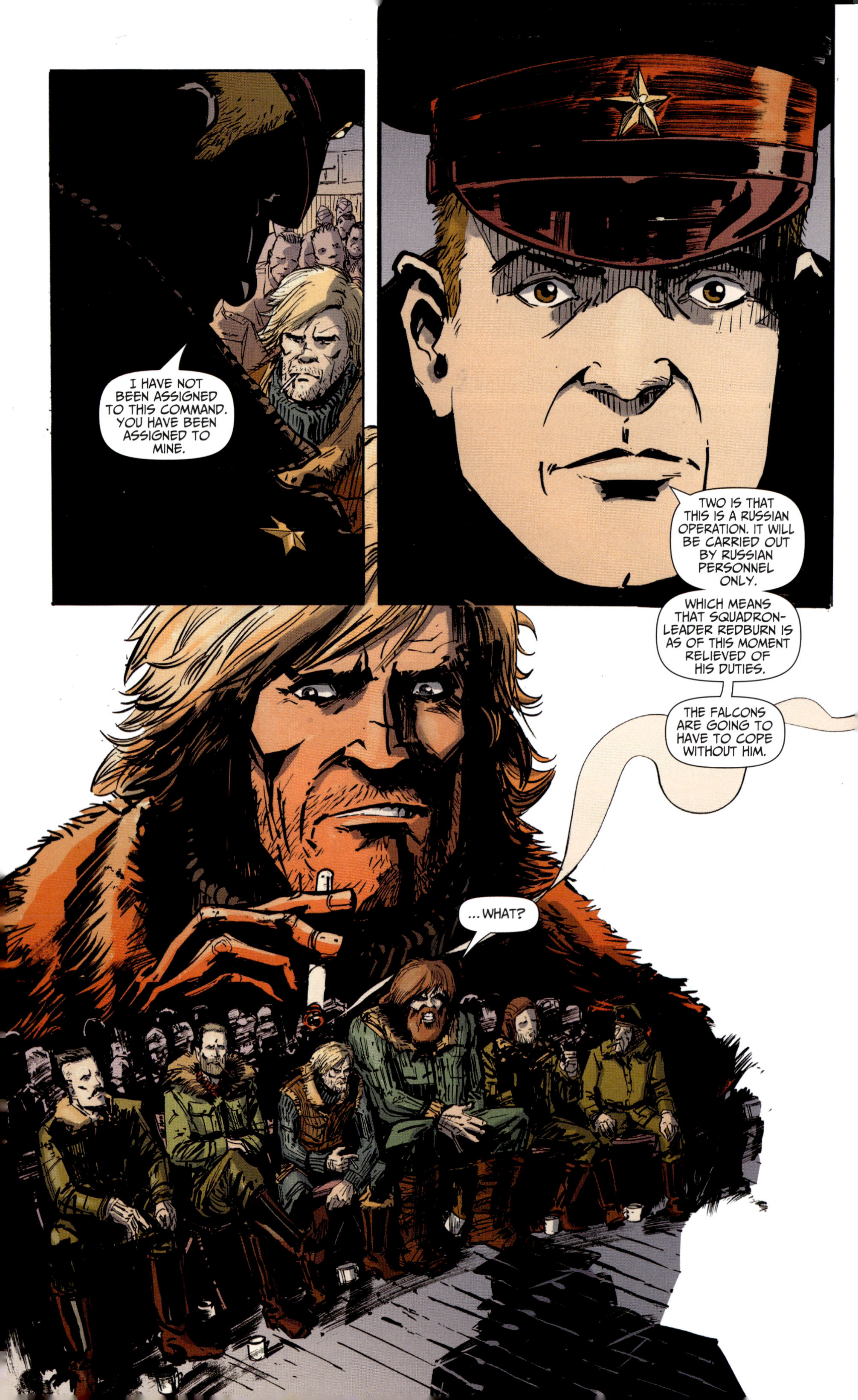
I HAVE NOT BEEN ASSIGNED TO THIS COMMAND. YOU HAVE BEEN ASSIGNED TO MINE.
TWO IS THAT THIS IS A RUSSIAN OPERATION. IT WILL BE CARRIED OUT BY RUSSIAN PERSONNEL ONLY.
WHICH MEANS THAT SQUADRON-LEADER REDBURN IS AS OF THIS MOMENT RELIEVED OF HIS DUTIES.
THE FALCONS ARE GOING TO HAVE TO COPE WITHOUT HIM.
...WHAT?

ISSUE THREE
Cover art by:
Keith Burns

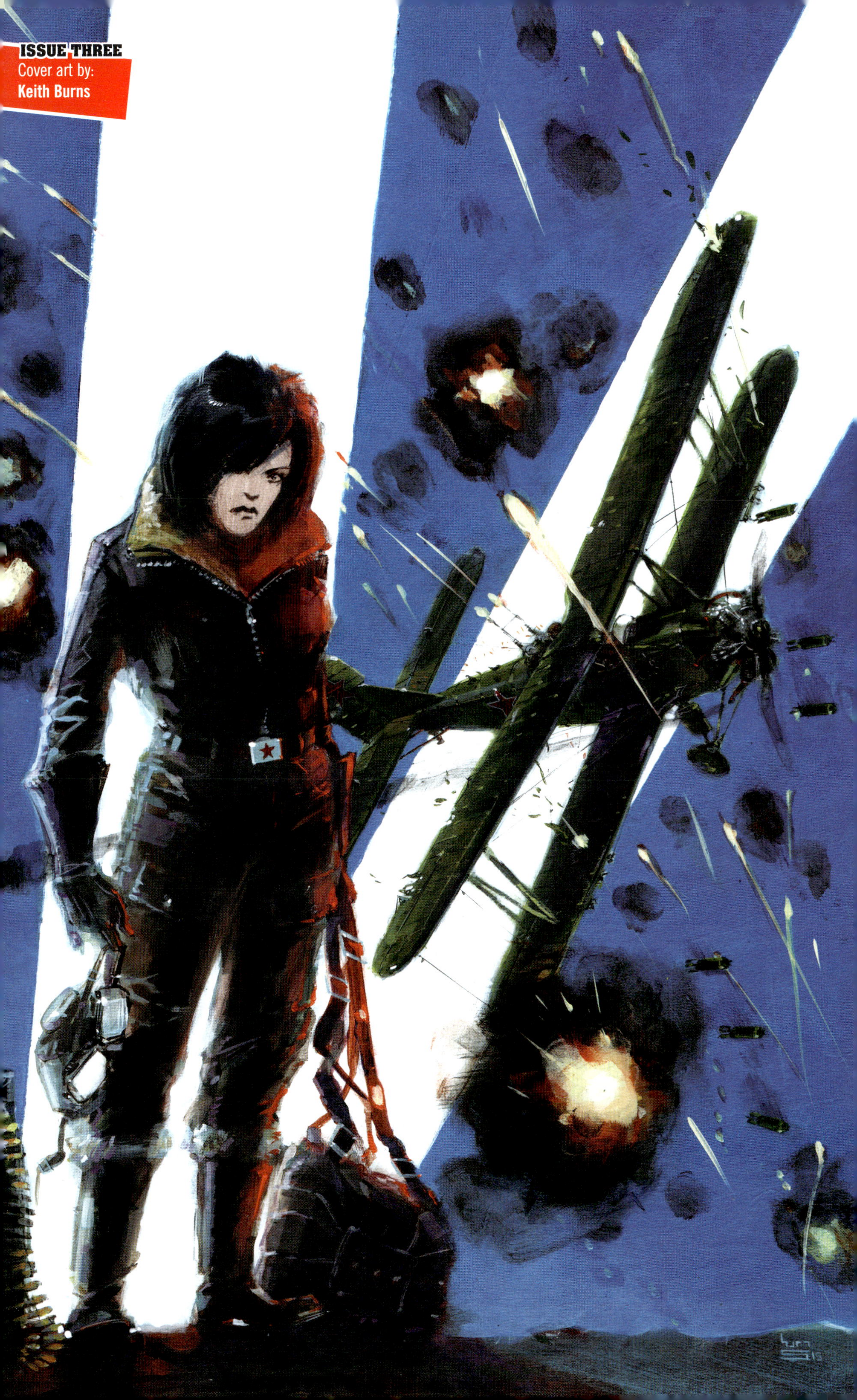

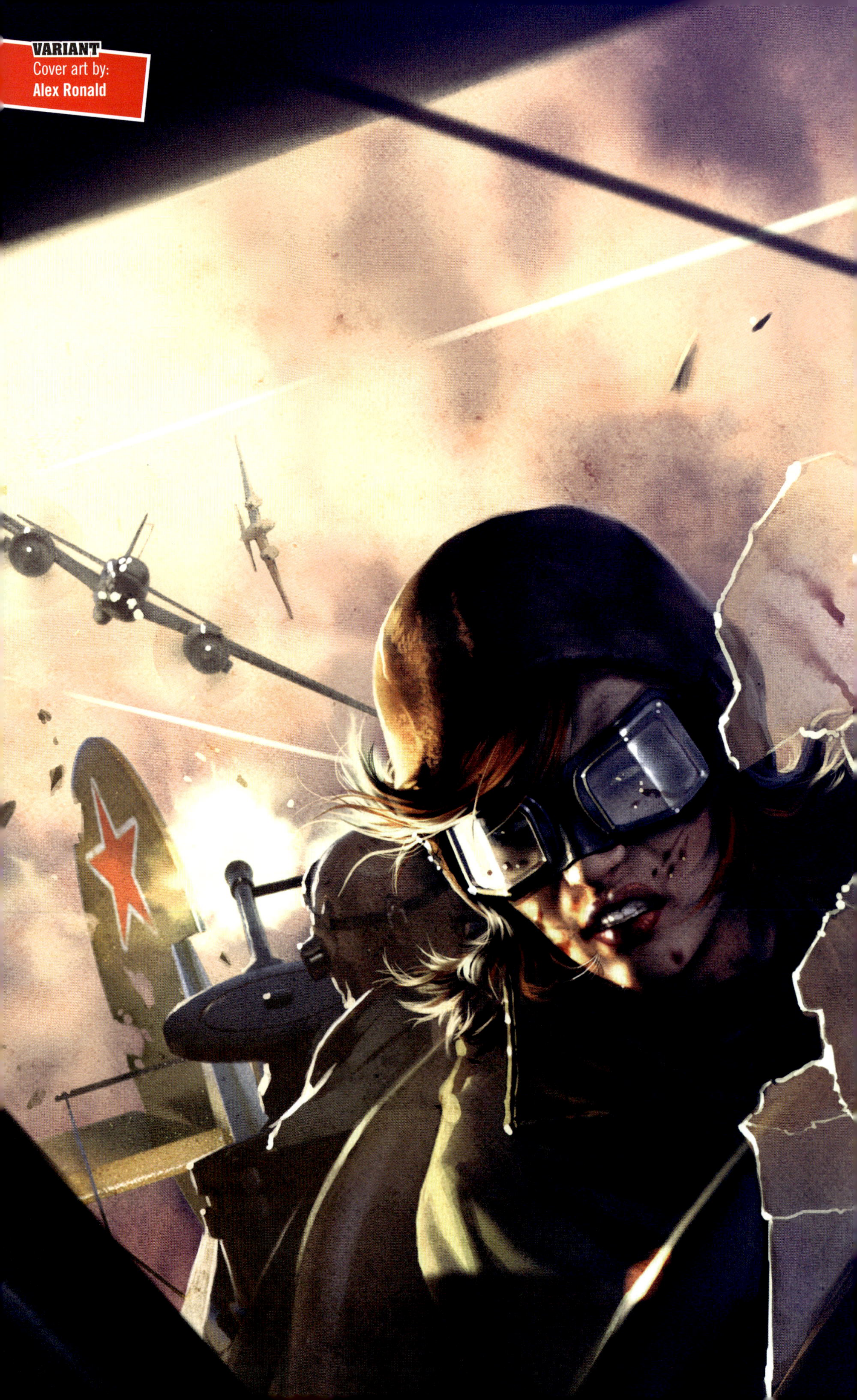

VARIANT
Cover art by:
Alex Ronald

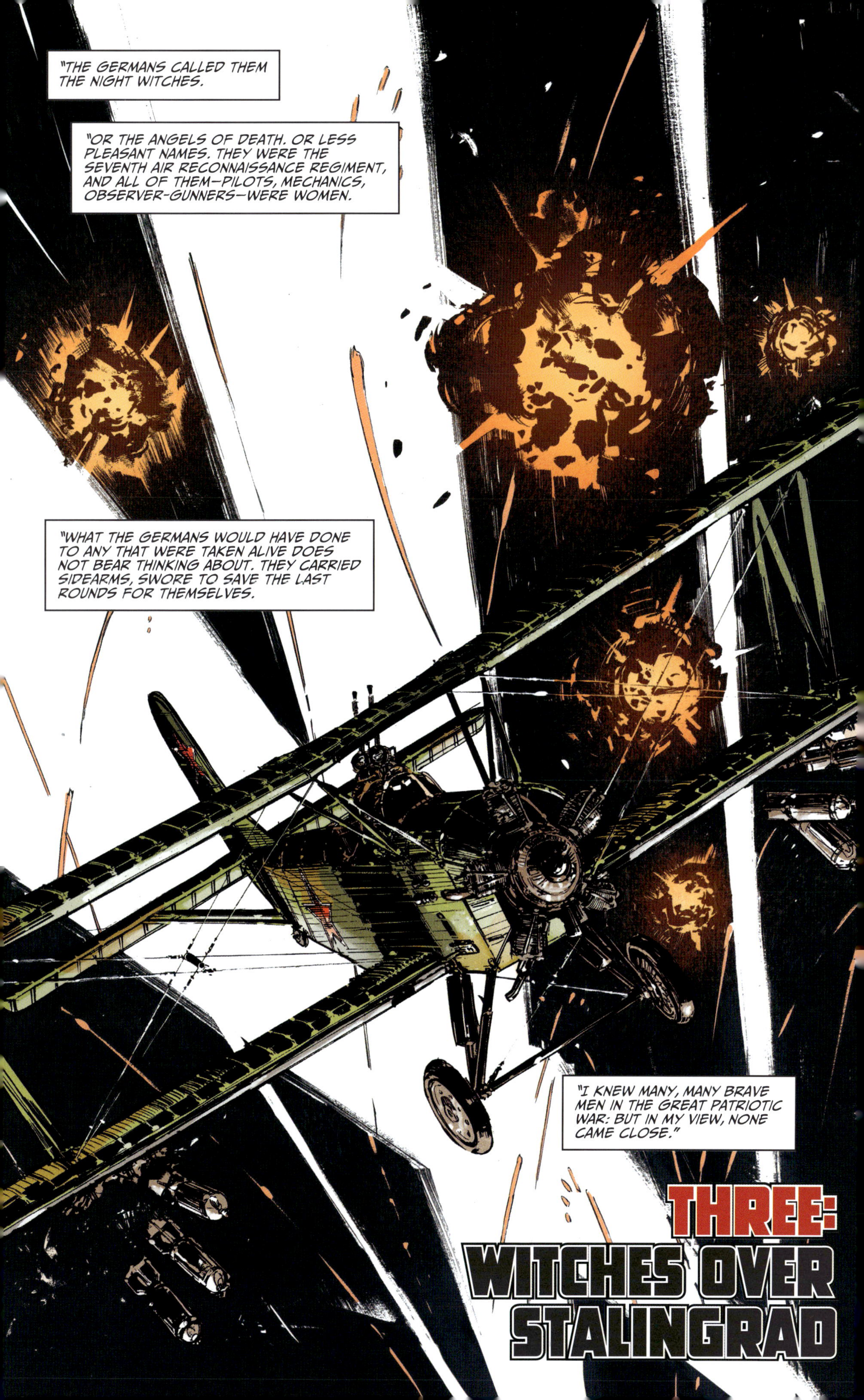
"THE GERMANS CALLED THEM THE NIGHT WITCHES.
"OR THE ANGELS OF DEATH. OR LESS PLEASANT NAMES. THEY WERE THE SEVENTH AIR RECONNAISSANCE REGIMENT, AND ALL OF THEM—PILOTS, MECHANICS, OBSERVER-GUNNERS—WERE WOMEN.
"WHAT THE GERMANS WOULD HAVE DONE TO ANY THAT WERE TAKEN ALIVE DOES NOT BEAR THINKING ABOUT. THEY CARRIED SIDEARMS, SWORE TO SAVE THE LAST ROUNDS FOR THEMSELVES.
"I KNEW MANY, MANY BRAVE MEN IN THE GREAT PATRIOTIC WAR: BUT IN MY VIEW, NONE CAME CLOSE."
THREE:
WITCHES OVER STALINGRAD

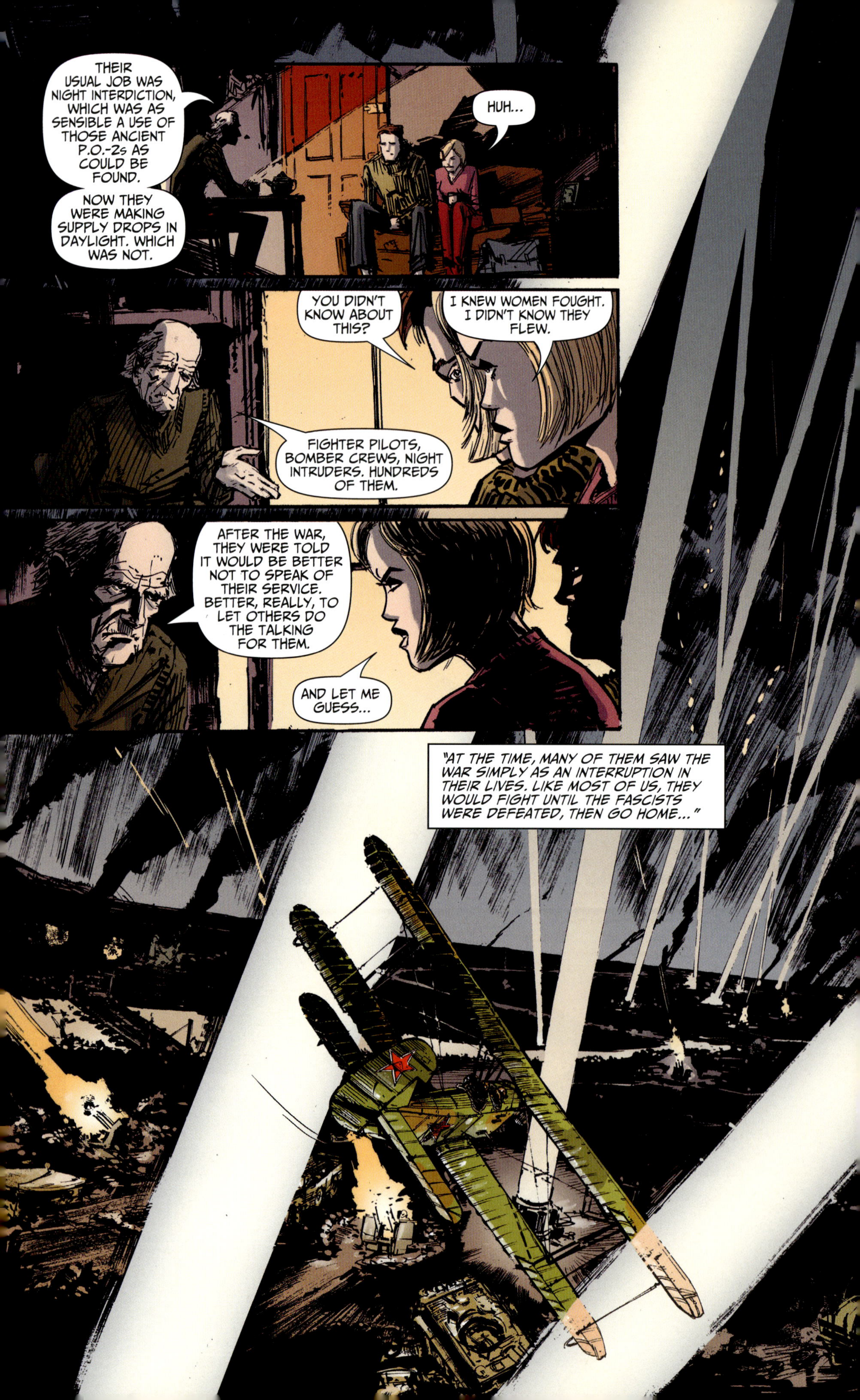

THEIR USUAL JOB WAS NIGHT INTERDICTION, WHICH WAS AS SENSIBLE A USE OF THOSE ANCIENT P.O.-2s AS COULD BE FOUND.
NOW THEY WERE MAKING SUPPLY DROPS IN DAYLIGHT. WHICH WAS NOT.
HUH...
YOU DIDN'T KNOW ABOUT THIS?
I KNEW WOMEN FOUGHT. I DIDN'T KNOW THEY FLEW.
FIGHTER PILOTS, BOMBER CREWS, NIGHT INTRUDERS. HUNDREDS OF THEM.
AFTER THE WAR, THEY WERE TOLD IT WOULD BE BETTER NOT TO SPEAK OF THEIR SERVICE. BETTER, REALLY, TO LET OTHERS DO THE TALKING FOR THEM.
AND LET ME GUESS...
"AT THE TIME, MANY OF THEM SAW THE WAR SIMPLY AS AN INTERRUPTION IN THEIR LIVES. LIKE MOST OF US, THEY WOULD FIGHT UNTIL THE FASCISTS WERE DEFEATED, THEN GO HOME..."

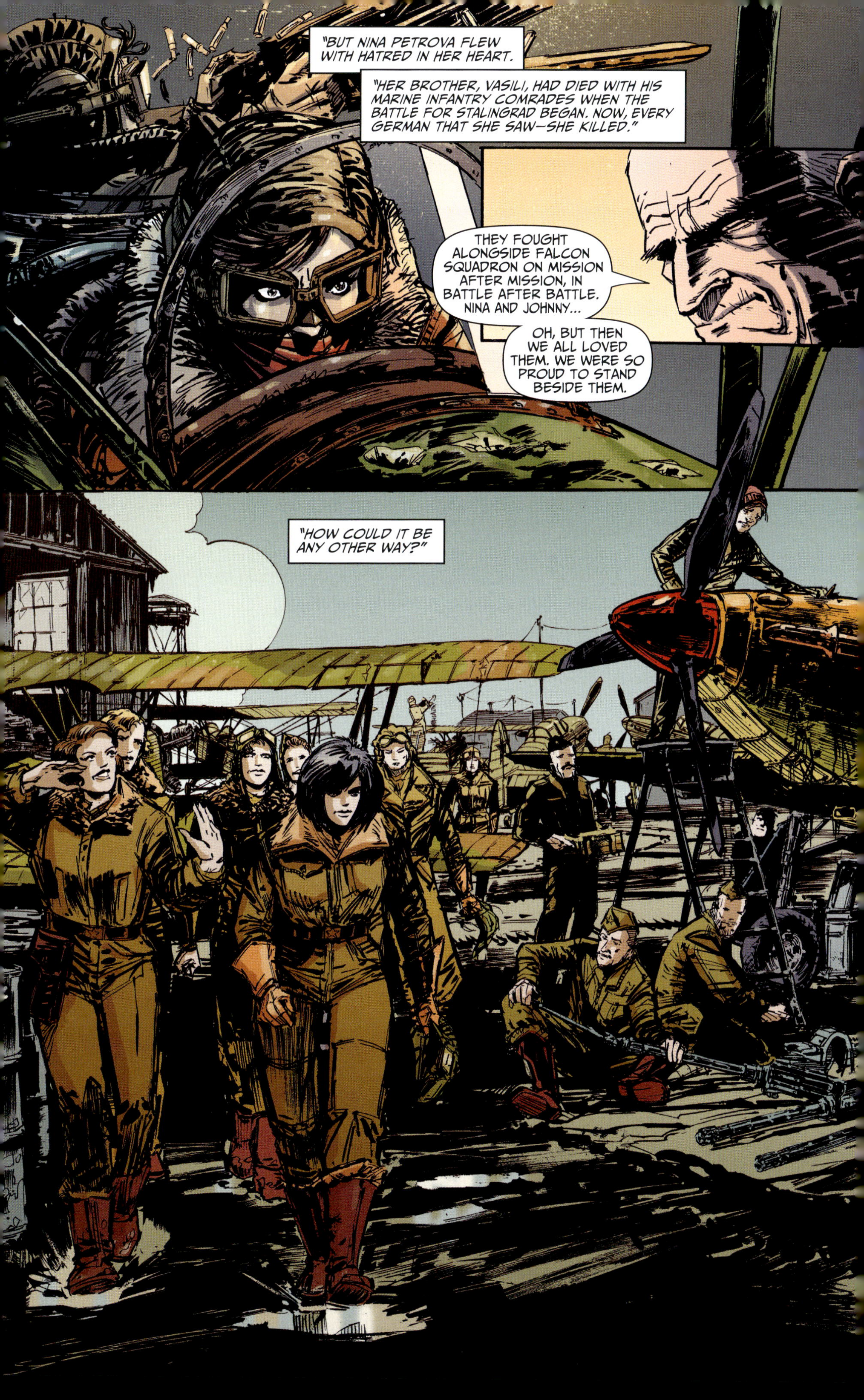
"BUT NINA PETROVA FLEW WITH HATRED IN HER HEART.
"HER BROTHER, VASILI, HAD DIED WITH HIS MARINE INFANTRY COMRADES WHEN THE BATTLE FOR STALINGRAD BEGAN. NOW, EVERY GERMAN THAT SHE SAW—SHE KILLED."
THEY FOUGHT ALONGSIDE FALCON SQUADRON ON MISSION AFTER MISSION, IN BATTLE AFTER BATTLE. NINA AND JOHNNY...
OH, BUT THEN WE ALL LOVED THEM. WE WERE SO PROUD TO STAND BESIDE THEM.
"HOW COULD IT BE ANY OTHER WAY?"

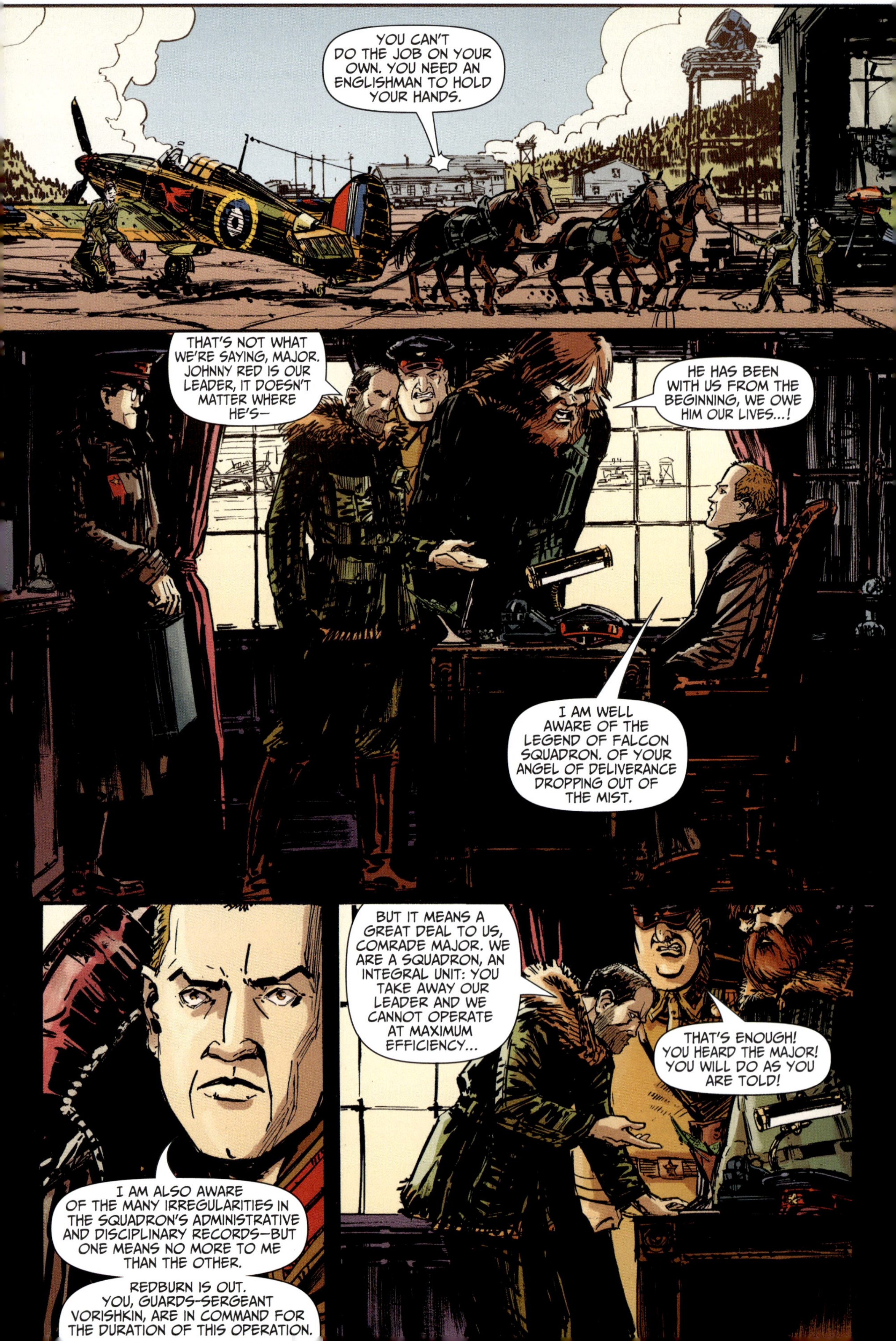
YOU CAN'T DO THE JOB ON YOUR OWN. YOU NEED AN ENGLISHMAN TO HOLD YOUR HANDS.
THAT'S NOT WHAT WE'RE SAYING, MAJOR. JOHNNY RED IS OUR LEADER, IT DOESN'T MATTER WHERE HE'S—
HE HAS BEEN WITH US FROM THE BEGINNING, WE OWE HIM OUR LIVES...!
I AM WELL AWARE OF THE LEGEND OF FALCON SQUADRON. OF YOUR ANGEL OF DELIVERANCE DROPPING OUT OF THE MIST.
I AM ALSO AWARE OF THE MANY IRREGULARITIES IN THE SQUADRON'S ADMINISTRATIVE AND DISCIPLINARY RECORDS—BUT ONE MEANS NO MORE TO ME THAN THE OTHER.
REDBURN IS OUT. YOU, GUARDS-SERGEANT VORISHKIN, ARE IN COMMAND FOR THE DURATION OF THIS OPERATION.
BUT IT MEANS A GREAT DEAL TO US, COMRADE MAJOR. WE ARE A SQUADRON, AN INTEGRAL UNIT: YOU TAKE AWAY OUR LEADER AND WE CANNOT OPERATE AT MAXIMUM EFFICIENCY...
THAT'S ENOUGH! YOU HEARD THE MAJOR! YOU WILL DO AS YOU ARE TOLD!

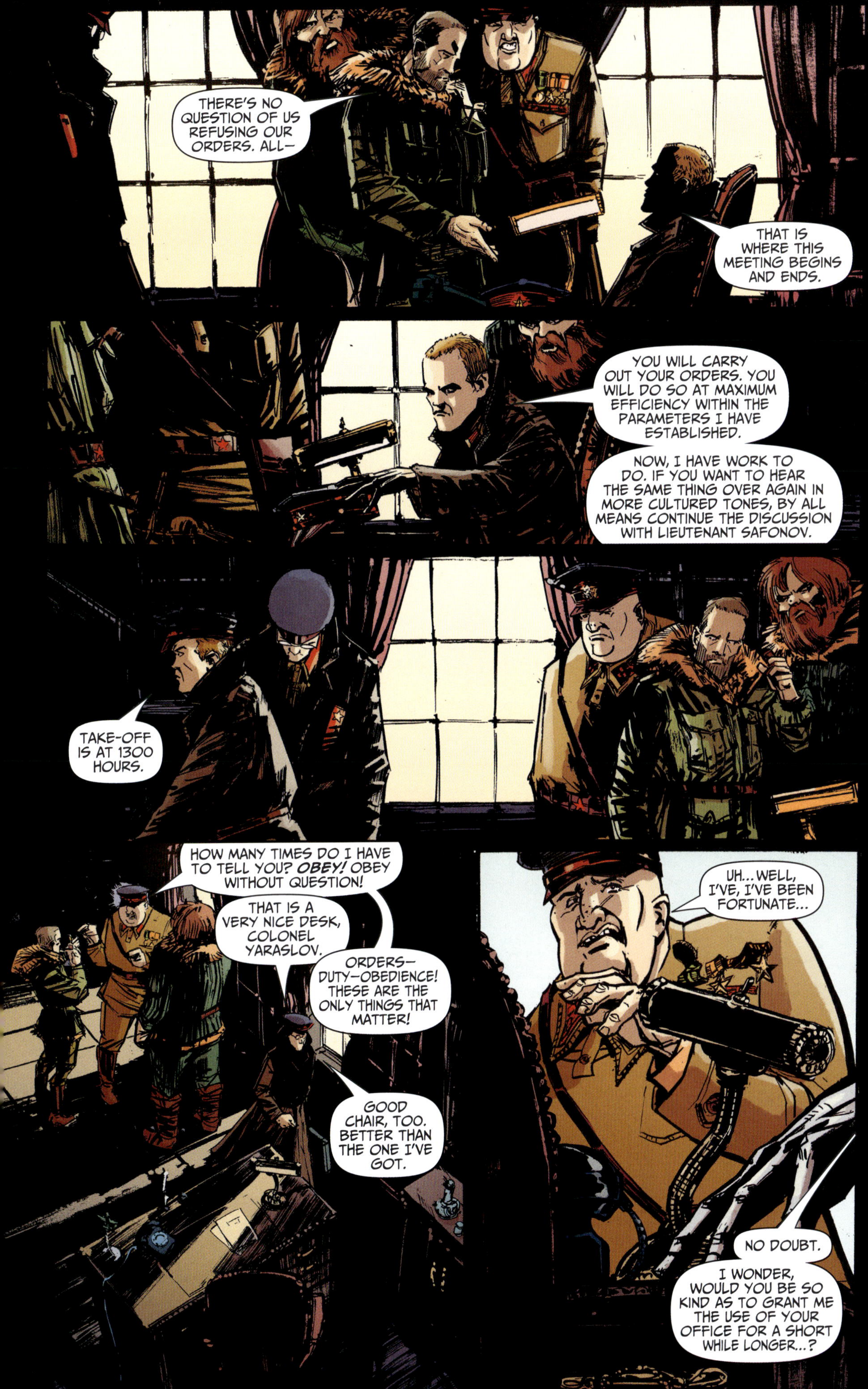
THERE'S NO QUESTION OF US REFUSING OUR ORDERS. ALL—
THAT IS WHERE THIS MEETING BEGINS AND ENDS.
YOU WILL CARRY OUT YOUR ORDERS. YOU WILL DO SO AT MAXIMUM EFFICIENCY WITHIN THE PARAMETERS I HAVE ESTABLISHED.
NOW, I HAVE WORK TO DO. IF YOU WANT TO HEAR THE SAME THING OVER AGAIN IN MORE CULTURED TONES, BY ALL MEANS CONTINUE THE DISCUSSION WITH LIEUTENANT SAFONOV.
TAKE-OFF IS AT 1300 HOURS.
HOW MANY TIMES DO I HAVE TO TELL YOU? *OBEY!* OBEY WITHOUT QUESTION!
THAT IS A VERY NICE DESK, COLONEL YARASLOV.
ORDERS—DUTY—OBEDIENCE! THESE ARE THE ONLY THINGS THAT MATTER!
GOOD CHAIR, TOO. BETTER THAN THE ONE I'VE GOT.
UH...WELL, I'VE, I'VE BEEN FORTUNATE...
NO DOUBT.
I WONDER, WOULD YOU BE SO KIND AS TO GRANT ME THE USE OF YOUR OFFICE FOR A SHORT WHILE LONGER...?

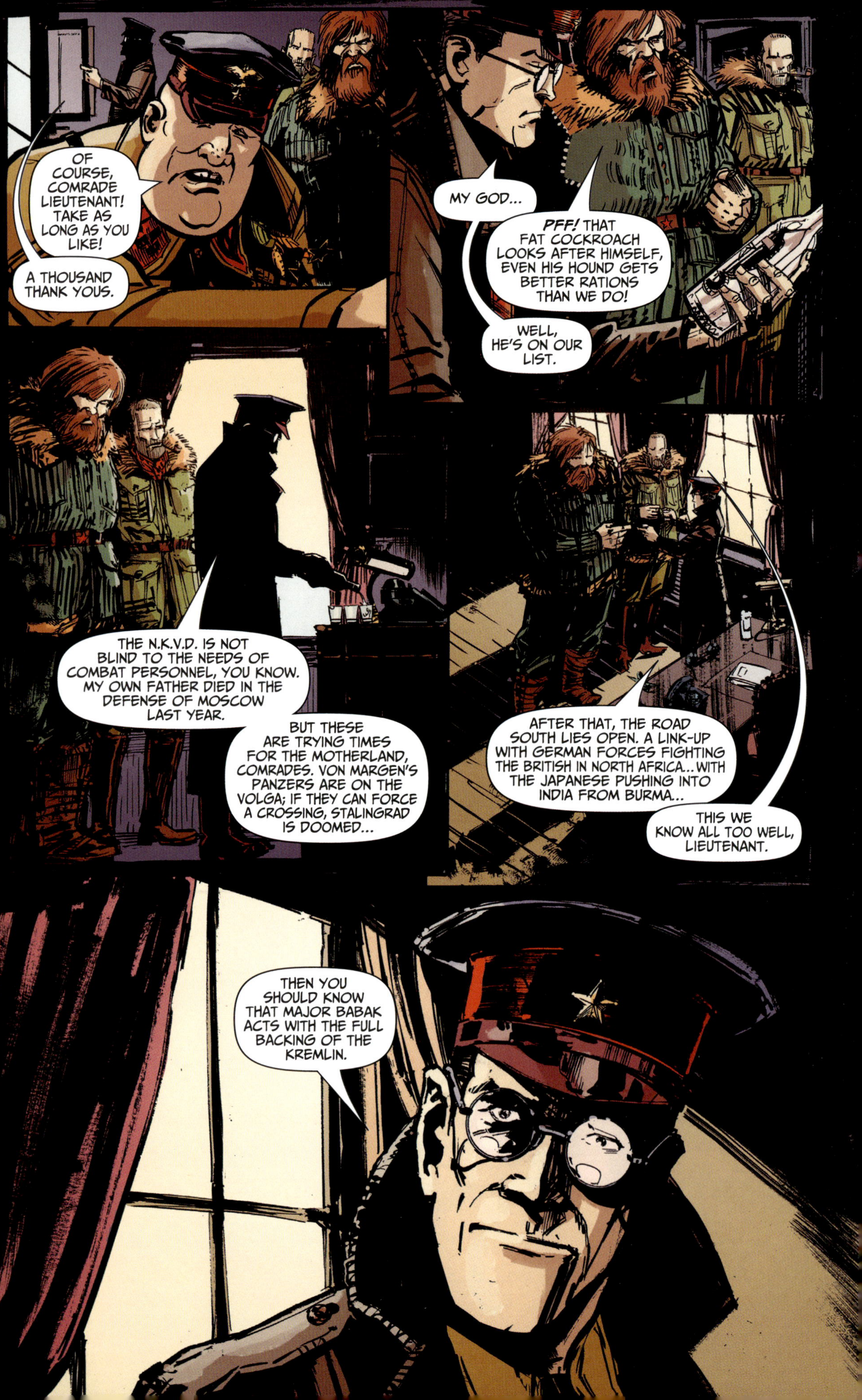
OF COURSE, COMRADE LIEUTENANT! TAKE AS LONG AS YOU LIKE!
A THOUSAND THANK YOUS.
MY GOD...
PFF! THAT FAT COCKROACH LOOKS AFTER HIMSELF, EVEN HIS HOUND GETS BETTER RATIONS THAN WE DO!
WELL, HE'S ON OUR LIST.
THE N.K.V.D. IS NOT BLIND TO THE NEEDS OF COMBAT PERSONNEL, YOU KNOW. MY OWN FATHER DIED IN THE DEFENSE OF MOSCOW LAST YEAR.
BUT THESE ARE TRYING TIMES FOR THE MOTHERLAND, COMRADES. VON MARGEN'S PANZERS ARE ON THE VOLGA; IF THEY CAN FORCE A CROSSING, STALINGRAD IS DOOMED...
AFTER THAT, THE ROAD SOUTH LIES OPEN. A LINK-UP WITH GERMAN FORCES FIGHTING THE BRITISH IN NORTH AFRICA...WITH THE JAPANESE PUSHING INTO INDIA FROM BURMA...
THIS WE KNOW ALL TOO WELL, LIEUTENANT.
THEN YOU SHOULD KNOW THAT MAJOR BABAK ACTS WITH THE FULL BACKING OF THE KREMLIN.

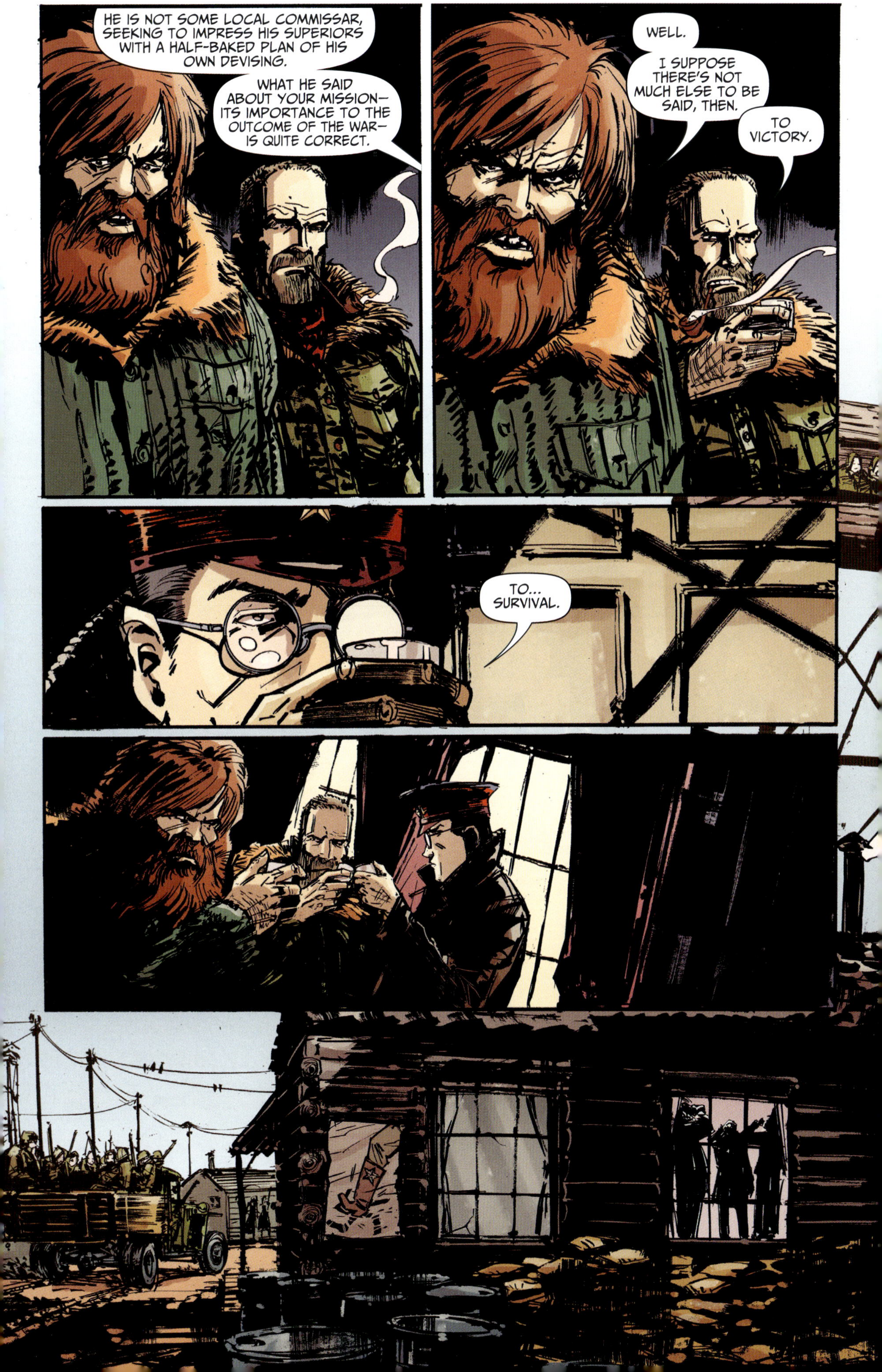
HE IS NOT SOME LOCAL COMMISSAR, SEEKING TO IMPRESS HIS SUPERIORS WITH A HALF-BAKED PLAN OF HIS OWN DEVISING.
WHAT HE SAID ABOUT YOUR MISSION— ITS IMPORTANCE TO THE OUTCOME OF THE WAR— IS QUITE CORRECT.
WELL.
I SUPPOSE THERE'S NOT MUCH ELSE TO BE SAID, THEN.
TO VICTORY.
TO... SURVIVAL.

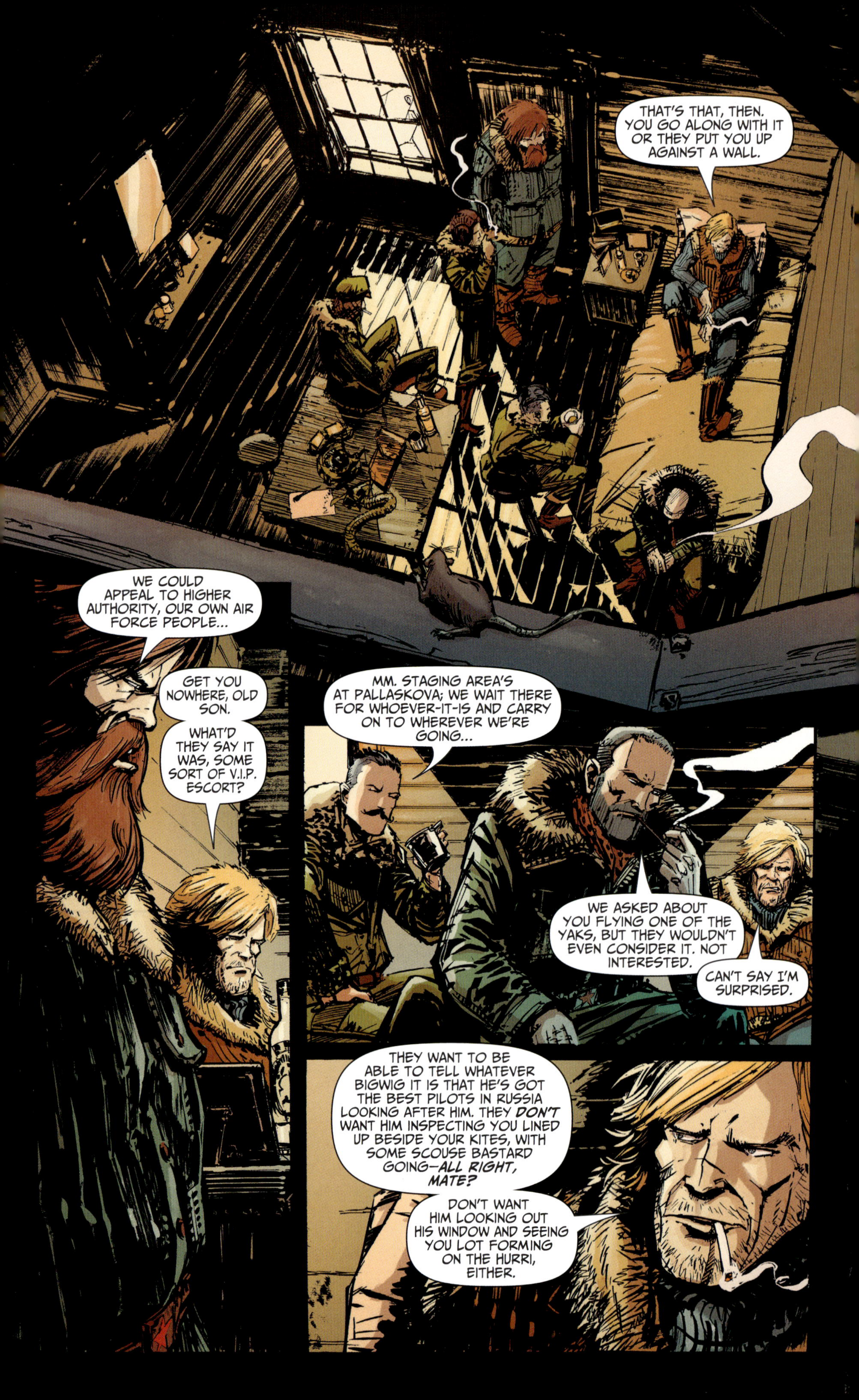
THAT'S THAT, THEN. YOU GO ALONG WITH IT OR THEY PUT YOU UP AGAINST A WALL.
WE COULD APPEAL TO HIGHER AUTHORITY, OUR OWN AIR FORCE PEOPLE...
GET YOU NOWHERE, OLD SON.
WHAT'D THEY SAY IT WAS, SOME SORT OF V.I.P. ESCORT?
MM. STAGING AREA'S AT PALLASKOVA; WE WAIT THERE FOR WHOEVER-IT-IS AND CARRY ON TO WHEREVER WE'RE GOING...
WE ASKED ABOUT YOU FLYING ONE OF THE YAKS, BUT THEY WOULDN'T EVEN CONSIDER IT. NOT INTERESTED.
CAN'T SAY I'M SURPRISED.
THEY WANT TO BE ABLE TO TELL WHATEVER BIGWIG IT IS THAT HE'S GOT THE BEST PILOTS IN RUSSIA LOOKING AFTER HIM. THEY DON'T WANT HIM INSPECTING YOU LINED UP BESIDE YOUR KITES, WITH SOME SCOUSE BASTARD GOING—ALL RIGHT, MATE?
DON'T WANT HIM LOOKING OUT HIS WINDOW AND SEEING YOU LOT FORMING ON THE HURRI, EITHER.

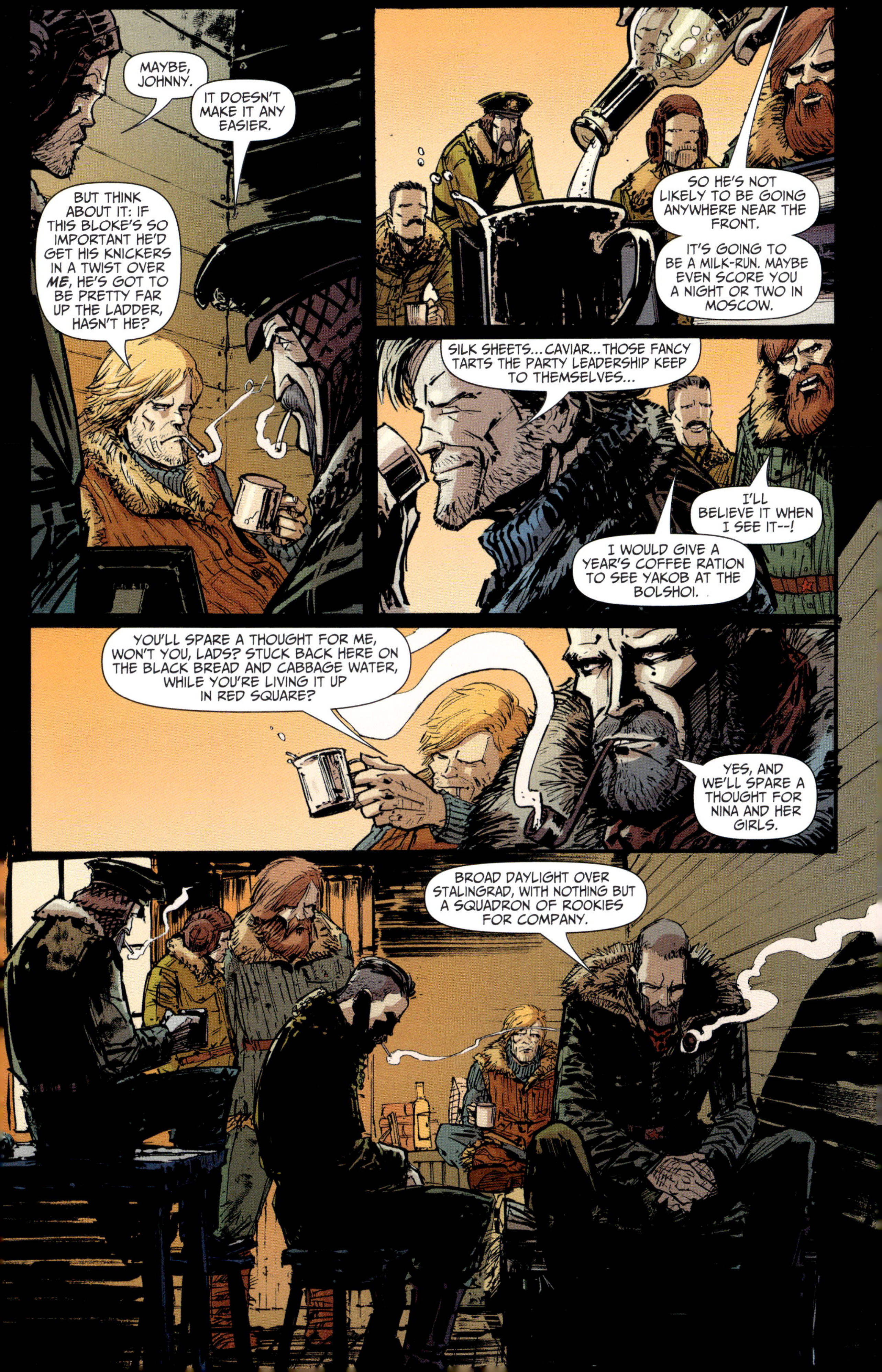
MAYBE, JOHNNY.
IT DOESN'T MAKE IT ANY EASIER.
BUT THINK ABOUT IT: IF THIS BLOKE'S SO IMPORTANT HE'D GET HIS KNICKERS IN A TWIST OVER *ME*, HE'S GOT TO BE PRETTY FAR UP THE LADDER, HASN'T HE?
SO HE'S NOT LIKELY TO BE GOING ANYWHERE NEAR THE FRONT.
IT'S GOING TO BE A MILK-RUN. MAYBE EVEN SCORE YOU A NIGHT OR TWO IN MOSCOW.
SILK SHEETS... CAVIAR... THOSE FANCY TARTS THE PARTY LEADERSHIP KEEP TO THEMSELVES...
I'LL BELIEVE IT WHEN I SEE IT--!
I WOULD GIVE A YEAR'S COFFEE RATION TO SEE YAKOB AT THE BOLSHOI.
YOU'LL SPARE A THOUGHT FOR ME, WON'T YOU, LADS? STUCK BACK HERE ON THE BLACK BREAD AND CABBAGE WATER, WHILE YOU'RE LIVING IT UP IN RED SQUARE?
YES, AND WE'LL SPARE A THOUGHT FOR NINA AND HER GIRLS.
BROAD DAYLIGHT OVER STALINGRAD, WITH NOTHING BUT A SQUADRON OF ROOKIES FOR COMPANY.

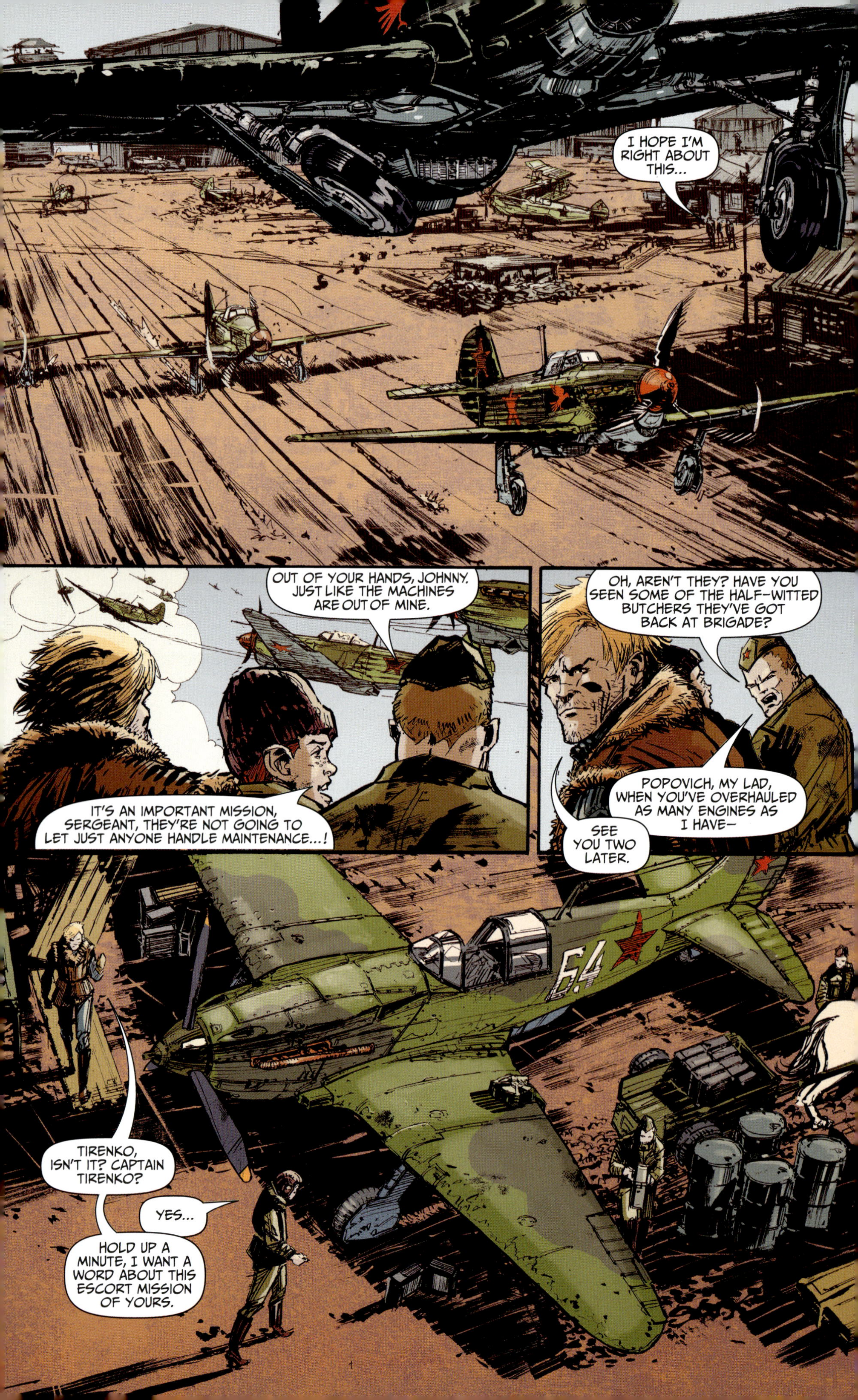
I HOPE I'M RIGHT ABOUT THIS...
OUT OF YOUR HANDS, JOHNNY. JUST LIKE THE MACHINES ARE OUT OF MINE.
IT'S AN IMPORTANT MISSION, SERGEANT, THEY'RE NOT GOING TO LET JUST ANYONE HANDLE MAINTENANCE...!
OH, AREN'T THEY? HAVE YOU SEEN SOME OF THE HALF-WITTED BUTCHERS THEY'VE GOT BACK AT BRIGADE?
POPOVICH, MY LAD, WHEN YOU'VE OVERHAULED AS MANY ENGINES AS I HAVE–
SEE YOU TWO LATER.
TIRENKO, ISN'T IT? CAPTAIN TIRENKO?
YES...
HOLD UP A MINUTE, I WANT A WORD ABOUT THIS ESCORT MISSION OF YOURS.
64

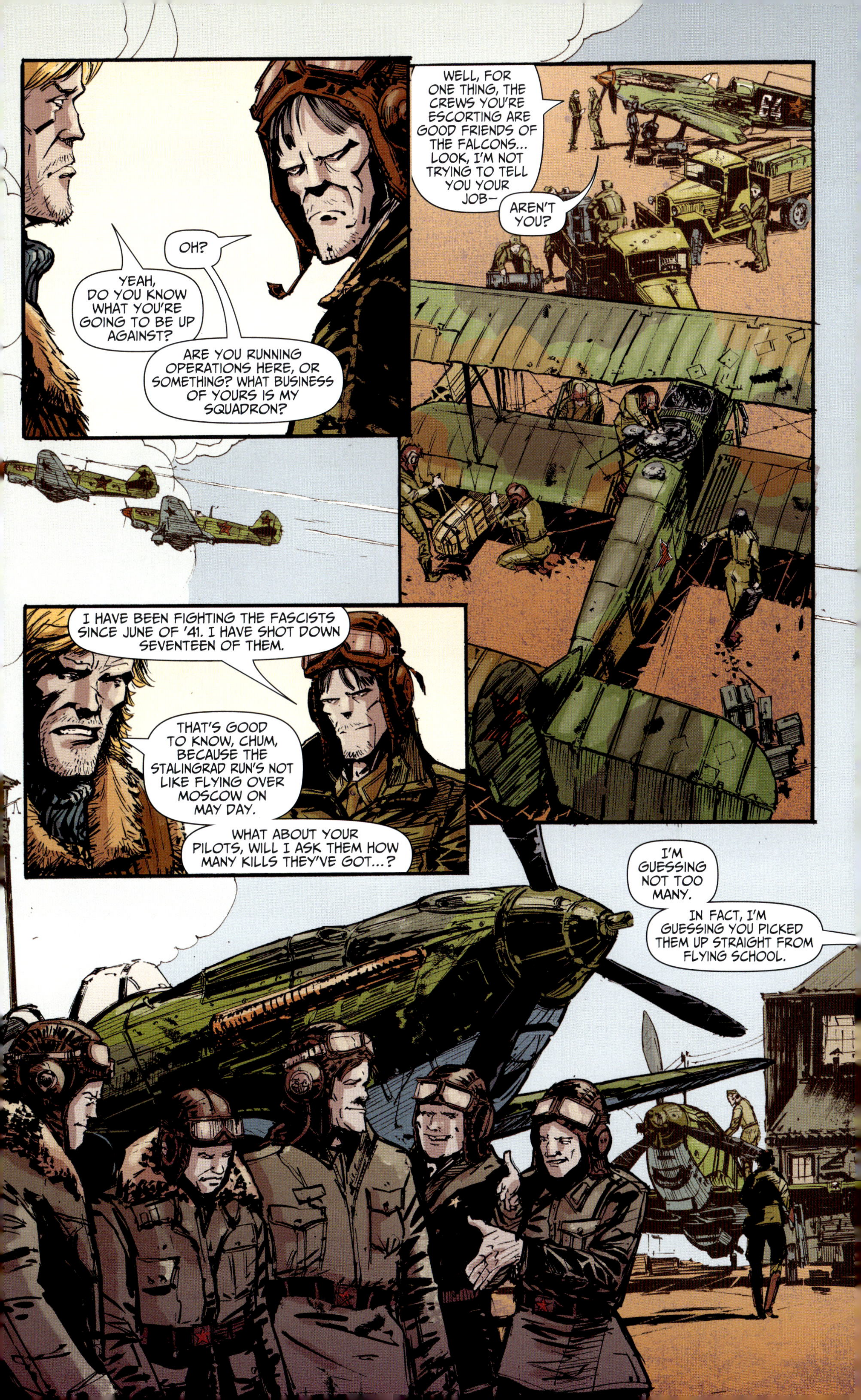
YEAH, DO YOU KNOW WHAT YOU'RE GOING TO BE UP AGAINST?
OH?
ARE YOU RUNNING OPERATIONS HERE, OR SOMETHING? WHAT BUSINESS OF YOURS IS MY SQUADRON?
WELL, FOR ONE THING, THE CREWS YOU'RE ESCORTING ARE GOOD FRIENDS OF THE FALCONS... LOOK, I'M NOT TRYING TO TELL YOU YOUR JOB—
AREN'T YOU?
I HAVE BEEN FIGHTING THE FASCISTS SINCE JUNE OF '41. I HAVE SHOT DOWN SEVENTEEN OF THEM.
THAT'S GOOD TO KNOW, CHUM, BECAUSE THE STALINGRAD RUN'S NOT LIKE FLYING OVER MOSCOW ON MAY DAY.
WHAT ABOUT YOUR PILOTS, WILL I ASK THEM HOW MANY KILLS THEY'VE GOT...?
I'M GUESSING NOT TOO MANY.
IN FACT, I'M GUESSING YOU PICKED THEM UP STRAIGHT FROM FLYING SCHOOL.

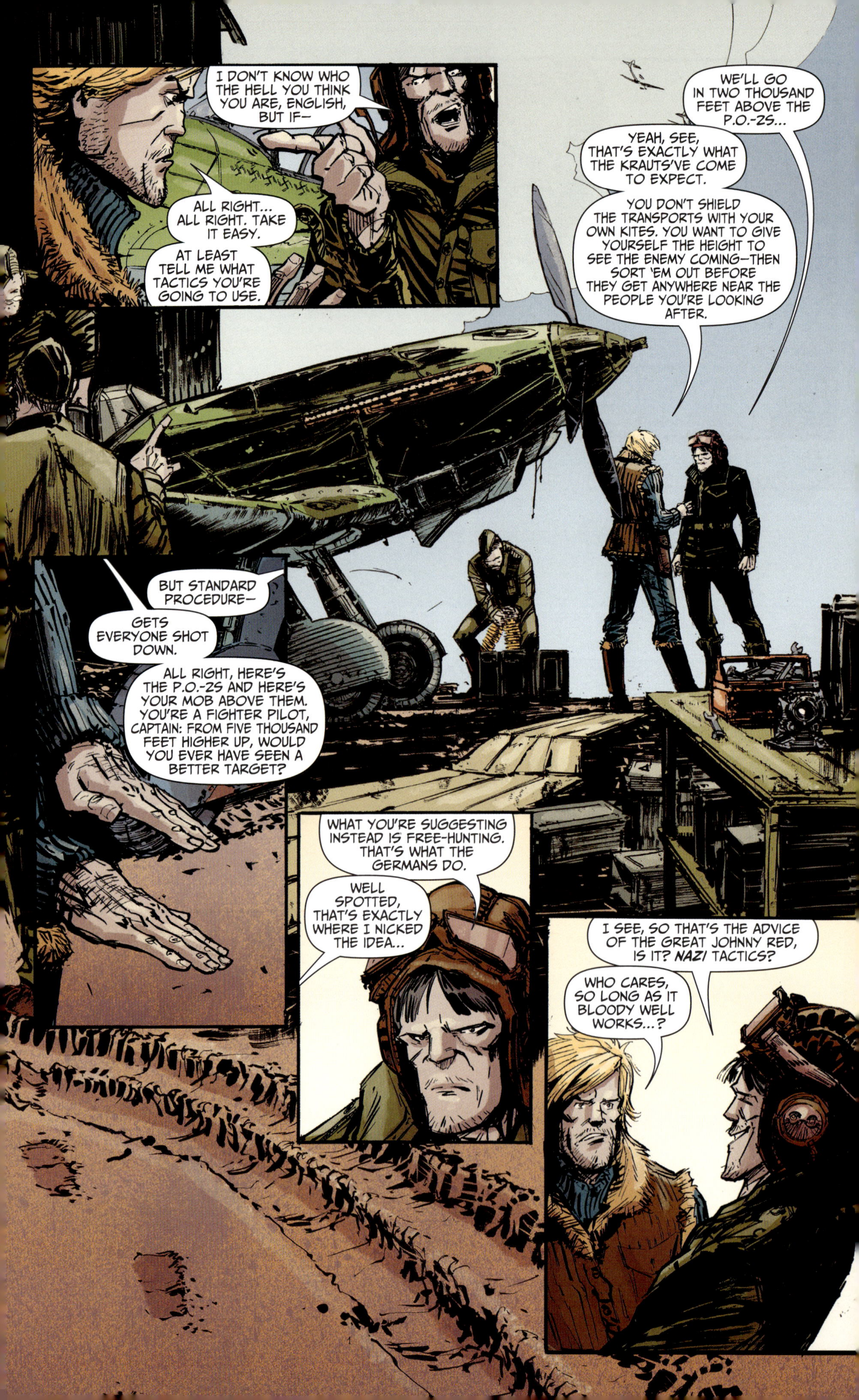
I DON'T KNOW WHO THE HELL YOU THINK YOU ARE, ENGLISH, BUT IF—
ALL RIGHT... ALL RIGHT. TAKE IT EASY.
AT LEAST TELL ME WHAT TACTICS YOU'RE GOING TO USE.
WE'LL GO IN TWO THOUSAND FEET ABOVE THE P.O.-2S...
YEAH, SEE, THAT'S EXACTLY WHAT THE KRAUTS'VE COME TO EXPECT.
YOU DON'T SHIELD THE TRANSPORTS WITH YOUR OWN KITES. YOU WANT TO GIVE YOURSELF THE HEIGHT TO SEE THE ENEMY COMING—THEN SORT 'EM OUT BEFORE THEY GET ANYWHERE NEAR THE PEOPLE YOU'RE LOOKING AFTER.
BUT STANDARD PROCEDURE—
GETS EVERYONE SHOT DOWN.
ALL RIGHT, HERE'S THE P.O.-2S AND HERE'S YOUR MOB ABOVE THEM. YOU'RE A FIGHTER PILOT, CAPTAIN: FROM FIVE THOUSAND FEET HIGHER UP, WOULD YOU EVER HAVE SEEN A BETTER TARGET?
WHAT YOU'RE SUGGESTING INSTEAD IS FREE-HUNTING. THAT'S WHAT THE GERMANS DO.
WELL SPOTTED, THAT'S EXACTLY WHERE I NICKED THE IDEA...
I SEE, SO THAT'S THE ADVICE OF THE GREAT JOHNNY RED, IS IT? *NAZI* TACTICS?
WHO CARES, SO LONG AS IT BLOODY WELL WORKS...?

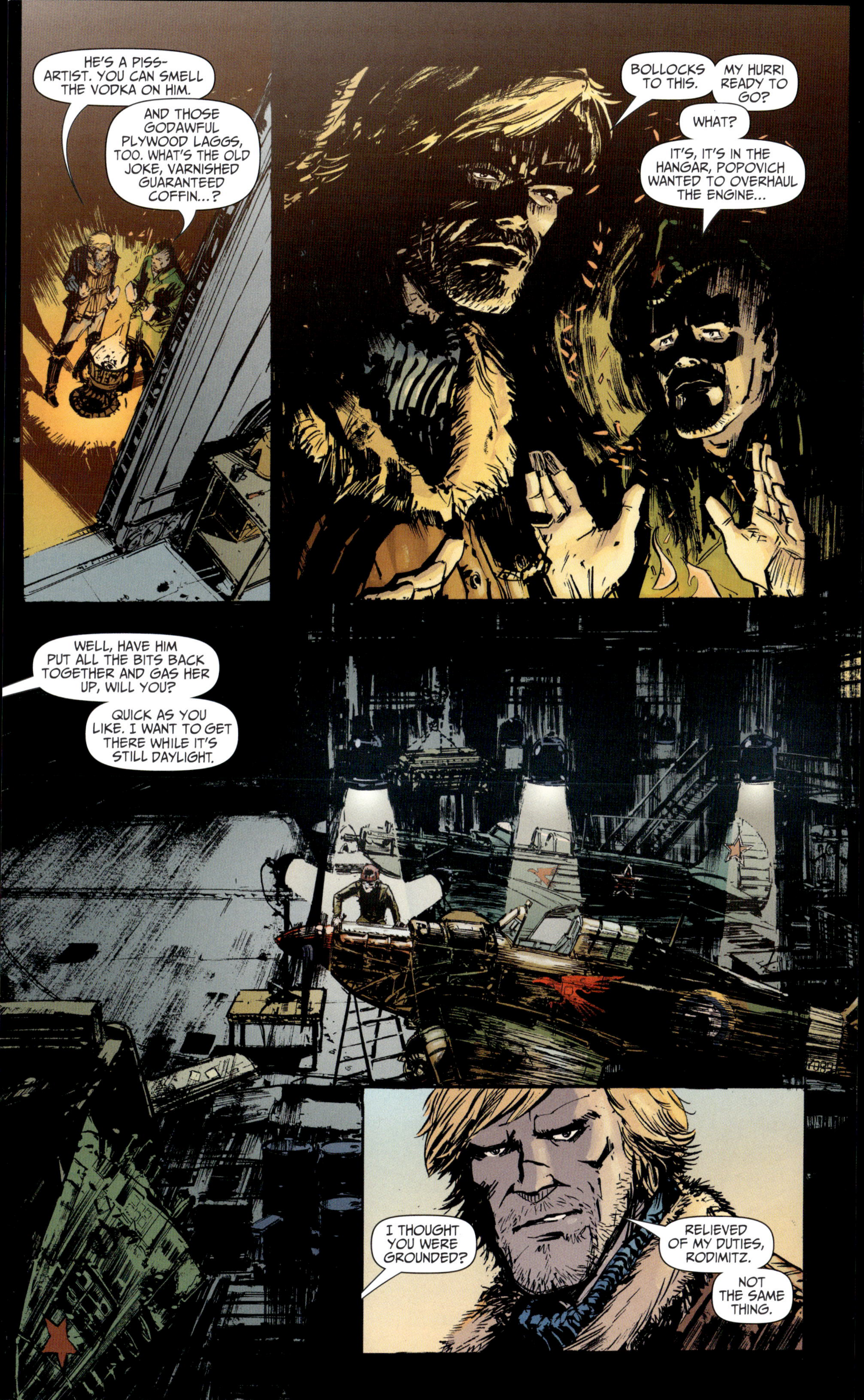
HE'S A PISS-ARTIST. YOU CAN SMELL THE VODKA ON HIM.
AND THOSE GODAWFUL PLYWOOD LAGGS, TOO. WHAT'S THE OLD JOKE, VARNISHED GUARANTEED COFFIN...?
BOLLOCKS TO THIS.
MY HURRI READY TO GO?
WHAT?
IT'S, IT'S IN THE HANGAR, POPOVICH WANTED TO OVERHAUL THE ENGINE...
WELL, HAVE HIM PUT ALL THE BITS BACK TOGETHER AND GAS HER UP, WILL YOU?
QUICK AS YOU LIKE. I WANT TO GET THERE WHILE IT'S STILL DAYLIGHT.
I THOUGHT YOU WERE GROUNDED?
RELIEVED OF MY DUTIES, RODIMITZ.
NOT THE SAME THING.

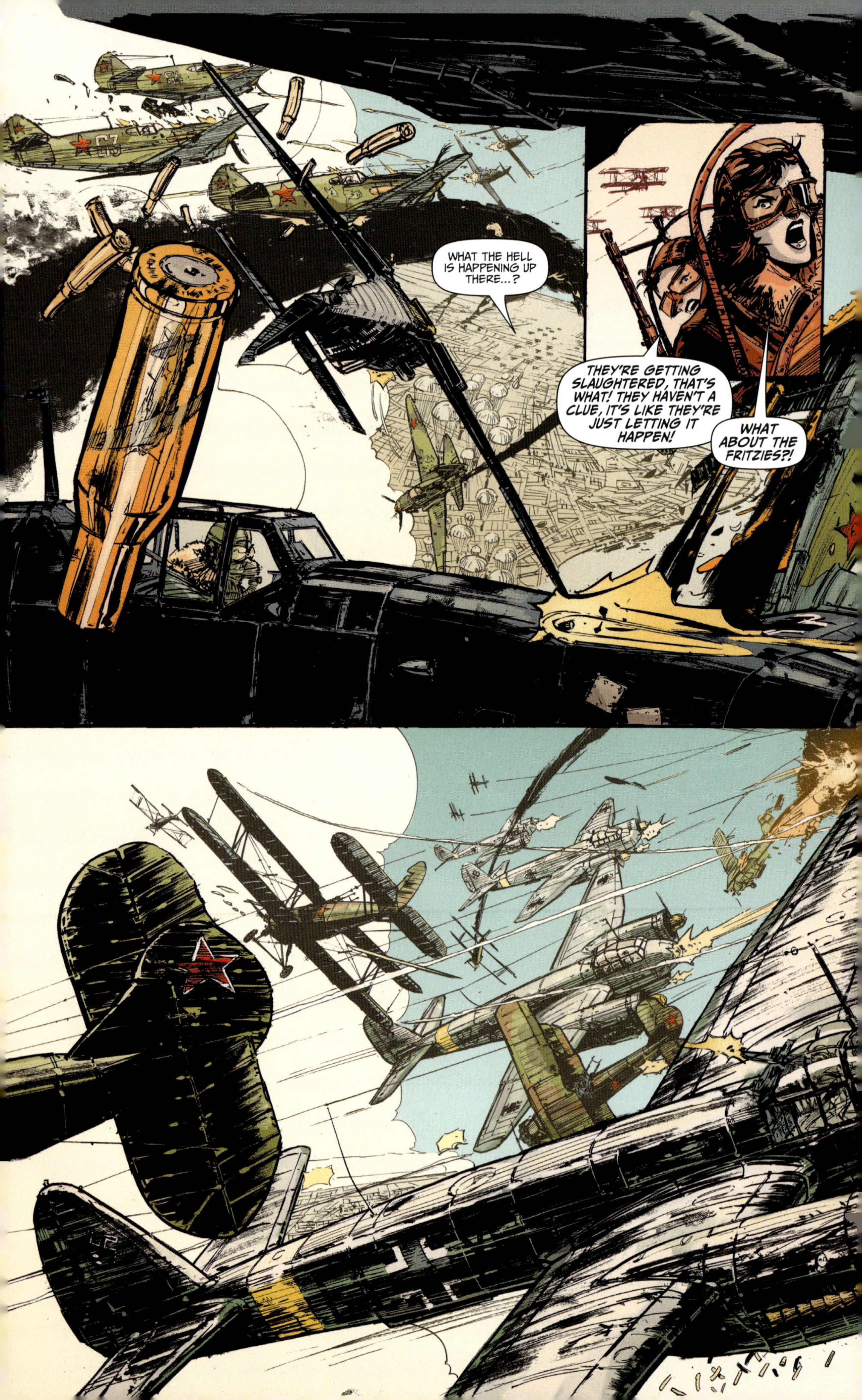
WHAT THE HELL IS HAPPENING UP THERE...?
THEY'RE GETTING SLAUGHTERED, THAT'S WHAT! THEY HAVEN'T A CLUE, IT'S LIKE THEY'RE JUST LETTING IT HAPPEN!
WHAT ABOUT THE FRITZIES?!

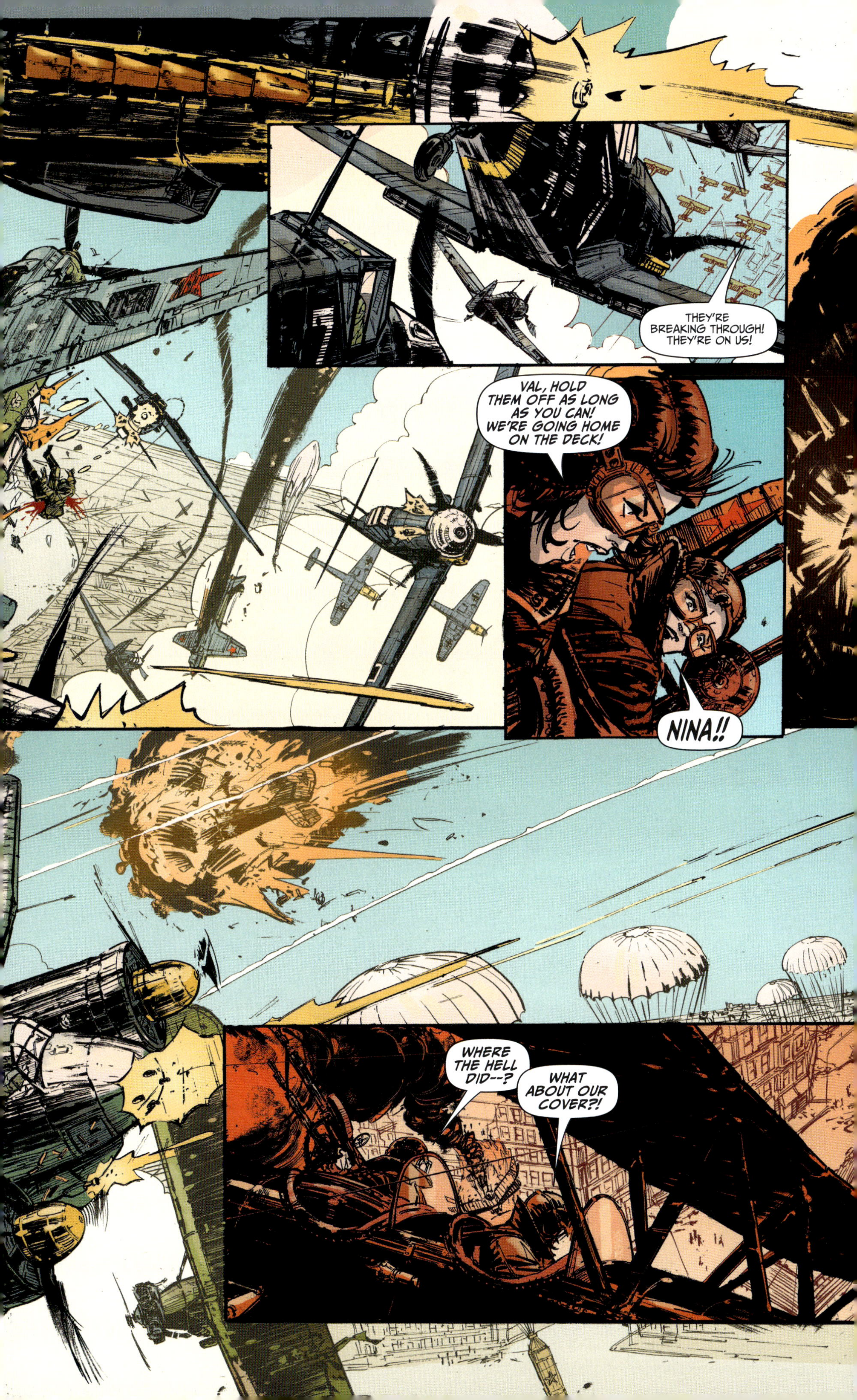

THEY'RE BREAKING THROUGH! THEY'RE ON US!
VAL, HOLD THEM OFF AS LONG AS YOU CAN! WE'RE GOING HOME ON THE DECK!
NINA!!
WHERE THE HELL DID--?
WHAT ABOUT OUR COVER?!

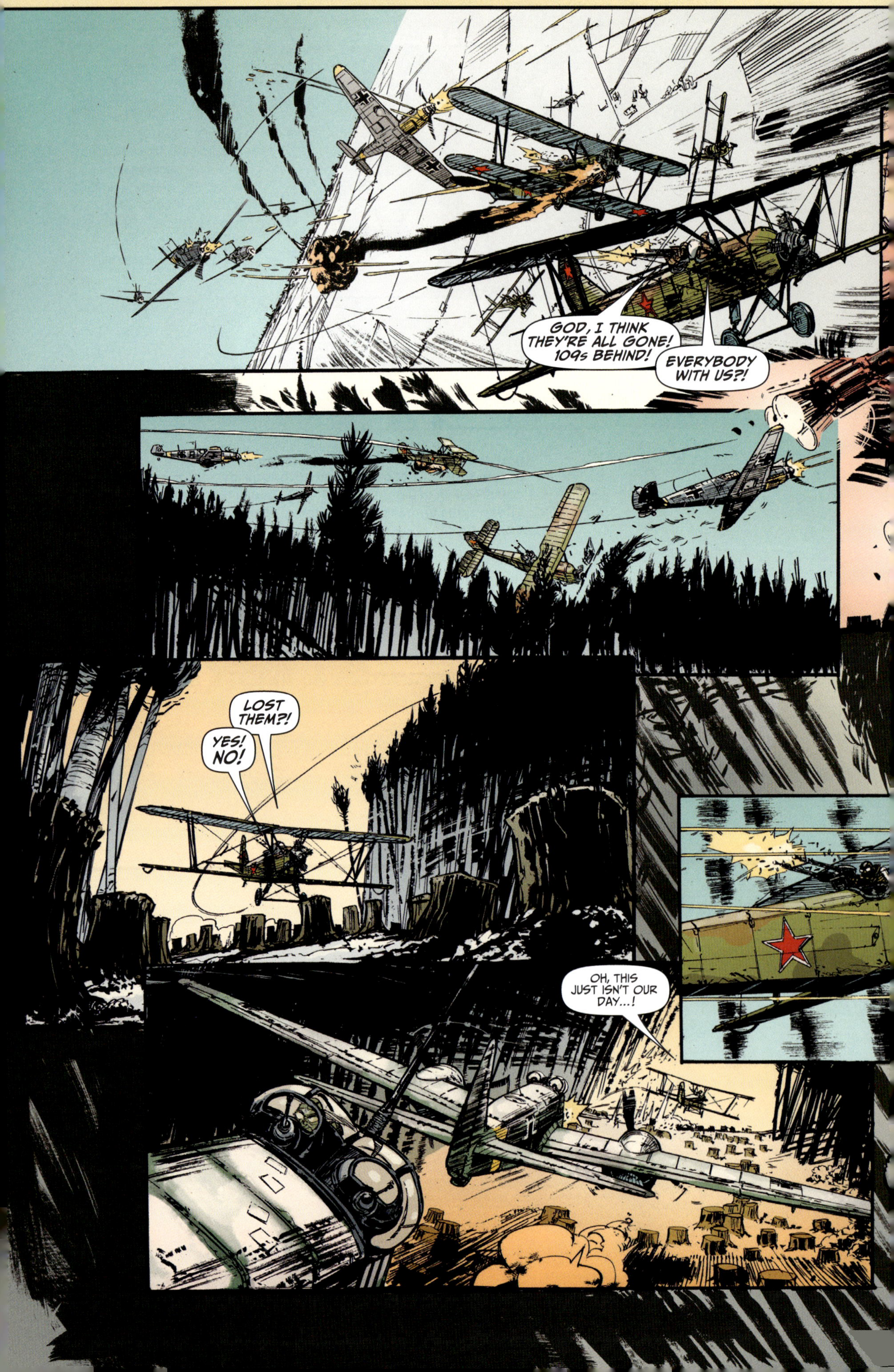
GOD, I THINK THEY'RE ALL GONE! 109s BEHIND!
EVERYBODY WITH US?!
LOST THEM?!
YES! NO!
OH, THIS JUST ISN'T OUR DAY...!

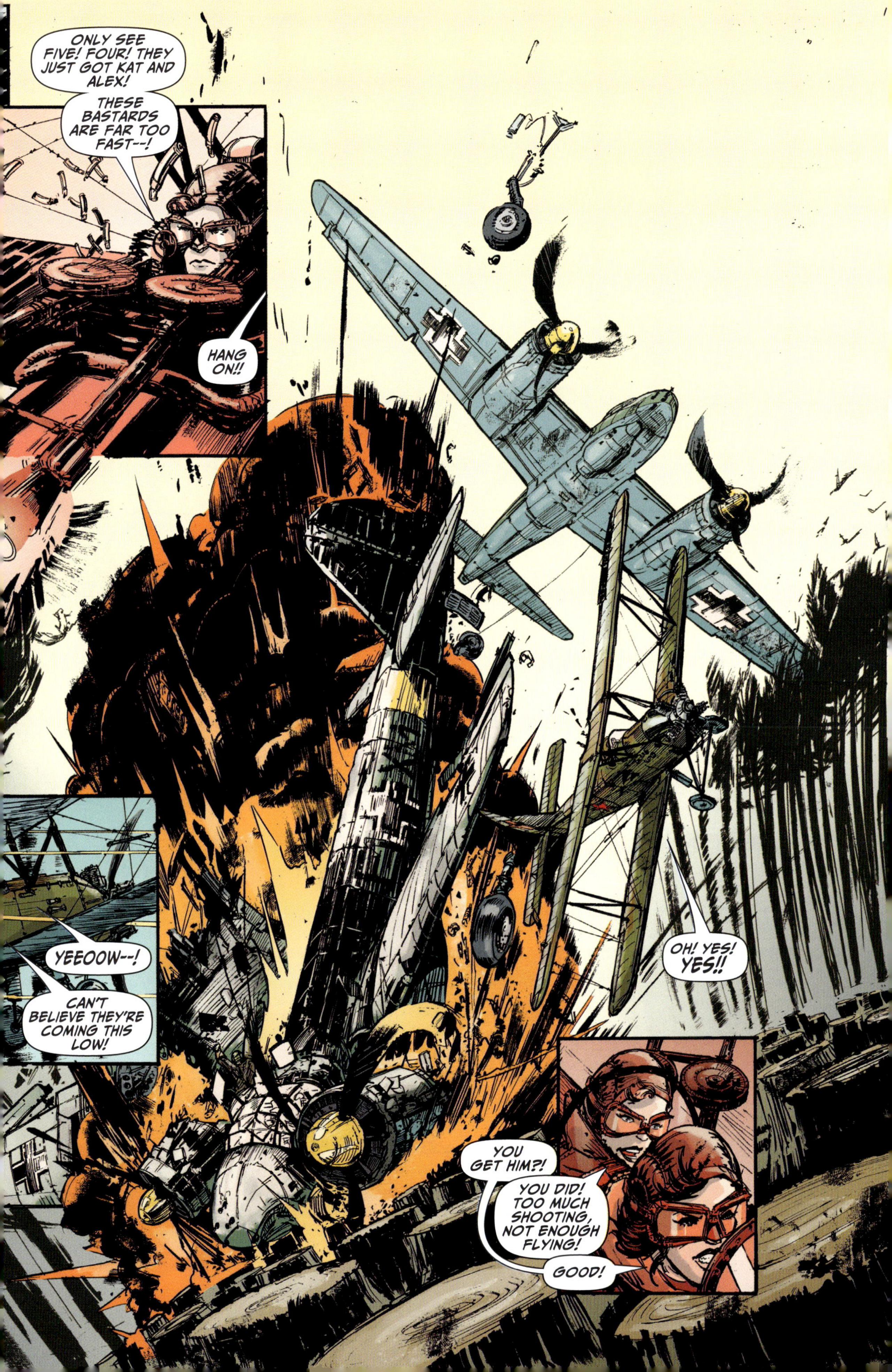
ONLY SEE FIVE! FOUR! THEY JUST GOT KAT AND ALEX!
THESE BASTARDS ARE FAR TOO FAST--!
HANG ON!!
YEEOOW--!
CAN'T BELIEVE THEY'RE COMING THIS LOW!
OH! YES! YES!!
YOU GET HIM?!
YOU DID! TOO MUCH SHOOTING, NOT ENOUGH FLYING!
GOOD!

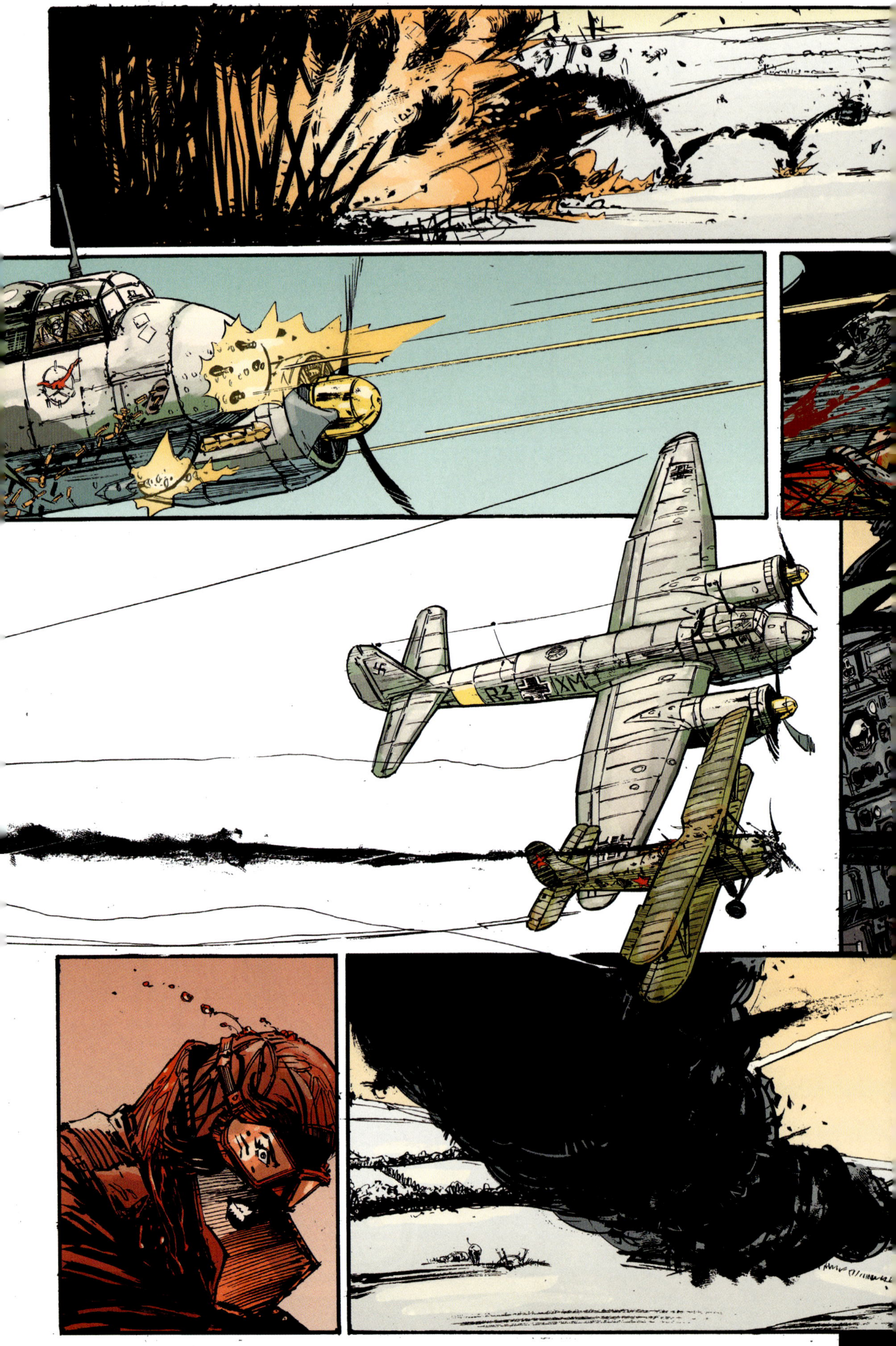

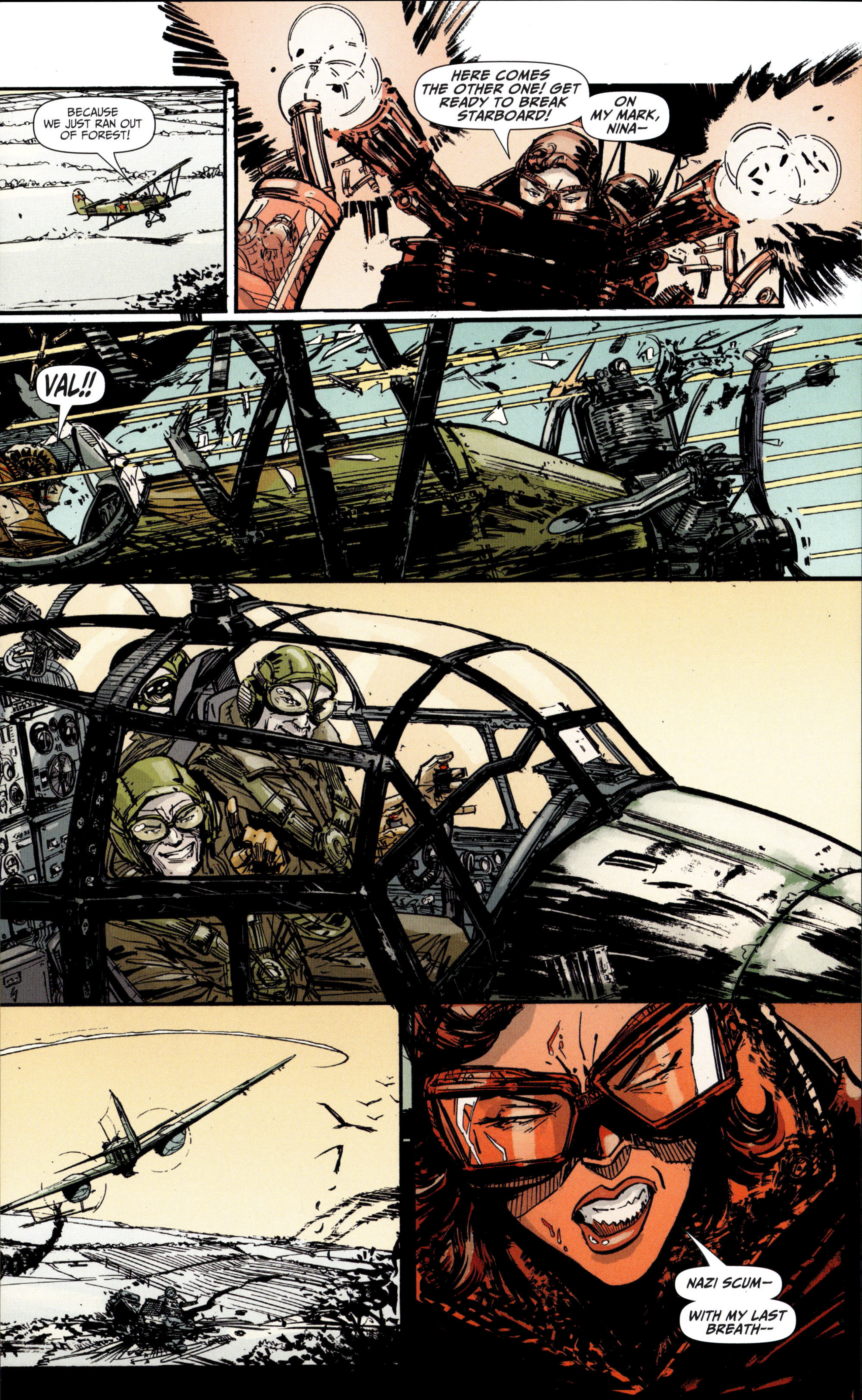

BECAUSE WE JUST RAN OUT OF FOREST!
HERE COMES THE OTHER ONE! GET READY TO BREAK STARBOARD!
ON MY MARK, NINA–
VAL!!
NAZI SCUM–
WITH MY LAST BREATH--

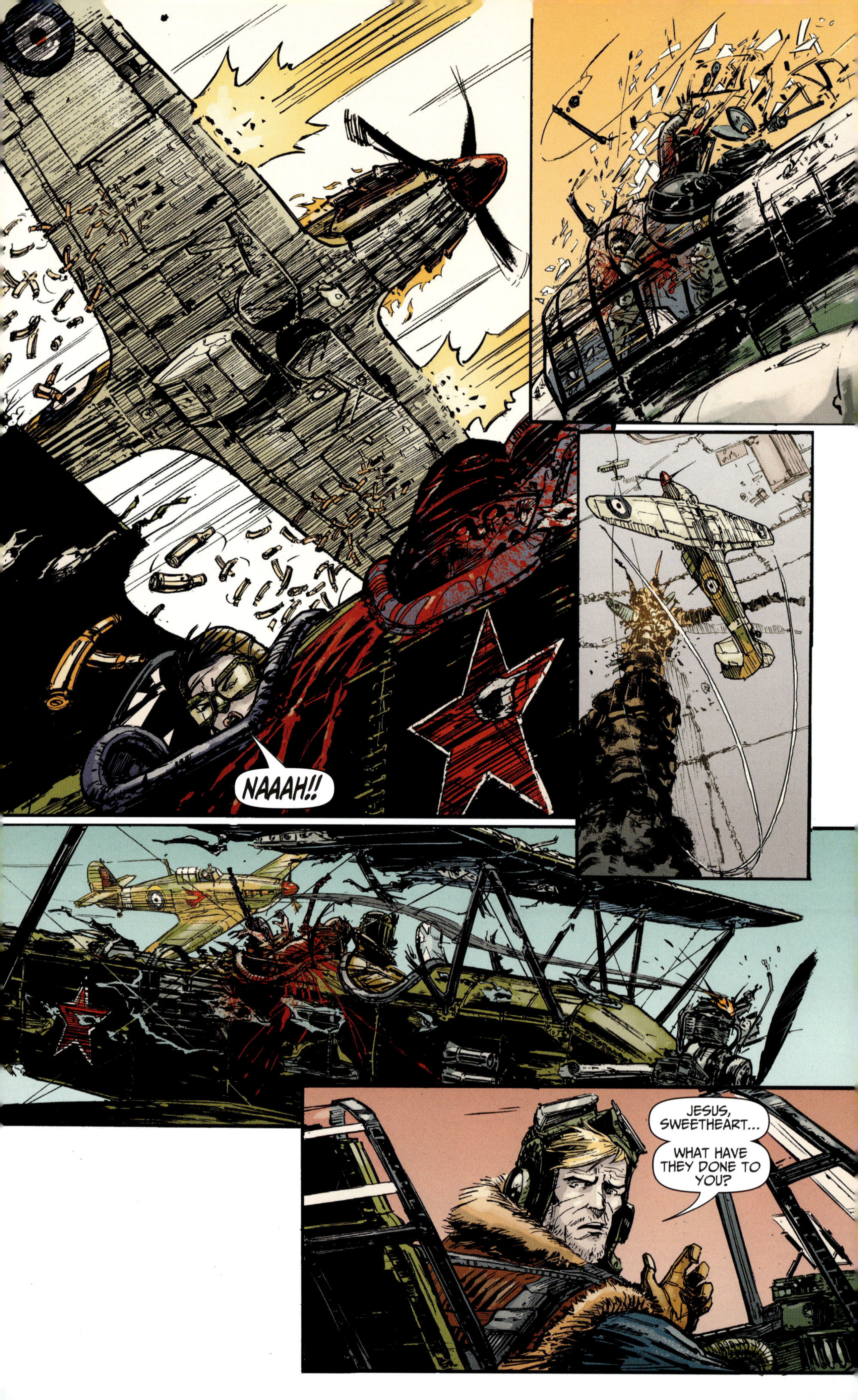
NAAAH!!
JESUS, SWEETHEART...
WHAT HAVE THEY DONE TO YOU?

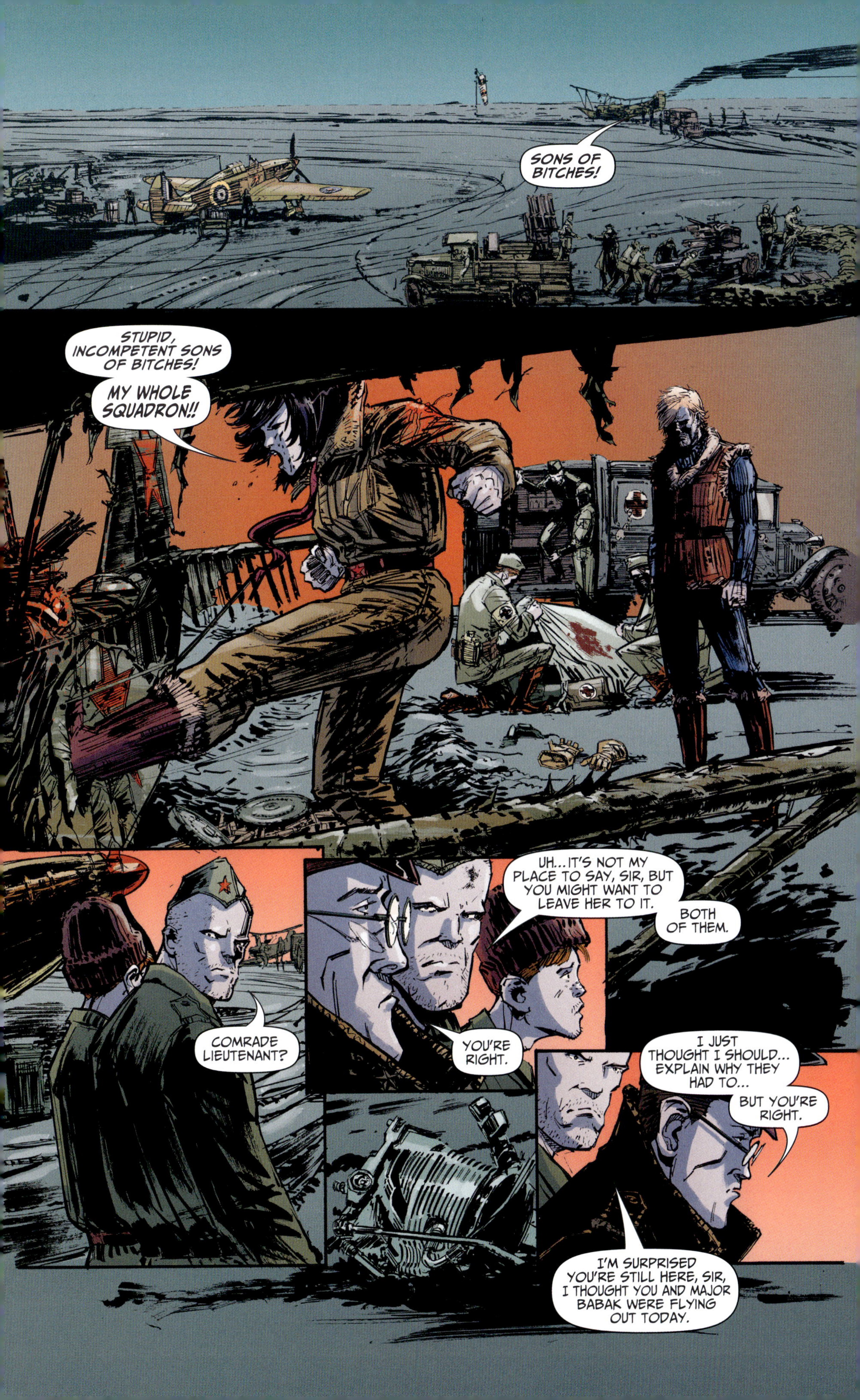
SONS OF BITCHES!
STUPID, INCOMPETENT SONS OF BITCHES!
MY WHOLE SQUADRON!!
COMRADE LIEUTENANT?
UH... IT'S NOT MY PLACE TO SAY, SIR, BUT YOU MIGHT WANT TO LEAVE HER TO IT.
BOTH OF THEM.
YOU'RE RIGHT.
I JUST THOUGHT I SHOULD... EXPLAIN WHY THEY HAD TO...
BUT YOU'RE RIGHT.
I'M SURPRISED YOU'RE STILL HERE, SIR, I THOUGHT YOU AND MAJOR BABAK WERE FLYING OUT TODAY.

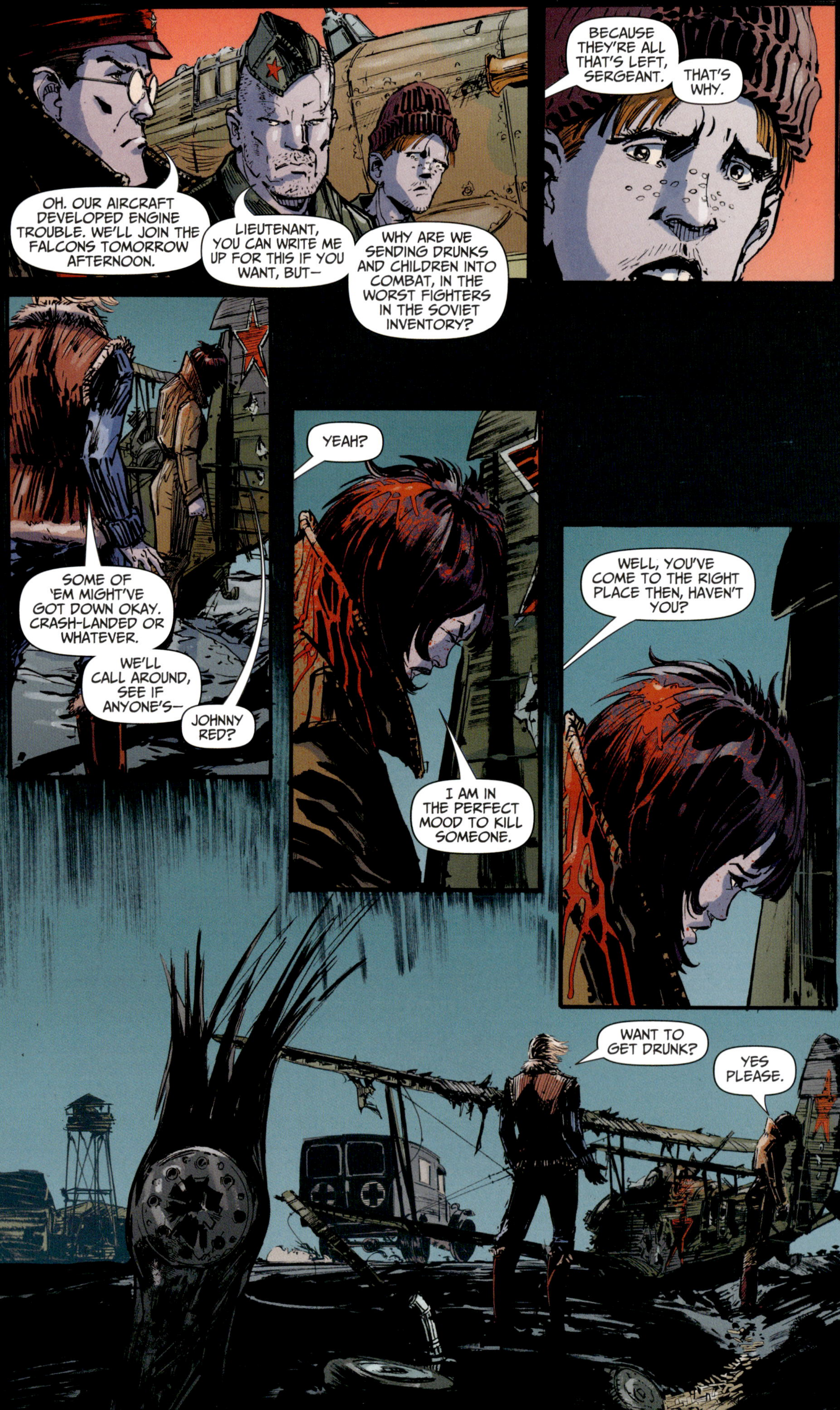
OH. OUR AIRCRAFT DEVELOPED ENGINE TROUBLE. WE'LL JOIN THE FALCONS TOMORROW AFTERNOON.
LIEUTENANT, YOU CAN WRITE ME UP FOR THIS IF YOU WANT, BUT—
WHY ARE WE SENDING DRUNKS AND CHILDREN INTO COMBAT, IN THE WORST FIGHTERS IN THE SOVIET INVENTORY?
BECAUSE THEY'RE ALL THAT'S LEFT, SERGEANT.
THAT'S WHY.
SOME OF 'EM MIGHT'VE GOT DOWN OKAY. CRASH-LANDED OR WHATEVER.
WE'LL CALL AROUND, SEE IF ANYONE'S—
JOHNNY RED?
YEAH?
I AM IN THE PERFECT MOOD TO KILL SOMEONE.
WELL, YOU'VE COME TO THE RIGHT PLACE THEN, HAVEN'T YOU?
WANT TO GET DRUNK?
YES PLEASE.

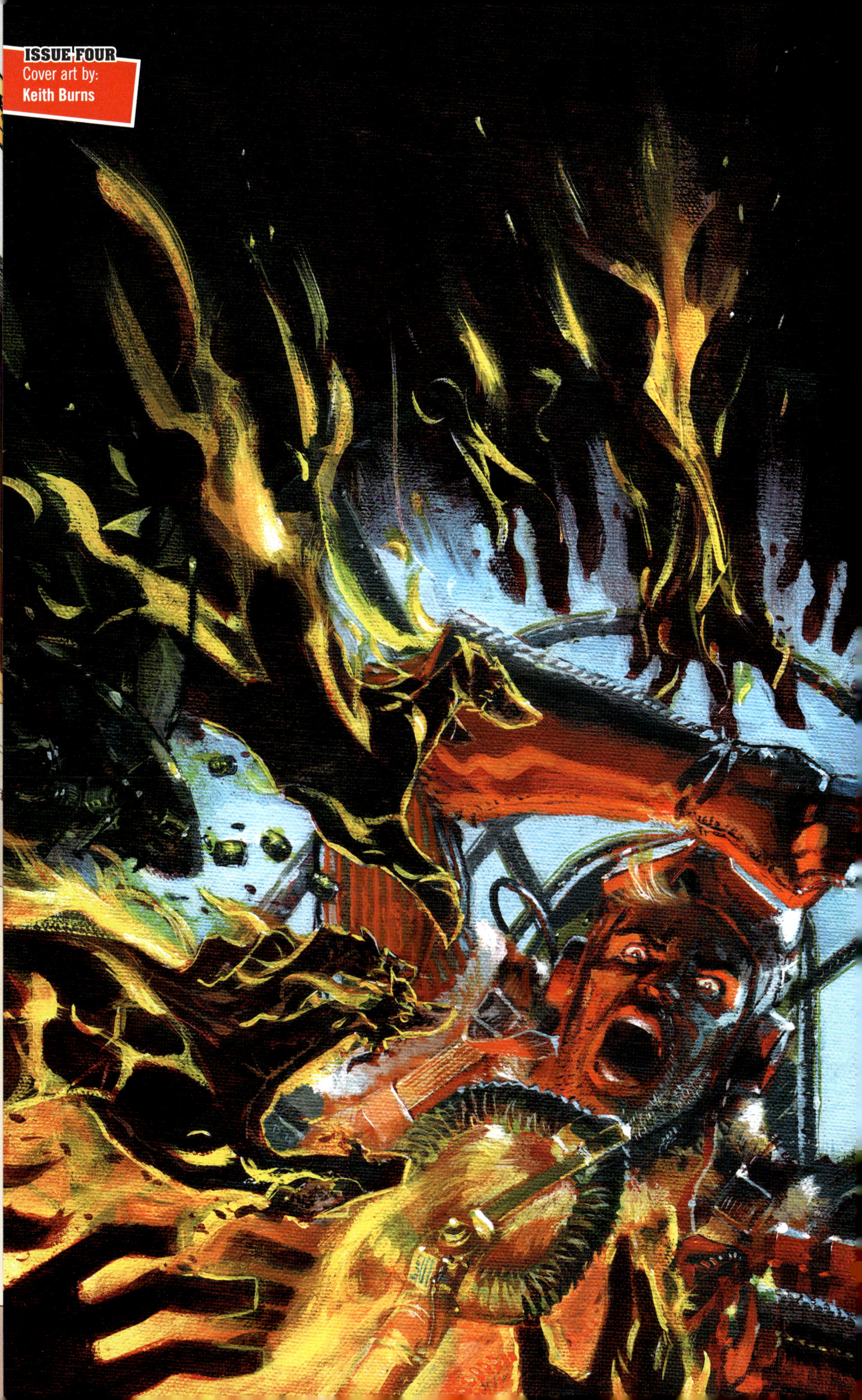

ISSUE FOUR
Cover art by:
Keith Burns

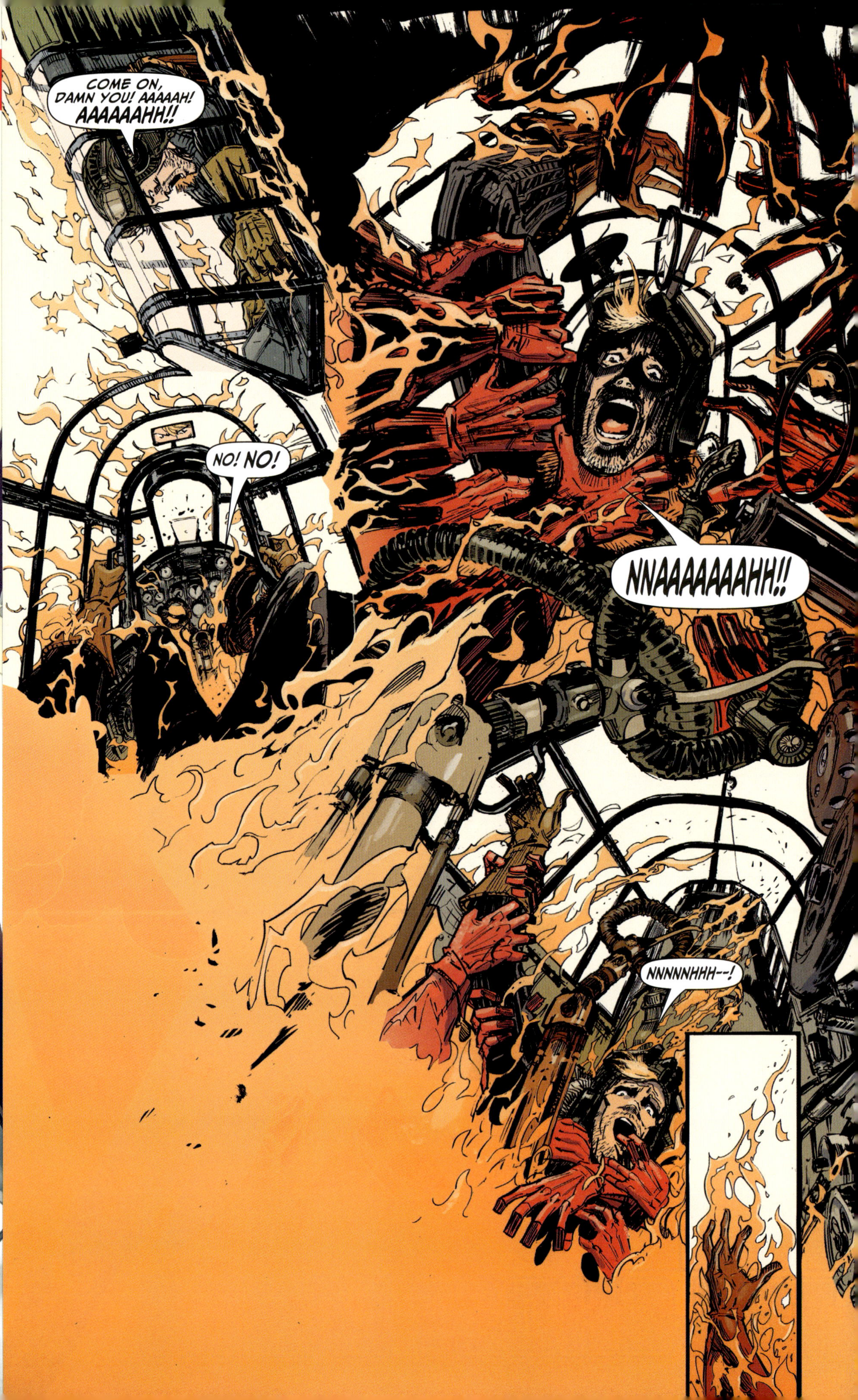
COME ON, DAMN YOU! AAAAAH! AAAAAAHH!!
NO! NO!
NNAAAAAAAHH!!
NNNNNHHH--!

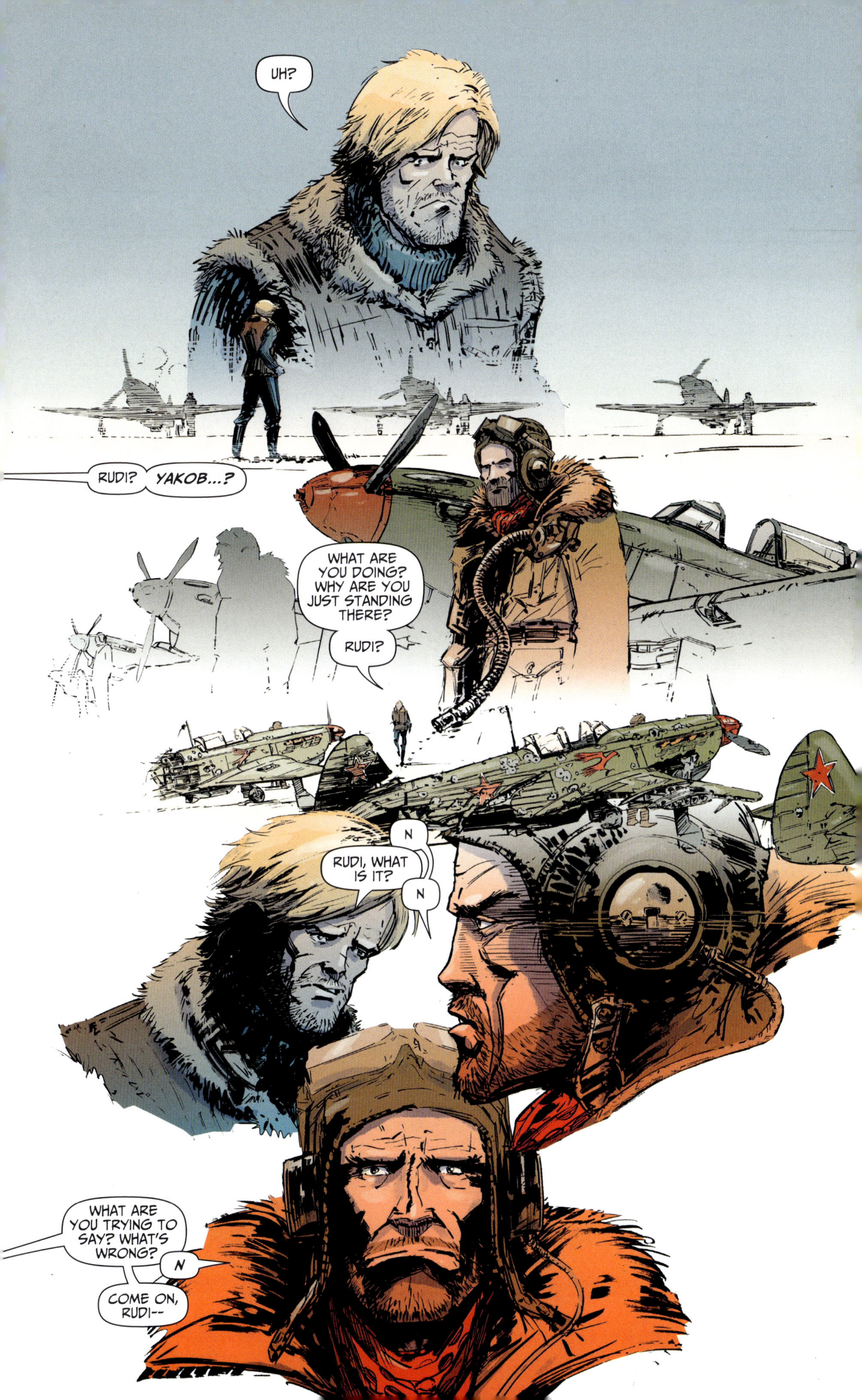
UH?
RUDI?
YAKOB...?
WHAT ARE YOU DOING? WHY ARE YOU JUST STANDING THERE?
RUDI?
N
RUDI, WHAT IS IT?
N
WHAT ARE YOU TRYING TO SAY? WHAT'S WRONG?
N
COME ON, RUDI--

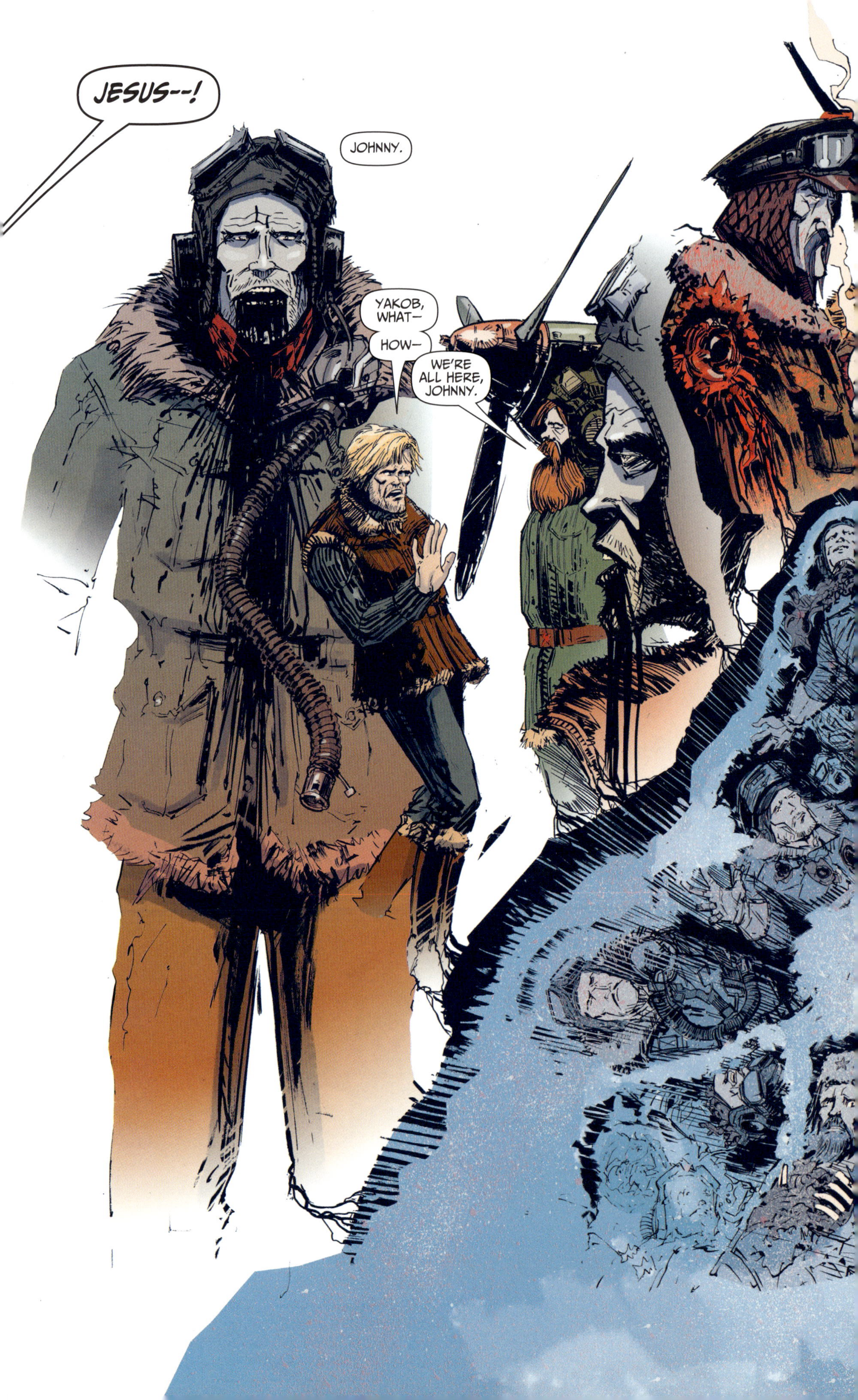
JESUS--!
JOHNNY.
YAKOB, WHAT—
HOW—
WE'RE ALL HERE, JOHNNY.

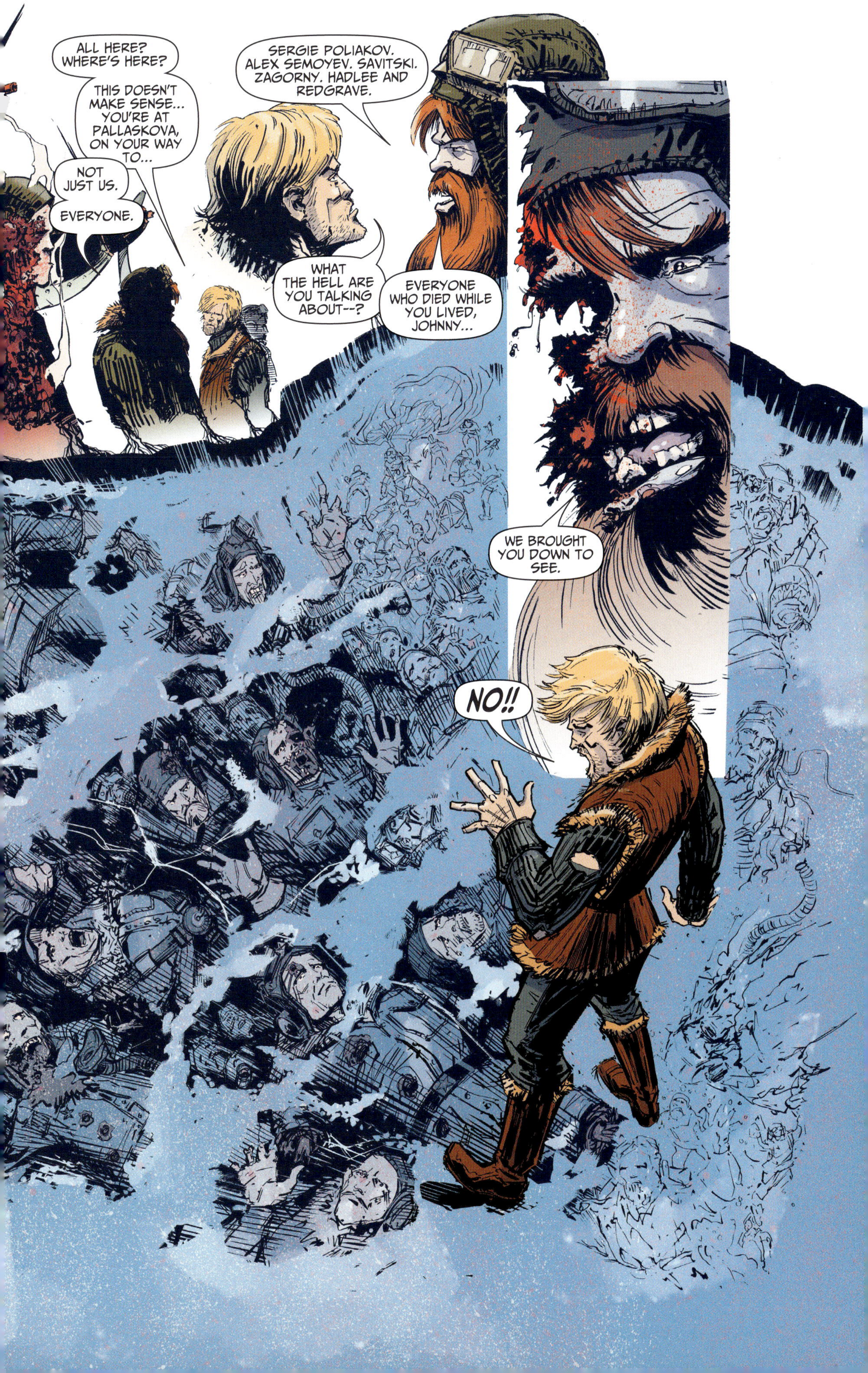

ALL HERE? WHERE'S HERE?
THIS DOESN'T MAKE SENSE... YOU'RE AT PALLASKOVA, ON YOUR WAY TO...
NOT JUST US.
EVERYONE.
SERGIE POLIAKOV. ALEX SEMOYEV. SAVITSKI. ZAGORNY. HADLEE AND REDGRAVE.
WHAT THE HELL ARE YOU TALKING ABOUT--?
EVERYONE WHO DIED WHILE YOU LIVED, JOHNNY...
WE BROUGHT YOU DOWN TO SEE.
NO!!

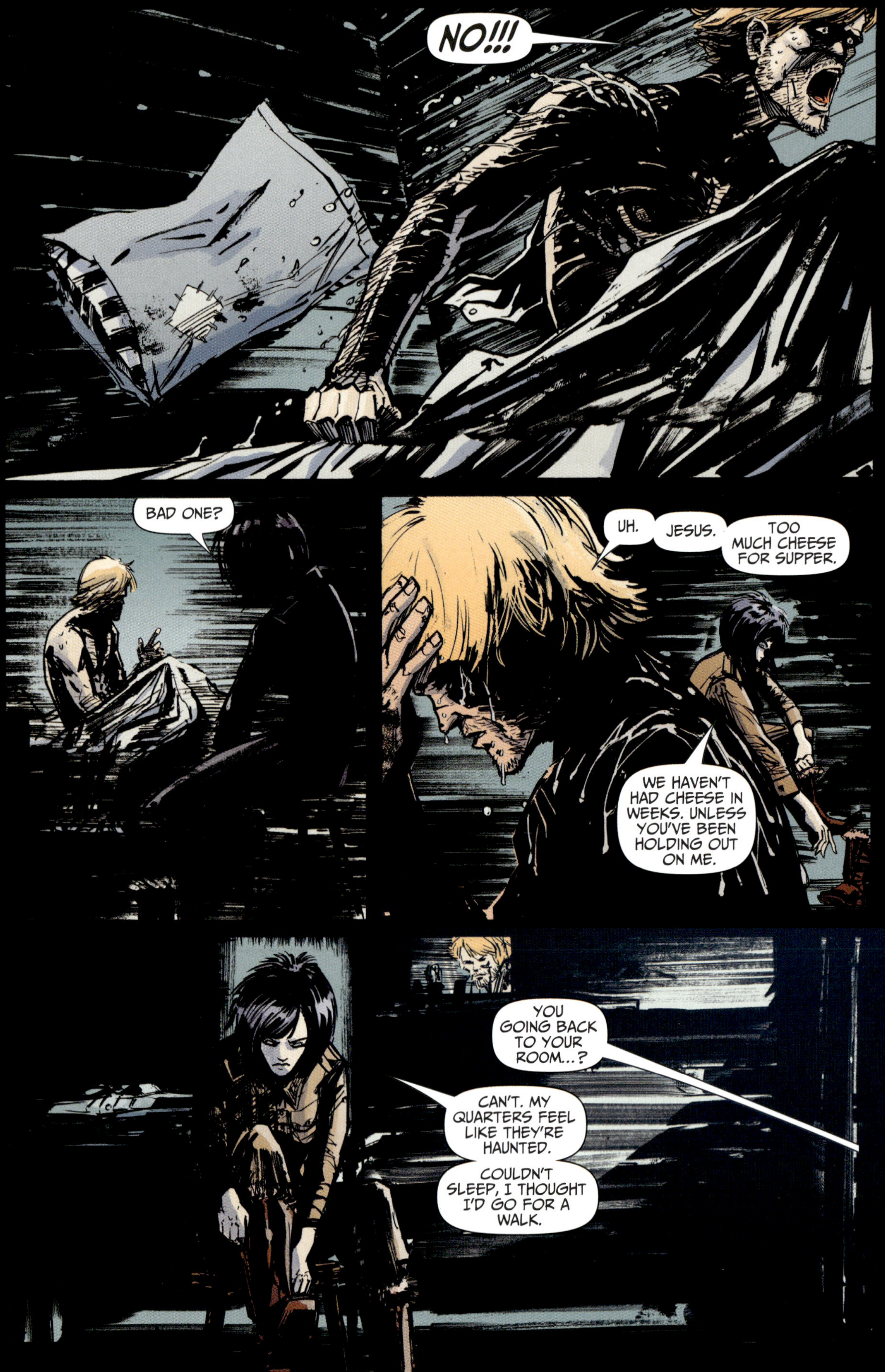
NO!!!
BAD ONE?
UH.
JESUS.
TOO MUCH CHEESE FOR SUPPER.
WE HAVEN'T HAD CHEESE IN WEEKS. UNLESS YOU'VE BEEN HOLDING OUT ON ME.
YOU GOING BACK TO YOUR ROOM...?
CAN'T. MY QUARTERS FEEL LIKE THEY'RE HAUNTED.
COULDN'T SLEEP, I THOUGHT I'D GO FOR A WALK.

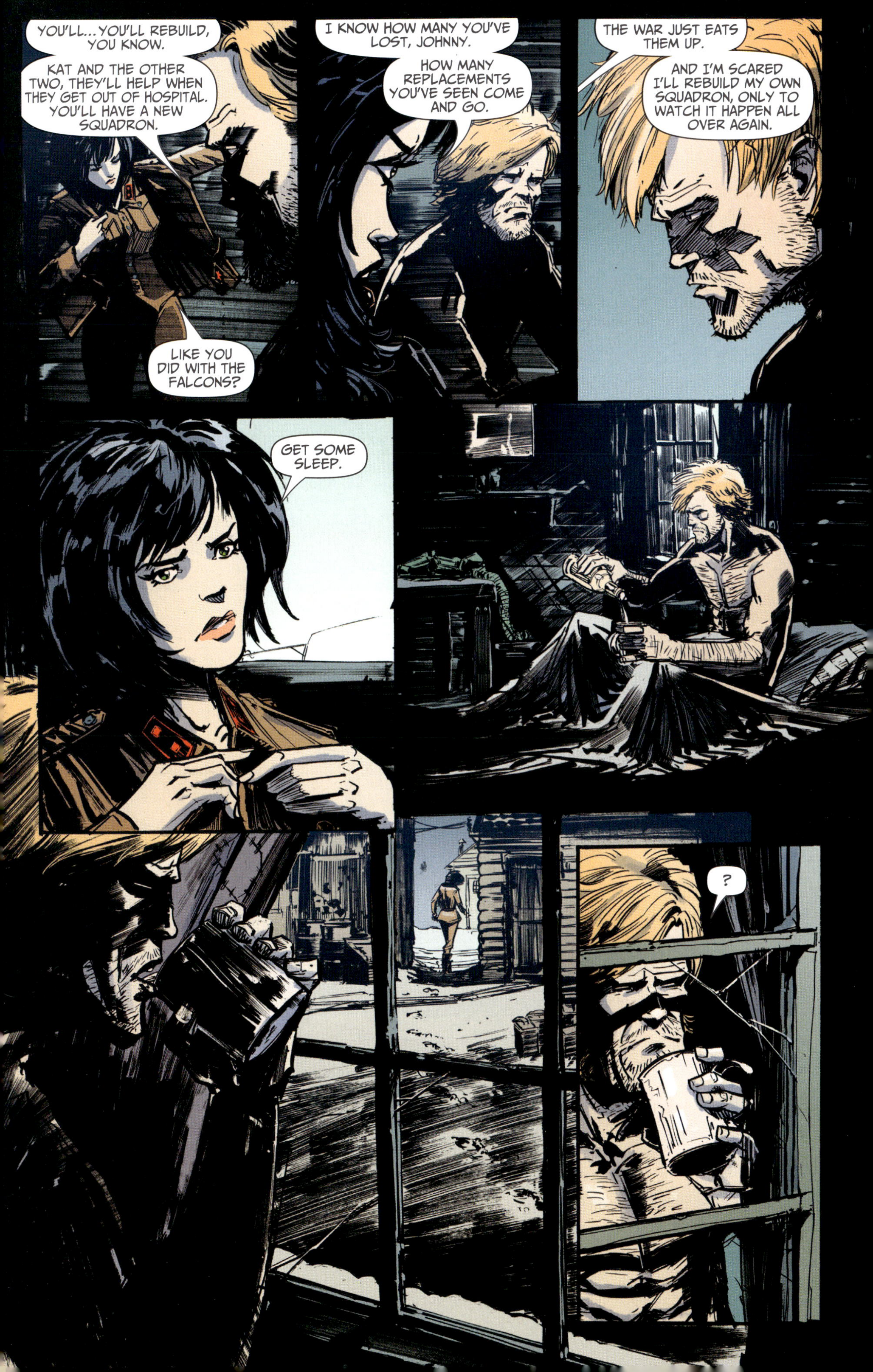
YOU'LL...YOU'LL REBUILD, YOU KNOW.
KAT AND THE OTHER TWO, THEY'LL HELP WHEN THEY GET OUT OF HOSPITAL. YOU'LL HAVE A NEW SQUADRON.
LIKE YOU DID WITH THE FALCONS?
I KNOW HOW MANY YOU'VE LOST, JOHNNY.
HOW MANY REPLACEMENTS YOU'VE SEEN COME AND GO.
THE WAR JUST EATS THEM UP.
AND I'M SCARED I'LL REBUILD MY OWN SQUADRON, ONLY TO WATCH IT HAPPEN ALL OVER AGAIN.
GET SOME SLEEP.
?

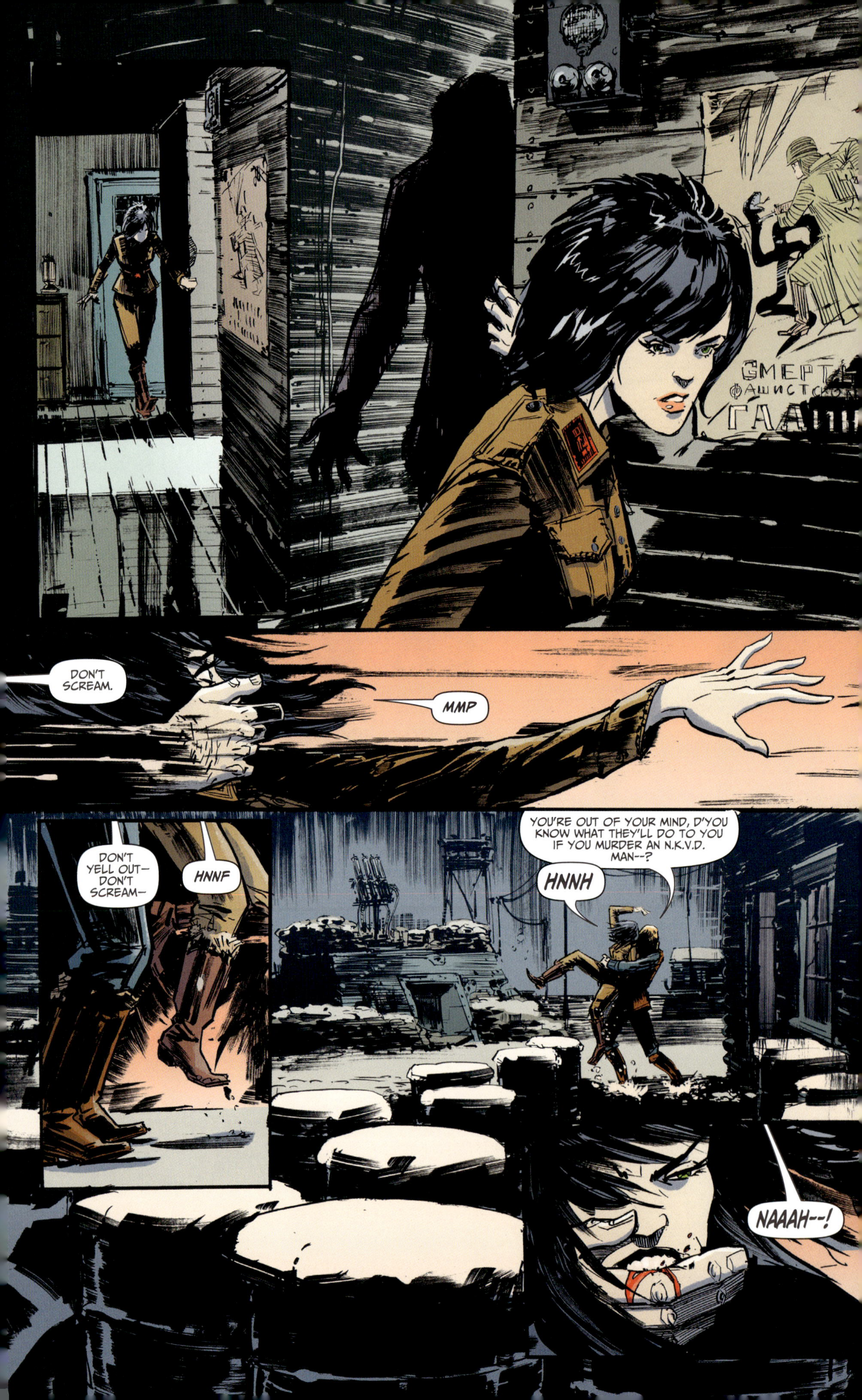
DON'T SCREAM.
MMP
DON'T YELL OUT— DON'T SCREAM—
HNNF
YOU'RE OUT OF YOUR MIND, D'YOU KNOW WHAT THEY'LL DO TO YOU IF YOU MURDER AN N.K.V.D. MAN--?
HNNH
NAAAH--!

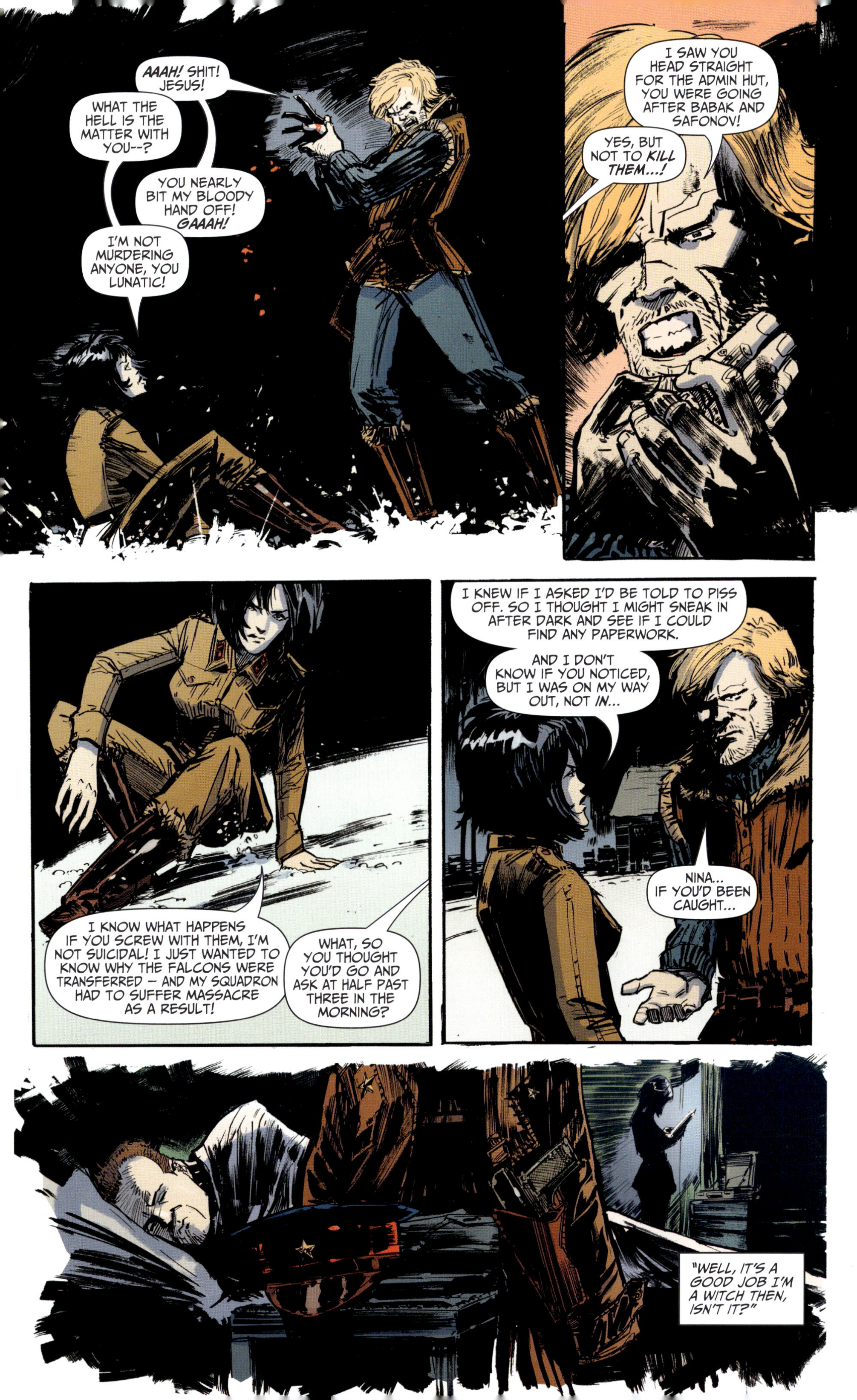
AAAH! SHIT! JESUS!
WHAT THE HELL IS THE MATTER WITH YOU--?
YOU NEARLY BIT MY BLOODY HAND OFF! GAAAH!
I'M NOT MURDERING ANYONE, YOU LUNATIC!
I SAW YOU HEAD STRAIGHT FOR THE ADMIN HUT, YOU WERE GOING AFTER BABAK AND SAFONOV!
YES, BUT NOT TO KILL THEM...!
I KNOW WHAT HAPPENS IF YOU SCREW WITH THEM, I'M NOT SUICIDAL! I JUST WANTED TO KNOW WHY THE FALCONS WERE TRANSFERRED – AND MY SQUADRON HAD TO SUFFER MASSACRE AS A RESULT!
WHAT, SO YOU THOUGHT YOU'D GO AND ASK AT HALF PAST THREE IN THE MORNING?
I KNEW IF I ASKED I'D BE TOLD TO PISS OFF. SO I THOUGHT I MIGHT SNEAK IN AFTER DARK AND SEE IF I COULD FIND ANY PAPERWORK.
AND I DON'T KNOW IF YOU NOTICED, BUT I WAS ON MY WAY OUT, NOT IN...
NINA... IF YOU'D BEEN CAUGHT...
"WELL, IT'S A GOOD JOB I'M A WITCH THEN, ISN'T IT?"

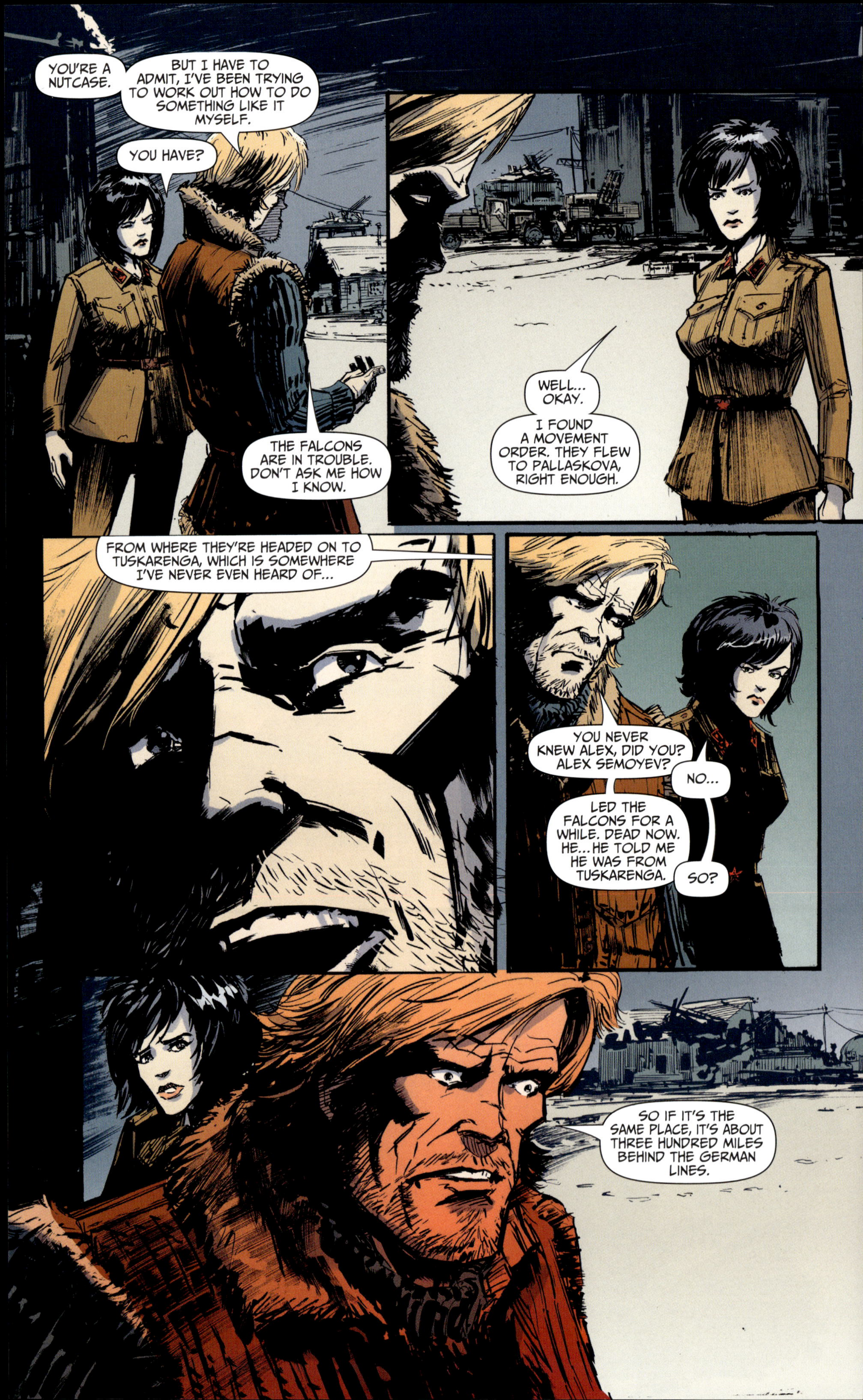
YOU'RE A NUTCASE.
BUT I HAVE TO ADMIT, I'VE BEEN TRYING TO WORK OUT HOW TO DO SOMETHING LIKE IT MYSELF.
YOU HAVE?
THE FALCONS ARE IN TROUBLE. DON'T ASK ME HOW I KNOW.
WELL... OKAY.
I FOUND A MOVEMENT ORDER. THEY FLEW TO PALLASKOVA, RIGHT ENOUGH.
FROM WHERE THEY'RE HEADED ON TO TUSKARENGA, WHICH IS SOMEWHERE I'VE NEVER EVEN HEARD OF...
YOU NEVER KNEW ALEX, DID YOU? ALEX SEMOYEV?
NO...
LED THE FALCONS FOR A WHILE. DEAD NOW. HE...HE TOLD ME HE WAS FROM TUSKARENGA.
SO?
SO IF IT'S THE SAME PLACE, IT'S ABOUT THREE HUNDRED MILES BEHIND THE GERMAN LINES.

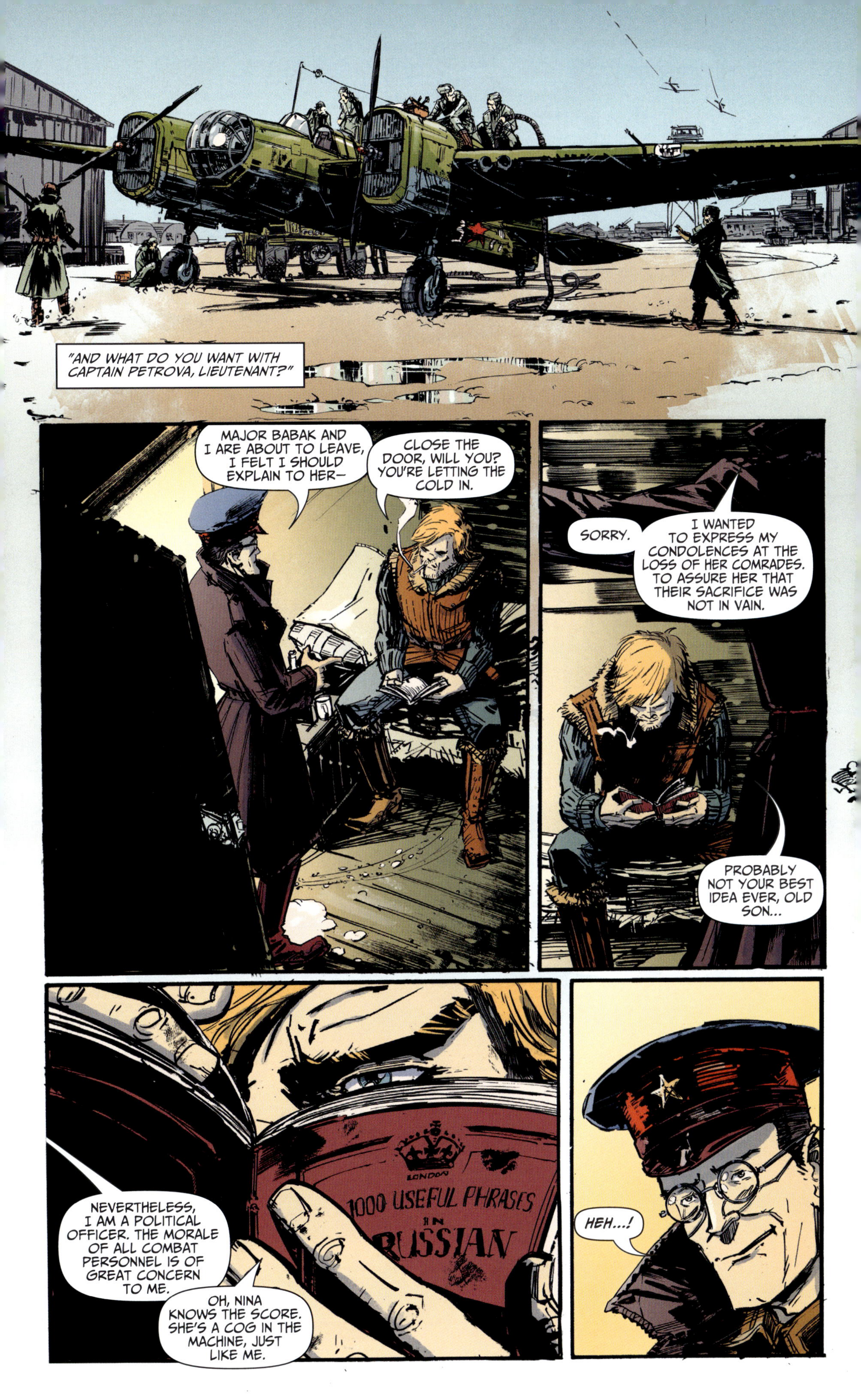
"AND WHAT DO YOU WANT WITH CAPTAIN PETROVA, LIEUTENANT?"
MAJOR BABAK AND I ARE ABOUT TO LEAVE, I FELT I SHOULD EXPLAIN TO HER—
CLOSE THE DOOR, WILL YOU? YOU'RE LETTING THE COLD IN.
SORRY.
I WANTED TO EXPRESS MY CONDOLENCES AT THE LOSS OF HER COMRADES. TO ASSURE HER THAT THEIR SACRIFICE WAS NOT IN VAIN.
PROBABLY NOT YOUR BEST IDEA EVER, OLD SON...
LONDON
1000 USEFUL PHRASES IN RUSSIAN
NEVERTHELESS, I AM A POLITICAL OFFICER. THE MORALE OF ALL COMBAT PERSONNEL IS OF GREAT CONCERN TO ME.
OH, NINA KNOWS THE SCORE. SHE'S A COG IN THE MACHINE, JUST LIKE ME.
HEH...!

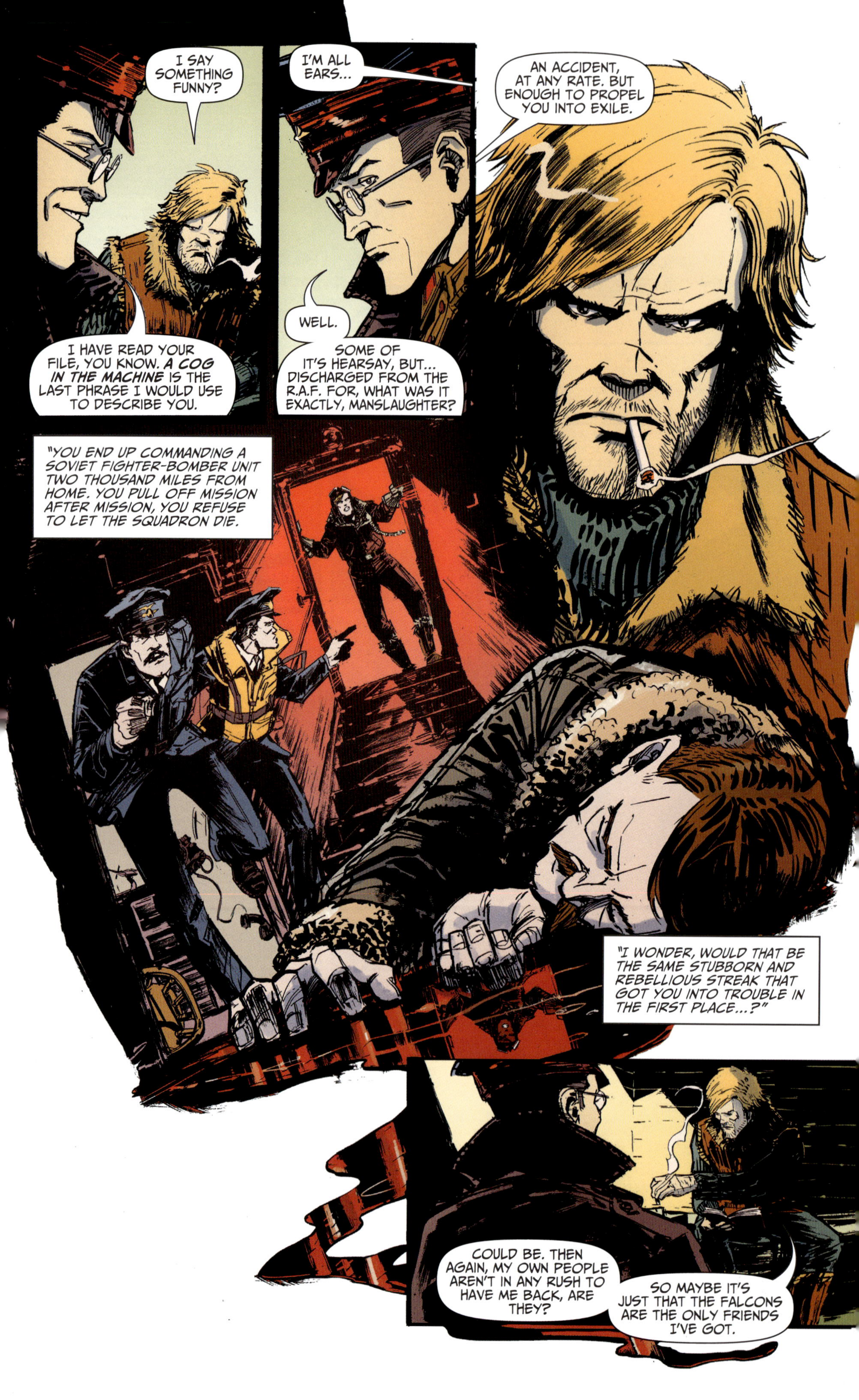
I SAY SOMETHING FUNNY?
I HAVE READ YOUR FILE, YOU KNOW. A COG IN THE MACHINE IS THE LAST PHRASE I WOULD USE TO DESCRIBE YOU.
I'M ALL EARS...
WELL.
SOME OF IT'S HEARSAY, BUT... DISCHARGED FROM THE R.A.F. FOR, WHAT WAS IT EXACTLY, MANSLAUGHTER?
AN ACCIDENT, AT ANY RATE. BUT ENOUGH TO PROPEL YOU INTO EXILE.
"YOU END UP COMMANDING A SOVIET FIGHTER-BOMBER UNIT TWO THOUSAND MILES FROM HOME. YOU PULL OFF MISSION AFTER MISSION, YOU REFUSE TO LET THE SQUADRON DIE.
"I WONDER, WOULD THAT BE THE SAME STUBBORN AND REBELLIOUS STREAK THAT GOT YOU INTO TROUBLE IN THE FIRST PLACE...?"
COULD BE. THEN AGAIN, MY OWN PEOPLE AREN'T IN ANY RUSH TO HAVE ME BACK, ARE THEY?
SO MAYBE IT'S JUST THAT THE FALCONS ARE THE ONLY FRIENDS I'VE GOT.

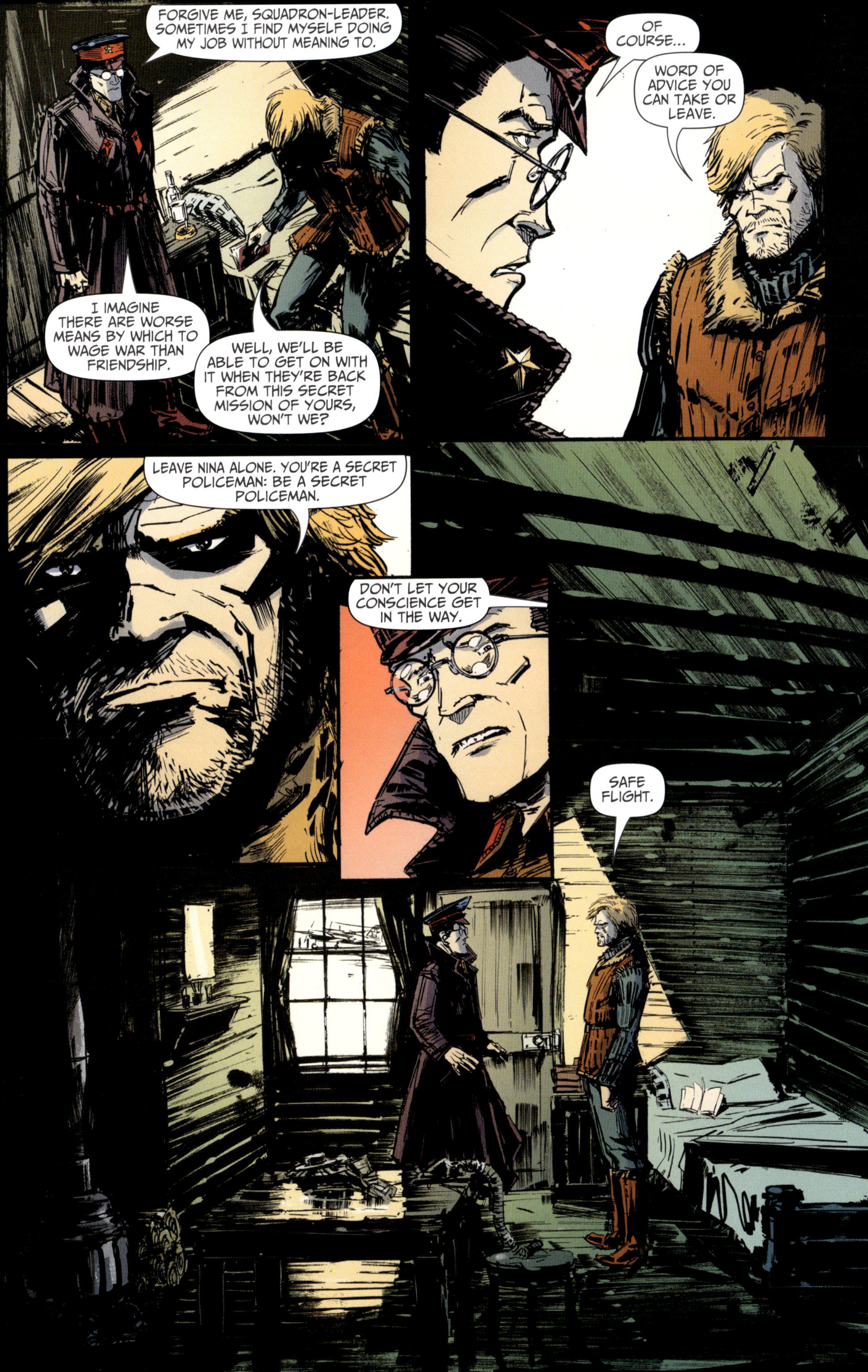
FORGIVE ME, SQUADRON-LEADER. SOMETIMES I FIND MYSELF DOING MY JOB WITHOUT MEANING TO.
I IMAGINE THERE ARE WORSE MEANS BY WHICH TO WAGE WAR THAN FRIENDSHIP.
WELL, WE'LL BE ABLE TO GET ON WITH IT WHEN THEY'RE BACK FROM THIS SECRET MISSION OF YOURS, WON'T WE?
OF COURSE...
WORD OF ADVICE YOU CAN TAKE OR LEAVE.
LEAVE NINA ALONE. YOU'RE A SECRET POLICEMAN: BE A SECRET POLICEMAN.
DON'T LET YOUR CONSCIENCE GET IN THE WAY.
SAFE FLIGHT.

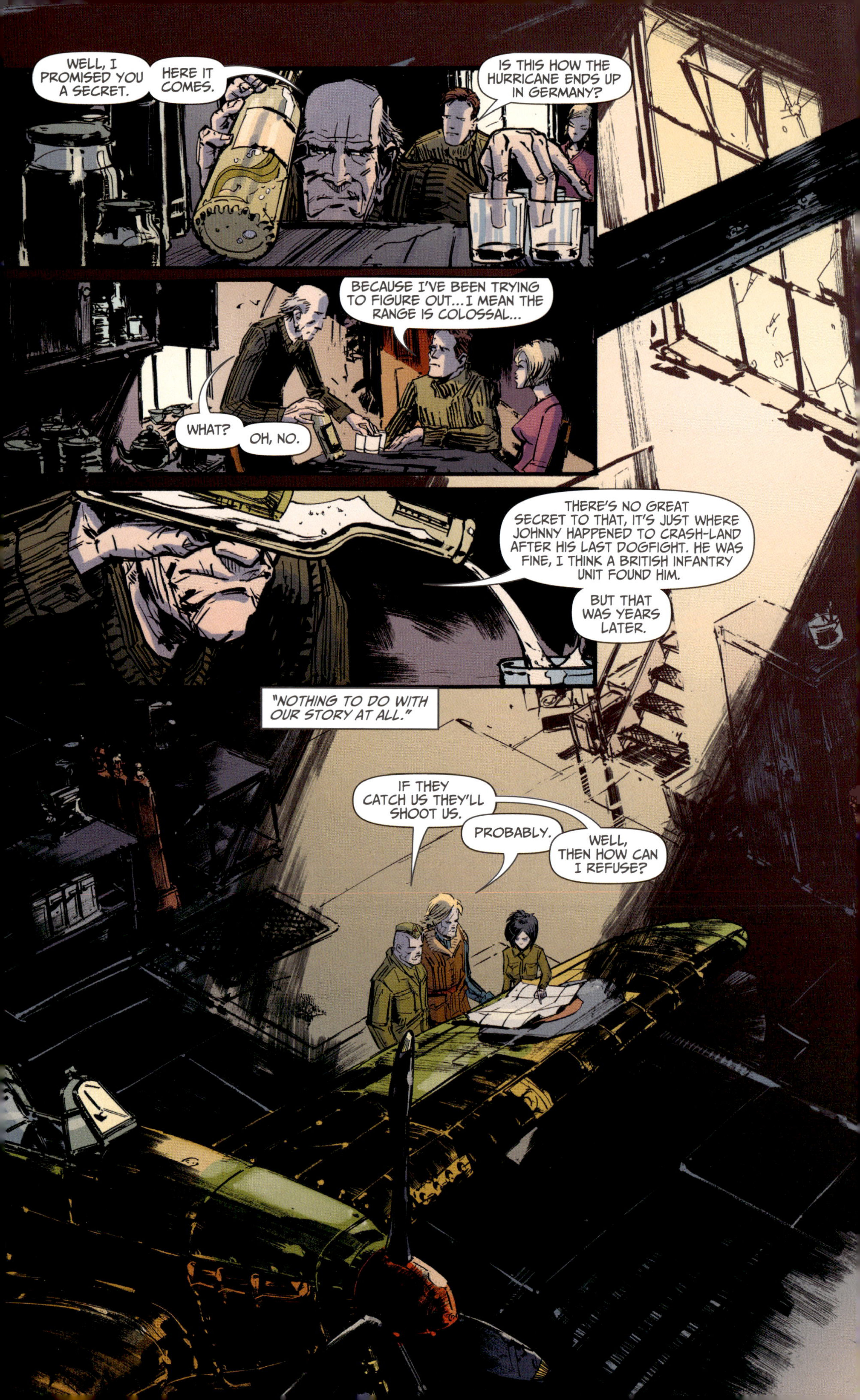
WELL, I PROMISED YOU A SECRET.
HERE IT COMES.
IS THIS HOW THE HURRICANE ENDS UP IN GERMANY?
BECAUSE I'VE BEEN TRYING TO FIGURE OUT... I MEAN THE RANGE IS COLOSSAL...
WHAT?
OH, NO.
THERE'S NO GREAT SECRET TO THAT, IT'S JUST WHERE JOHNNY HAPPENED TO CRASH-LAND AFTER HIS LAST DOGFIGHT. HE WAS FINE, I THINK A BRITISH INFANTRY UNIT FOUND HIM.
BUT THAT WAS YEARS LATER.
"NOTHING TO DO WITH OUR STORY AT ALL."
IF THEY CATCH US THEY'LL SHOOT US.
PROBABLY.
WELL, THEN HOW CAN I REFUSE?

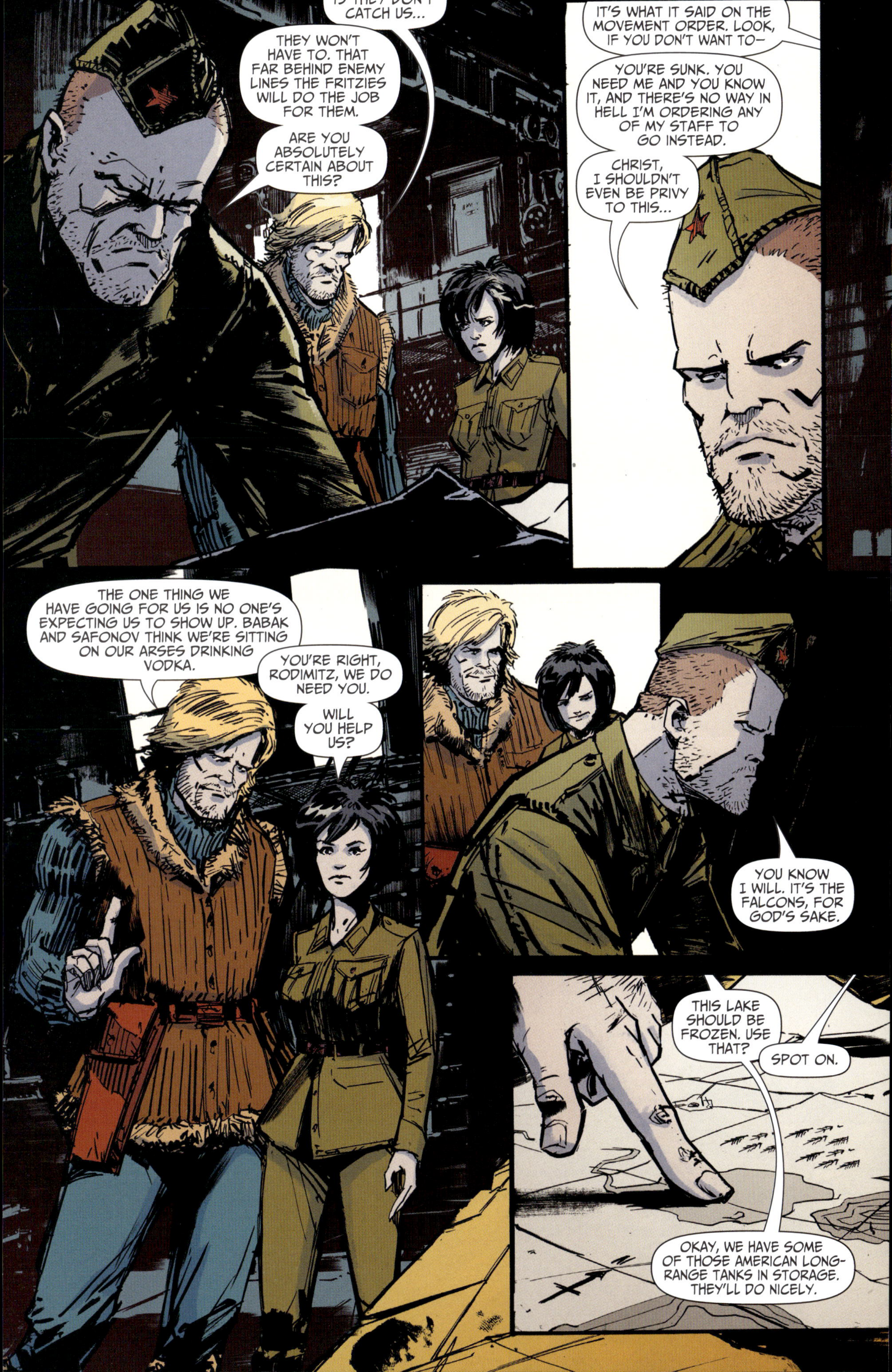
CATCH US...
THEY WON'T HAVE TO. THAT FAR BEHIND ENEMY LINES THE FRITZIES WILL DO THE JOB FOR THEM.
ARE YOU ABSOLUTELY CERTAIN ABOUT THIS?
IT'S WHAT IT SAID ON THE MOVEMENT ORDER. LOOK, IF YOU DON'T WANT TO—
YOU'RE SUNK. YOU NEED ME AND YOU KNOW IT, AND THERE'S NO WAY IN HELL I'M ORDERING ANY OF MY STAFF TO GO INSTEAD.
CHRIST, I SHOULDN'T EVEN BE PRIVY TO THIS...
THE ONE THING WE HAVE GOING FOR US IS NO ONE'S EXPECTING US TO SHOW UP. BABAK AND SAFONOV THINK WE'RE SITTING ON OUR ARSES DRINKING VODKA.
YOU'RE RIGHT, RODIMITZ, WE DO NEED YOU.
WILL YOU HELP US?
YOU KNOW I WILL. IT'S THE FALCONS, FOR GOD'S SAKE.
THIS LAKE SHOULD BE FROZEN. USE THAT?
SPOT ON.
OKAY, WE HAVE SOME OF THOSE AMERICAN LONG-RANGE TANKS IN STORAGE. THEY'LL DO NICELY.

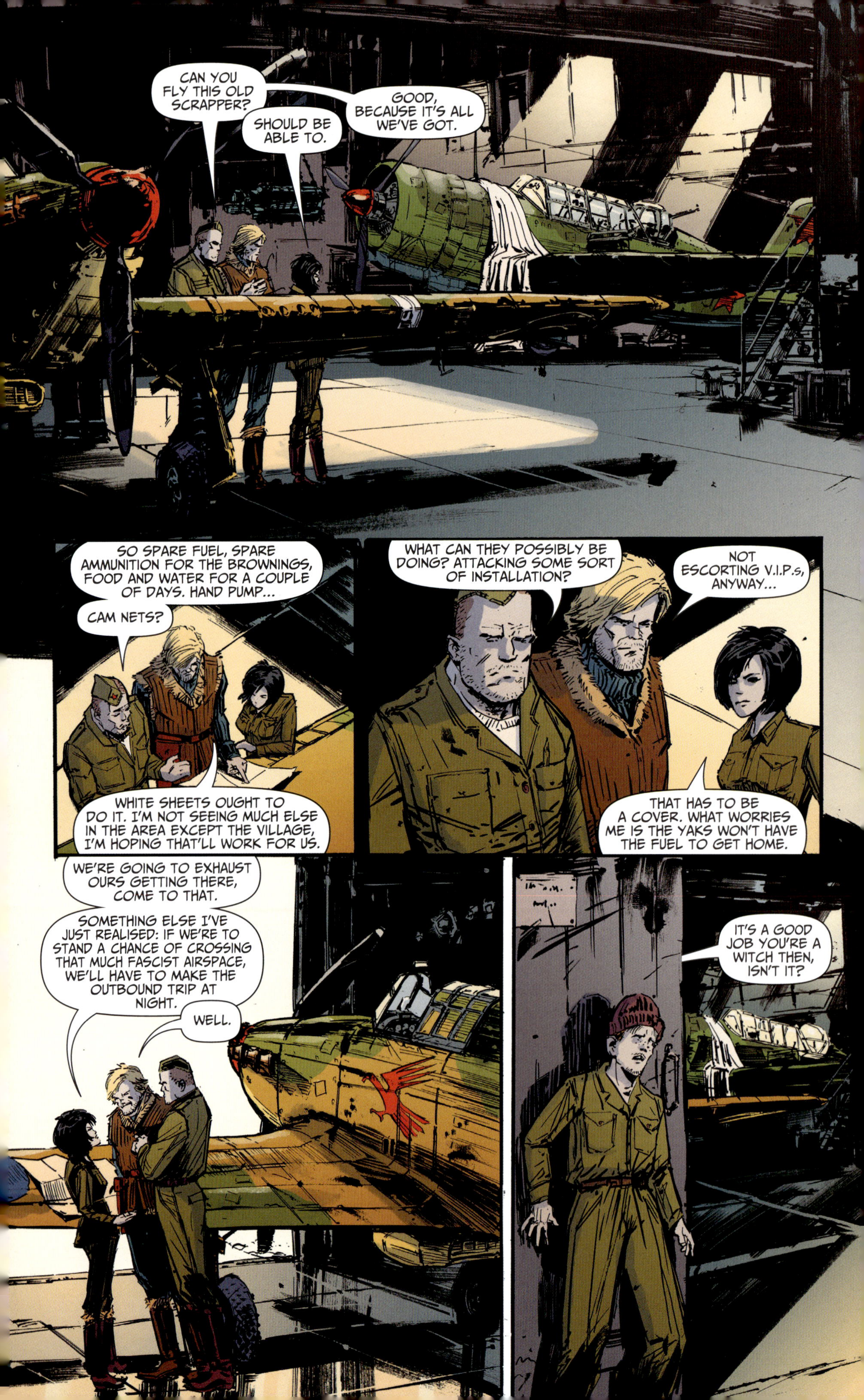

CAN YOU FLY THIS OLD SCRAPPER?
SHOULD BE ABLE TO.
GOOD, BECAUSE IT'S ALL WE'VE GOT.
SO SPARE FUEL, SPARE AMMUNITION FOR THE BROWNINGS, FOOD AND WATER FOR A COUPLE OF DAYS. HAND PUMP...
CAM NETS?
WHITE SHEETS OUGHT TO DO IT. I'M NOT SEEING MUCH ELSE IN THE AREA EXCEPT THE VILLAGE, I'M HOPING THAT'LL WORK FOR US.
WHAT CAN THEY POSSIBLY BE DOING? ATTACKING SOME SORT OF INSTALLATION?
NOT ESCORTING V.I.P.s, ANYWAY...
THAT HAS TO BE A COVER. WHAT WORRIES ME IS THE YAKS WON'T HAVE THE FUEL TO GET HOME.
WE'RE GOING TO EXHAUST OURS GETTING THERE, COME TO THAT.
SOMETHING ELSE I'VE JUST REALISED: IF WE'RE TO STAND A CHANCE OF CROSSING THAT MUCH FASCIST AIRSPACE, WE'LL HAVE TO MAKE THE OUTBOUND TRIP AT NIGHT.
WELL.
IT'S A GOOD JOB YOU'RE A WITCH THEN, ISN'T IT?

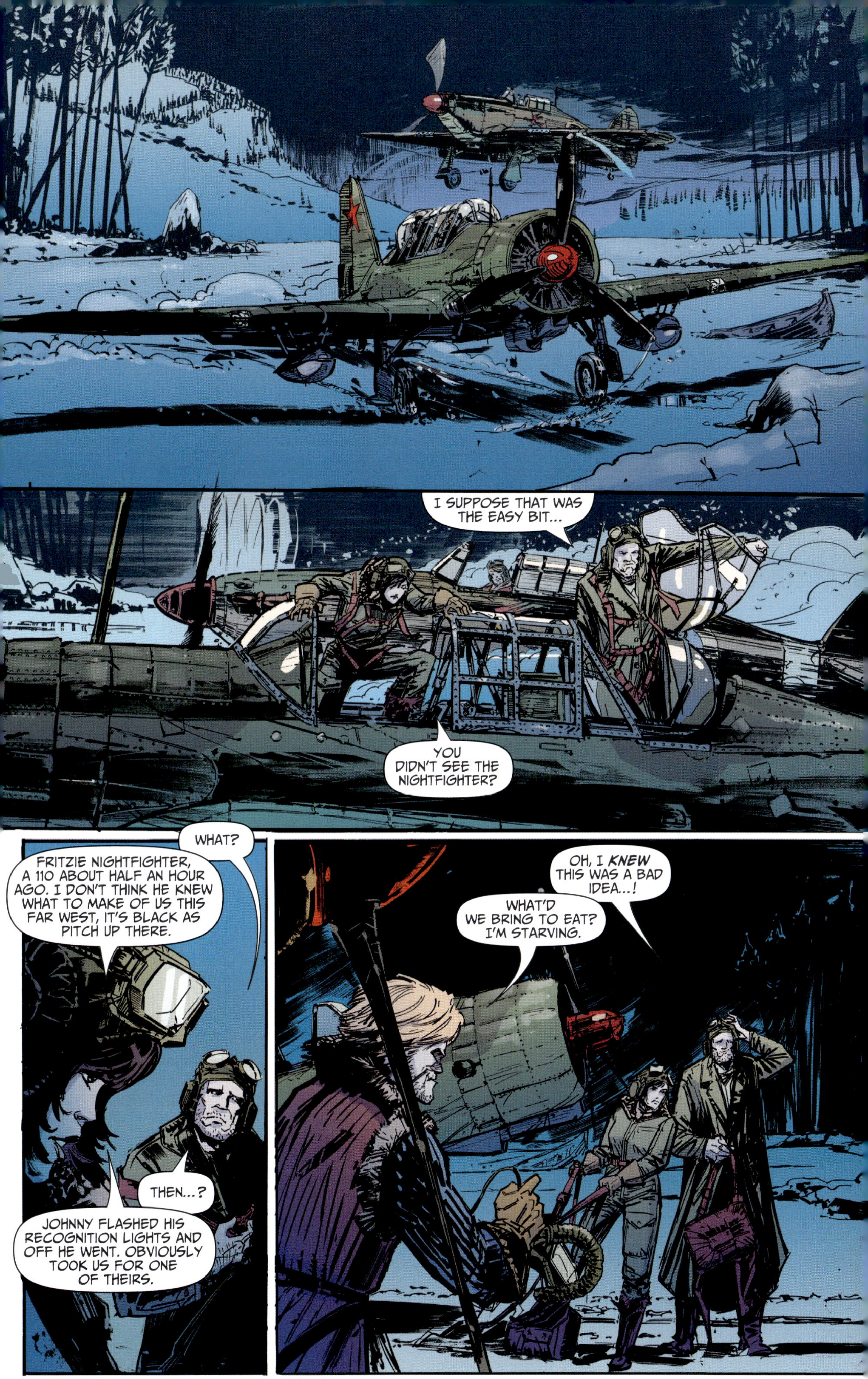
I SUPPOSE THAT WAS THE EASY BIT...
YOU DIDN'T SEE THE NIGHTFIGHTER?
WHAT?
FRITZIE NIGHTFIGHTER, A 110 ABOUT HALF AN HOUR AGO. I DON'T THINK HE KNEW WHAT TO MAKE OF US THIS FAR WEST, IT'S BLACK AS PITCH UP THERE.
THEN...?
JOHNNY FLASHED HIS RECOGNITION LIGHTS AND OFF HE WENT. OBVIOUSLY TOOK US FOR ONE OF THEIRS.
WHAT'D WE BRING TO EAT? I'M STARVING.
OH, I *KNEW* THIS WAS A BAD IDEA...!

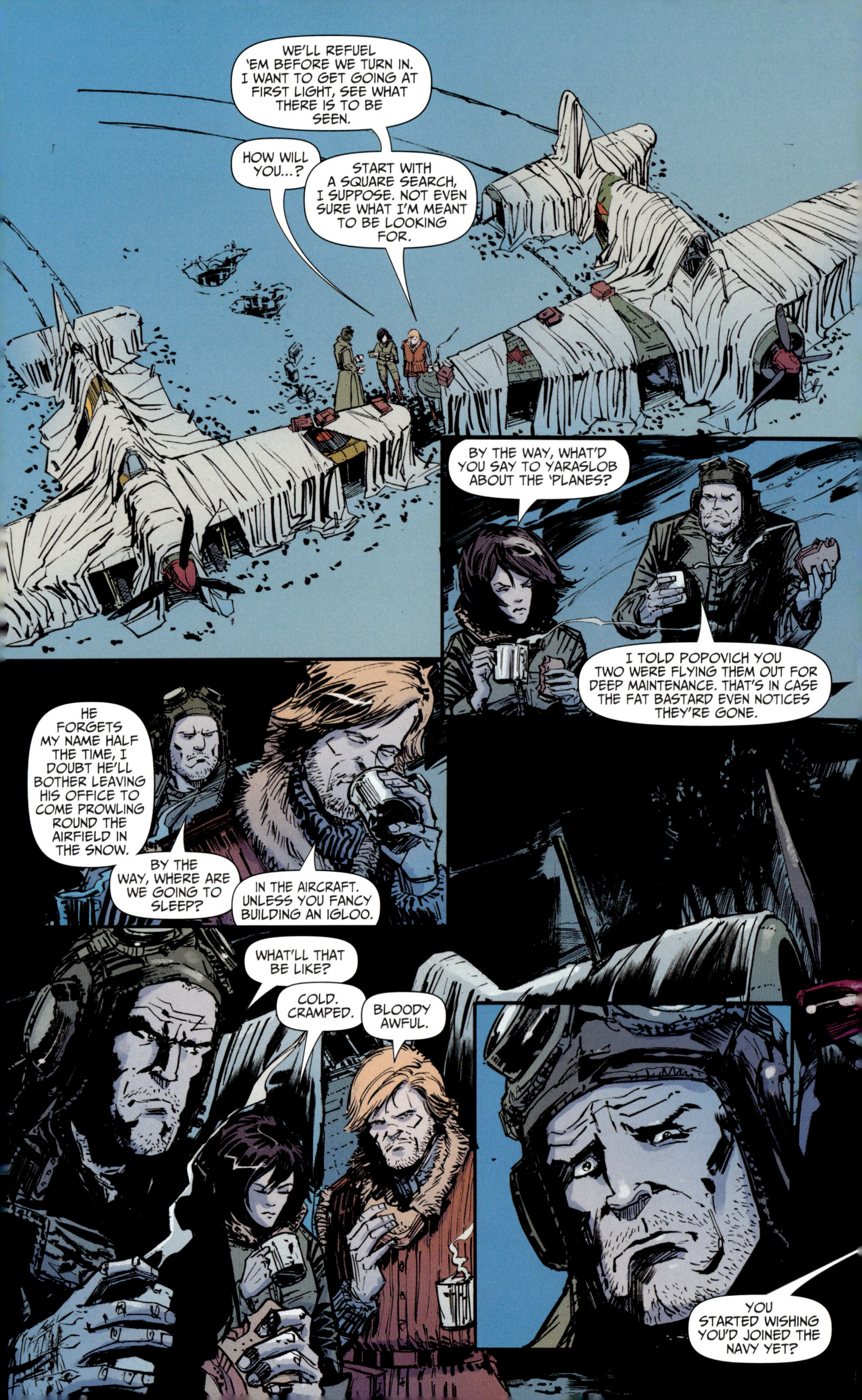
WE'LL REFUEL 'EM BEFORE WE TURN IN. I WANT TO GET GOING AT FIRST LIGHT, SEE WHAT THERE IS TO BE SEEN.
HOW WILL YOU...?
START WITH A SQUARE SEARCH, I SUPPOSE. NOT EVEN SURE WHAT I'M MEANT TO BE LOOKING FOR.
BY THE WAY, WHAT'D YOU SAY TO YARASLOB ABOUT THE 'PLANES?
I TOLD POPOVICH YOU TWO WERE FLYING THEM OUT FOR DEEP MAINTENANCE. THAT'S IN CASE THE FAT BASTARD EVEN NOTICES THEY'RE GONE.
HE FORGETS MY NAME HALF THE TIME, I DOUBT HE'LL BOTHER LEAVING HIS OFFICE TO COME PROWLING ROUND THE AIRFIELD IN THE SNOW.
BY THE WAY, WHERE ARE WE GOING TO SLEEP?
IN THE AIRCRAFT. UNLESS YOU FANCY BUILDING AN IGLOO.
WHAT'LL THAT BE LIKE?
COLD. CRAMPED.
BLOODY AWFUL.
YOU STARTED WISHING YOU'D JOINED THE NAVY YET?

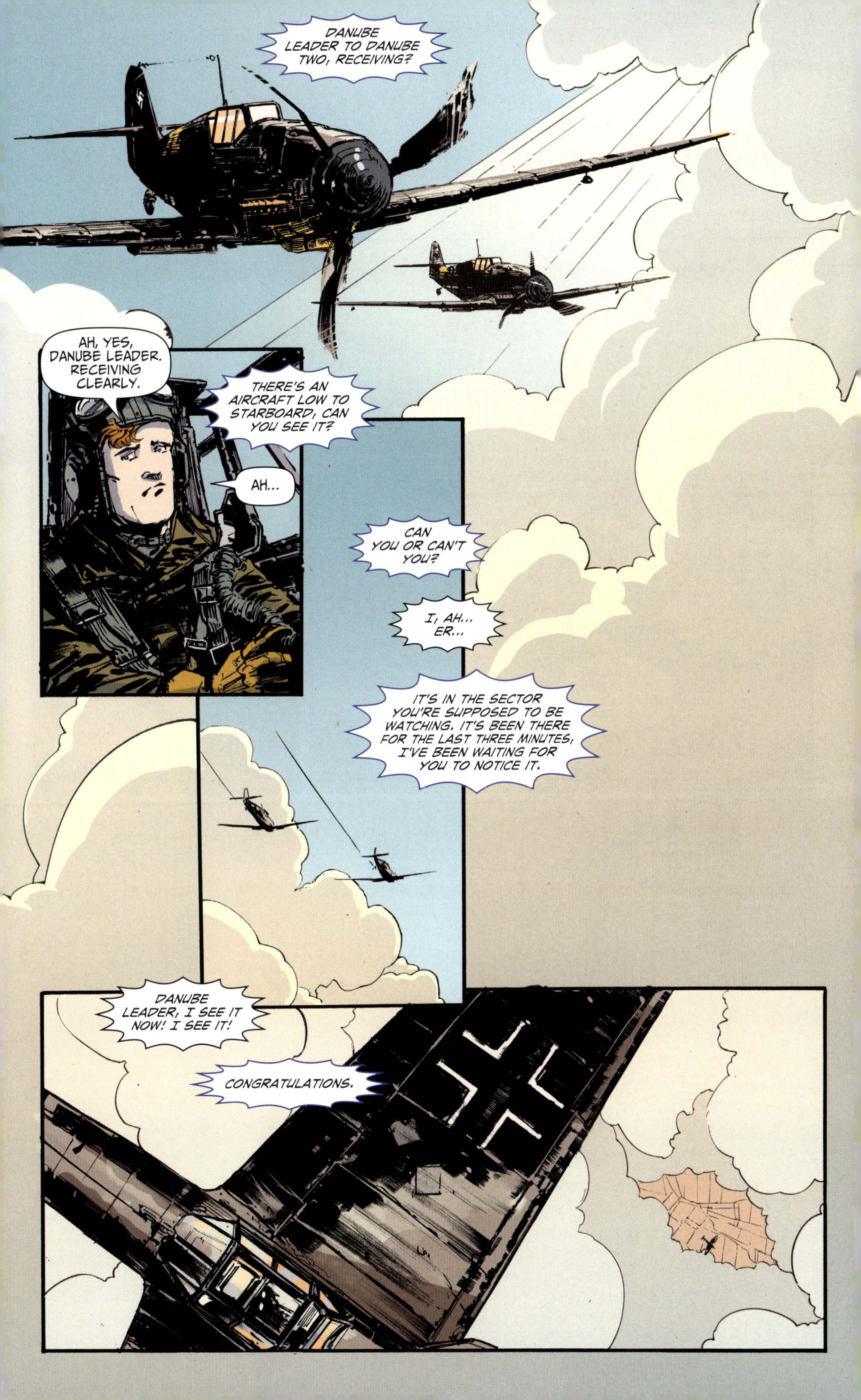
DANUBE LEADER TO DANUBE TWO, RECEIVING?
AH, YES, DANUBE LEADER. RECEIVING CLEARLY.
THERE'S AN AIRCRAFT LOW TO STARBOARD, CAN YOU SEE IT?
AH...
CAN YOU OR CAN'T YOU?
I, AH... ER...
IT'S IN THE SECTOR YOU'RE SUPPOSED TO BE WATCHING. IT'S BEEN THERE FOR THE LAST THREE MINUTES, I'VE BEEN WAITING FOR YOU TO NOTICE IT.
DANUBE LEADER, I SEE IT NOW! I SEE IT!
CONGRATULATIONS.

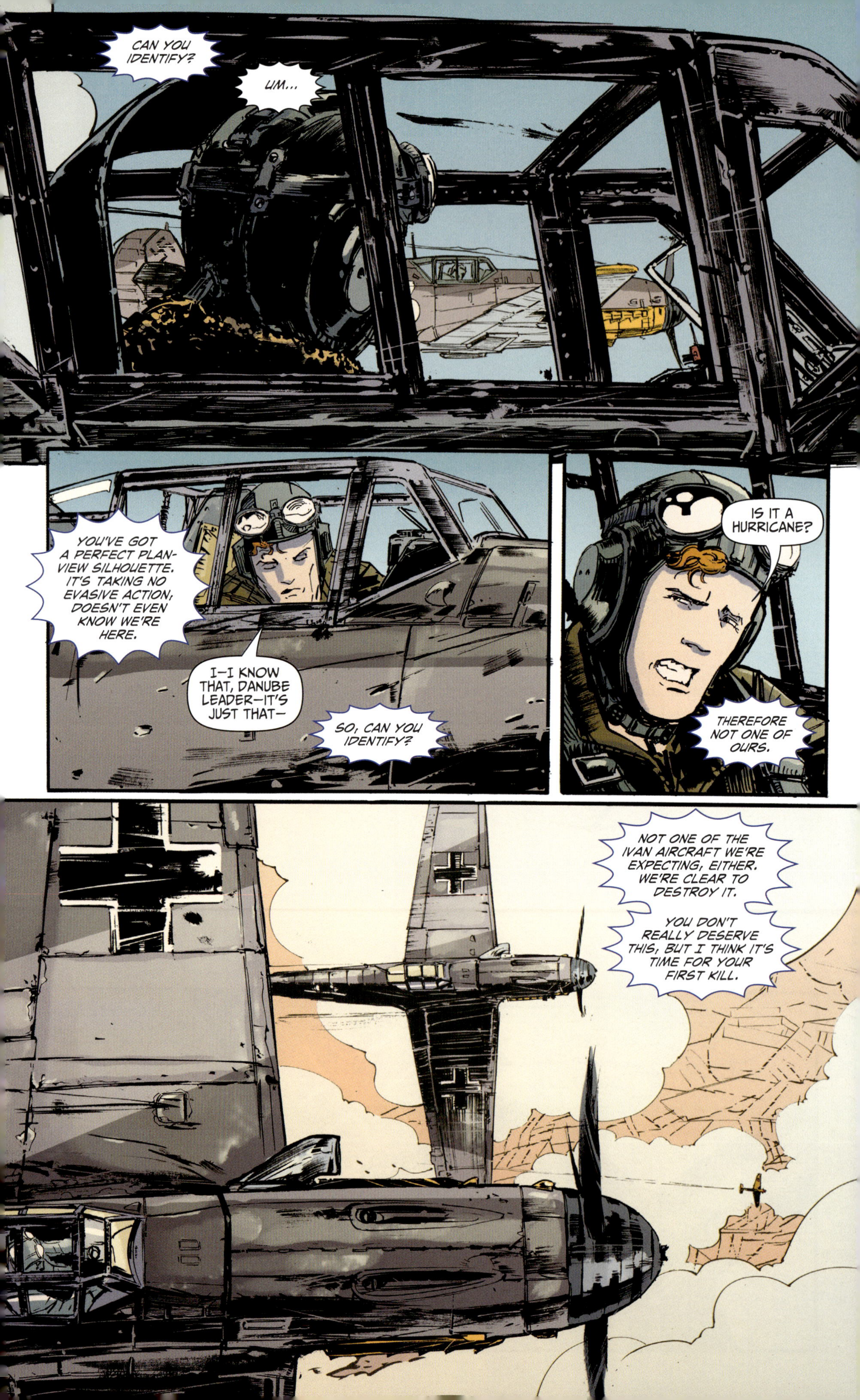
CAN YOU IDENTIFY?
UM...
YOU'VE GOT A PERFECT PLAN-VIEW SILHOUETTE. IT'S TAKING NO EVASIVE ACTION, DOESN'T EVEN KNOW WE'RE HERE.
I—I KNOW THAT, DANUBE LEADER—IT'S JUST THAT—
SO, CAN YOU IDENTIFY?
IS IT A HURRICANE?
THEREFORE NOT ONE OF OURS.
NOT ONE OF THE IVAN AIRCRAFT WE'RE EXPECTING, EITHER. WE'RE CLEAR TO DESTROY IT.
YOU DON'T REALLY DESERVE THIS, BUT I THINK IT'S TIME FOR YOUR FIRST KILL.

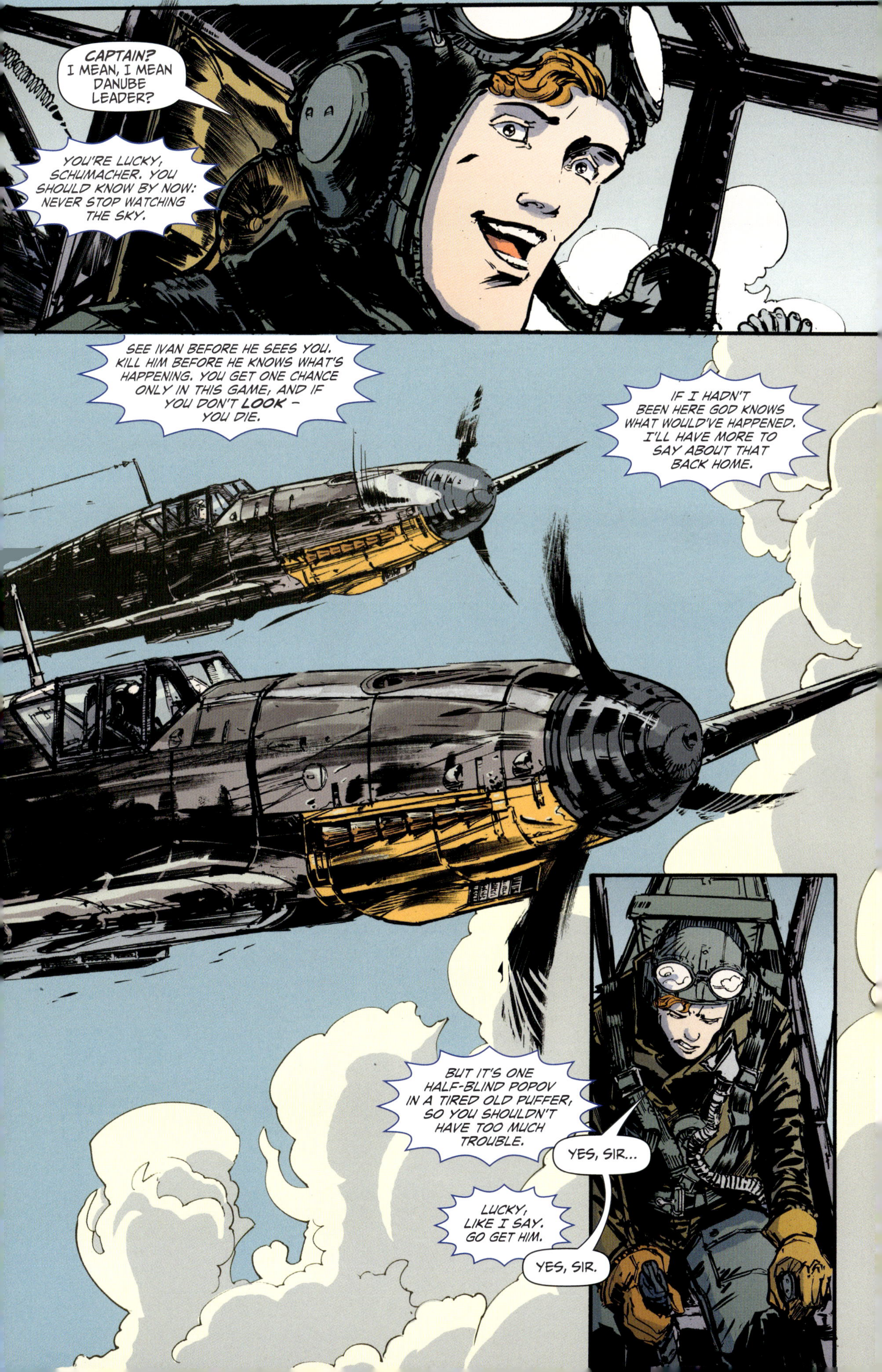
CAPTAIN? I MEAN, I MEAN DANUBE LEADER?
YOU'RE LUCKY, SCHUMACHER. YOU SHOULD KNOW BY NOW: NEVER STOP WATCHING THE SKY.
SEE IVAN BEFORE HE SEES YOU. KILL HIM BEFORE HE KNOWS WHAT'S HAPPENING. YOU GET ONE CHANCE ONLY IN THIS GAME, AND IF YOU DON'T LOOK – YOU DIE.
IF I HADN'T BEEN HERE GOD KNOWS WHAT WOULD'VE HAPPENED. I'LL HAVE MORE TO SAY ABOUT THAT BACK HOME.
BUT IT'S ONE HALF-BLIND POPOV IN A TIRED OLD PUFFER, SO YOU SHOULDN'T HAVE TOO MUCH TROUBLE.
YES, SIR...
LUCKY, LIKE I SAY. GO GET HIM.
YES, SIR.

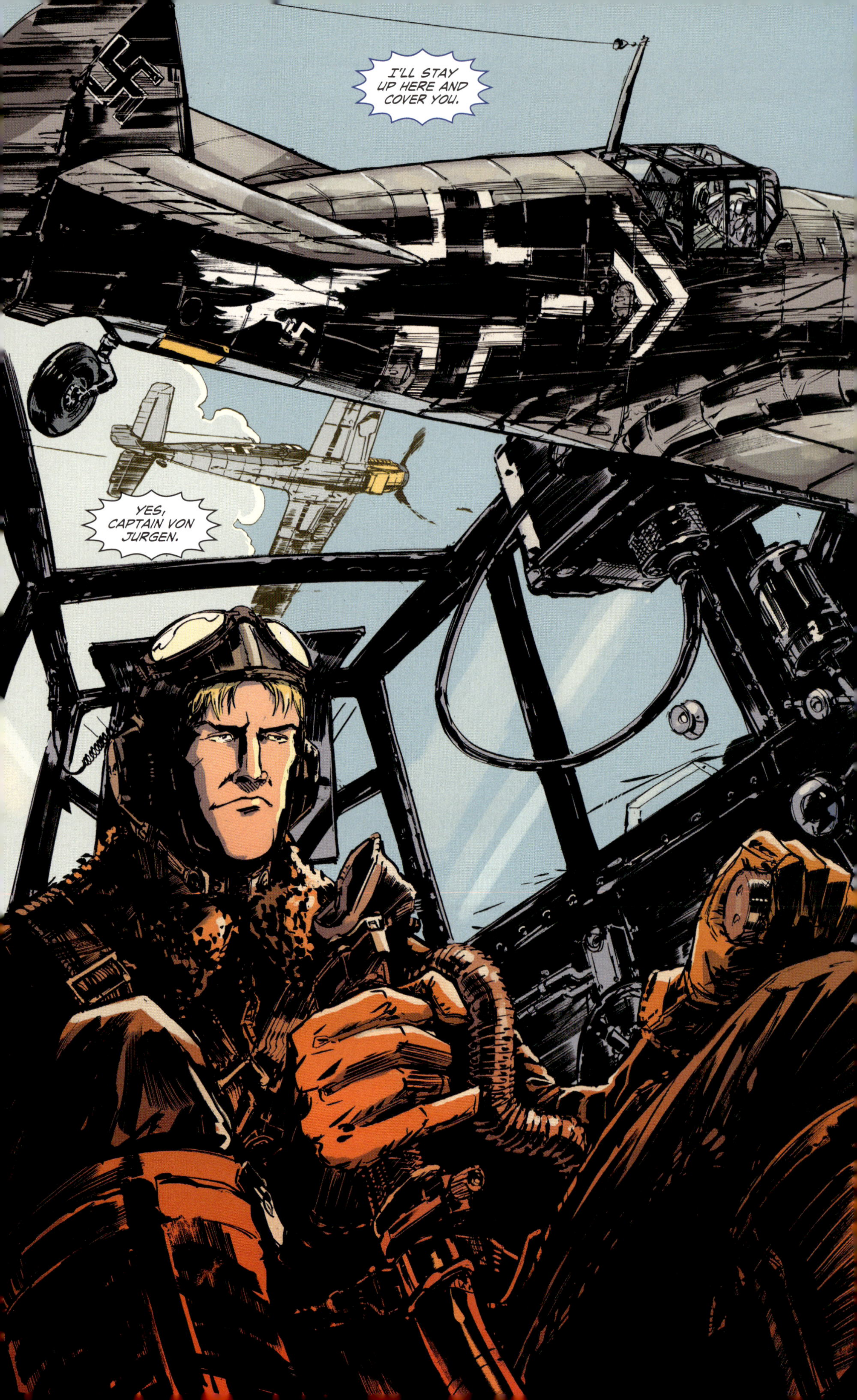
I'LL STAY UP HERE AND COVER YOU.
YES, CAPTAIN VON JURGEN.

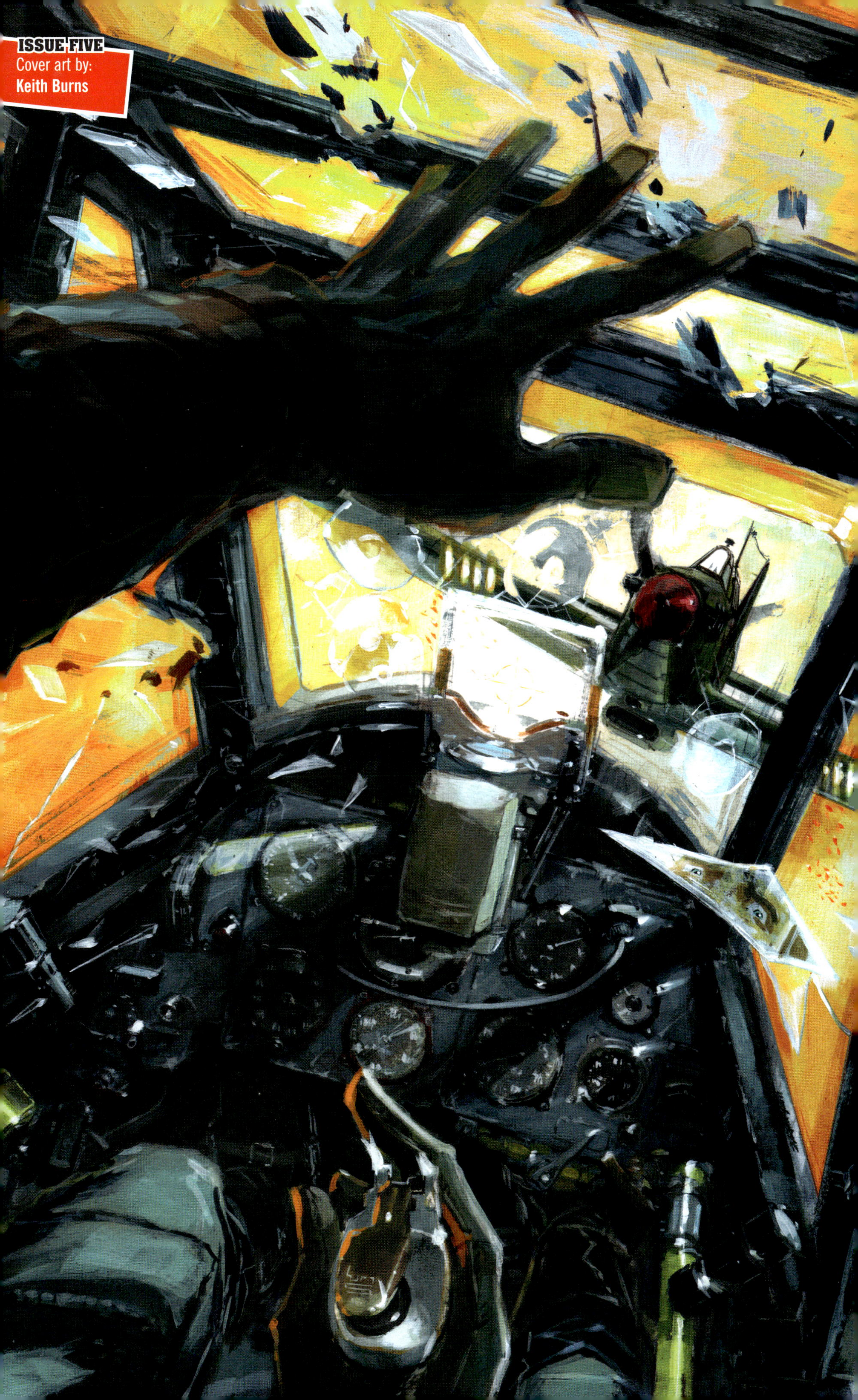

ISSUE FIVE
Cover art by:
Keith Burns

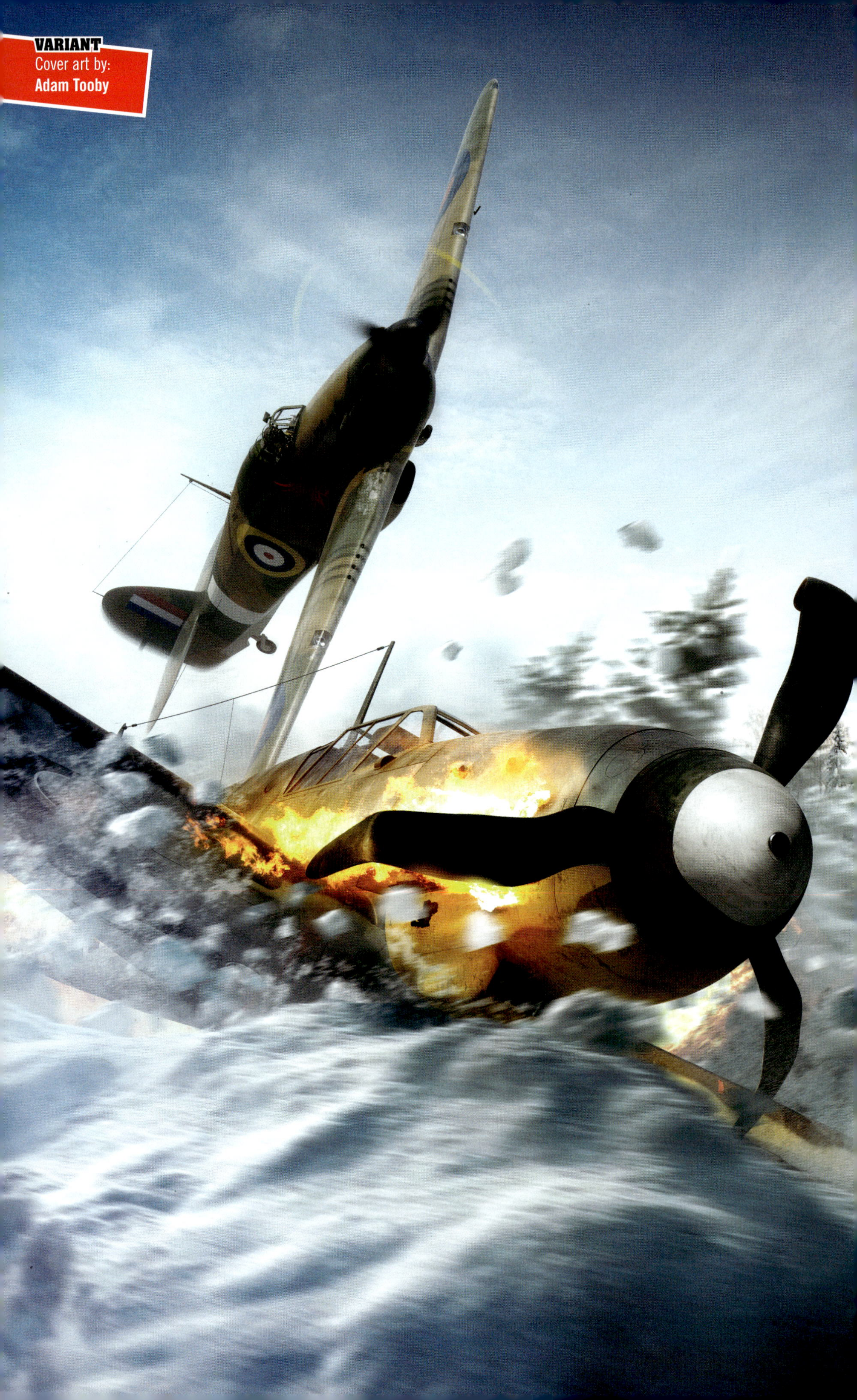

VARIANT
Cover art by:
Adam Tooby

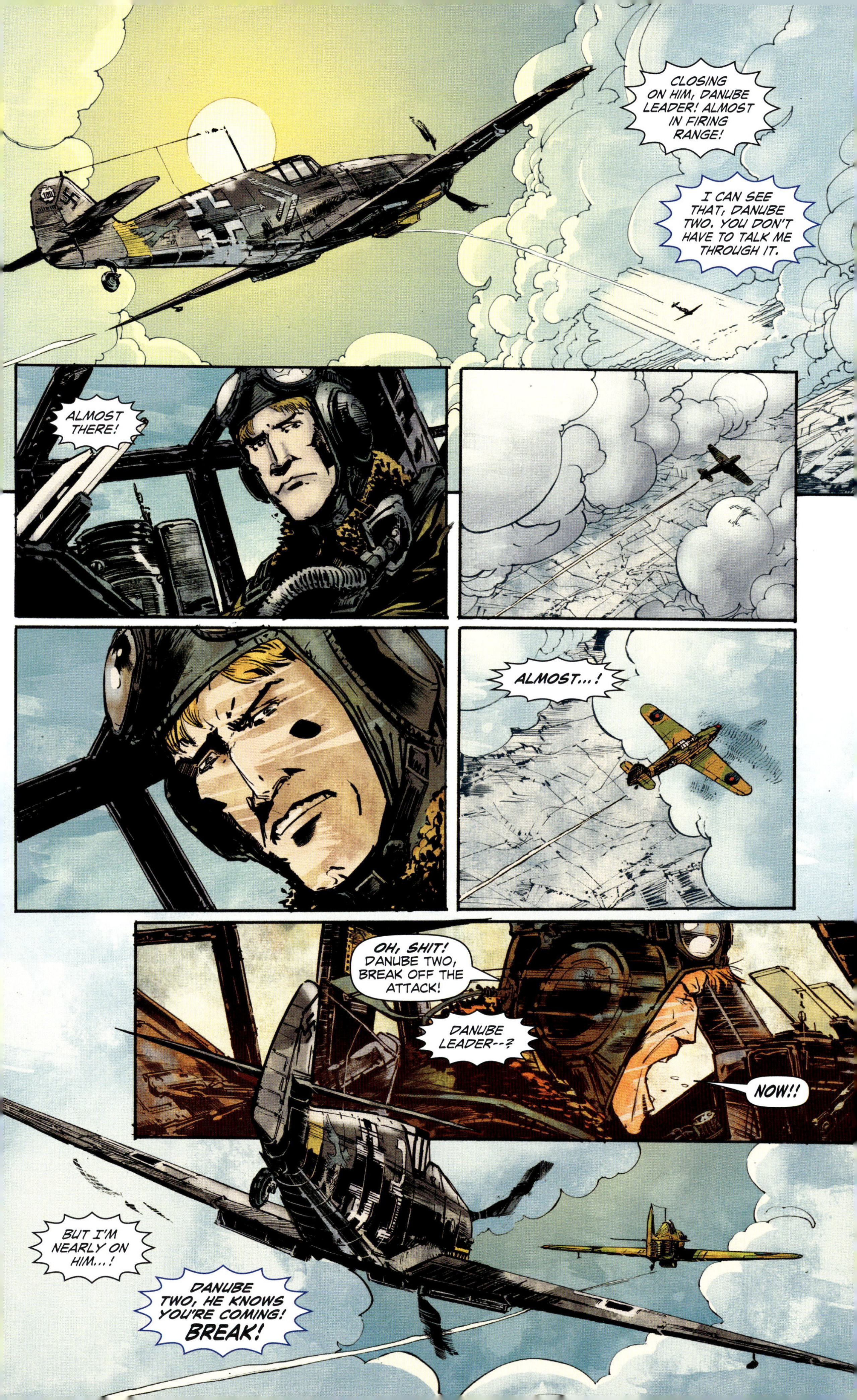
CLOSING ON HIM, DANUBE LEADER! ALMOST IN FIRING RANGE!
I CAN SEE THAT, DANUBE TWO. YOU DON'T HAVE TO TALK ME THROUGH IT.
ALMOST THERE!
ALMOST...!
OH, SHIT! DANUBE TWO, BREAK OFF THE ATTACK!
DANUBE LEADER--?
NOW!!
BUT I'M NEARLY ON HIM...!
DANUBE TWO, HE KNOWS YOU'RE COMING! BREAK!

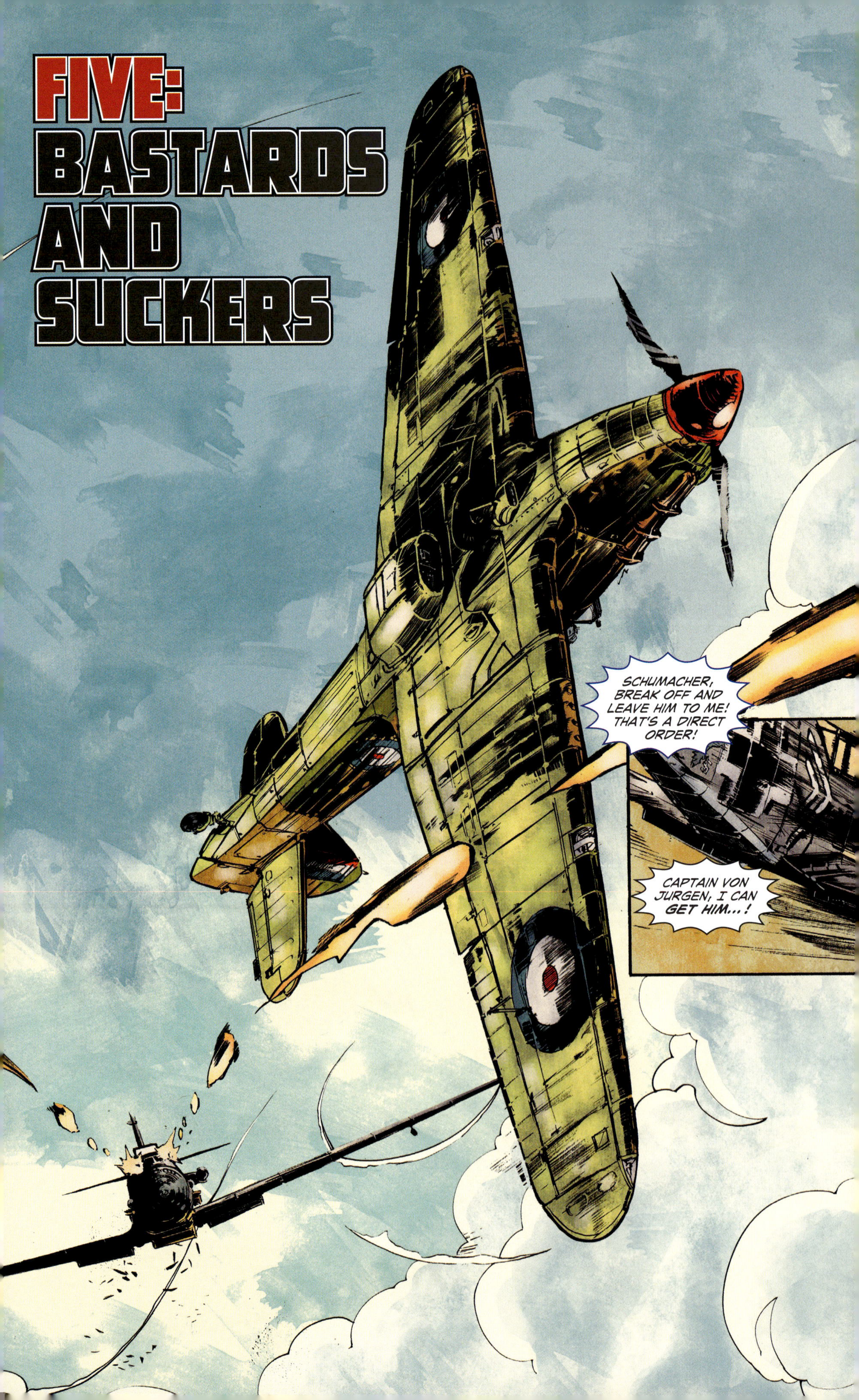
FIVE: BASTARDS AND SUCKERS
SCHUMACHER, BREAK OFF AND LEAVE HIM TO ME! THAT'S A DIRECT ORDER!
CAPTAIN VON JURGEN, I CAN GET HIM...!

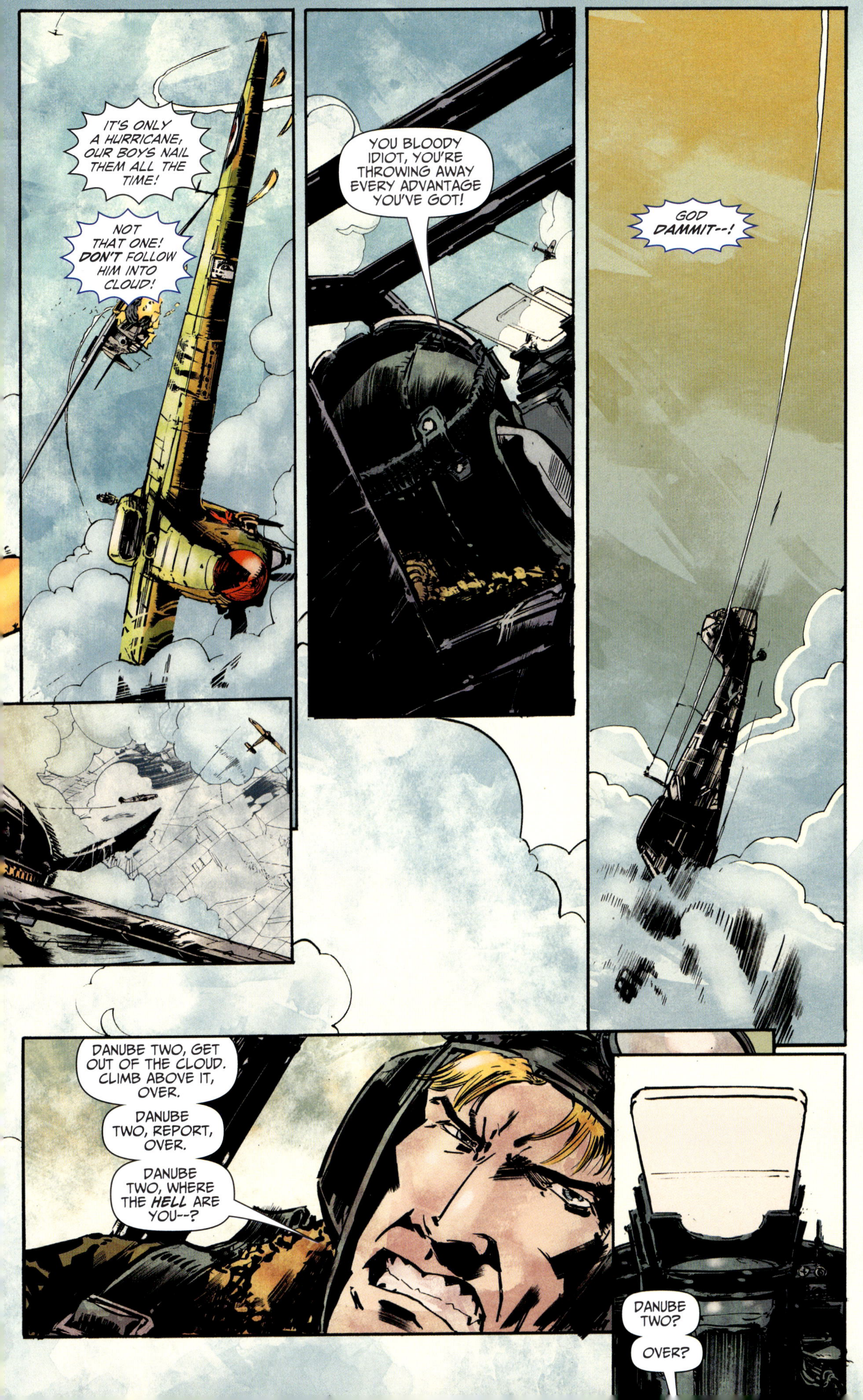
IT'S ONLY A HURRICANE, OUR BOYS NAIL THEM ALL THE TIME!
NOT THAT ONE! **DON'T** FOLLOW HIM INTO CLOUD!
YOU BLOODY IDIOT, YOU'RE THROWING AWAY EVERY ADVANTAGE YOU'VE GOT!
GOD **DAMMIT--!**
DANUBE TWO, GET OUT OF THE CLOUD. CLIMB ABOVE IT, OVER.
DANUBE TWO, REPORT, OVER.
DANUBE TWO, WHERE THE **HELL** ARE YOU--?
DANUBE TWO?
OVER?

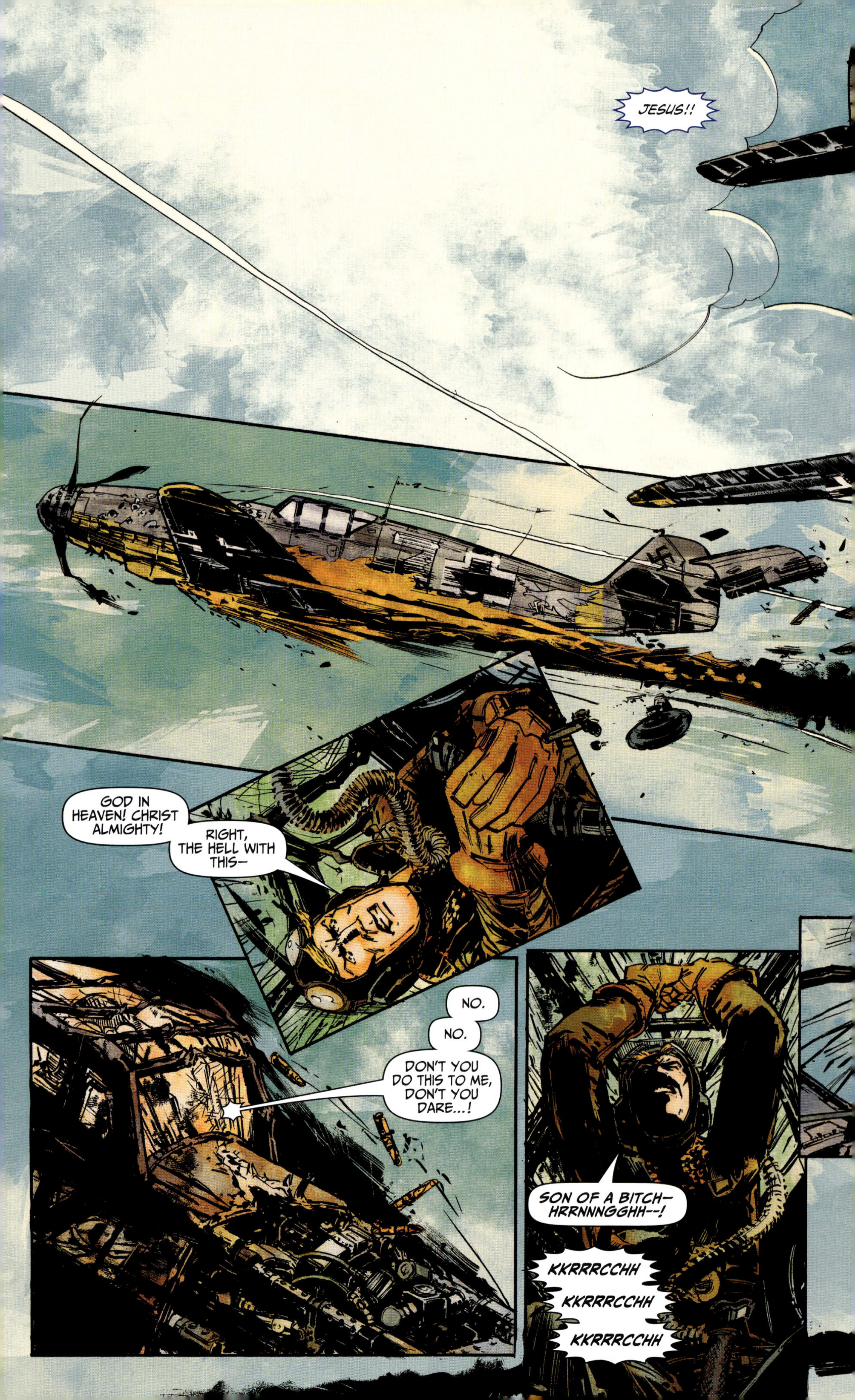
JESUS!!
GOD IN HEAVEN! CHRIST ALMIGHTY!
RIGHT, THE HELL WITH THIS—
NO.
NO.
DON'T YOU DO THIS TO ME, DON'T YOU DARE...!
SON OF A BITCH— HRRNNNGGHH--!
KKRRRCCHH
KKRRRCCHH
KKRRRCCHH

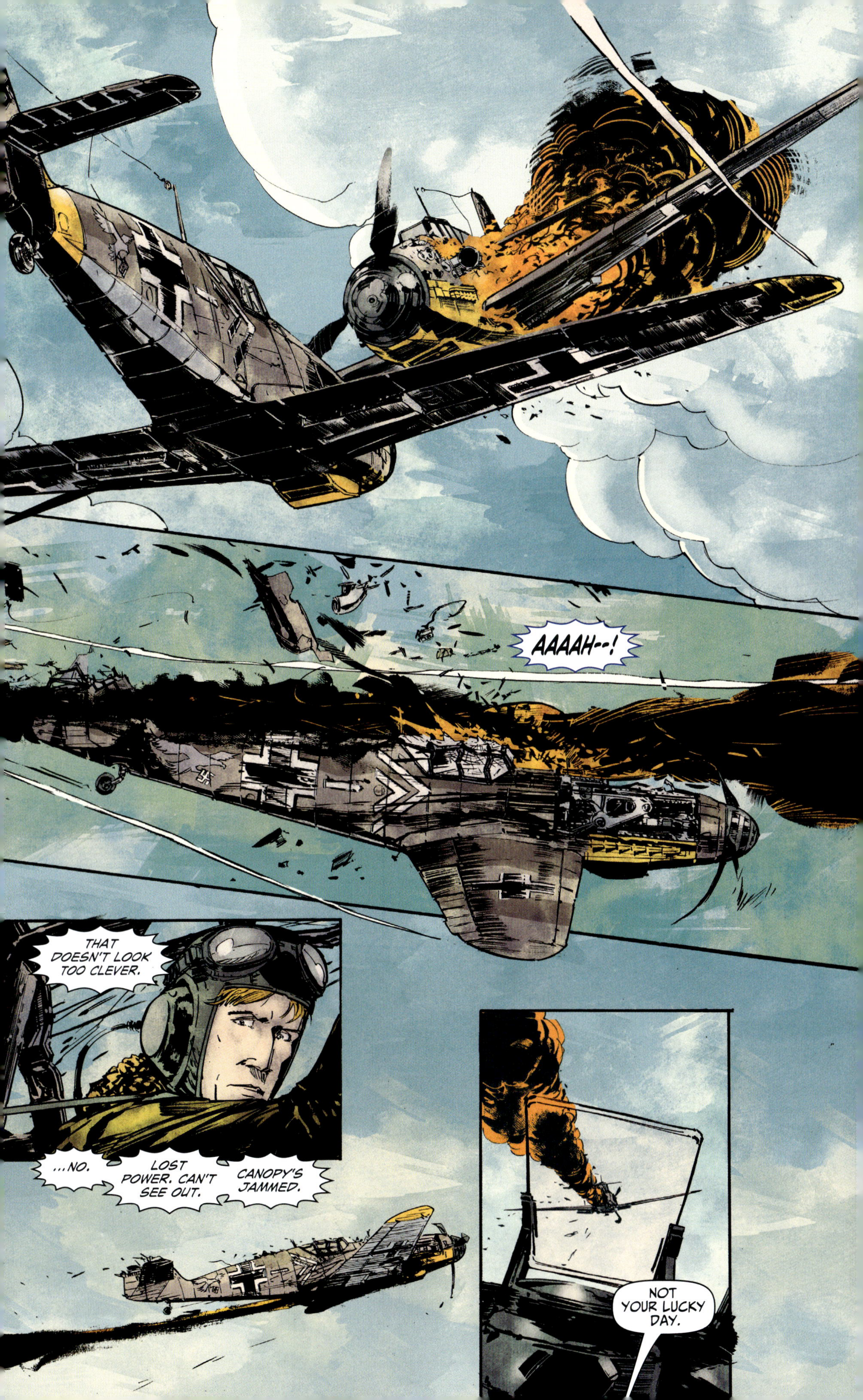
AAAAH--!
THAT DOESN'T LOOK TOO CLEVER.
...NO.
LOST POWER. CAN'T SEE OUT.
CANOPY'S JAMMED.
NOT YOUR LUCKY DAY.

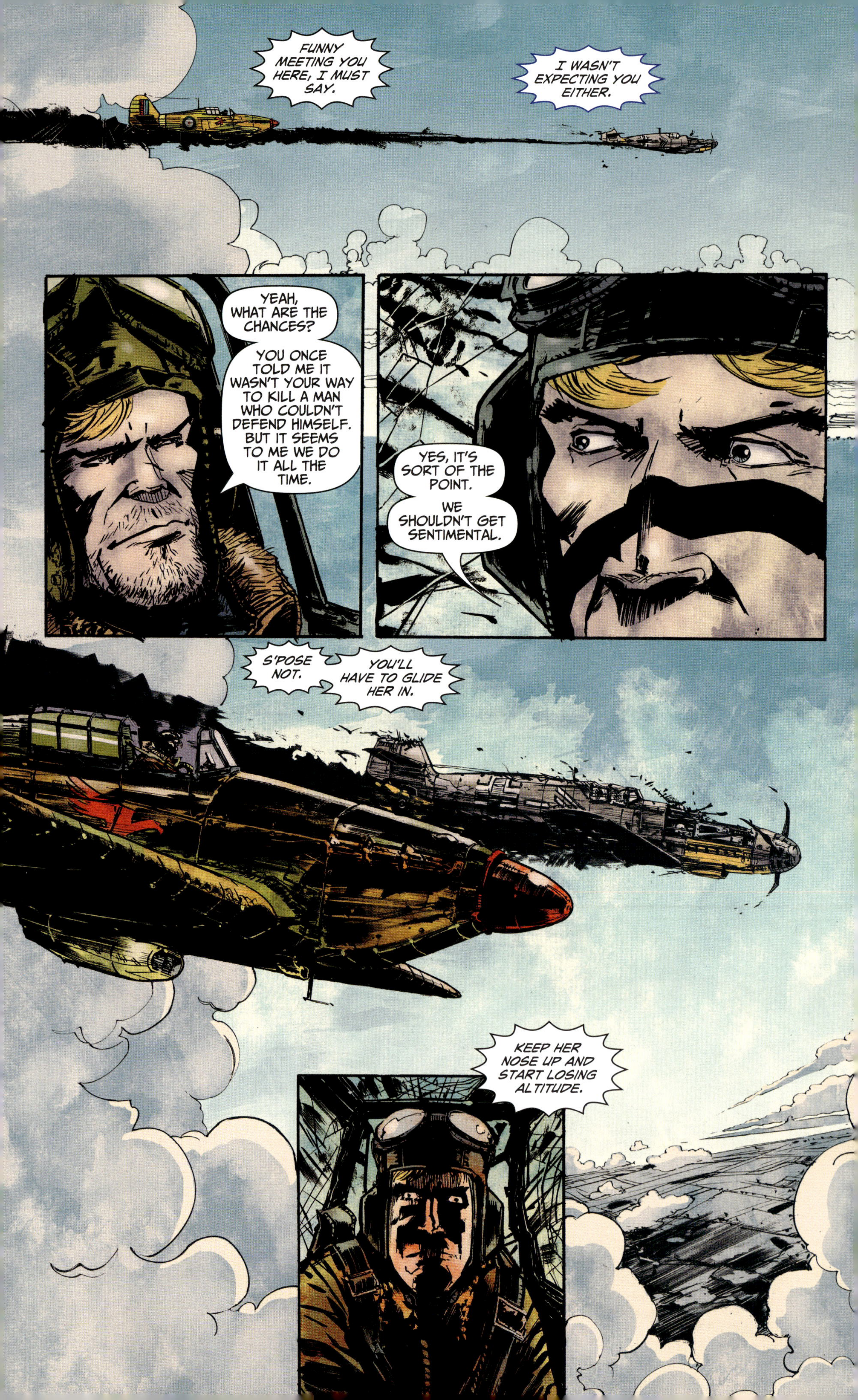
FUNNY MEETING YOU HERE, I MUST SAY.
I WASN'T EXPECTING YOU EITHER.
YEAH, WHAT ARE THE CHANCES?
YOU ONCE TOLD ME IT WASN'T YOUR WAY TO KILL A MAN WHO COULDN'T DEFEND HIMSELF. BUT IT SEEMS TO ME WE DO IT ALL THE TIME.
YES, IT'S SORT OF THE POINT.
WE SHOULDN'T GET SENTIMENTAL.
S'POSE NOT.
YOU'LL HAVE TO GLIDE HER IN.
KEEP HER NOSE UP AND START LOSING ALTITUDE.

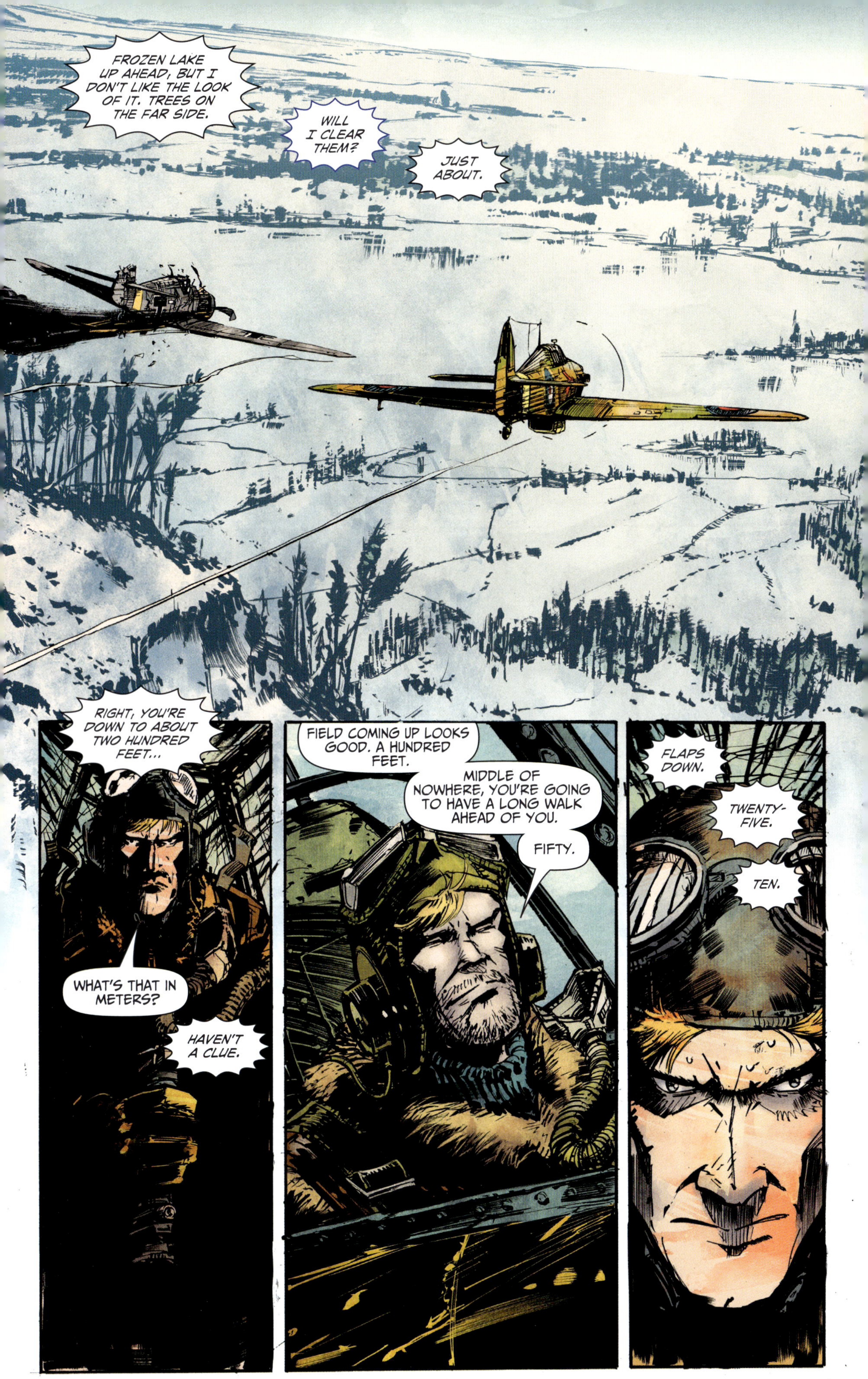

FROZEN LAKE UP AHEAD, BUT I DON'T LIKE THE LOOK OF IT. TREES ON THE FAR SIDE.
WILL I CLEAR THEM?
JUST ABOUT.
RIGHT, YOU'RE DOWN TO ABOUT TWO HUNDRED FEET...
WHAT'S THAT IN METERS?
HAVEN'T A CLUE.
FIELD COMING UP LOOKS GOOD. A HUNDRED FEET.
MIDDLE OF NOWHERE, YOU'RE GOING TO HAVE A LONG WALK AHEAD OF YOU.
FIFTY.
FLAPS DOWN.
TWENTY-FIVE.
TEN.

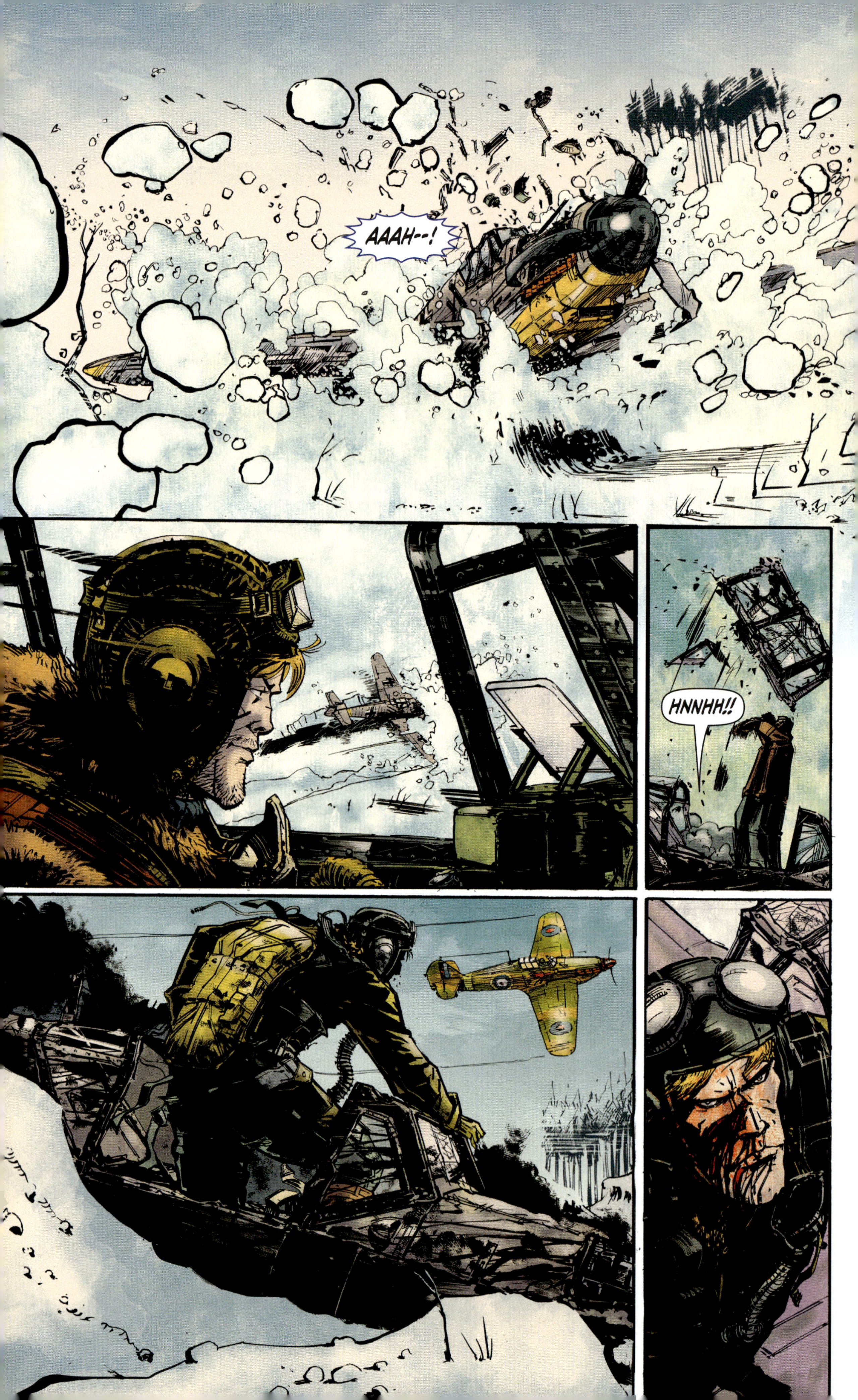
AAAH--!
HNNHH!!

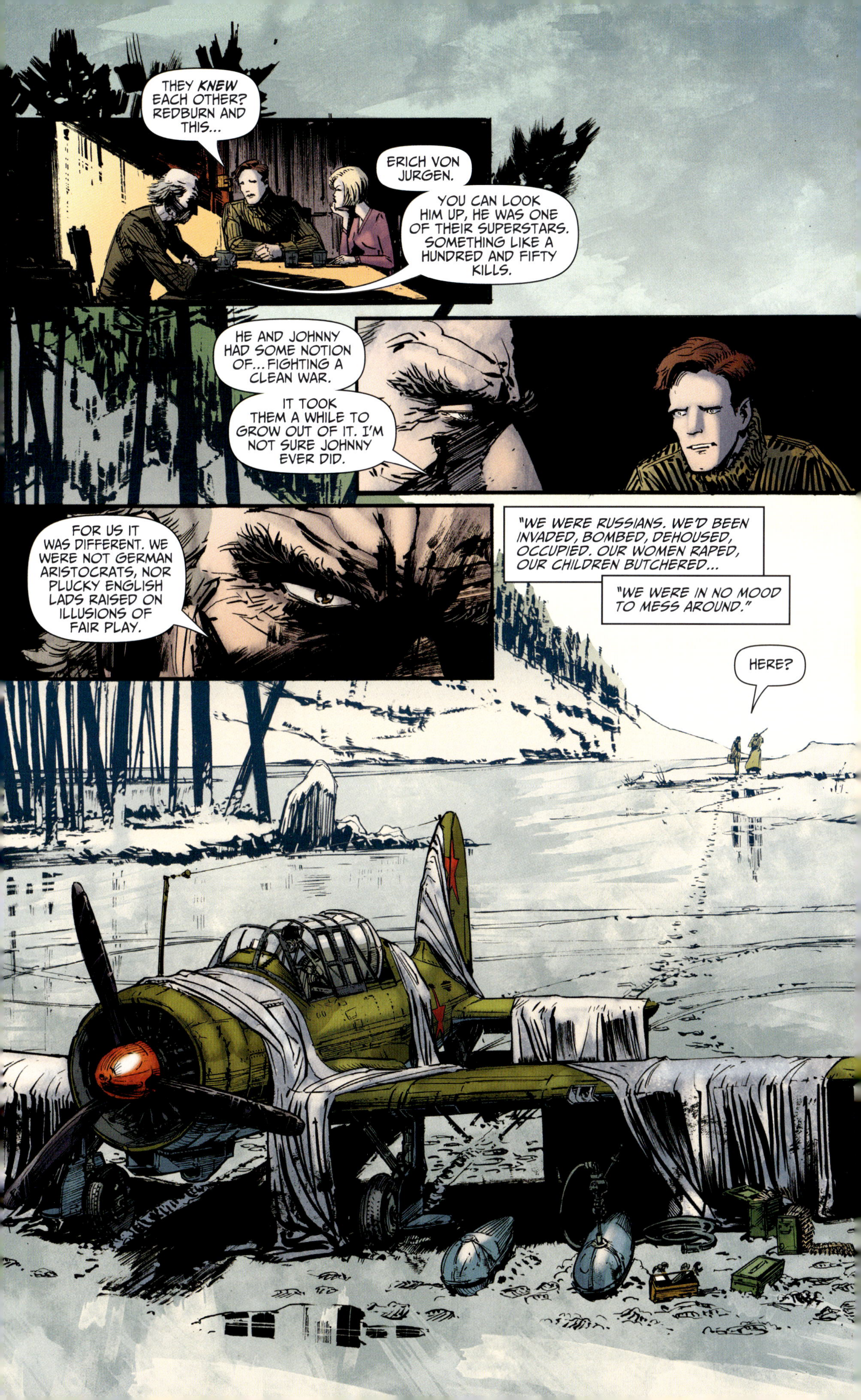

THEY *KNEW* EACH OTHER? REDBURN AND THIS...
ERICH VON JURGEN.
YOU CAN LOOK HIM UP, HE WAS ONE OF THEIR SUPERSTARS. SOMETHING LIKE A HUNDRED AND FIFTY KILLS.
HE AND JOHNNY HAD SOME NOTION OF... FIGHTING A CLEAN WAR.
IT TOOK THEM A WHILE TO GROW OUT OF IT. I'M NOT SURE JOHNNY EVER DID.
FOR US IT WAS DIFFERENT. WE WERE NOT GERMAN ARISTOCRATS, NOR PLUCKY ENGLISH LADS RAISED ON ILLUSIONS OF FAIR PLAY.
"WE WERE RUSSIANS. WE'D BEEN INVADED, BOMBED, DEHOUSED, OCCUPIED. OUR WOMEN RAPED, OUR CHILDREN BUTCHERED...
"WE WERE IN NO MOOD TO MESS AROUND."
HERE?

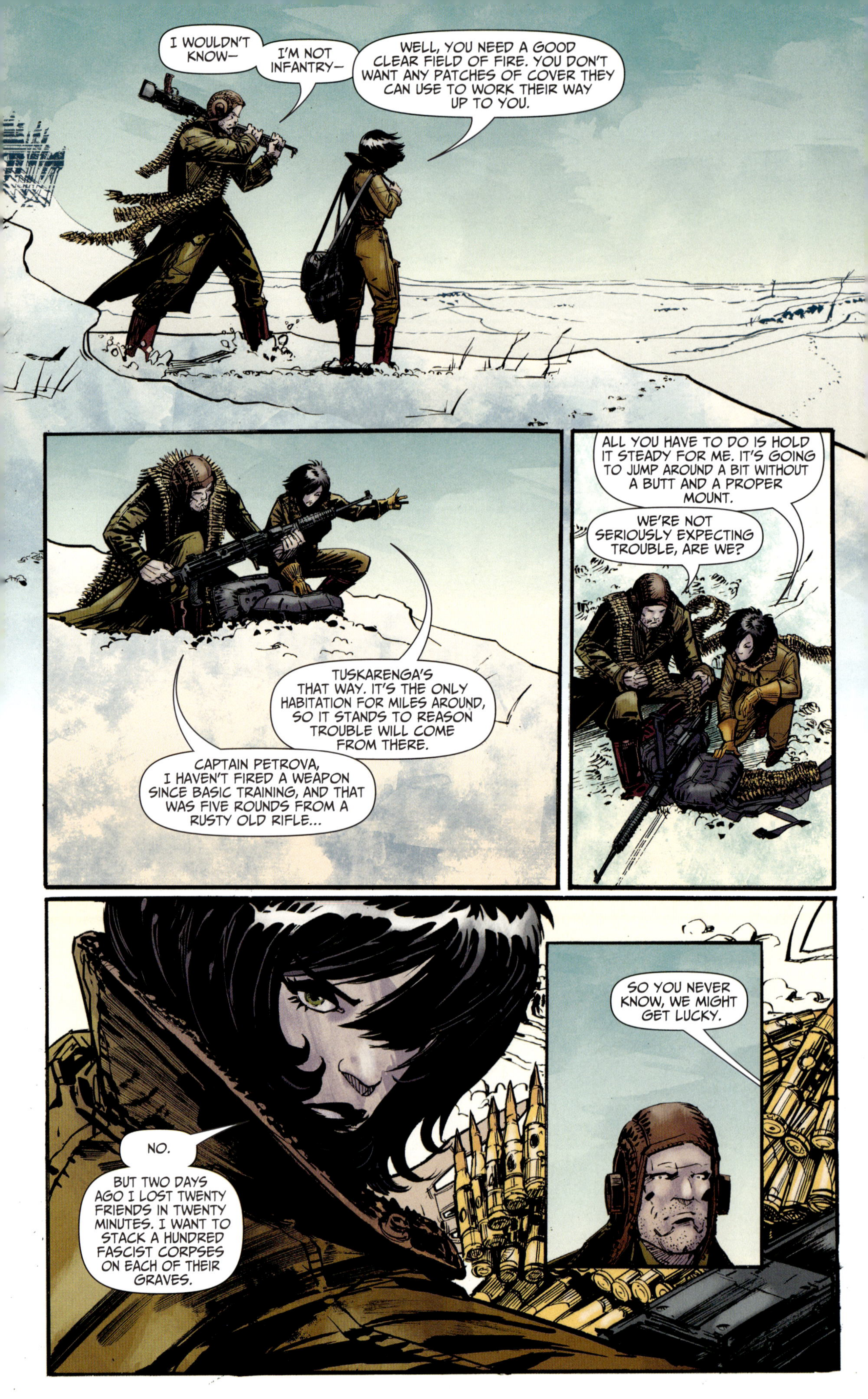
I WOULDN'T KNOW—
I'M NOT INFANTRY—
WELL, YOU NEED A GOOD CLEAR FIELD OF FIRE. YOU DON'T WANT ANY PATCHES OF COVER THEY CAN USE TO WORK THEIR WAY UP TO YOU.
TUSKARENGA'S THAT WAY. IT'S THE ONLY HABITATION FOR MILES AROUND, SO IT STANDS TO REASON TROUBLE WILL COME FROM THERE.
CAPTAIN PETROVA, I HAVEN'T FIRED A WEAPON SINCE BASIC TRAINING, AND THAT WAS FIVE ROUNDS FROM A RUSTY OLD RIFLE...
ALL YOU HAVE TO DO IS HOLD IT STEADY FOR ME. IT'S GOING TO JUMP AROUND A BIT WITHOUT A BUTT AND A PROPER MOUNT.
WE'RE NOT SERIOUSLY EXPECTING TROUBLE, ARE WE?
NO.
BUT TWO DAYS AGO I LOST TWENTY FRIENDS IN TWENTY MINUTES. I WANT TO STACK A HUNDRED FASCIST CORPSES ON EACH OF THEIR GRAVES.
SO YOU NEVER KNOW, WE MIGHT GET LUCKY.

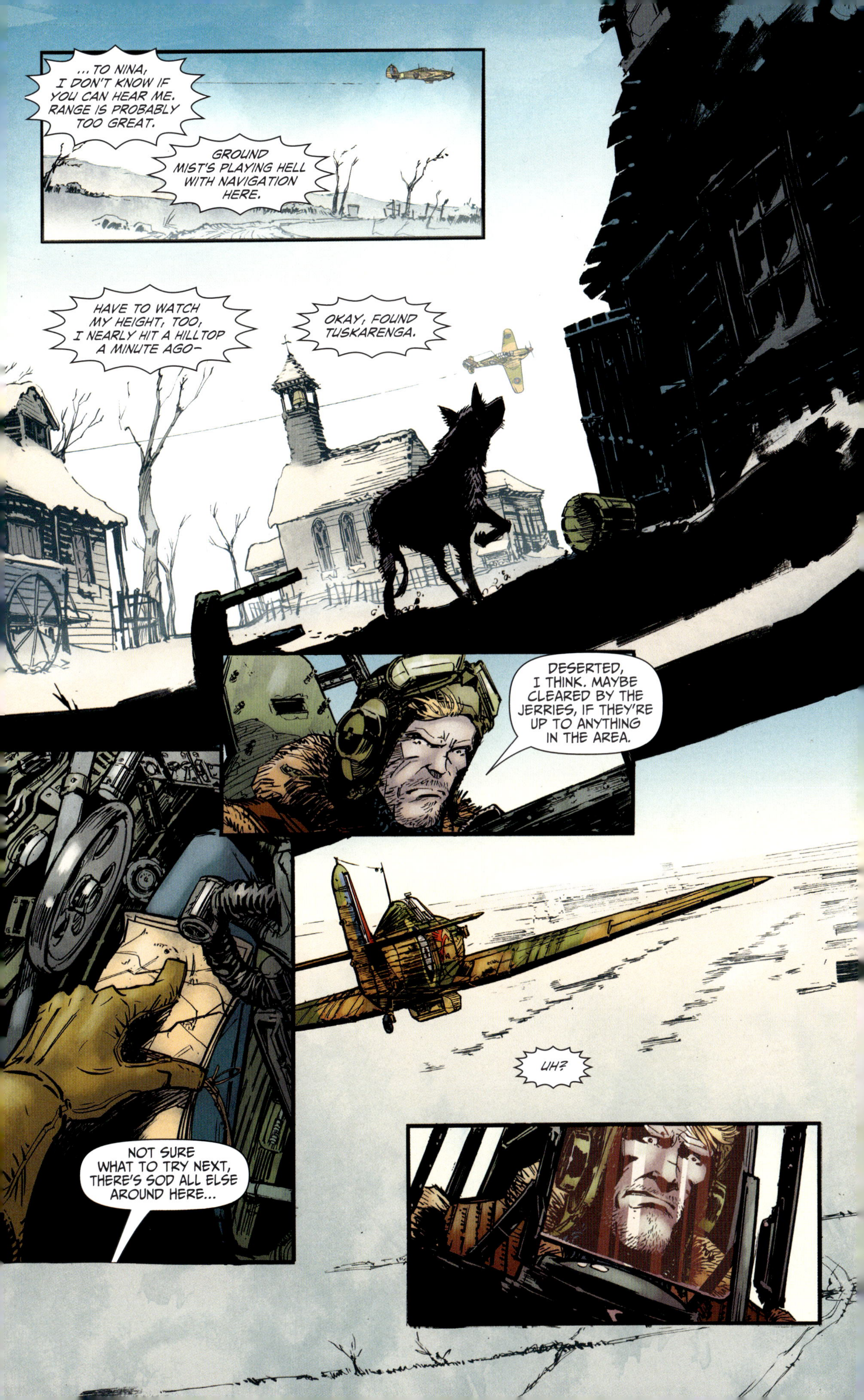
...TO NINA, I DON'T KNOW IF YOU CAN HEAR ME. RANGE IS PROBABLY TOO GREAT.
GROUND MIST'S PLAYING HELL WITH NAVIGATION HERE.
HAVE TO WATCH MY HEIGHT, TOO, I NEARLY HIT A HILLTOP A MINUTE AGO–
OKAY, FOUND TUSKARENGA.
DESERTED, I THINK. MAYBE CLEARED BY THE JERRIES, IF THEY'RE UP TO ANYTHING IN THE AREA.
NOT SURE WHAT TO TRY NEXT, THERE'S SOD ALL ELSE AROUND HERE...
UH?

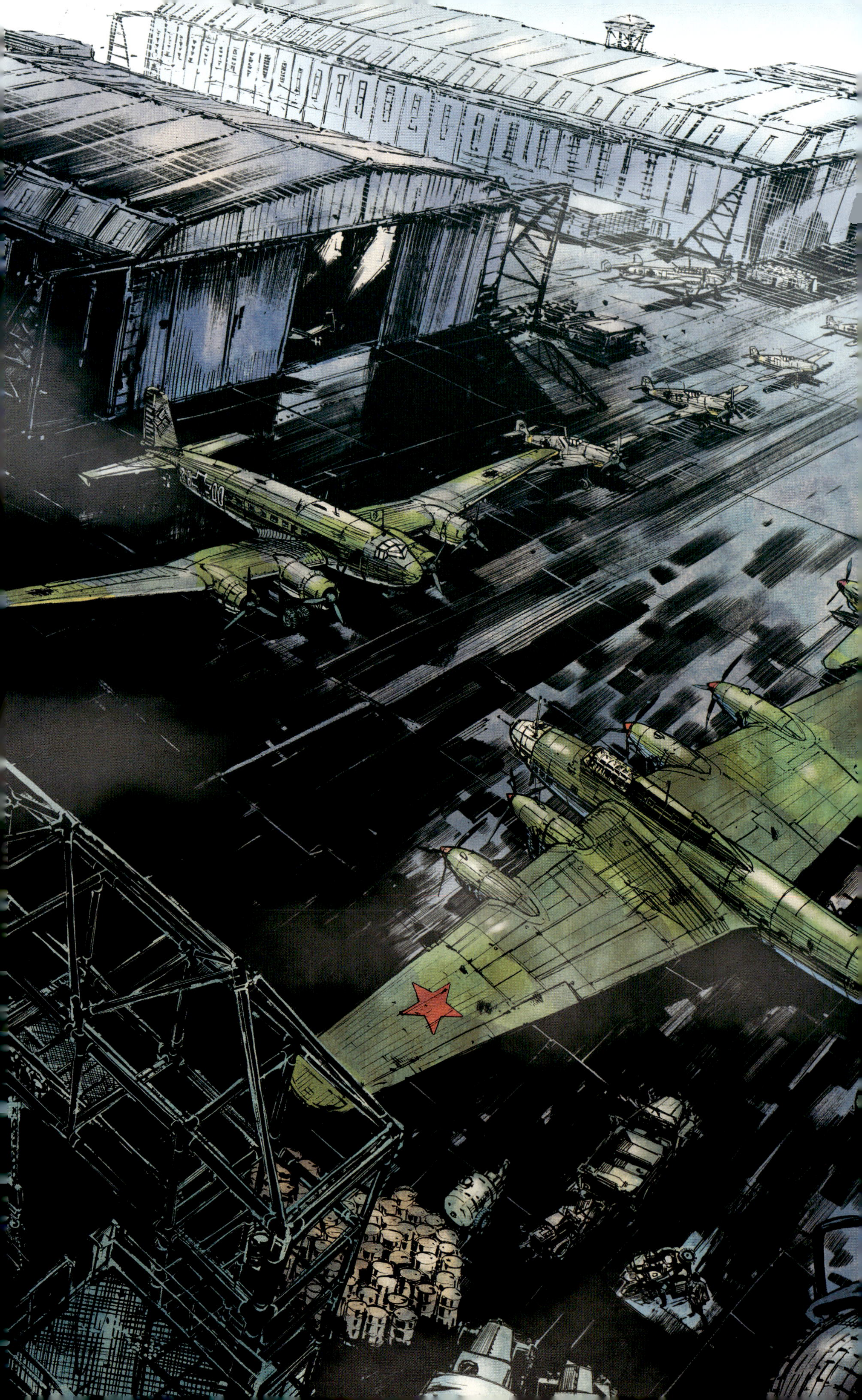

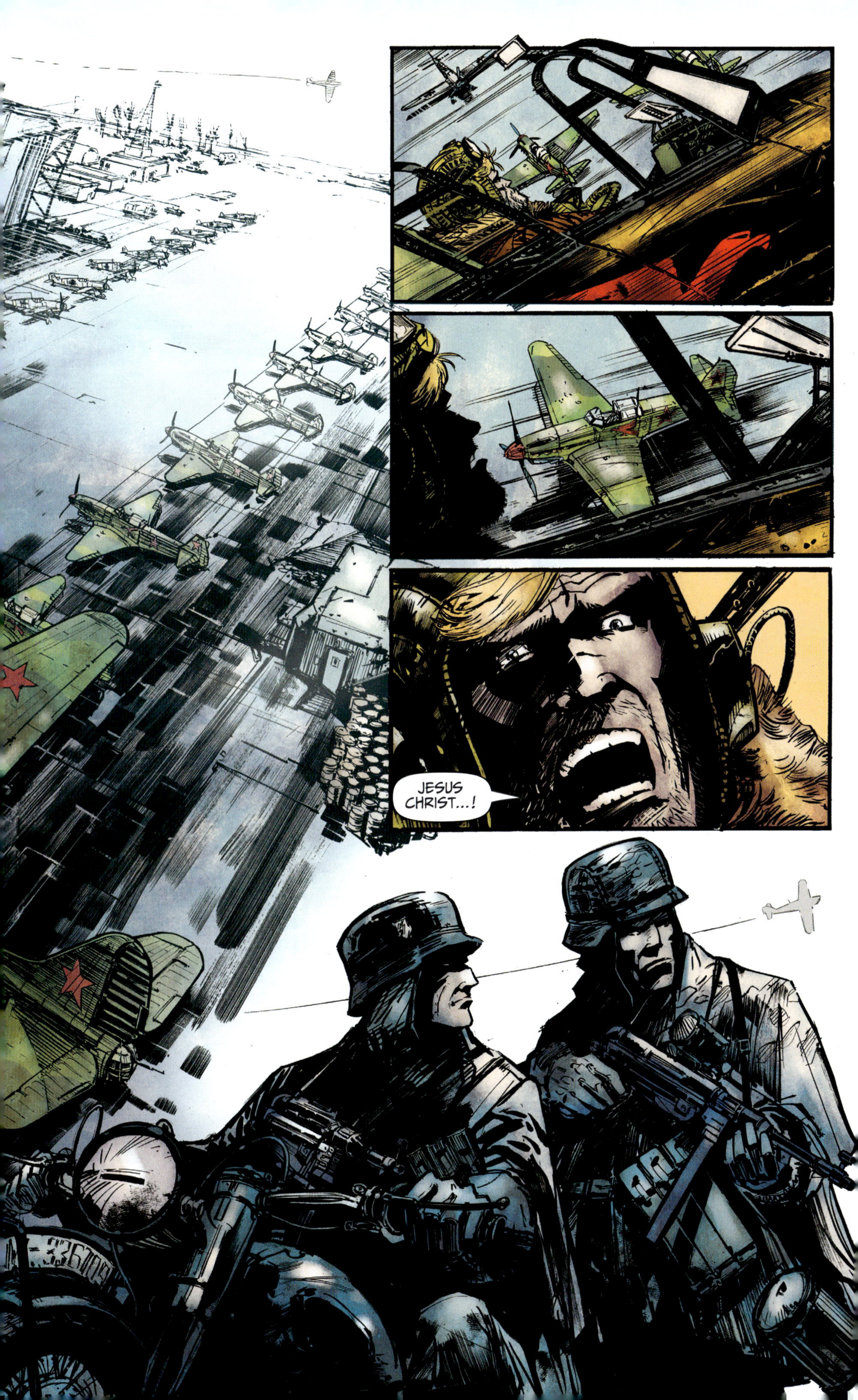
JESUS CHRIST...!

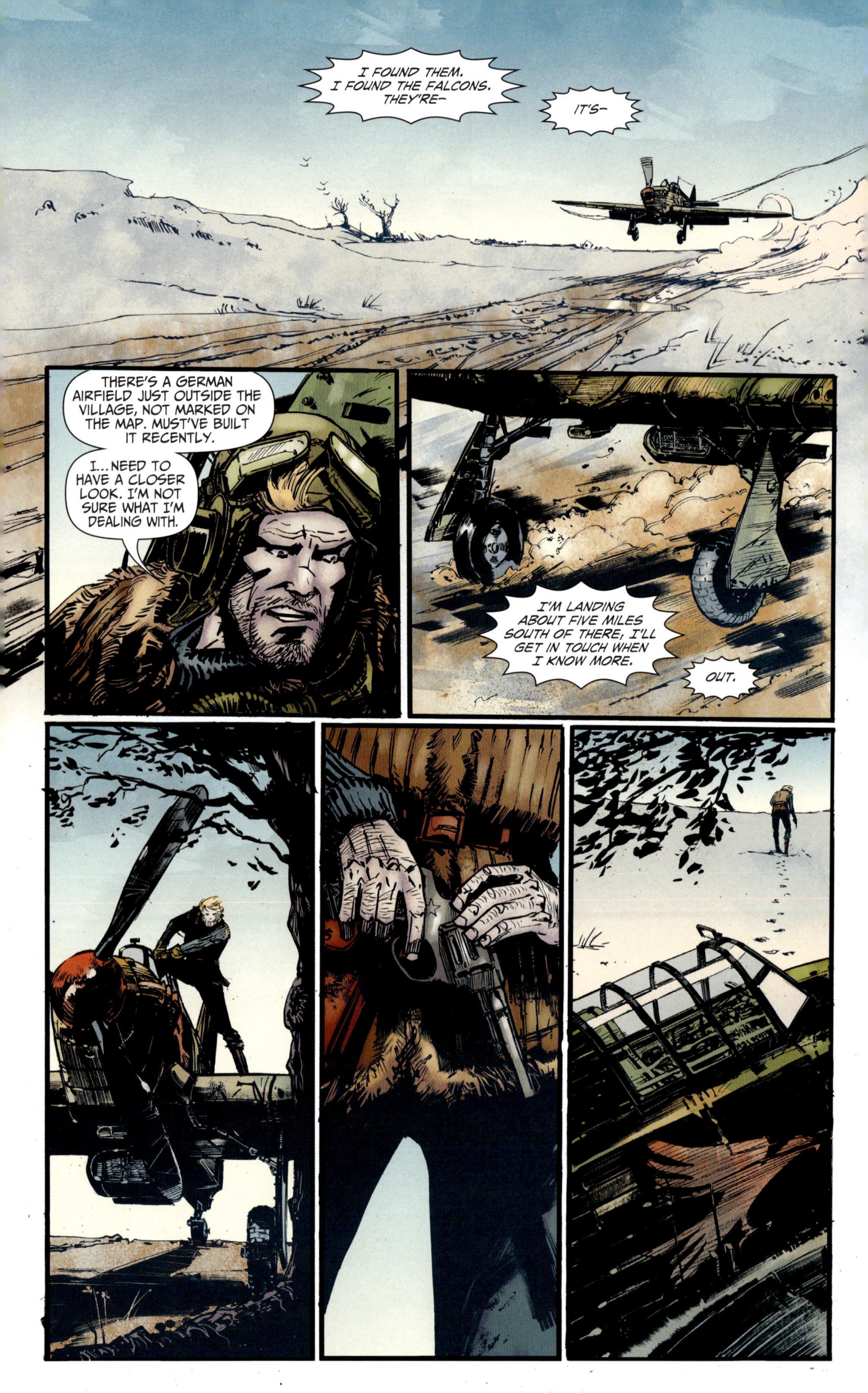
I FOUND THEM. I FOUND THE FALCONS. THEY'RE-
IT'S-
THERE'S A GERMAN AIRFIELD JUST OUTSIDE THE VILLAGE, NOT MARKED ON THE MAP. MUST'VE BUILT IT RECENTLY.
I...NEED TO HAVE A CLOSER LOOK. I'M NOT SURE WHAT I'M DEALING WITH.
I'M LANDING ABOUT FIVE MILES SOUTH OF THERE; I'LL GET IN TOUCH WHEN I KNOW MORE.
OUT.

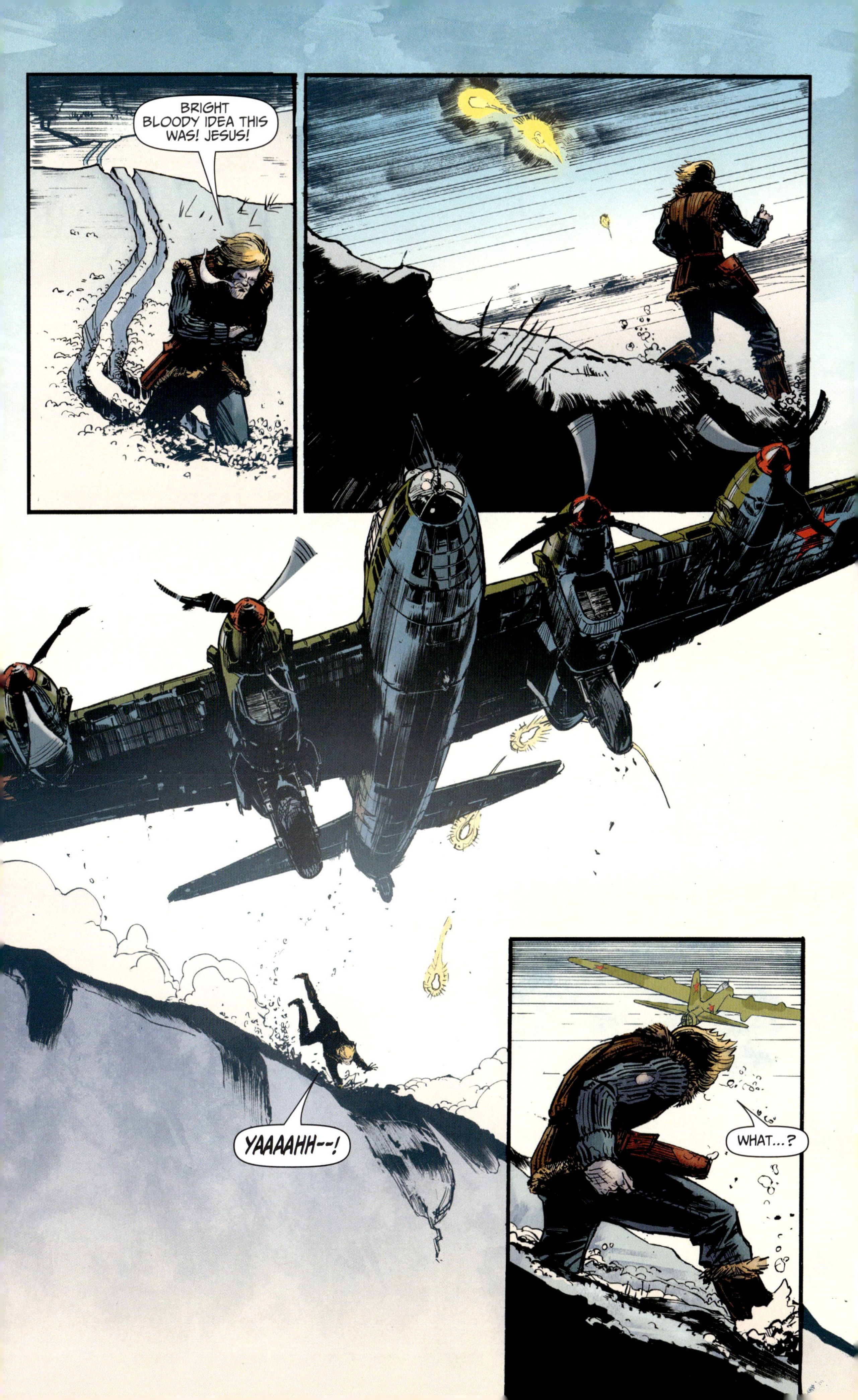
BRIGHT BLOODY IDEA THIS WAS! JESUS!
YAAAAHH--!
WHAT...?

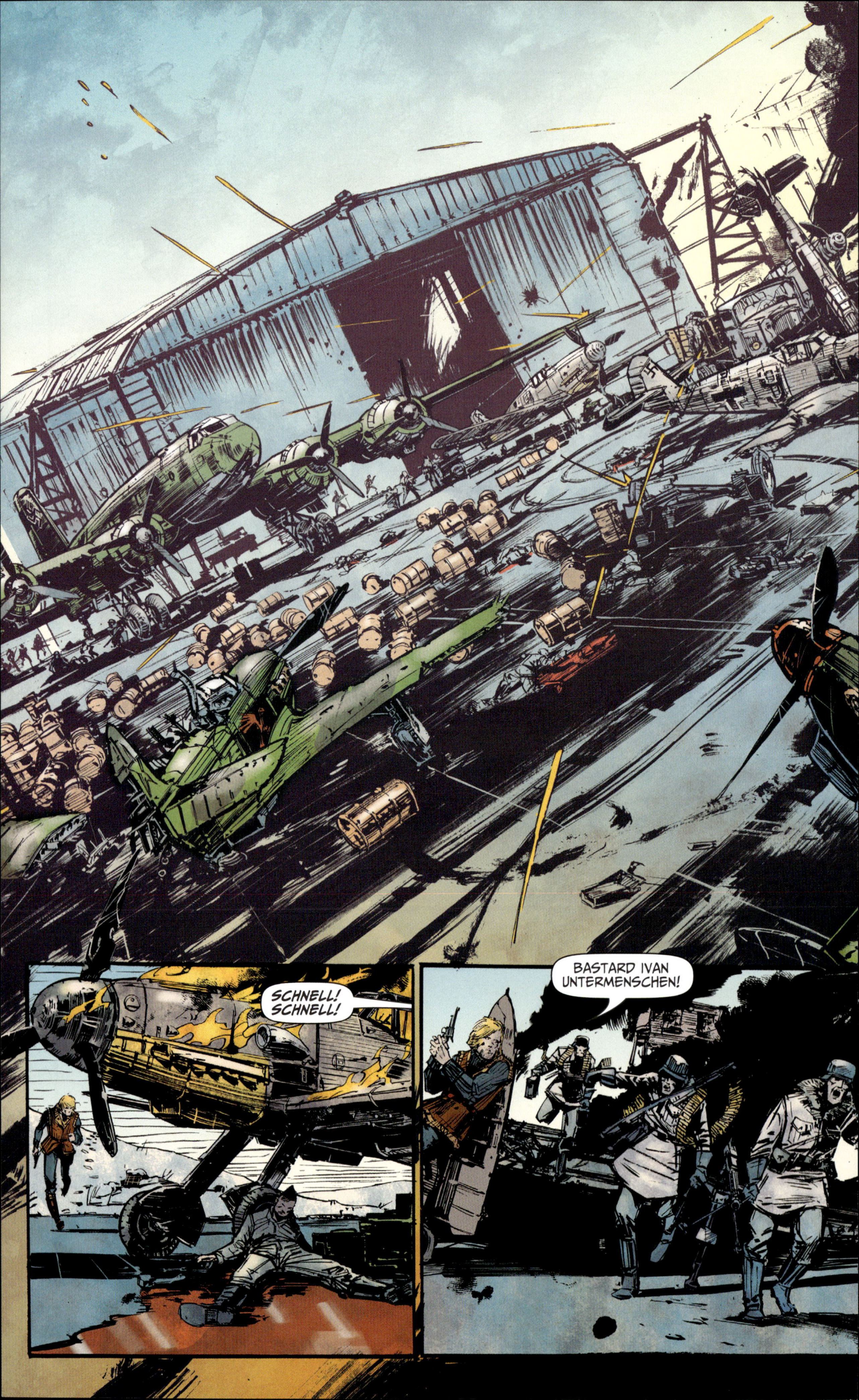
SCHNELL! SCHNELL!
BASTARD IVAN UNTERMENSCHEN!

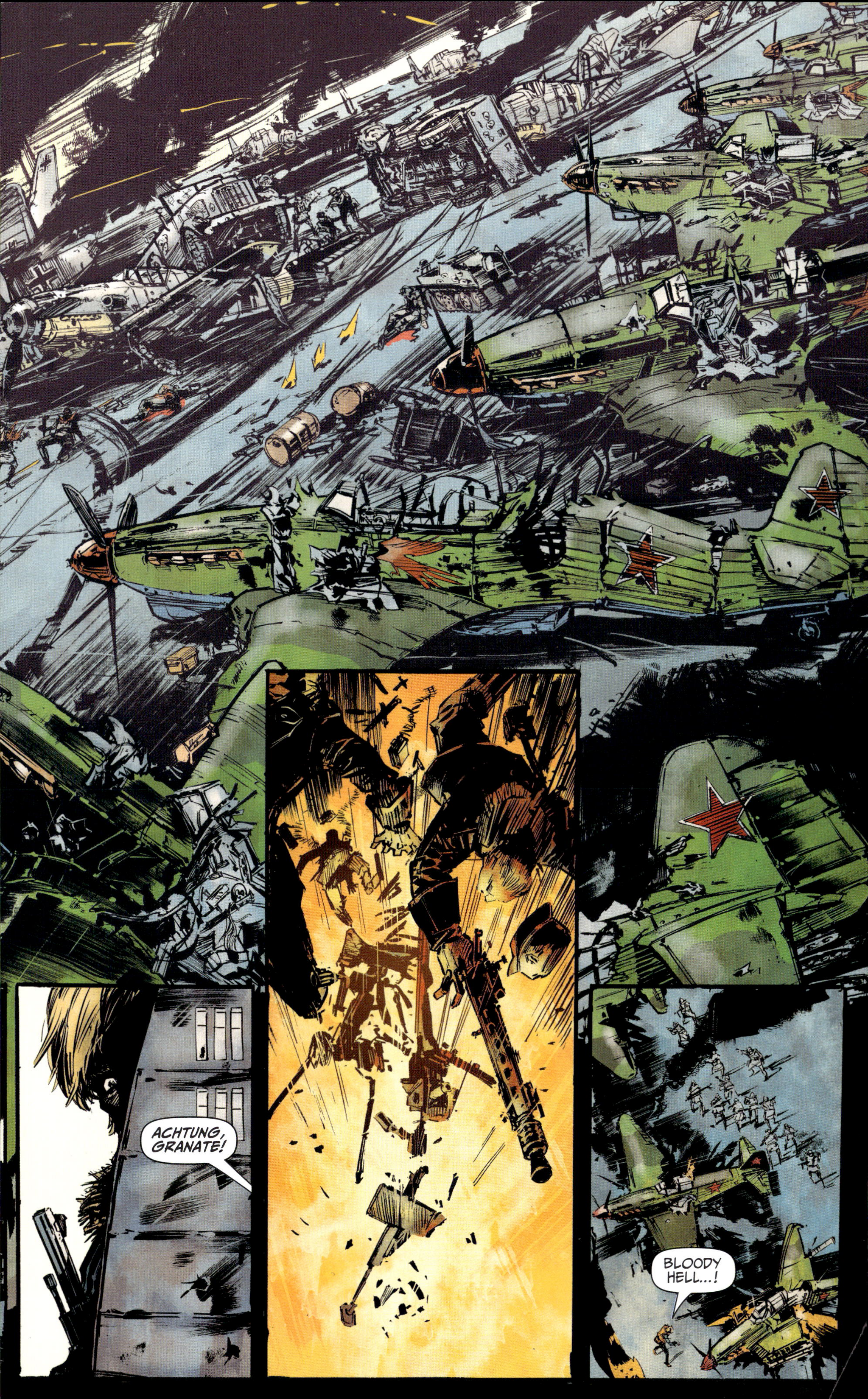
ACHTUNG, GRANATE!
BLOODY HELL...!

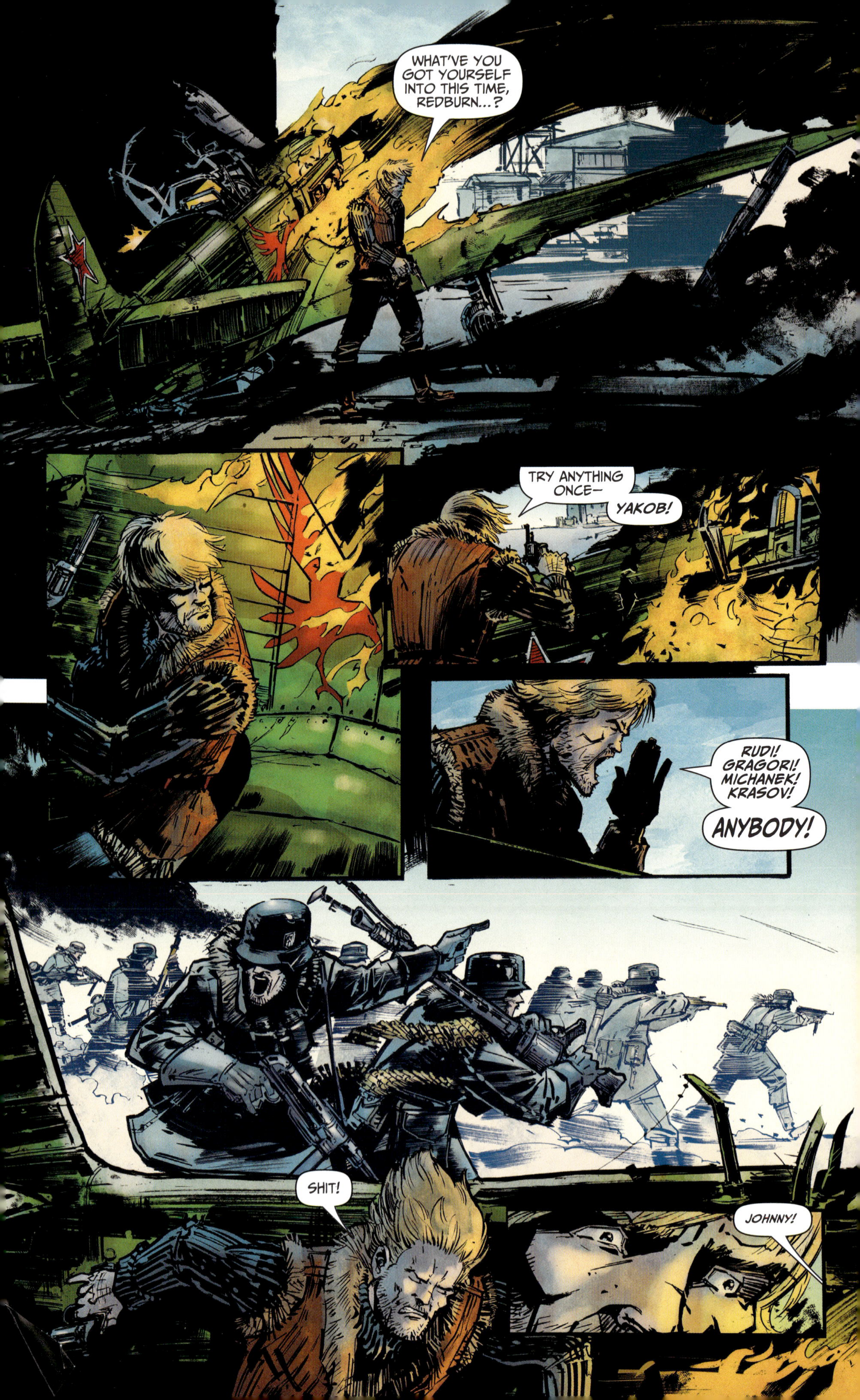
WHAT'VE YOU GOT YOURSELF INTO THIS TIME, REDBURN...?
TRY ANYTHING ONCE–
YAKOB!
RUDI! GRAGORI! MICHANEK! KRASOV!
ANYBODY!
SHIT!
JOHNNY!

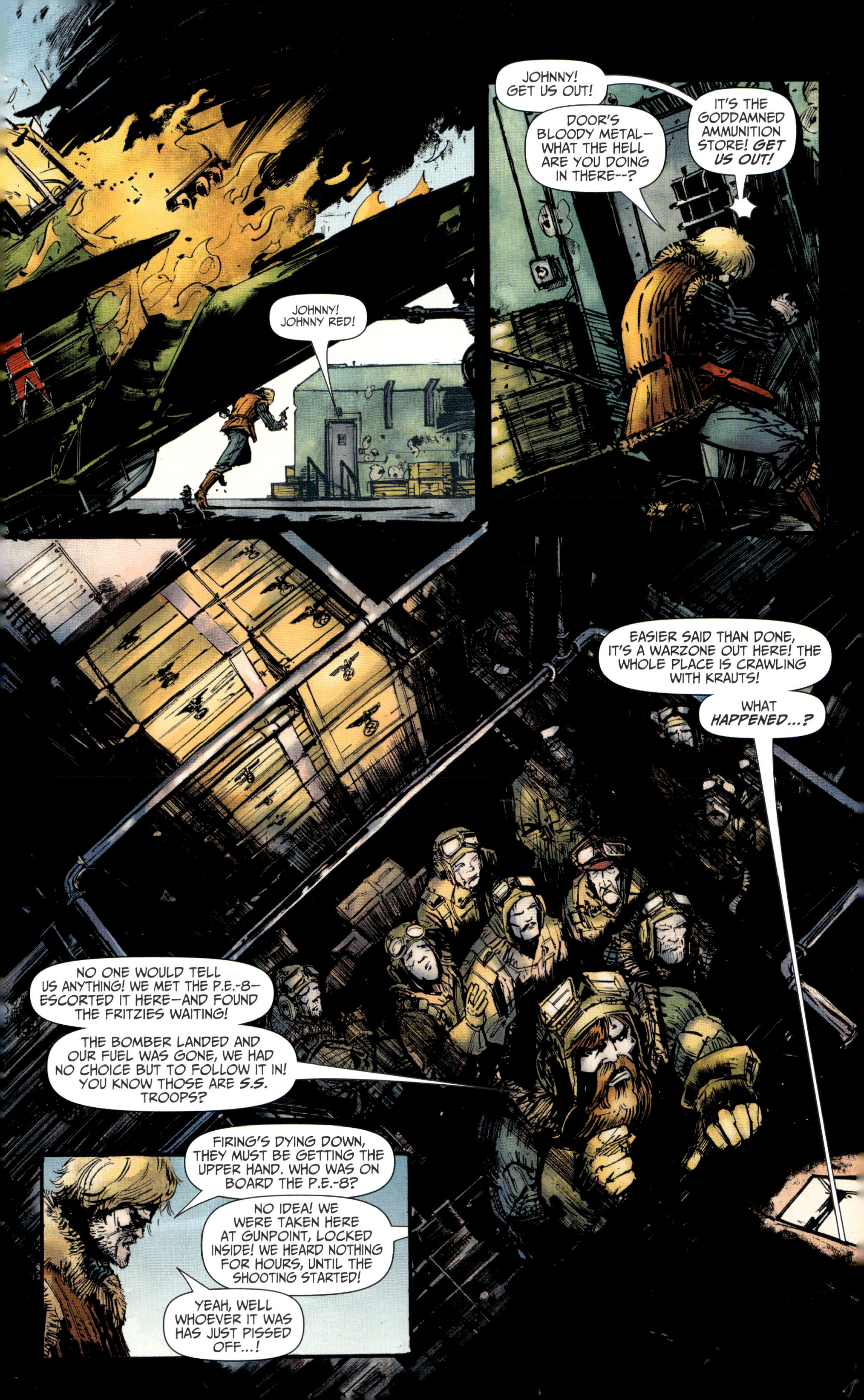
JOHNNY! JOHNNY RED!
JOHNNY! GET US OUT!
DOOR'S BLOODY METAL— WHAT THE HELL ARE YOU DOING IN THERE--?
IT'S THE GODDAMNED AMMUNITION STORE! GET US OUT!
EASIER SAID THAN DONE, IT'S A WARZONE OUT HERE! THE WHOLE PLACE IS CRAWLING WITH KRAUTS!
WHAT HAPPENED...?
NO ONE WOULD TELL US ANYTHING! WE MET THE P.E.-8— ESCORTED IT HERE—AND FOUND THE FRITZIES WAITING!
THE BOMBER LANDED AND OUR FUEL WAS GONE, WE HAD NO CHOICE BUT TO FOLLOW IT IN! YOU KNOW THOSE ARE S.S. TROOPS?
FIRING'S DYING DOWN, THEY MUST BE GETTING THE UPPER HAND. WHO WAS ON BOARD THE P.E.-8?
NO IDEA! WE WERE TAKEN HERE AT GUNPOINT, LOCKED INSIDE! WE HEARD NOTHING FOR HOURS, UNTIL THE SHOOTING STARTED!
YEAH, WELL WHOEVER IT WAS HAS JUST PISSED OFF...!

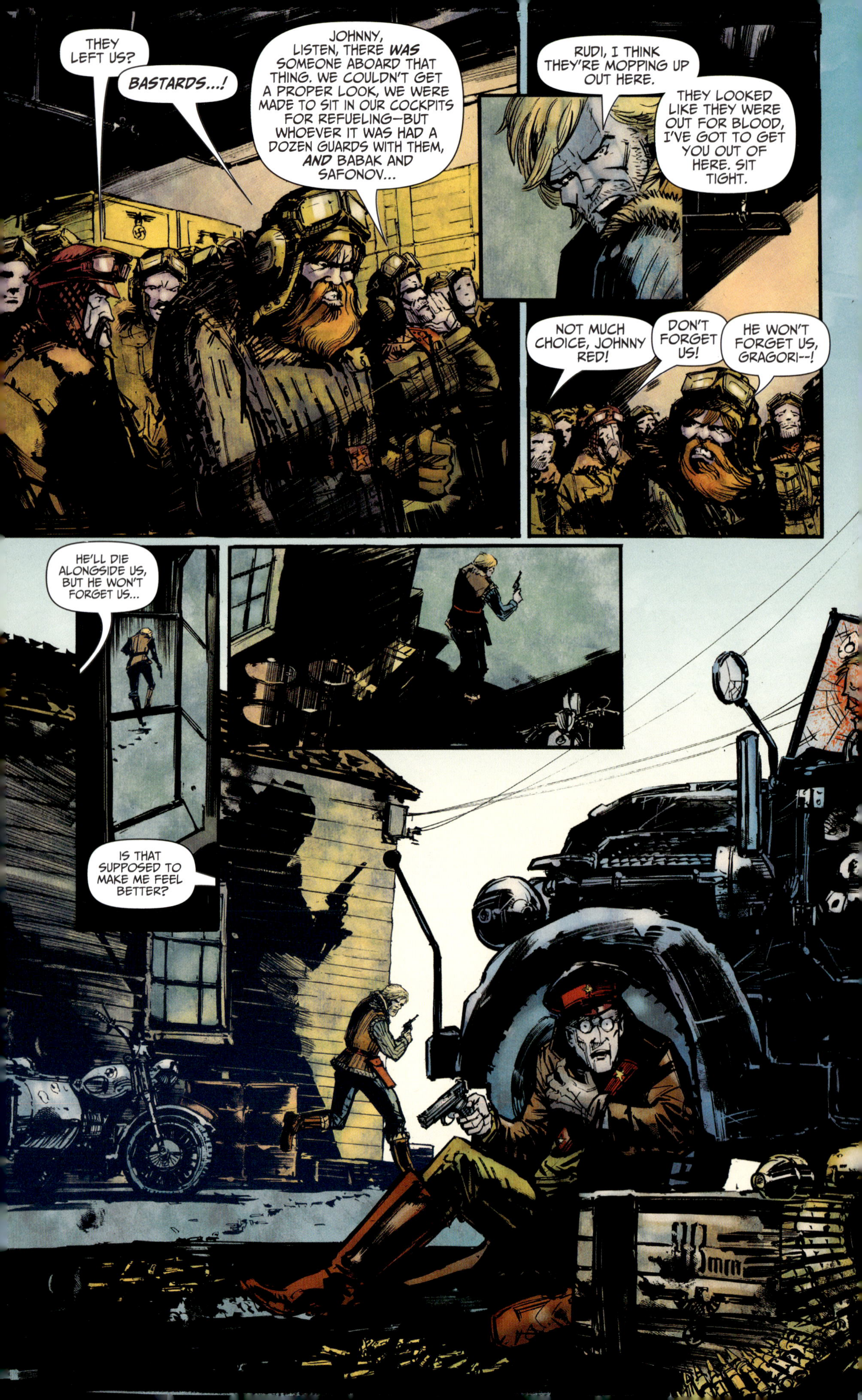
THEY LEFT US?
BASTARDS...!
JOHNNY, LISTEN, THERE WAS SOMEONE ABOARD THAT THING. WE COULDN'T GET A PROPER LOOK, WE WERE MADE TO SIT IN OUR COCKPITS FOR REFUELING—BUT WHOEVER IT WAS HAD A DOZEN GUARDS WITH THEM, AND BABAK AND SAFONOV...
RUDI, I THINK THEY'RE MOPPING UP OUT HERE.
THEY LOOKED LIKE THEY WERE OUT FOR BLOOD, I'VE GOT TO GET YOU OUT OF HERE. SIT TIGHT.
NOT MUCH CHOICE, JOHNNY RED!
DON'T FORGET US!
HE WON'T FORGET US, GRAGORI--!
HE'LL DIE ALONGSIDE US, BUT HE WON'T FORGET US...
IS THAT SUPPOSED TO MAKE ME FEEL BETTER?

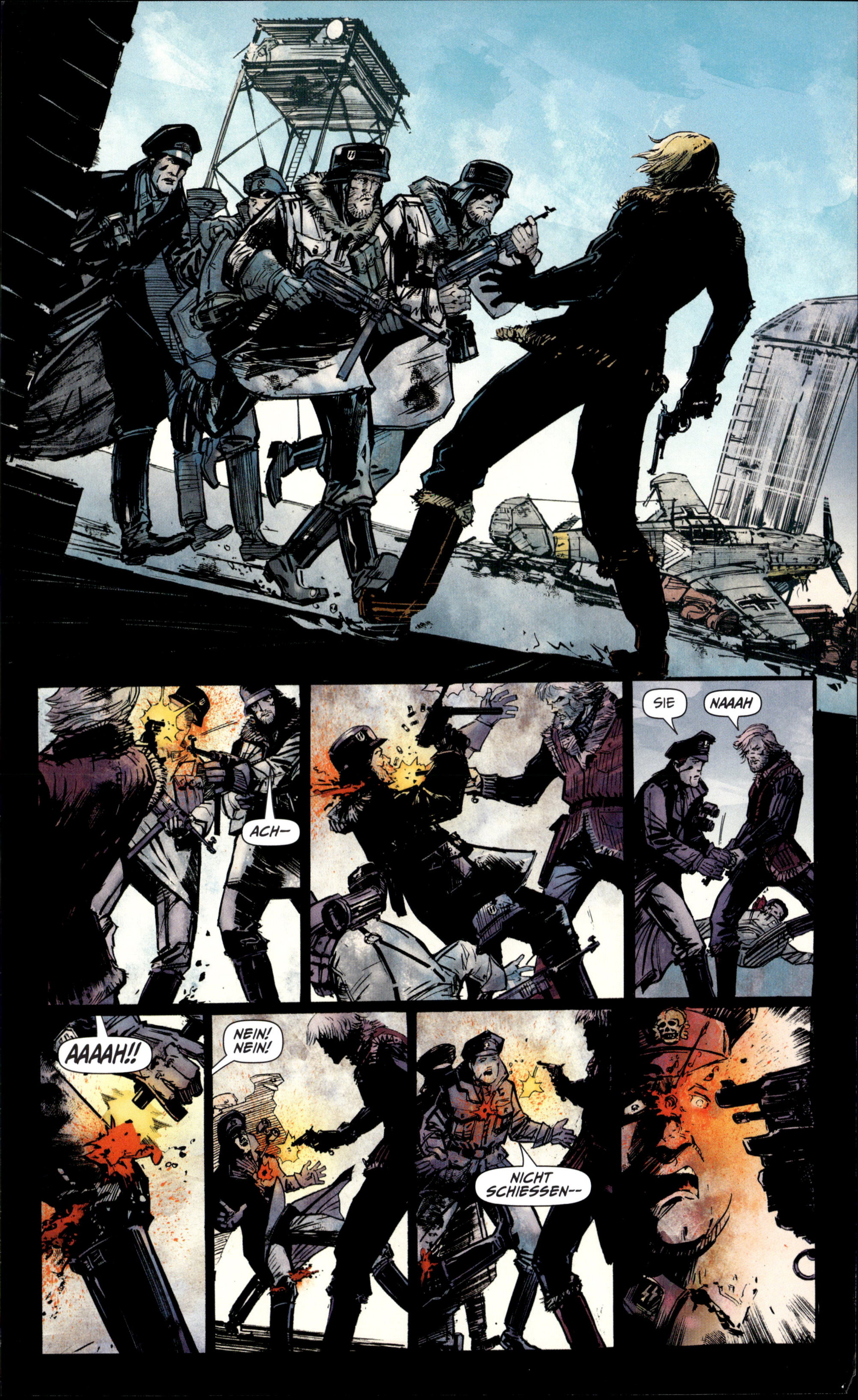
ACH–
SIE
NAAAH
AAAAH!!
NEIN! NEIN!
NICHT SCHIESSEN--

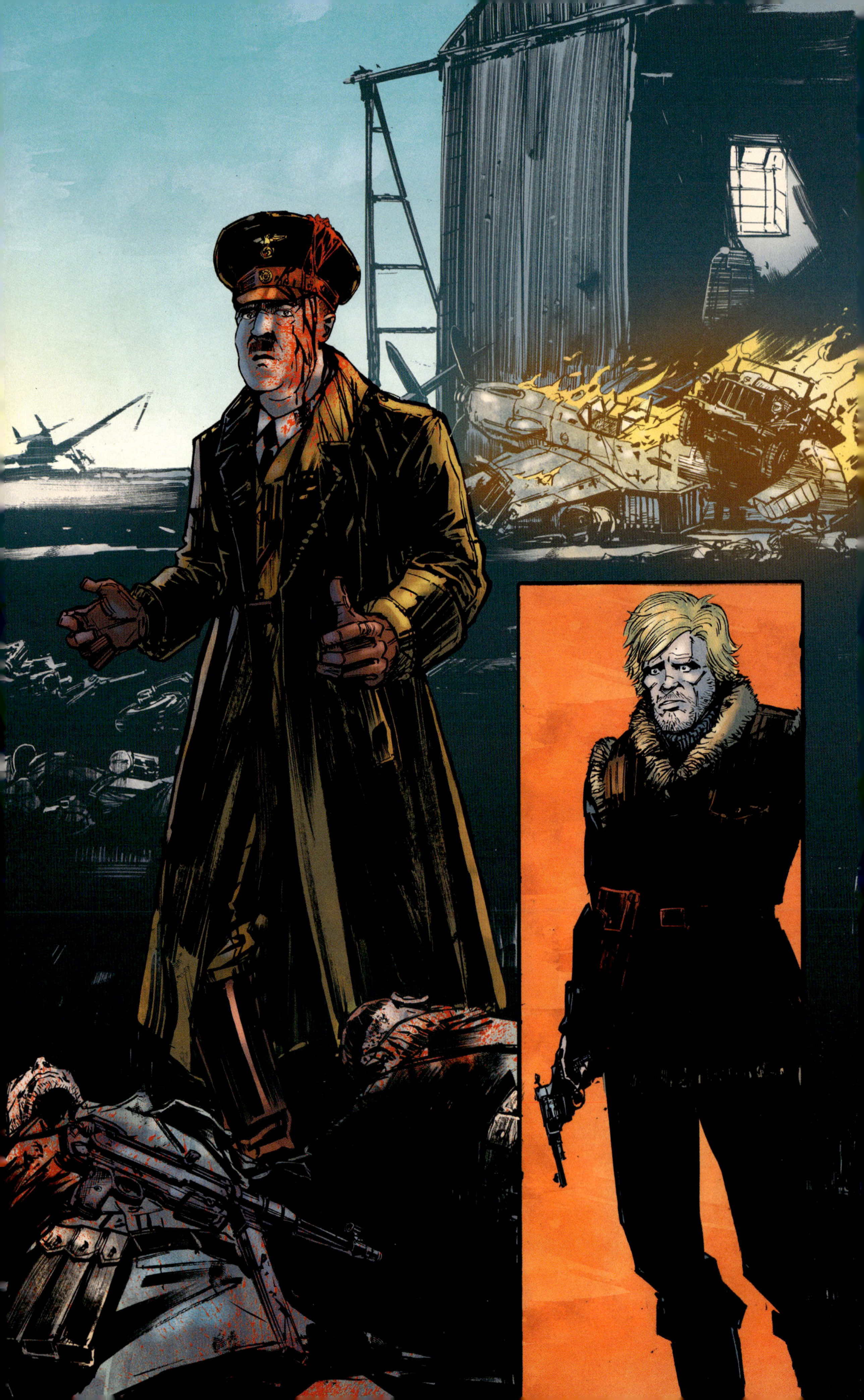

ISSUE SIX
Cover art by:
Keith Burns

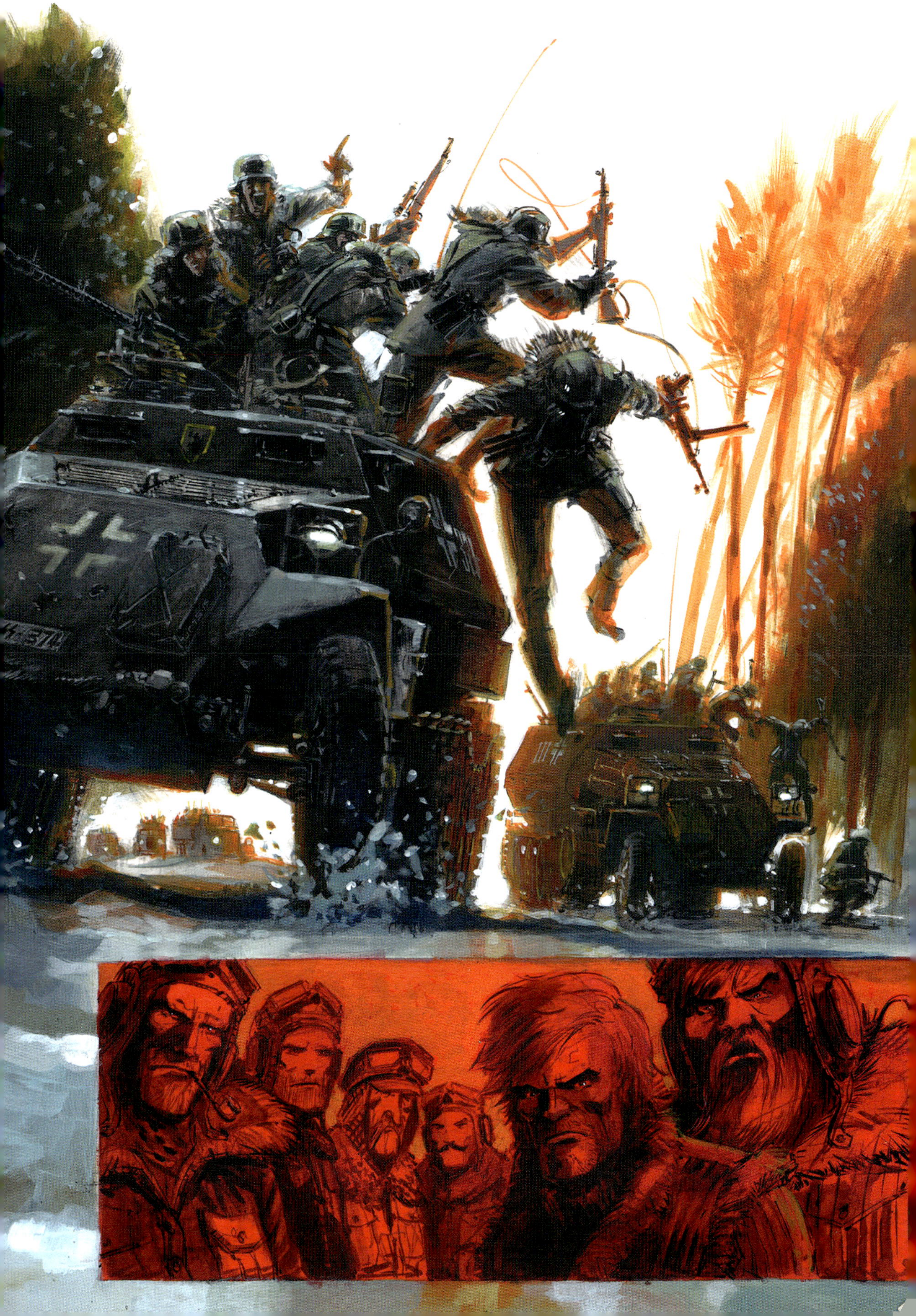

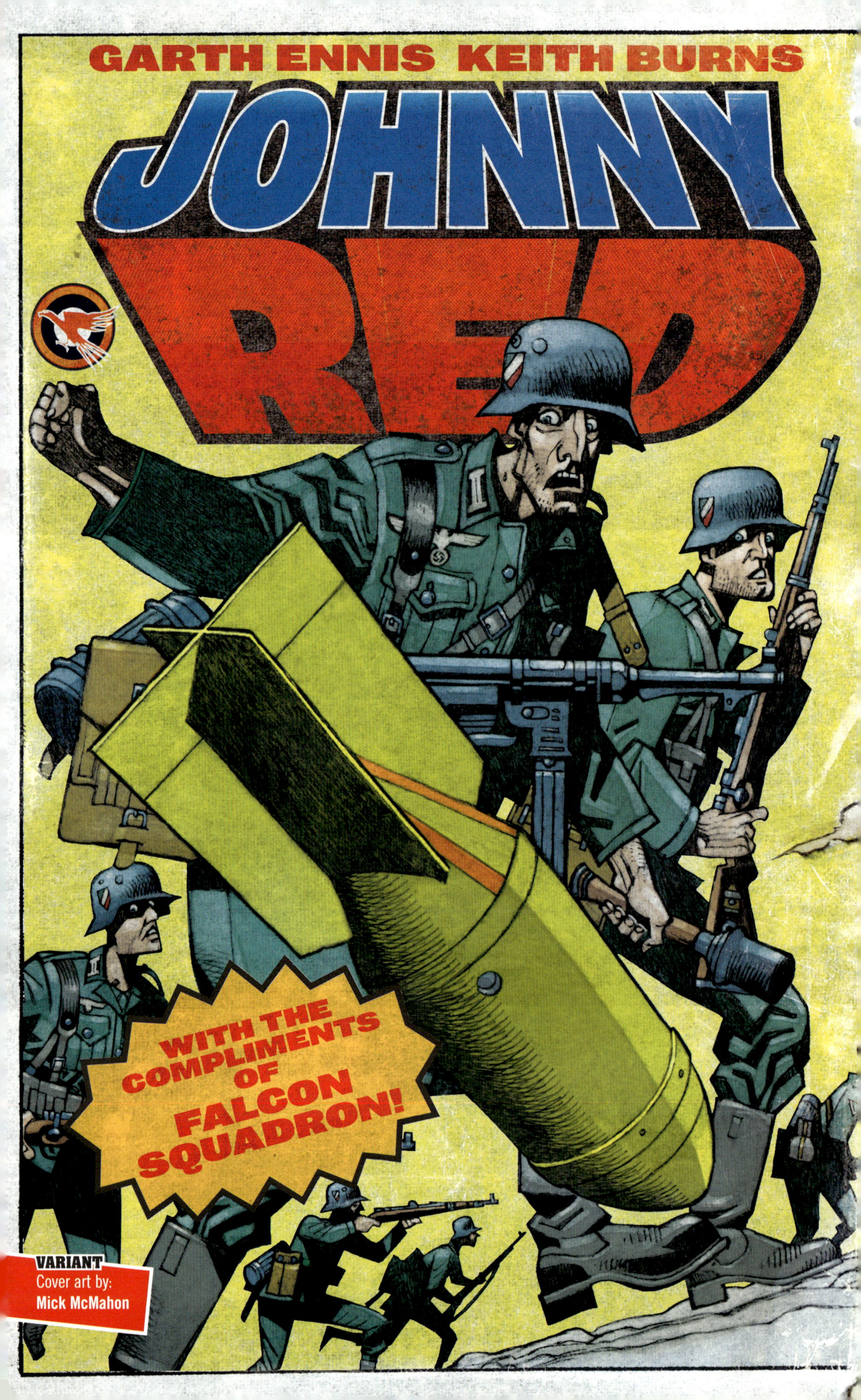
GARTH ENNIS KEITH BURNS
JOHNNY RED
WITH THE COMPLIMENTS OF FALCON SQUADRON!
VARIANT
Cover art by:
Mick McMahon

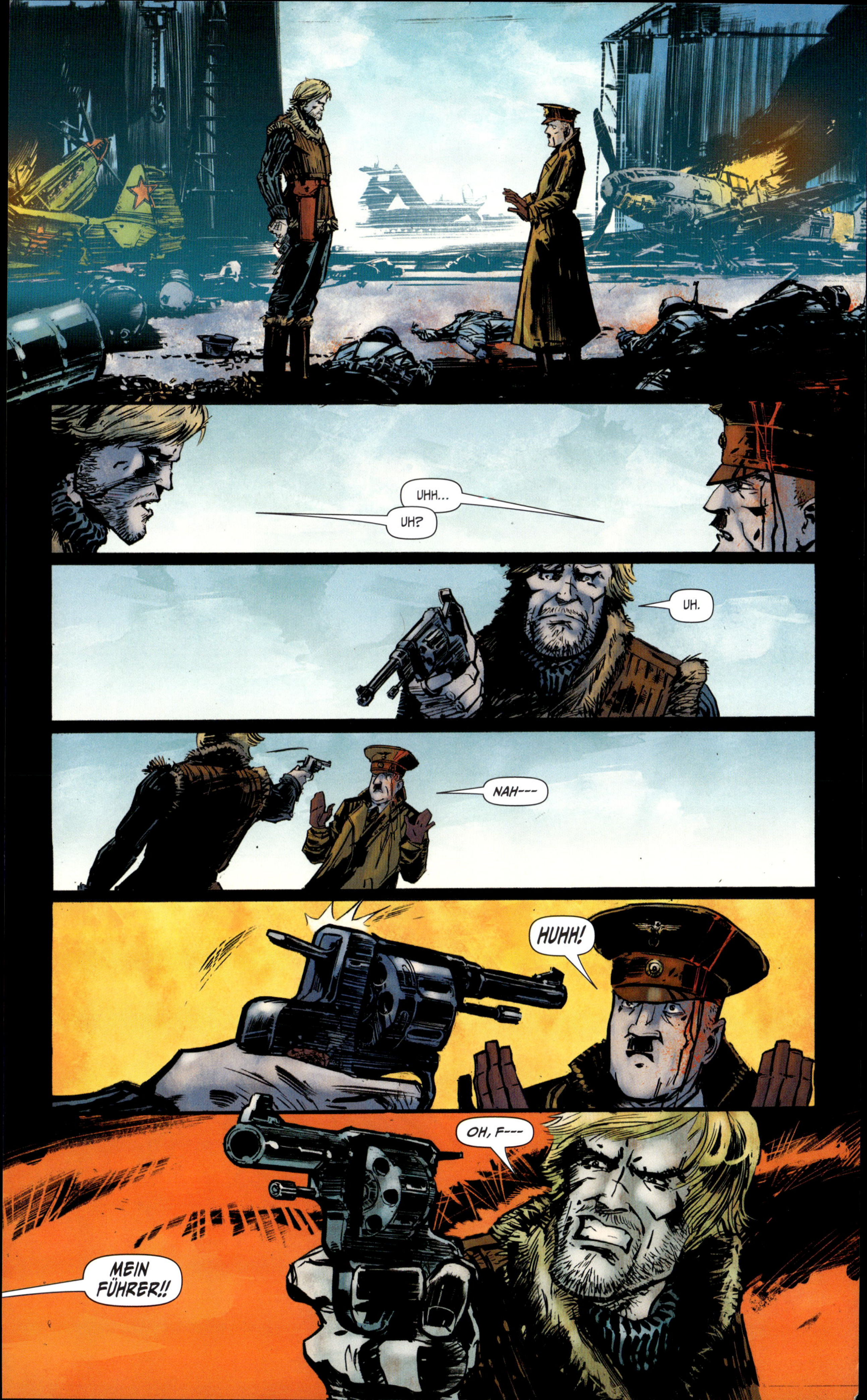
UHH...
UH?
UH.
NAH---
HUHH!
OH, F---
MEIN FÜHRER!!

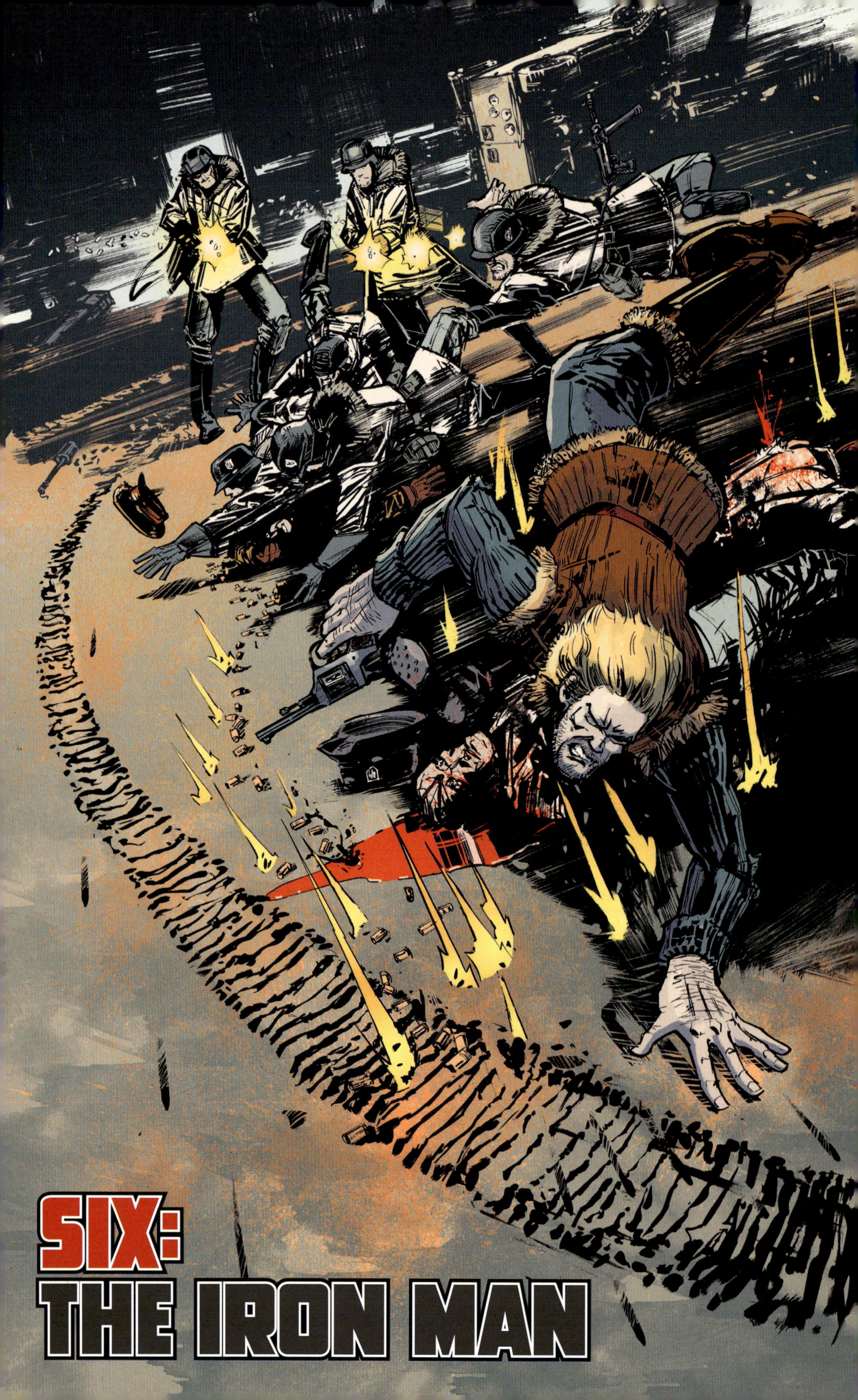
SIX:
THE IRON MAN

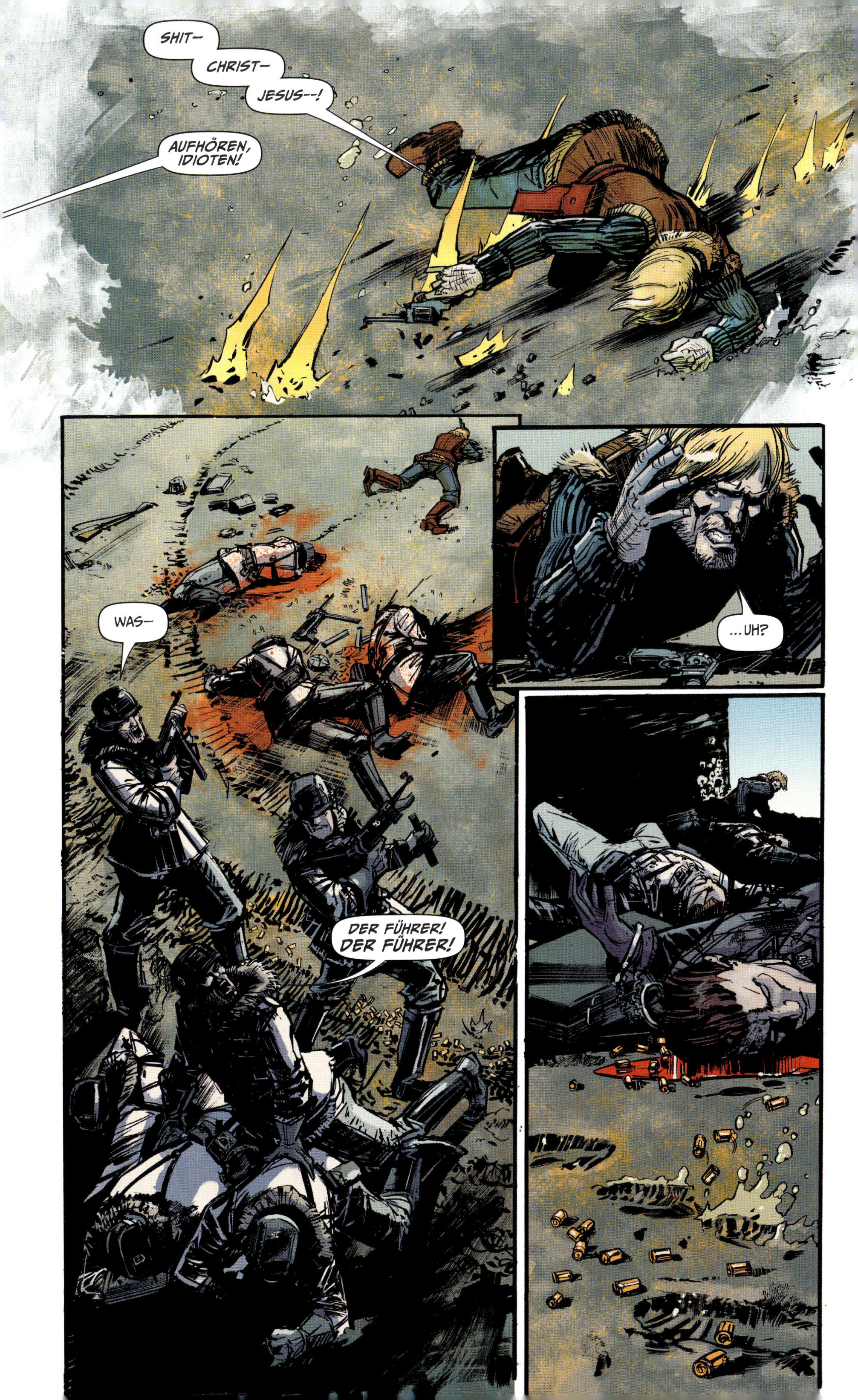
SHIT–
CHRIST–
JESUS––!
AUFHÖREN, IDIOTEN!
WAS–
...UH?
DER FÜHRER! DER FÜHRER!

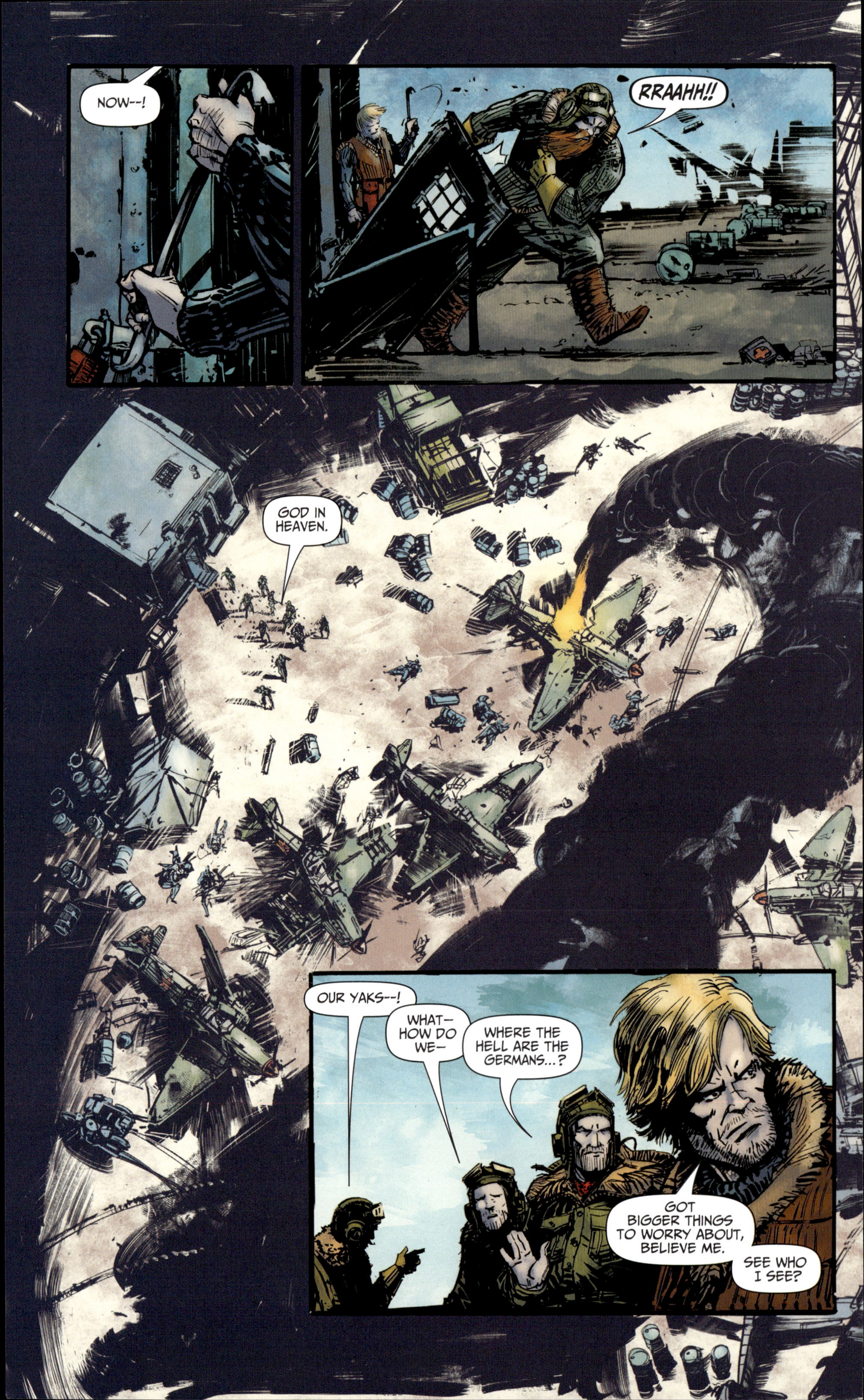
NOW--!
RRAAHH!!
GOD IN HEAVEN.
OUR YAKS--!
WHAT— HOW DO WE—
WHERE THE HELL ARE THE GERMANS...?
GOT BIGGER THINGS TO WORRY ABOUT, BELIEVE ME.
SEE WHO I SEE?

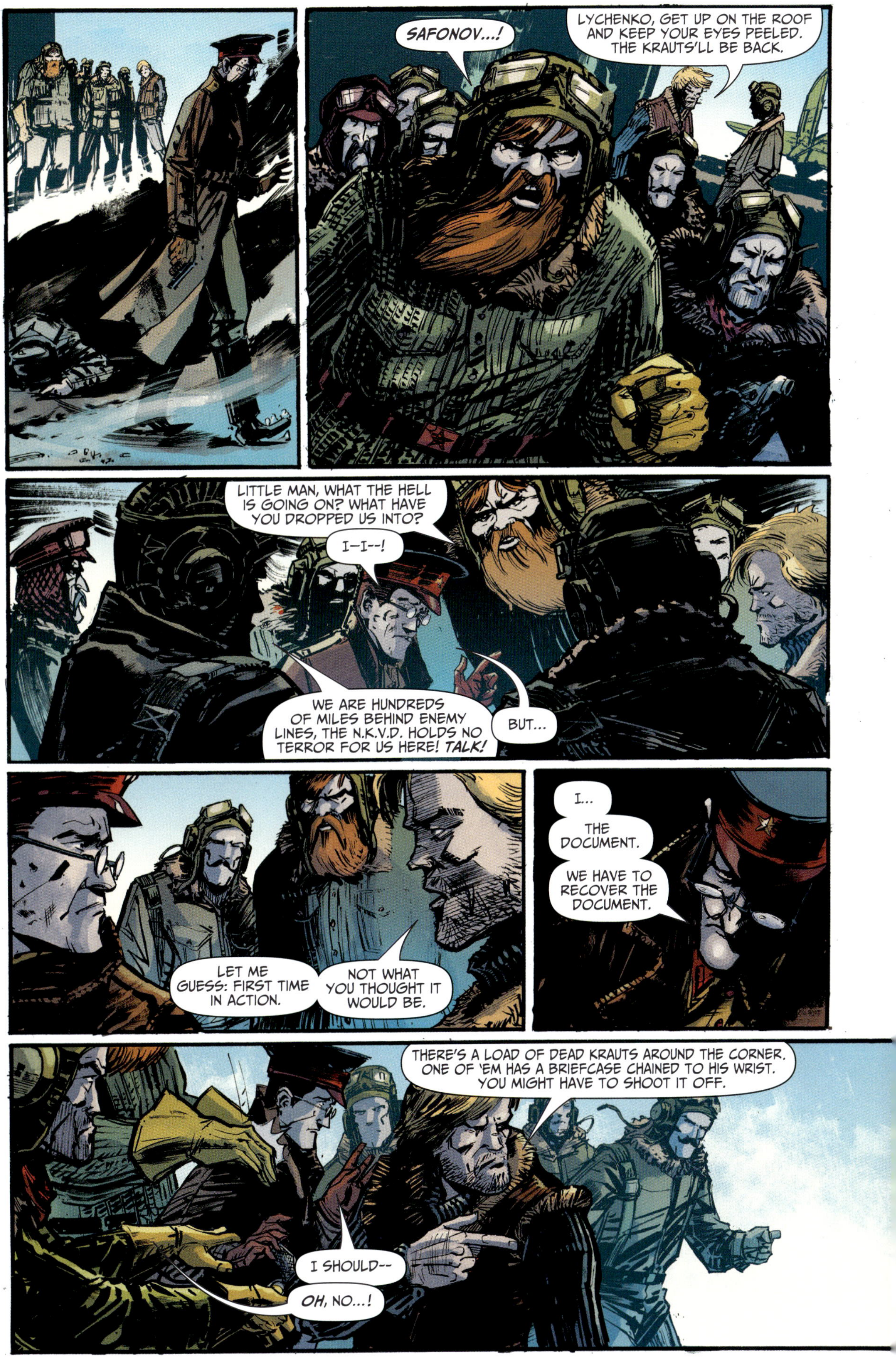
SAFONOV...!
LYCHENKO, GET UP ON THE ROOF AND KEEP YOUR EYES PEELED. THE KRAUTS'LL BE BACK.
LITTLE MAN, WHAT THE HELL IS GOING ON? WHAT HAVE YOU DROPPED US INTO?
I--I--!
WE ARE HUNDREDS OF MILES BEHIND ENEMY LINES, THE N.K.V.D. HOLDS NO TERROR FOR US HERE! TALK!
BUT...
LET ME GUESS: FIRST TIME IN ACTION.
NOT WHAT YOU THOUGHT IT WOULD BE.
I...
THE DOCUMENT.
WE HAVE TO RECOVER THE DOCUMENT.
THERE'S A LOAD OF DEAD KRAUTS AROUND THE CORNER. ONE OF 'EM HAS A BRIEFCASE CHAINED TO HIS WRIST. YOU MIGHT HAVE TO SHOOT IT OFF.
I SHOULD--
OH, NO...!

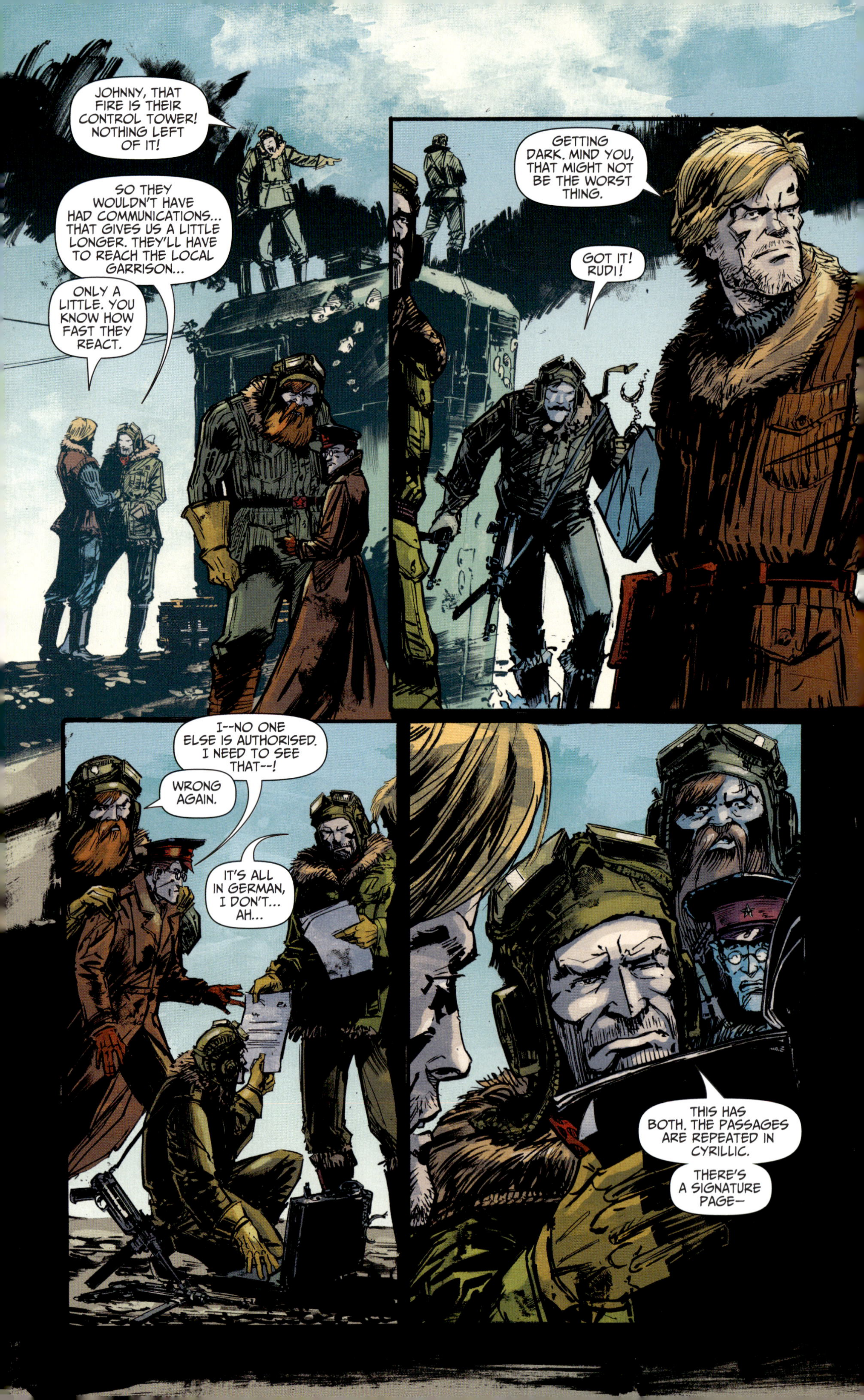
JOHNNY, THAT FIRE IS THEIR CONTROL TOWER! NOTHING LEFT OF IT!
SO THEY WOULDN'T HAVE HAD COMMUNICATIONS... THAT GIVES US A LITTLE LONGER. THEY'LL HAVE TO REACH THE LOCAL GARRISON...
ONLY A LITTLE. YOU KNOW HOW FAST THEY REACT.
GETTING DARK. MIND YOU, THAT MIGHT NOT BE THE WORST THING.
GOT IT! RUDI!
I--NO ONE ELSE IS AUTHORISED. I NEED TO SEE THAT--!
WRONG AGAIN.
IT'S ALL IN GERMAN, I DON'T... AH...
THIS HAS BOTH. THE PASSAGES ARE REPEATED IN CYRILLIC.
THERE'S A SIGNATURE PAGE—

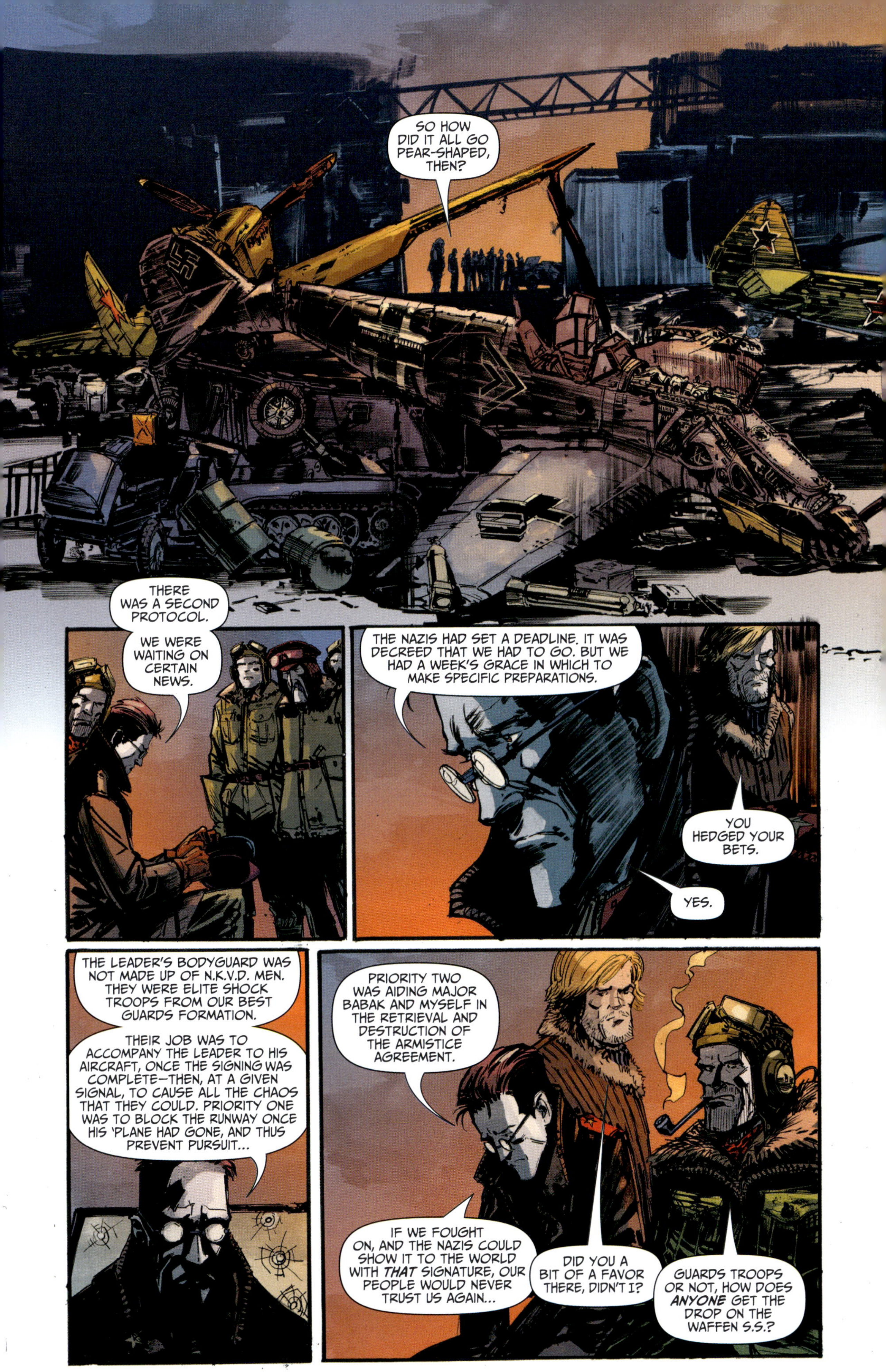
SO HOW DID IT ALL GO PEAR-SHAPED, THEN?
THERE WAS A SECOND PROTOCOL.
WE WERE WAITING ON CERTAIN NEWS.
THE NAZIS HAD SET A DEADLINE. IT WAS DECREED THAT WE HAD TO GO. BUT WE HAD A WEEK'S GRACE IN WHICH TO MAKE SPECIFIC PREPARATIONS.
YOU HEDGED YOUR BETS.
YES.
THE LEADER'S BODYGUARD WAS NOT MADE UP OF N.K.V.D. MEN. THEY WERE ELITE SHOCK TROOPS FROM OUR BEST GUARDS FORMATION.
THEIR JOB WAS TO ACCOMPANY THE LEADER TO HIS AIRCRAFT, ONCE THE SIGNING WAS COMPLETE—THEN, AT A GIVEN SIGNAL, TO CAUSE ALL THE CHAOS THAT THEY COULD. PRIORITY ONE WAS TO BLOCK THE RUNWAY ONCE HIS 'PLANE HAD GONE, AND THUS PREVENT PURSUIT...
PRIORITY TWO WAS AIDING MAJOR BABAK AND MYSELF IN THE RETRIEVAL AND DESTRUCTION OF THE ARMISTICE AGREEMENT.
IF WE FOUGHT ON, AND THE NAZIS COULD SHOW IT TO THE WORLD WITH *THAT* SIGNATURE, OUR PEOPLE WOULD NEVER TRUST US AGAIN...
DID YOU A BIT OF A FAVOR THERE, DIDN'T I?
GUARDS TROOPS OR NOT, HOW DOES *ANYONE* GET THE DROP ON THE WAFFEN S.S.?

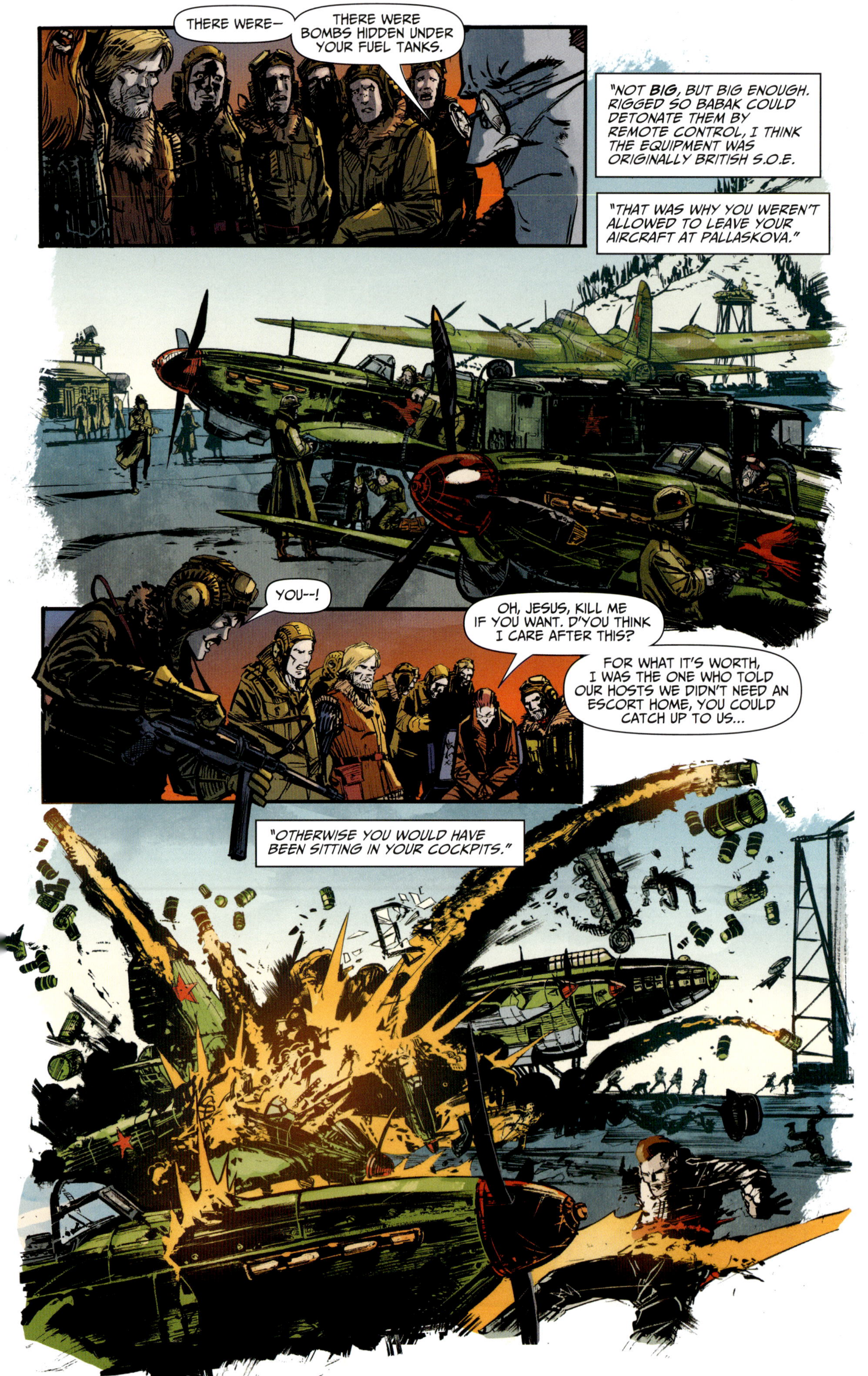
THERE WERE—
THERE WERE BOMBS HIDDEN UNDER YOUR FUEL TANKS.
"NOT BIG, BUT BIG ENOUGH. RIGGED SO BABAK COULD DETONATE THEM BY REMOTE CONTROL, I THINK THE EQUIPMENT WAS ORIGINALLY BRITISH S.O.E.
"THAT WAS WHY YOU WEREN'T ALLOWED TO LEAVE YOUR AIRCRAFT AT PALLASKOVA."
YOU--!
OH, JESUS, KILL ME IF YOU WANT. D'YOU THINK I CARE AFTER THIS?
FOR WHAT IT'S WORTH, I WAS THE ONE WHO TOLD OUR HOSTS WE DIDN'T NEED AN ESCORT HOME, YOU COULD CATCH UP TO US...
"OTHERWISE YOU WOULD HAVE BEEN SITTING IN YOUR COCKPITS."

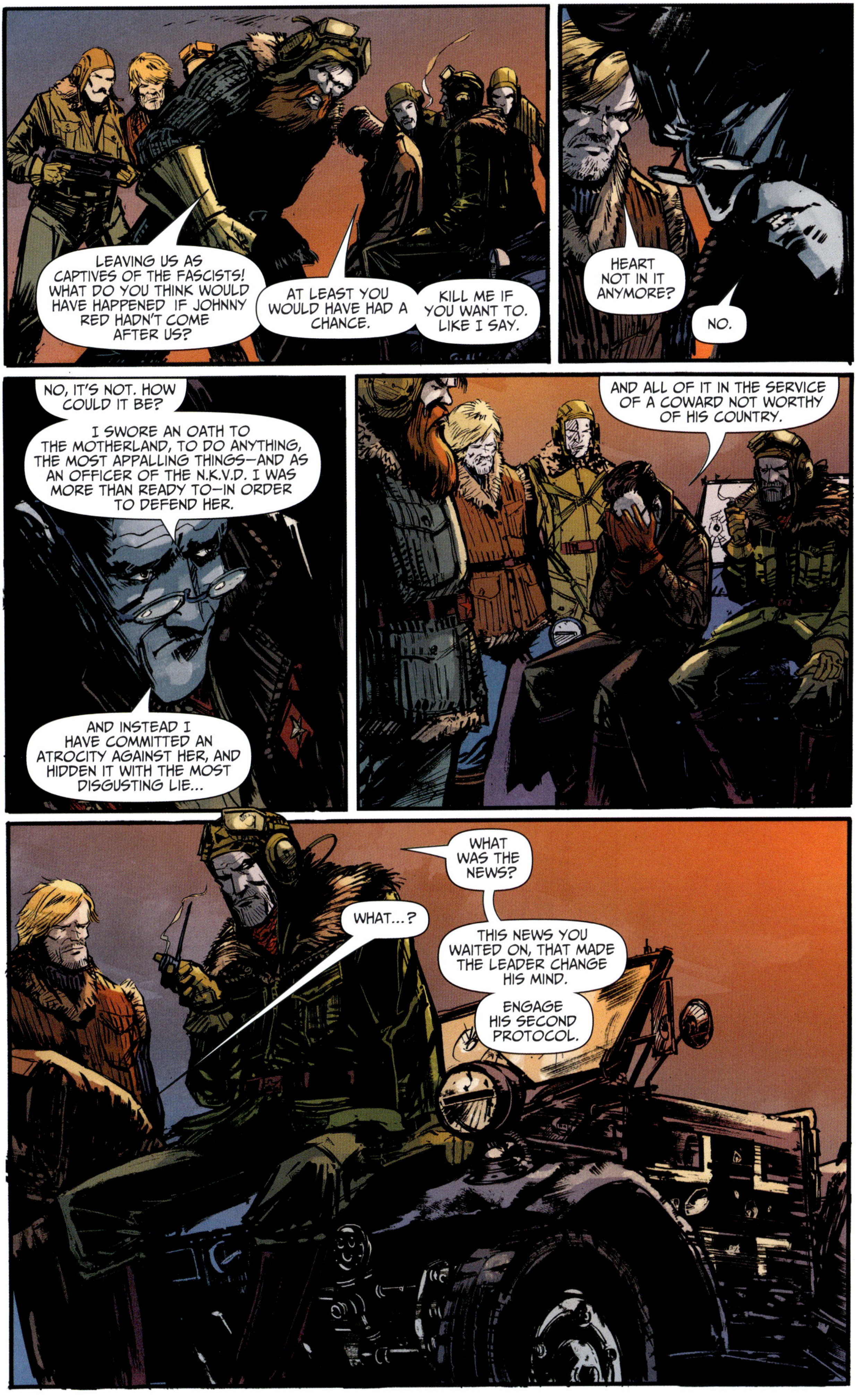
LEAVING US AS CAPTIVES OF THE FASCISTS! WHAT DO YOU THINK WOULD HAVE HAPPENED IF JOHNNY RED HADN'T COME AFTER US?
AT LEAST YOU WOULD HAVE HAD A CHANCE.
KILL ME IF YOU WANT TO. LIKE I SAY.
HEART NOT IN IT ANYMORE?
NO.
NO, IT'S NOT. HOW COULD IT BE?
I SWORE AN OATH TO THE MOTHERLAND, TO DO ANYTHING, THE MOST APPALLING THINGS—AND AS AN OFFICER OF THE N.K.V.D. I WAS MORE THAN READY TO—IN ORDER TO DEFEND HER.
AND INSTEAD I HAVE COMMITTED AN ATROCITY AGAINST HER, AND HIDDEN IT WITH THE MOST DISGUSTING LIE...
AND ALL OF IT IN THE SERVICE OF A COWARD NOT WORTHY OF HIS COUNTRY.
WHAT...?
WHAT WAS THE NEWS?
THIS NEWS YOU WAITED ON, THAT MADE THE LEADER CHANGE HIS MIND.
ENGAGE HIS SECOND PROTOCOL.

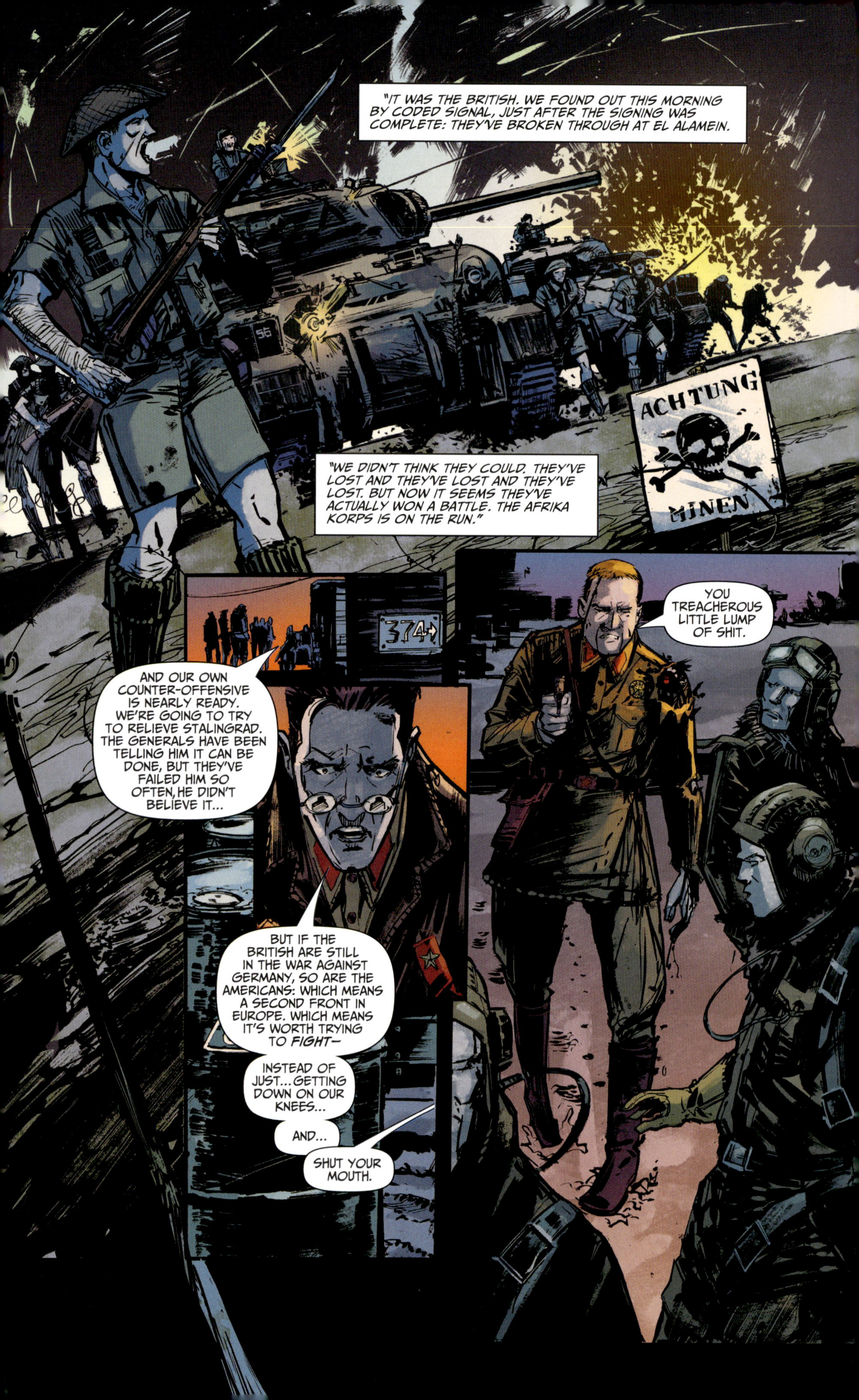
"IT WAS THE BRITISH. WE FOUND OUT THIS MORNING BY CODED SIGNAL, JUST AFTER THE SIGNING WAS COMPLETE: THEY'VE BROKEN THROUGH AT EL ALAMEIN.
56
ACHTUNG
MINEN
"WE DIDN'T THINK THEY COULD. THEY'VE LOST AND THEY'VE LOST AND THEY'VE LOST. BUT NOW IT SEEMS THEY'VE ACTUALLY WON A BATTLE. THE AFRIKA KORPS IS ON THE RUN."
374
AND OUR OWN COUNTER-OFFENSIVE IS NEARLY READY. WE'RE GOING TO TRY TO RELIEVE STALINGRAD. THE GENERALS HAVE BEEN TELLING HIM IT CAN BE DONE, BUT THEY'VE FAILED HIM SO OFTEN, HE DIDN'T BELIEVE IT...
BUT IF THE BRITISH ARE STILL IN THE WAR AGAINST GERMANY, SO ARE THE AMERICANS: WHICH MEANS A SECOND FRONT IN EUROPE. WHICH MEANS IT'S WORTH TRYING TO *FIGHT*—
INSTEAD OF JUST... GETTING DOWN ON OUR KNEES...
AND...
YOU TREACHEROUS LITTLE LUMP OF SHIT.
SHUT YOUR MOUTH.

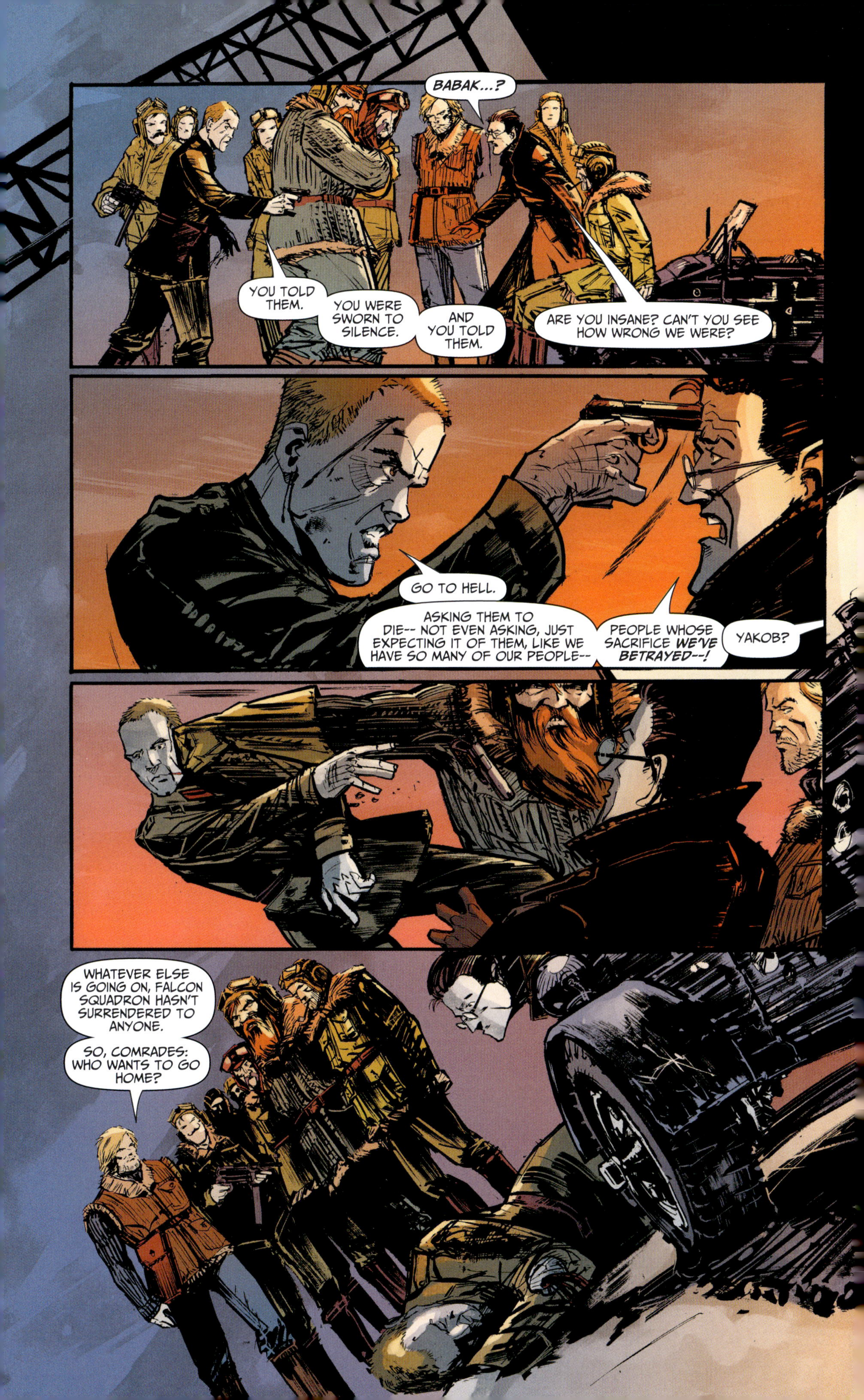
BABAK...?
YOU TOLD THEM.
YOU WERE SWORN TO SILENCE.
AND YOU TOLD THEM.
ARE YOU INSANE? CAN'T YOU SEE HOW WRONG WE WERE?
GO TO HELL.
ASKING THEM TO DIE-- NOT EVEN ASKING, JUST EXPECTING IT OF THEM, LIKE WE HAVE SO MANY OF OUR PEOPLE--
PEOPLE WHOSE SACRIFICE *WE'VE BETRAYED--!*
YAKOB?
WHATEVER ELSE IS GOING ON, FALCON SQUADRON HASN'T SURRENDERED TO ANYONE.
SO, COMRADES: WHO WANTS TO GO HOME?

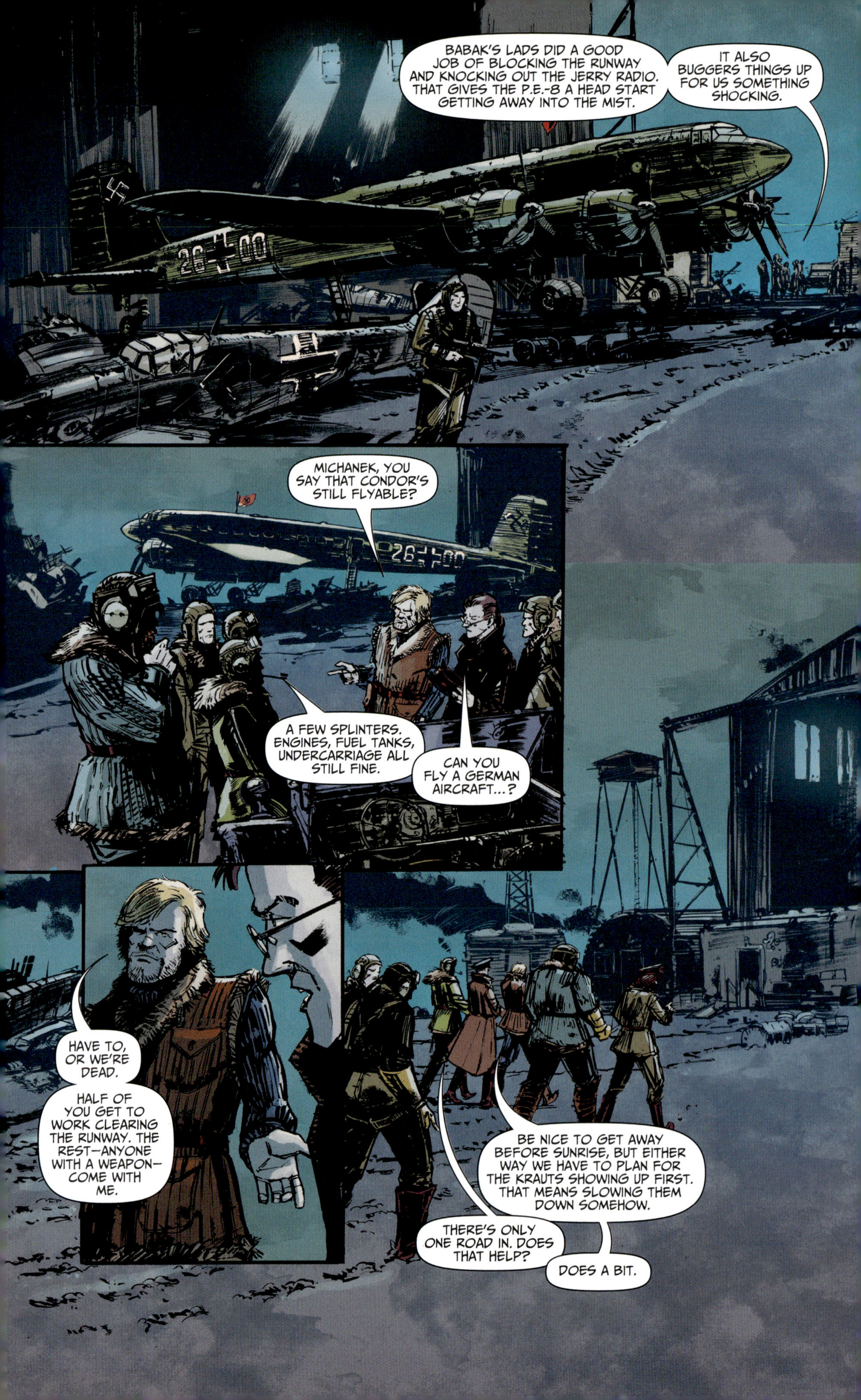
BABAK'S LADS DID A GOOD JOB OF BLOCKING THE RUNWAY AND KNOCKING OUT THE JERRY RADIO. THAT GIVES THE P.E.-8 A HEAD START GETTING AWAY INTO THE MIST.
IT ALSO BUGGERS THINGS UP FOR US SOMETHING SHOCKING.
26+00
MICHANEK, YOU SAY THAT CONDOR'S STILL FLYABLE?
A FEW SPLINTERS. ENGINES, FUEL TANKS, UNDERCARRIAGE ALL STILL FINE.
CAN YOU FLY A GERMAN AIRCRAFT...?
HAVE TO, OR WE'RE DEAD.
HALF OF YOU GET TO WORK CLEARING THE RUNWAY. THE REST—ANYONE WITH A WEAPON—COME WITH ME.
BE NICE TO GET AWAY BEFORE SUNRISE, BUT EITHER WAY WE HAVE TO PLAN FOR THE KRAUTS SHOWING UP FIRST. THAT MEANS SLOWING THEM DOWN SOMEHOW.
THERE'S ONLY ONE ROAD IN. DOES THAT HELP?
DOES A BIT.

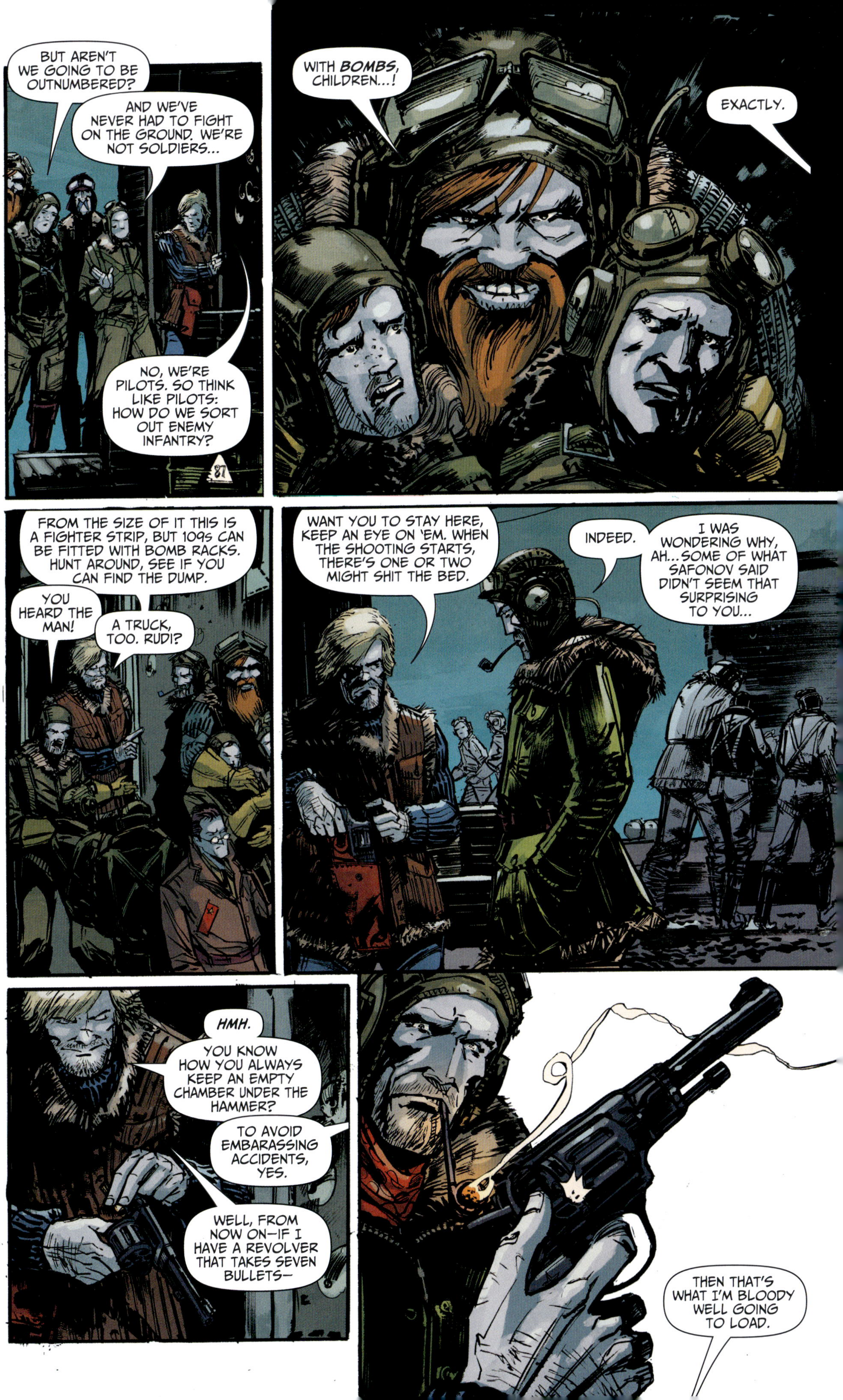
BUT AREN'T WE GOING TO BE OUTNUMBERED?
AND WE'VE NEVER HAD TO FIGHT ON THE GROUND. WE'RE NOT SOLDIERS...
NO, WE'RE PILOTS. SO THINK LIKE PILOTS: HOW DO WE SORT OUT ENEMY INFANTRY?
87
WITH BOMBS, CHILDREN...!
EXACTLY.
FROM THE SIZE OF IT THIS IS A FIGHTER STRIP, BUT 109s CAN BE FITTED WITH BOMB RACKS. HUNT AROUND, SEE IF YOU CAN FIND THE DUMP.
YOU HEARD THE MAN!
A TRUCK, TOO. RUDI?
WANT YOU TO STAY HERE, KEEP AN EYE ON 'EM. WHEN THE SHOOTING STARTS, THERE'S ONE OR TWO MIGHT SHIT THE BED.
INDEED.
I WAS WONDERING WHY, AH...SOME OF WHAT SAFONOV SAID DIDN'T SEEM THAT SURPRISING TO YOU...
HMH.
YOU KNOW HOW YOU ALWAYS KEEP AN EMPTY CHAMBER UNDER THE HAMMER?
TO AVOID EMBARASSING ACCIDENTS, YES.
WELL, FROM NOW ON—IF I HAVE A REVOLVER THAT TAKES SEVEN BULLETS—
THEN THAT'S WHAT I'M BLOODY WELL GOING TO LOAD.

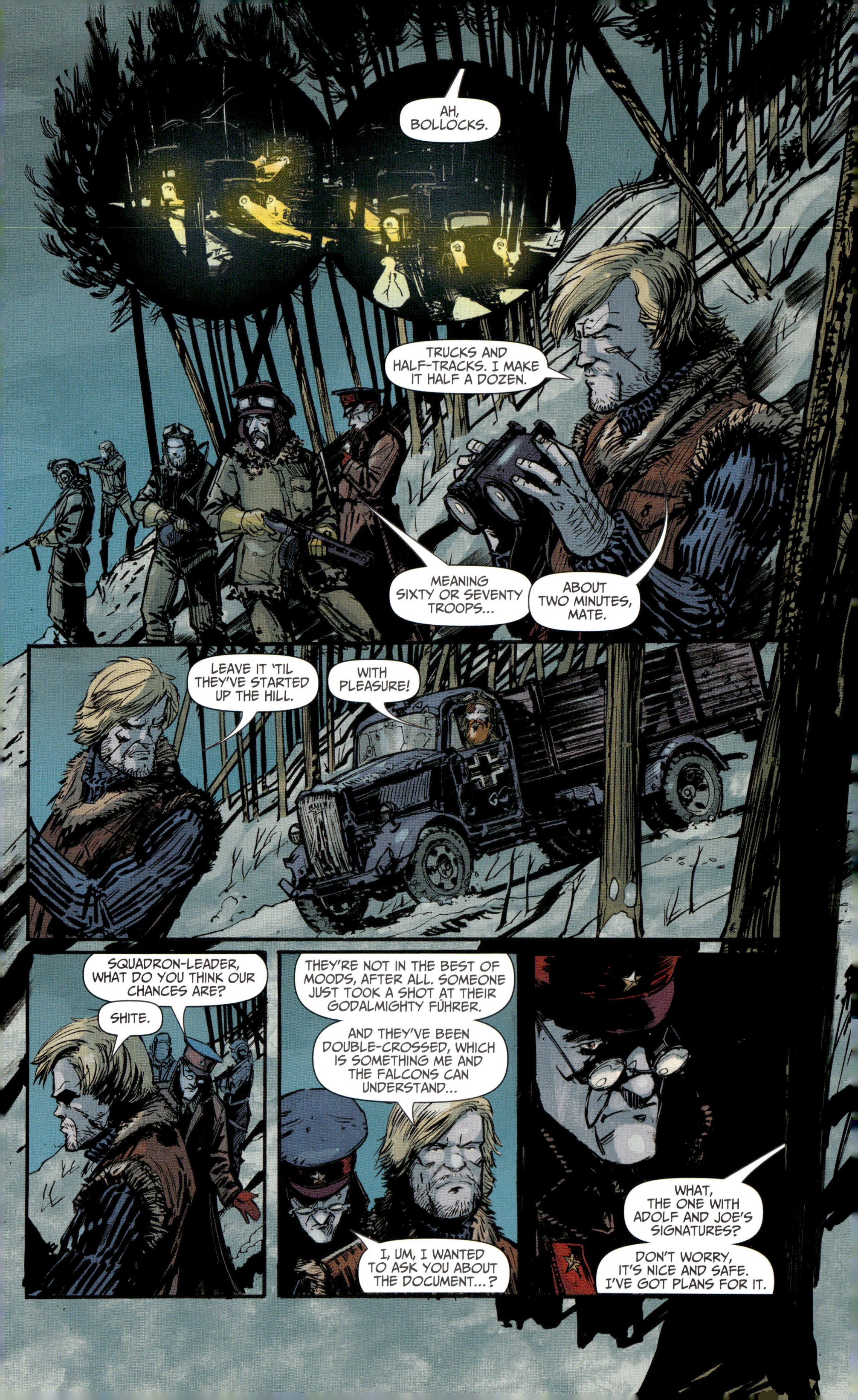
AH, BOLLOCKS.
TRUCKS AND HALF-TRACKS. I MAKE IT HALF A DOZEN.
MEANING SIXTY OR SEVENTY TROOPS...
ABOUT TWO MINUTES, MATE.
LEAVE IT 'TIL THEY'VE STARTED UP THE HILL.
WITH PLEASURE!
SQUADRON-LEADER, WHAT DO YOU THINK OUR CHANCES ARE?
SHITE.
THEY'RE NOT IN THE BEST OF MOODS, AFTER ALL. SOMEONE JUST TOOK A SHOT AT THEIR GODALMIGHTY FÜHRER.
AND THEY'VE BEEN DOUBLE-CROSSED, WHICH IS SOMETHING ME AND THE FALCONS CAN UNDERSTAND...
I, UM, I WANTED TO ASK YOU ABOUT THE DOCUMENT...?
WHAT, THE ONE WITH ADOLF AND JOE'S SIGNATURES?
DON'T WORRY, IT'S NICE AND SAFE. I'VE GOT PLANS FOR IT.

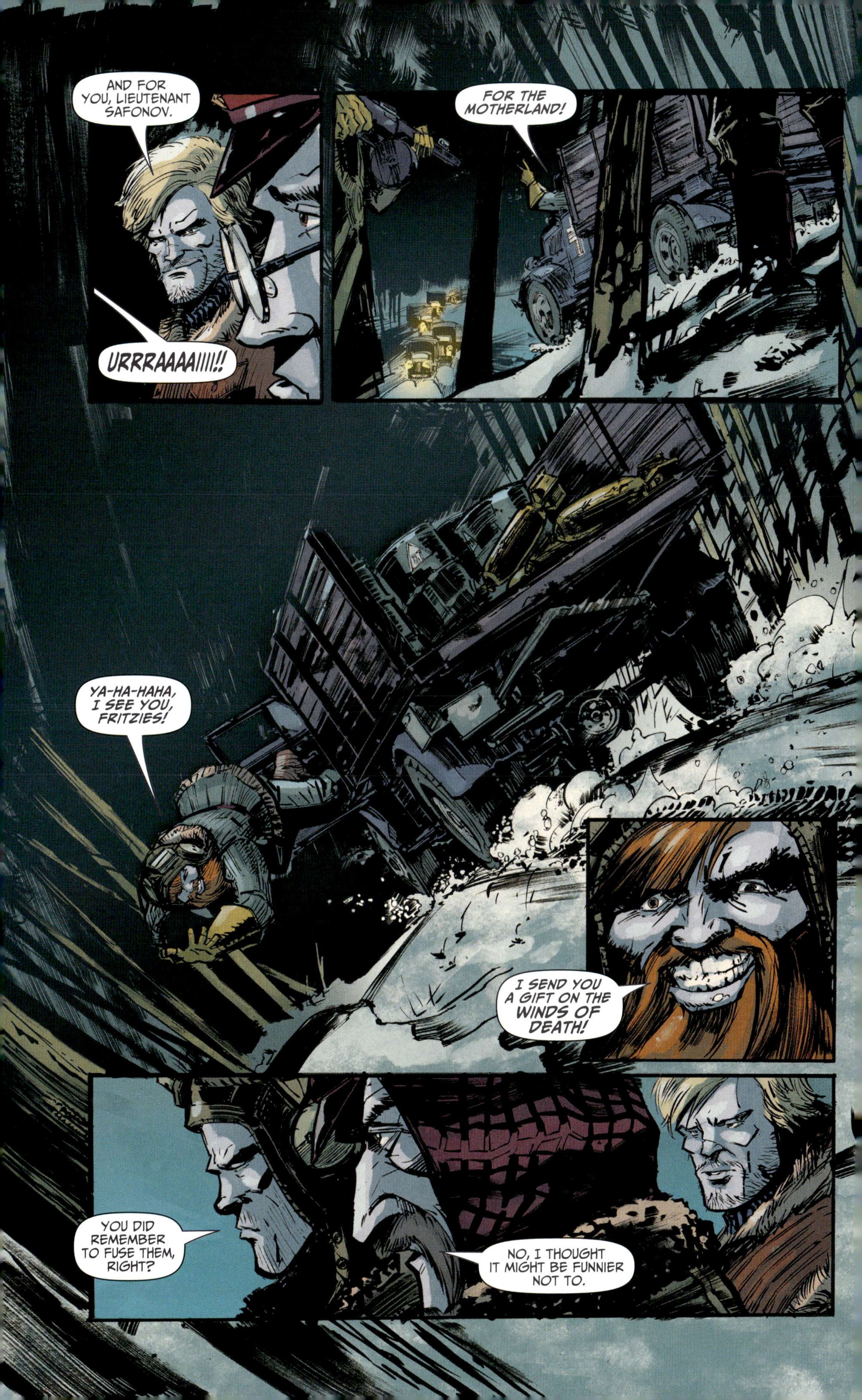
AND FOR YOU, LIEUTENANT SAFONOV.
URRRAAAAIIII!!
FOR THE MOTHERLAND!
YA-HA-HAHA, I SEE YOU, FRITZIES!
I SEND YOU A GIFT ON THE WINDS OF DEATH!
YOU DID REMEMBER TO FUSE THEM, RIGHT?
NO, I THOUGHT IT MIGHT BE FUNNIER NOT TO.

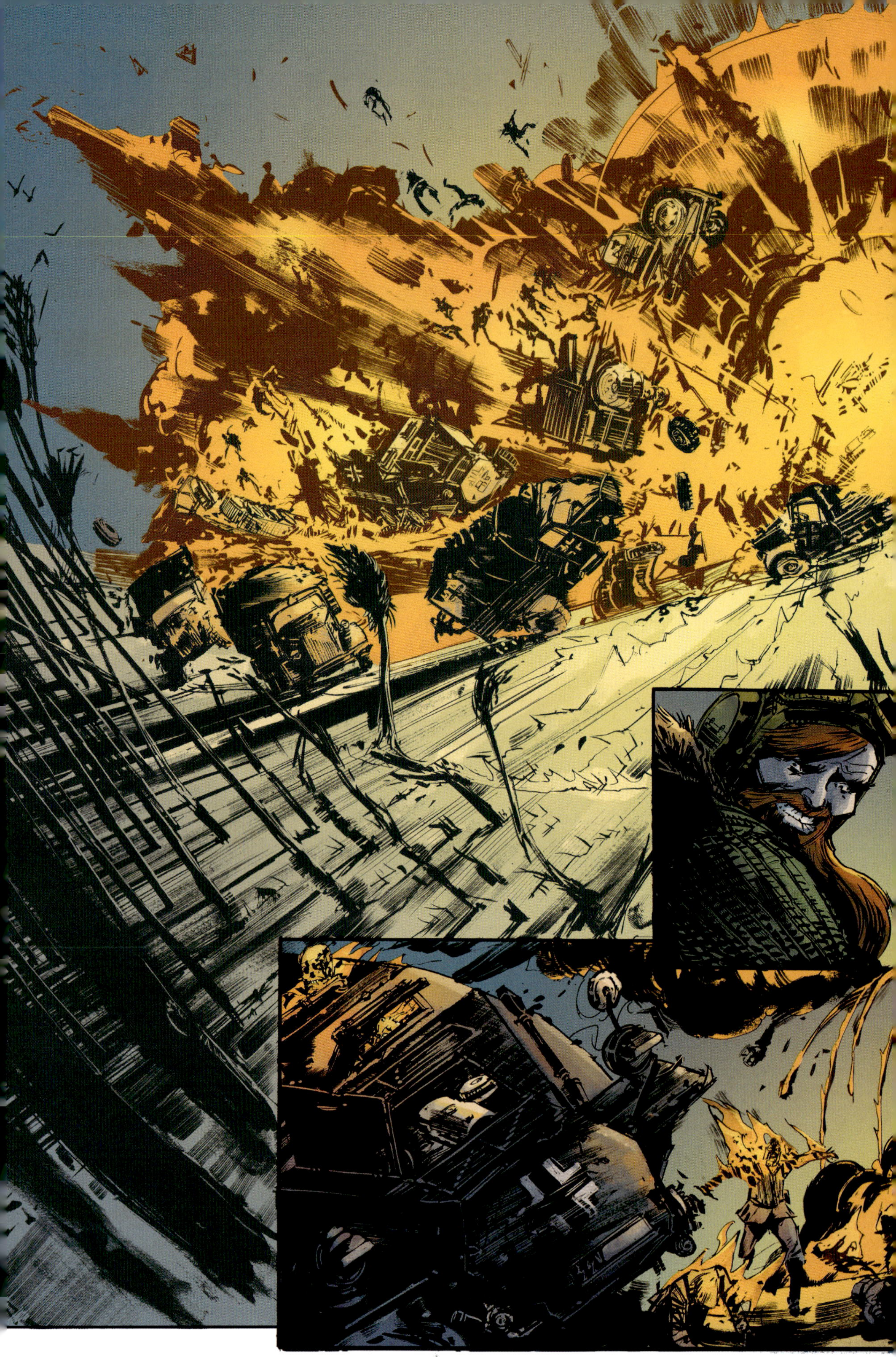

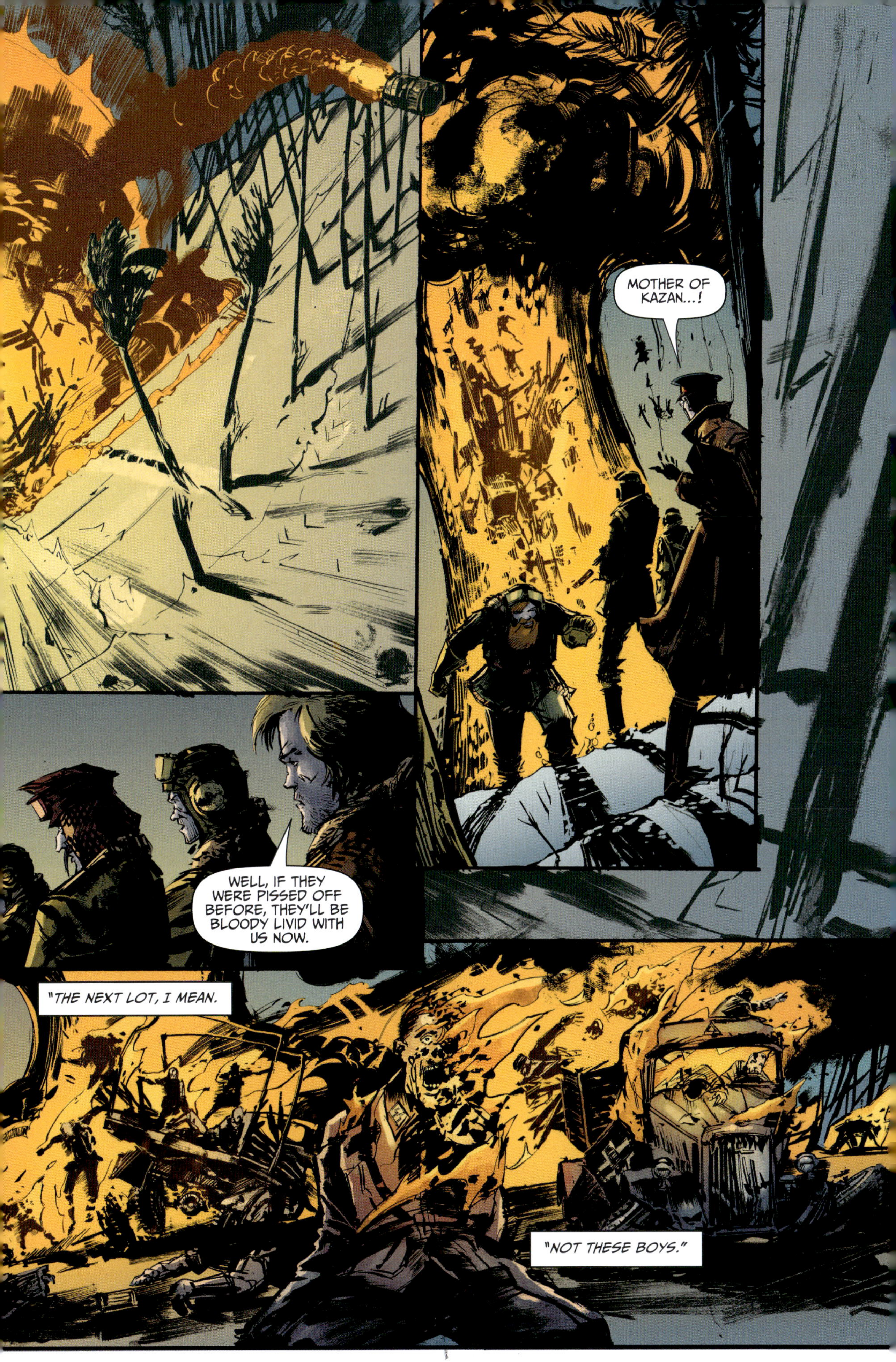
MOTHER OF KAZAN...!
WELL, IF THEY WERE PISSED OFF BEFORE, THEY'LL BE BLOODY LIVID WITH US NOW.
"THE NEXT LOT, I MEAN.
"NOT THESE BOYS."

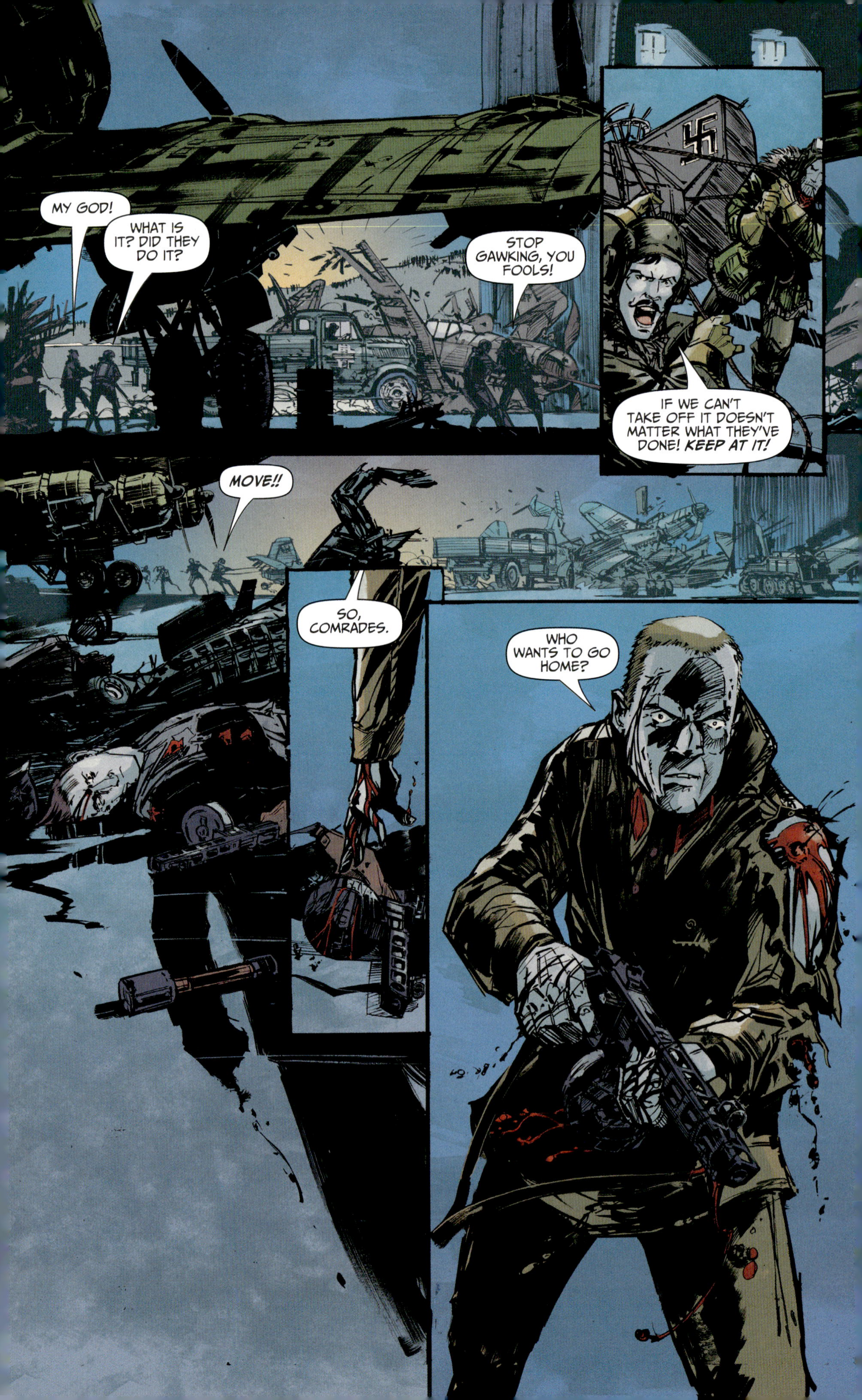
MY GOD!
WHAT IS IT? DID THEY DO IT?
STOP GAWKING, YOU FOOLS!
IF WE CAN'T TAKE OFF IT DOESN'T MATTER WHAT THEY'VE DONE! KEEP AT IT!
MOVE!!
SO, COMRADES.
WHO WANTS TO GO HOME?

ISSUE SEVEN
Cover art by:
Keith Burns

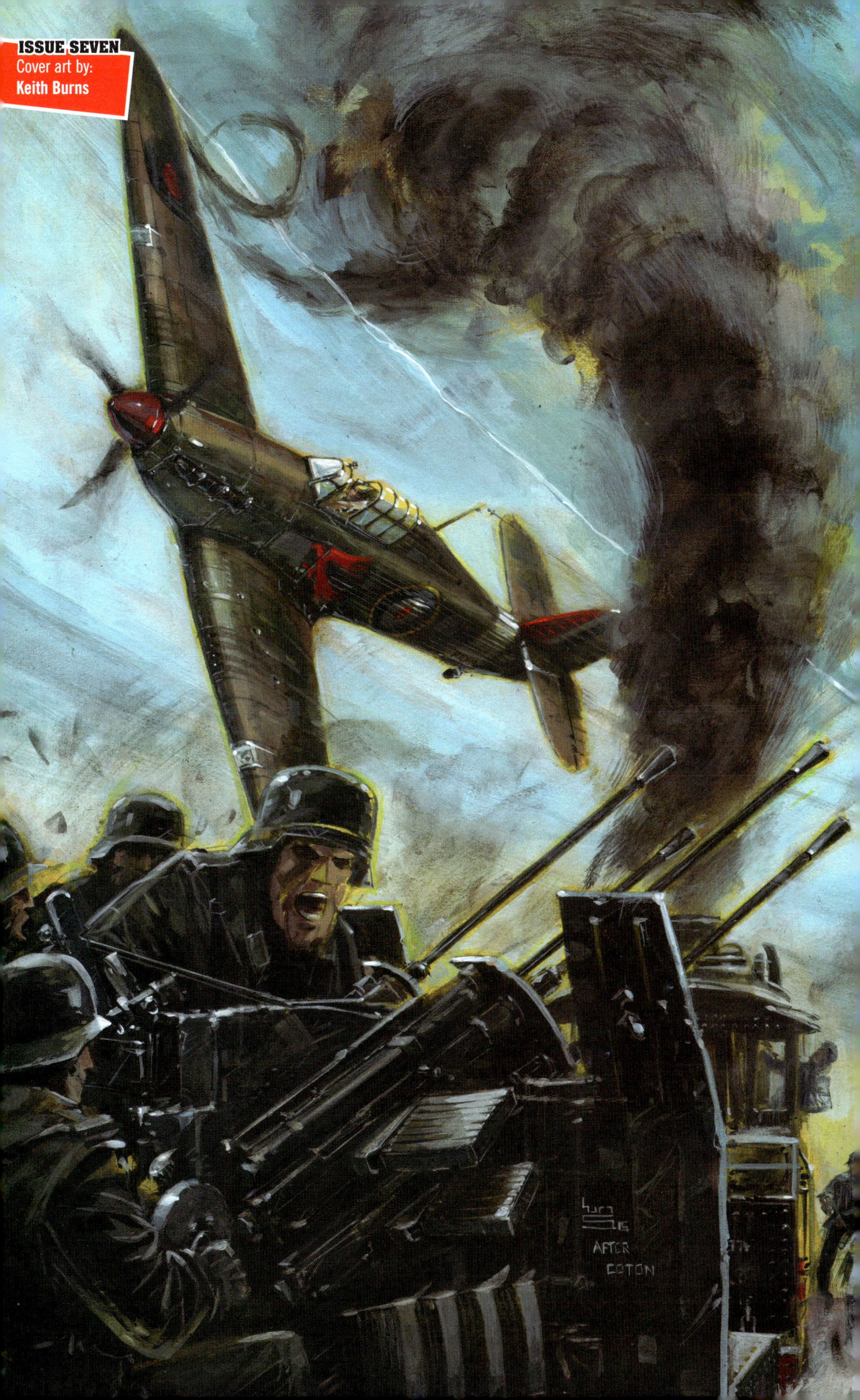
AFTER
COTON

VARIANT
Cover art by:
Mike Perkins

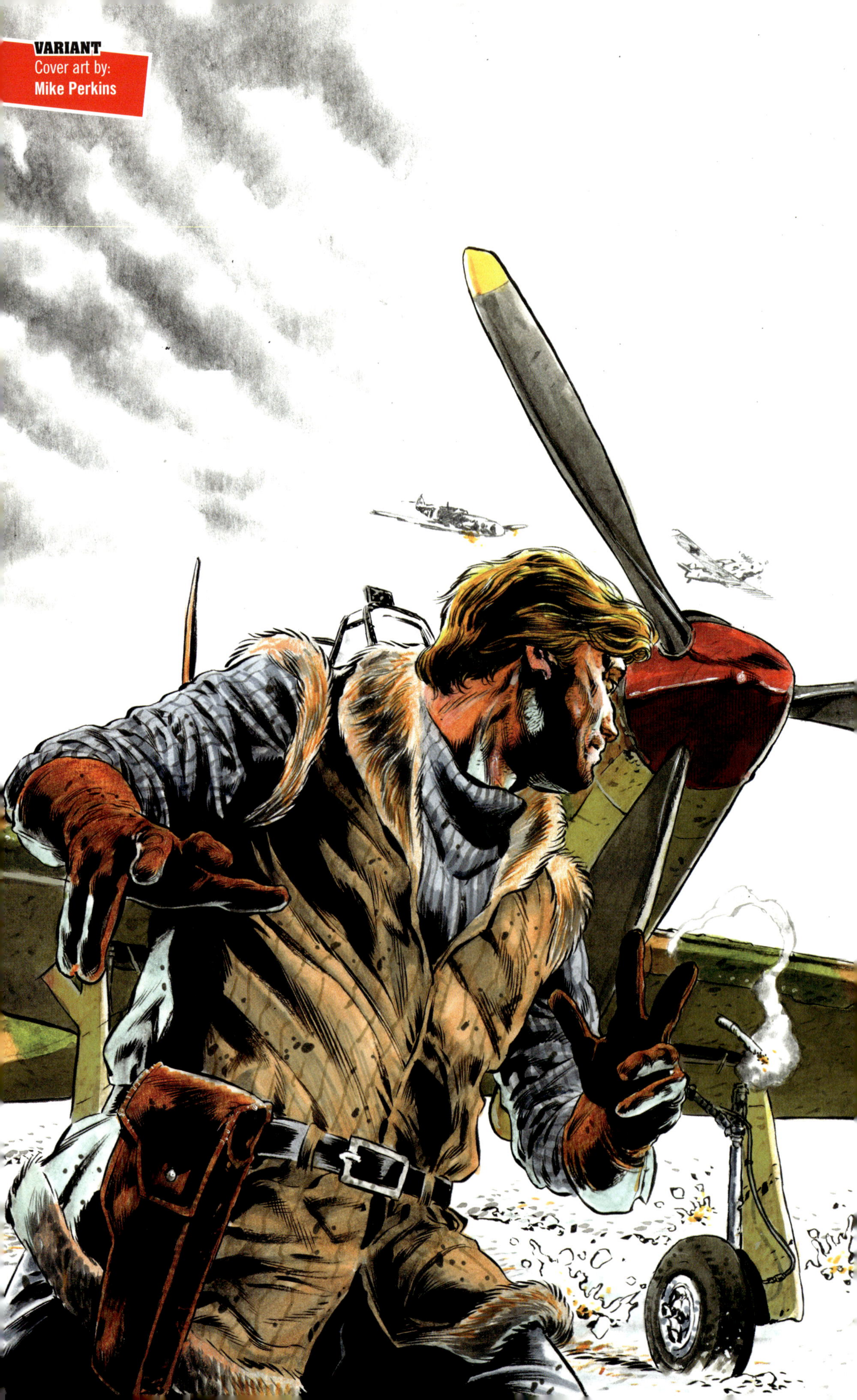

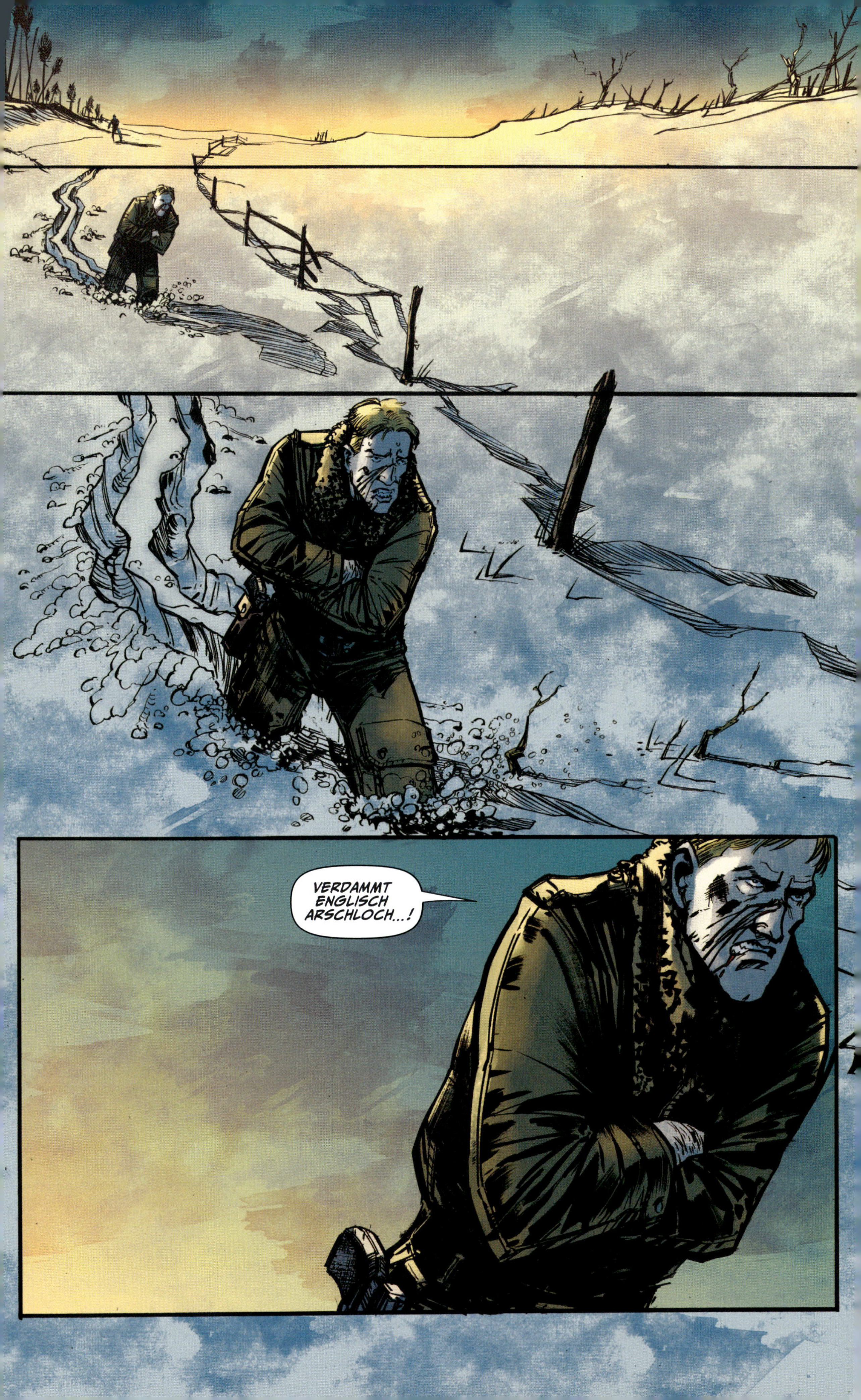
VERDAMMT ENGLISCH ARSCHLOCH...!

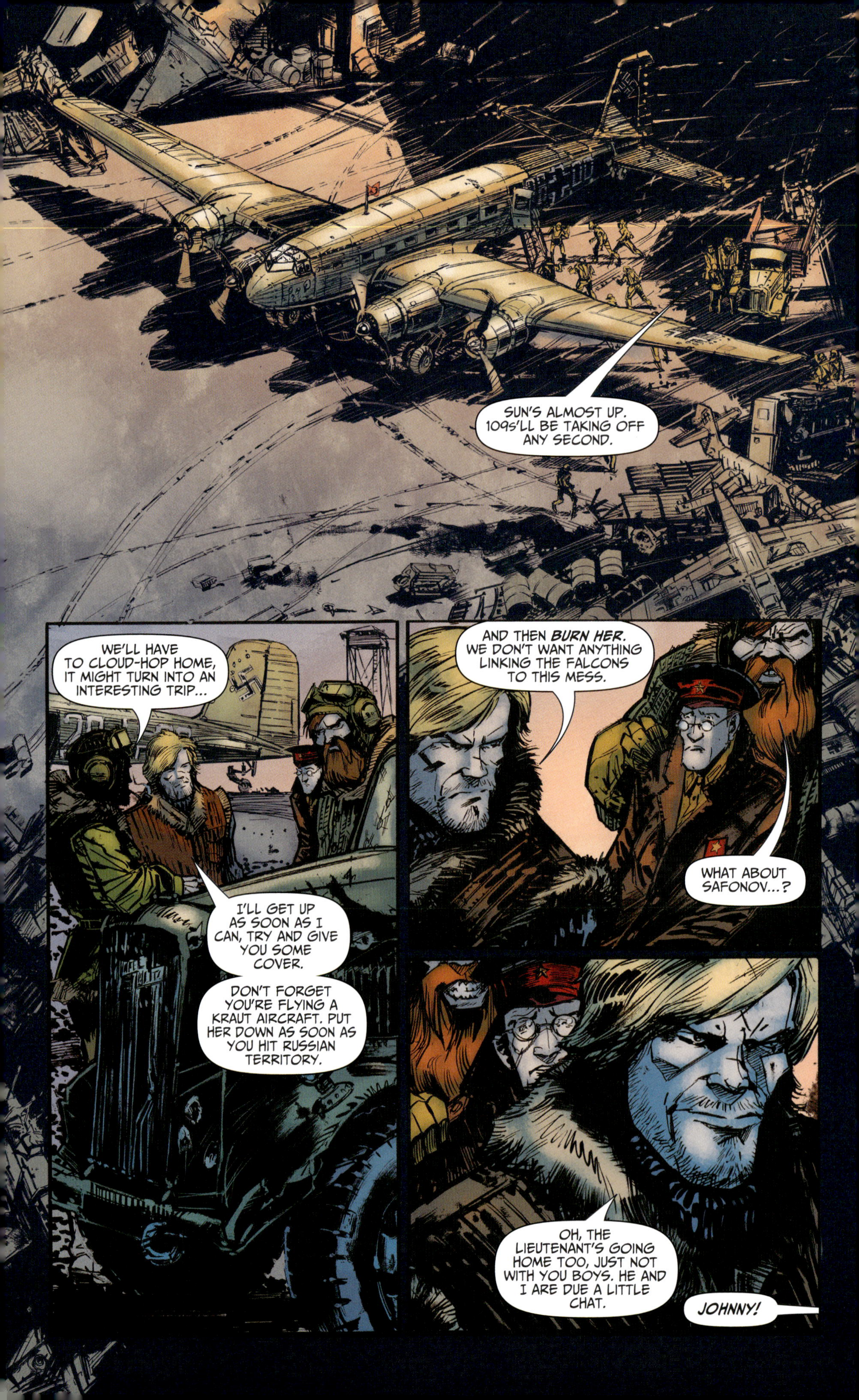

SUN'S ALMOST UP. 109s'LL BE TAKING OFF ANY SECOND.
WE'LL HAVE TO CLOUD-HOP HOME, IT MIGHT TURN INTO AN INTERESTING TRIP...
I'LL GET UP AS SOON AS I CAN, TRY AND GIVE YOU SOME COVER.
DON'T FORGET YOU'RE FLYING A KRAUT AIRCRAFT. PUT HER DOWN AS SOON AS YOU HIT RUSSIAN TERRITORY.
AND THEN ***BURN HER***. WE DON'T WANT ANYTHING LINKING THE FALCONS TO THIS MESS.
WHAT ABOUT SAFONOV...?
OH, THE LIEUTENANT'S GOING HOME TOO, JUST NOT WITH YOU BOYS. HE AND I ARE DUE A LITTLE CHAT.
JOHNNY!

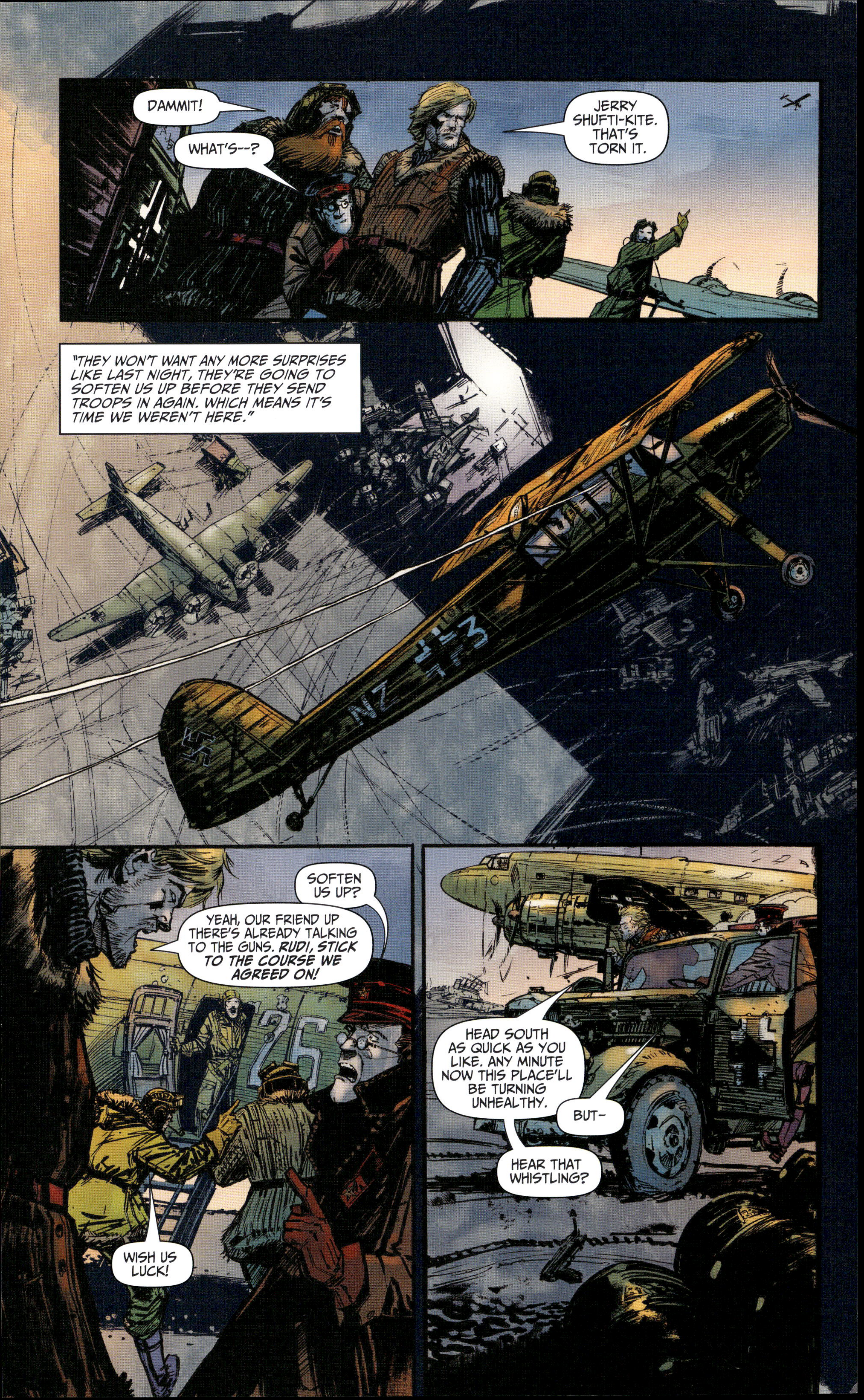
DAMMIT!
WHAT'S--?
JERRY SHUFTI-KITE. THAT'S TORN IT.
"THEY WON'T WANT ANY MORE SURPRISES LIKE LAST NIGHT, THEY'RE GOING TO SOFTEN US UP BEFORE THEY SEND TROOPS IN AGAIN. WHICH MEANS IT'S TIME WE WEREN'T HERE."
NZ
SOFTEN US UP?
YEAH, OUR FRIEND UP THERE'S ALREADY TALKING TO THE GUNS. RUDI, STICK TO THE COURSE WE AGREED ON!
26
WISH US LUCK!
HEAD SOUTH AS QUICK AS YOU LIKE. ANY MINUTE NOW THIS PLACE'LL BE TURNING UNHEALTHY.
BUT-
HEAR THAT WHISTLING?

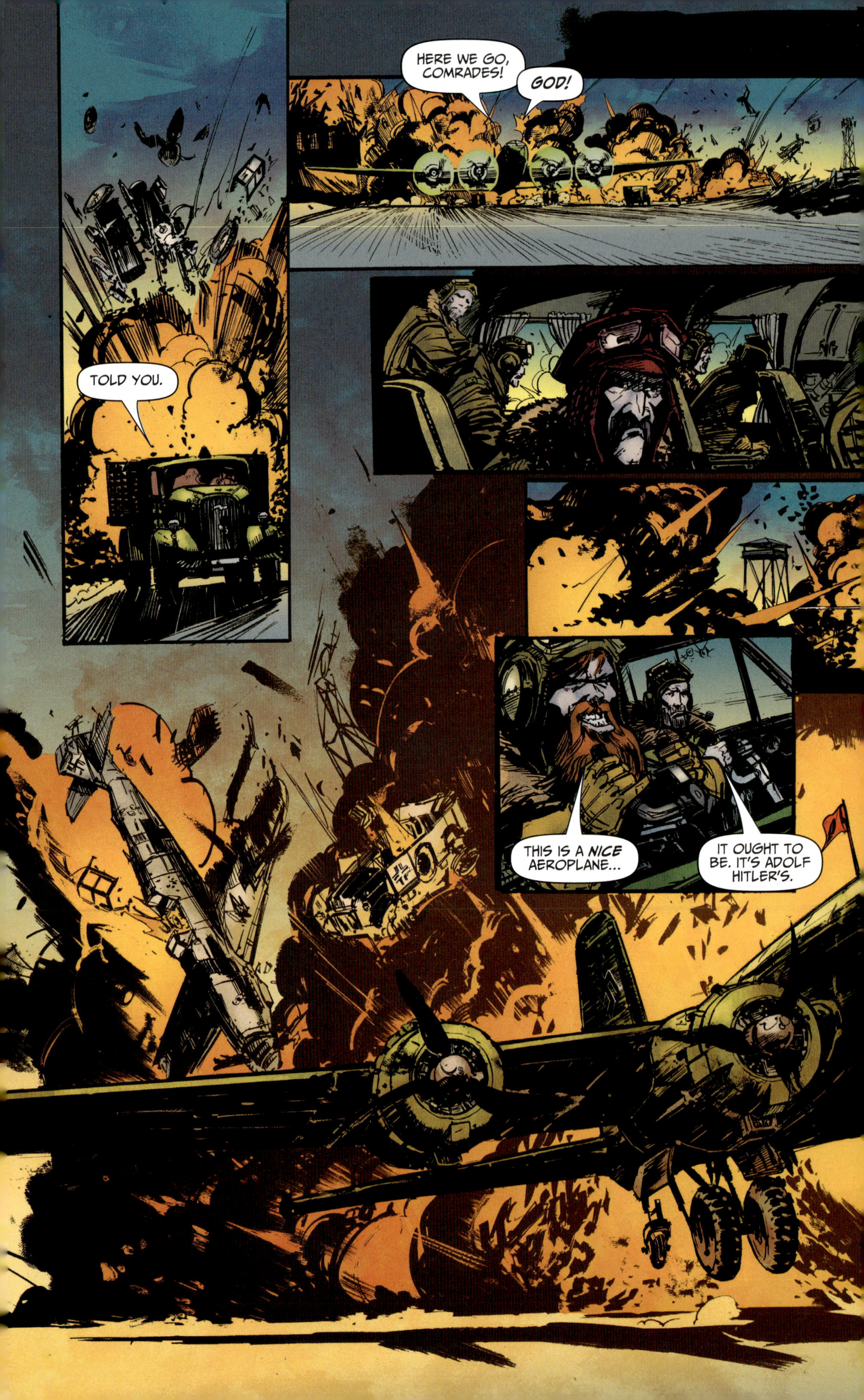
HERE WE GO, COMRADES!
GOD!
TOLD YOU.
THIS IS A NICE AEROPLANE...
IT OUGHT TO BE. IT'S ADOLF HITLER'S.

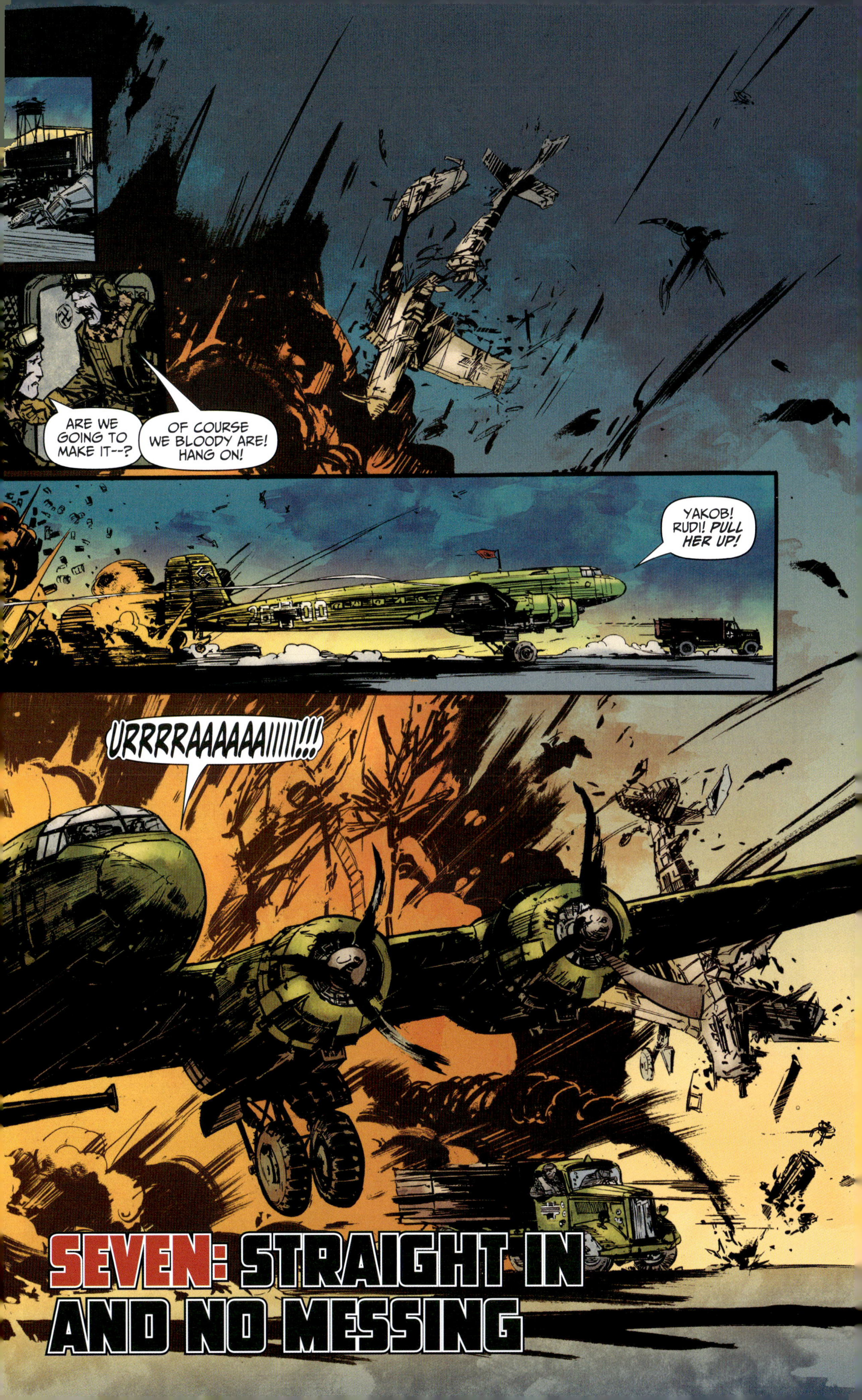

ARE WE GOING TO MAKE IT--?
OF COURSE WE BLOODY ARE! HANG ON!
YAKOB! RUDI! PULL HER UP!
URRRRAAAAAAIIIIII!!!
SEVEN: STRAIGHT IN AND NO MESSING

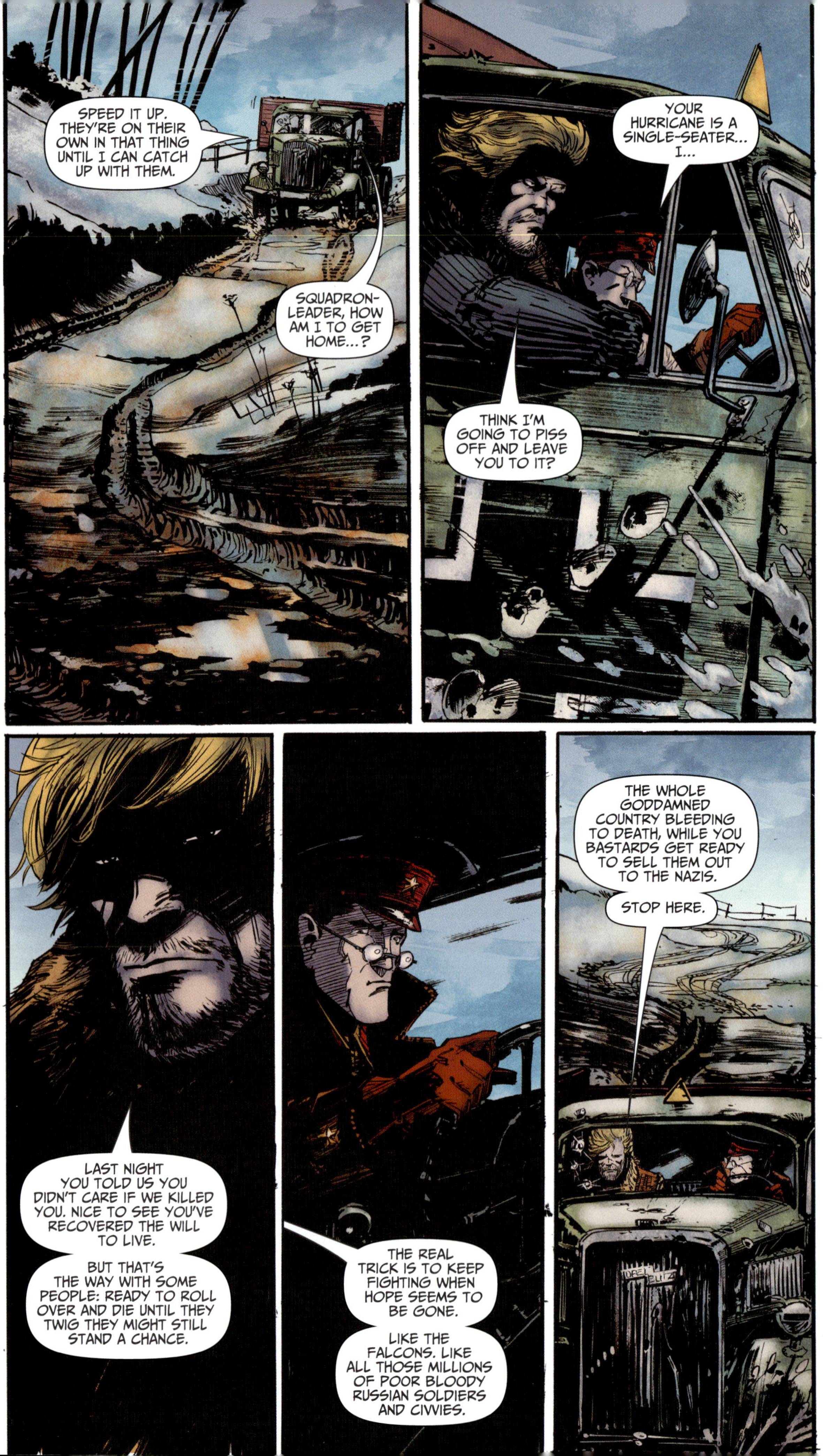
SPEED IT UP. THEY'RE ON THEIR OWN IN THAT THING UNTIL I CAN CATCH UP WITH THEM.
SQUADRON-LEADER, HOW AM I TO GET HOME...?
YOUR HURRICANE IS A SINGLE-SEATER... I...
THINK I'M GOING TO PISS OFF AND LEAVE YOU TO IT?
LAST NIGHT YOU TOLD US YOU DIDN'T CARE IF WE KILLED YOU. NICE TO SEE YOU'VE RECOVERED THE WILL TO LIVE.
BUT THAT'S THE WAY WITH SOME PEOPLE: READY TO ROLL OVER AND DIE UNTIL THEY TWIG THEY MIGHT STILL STAND A CHANCE.
THE REAL TRICK IS TO KEEP FIGHTING WHEN HOPE SEEMS TO BE GONE.
LIKE THE FALCONS. LIKE ALL THOSE MILLIONS OF POOR BLOODY RUSSIAN SOLDIERS AND CIVVIES.
THE WHOLE GODDAMNED COUNTRY BLEEDING TO DEATH, WHILE YOU BASTARDS GET READY TO SELL THEM OUT TO THE NAZIS.
STOP HERE.

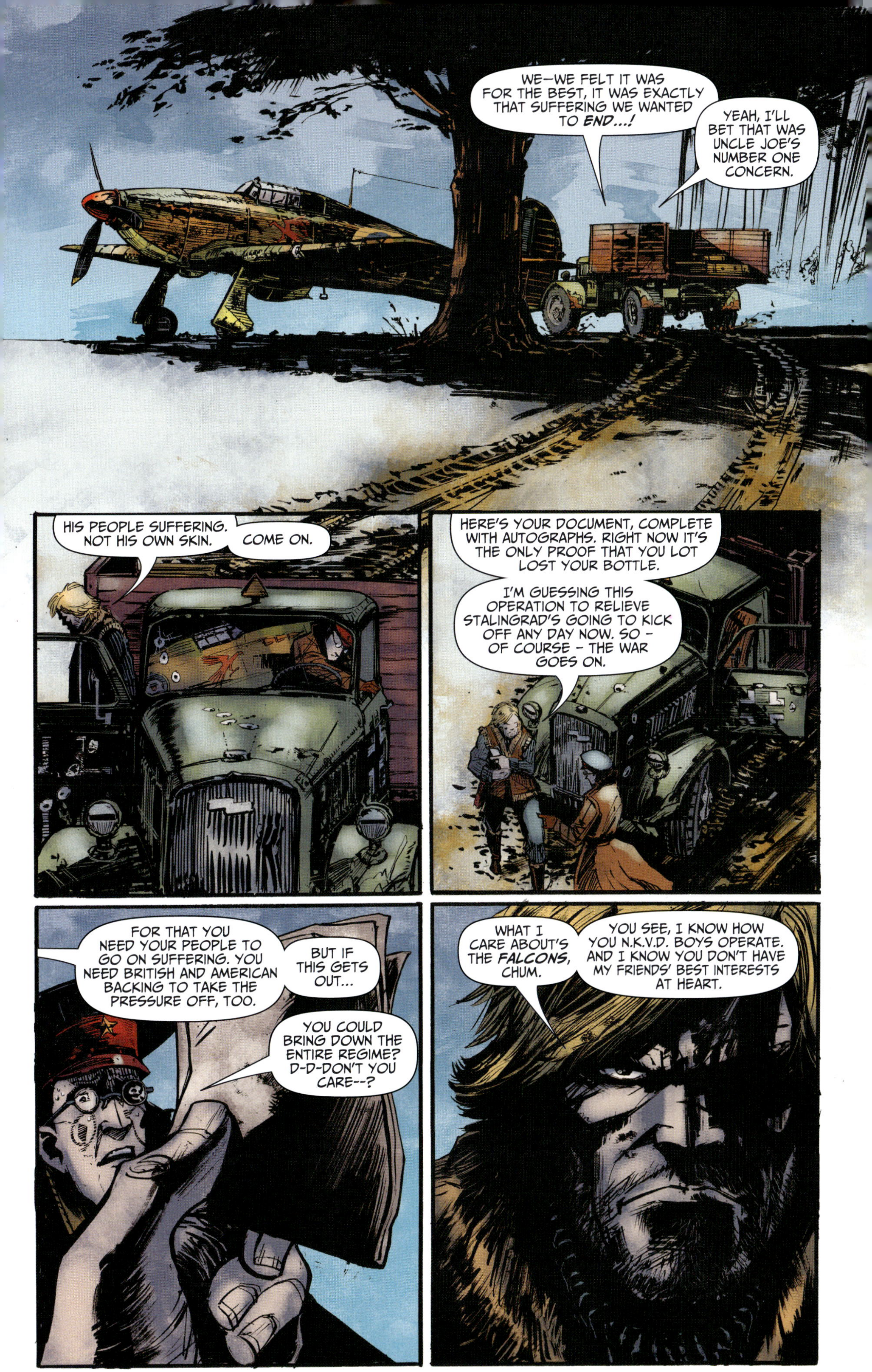
WE—WE FELT IT WAS FOR THE BEST, IT WAS EXACTLY THAT SUFFERING WE WANTED TO *END...!*
YEAH, I'LL BET THAT WAS UNCLE JOE'S NUMBER ONE CONCERN.
HIS PEOPLE SUFFERING. NOT HIS OWN SKIN.
COME ON.
HERE'S YOUR DOCUMENT, COMPLETE WITH AUTOGRAPHS. RIGHT NOW IT'S THE ONLY PROOF THAT YOU LOT LOST YOUR BOTTLE.
I'M GUESSING THIS OPERATION TO RELIEVE STALINGRAD'S GOING TO KICK OFF ANY DAY NOW. SO - OF COURSE - THE WAR GOES ON.
FOR THAT YOU NEED YOUR PEOPLE TO GO ON SUFFERING. YOU NEED BRITISH AND AMERICAN BACKING TO TAKE THE PRESSURE OFF, TOO.
BUT IF THIS GETS OUT...
YOU COULD BRING DOWN THE ENTIRE REGIME? D-D-DON'T YOU CARE--?
WHAT I CARE ABOUT'S THE *FALCONS,* CHUM.
YOU SEE, I KNOW HOW YOU N.K.V.D. BOYS OPERATE. AND I KNOW YOU DON'T HAVE MY FRIENDS' BEST INTERESTS AT HEART.

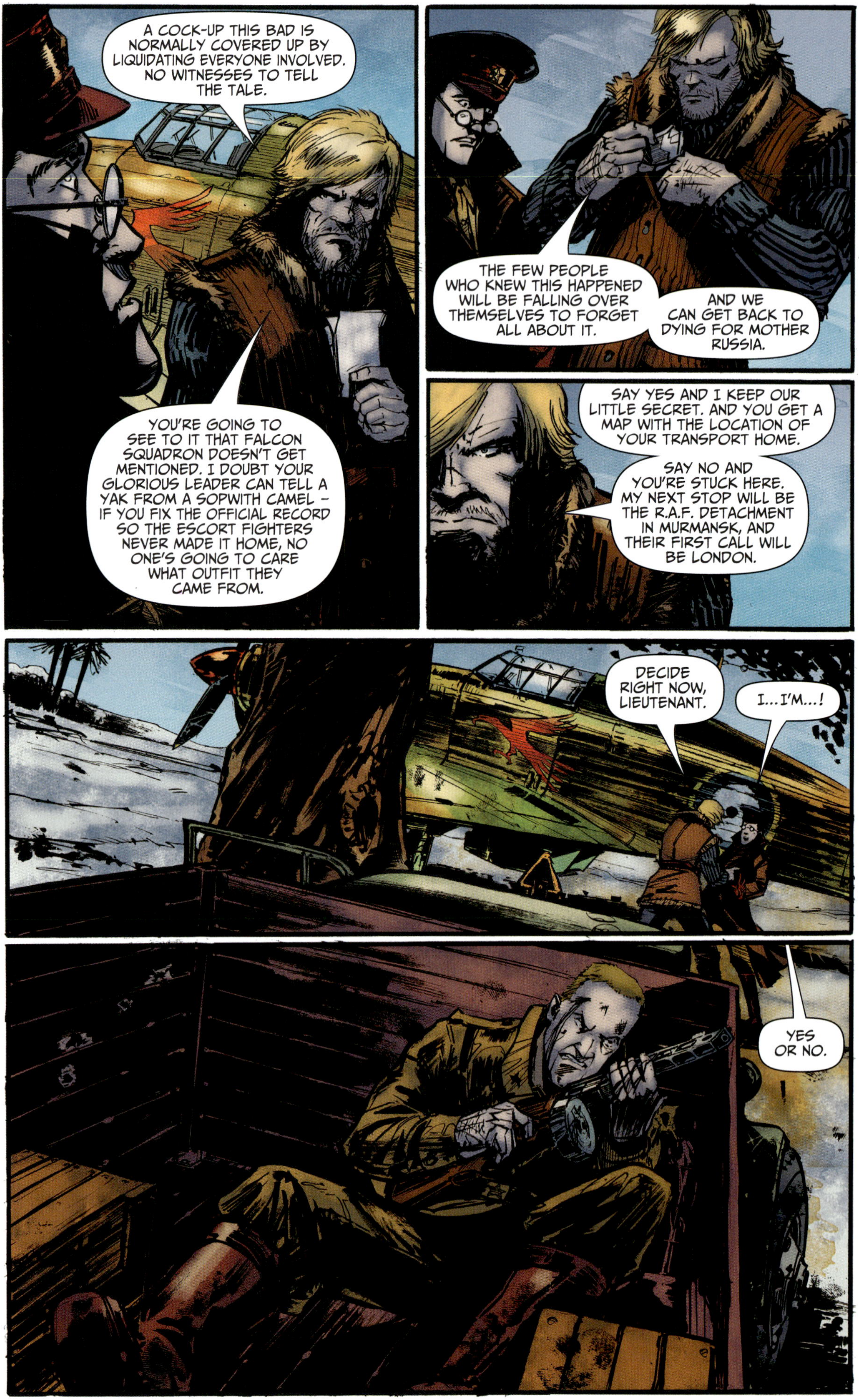
A COCK-UP THIS BAD IS NORMALLY COVERED UP BY LIQUIDATING EVERYONE INVOLVED. NO WITNESSES TO TELL THE TALE.
YOU'RE GOING TO SEE TO IT THAT FALCON SQUADRON DOESN'T GET MENTIONED. I DOUBT YOUR GLORIOUS LEADER CAN TELL A YAK FROM A SOPWITH CAMEL – IF YOU FIX THE OFFICIAL RECORD SO THE ESCORT FIGHTERS NEVER MADE IT HOME, NO ONE'S GOING TO CARE WHAT OUTFIT THEY CAME FROM.
THE FEW PEOPLE WHO KNEW THIS HAPPENED WILL BE FALLING OVER THEMSELVES TO FORGET ALL ABOUT IT.
AND WE CAN GET BACK TO DYING FOR MOTHER RUSSIA.
SAY YES AND I KEEP OUR LITTLE SECRET. AND YOU GET A MAP WITH THE LOCATION OF YOUR TRANSPORT HOME.
SAY NO AND YOU'RE STUCK HERE. MY NEXT STOP WILL BE THE R.A.F. DETACHMENT IN MURMANSK, AND THEIR FIRST CALL WILL BE LONDON.
DECIDE RIGHT NOW, LIEUTENANT.
I...I'M...!
YES OR NO.

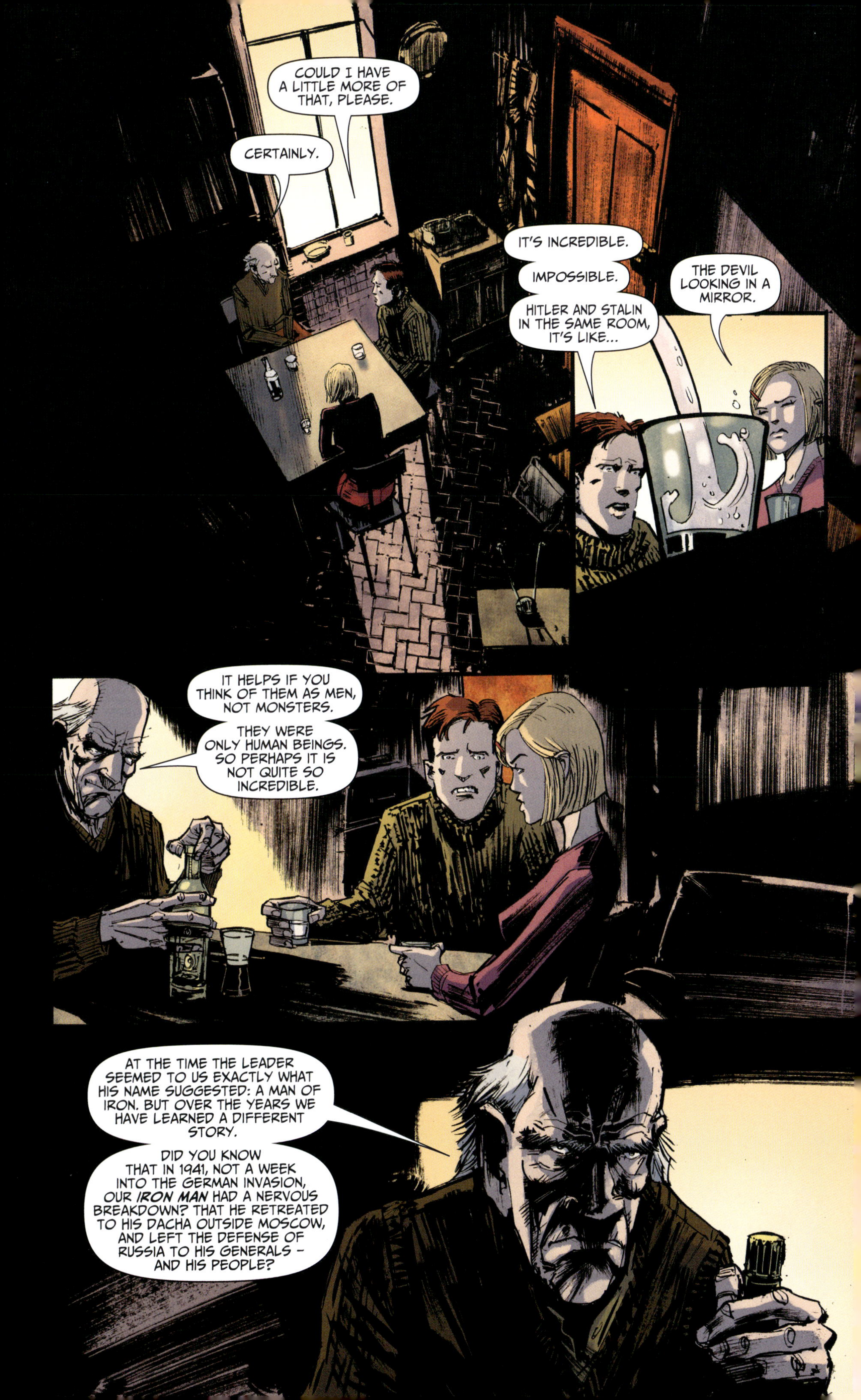
COULD I HAVE A LITTLE MORE OF THAT, PLEASE.
CERTAINLY.
IT'S INCREDIBLE.
IMPOSSIBLE.
HITLER AND STALIN IN THE SAME ROOM, IT'S LIKE...
THE DEVIL LOOKING IN A MIRROR.
IT HELPS IF YOU THINK OF THEM AS MEN, NOT MONSTERS.
THEY WERE ONLY HUMAN BEINGS. SO PERHAPS IT IS NOT QUITE SO INCREDIBLE.
AT THE TIME THE LEADER SEEMED TO US EXACTLY WHAT HIS NAME SUGGESTED: A MAN OF IRON. BUT OVER THE YEARS WE HAVE LEARNED A DIFFERENT STORY.
DID YOU KNOW THAT IN 1941, NOT A WEEK INTO THE GERMAN INVASION, OUR *IRON MAN* HAD A NERVOUS BREAKDOWN? THAT HE RETREATED TO HIS DACHA OUTSIDE MOSCOW, AND LEFT THE DEFENSE OF RUSSIA TO HIS GENERALS – AND HIS PEOPLE?

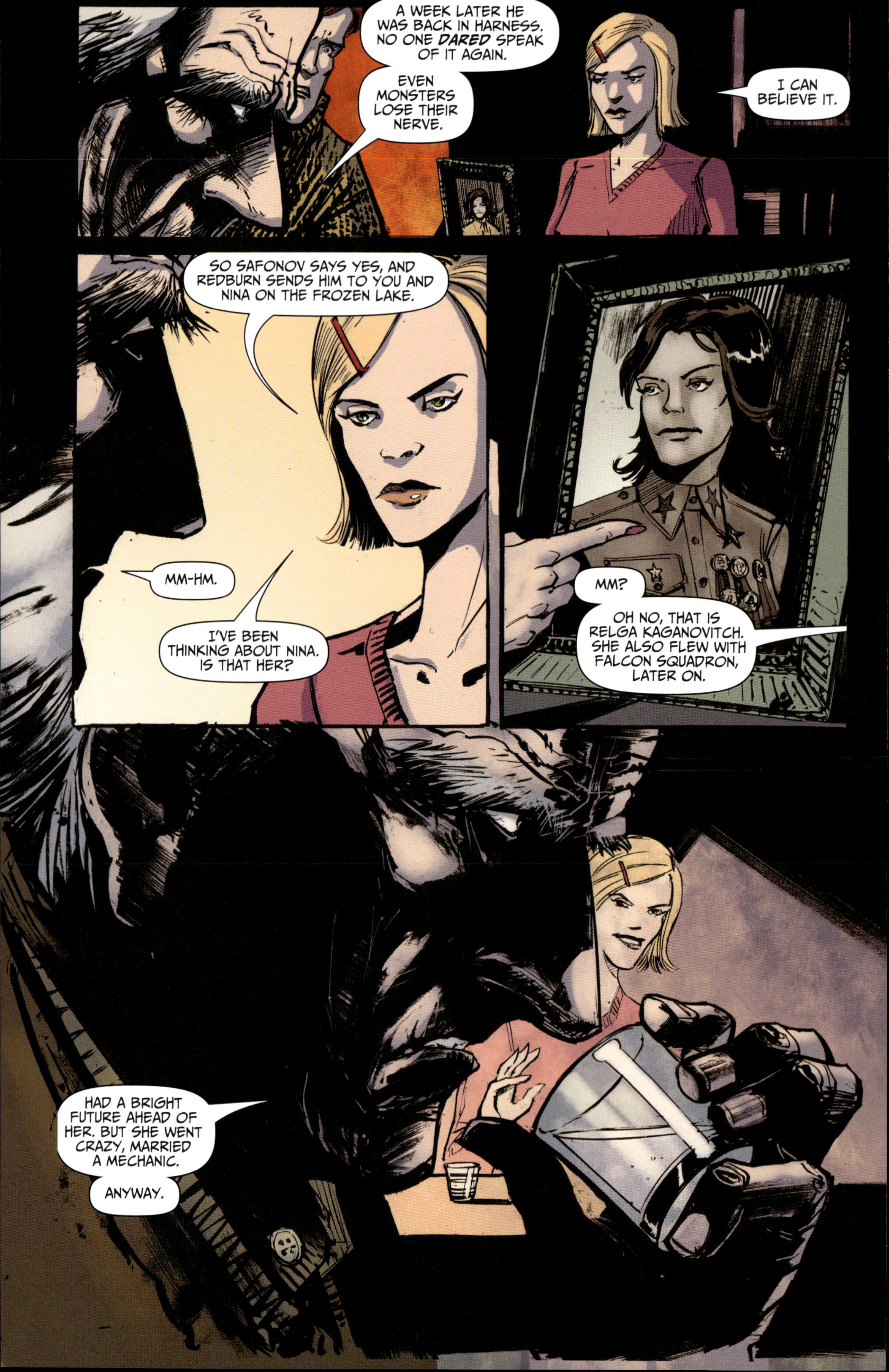

A WEEK LATER HE WAS BACK IN HARNESS. NO ONE *DARED* SPEAK OF IT AGAIN.
EVEN MONSTERS LOSE THEIR NERVE.
I CAN BELIEVE IT.
SO SAFONOV SAYS YES, AND REDBURN SENDS HIM TO YOU AND NINA ON THE FROZEN LAKE.
MM-HM.
I'VE BEEN THINKING ABOUT NINA. IS THAT HER?
MM?
OH NO, THAT IS RELGA KAGANOVITCH. SHE ALSO FLEW WITH FALCON SQUADRON, LATER ON.
HAD A BRIGHT FUTURE AHEAD OF HER. BUT SHE WENT CRAZY, MARRIED A MECHANIC.
ANYWAY.

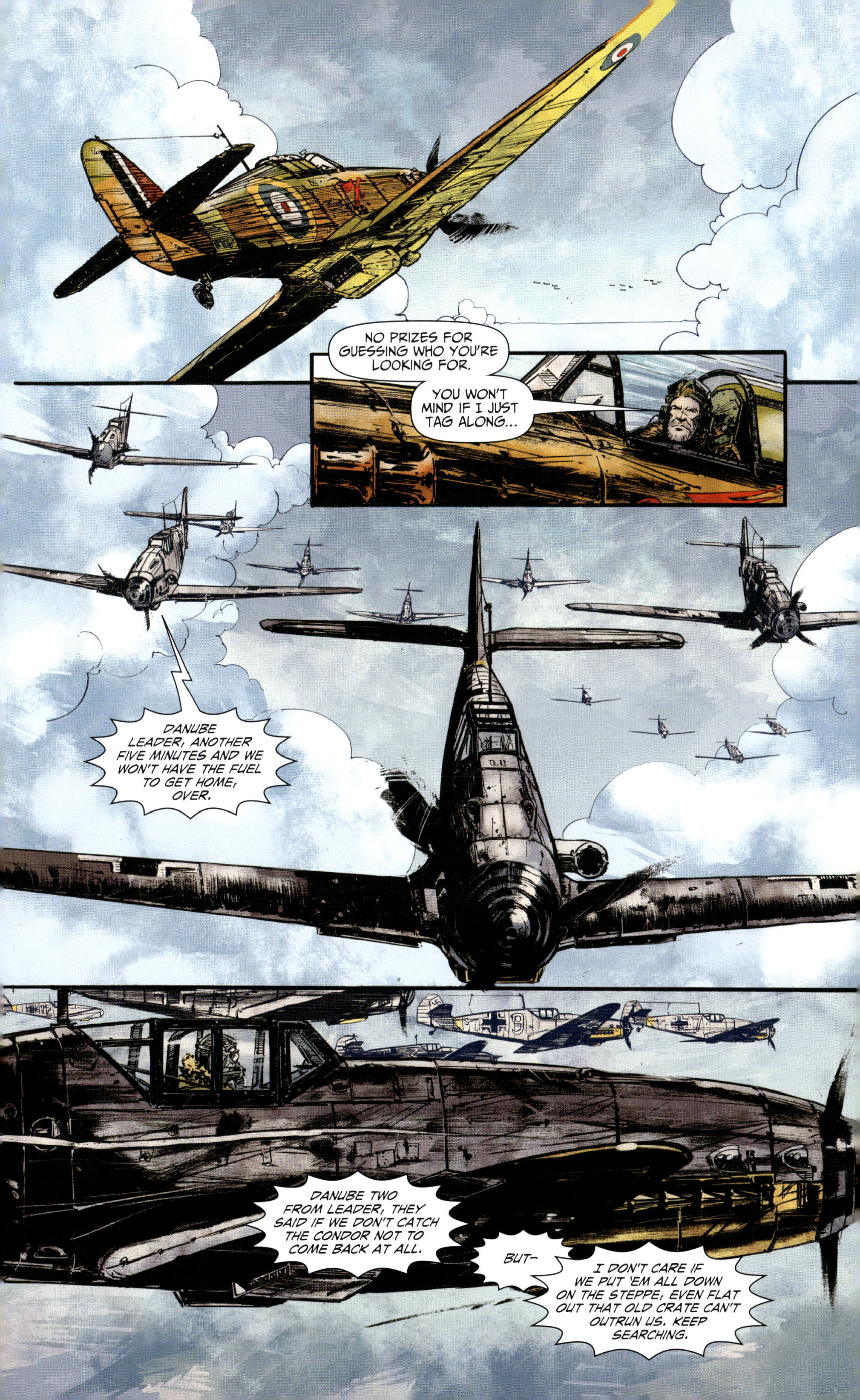
NO PRIZES FOR GUESSING WHO YOU'RE LOOKING FOR.
YOU WON'T MIND IF I JUST TAG ALONG...
DANUBE LEADER, ANOTHER FIVE MINUTES AND WE WON'T HAVE THE FUEL TO GET HOME, OVER.
DANUBE TWO FROM LEADER, THEY SAID IF WE DON'T CATCH THE CONDOR NOT TO COME BACK AT ALL.
BUT–
I DON'T CARE IF WE PUT 'EM ALL DOWN ON THE STEPPE, EVEN FLAT OUT THAT OLD CRATE CAN'T OUTRUN US. KEEP SEARCHING.

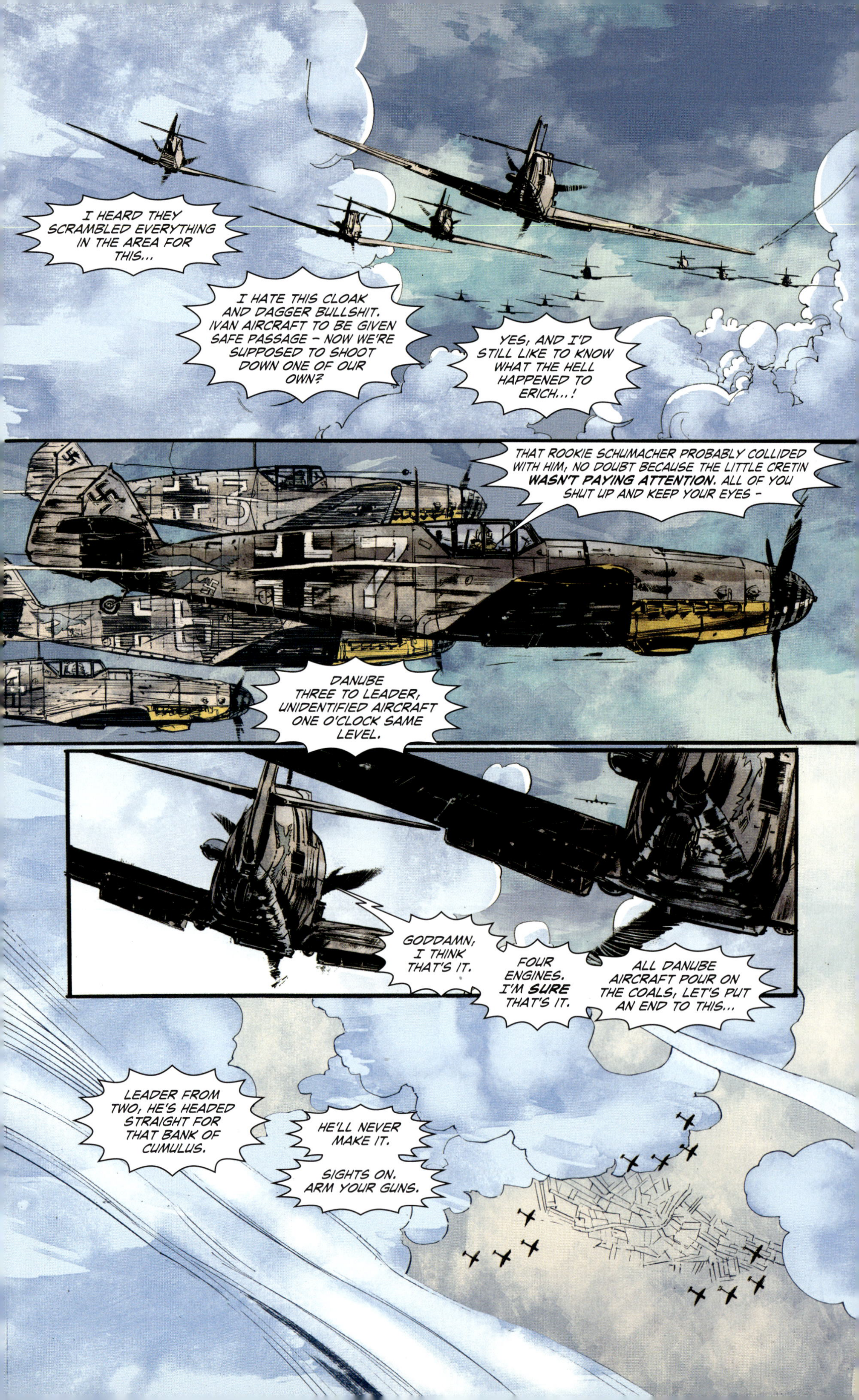
I HEARD THEY SCRAMBLED EVERYTHING IN THE AREA FOR THIS...
I HATE THIS CLOAK AND DAGGER BULLSHIT. IVAN AIRCRAFT TO BE GIVEN SAFE PASSAGE – NOW WE'RE SUPPOSED TO SHOOT DOWN ONE OF OUR OWN?
YES, AND I'D STILL LIKE TO KNOW WHAT THE HELL HAPPENED TO ERICH...!
THAT ROOKIE SCHUMACHER PROBABLY COLLIDED WITH HIM, NO DOUBT BECAUSE THE LITTLE CRETIN **WASN'T PAYING ATTENTION**. ALL OF YOU SHUT UP AND KEEP YOUR EYES –
DANUBE THREE TO LEADER, UNIDENTIFIED AIRCRAFT ONE O'CLOCK SAME LEVEL.
GODDAMN, I THINK THAT'S IT.
FOUR ENGINES. I'M **SURE** THAT'S IT.
ALL DANUBE AIRCRAFT POUR ON THE COALS, LET'S PUT AN END TO THIS...
LEADER FROM TWO, HE'S HEADED STRAIGHT FOR THAT BANK OF CUMULUS.
HE'LL NEVER MAKE IT.
SIGHTS ON. ARM YOUR GUNS.

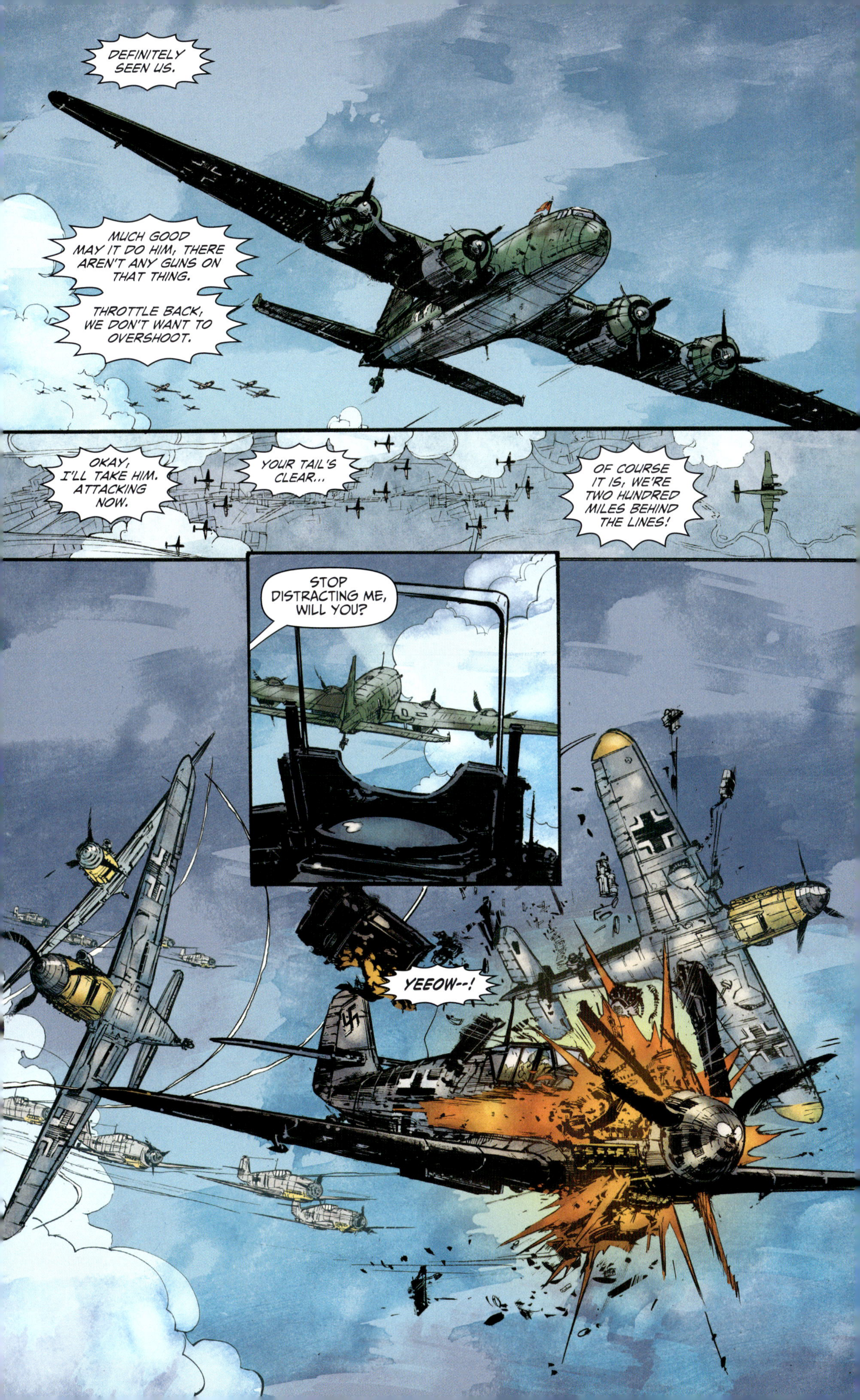
DEFINITELY SEEN US.
MUCH GOOD MAY IT DO HIM, THERE AREN'T ANY GUNS ON THAT THING.
THROTTLE BACK; WE DON'T WANT TO OVERSHOOT.
OKAY; I'LL TAKE HIM. ATTACKING NOW.
YOUR TAIL'S CLEAR...
OF COURSE IT IS, WE'RE TWO HUNDRED MILES BEHIND THE LINES!
STOP DISTRACTING ME, WILL YOU?
YEEOW--!

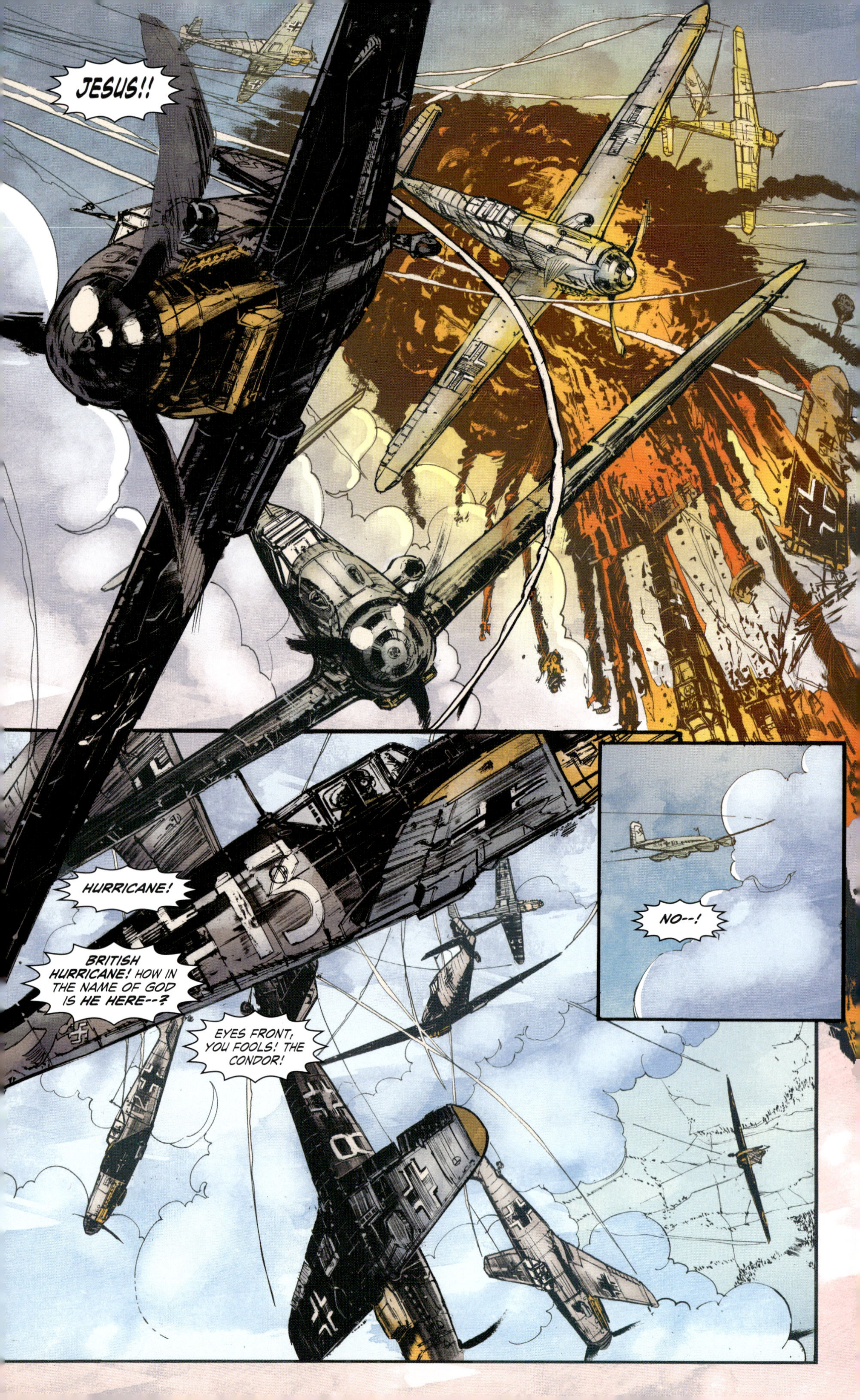
JESUS!!
HURRICANE!
BRITISH HURRICANE! HOW IN THE NAME OF GOD IS HE HERE--?
EYES FRONT, YOU FOOLS! THE CONDOR!
NO--!

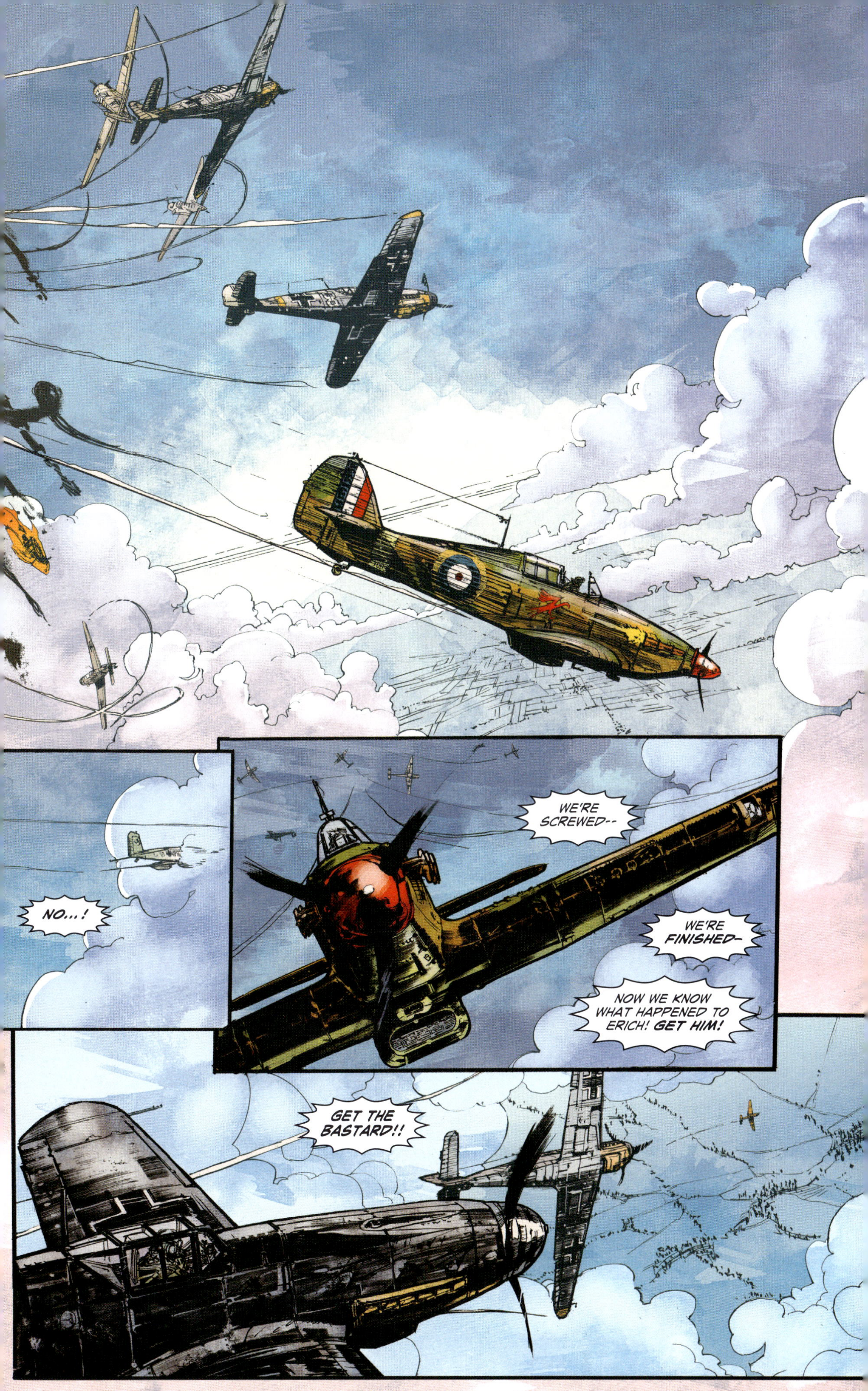

NO...!
WE'RE SCREWED--
WE'RE FINISHED-
NOW WE KNOW WHAT HAPPENED TO ERICH! GET HIM!
GET THE BASTARD!!

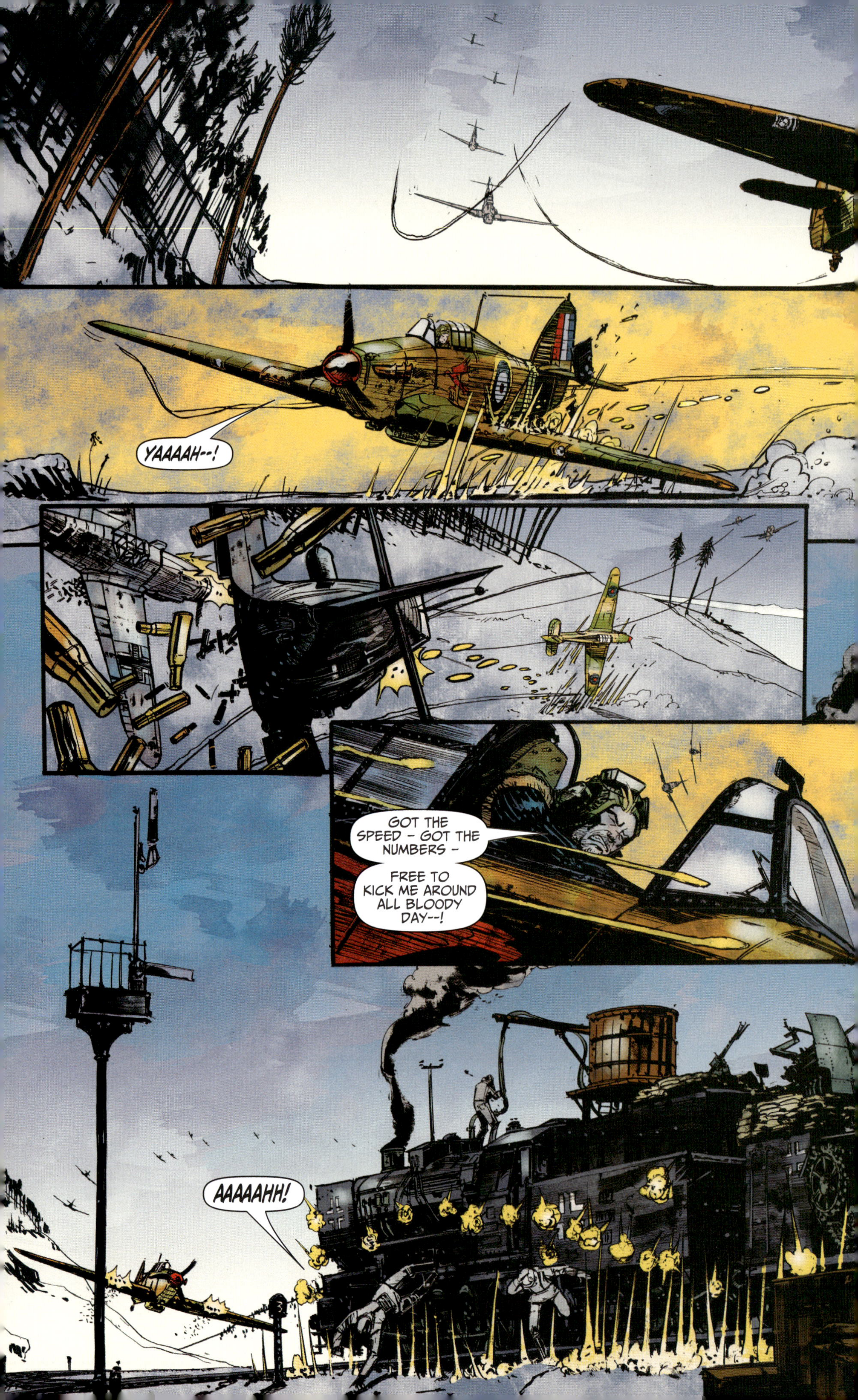
YAAAAH--!
GOT THE SPEED – GOT THE NUMBERS –
FREE TO KICK ME AROUND ALL BLOODY DAY--!
AAAAAHH!

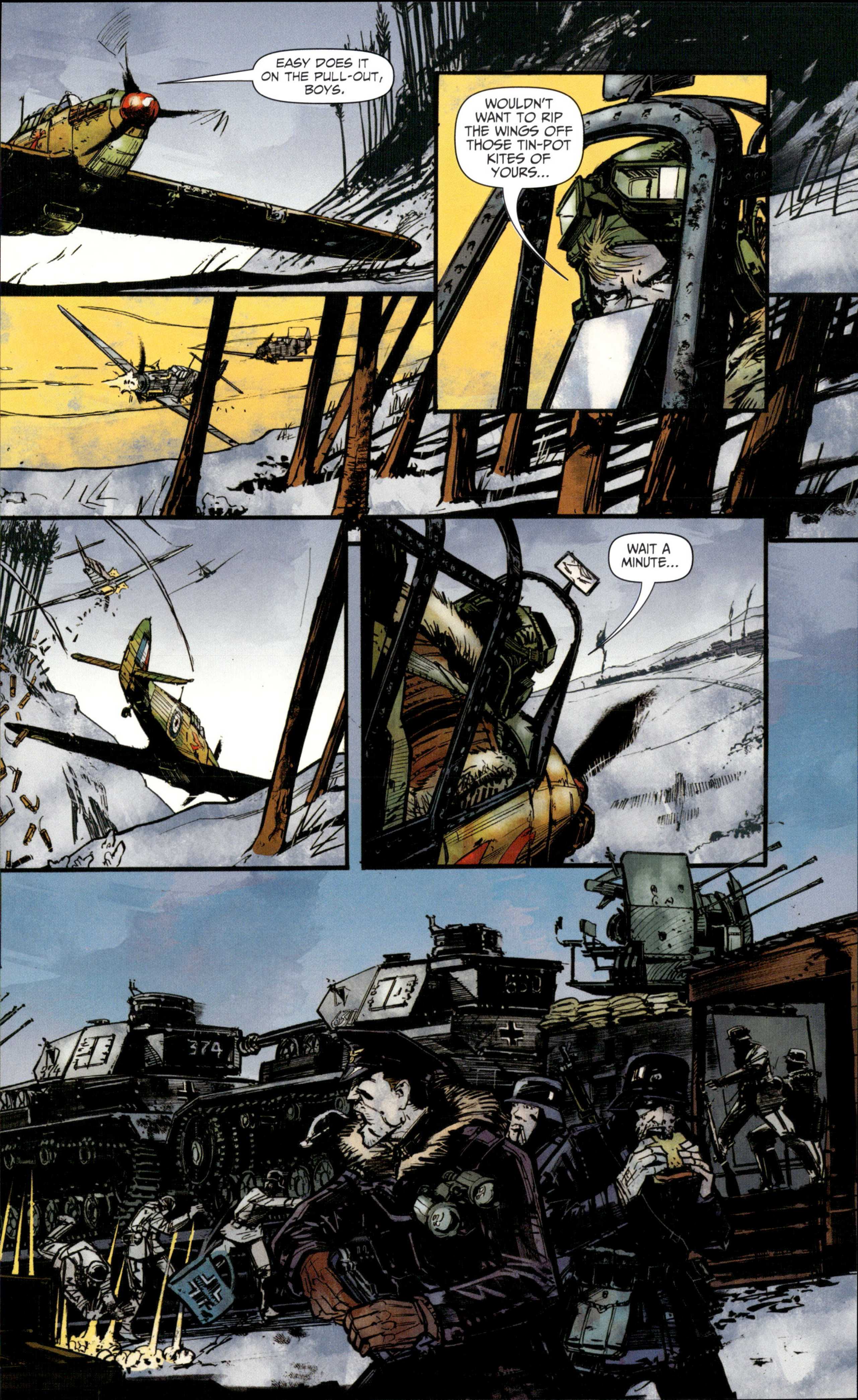
EASY DOES IT ON THE PULL-OUT, BOYS.
WOULDN'T WANT TO RIP THE WINGS OFF THOSE TIN-POT KITES OF YOURS...
WAIT A MINUTE...

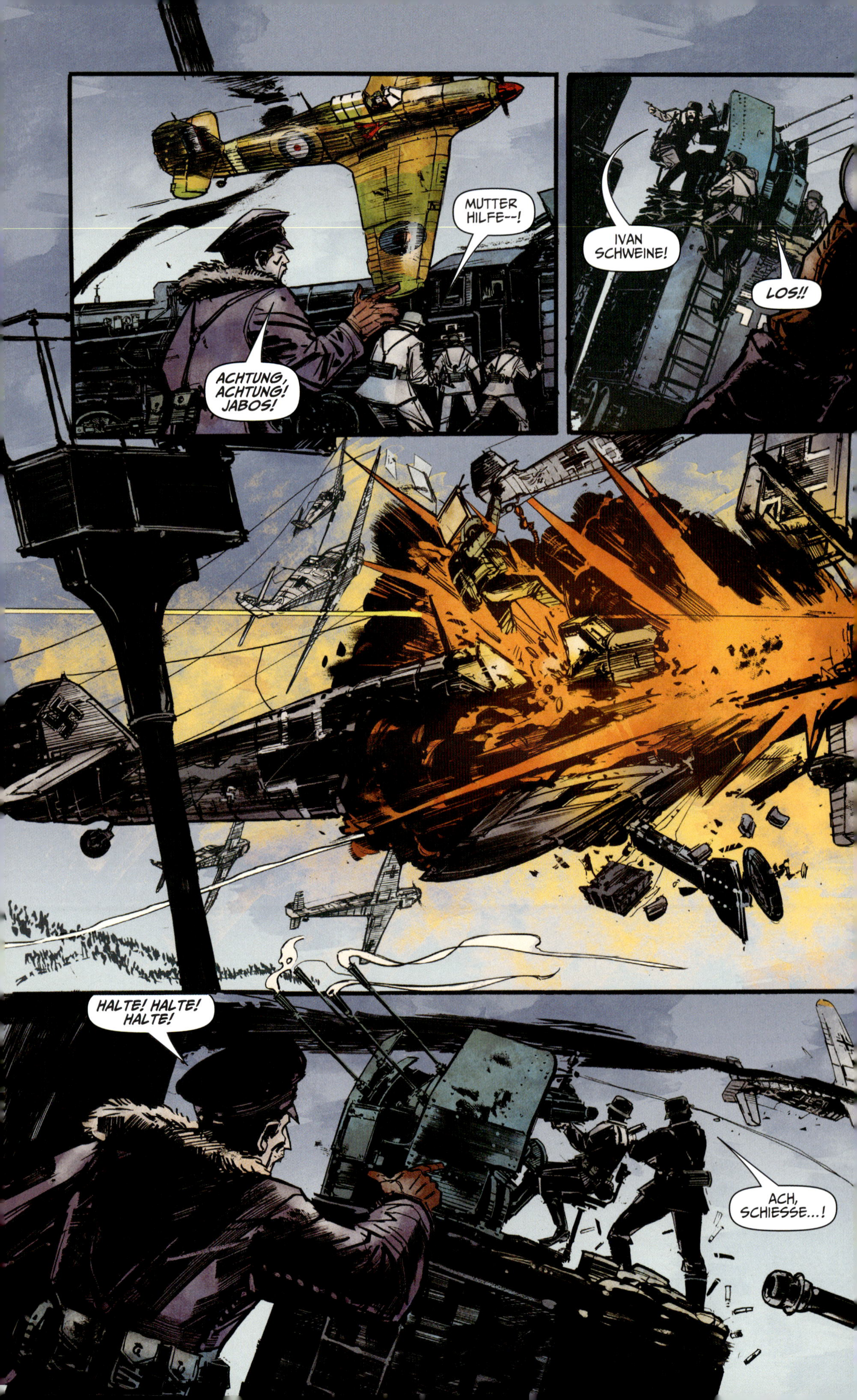
MUTTER HILFE--!
ACHTUNG, ACHTUNG! JABOS!
IVAN SCHWEINE!
LOS!!
HALTE! HALTE! HALTE!
ACH, SCHIESSE...!

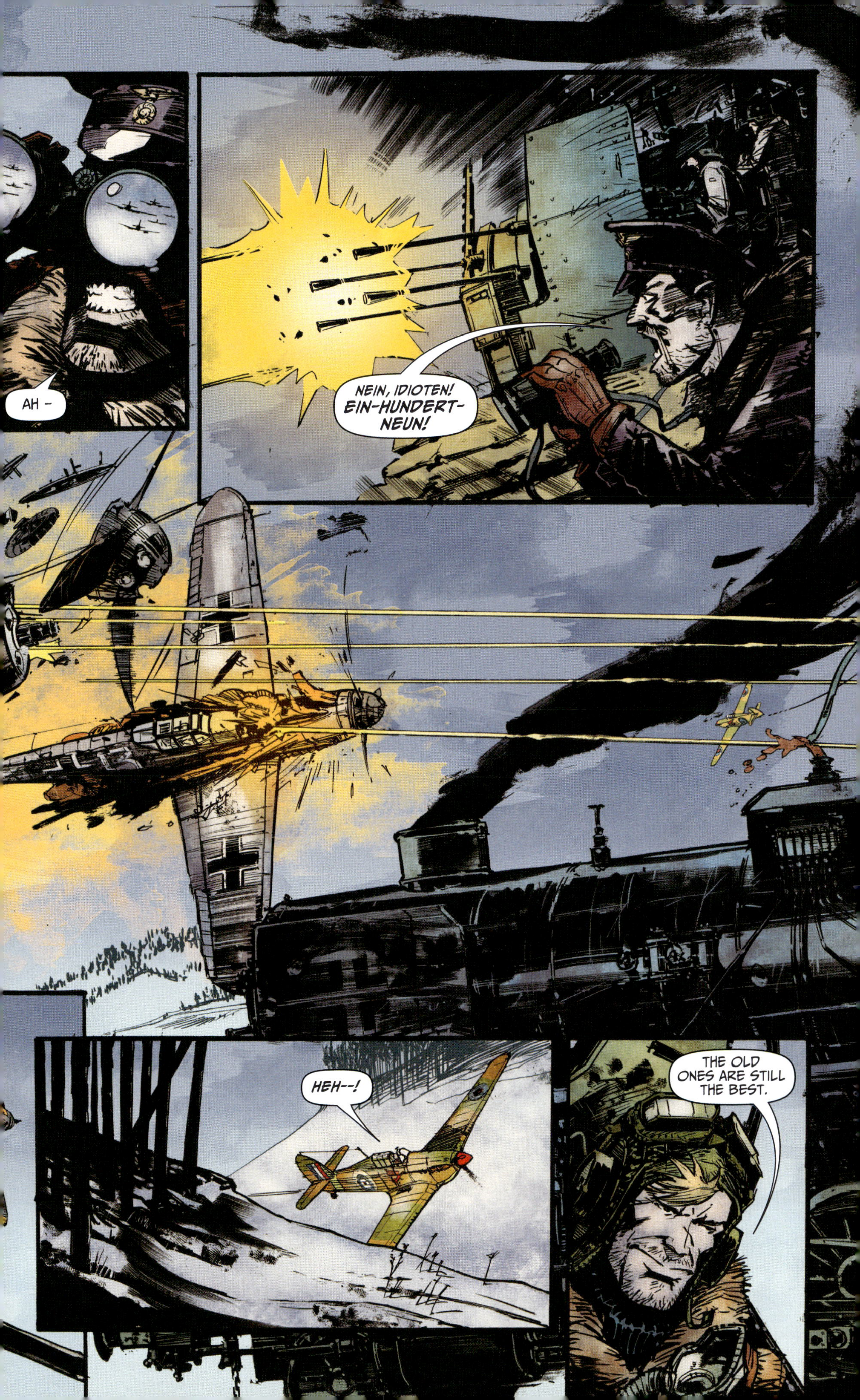
AH -
NEIN, IDIOTEN! EIN-HUNDERT-NEUN!
HEH--!
THE OLD ONES ARE STILL THE BEST.

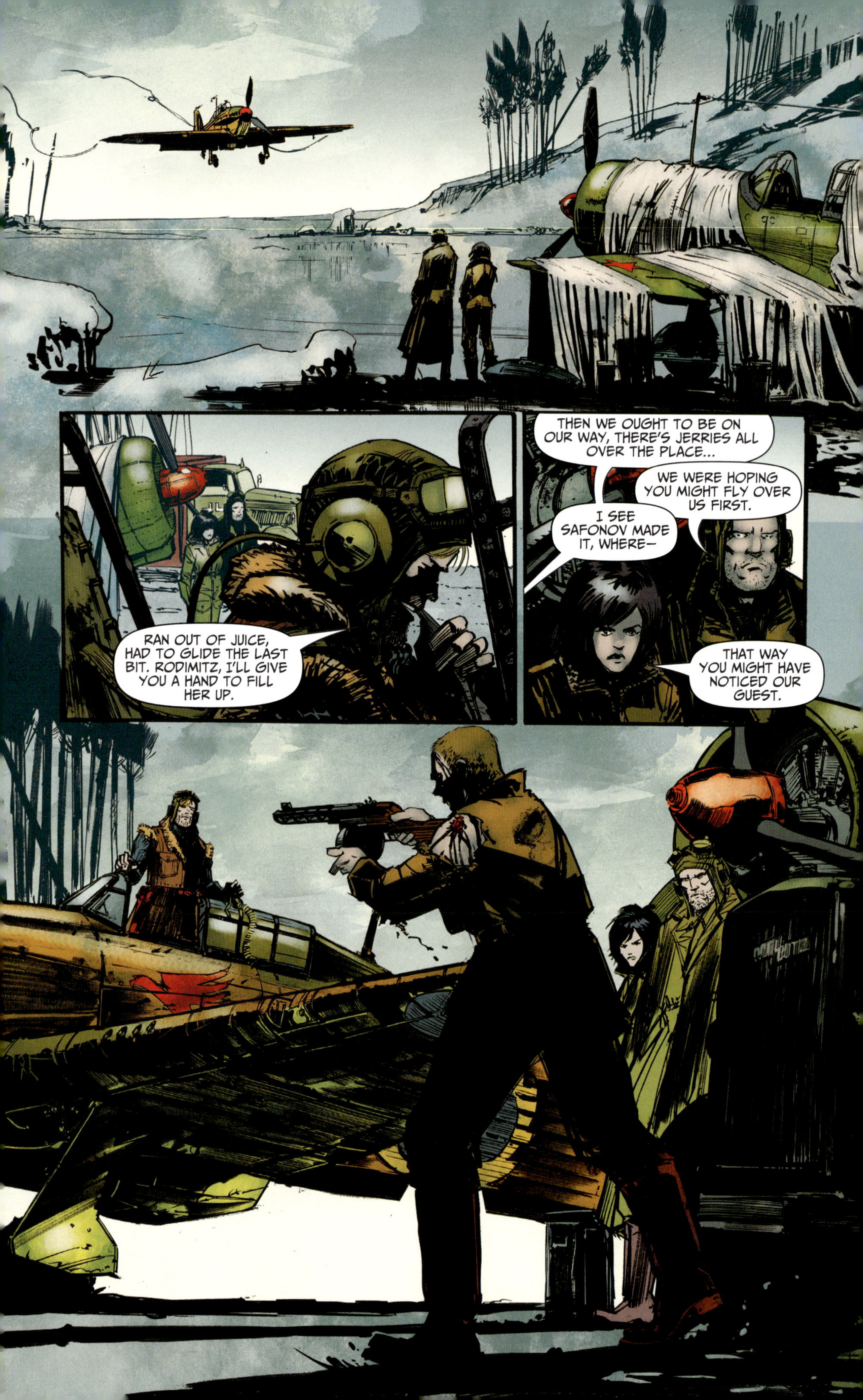
RAN OUT OF JUICE, HAD TO GLIDE THE LAST BIT. RODIMITZ, I'LL GIVE YOU A HAND TO FILL HER UP.
THEN WE OUGHT TO BE ON OUR WAY, THERE'S JERRIES ALL OVER THE PLACE...
I SEE SAFONOV MADE IT, WHERE–
WE WERE HOPING YOU MIGHT FLY OVER US FIRST.
THAT WAY YOU MIGHT HAVE NOTICED OUR GUEST.

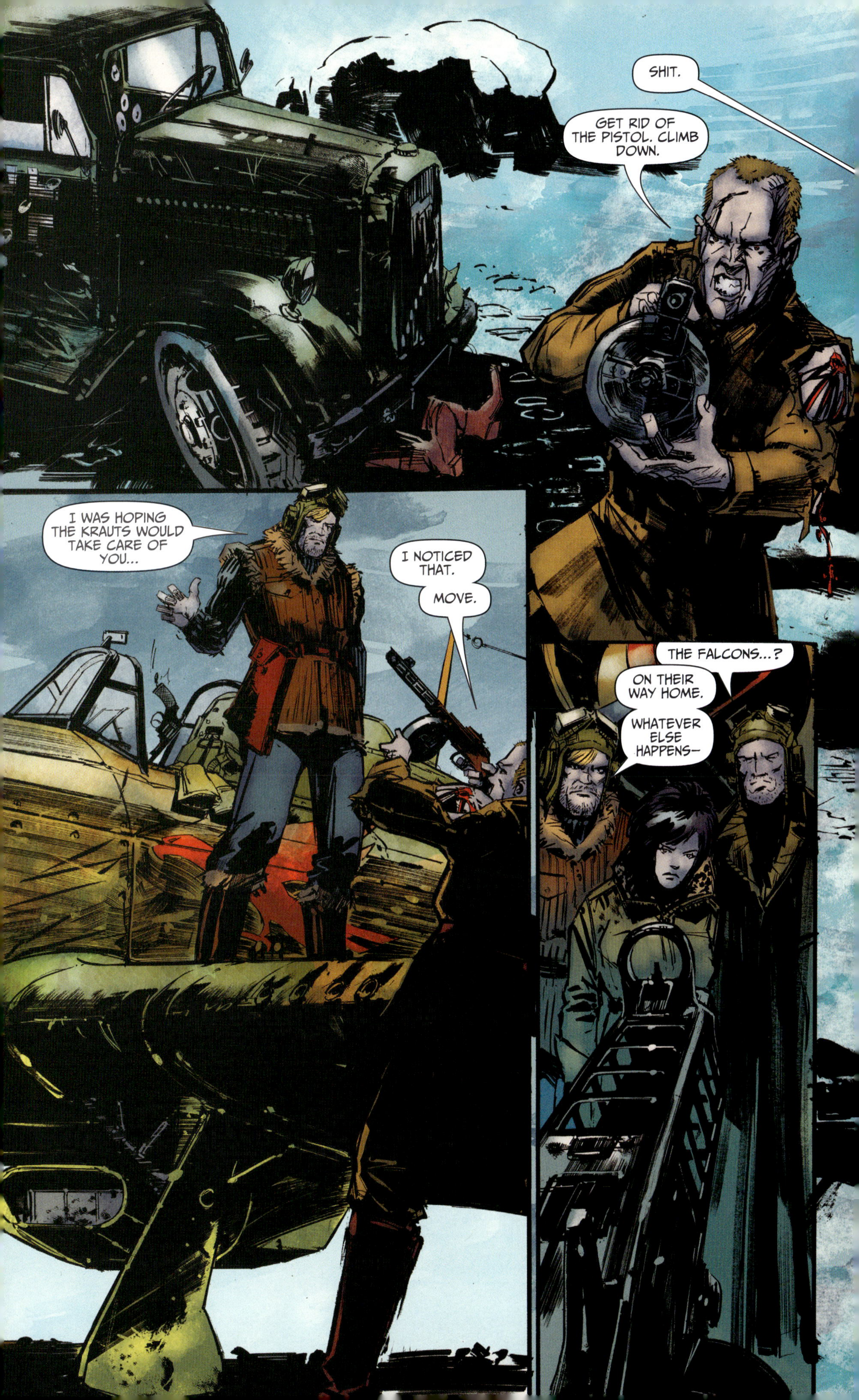
SHIT.
GET RID OF THE PISTOL. CLIMB DOWN.
I WAS HOPING THE KRAUTS WOULD TAKE CARE OF YOU...
I NOTICED THAT.
MOVE.
THE FALCONS...?
ON THEIR WAY HOME.
WHATEVER ELSE HAPPENS—

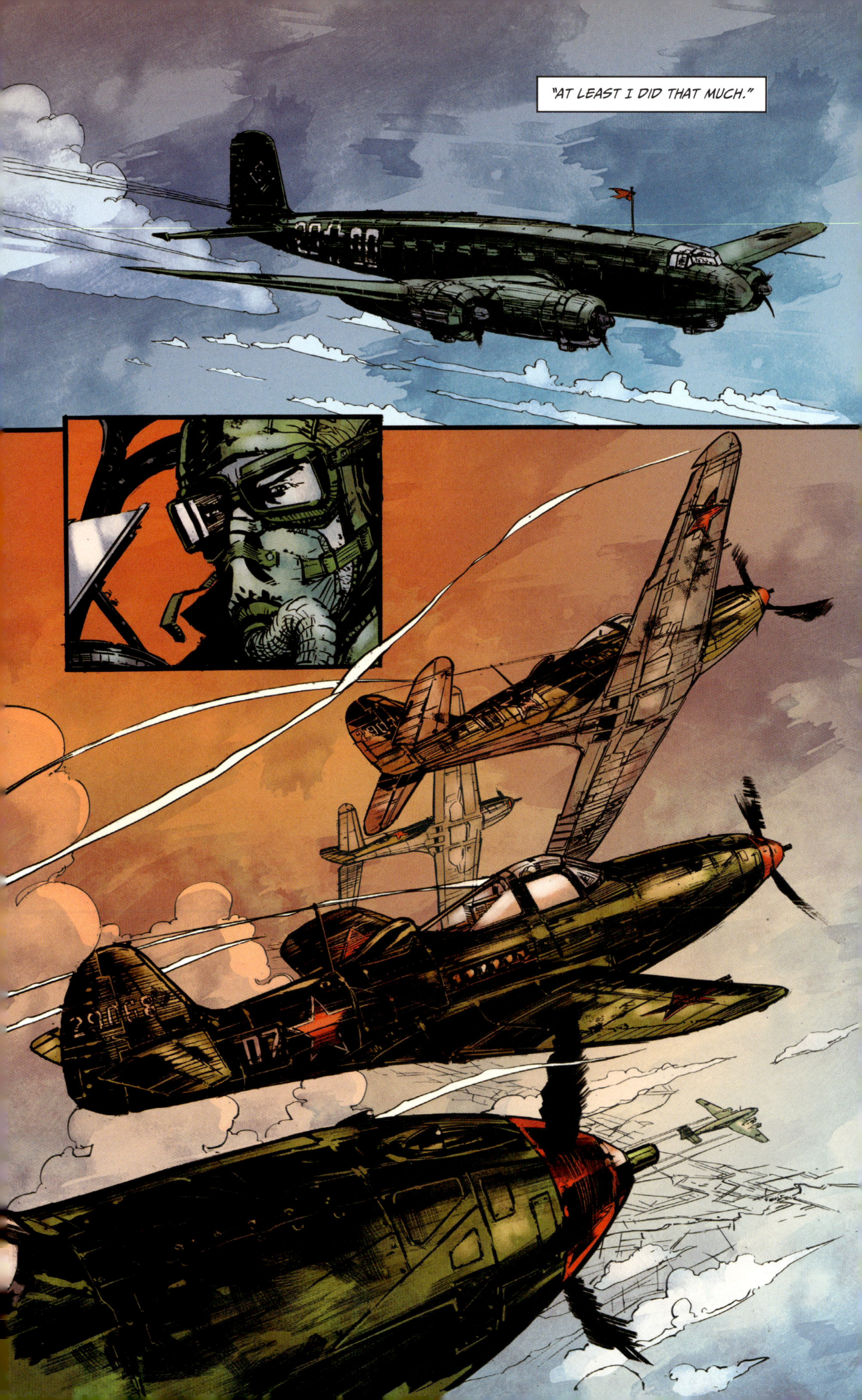
"AT LEAST I DID THAT MUCH."

ISSUE EIGHT
Cover art by:
Keith Burns

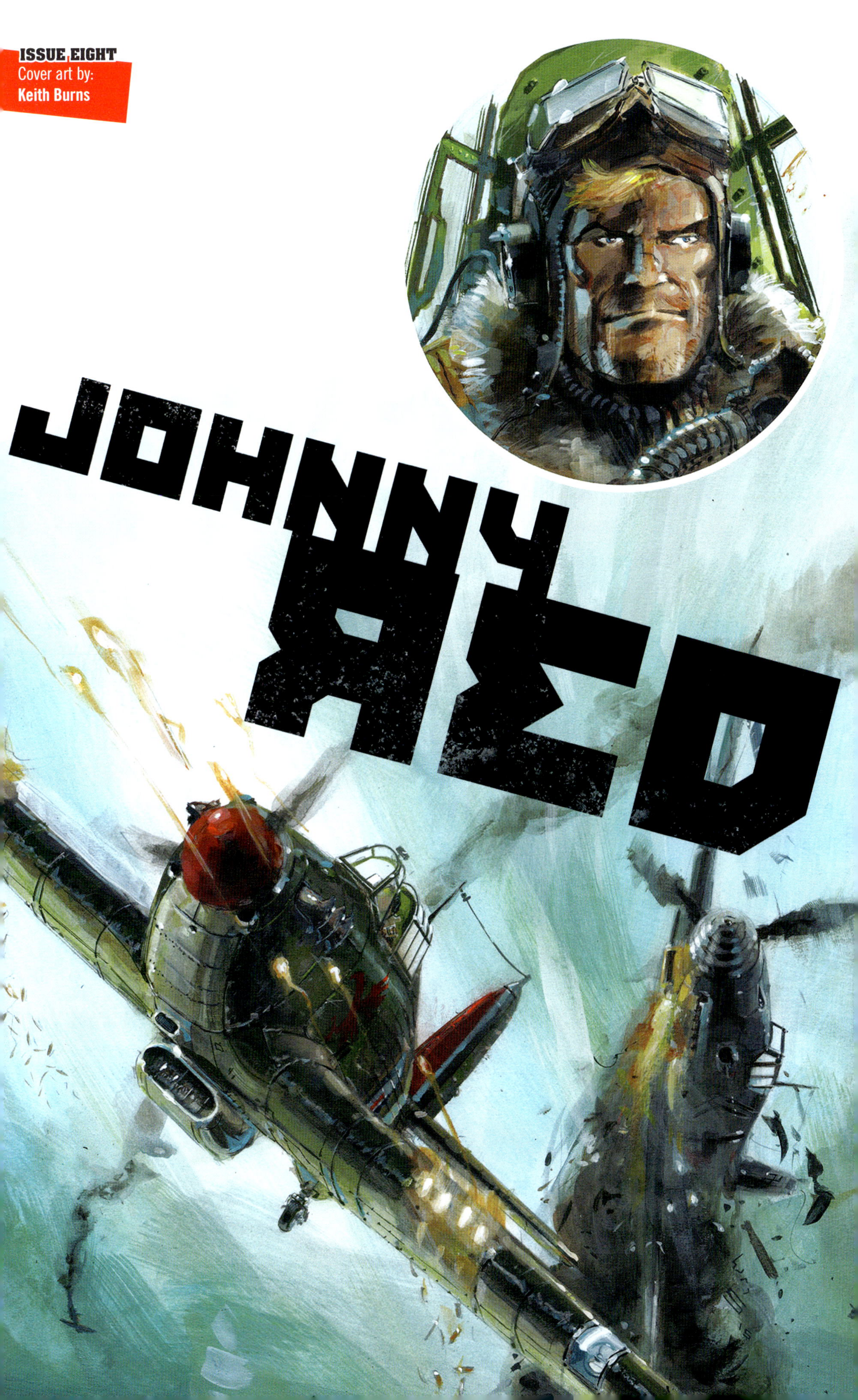
JOHNNY RED

VARIANT
Cover art by:
Ian Kennedy

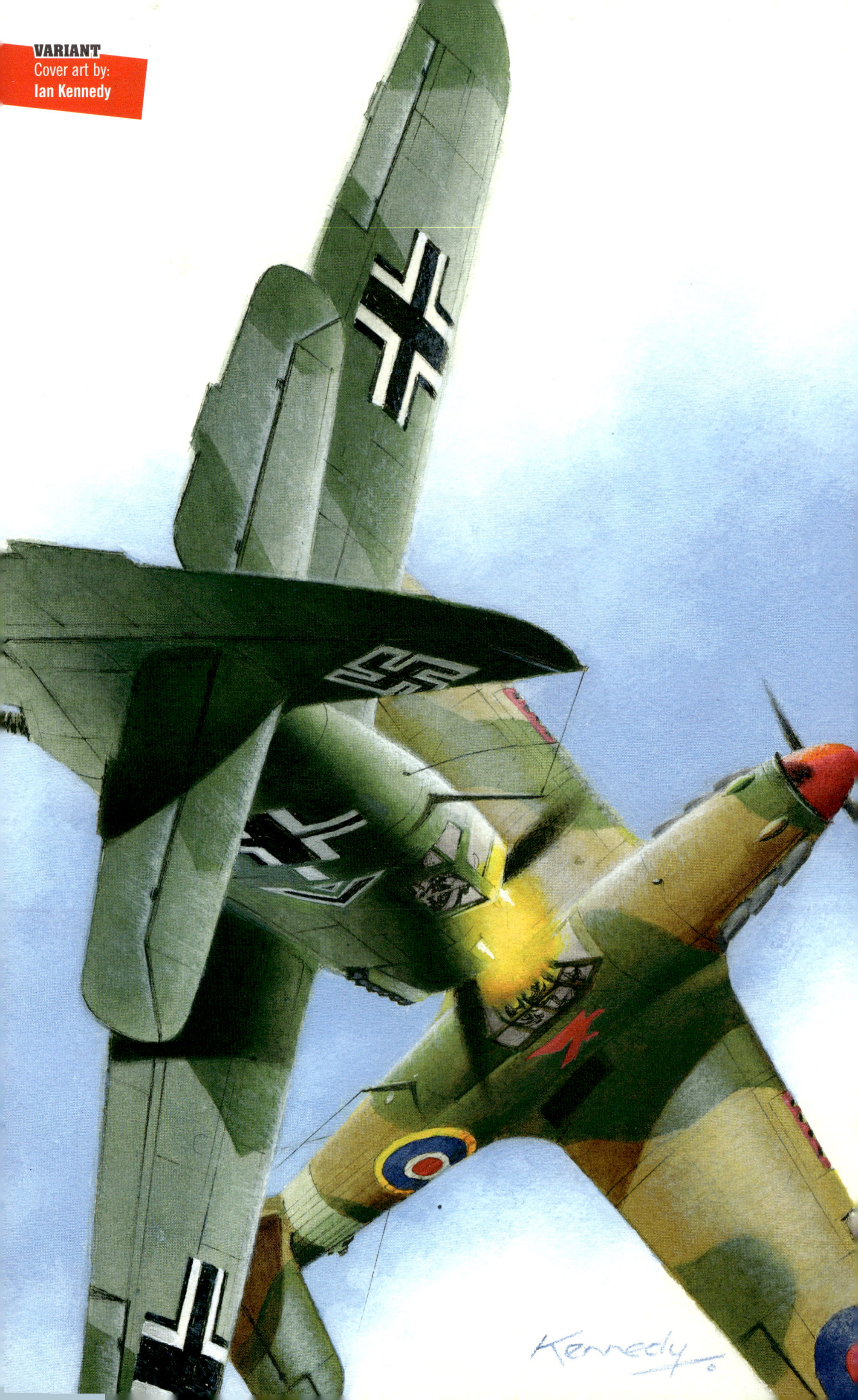
Kennedy

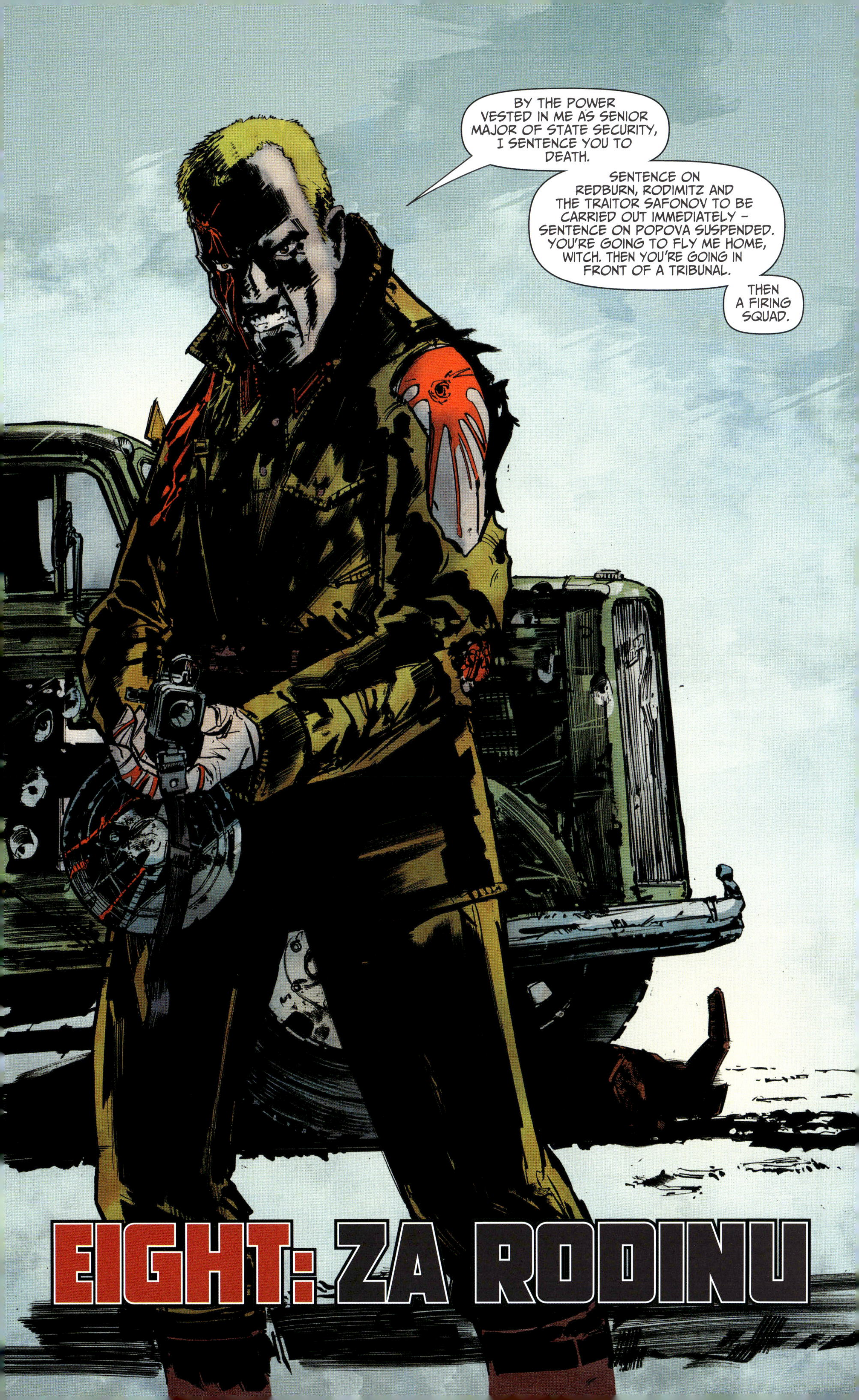
BY THE POWER VESTED IN ME AS SENIOR MAJOR OF STATE SECURITY, I SENTENCE YOU TO DEATH.
SENTENCE ON REDBURN, RODIMITZ AND THE TRAITOR SAFONOV TO BE CARRIED OUT IMMEDIATELY – SENTENCE ON POPOVA SUSPENDED. YOU'RE GOING TO FLY ME HOME, WITCH. THEN YOU'RE GOING IN FRONT OF A TRIBUNAL.
THEN A FIRING SQUAD.
EIGHT: ZA RODINU

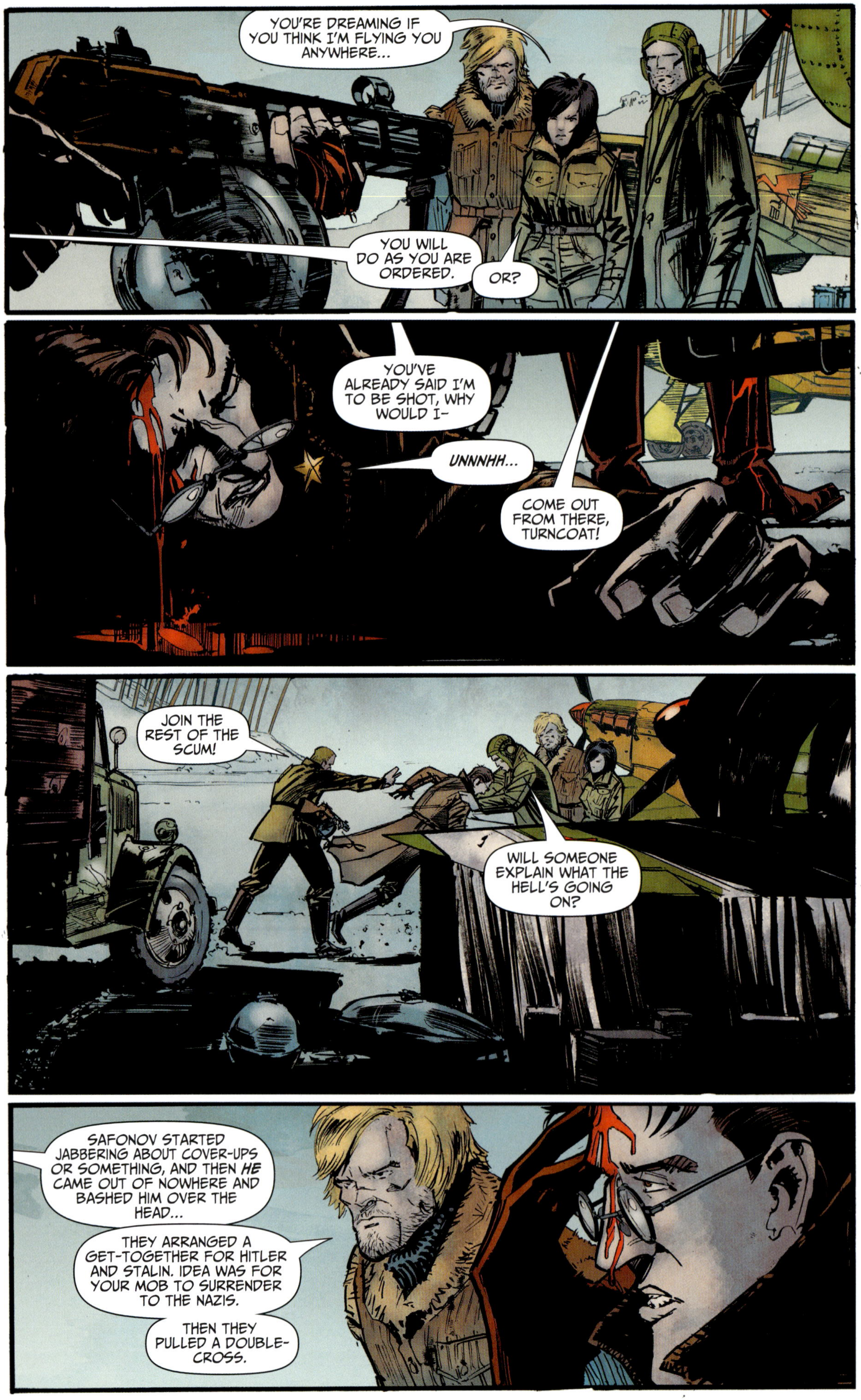

YOU'RE DREAMING IF YOU THINK I'M FLYING YOU ANYWHERE...
YOU WILL DO AS YOU ARE ORDERED.
OR?
YOU'VE ALREADY SAID I'M TO BE SHOT, WHY WOULD I-
UNNNHH...
COME OUT FROM THERE, TURNCOAT!
JOIN THE REST OF THE SCUM!
WILL SOMEONE EXPLAIN WHAT THE HELL'S GOING ON?
SAFONOV STARTED JABBERING ABOUT COVER-UPS OR SOMETHING, AND THEN HE CAME OUT OF NOWHERE AND BASHED HIM OVER THE HEAD...
THEY ARRANGED A GET-TOGETHER FOR HITLER AND STALIN. IDEA WAS FOR YOUR MOB TO SURRENDER TO THE NAZIS.
THEN THEY PULLED A DOUBLE-CROSS.

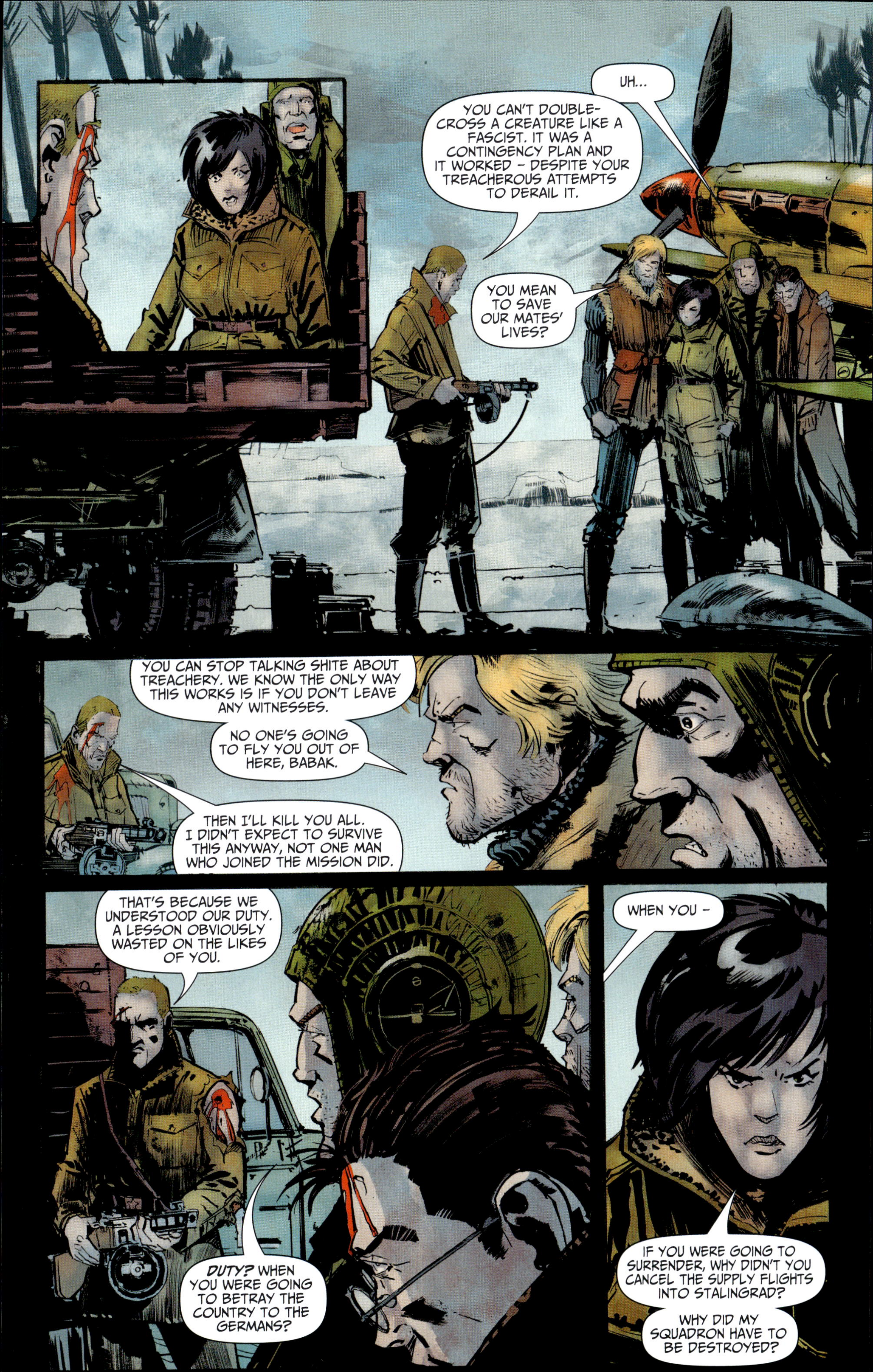
UH...
YOU CAN'T DOUBLE-CROSS A CREATURE LIKE A FASCIST. IT WAS A CONTINGENCY PLAN AND IT WORKED – DESPITE YOUR TREACHEROUS ATTEMPTS TO DERAIL IT.
YOU MEAN TO SAVE OUR MATES' LIVES?
YOU CAN STOP TALKING SHITE ABOUT TREACHERY. WE KNOW THE ONLY WAY THIS WORKS IS IF YOU DON'T LEAVE ANY WITNESSES.
NO ONE'S GOING TO FLY YOU OUT OF HERE, BABAK.
THEN I'LL KILL YOU ALL. I DIDN'T EXPECT TO SURVIVE THIS ANYWAY, NOT ONE MAN WHO JOINED THE MISSION DID.
THAT'S BECAUSE WE UNDERSTOOD OUR DUTY. A LESSON OBVIOUSLY WASTED ON THE LIKES OF YOU.
DUTY? WHEN YOU WERE GOING TO BETRAY THE COUNTRY TO THE GERMANS?
WHEN YOU –
IF YOU WERE GOING TO SURRENDER, WHY DIDN'T YOU CANCEL THE SUPPLY FLIGHTS INTO STALINGRAD?
WHY DID MY SQUADRON HAVE TO BE DESTROYED?

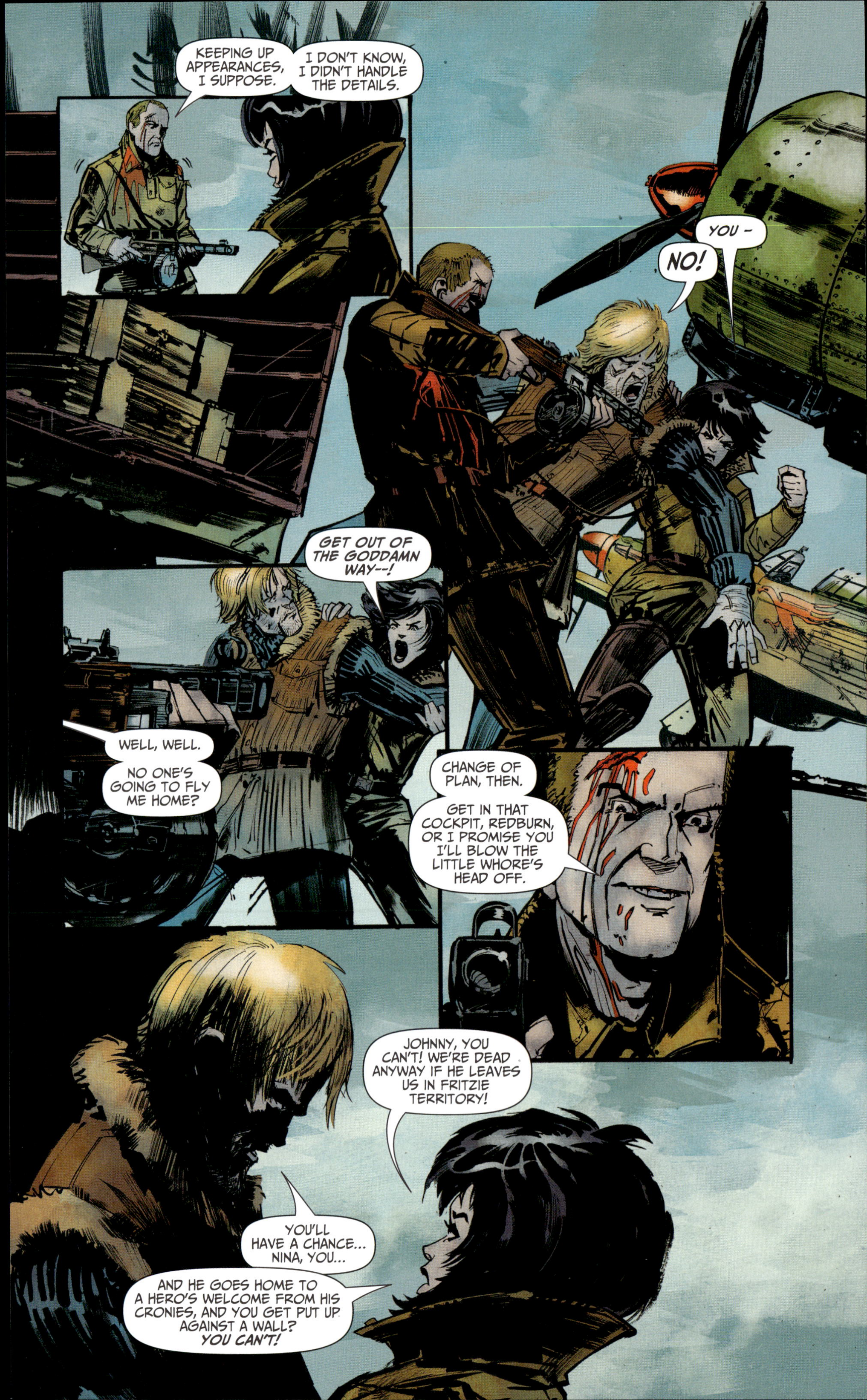
KEEPING UP APPEARANCES, I SUPPOSE.
I DON'T KNOW, I DIDN'T HANDLE THE DETAILS.
YOU -
NO!
GET OUT OF THE GODDAMN WAY--!
WELL, WELL.
NO ONE'S GOING TO FLY ME HOME?
CHANGE OF PLAN, THEN.
GET IN THAT COCKPIT, REDBURN, OR I PROMISE YOU I'LL BLOW THE LITTLE WHORE'S HEAD OFF.
JOHNNY, YOU CAN'T! WE'RE DEAD ANYWAY IF HE LEAVES US IN FRITZIE TERRITORY!
YOU'LL HAVE A CHANCE... NINA, YOU...
AND HE GOES HOME TO A HERO'S WELCOME FROM HIS CRONIES, AND YOU GET PUT UP AGAINST A WALL? YOU CAN'T!

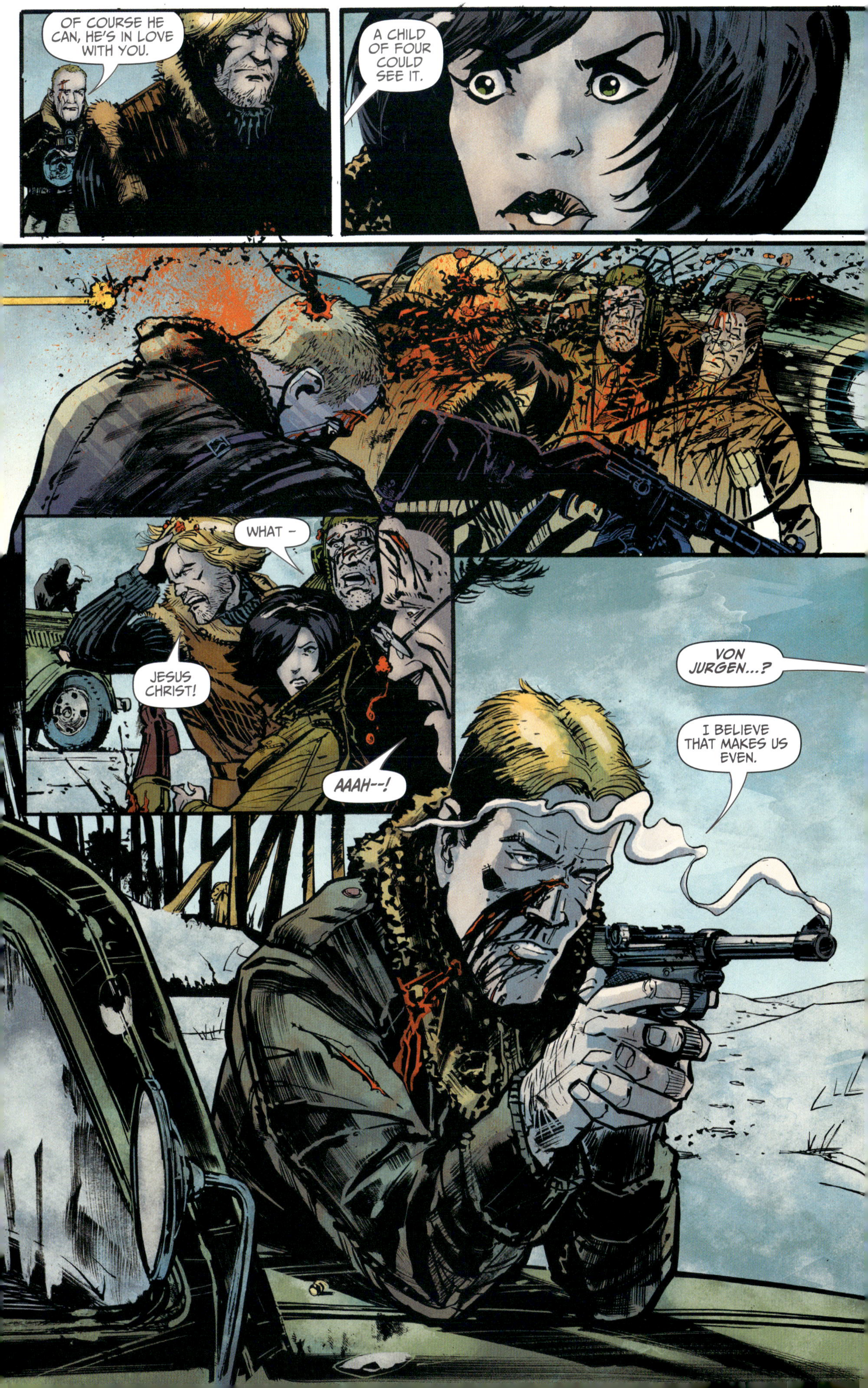
OF COURSE HE CAN, HE'S IN LOVE WITH YOU.
A CHILD OF FOUR COULD SEE IT.
WHAT –
JESUS CHRIST!
AAAH--!
VON JURGEN...?
I BELIEVE THAT MAKES US EVEN.

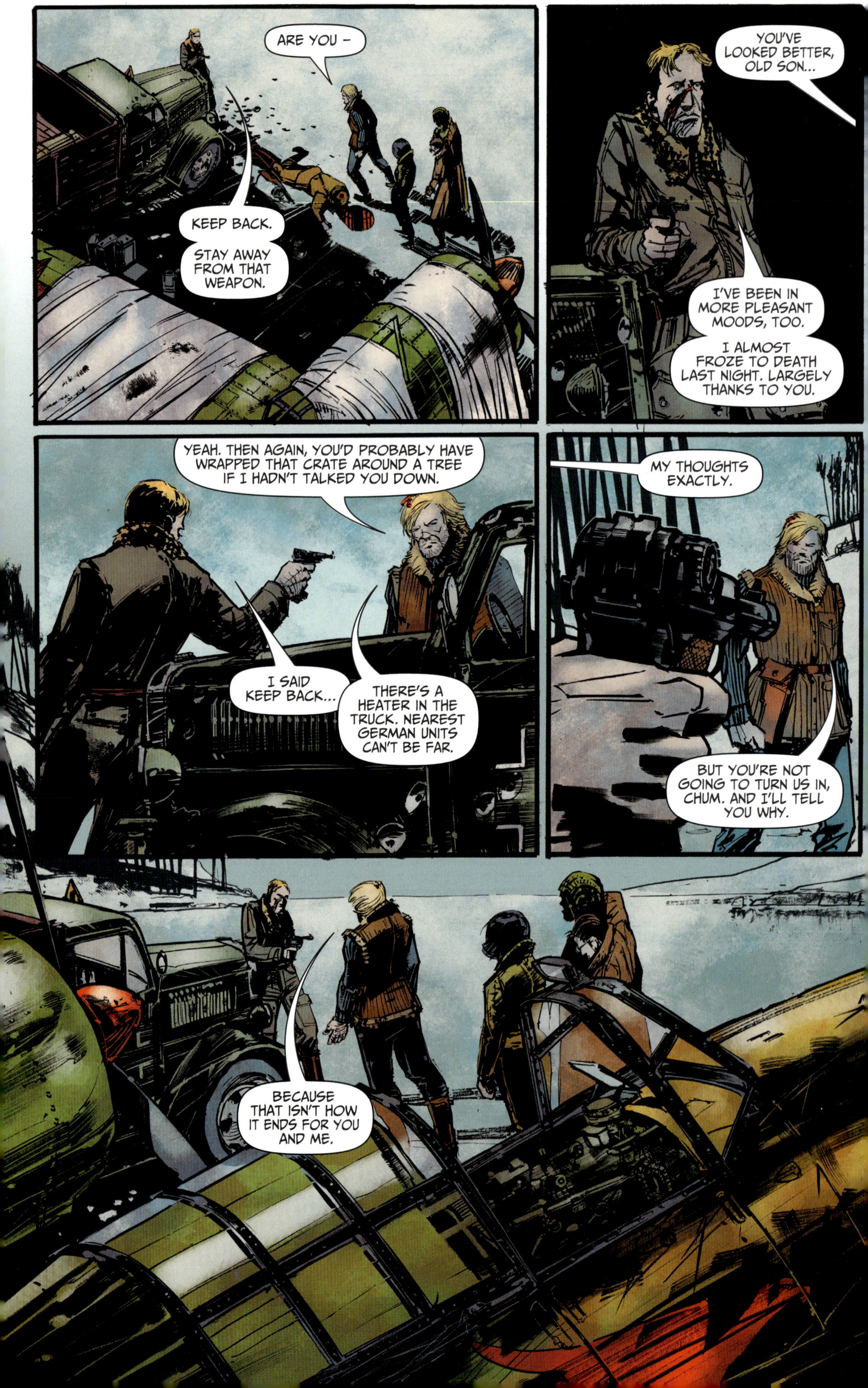
ARE YOU –
KEEP BACK.
STAY AWAY FROM THAT WEAPON.
YOU'VE LOOKED BETTER, OLD SON...
I'VE BEEN IN MORE PLEASANT MOODS, TOO.
I ALMOST FROZE TO DEATH LAST NIGHT. LARGELY THANKS TO YOU.
YEAH. THEN AGAIN, YOU'D PROBABLY HAVE WRAPPED THAT CRATE AROUND A TREE IF I HADN'T TALKED YOU DOWN.
I SAID KEEP BACK...
THERE'S A HEATER IN THE TRUCK. NEAREST GERMAN UNITS CAN'T BE FAR.
MY THOUGHTS EXACTLY.
BUT YOU'RE NOT GOING TO TURN US IN, CHUM. AND I'LL TELL YOU WHY.
BECAUSE THAT ISN'T HOW IT ENDS FOR YOU AND ME.

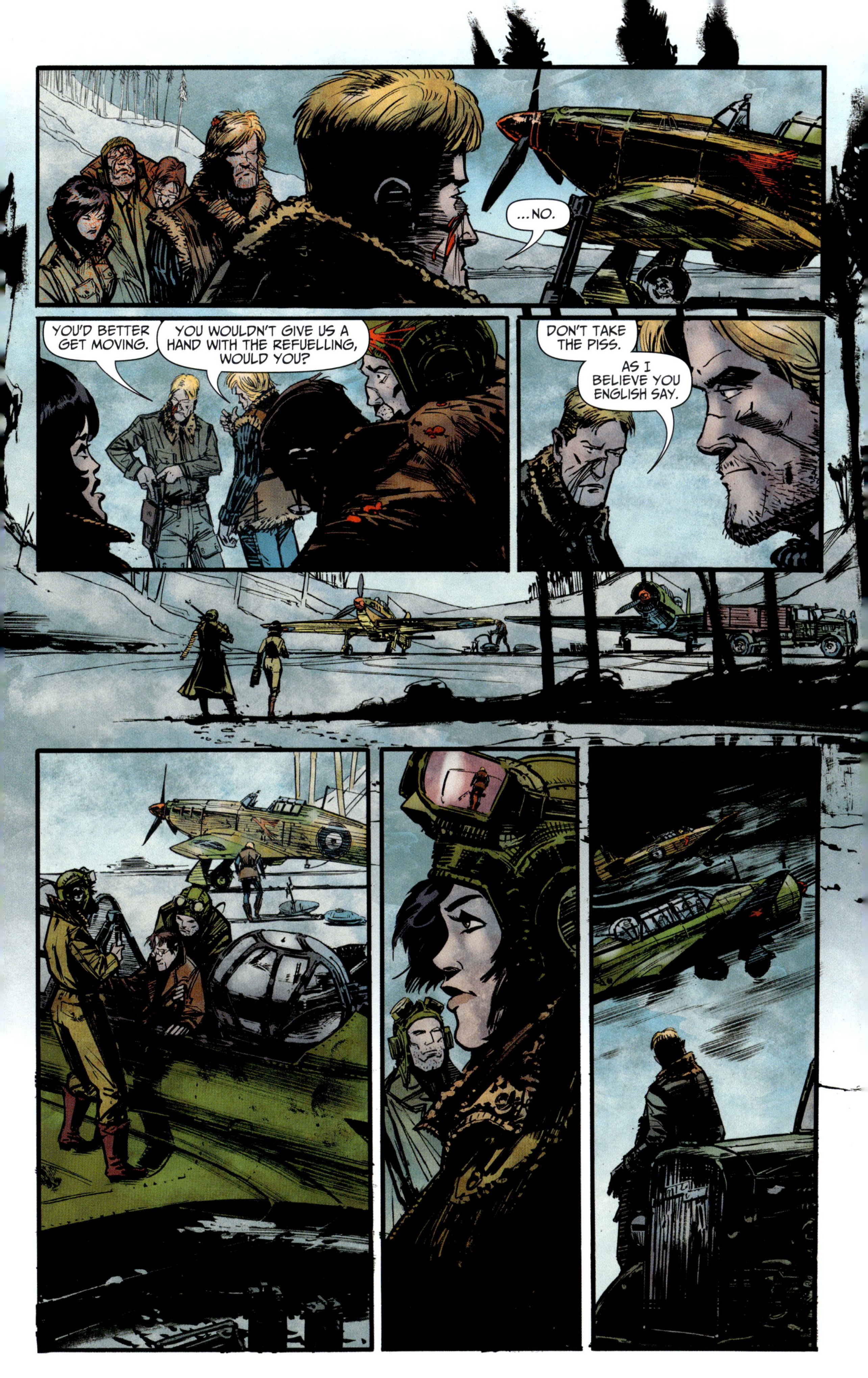
...NO.
YOU'D BETTER GET MOVING.
YOU WOULDN'T GIVE US A HAND WITH THE REFUELLING, WOULD YOU?
DON'T TAKE THE PISS.
AS I BELIEVE YOU ENGLISH SAY.

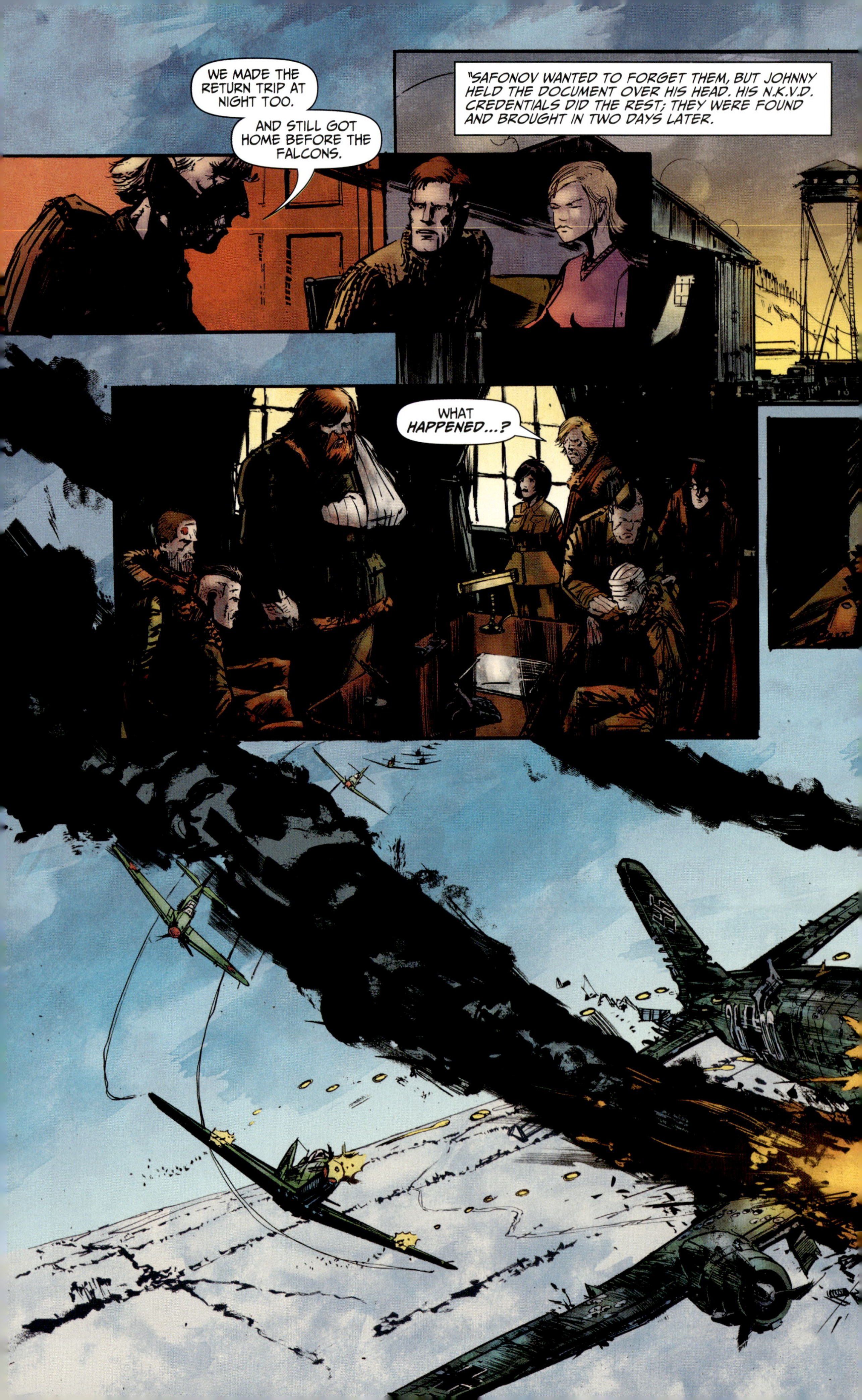
WE MADE THE RETURN TRIP AT NIGHT TOO.
AND STILL GOT HOME BEFORE THE FALCONS.
"SAFONOV WANTED TO FORGET THEM, BUT JOHNNY HELD THE DOCUMENT OVER HIS HEAD. HIS N.K.V.D. CREDENTIALS DID THE REST; THEY WERE FOUND AND BROUGHT IN TWO DAYS LATER.
WHAT HAPPENED...?

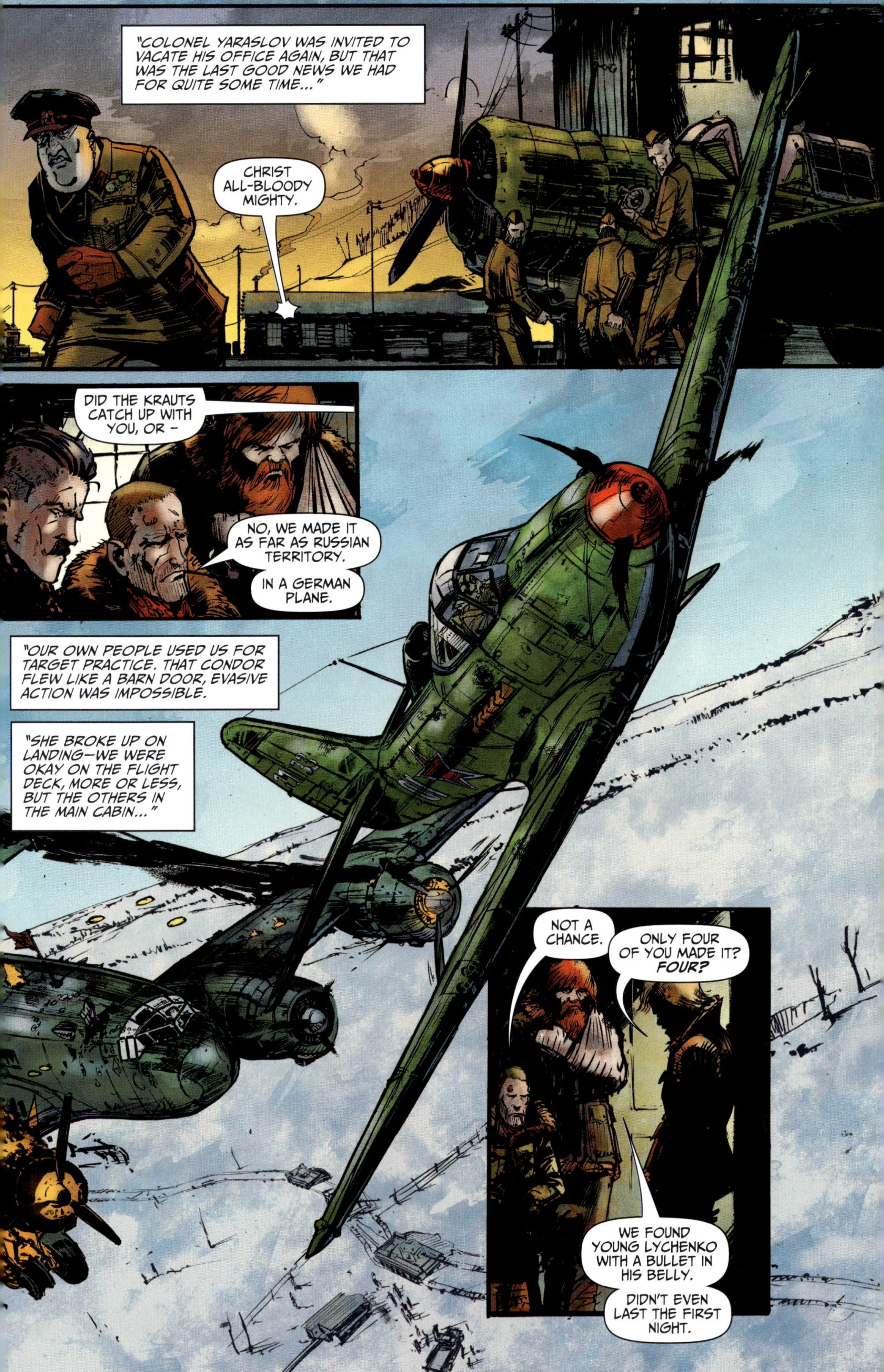
"COLONEL YARASLOV WAS INVITED TO VACATE HIS OFFICE AGAIN, BUT THAT WAS THE LAST GOOD NEWS WE HAD FOR QUITE SOME TIME..."
CHRIST ALL-BLOODY MIGHTY.
DID THE KRAUTS CATCH UP WITH YOU, OR –
NO, WE MADE IT AS FAR AS RUSSIAN TERRITORY.
IN A GERMAN PLANE.
"OUR OWN PEOPLE USED US FOR TARGET PRACTICE. THAT CONDOR FLEW LIKE A BARN DOOR, EVASIVE ACTION WAS IMPOSSIBLE.
"SHE BROKE UP ON LANDING—WE WERE OKAY ON THE FLIGHT DECK, MORE OR LESS, BUT THE OTHERS IN THE MAIN CABIN..."
ONLY FOUR OF YOU MADE IT? *FOUR?*
NOT A CHANCE.
WE FOUND YOUNG LYCHENKO WITH A BULLET IN HIS BELLY.
DIDN'T EVEN LAST THE FIRST NIGHT.

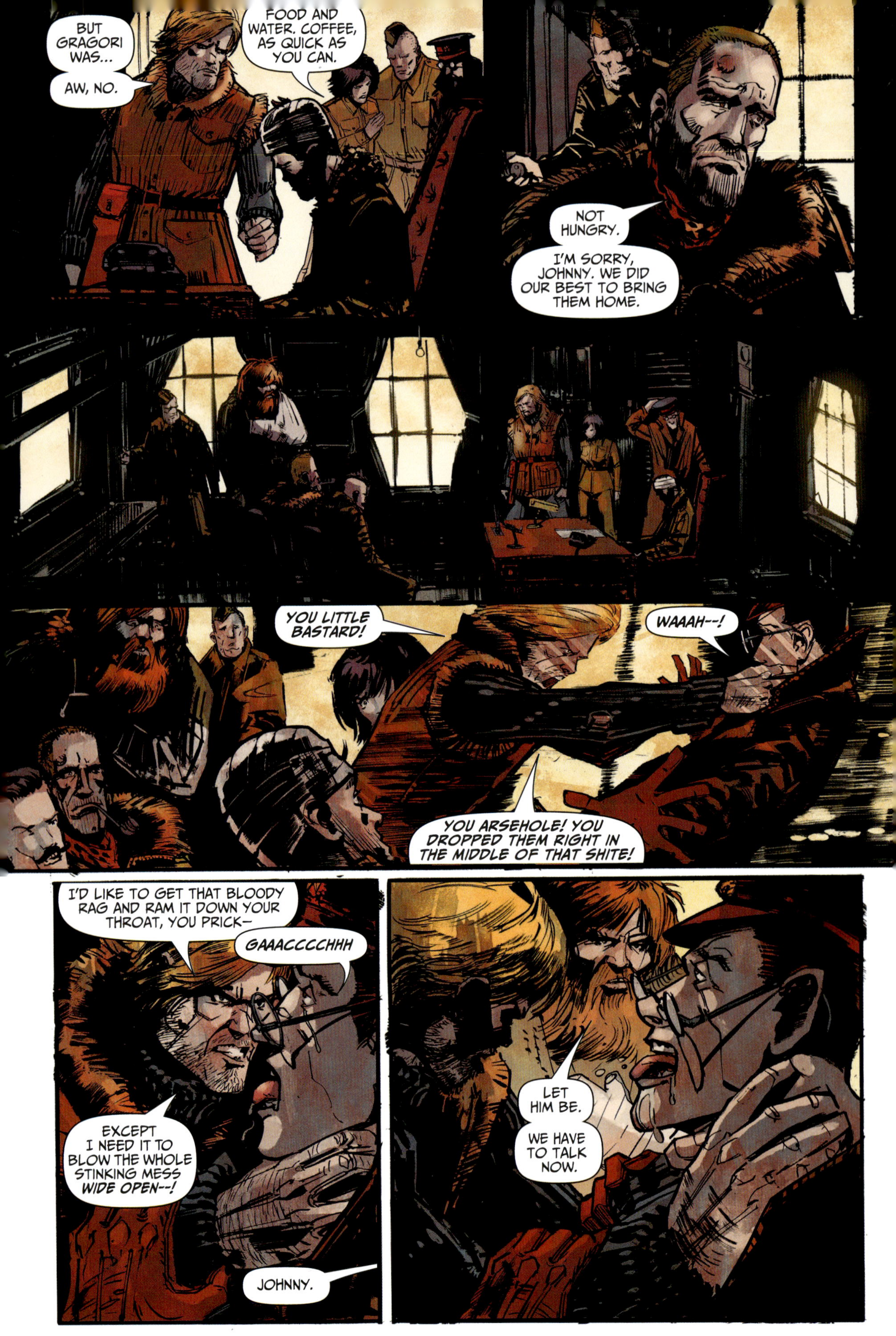
BUT GRAGORI WAS...
AW, NO.
FOOD AND WATER. COFFEE, AS QUICK AS YOU CAN.
NOT HUNGRY.
I'M SORRY, JOHNNY. WE DID OUR BEST TO BRING THEM HOME.
YOU LITTLE BASTARD!
WAAAH--!
YOU ARSEHOLE! YOU DROPPED THEM RIGHT IN THE MIDDLE OF THAT SHITE!
I'D LIKE TO GET THAT BLOODY RAG AND RAM IT DOWN YOUR THROAT, YOU PRICK–
GAAACCCCHHH
EXCEPT I NEED IT TO BLOW THE WHOLE STINKING MESS WIDE OPEN--!
JOHNNY.
LET HIM BE.
WE HAVE TO TALK NOW.

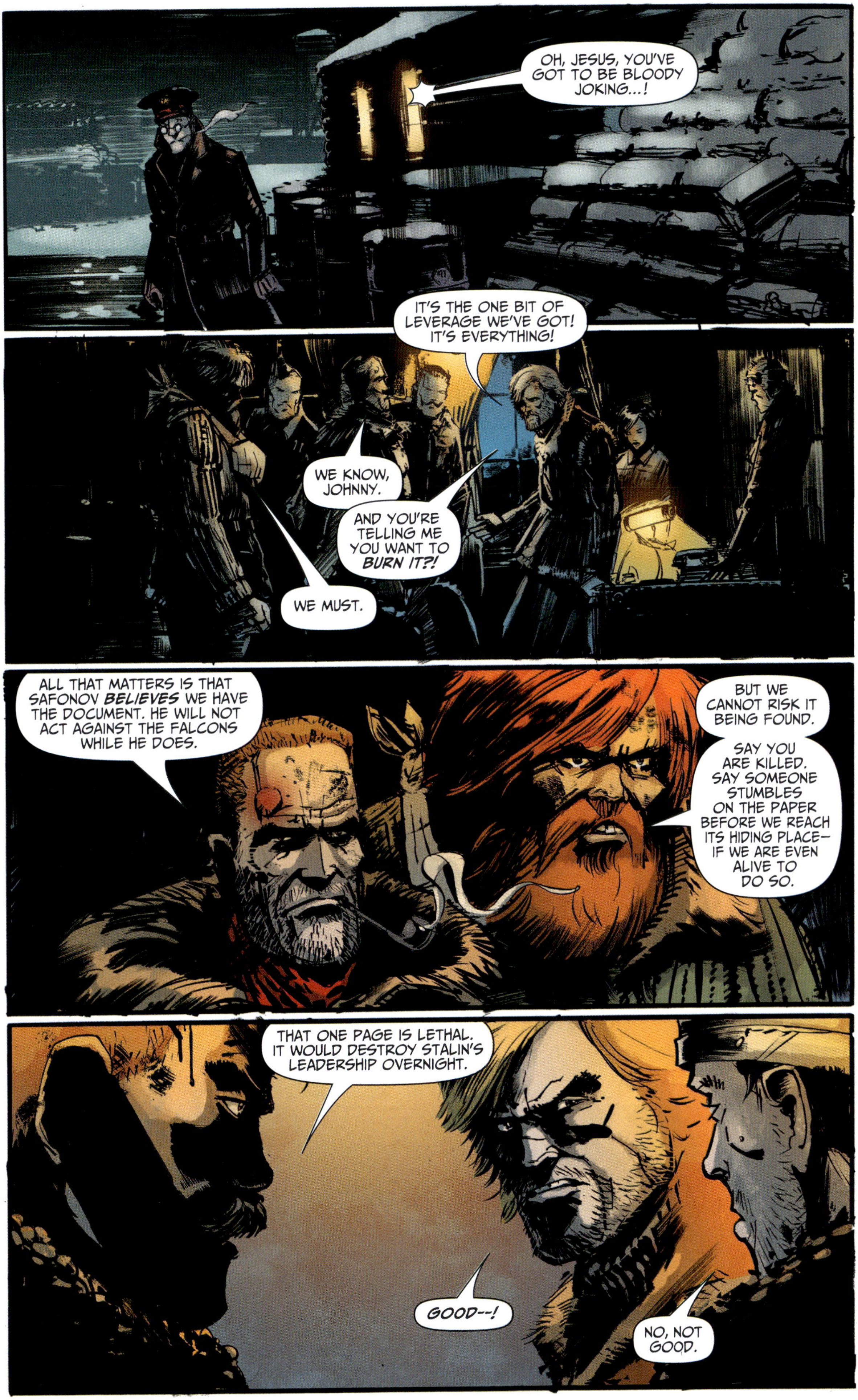
OH, JESUS, YOU'VE GOT TO BE BLOODY JOKING...!
IT'S THE ONE BIT OF LEVERAGE WE'VE GOT! IT'S EVERYTHING!
WE KNOW, JOHNNY.
AND YOU'RE TELLING ME YOU WANT TO *BURN IT?!*
WE MUST.
ALL THAT MATTERS IS THAT SAFONOV *BELIEVES* WE HAVE THE DOCUMENT. HE WILL NOT ACT AGAINST THE FALCONS WHILE HE DOES.
BUT WE CANNOT RISK IT BEING FOUND.
SAY YOU ARE KILLED. SAY SOMEONE STUMBLES ON THE PAPER BEFORE WE REACH ITS HIDING PLACE— IF WE ARE EVEN ALIVE TO DO SO.
THAT ONE PAGE IS LETHAL. IT WOULD DESTROY STALIN'S LEADERSHIP OVERNIGHT.
GOOD--!
NO, NOT GOOD.

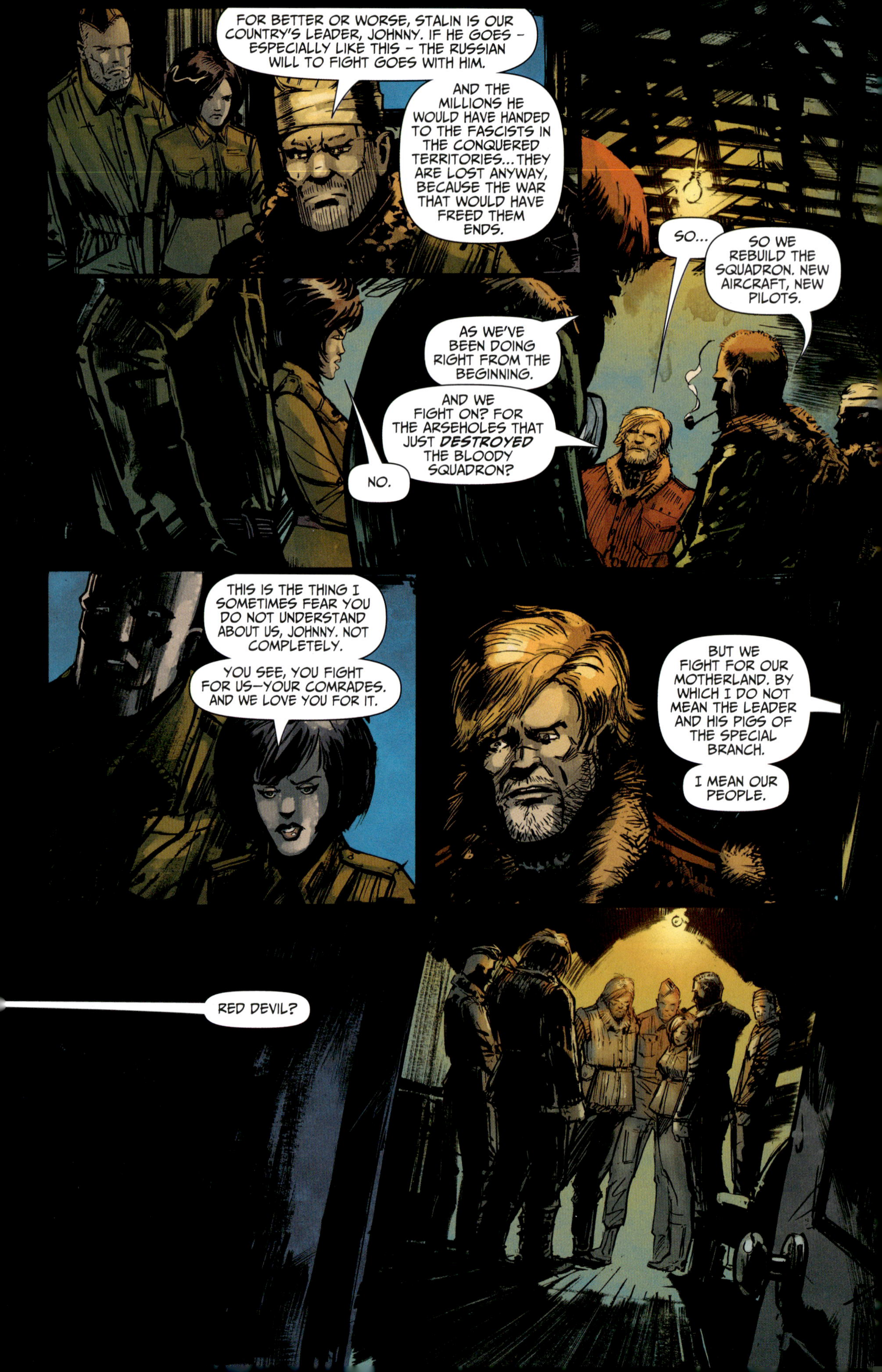
FOR BETTER OR WORSE, STALIN IS OUR COUNTRY'S LEADER, JOHNNY. IF HE GOES – ESPECIALLY LIKE THIS – THE RUSSIAN WILL TO FIGHT GOES WITH HIM.
AND THE MILLIONS HE WOULD HAVE HANDED TO THE FASCISTS IN THE CONQUERED TERRITORIES... THEY ARE LOST ANYWAY, BECAUSE THE WAR THAT WOULD HAVE FREED THEM ENDS.
SO...
SO WE REBUILD THE SQUADRON. NEW AIRCRAFT, NEW PILOTS.
AS WE'VE BEEN DOING RIGHT FROM THE BEGINNING.
AND WE FIGHT ON? FOR THE ARSEHOLES THAT JUST DESTROYED THE BLOODY SQUADRON?
NO.
THIS IS THE THING I SOMETIMES FEAR YOU DO NOT UNDERSTAND ABOUT US, JOHNNY. NOT COMPLETELY.
YOU SEE, YOU FIGHT FOR US—YOUR COMRADES. AND WE LOVE YOU FOR IT.
BUT WE FIGHT FOR OUR MOTHERLAND. BY WHICH I DO NOT MEAN THE LEADER AND HIS PIGS OF THE SPECIAL BRANCH.
I MEAN OUR PEOPLE.
RED DEVIL?

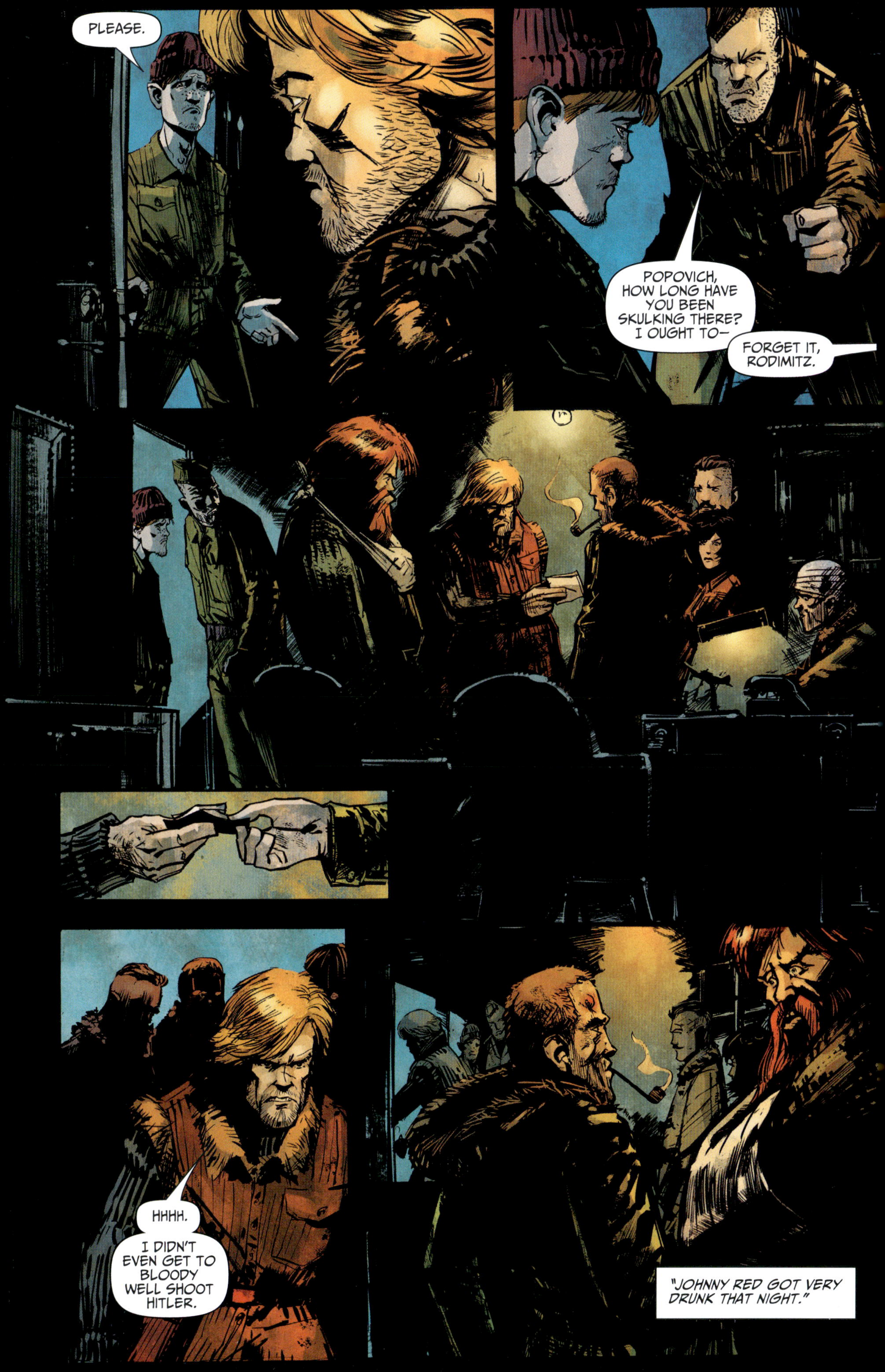
PLEASE.
POPOVICH, HOW LONG HAVE YOU BEEN SKULKING THERE? I OUGHT TO—
FORGET IT, RODIMITZ.
HHHH.
I DIDN'T EVEN GET TO BLOODY WELL SHOOT HITLER.
"JOHNNY RED GOT VERY DRUNK THAT NIGHT."

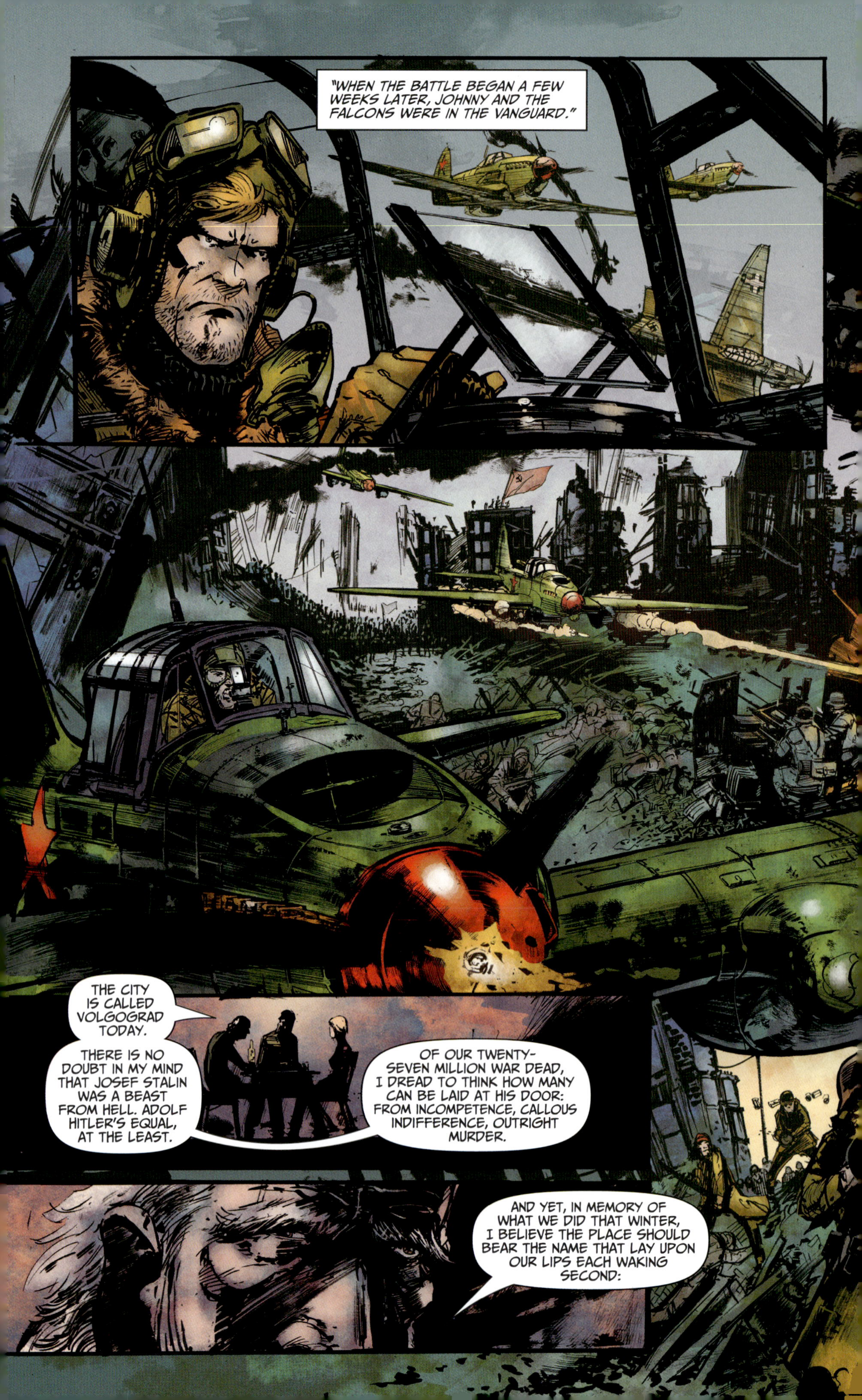
"WHEN THE BATTLE BEGAN A FEW WEEKS LATER, JOHNNY AND THE FALCONS WERE IN THE VANGUARD."
THE CITY IS CALLED VOLGOGRAD TODAY.
THERE IS NO DOUBT IN MY MIND THAT JOSEF STALIN WAS A BEAST FROM HELL. ADOLF HITLER'S EQUAL, AT THE LEAST.
OF OUR TWENTY-SEVEN MILLION WAR DEAD, I DREAD TO THINK HOW MANY CAN BE LAID AT HIS DOOR: FROM INCOMPETENCE, CALLOUS INDIFFERENCE, OUTRIGHT MURDER.
AND YET, IN MEMORY OF WHAT WE DID THAT WINTER, I BELIEVE THE PLACE SHOULD BEAR THE NAME THAT LAY UPON OUR LIPS EACH WAKING SECOND:

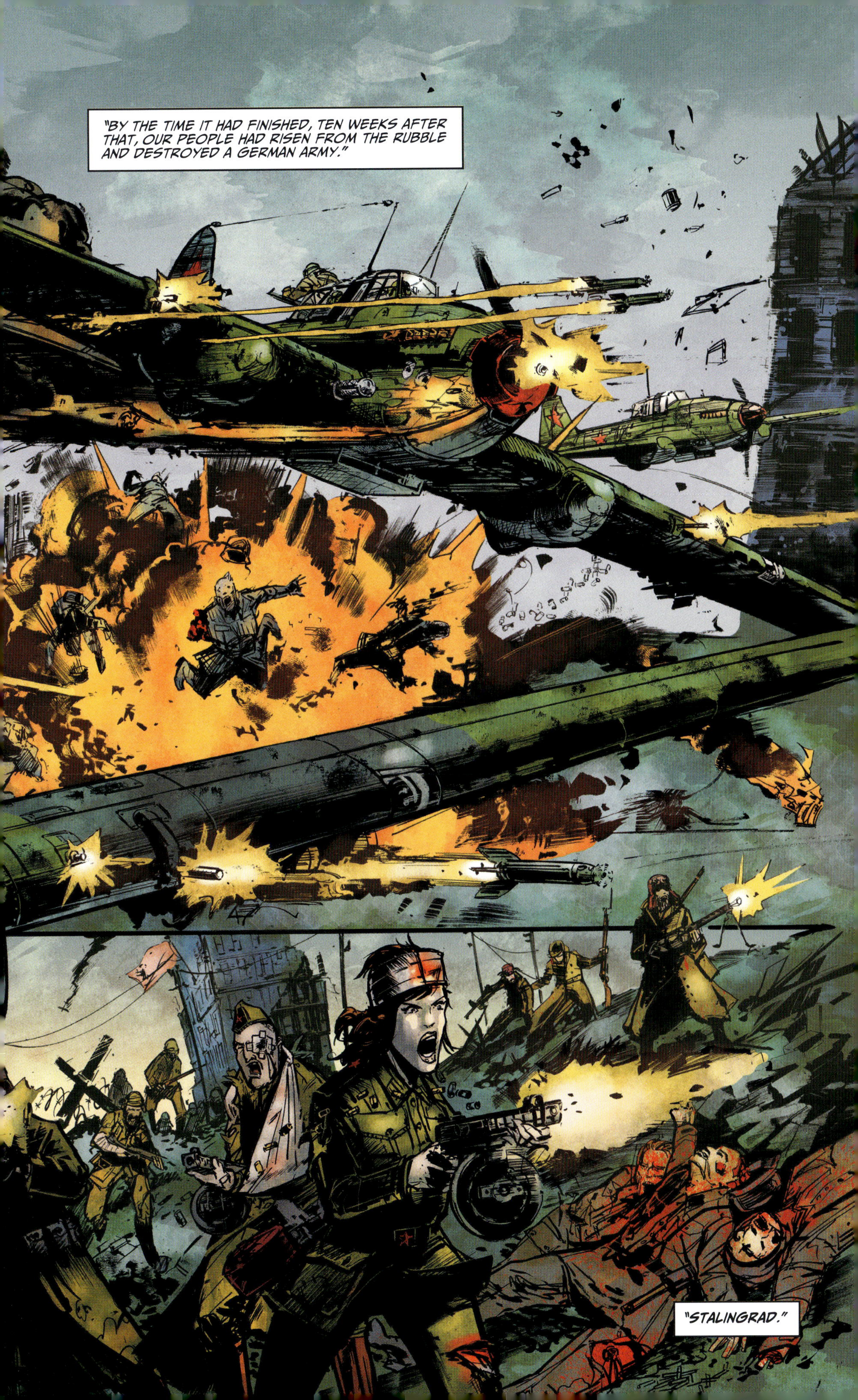
"BY THE TIME IT HAD FINISHED, TEN WEEKS AFTER THAT, OUR PEOPLE HAD RISEN FROM THE RUBBLE AND DESTROYED A GERMAN ARMY."
"STALINGRAD."

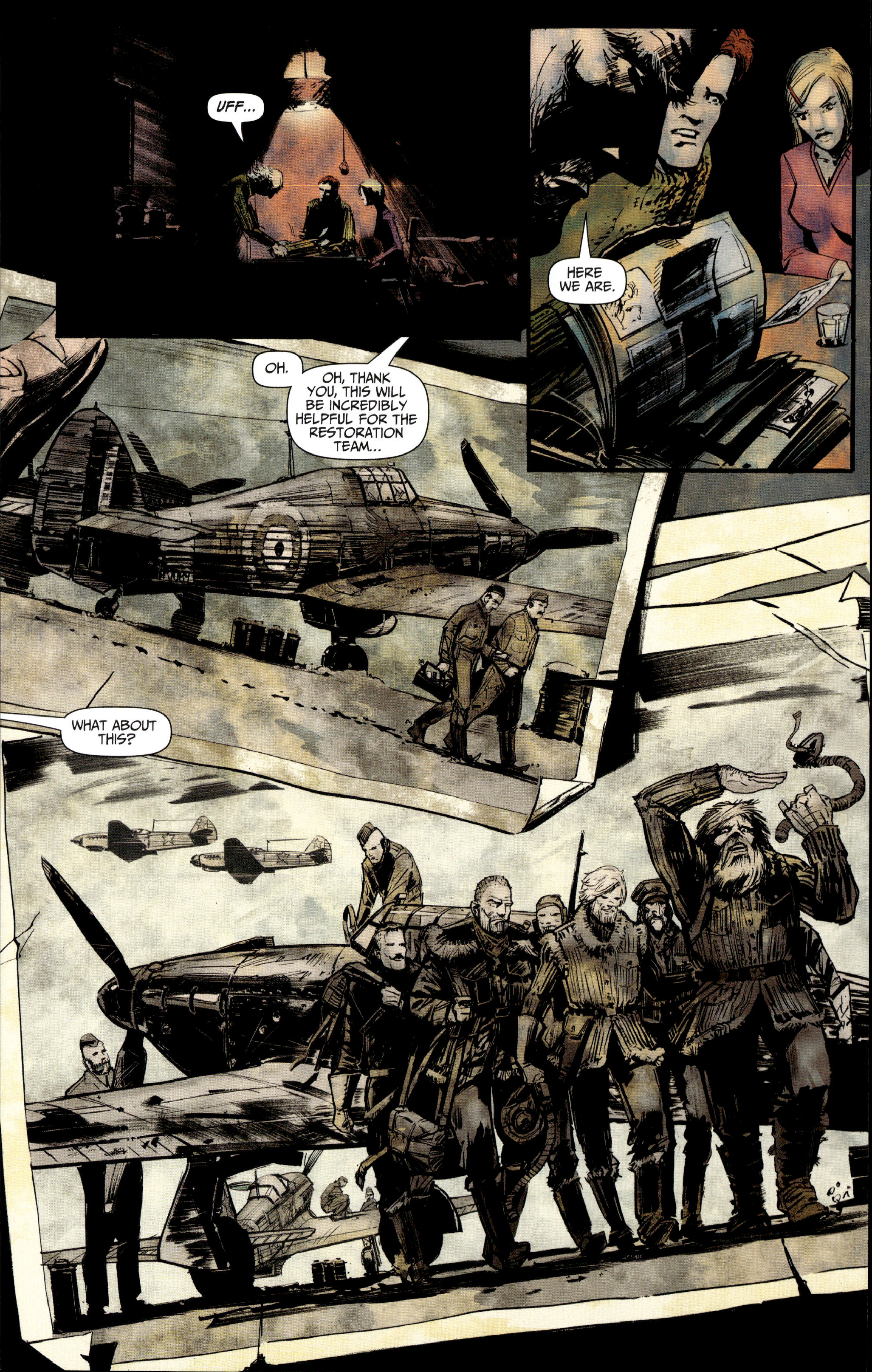
UFF...
HERE WE ARE.
OH.
OH, THANK YOU, THIS WILL BE INCREDIBLY HELPFUL FOR THE RESTORATION TEAM...
WHAT ABOUT THIS?

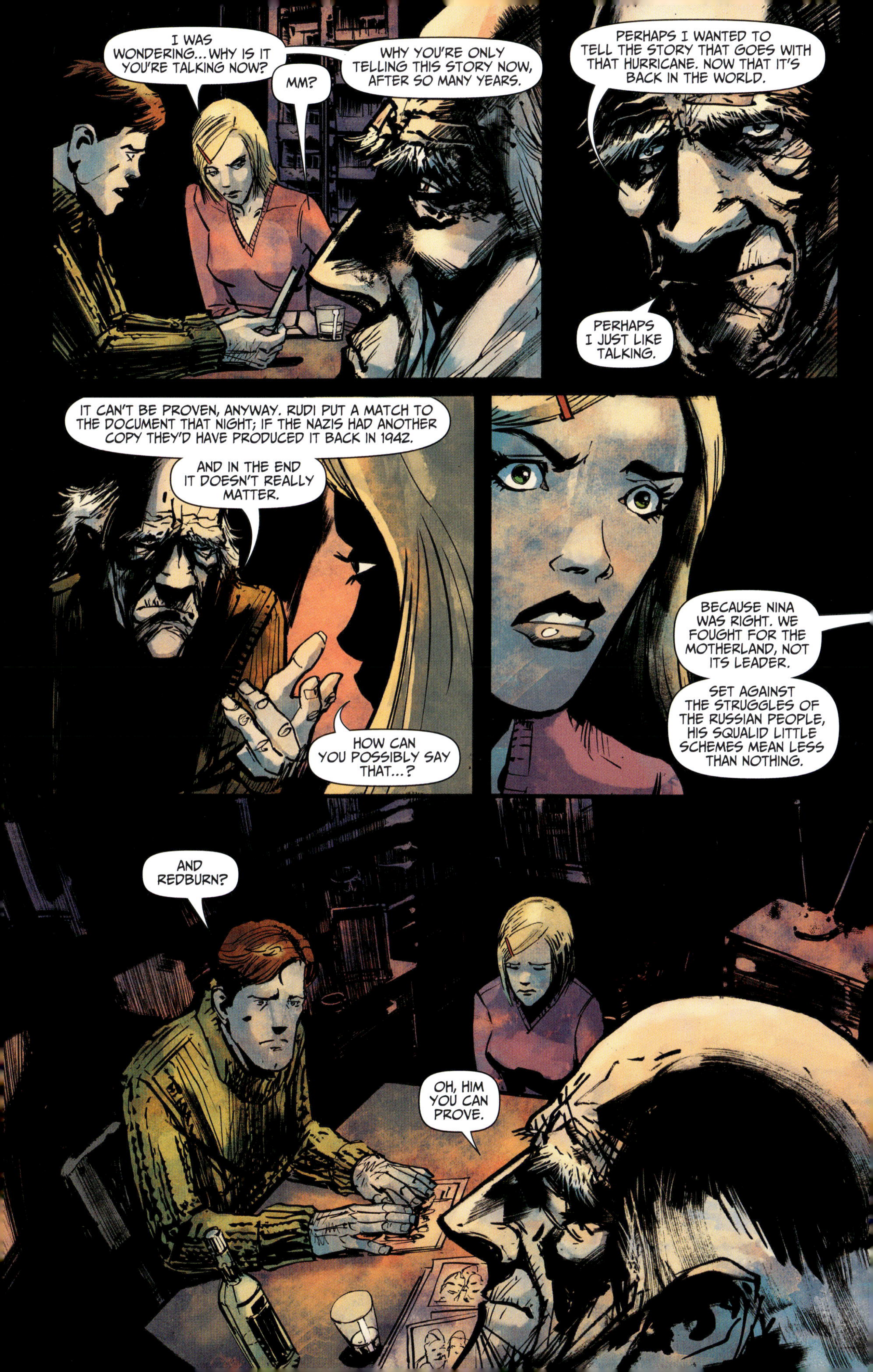
I WAS WONDERING... WHY IS IT YOU'RE TALKING NOW?
MM?
WHY YOU'RE ONLY TELLING THIS STORY NOW, AFTER SO MANY YEARS.
PERHAPS I WANTED TO TELL THE STORY THAT GOES WITH THAT HURRICANE. NOW THAT IT'S BACK IN THE WORLD.
PERHAPS I JUST LIKE TALKING.
IT CAN'T BE PROVEN, ANYWAY. RUDI PUT A MATCH TO THE DOCUMENT THAT NIGHT; IF THE NAZIS HAD ANOTHER COPY THEY'D HAVE PRODUCED IT BACK IN 1942.
AND IN THE END IT DOESN'T REALLY MATTER.
HOW CAN YOU POSSIBLY SAY THAT...?
BECAUSE NINA WAS RIGHT. WE FOUGHT FOR THE MOTHERLAND, NOT ITS LEADER.
SET AGAINST THE STRUGGLES OF THE RUSSIAN PEOPLE, HIS SQUALID LITTLE SCHEMES MEAN LESS THAN NOTHING.
AND REDBURN?
OH, HIM YOU CAN PROVE.

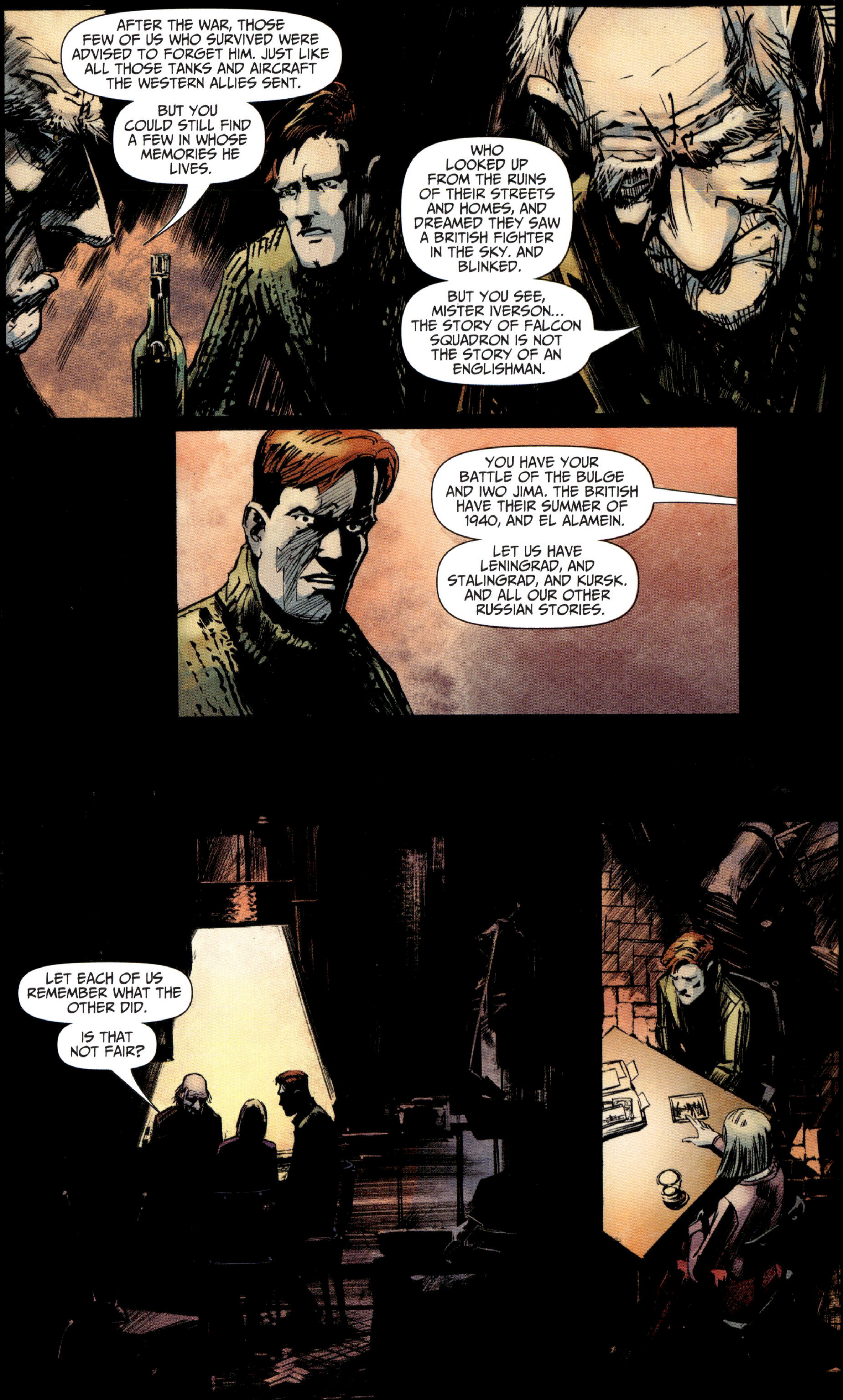
AFTER THE WAR, THOSE FEW OF US WHO SURVIVED WERE ADVISED TO FORGET HIM. JUST LIKE ALL THOSE TANKS AND AIRCRAFT THE WESTERN ALLIES SENT.
BUT YOU COULD STILL FIND A FEW IN WHOSE MEMORIES HE LIVES.
WHO LOOKED UP FROM THE RUINS OF THEIR STREETS AND HOMES, AND DREAMED THEY SAW A BRITISH FIGHTER IN THE SKY. AND BLINKED.
BUT YOU SEE, MISTER IVERSON... THE STORY OF FALCON SQUADRON IS NOT THE STORY OF AN ENGLISHMAN.
YOU HAVE YOUR BATTLE OF THE BULGE AND IWO JIMA. THE BRITISH HAVE THEIR SUMMER OF 1940, AND EL ALAMEIN.
LET US HAVE LENINGRAD, AND STALINGRAD, AND KURSK. AND ALL OUR OTHER RUSSIAN STORIES.
LET EACH OF US REMEMBER WHAT THE OTHER DID.
IS THAT NOT FAIR?

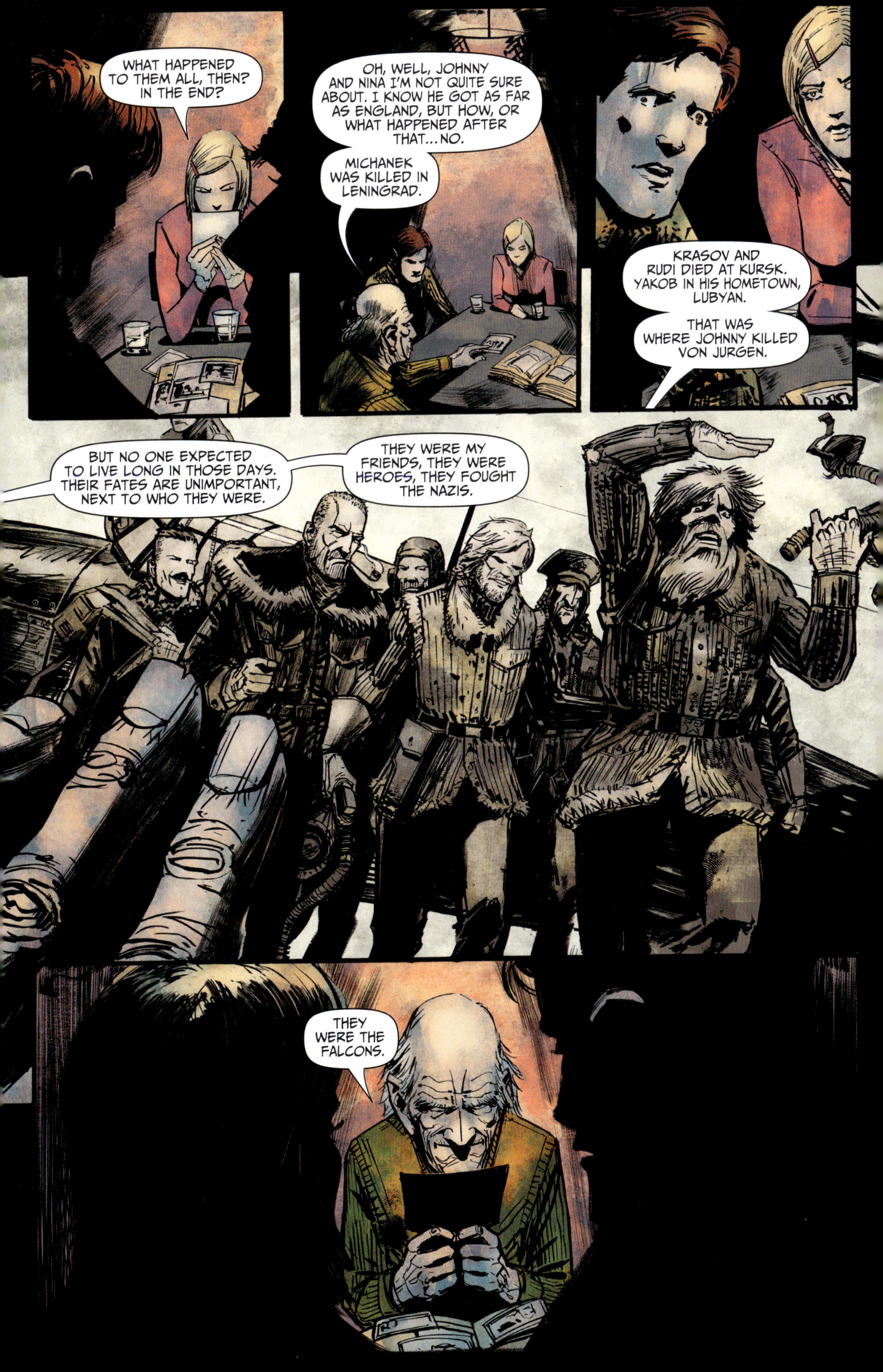
WHAT HAPPENED TO THEM ALL, THEN? IN THE END?
OH, WELL, JOHNNY AND NINA I'M NOT QUITE SURE ABOUT. I KNOW HE GOT AS FAR AS ENGLAND, BUT HOW, OR WHAT HAPPENED AFTER THAT... NO.
MICHANEK WAS KILLED IN LENINGRAD.
KRASOV AND RUDI DIED AT KURSK. YAKOB IN HIS HOMETOWN, LUBYAN.
THAT WAS WHERE JOHNNY KILLED VON JURGEN.
BUT NO ONE EXPECTED TO LIVE LONG IN THOSE DAYS. THEIR FATES ARE UNIMPORTANT, NEXT TO WHO THEY WERE.
THEY WERE MY FRIENDS, THEY WERE HEROES, THEY FOUGHT THE NAZIS.
THEY WERE THE FALCONS.

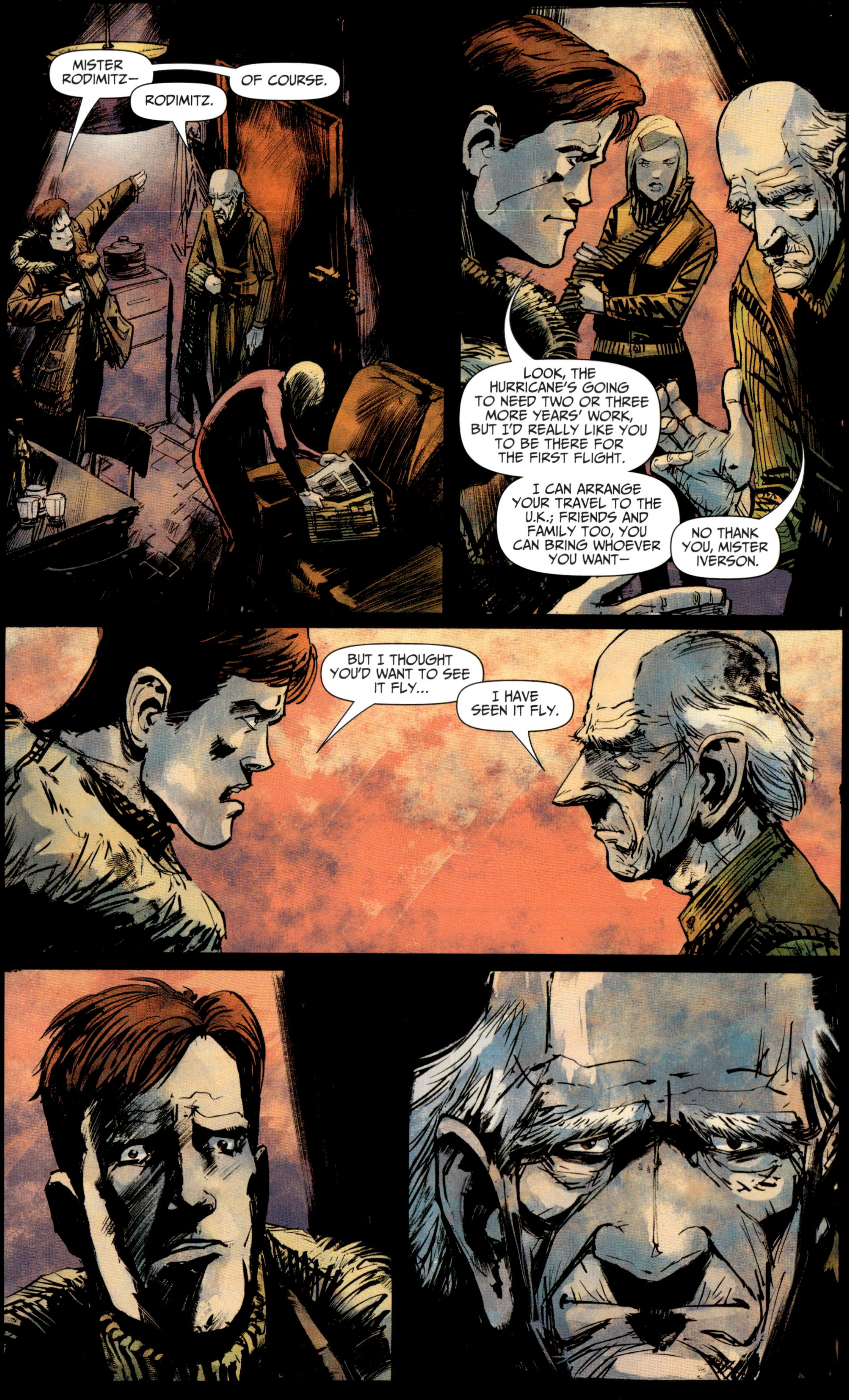
MISTER RODIMITZ—
RODIMITZ.
OF COURSE.
LOOK, THE HURRICANE'S GOING TO NEED TWO OR THREE MORE YEARS' WORK, BUT I'D REALLY LIKE YOU TO BE THERE FOR THE FIRST FLIGHT.
I CAN ARRANGE YOUR TRAVEL TO THE U.K.; FRIENDS AND FAMILY TOO, YOU CAN BRING WHOEVER YOU WANT—
NO THANK YOU, MISTER IVERSON.
BUT I THOUGHT YOU'D WANT TO SEE IT FLY...
I HAVE SEEN IT FLY.

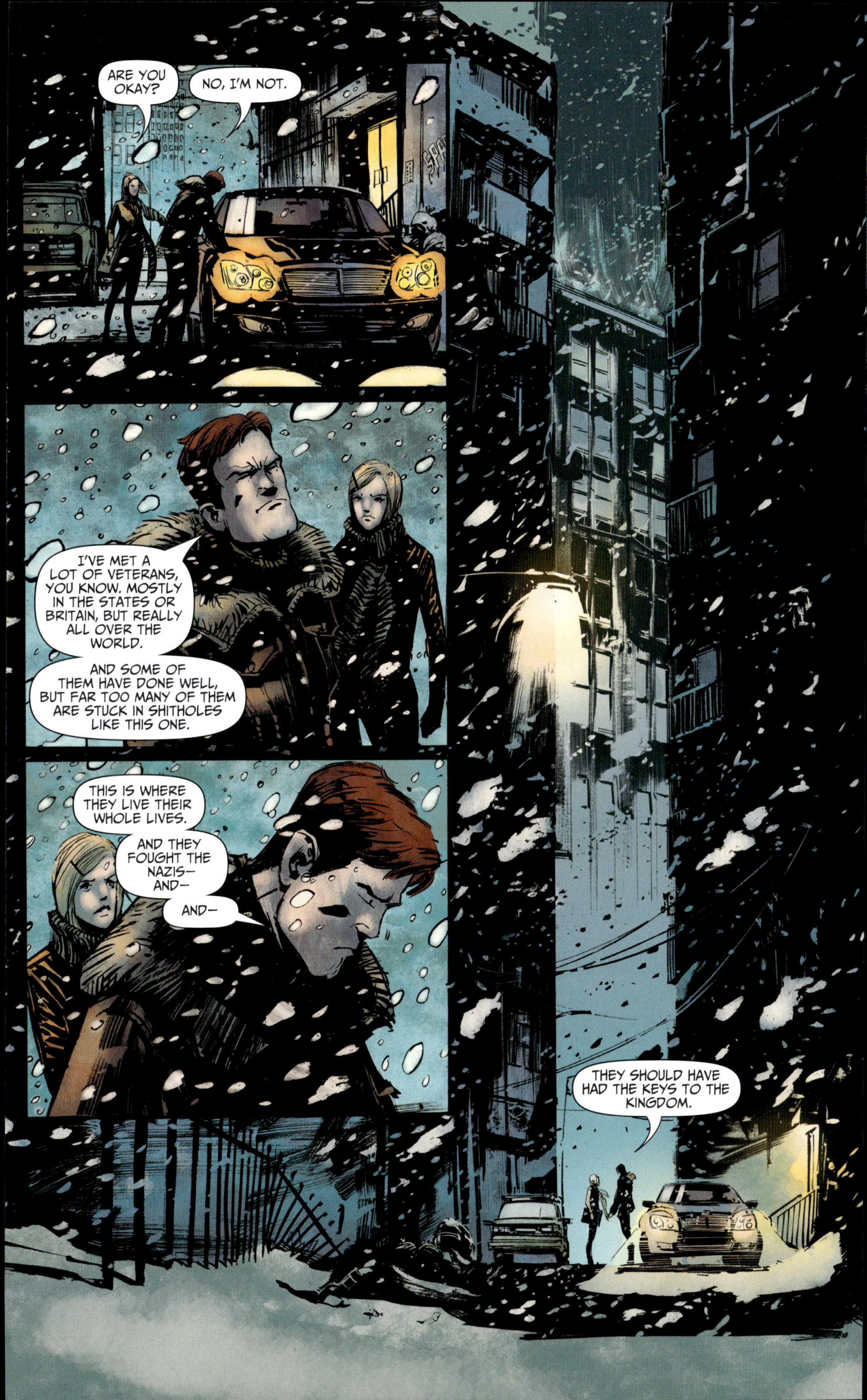
ARE YOU OKAY?
NO, I'M NOT.
I'VE MET A LOT OF VETERANS, YOU KNOW. MOSTLY IN THE STATES OR BRITAIN, BUT REALLY ALL OVER THE WORLD.
AND SOME OF THEM HAVE DONE WELL, BUT FAR TOO MANY OF THEM ARE STUCK IN SHITHOLES LIKE THIS ONE.
THIS IS WHERE THEY LIVE THEIR WHOLE LIVES.
AND THEY FOUGHT THE NAZIS— AND—
AND—
THEY SHOULD HAVE HAD THE KEYS TO THE KINGDOM.

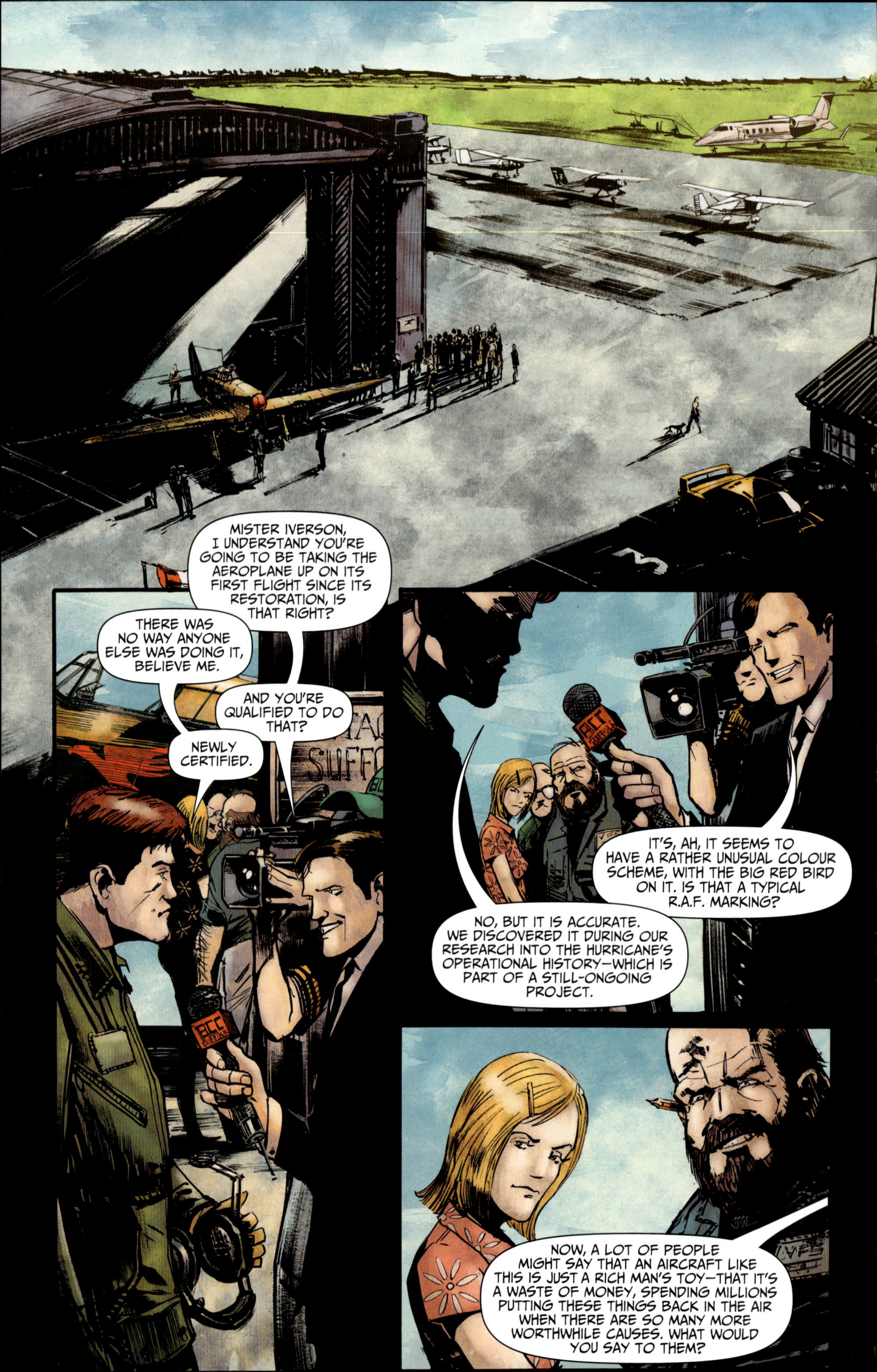
MISTER IVERSON, I UNDERSTAND YOU'RE GOING TO BE TAKING THE AEROPLANE UP ON ITS FIRST FLIGHT SINCE ITS RESTORATION, IS THAT RIGHT?
THERE WAS NO WAY ANYONE ELSE WAS DOING IT, BELIEVE ME.
AND YOU'RE QUALIFIED TO DO THAT?
NEWLY CERTIFIED.
IT'S, AH, IT SEEMS TO HAVE A RATHER UNUSUAL COLOUR SCHEME, WITH THE BIG RED BIRD ON IT. IS THAT A TYPICAL R.A.F. MARKING?
NO, BUT IT IS ACCURATE. WE DISCOVERED IT DURING OUR RESEARCH INTO THE HURRICANE'S OPERATIONAL HISTORY—WHICH IS PART OF A STILL-ONGOING PROJECT.
NOW, A LOT OF PEOPLE MIGHT SAY THAT AN AIRCRAFT LIKE THIS IS JUST A RICH MAN'S TOY—THAT IT'S A WASTE OF MONEY, SPENDING MILLIONS PUTTING THESE THINGS BACK IN THE AIR WHEN THERE ARE SO MANY MORE WORTHWHILE CAUSES. WHAT WOULD YOU SAY TO THEM?

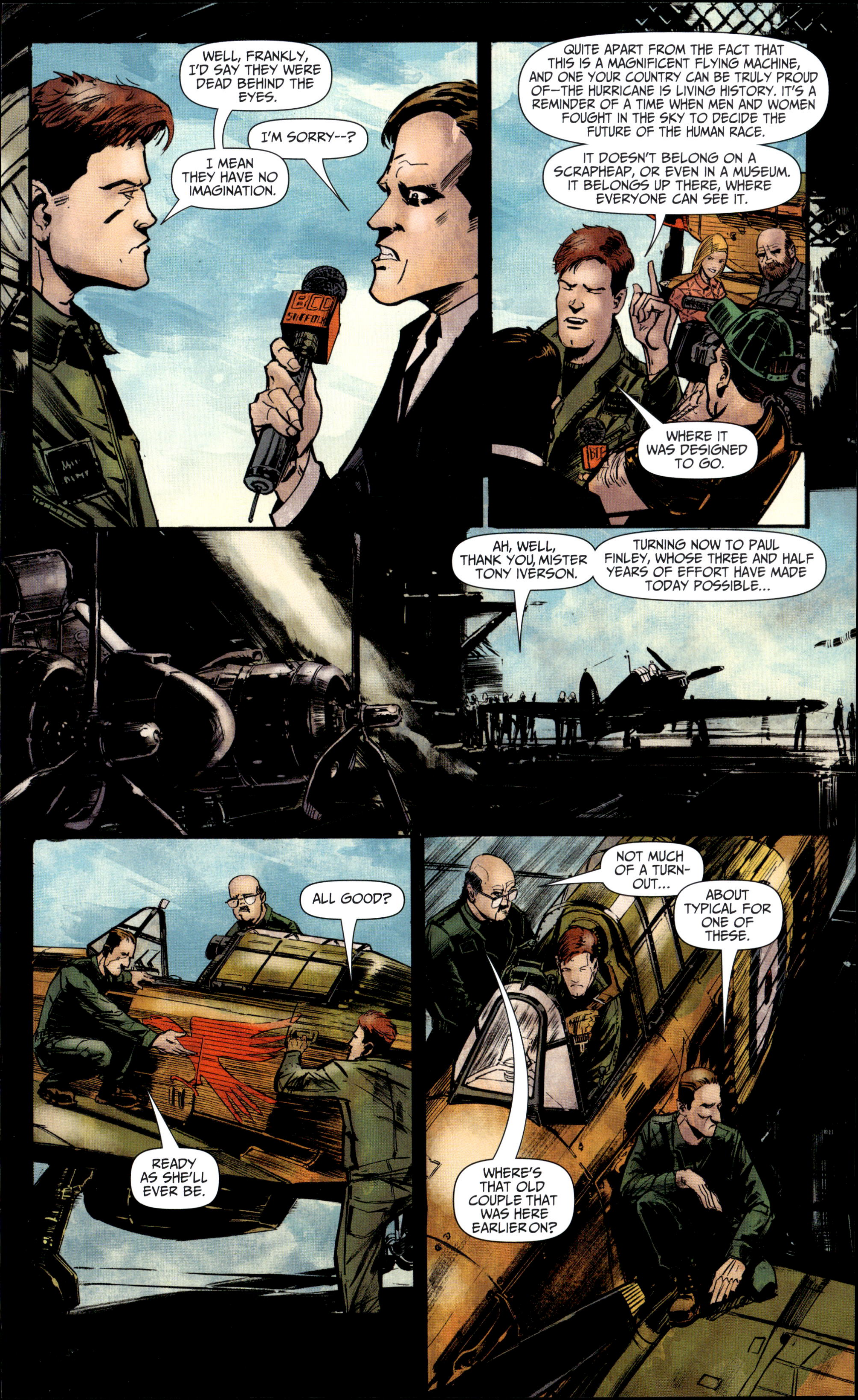
WELL, FRANKLY, I'D SAY THEY WERE DEAD BEHIND THE EYES.
I'M SORRY--?
I MEAN THEY HAVE NO IMAGINATION.
QUITE APART FROM THE FACT THAT THIS IS A MAGNIFICENT FLYING MACHINE, AND ONE YOUR COUNTRY CAN BE TRULY PROUD OF—THE HURRICANE IS LIVING HISTORY. IT'S A REMINDER OF A TIME WHEN MEN AND WOMEN FOUGHT IN THE SKY TO DECIDE THE FUTURE OF THE HUMAN RACE.
IT DOESN'T BELONG ON A SCRAPHEAP, OR EVEN IN A MUSEUM. IT BELONGS UP THERE, WHERE EVERYONE CAN SEE IT.
WHERE IT WAS DESIGNED TO GO.
AH, WELL, THANK YOU, MISTER TONY IVERSON.
TURNING NOW TO PAUL FINLEY, WHOSE THREE AND HALF YEARS OF EFFORT HAVE MADE TODAY POSSIBLE...
ALL GOOD?
READY AS SHE'LL EVER BE.
NOT MUCH OF A TURN-OUT...
ABOUT TYPICAL FOR ONE OF THESE.
WHERE'S THAT OLD COUPLE THAT WAS HERE EARLIER ON?

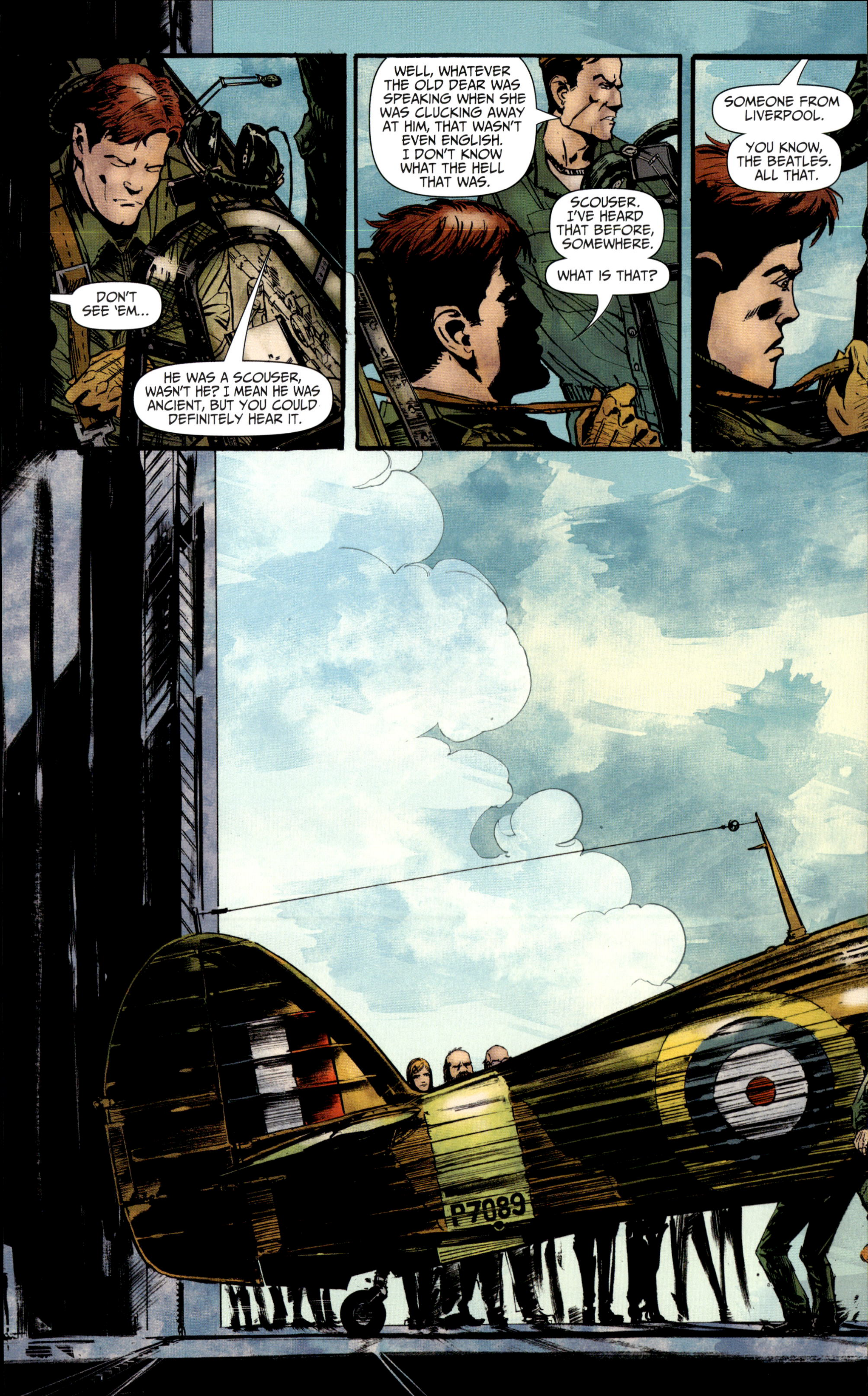
DON'T SEE 'EM...
HE WAS A SCOUSER, WASN'T HE? I MEAN HE WAS ANCIENT, BUT YOU COULD DEFINITELY HEAR IT.
WELL, WHATEVER THE OLD DEAR WAS SPEAKING WHEN SHE WAS CLUCKING AWAY AT HIM, THAT WASN'T EVEN ENGLISH. I DON'T KNOW WHAT THE HELL THAT WAS.
SCOUSER. I'VE HEARD THAT BEFORE, SOMEWHERE.
WHAT IS THAT?
SOMEONE FROM LIVERPOOL.
YOU KNOW, THE BEATLES. ALL THAT.
P7089

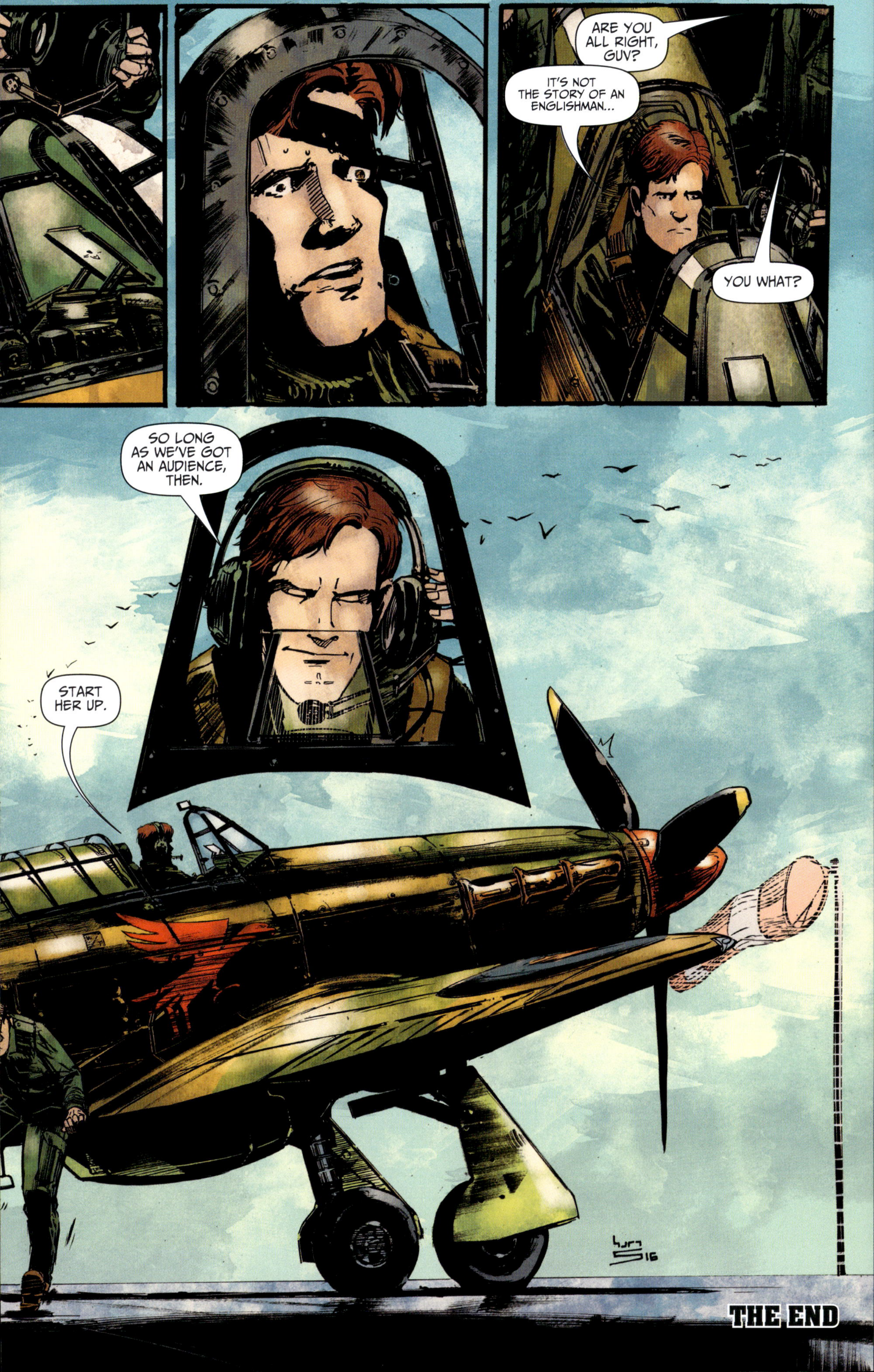
ARE YOU ALL RIGHT, GUV?
IT'S NOT THE STORY OF AN ENGLISHMAN...
YOU WHAT?
SO LONG AS WE'VE GOT AN AUDIENCE, THEN.
START HER UP.
THE END

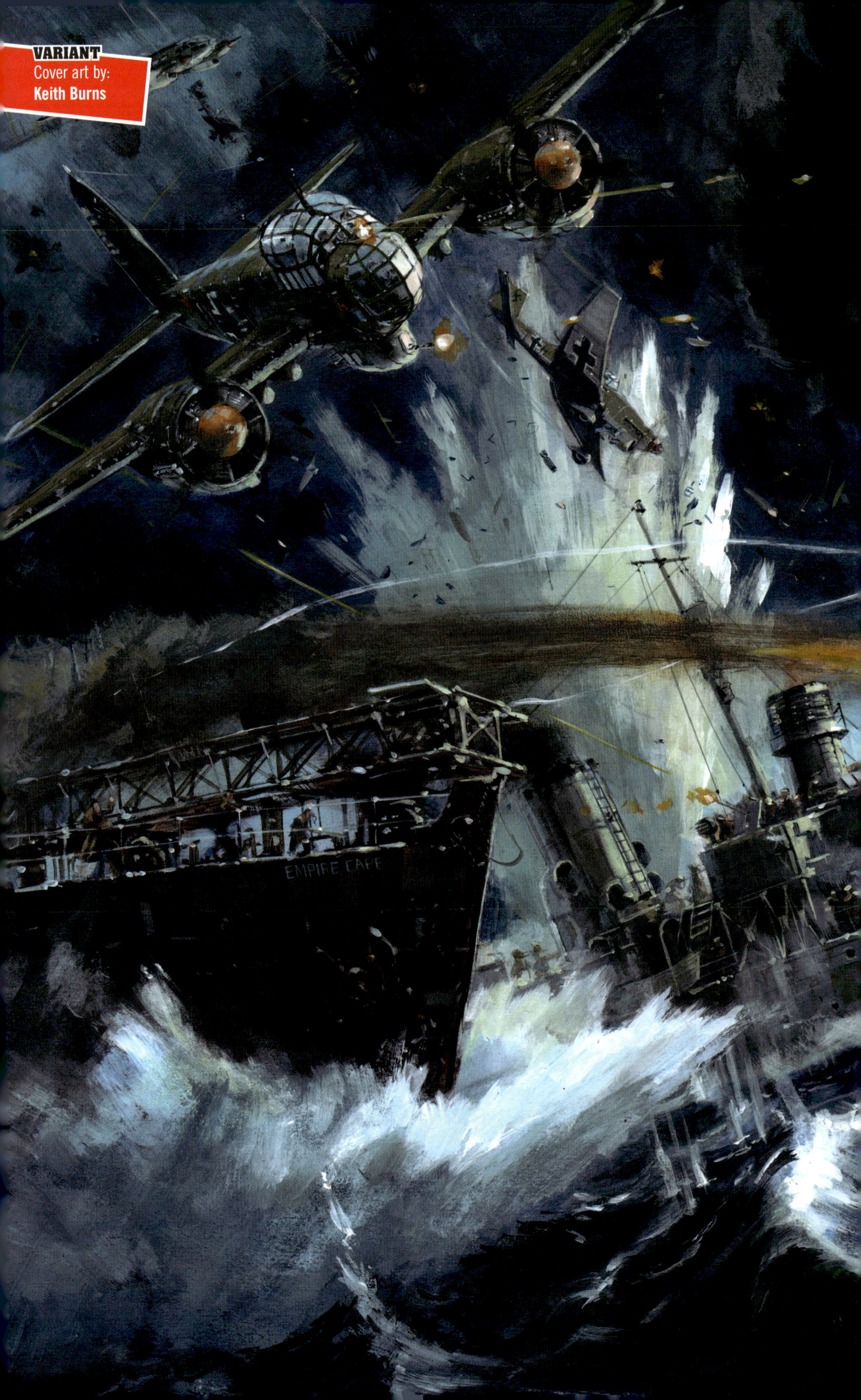

VARIANT
Cover art by:
Keith Burns

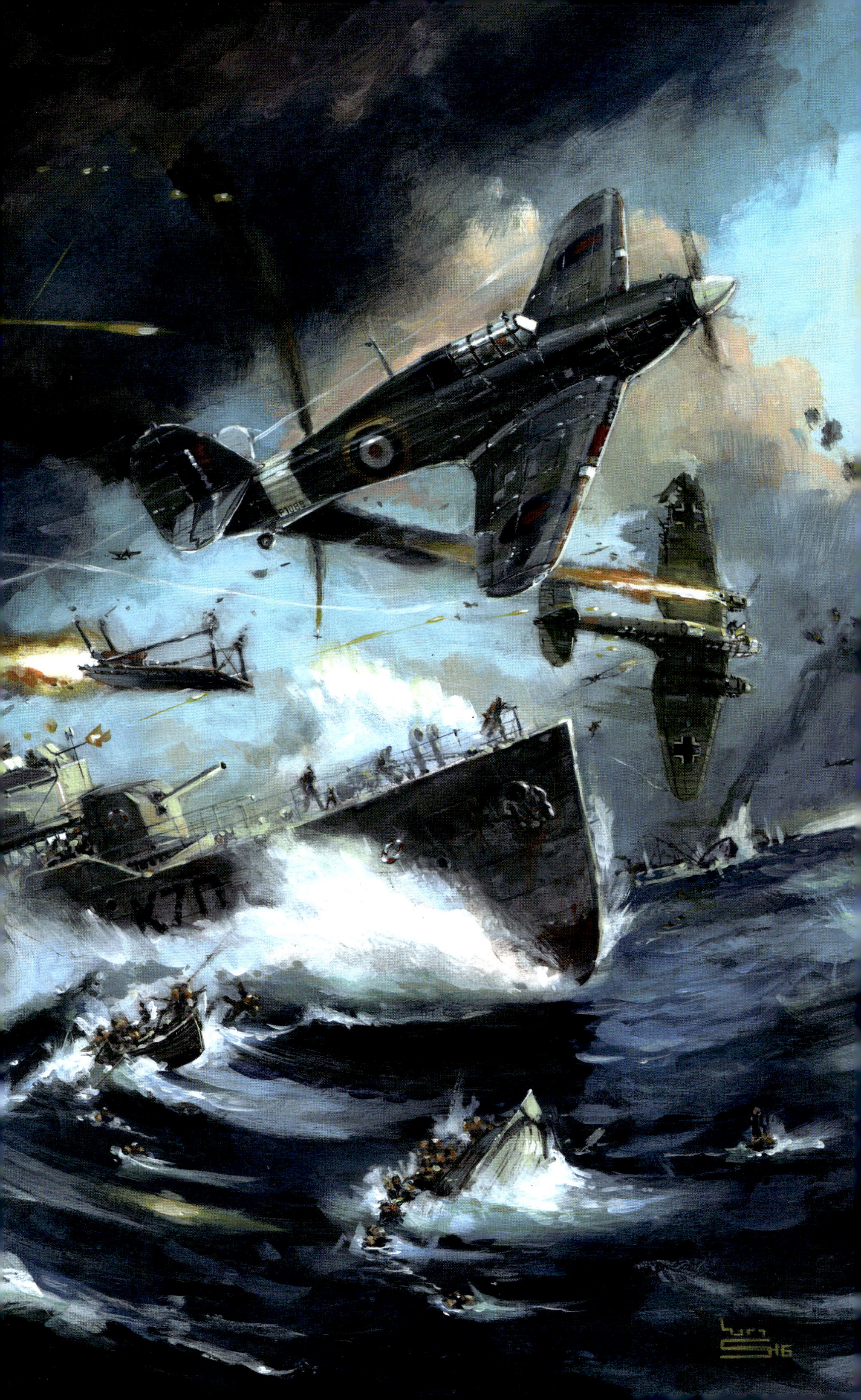

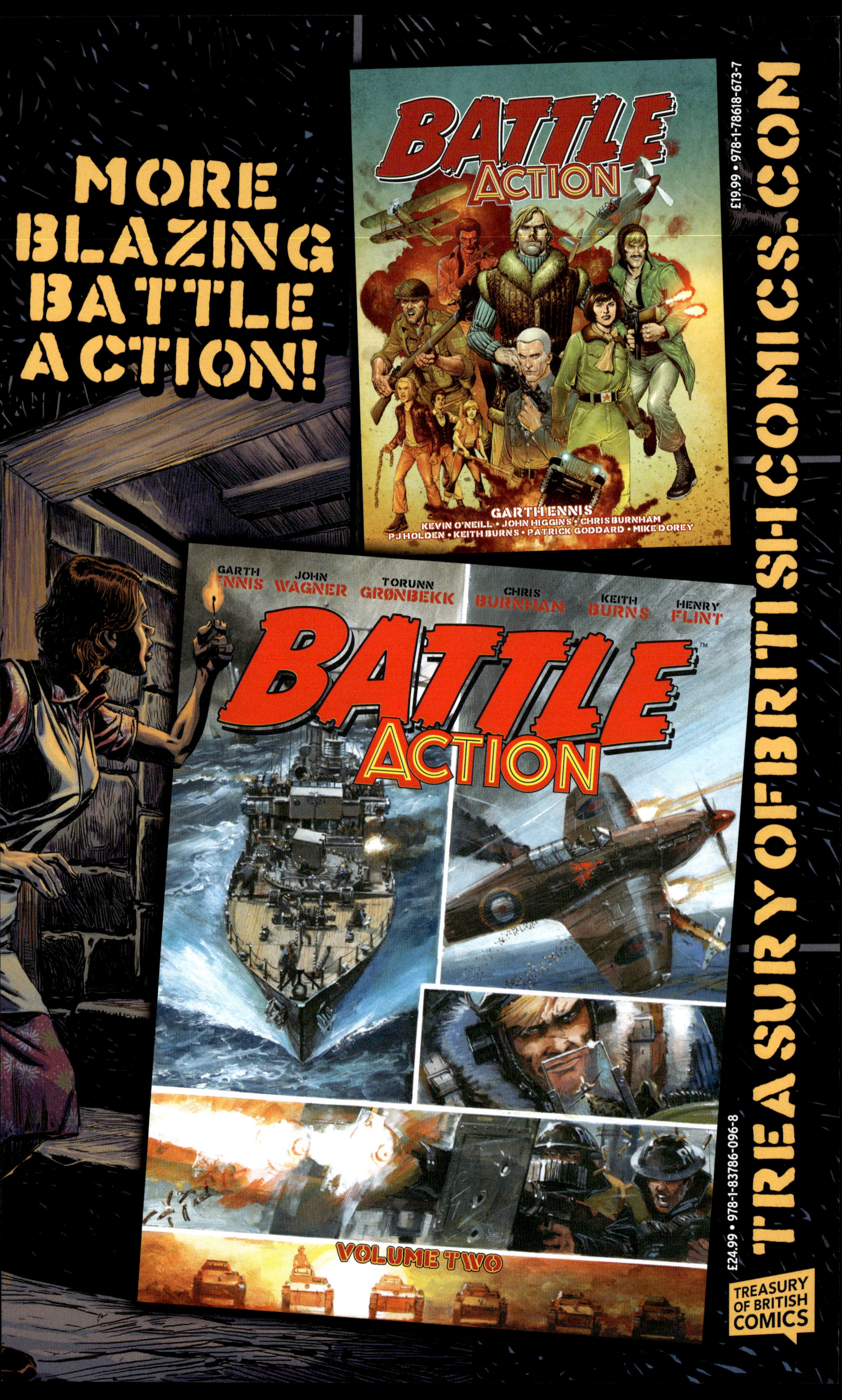
MORE BLAZING BATTLE ACTION!
BATTLE ACTION
GARTH ENNIS
KEVIN O'NEILL • JOHN HIGGINS • CHRIS BURNHAM
PJ HOLDEN • KEITH BURNS • PATRICK GODDARD • MIKE DOREY
£19.99 • 978-1-78618-673-7
GARTH ENNIS
JOHN WAGNER
TORUNN GRØNBEKK
CHRIS BURNHAM
KEITH BURNS
HENRY FLINT
BATTLE ACTION
VOLUME TWO
£24.99 • 978-1-83786-096-8
TREASURYOFBRITISHCOMICS.COM
TREASURY OF BRITISH COMICS

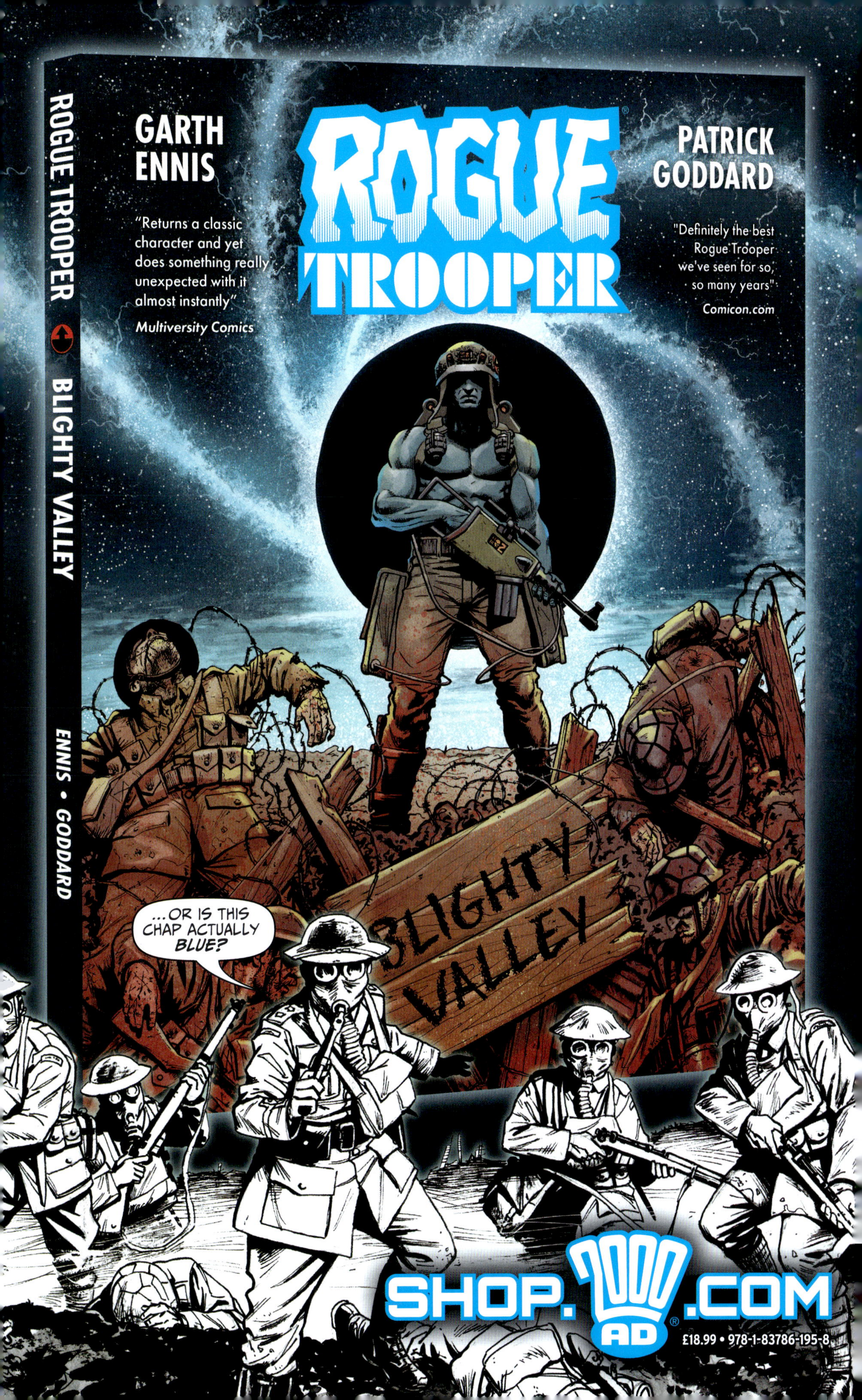
ROGUE TROOPER
BLIGHTY VALLEY
ENNIS • GODDARD
GARTH ENNIS
"Returns a classic character and yet does something really unexpected with it almost instantly"
Multiversity Comics
ROGUE TROOPER
PATRICK GODDARD
"Definitely the best Rogue Trooper we've seen for so, so many years"
Comicon.com
BLIGHTY VALLEY
...OR IS THIS CHAP ACTUALLY BLUE?
SHOP.2000AD.COM
£18.99 • 978-1-83786-195-8

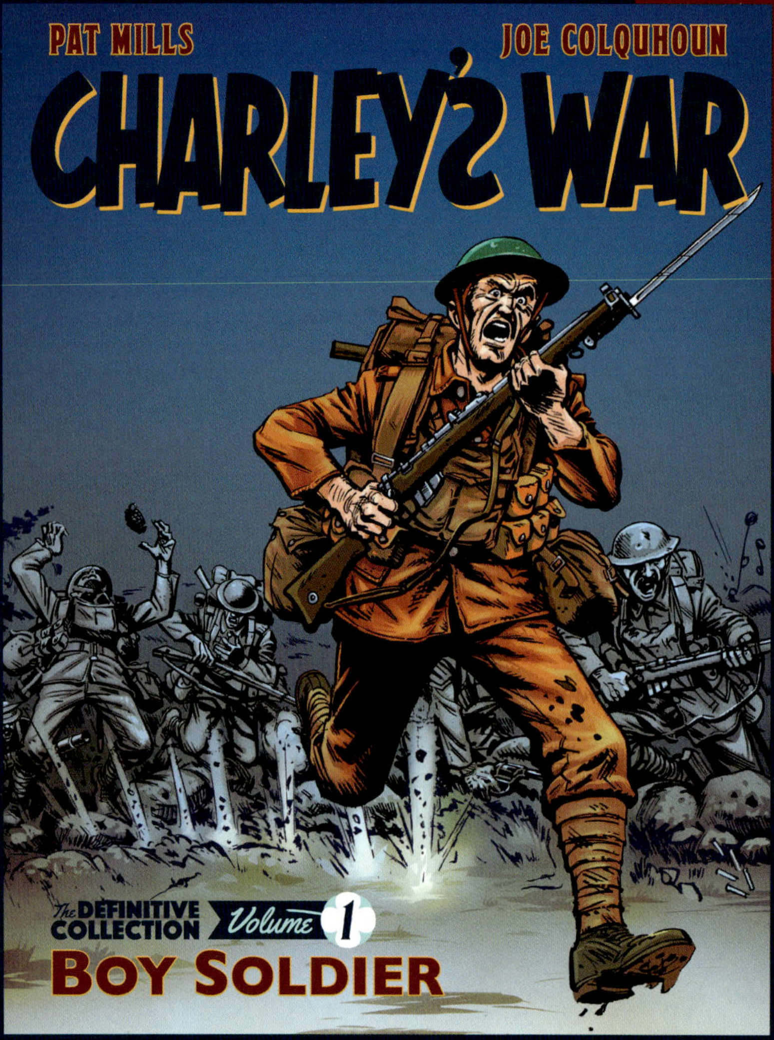
PAT MILLS
JOE COLQUHOUN
CHARLEY'S WAR
The DEFINITIVE COLLECTION
Volume 1
BOY SOLDIER

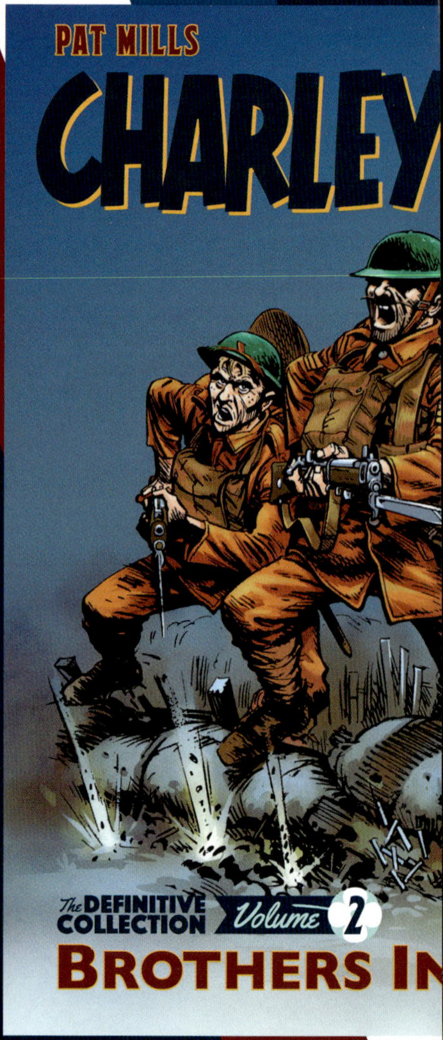
PAT MILLS
CHARLEY
The DEFINITIVE COLLECTION
Volume 2
BROTHERS I

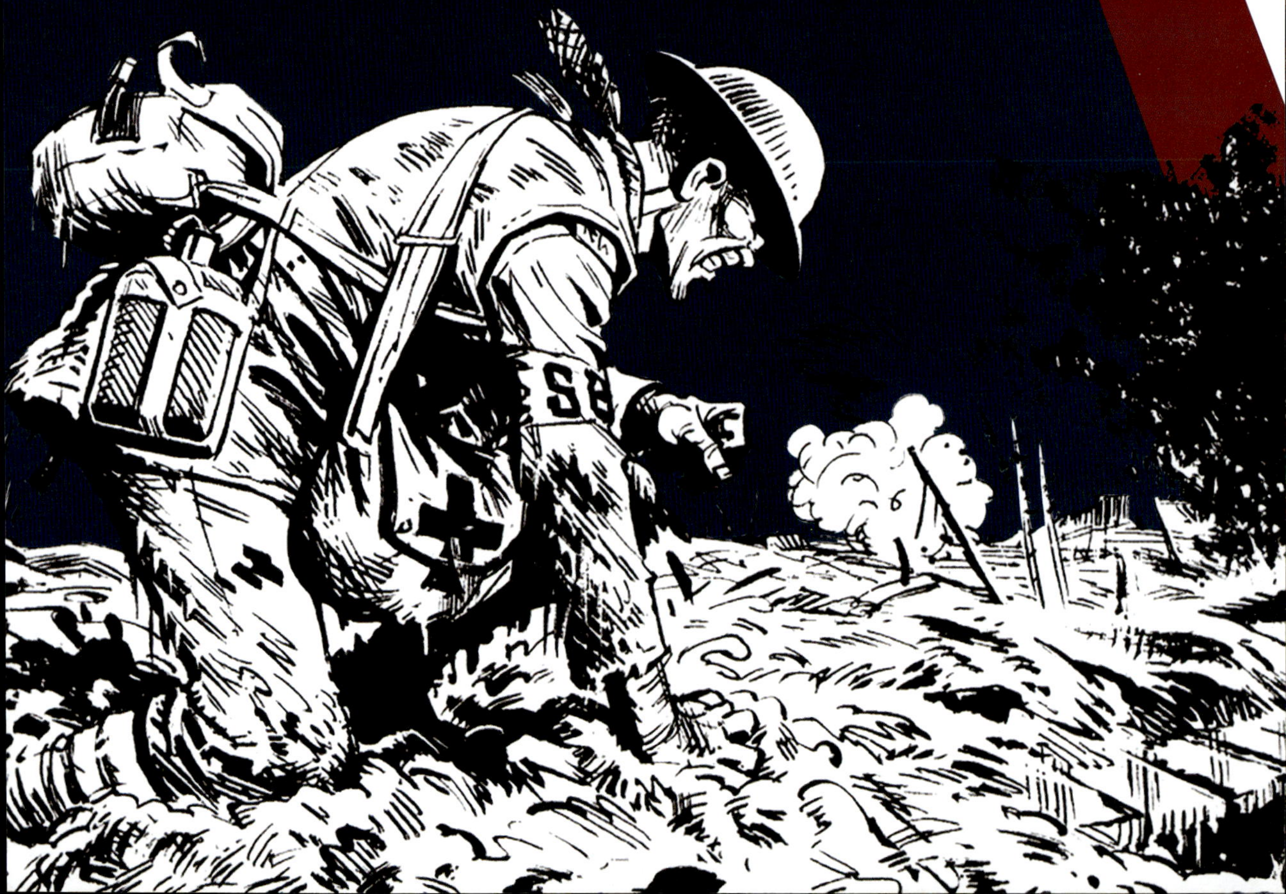
SB

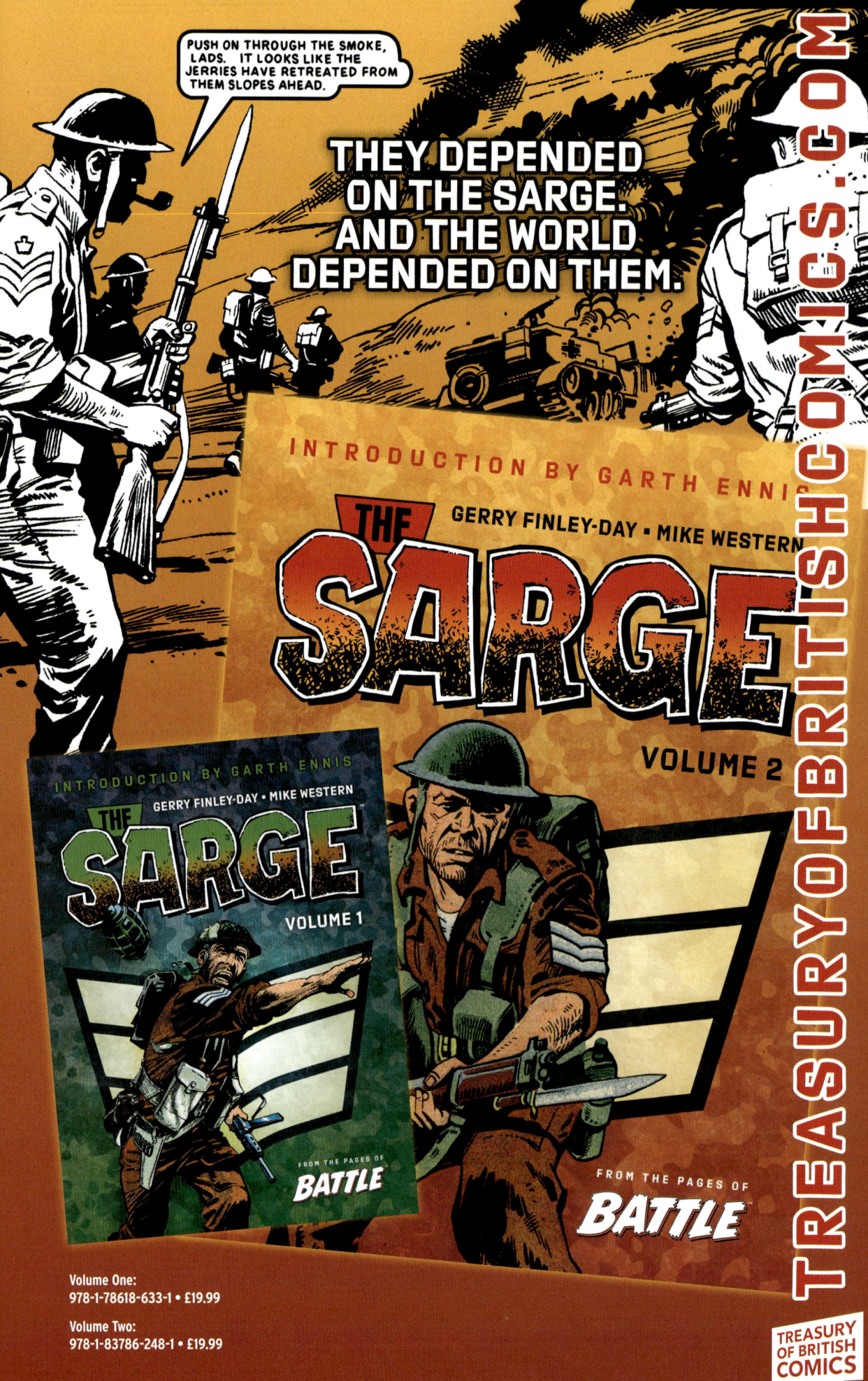

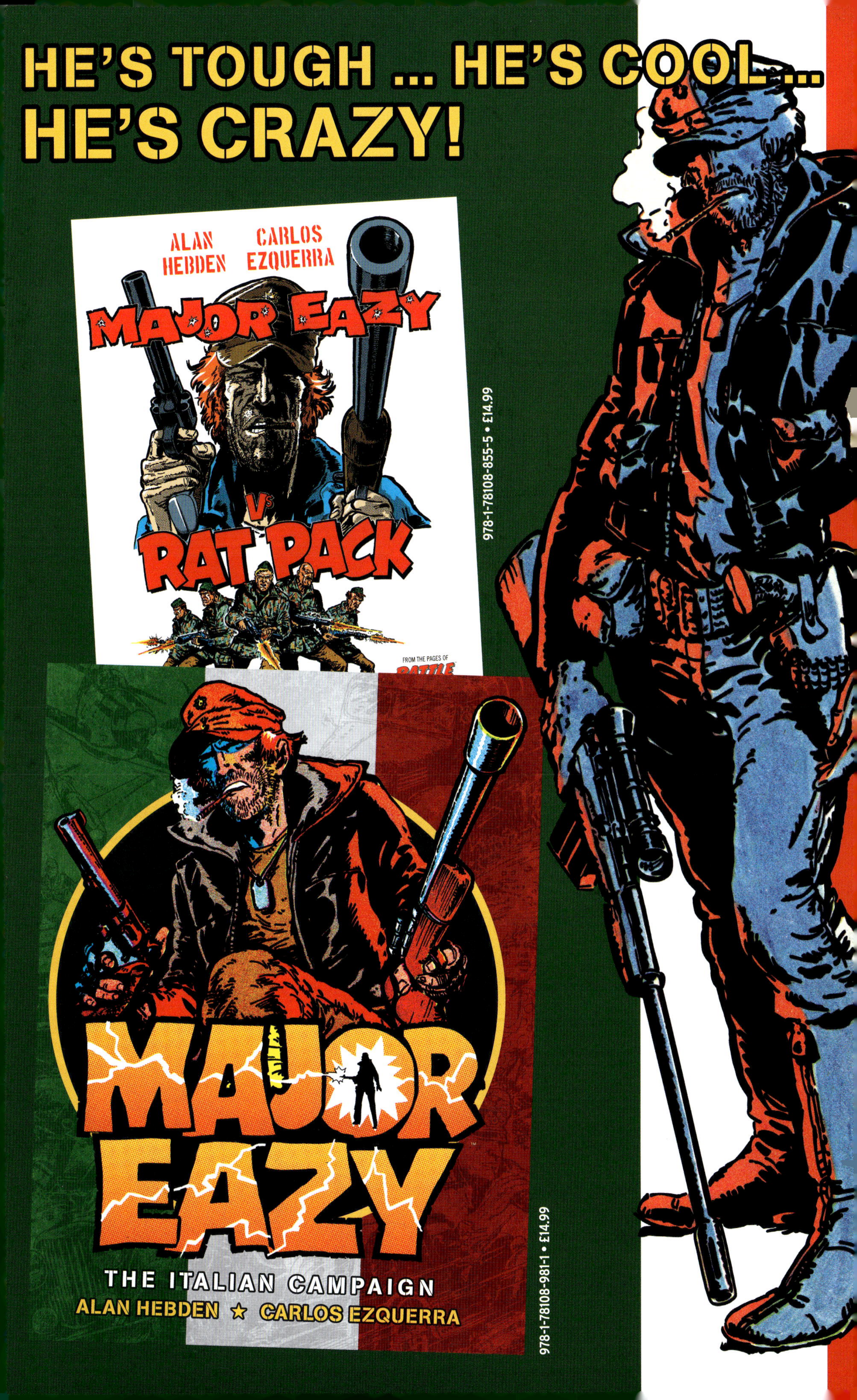
HE'S TOUGH ... HE'S COOL ...
HE'S CRAZY!
ALAN HEBDEN
CARLOS EZQUERRA
MAJOR EAZY
VS
RAT PACK
FROM THE PAGES OF
978-1-78108-855-5 • £14.99
MAJOR EAZY
THE ITALIAN CAMPAIGN
ALAN HEBDEN ★ CARLOS EZQUERRA
978-1-78108-981-1 • £14.99

HELLMAN ON THE RUSSIAN FRONT!

Hammer Force:
978-1-78108-942-2 • £12.99

Downfall:
978-1-83786-098-2 • £14.99

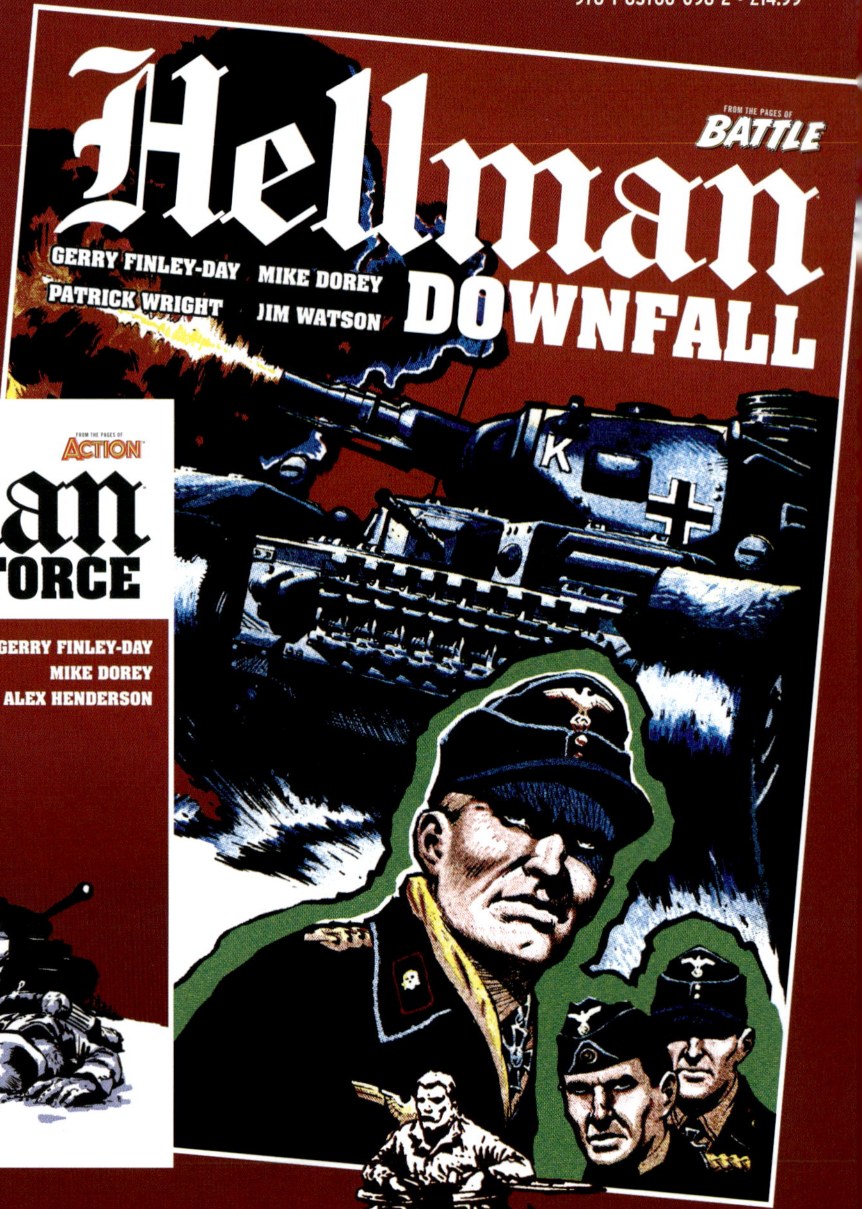

FROM THE PAGES OF
BATTLE
Hellman
GERRY FINLEY-DAY
MIKE DOREY
PATRICK WRIGHT
JIM WATSON
DOWNFALL

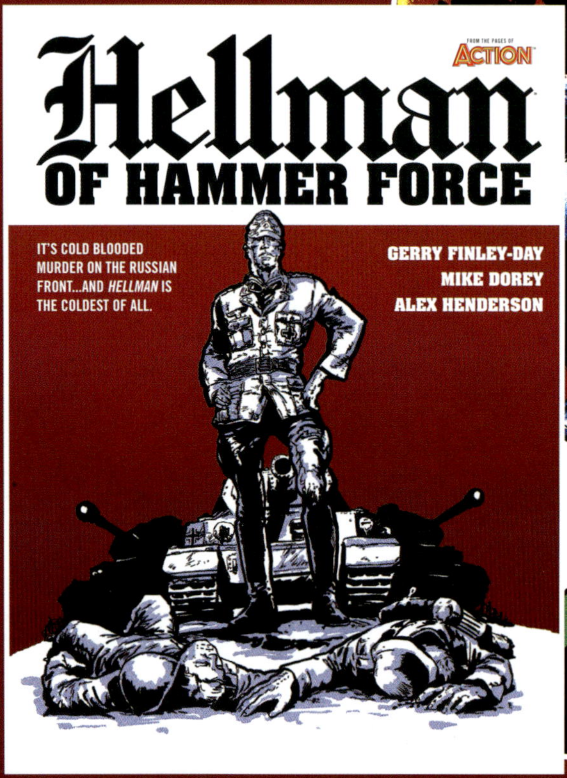

FROM THE PAGES OF
ACTION
Hellman
OF HAMMER FORCE
IT'S COLD BLOODED MURDER ON THE RUSSIAN FRONT...AND HELLMAN IS THE COLDEST OF ALL.
GERRY FINLEY-DAY
MIKE DOREY
ALEX HENDERSON

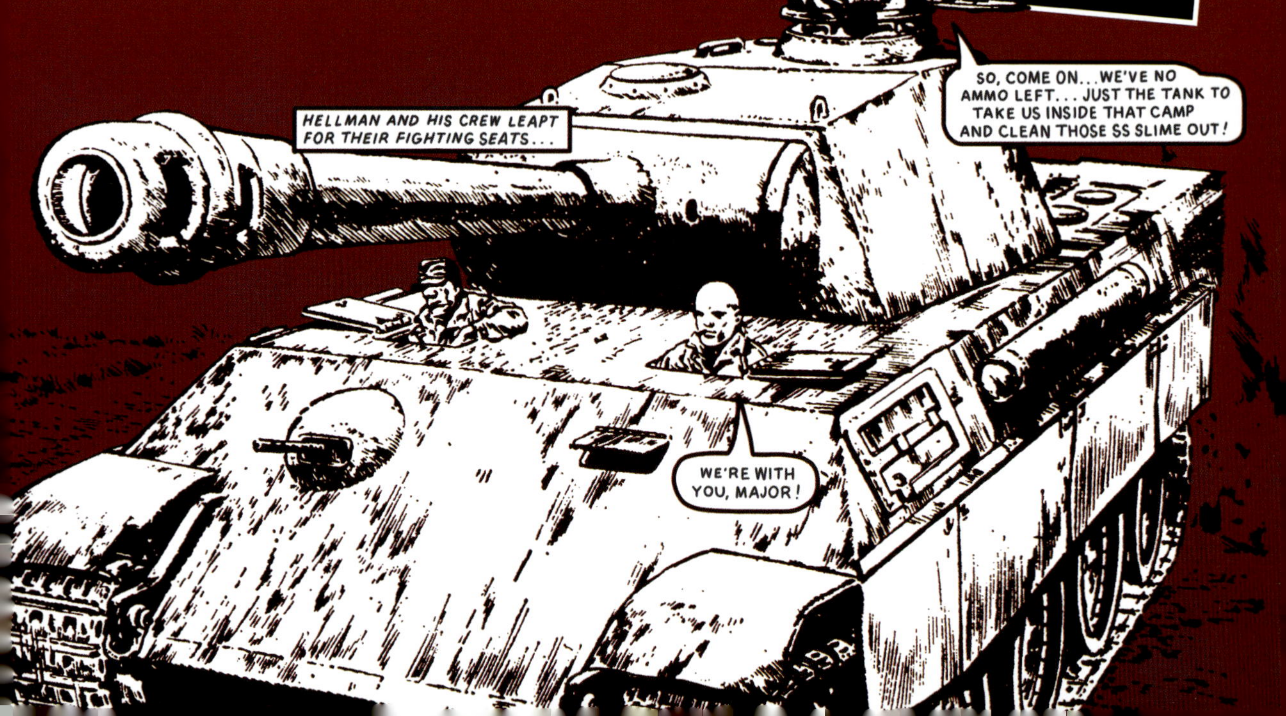

HELLMAN AND HIS CREW LEAPT FOR THEIR FIGHTING SEATS...
SO, COME ON...WE'VE NO AMMO LEFT... JUST THE TANK TO TAKE US INSIDE THAT CAMP AND CLEAN THOSE SS SLIME OUT!
WE'RE WITH YOU, MAJOR!

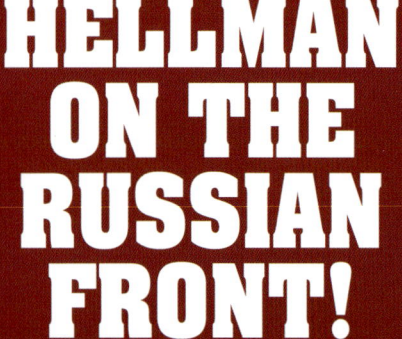

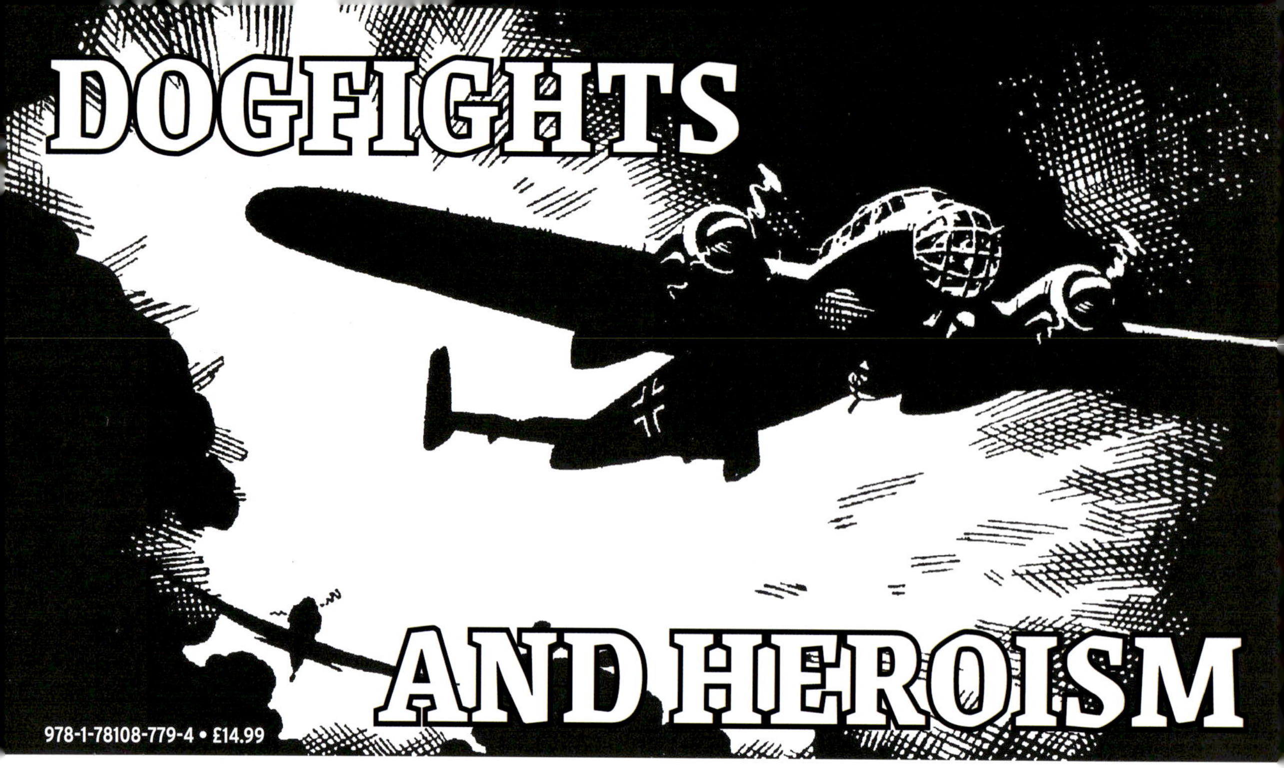
DOGFIGHTS
AND HEROISM
978-1-78108-779-4 • £14.99

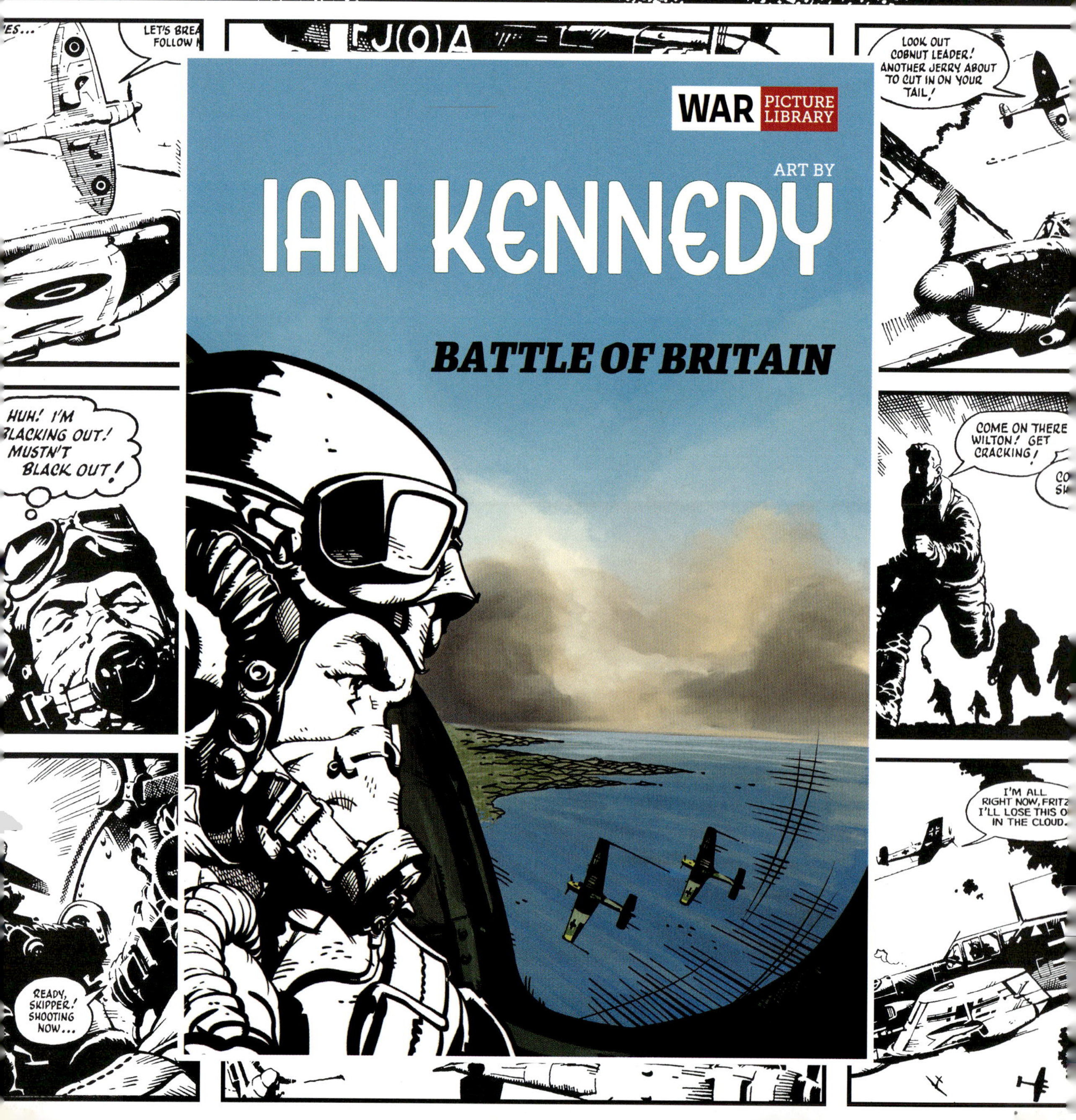
LOOK OUT COBNUT LEADER! ANOTHER JERRY ABOUT TO CUT IN ON YOUR TAIL!
WAR PICTURE LIBRARY
ART BY
IAN KENNEDY
BATTLE OF BRITAIN
COME ON THERE WILTON! GET CRACKING!
I'M ALL RIGHT NOW, FRITZ
READY, SKIPPER! SHOOTING NOW...

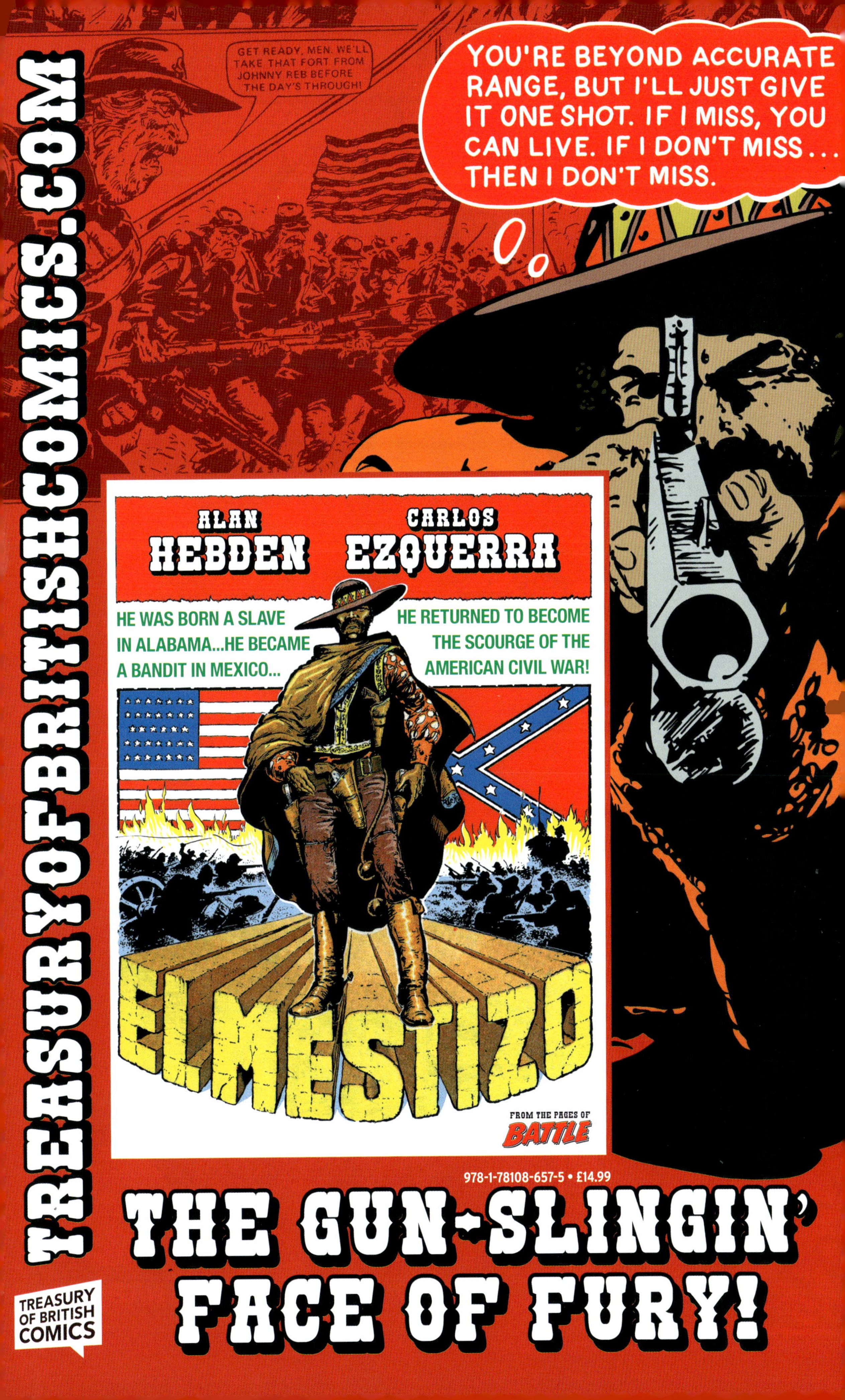

GET READY, MEN. WE'LL TAKE THAT FORT FROM JOHNNY REB BEFORE THE DAY'S THROUGH!
YOU'RE BEYOND ACCURATE RANGE, BUT I'LL JUST GIVE IT ONE SHOT. IF I MISS, YOU CAN LIVE. IF I DON'T MISS... THEN I DON'T MISS.
TREASURYOFBRITISHCOMICS.COM
ALAN HEBDEN
CARLOS EZQUERRA
HE WAS BORN A SLAVE IN ALABAMA...HE BECAME A BANDIT IN MEXICO...
HE RETURNED TO BECOME THE SCOURGE OF THE AMERICAN CIVIL WAR!
EL MESTIZO
FROM THE PAGES OF BATTLE
978-1-78108-657-5 • £14.99
THE GUN-SLINGIN' FACE OF FURY!
TREASURY OF BRITISH COMICS

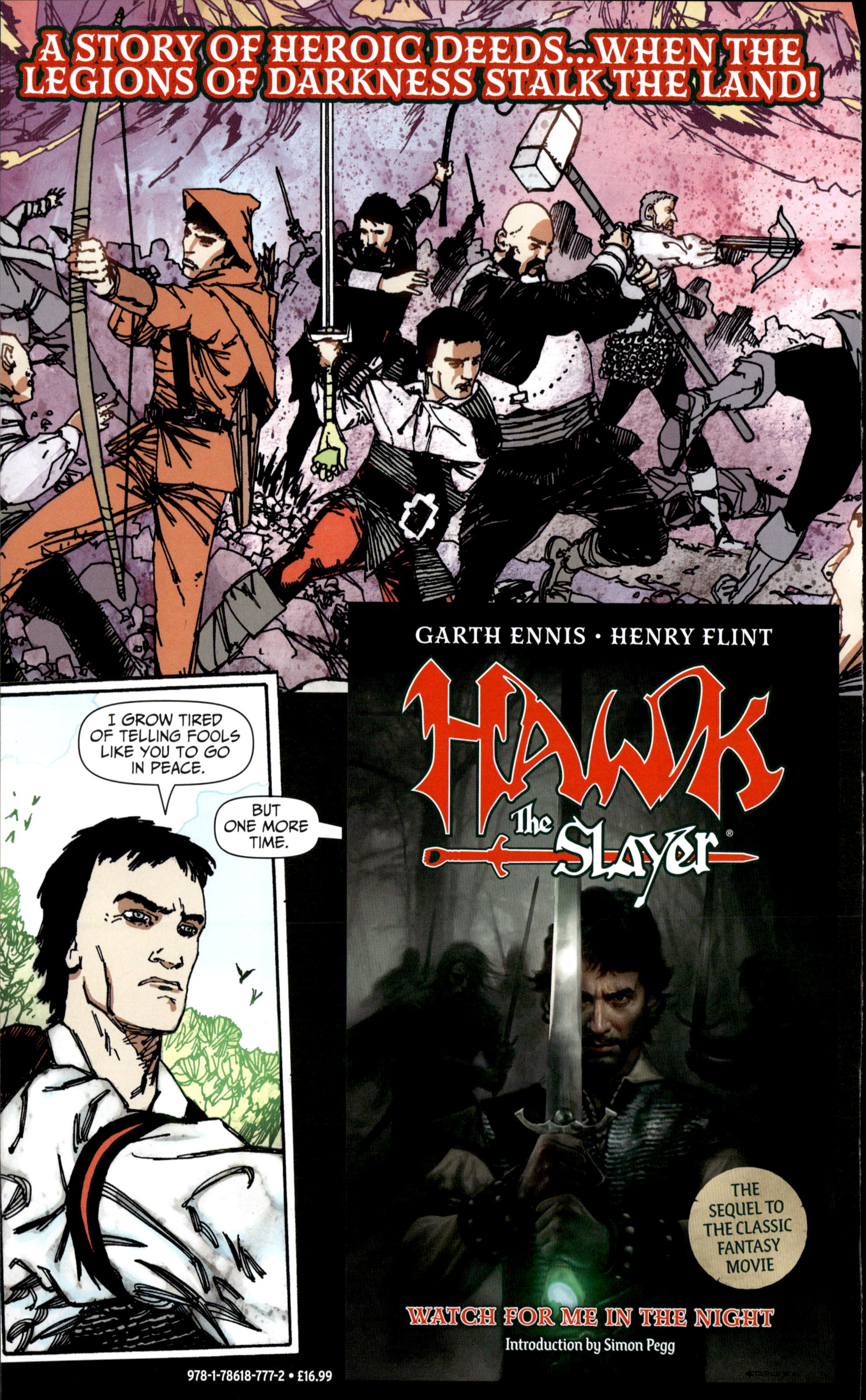
A STORY OF HEROIC DEEDS...WHEN THE LEGIONS OF DARKNESS STALK THE LAND!
I GROW TIRED OF TELLING FOOLS LIKE YOU TO GO IN PEACE.
BUT ONE MORE TIME.
GARTH ENNIS • HENRY FLINT
HAWK The Slayer®
THE SEQUEL TO THE CLASSIC FANTASY MOVIE
WATCH FOR ME IN THE NIGHT
Introduction by Simon Pegg
978-1-78618-777-2 • £16.99

Garth Ennis

For **2000 AD** Garth Ennis has written *Rogue Trooper, Judge Dredd vs Robo Hunter*, and *Bonjo From Beyond The Stars*, and is also part of the ongoing revival of **Battle Action**, for which he writes *Johnny Red*. Outside of the Galaxy's Greatest he is known for **Preacher**, **The Boys**, **Hitman**, **The Punisher** and a great many war comics, including **War Stories**, **Battlefields**, **The Stringbags**, **Sara** and **Partisan**.

Keith Burns

Keith Burns is a member of the Guild of Aviation Artists, and has previously worked on *Rat Pack* for **Battle**, and is busy drawing the upcoming *Johnny Red* storyline.

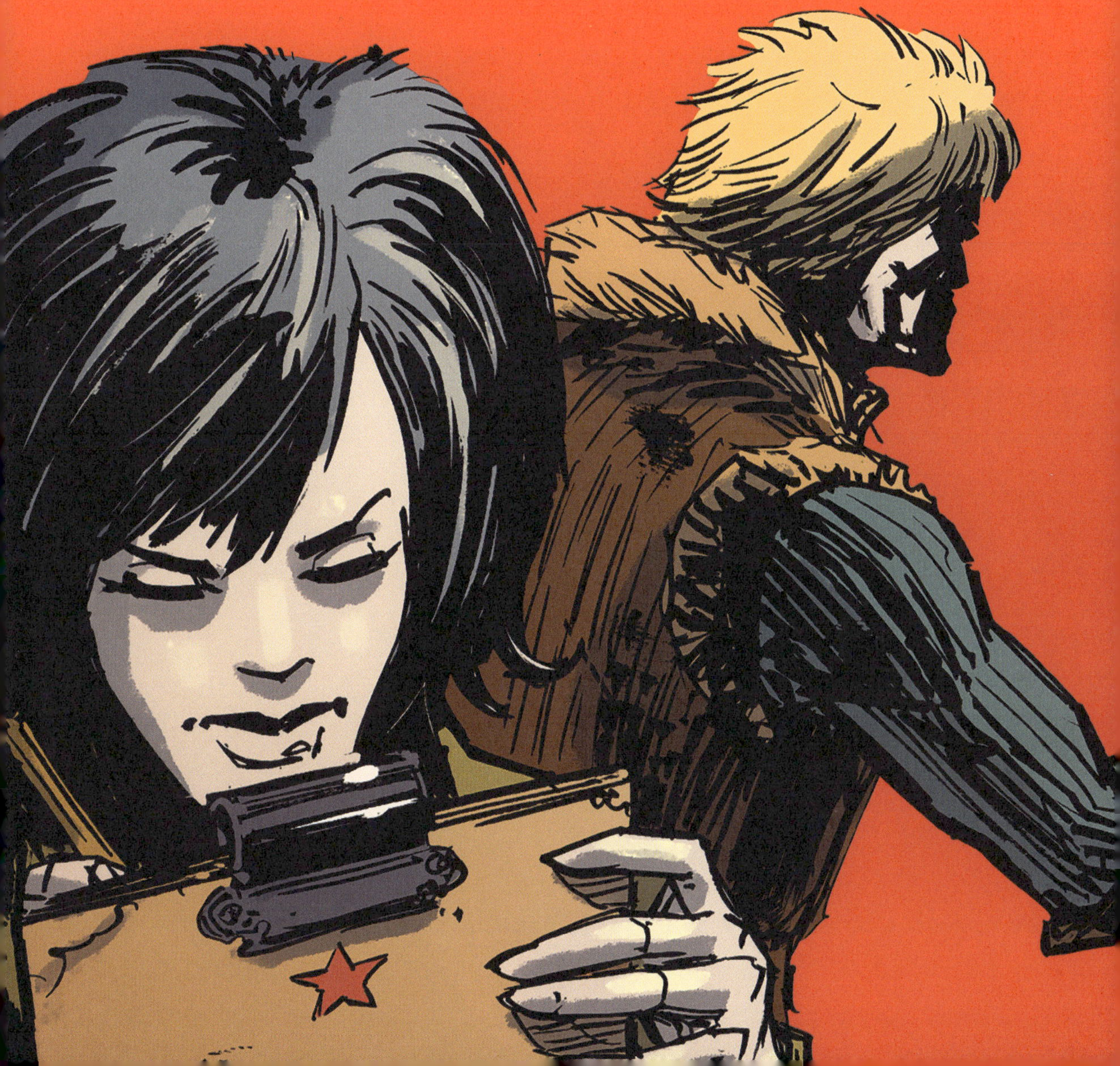

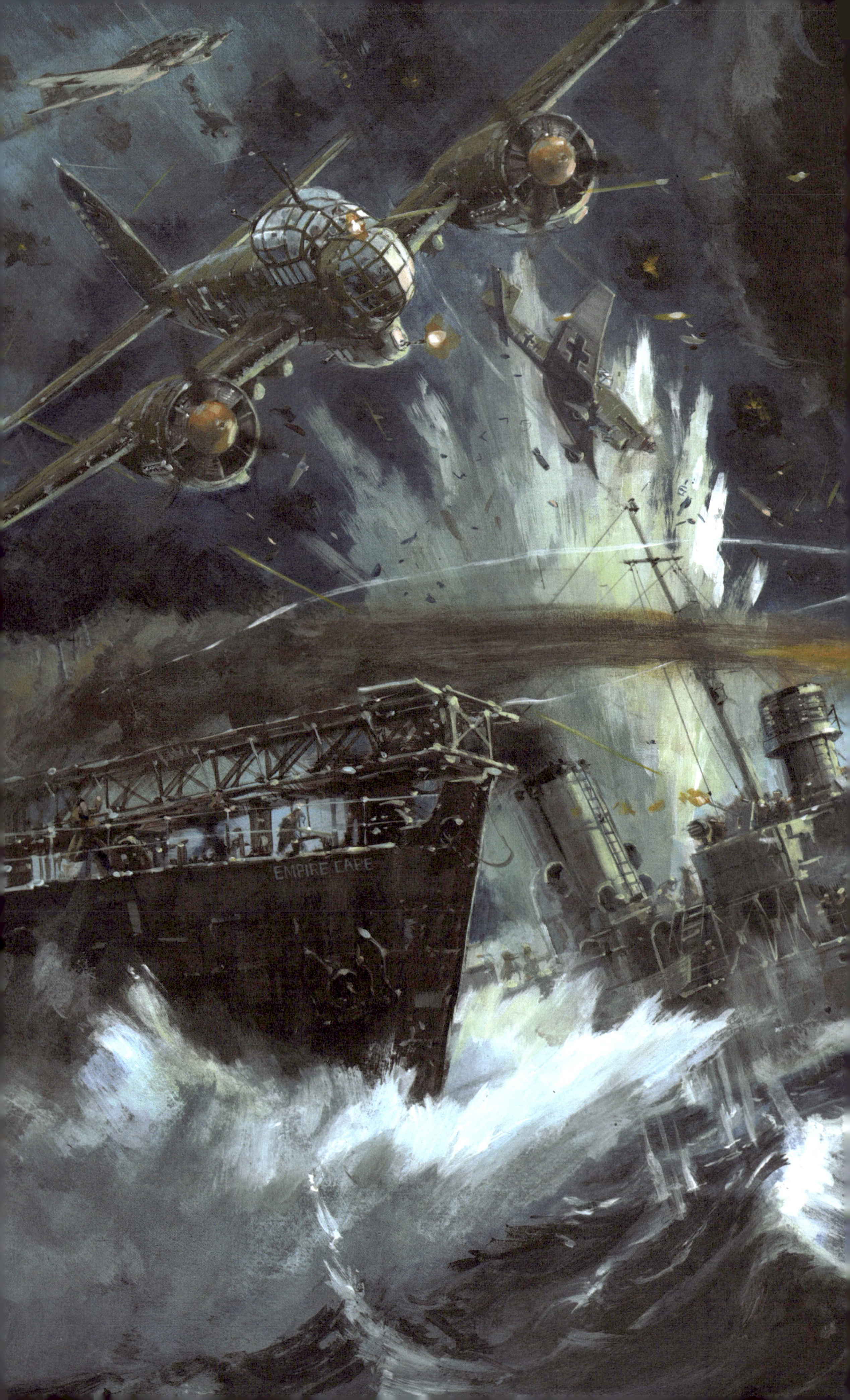
EMPIRE